PARALLEL LIVES

EXILED INNOCENCE

Enjoy,

JR Liba

PARALLEL LIVES

Exiled Innocence

by

TR Liles

For information, contact:

Impressionist Publishing
7432 Deframe St.
Arvada, CO 80005-2857

LCCN: Pending
ISBN: 0-9747015-0-5

All the characters in this book are fictional, and any resemblance to
actual persons living or dead is purely coincidental. Although the story
alludes to eras, locations, and events, it is not to be misconstrued as
historically or technically accurate.

Book Design by author
Cover Artist — Kayla Remus
Cover Layout & Design — MacGraphics Services
                        - Karen Saunders
Printing and Binding — KIMCO
                    -   Scott Laudenslager

Printed in the United States of America
1 3 5 7 9 10 8 6 4 2

This book is dedicated to my children:
Tamara, Lisa, Kevin, Kimberly, & Ty

ACKNOWLEDGEMENTS

Thanks to the many people who reviewed various drafts of the manuscript and/or contributed to the present form of the story and reinforced my commitment to present this novel for publication. Special mention goes to: Sharon Liles, Lyle and Teresa Horner, Jack Clark, Phil & Lisa Colwell, Mike and Donna Hoephner, Pauleta Maggard, Tiffaney Cooper, Tamara Gable, Dean and Vivian Sanderson, Carol Christensen, Harold and Lora Lee Liles, Margaret Liles, Chet Maggard, Kevin and Nancy Saquilan, Barbara Villasenor, Myra Westphall, Oscar and Barbara Casey, Don and Gina Jantz, Richard and Ginger Spady, Jim Hall, Robert Chase, Cary and Angie German, Danny and Beth Vierra, Al Jamison, Mary Agpawa, Cam Anderson, Karen Saunders, Glenn Arnold, John Gomez, Kayla Remus, Karen Saunders, Scott Laudenslager, Ilse Schmitt, Rick and Dottie Childress, Jack and Carol Messick, Doris Mays, Ken and Fran Sluggett, Derek Colwell, Jordan Colwell, Henrietta Foster, Steve Olson....

PARALLEL LIVES — Exiled Innocence

by TR Liles

Lost Innocence

Born, Randall T. Ferris, he grew up in the southwest during the early 60s. Low rolling mountains, referred to as hills by relatives from Colorado, surrounded his home located in a wide valley. Eons ago a gigantic granite asteroid hit the limestone plains laid down even more eons ago by a shallow sea. The resulting shock waves from the earth-shattering impact created harmonic pressure nodes in the earth's surface where mountains of limestone popped up among the newly deposited flint-gray granite mountains.

After a hundred million years of erosion, the mountains were now old and eroded residuals of the majestic range that had once been home to roving dinosaurs. The erosion had caused the granite to turn into a rich black clay-loam soil—lamented by locals as *gumbo*. During a rain the gumbo became a sticky tenacious mud. However, the rich soil was the reason that Randy's recent ancestors had settled this valley. When the rains were gentle and frequent, a farmer-rancher harvested bumper crops of wheat and cotton. As an added bonus, he could usually cut enough alfalfa hay to feed a herd of beef cattle over the winter.

This year, Randy's seventeenth year, the spring rains had been gentle and frequent. The flowing waves of ripening grain resembled giant carpets stretching and waving toward the mountains in the distance. The wheat was almost ready for the grain combines that appeared each year in convoys, like traveling bands of Gypsies. From a distance the grain combines resembled giant dragonflies chasing each other around the fields—devouring the golden grain and excreting the straw out the rear.

Randy was a part of this socioeconomic and ecological system; the only life that he had ever known. Twenty acres of this year's harvest were his; the culmination of an FFA (Future Farmers of America) project started last winter.

Working in the fields had been long and arduous. His muscled torso reflected the healthy sheen and vibrancy of youth. He was seventeen—*knew everything there was to know about anything and was restless to challenge the world for all that would be his.*

The distant horizons pulled at his soul—wanderlust reinforced by endless hours spent on a tractor working the never-ending fields. Soon, his world would be open to adventure and discovery. He just needed to complete his last year of high school to be free—free to choose his own special path in life that would sculpt his destiny.

His *seventeenth summer* was a major turning point in Randy's life. He had picked up his girlfriend, Sherrill (*Cheryl*), in his dad's Chevy pick-up truck. Their destination was Craterville, an amusement park near Lake Altus. Every Independence Day the amusement park had a gargantuan fireworks display and the G-force rides were always exhilarating. With Sherrill holding onto him tightly, they would scream in unison as the roller coaster roared hell-bent-for-disaster over the steel tracks.

Today, their anticipation was high for another fun day together. However, approaching out in the west was one of those glorious infamous "Great Plains Thunderstorms"—now positioned over Lake Altus. Thunderstorms in the southwest were an event of their own—nature at its grandest. Warm moist air flowing in from the Gulf of Mexico, swirling over Texas, and colliding with a cold front from the Colorado Rockies created a pyrotechnic display of lightning and thunder grander than any fireworks display. The electrified towering tempest would then sweep north and eastward across tornado alley.

Not wishing to test fate with a possible lightning strike on the steel rails of a roller coaster, Randy and Sherrill had decided to stop on a hill close to his home and wait out the approaching storm. The vista extended from twenty to thirty miles in all directions. Randy's wheat field was just at the base of the knoll. The young couple sat back quietly and took in the view. Few words needed to pass between them. Just being in each other's company was gratifying and an occasional uttered phrase between them communicated paragraphs of thoughts.

Randy stretched and breathed in deeply, savoring the fresh scent of ripening wheat mixed with wafts of cool moist air from the approaching rain.

"*Ah, life is good,*" he congratulated himself. Snuggled up next to him was the best looking sexiest girl in high school. Her name was Sherrill Lindstrom and she was beautiful beyond his wildest dreams of the perfect girl. They loved each other and planned to marry some day, but that was in the future—a long way into the future.

Randy and Sherrill's religious and ingrained ethics had prevented them from going beyond the exploratory stages of courtship. Recently however, the moments of passionate kissing and caressing had taken them to new heights of erotic desire. The decision to pull away from the edge had become harder and their lingering passion had lasted longer and longer. For now, they were satisfying themselves with exploring exotic areas with planned but seemingly innocent touches and caresses.

Growing up in a ranch environment had afforded them, many times, to observe the act of breeding among their farm animals. When the female seasonally came into heat, the males of the specie, eyes dilated and mouth foaming from arousal by the smell of pheromones, mounted the female. The sexual copulation lasted less than 10 seconds. After dismounting, the male stumbled around stiff legged with his nose extended, sniffing the air with a quizzical expression—as if to say, "Is that all there is to it? I was expecting more!"

Randy sometimes experienced voyeur empathy in those antics and occasionally walked away with an embarrassing boner. At other times that boner would unexpectedly reappear at the most inopportune time— as if it had an independent life of its own. It might even spring to attention when a girl dressed in shorts for gym class, simply bent over to pick up a basketball.

It could cause an embarrassing bulge in his jeans if he just watched a girl jogging around the perimeter of the basketball court; her supple young nipples pressing against her gym top grabbing his attention until his gaze was drawn to her tight rounded butt forming a mesmerizing rhythmic display of cloth tugging against cloth. The seams of her gym shorts seemed barely able to endure her energy. The sight was enough to cause the blood to drain from his red-blooded American boy's brain. A worldly uncle had once sagely observed, "God giveth a young man two heads, but a blood supply to think with only one head at a time."

Sherrill at 5' 10" was a star on the girl's basketball team and Randy was captain of the boy's basketball team. At 6' 2", he was above average height and played center most of the time, but he also had the speed and athletic ability to play as a forward or guard.

It was during those wonderful nights, riding back home on the bus after a vigorously contested game, that they found the most opportunity to discover each other. Their bodies were already stimulated by the

3

exertion of the game, but they had the secure feeling of *not* going too far, since they were surrounded by their teammates.

They snuggled together in the back seat of the bus with Randy's big sports jacket pulled across them, shielding them from prying eyes. They began exploring and experiencing the joy of touching and being touched. These experiences started forming bonds of trust and heightened desire that they felt could be safely controlled under most circumstances.

Their hometown was a typical small community. It was a town where the gossip wags knew what you were going to do before you did it. Moreover, even if you didn't do it, they would gossip that you did it anyway. Often, the men were far worse in their gossiping than the women.

One time in particular, Randy had taken a set of plowshares to Staples Blacksmith & Garage to have the edges hardened. The garage was a favorite hang out for men, who had idle hours to spend talking about the weather and women, while playing cards and dominoes. The owner, Bud Staples, liked Randy and teased him good-naturedly, but almost always with sexual innuendos. "Hey, Mr. Towel Rack," he called out so all could hear as Randy entered the shop. "How've ya been? We heard that you borrowed your Uncle Fred's convertible and took your girlfriend out to the lake."

Pausing for a moment to project innocence in his statement, he continued just as loudly, "We also heard that you brought it back smelling like fish." That got everybody's attention.

When Randy innocently replied, "Yes, we went to the lake, but we didn't go fishing," the whole crowd of geezers broke into knee slapping laughter. Randy didn't have a clue why they were laughing, until later, when his uncle explained it all to him in pornographic terms.

Randy was well aware that many a girl's reputation had been tarnished by slanderous talk and whispered innuendoes inferring that she was *loose* and *free*. Those girls couldn't get dates with boys from *decent* families and often had moved out of the community to escape discrimination and persecution.

He didn't want gossip and innuendoes to compromise Sherrill's reputation. For these reasons, he preferred to double date with his younger sister Leta, who was one school grade below him. She had cute girlfriends, providing opportunities for flirtatious banter; but Sherrill was his age and all other girls paled in her shadow.

Today, Sherrill and he had planned to go to Craterville with his sister and her boyfriend David, who was Randy's best friend. Conflicting schedules had forced them to take separate vehicles. Hence, here they were alone together watching the approaching storm and feeling the ionic electricity in the air.

Sheets of rain draped down from the clouds to the ground; the clouds had a strange roiling motion. White swirling scuds of clouds appeared to slide down the front of the rain wall, disappeared, and then reappeared thousands of feet up to repeat the cycle. Abruptly the storm spawned a tornado and then spontaneously, two more sister funnels appeared.

The rare sight of three twisters on the ground excited Randy and Sherrill's adventurous nature, but didn't alarm them unnecessarily, since the sight of a tornado was just another of nature's majestic displays. As long as they were not in the direct path of a tornado, they could appreciate the beauty and admire the strength of such an awesome sight.

The twisters resembled gigantic elephant trunks dangling down from the dark clouds, with the head of the elephants hidden in the blackness of the clouds. The flipping twisting trunks fed across the plains for almost ten minutes, and then disappeared back into the clouds.

Tornadoes, they had learned at an early age, were not always a threat to safety. As long as you could see them, then you could usually evade them. If you couldn't evade them, then the prudent choice was to take shelter in a storm cellar until the storm's fury had passed and nature returned back to normalcy.

The approaching storm was now about five miles away when the skies turned an ominous shade of tarnished green. Randy studied the clouds and prophesied, "Those storm clouds have hail in them—there's not a darn thing we can do." He wrapped his arm around Sherrill as she nestled into the safety of his embrace. Together, they apprehensively watched as the storm swept ever closer.

At first, the hail beat an intermittent thump-ping on the cab and hood of the pickup. Then, like the demons of hell had been loosened, the staccato of Gatling guns beat down upon them. Randy's anxiety culminated into feelings of devastation as he saw his small financial future flattened in front of his eyes.

The deluge became so thick that they couldn't even see the hood ornament. It seemed unceasing—then as suddenly as it had started—it stopped. The air cleared and there were four inches of steaming ice on the hood of the pickup truck, quickly thawing in the summer heat—but the damage had been extensive. There was not a single green blade of wheat poking through the thick white carpet of icy pellets.

Randy stared in denial at the devastation. He had planned to use the money from the harvest to buy a car and put the rest into savings for college. Now he had nothing to show for the money already spent and the labor expended to get the anticipated wheat harvest.

Sherrill pressed her forehead against Randy's cheek; big tears welled up in her eyes and ran down her cheeks. Compassionately, she intoned, "Oh, Randy, I know how you were looking forward to the money from this wheat crop—now it's wiped out."

Randy moaned, "I feel my whole life has just been wiped out." He started kissing away his own tears that had touched her forehead, and then kissed her tears on her cheek. The salty sweet taste of tears in his mouth made him thirsty for her lips. He whispered, "Sherrill, I'm glad you're here—for me."

At first, he kissed the edges of her mouth, and then her lower lip, and then her upper lip. Her lips parted slightly, a little moan of grief and rising passion emanated from deep within her body. Her moan and hot breath were a catalyst to his feelings of devastation. Finding a life buoy in her kisses, his lips clung to hers like a drowning man clinging to a life vest.

Her breath was hot and moist, adding to the fog of his breath that condensed on the windows supercooled by the hail. The fogged up windows blocked out a view of the outside and created an eerie sensation that they were the only two people left in the world.

He felt her body tremor slightly as his tongue slipped inside her mouth and searched out the delicious taste of a woman in the moments of arousal. This added fervor to his own rising passion and the fiery fever of his long suppressed desires.

He could feel her fingernails flex and dig into the nape of his neck. The pricks of pain were delightfully stimulating. His lips slid down to the softness of her neck. He bit down; just before his teeth touched, he let go. He soothingly brushed his lips back and forth across the tortured flesh, and then tenderly kissed the blemished spot.

Her fingernails dug deeper into his neck. Her free hand cupped his exposed ear, which she rolled and crumpled between her palm and fingers. She thrust out her chest. His chin caught on the v-shaped cut in her blouse, popping open the top button. This was familiar territory to the touch of his hands, but the first time his lips had been this far.

He paused for a moment as he felt stiffness in her back. Then as she relaxed, he took this as implied consent to voyage further into the unknown. His lips kissed and slid across the fullness of her breasts. Their breathing increased in frequency and came out in little rasping gasps.

She shifted slightly, as if on queue, like on the night bus returning from a basketball game, slipped her blouse out of her Bermuda shorts, and unsnapped the clasps from her bra. His fingertips moved up under her bra and found her perfectly formed virginal breast.

His passion began beating in his head as he gently but firmly rolled her nipples between his forefinger and thumb. Without seeming to move, she slipped off her blouse and her bra fell across his arms. The sight of his two hands appearing from under the bra and caressing her breast gave him the sensation of an out of body experience. It was as if someone else was caressing her breast and he was just a close onlooker.

A little voice in his head whispered, *warning—warning; you are getting too close to the edge*, but the voice was overpowered by his intermixed feelings of devastation and desire. As she pulled the bra away, he was suddenly brought back to a reality that could best be described as *unreality*.

Her breasts were the twin images of the most fantastic sight that he had ever seen. He didn't know which to kiss first. Upon kissing the first for a moment, there was a compelling attraction by the other for his lips. He kissed the second for only short moments when the first beckoned his attention to make sure that it hadn't escaped back into a dream world.

Floods of desire filled their bodies and he could feel her respond. His mouth formed around her nipple and like a suckling babe, his tongue started undulating, as if he was licking a spoon dipped into honey. The taste of her body was sweeter than any honey he had ever tasted and the scent of her body was sweeter than any rose, yet was more intoxicating than any wine he had ever tasted.

Their lovemaking became ritualized, as if they had rehearsed a thousand times. As he kissed her breast, she unbuttoned his shirt. His arm flared back in complete rhythm with her removing the sleeve. His other arm flared back to complete the removal of his shirt. As the shirt collar touched his fingertips, she released it. He draped the shirt, without looking, across the steering wheel.

As she reclined down across the seat, he unzipped her shorts. With only a slight resistance formed by the roundness of her buttocks, her shorts and panties slid off together. Her head seemed oddly downhill, so he folded the garments and positioned them as a pillow. His eyes cascaded down her body. He literally felt that he had ascended to heaven. She was the most beautiful creature that he had ever seen. He uttered, "Sherrill, you are beautiful!"

He had three sisters and had caught an occasional glimpse of their nudity, but here before him lay a creature that only the gods should have. The throbbing erection inside his blue jeans felt like it had godlike proportions; he had to release it from its solitary confinement. Rather clumsily, but hurriedly, he removed his boots and jeans. His knees never left from between her legs and a moment later he was as naked. Sherrill glanced down at his manhood; reactively spreading her legs further apart to accept him. She had only seen the male organ in its flaccid state, and stared wide-eyed at how big it became when erected; it had a regal bearing with kingly dimensions.

Randy had fantasized this moment many times and had the impulse to enter her immediately, but thought that if he did, the dream would evaporate. On the other hand, he thought that if he stopped to think then it might never happen. The passion of the moment was such that he wanted this moment to last forever, but he wanted it to happen now!

He drew encouragement from the misty desire in her beautiful green eyes. Her lips parted slightly and she whispered huskily, "Randy, I want you more than anything that I have ever wanted in my life—I want you inside me—take me now—please!"

He yearned to be inside her immediately, but he knew, without knowing for sure, that as soon as his manhood touched her womanhood that he would prematurely ejaculate. He wanted this wondrous experience to last more than just a fleeting moment. He started distracting himself by kissing her lips for long moments. Sliding his lips down her face, down her neck, he rediscovered each of her breasts. He took and gave pleasure through his kisses and through the pulsation of his tongue on her nipples.

As he kissed her breast, there was a faint erotic scent—he had to find the source. His lips slid down across her firm abs to her belly button, where his tongue explored the indention, and then down across her lower belly to the soft pubic hair between her legs. Here was the source of the erotic musk aroma of butter-basted truffles. As he kissed the inside of each thigh, he got closer to the source. However, inexperience of what to do or where to go or how far to go would have to wait for the future. He knew the mechanics of lovemaking, but had yet to discover the finesse that experience would bring.

She alternately squeezed and released his head with her thighs, as if to say, "I want you to, but I don't want you to do what ever it is you're doing that's driving me crazy with desire."

He kissed back up to her lips and felt that he had conquered his erection. It was still enormous, but the pulsation had slowed to a throb. He was sure that he had gained another plateau of control over his body. He let his staff lie lightly across her pubic bone. Resting amongst her pubic hair, he felt strangely like a *poppa bird* on the nest.

He smiled, realizing that mixing humor and passion was like mixing oil and water—they don't mix. But he discovered that a small amount of humor to oneself seemed to bring his passion to a controllable level. Although they both were straining and yearning with desire, he now felt that he was over the first hurdle and vowed to make this moment last longer than ten seconds.

Sherrill only flinched slightly and moaned more from pleasure than pain as he slowly manipulated his manhood into the opening of her vagina. He stroked the soft swollen hot-wet lips of her femininity. He didn't know why, but the technique felt natural; he went with sensation rather than logic.

He had been advised by an older boy to bite the earlobe of a virgin. Therefore, she would concentrate on that pain, rather than the pain of losing her maidenhead. He decided this was good advice. Kissing her, he whispered, "Sherrill, I love you." Biting her earlobe, he gave a short thrust and plunged into her body.

Her eyes widened and she exclaimed, "Oh, my God!" Biting her lower lip, tears of pain and ecstasy filled her eyes. He felt his own pulse racing and had to pause for a moment to maintain control. Then as the pulsation slowed, he probed farther and deeper into her body. As he reached the extent of her vagina, he felt something soft and supple encircle the head of his manhood and hold for a moment. Their bodies started undulating together in the rhythmic ageless bliss of lovemaking.

Their rhythm quickened; he pushed off her with arms extended on either side of her and his hands pressed against the seat. Her fingers wrapped around the back of his arms and her fingernails pressed hard against his skin.

He had full view of her body and the swollen nipples of her breast swirled in tight restrained rhythmic circles. Each of his eyes tried, independently, to follow each nipple's motion; he felt a strange disorientation, as though he were under a hypnotic spell.

The cab of the truck had its own darkness around him, but he saw her clearly. His brain wasn't thinking, but his thoughts were clear—except there was nothing there. Nothing, except for this exquisite creature beneath him—giving herself to him—her first man, and he, giving himself to her—his first woman.

As he felt himself climax inside her, he dreaded that it was over—this would be the end. But he underestimated the stamina of a 17-year-old boy in the prime of his manhood. The pulsation stopped after a few moments, but the erection stayed up and their bodies clashed together like titans grappling for position. The sweat from their bodies mingled together, creating a sauna effect of wild wet submersion into a tropical lagoon.

Suddenly her eyes focused on his and he felt her shudder. Her lips parted and she sucked in air through clinched teeth. Her legs sprang up and crisscrossed his back. Her heels pressed hard into his back; he felt the cascading domino effect of his vertebrae popping.

She felt a warm release deep in her abdomen that flowed up to her nipples and raced down to the tips of her toes. The sensation rebounded and rushed up her legs to overtake the waves of sensation flowing across her breast. The doubled waves cascaded into the secret recesses of her mind, creating a carillon of bells and bursting skyrockets. Resisting the explosion of emotions, she bit her lip—then unable to resist any longer, she screamed in sheer ecstasy as the waves flooded and flowed to the extremities of her body—to the extremities of her soul.

Randy felt her inner contractions pulsating around the head of his manhood, as if she were trying to draw him deeper into her. The stimulation caused him to climax again then his body lost all strength. He experienced the rush of running a marathon race; coming in the winner—exhausted, but ultimately rewarded.

They blissfully lay together in each other's arms for almost a half-hour. He held his full weight off her by supporting his elbows against the seat. Sherrill caressed him with her fingertips tracing each muscle in his back. Little murmurs of satisfaction whispered from her lips.

When he commented that she had an angelic glow in her face and a look in her eyes as if she had had a religious experience, she replied, "I have—and I'll be a convert forever!"

Randy felt as though he had soared among the heavens and she was his own special earth angel. He looked deeply into her eyes and vowed, "Forever—I love you, Sherrill." Moving his lips closer to her cheek, he whispered *sweet nothings* in her ear.

The drone of an airplane in the distance brought them back to the reality of a world existing outside their own. Randy fully expected to feel shame and black remorse—this was what their upbringing had demanded. But he could find little fault and even less sin in their discovering love and contentment in each other.

Sherrill had a fleeting moment of modesty and guilt, she moaned, "Oh, Randy, what have we done?" He cradled her face between his hands and tenderly kissed her lips.

She resolved the conflict in her mind and stated, "My lover—you are my god of gods in human form and you have my love and body forever. But I'll still retain the eternal God for safe keeping of my soul and hope that he can appreciate the love that we have for each other and bless us with his love for the rest of our lives."

The young lovers arrived at Craterville in a state of euphoria. Their flushed cheeks and effervescent glow in their faces caused Randy's sister Leta, who adored her big brother and was usually tuned into his innermost thoughts, to probe, "What have you two been up to?"

Randy was caught off guard, and stammered, "We, uh, we saw three tornadoes touch down at the same time—it was awesome!"

Even though both Randy and Leta had seen this rare event before, it was the only thing that he could think of at the moment. He didn't want to share with anyone, not even his sister from whom he kept nothing, the experience that had happened only an hour ago. He only wanted Sherrill and himself to have the common secret of the most fantastic experience of his—their lives.

He had awakened this morning a mere boy and now, not 10 hours later, he was a man. He felt 3 inches taller—as if he were walking on air; 4 years older—as if the problems of a teenager seemed remote and diminished; 5 years wiser—as if he had joined the ranks of his idols and had become an equal with them.

Sherrill also sensed the change in him and gave a squeeze to his hand to transmit a silent message that she liked what she saw. She had always admired Randy as they were growing up, but now here stood the man that had transformed her into a woman and she felt the love flowing within her veins like hot spicy apple cider.

David, Leta's boyfriend, feeling left out of the inner circle of intrigue, suggested, "Let's go on the Tilt-a-Whirl."

Sherrill declined, "Maybe later." She wanted to be alone with Randy, to give them a chance to come to terms with their newly found experience of each other.

Randy quickly agreed, "You two go ahead. Sherrill and I are going on the Ferris wheel—we'll catch up with you later." On the Ferris wheel, high above the masses, they would be a part of the gala crowd and yet, isolated from it.

Somehow it seemed fitting that a distant ancestral cousin had invented the first Ferris wheel back in the nineteenth century. It had made its debut at the Chicago World's Fair Midway as an amusement ride with a giant vertical power-driven steel wheel, 250 feet in diameter, supporting 36 cars with each car seating 40 people. The Ferris wheel at Craterville was a diminished version, but still provided chills and thrills when it stopped at the top of its rotation, rocking passengers back and forth suspended in air. They tightly gripped the restraining bar in anticipation of the sudden acceleration and exhilaration that would take them back to earth, to begin the skyward cycle again.

Randy and Sherrill rode the Ferris wheel a dozen times that evening; it was the only ride that could physically take them upward to mingle with their high spirit of elation of being alive and being together. Between rides, they walked hand in hand through the midway, occasionally stopping to chat with friends. They shared drinks and hamburgers with David and Leta, but the Ferris wheel kept beckoning them back; only it could approach the height of their feelings of loving and being in love.

Isolated above the crowd, they tenderly kissed and nestled their cheeks together. The warm summer breeze wafted Sherrill's hair around them, giving them the impression that they were being encapsulated together in a cocoon of gossamer strands of silk.

The ride operator noticed their repeated attendance in the waiting line and when the 4th of July fireworks started, he stopped the wheel with their chair at its apogee. He didn't restart the wheel again until the fireworks ended.

Randy and Sherrill couldn't believe their good fortune and savored the view. During the grand finale, Randy turned to Sherrill and whispered into her ear, "The fireworks are awesome, but they don't compare to the fireworks that went off in my head today, while I was in your arms."

Sherrill snuggled closer, kissed him tenderly on the mouth, and whispered with empathy, "Yes, my love, I know. You have awoken the woman in me, and I want this feeling to last forever."

They drove home slowly that night, wanting the day to never end. Having discovered the joys of each other, they didn't want to be apart. They wanted to be together forever, forget the rest of the world, and live in their own world. However, all moments pass and finally, reluctantly, Randy walked Sherrill to her door. He started to kiss her, and the porch light came on.

The door opened and her mom good-naturedly called through the screen, "You all are a little late, but I hope you had a good time. Now, Sherrill, you come on inside. It's past bedtime and we have lots of chores to do tomorrow."

Their hands slipped away, fingers sliding to fingertips then breaking contact. Randy felt something precious being taken from him. With his hand still extended, he whispered, "Good night, my love." Turning, he walked numbly back to his vehicle.

During the drive home, he tried to recapture the day in his thoughts, but his feelings were so intense and convoluted that he couldn't think of complete words or phrases that might even come close to describing his emotions and love for Sherrill.

When he arrived home, the rest of his family was already in bed and the house was dark. He entered his room without turning on the light, undressed, and slid nude into his bed. The cool sheets gave respite to his body and he lay there for long moments until sleep finally overcame him. He drifted off into a twisting turning erotic exotic dream—with Sherrill as the central character.

Harvest

Randy had not been able to see Sherrill for over six weeks. During harvest, bringing in the crops before more storms passed through the area always preempted social life on the farm. Preparations for harvest began well before sunup and the evening chores extended the workday well past sundown.

The young lovers shared a daily phone call, but their conversations were severely limited by being on a party line. The party line rang 'long and short' rings to identify which rural family the call was directed.

Often, during a conversation, clicks on the line indicated that nosey gossip wags were picking up their phones and eavesdropping. Therefore, Randy and Sherrill couldn't say what they wanted to say to each other and had to limit their conversations to small talk about the activities of farm life.

The phone system had a three-minute timer, which cut the call short so other people could use the line. A call back often got a busy signal because another subscriber on the line had placed or received a call. For teenagers, this limitation severely handicapped their social lives.

Today, Sherrill had called Randy. She casually suggested, "Randy, ask your father for a day off this coming Sunday. We can pack a picnic basket and go for a drive."

Randy cupped his hand over the mouthpiece and hollered, "Hey, Dad! Can I have Sunday off to go for a drive with Sherrill?"

Frank thought for a moment and considered, "All the smaller fields have been combined, and the contract combiners are finishing up the larger fields." He replied, "Sure, Son, you've worked hard. The plowing of the wheat stubble can wait another day."

Randy excitedly informed Sherrill, "Dad said, 'Yes!' I'll pick you up at your church after services." They continued their conversation until the three-minute timer cut them off. Randy hung up the phone and daydreamed. He had been looking forward to being with Sherrill. He had dreamed of nothing else, since their 4th of July together.

He thought back to the couple of times during the harvest that his daydreaming lapses had brought forth verbal reprimanded from his father. He had even accidentally broken off the side mirror of the truck with the combine header. *All work and no play makes a dull boy.* He was definitely feeling dull from the monotony of all work and no play.

Sunday, he picked Sherrill up in front of the Baptist Church. Generally, the majority of people north of town were Baptist; and, like Randy's family, the majority of the people south of town attended the First Christian Church; the people in between mostly were Nazarenes. Demographically, the difference of dogma in church doctrines seemed to mean less to the congregations than their proximity to a church that provided a community cornerstone for the fabric of a family's religious and social life.

At seeing Randy, Sherrill's face lit up as she smiled revealing perfectly formed white teeth and full sensual lips. A light-yellow sundress and a yellow ribbon in her hair complemented her lightly tanned face and arms. Her long golden hair highlighted with soft streaks of red caught the rays of sunshine and formed an aura around her face—a Nordic face with a broad intelligent forehead and high cheekbones that tapered gently to a strong jaw that projected both femininity and determination.

Randy felt that he was picking up an angel. She was an angel—the most divine creature on God's green earth. He felt humbled in her presence and his eyes adored her. Her face and skin had a youthful healthy glow, but little crinkles at the edge of her eyes gave the impression that she had been crying. He couldn't think of any reason why she would be unhappy, so he quickly dismissed it from his mind. Sherrill slid in next to him and they were off for the long sought day of being together.

"Where would my little earth angel like to go?" he asked lightly, expecting to hear her say—*Lake Altus*.

Instead, she responded, "Mount Scott."

Located on the eastern border of the Wild Life Refuge, Mount Scott was a favorite destination for sightseers and lovers. The surrounding vista included several bass fishing lakes that provided water recreation for Lawton, Fort Sill, and surrounding communities. Herds of buffalo, long horned cattle, prairie dogs, coyotes, deer, and an occasional rare elk rewarded visitors who drove through the Wild Life Refuge. Many picnic grounds and dams built by the CCC (Civilian Conservation Corps) in the 1930s provided *the place to go* when relatives were visiting. Randy and Sherrill had learned to swim in these cool deep pools on hot summer days.

The family picnics were memorable with all the delicious food and Rush Springs' watermelons. Their Black Diamond Melons were the best in the world. Cooled to 34 degrees in icehouses, the melons literally popped open at the touch of a knife. Their sweet juicy cores were like eating a snow cone on a hot summer day—except a hundred times better!

Rock climbing, another favorite diversion for all ages, was more like hill climbing on rock outcroppings. The ledges and crannies provided some isolation for lovers, and it wasn't unusual to climb over a rise and suddenly come upon two lovers. If they saw you, it was hard to tell who was the most embarrassed—them or you. If the lovers were oblivious to your presence then a quick glance usually satisfied your curiosity and you discretely took another trail on your adventure.

During the drive to Mount Scott, Sherrill was uncharacteristically quiet and only responded to conversation, instead of being an equal participant. Randy, on the other hand, was in high spirits. He was with the one he loved and was just bursting with life. He talked on about any anecdote that came to mind and was only slightly aware of Sherrill's out of character quietness.

When they reached the base of Mount Scott, Randy was surprised that they were there already. The time had passed so quickly that it seemed only moments had passed since he had picked Sherrill up in front of the church, instead of almost an hour. He hadn't consciously been aware of going over the cattle guards at the entrance or exit of the Refuge, or even the ones dispersed throughout the refuge to keep the buffalo and the herds of Texas Long-horned Cattle from roaming about and getting to areas that might cause conflicts with campers and picnickers.

He had borrowed his youngest uncle's convertible for this special day. Pulling the shift lever to low range, he followed the road that spiraled like a barber pole up to the top of Mount Scott. On top, the mountain was one huge flat parking lot. He parked the car, facing toward Lake Thomas and Lake Latonka in the distance, and turned off the ignition.

Sherrill's hand met his lowered hand halfway. Despite the heat, her hand was strangely moist and clammy. However, Randy was oblivious to this unnatural state because he was a man in love and was finally alone with the one person that he loved the most. The electricity of her touch sent thrills up his arm and made his whole body tingle. As they gazed into the distance, each was preoccupied with thoughts of the other. He finally turned to face her. Reaching out and touching her cheek with his fingertips, their lips met lightly. He whispered, "Sherrill, my angel, I love you."

She whispered hoarsely, "Randy, I love you too," then she burst into tears.

He knew from experience that women were emotional; after all, he had three sisters. Nevertheless, even *they* usually gave warning that an outburst of tears was on its way.

Sherrill's response to "I love you," had totally caught him off guard. However, as he sat trying to figure out what had just happened, this did little to prepare him that he was going to get smacked by the realities of life. He tried to comfort her and shush her tears, but finally resigned himself to just holding her in his arms until the sobbing ceased.

When she finally stopped crying, she dried her tears with Randy's handkerchief. Reaching out and holding both of his hands, she looked deeply into his eyes and heart, "Randy, do you really love me? Will you always love me—no matter what?"

Randy had a fleeting impulse to look away and collect his thoughts, but her pleading eyes held his and he realized her need for unbroken unbridled reassurance of his love.

He replied without blinking, "Yes, Sherrill, you're the only girl in my life and the only girl that I will ever love throughout eternity. Now, Honey, tell me, what is wrong. Why are you so sad?"

Sherrill sniffed, "I am not sad—I'm, I'm happy—but afraid. I'm afraid that what I am going to tell you will drive a wedge between us. I could never stand for that to happen. I could never bear to face life without you."

A million thoughts ran through Randy's mind, but he couldn't think of anything.... Then—suddenly the realization hit him. He uttered the marriage proposal that thousands of teenagers before him have stated with the same disbelief, "*You're what—!*"

A nod from her was confirmation of the most dreaded circumstances that unmarried couples could face, "Yes, Randy—I'm seven weeks pregnant."

It was little consolation that he had figured it out before being told. He sat stunned, unable to move, unable to respond. When Sherrill and he had made love, he had felt ageless. Now, he felt like a little boy, hurt and afraid, desperately wanting to run to his mother for consolation. But now he was being held accountable for a man's actions that dictated a man's response. He quickly thought of alternative answers—discarding them. He took Sherrill into his arms and tenderly whispered, "Darling, I love you."

Moving back to look into her eyes, he excitedly assuaged any doubts, "This is wonderful, Babe! We're going to have a baby! We'll get married and have our baby."

She beseeched, "Randy, are you sure? Are you really—really sure—you still want me?"

Not being really sure of the future, but being sure of his love for her, he confirmed, "Yes, My Love, I'm really sure."

She wrapped her arms around his neck and kissed him long and passionately on the lips. Pressing her body against his until their bodies become one outline against the backdrop of the blue horizon, Sherrill coaxed, "Randy, I want you again, just like before. I've dreamed of that day ever since and I get wet between my legs just thinking of it."

Randy glanced around to see that no one else was on the mountain. Not wanting to delay their confirmation of love, they quickly took off their own clothing and dropped them onto the floorboard of the car. Randy entered her quickly and was immediately lost in the abyss of their lovemaking. He was lost from all thought of his surroundings. Their bodies hungrily sought succor in each other.

As firmly as he pushed, he couldn't penetrate deep enough inside her; something firm and unyielding blocked his way. The first time they had made love, the depth of her had been soft and supple, now something stopped him an inch before he was in all the way. Then he remembered the baby. "Oh, my God," he whispered hoarsely. "What if I'm hurting the baby?"

He started to pull away, but Sherrill stopped him. Her yearning was unabated and she moaned, "What's wrong?"

He uttered pointedly, "The baby!"

She relaxed and laughed lightly, "Don't worry, you're not going to hurt the baby. My aunt Jenny, told me that a woman can have sex up to the eighth month of her pregnancy."

With this reassurance, but not being sure that all old wives' tales were the gospel, Randy resumed their lovemaking with slower shorter strokes.

Sherrill climaxed first. Her screams of pleasure reverberated over the mountaintop. They were unrestrained expressions of pleasure and a release of the pent-up weeks of worry from when she first suspected that she was pregnant.

Randy climaxed a moment later, interrupted by a thunderous rap of a billy club against the top of the driver's door. His scrotum sucked up and his penis went limp in mid-stroke.

A part-time park official with an ill-fitting soiled uniform and a sweat-stained hat had been inspecting a picnic area at one of the turnouts just below the top. He had routinely scrutinized the cars going by; waiting for a young couple to be the only ones on top. He would wait until he figured enough time had passed to allow them to get into a compromising position, and then he would bust them.

Randy had been lulled into a false sense of security by the knowledge that he would hear a car coming up the mountain. He reasoned that if that happened then they should have time to quickly get dressed to the point of appearing clothed.

Now he was bare-assed naked and so was Sherrill. His back was toward his nemesis and if he got up, Sherrill would be exposed. He laid there for a long moment, trying to gather his thoughts on what to do next. He had never been in such a vulnerable position and never wanted a repeat performance.

The official with a two-day-old beard snickered and snidely inquired, "That boy there hurting you, girlie?" The sarcasm dripped from his voice as he belittled Randy. "Let me see your license, Sonny Boy. Oh, you don't have any pockets—guess you can't show me your ID.

"Maybe you'd better get up off that there girl before that little white ass of yours gets all sunburned. I hear'd that a butt peel is the worst kind of sunburn. You ol' boys would have to sleep on your bellies. Then your mamas would get mad at you for poking holes in the mattress with your little dingies." The tirade of insulting remarks was interspersed with self-satisfied guffaws and snickers.

Randy realized that he had to do something—anything. His inaction only encouraged this weenie official to continue. He quickly grabbed the clothes and pushed them over Sherrill's private areas. Swinging to a sit-up position, he lifted so Sherrill could close her legs and swing them sideways with her heels against the front of the seat and her toes touching the carpet on the floor.

Randy could see that they were at a distinct disadvantage. The officer was standing over them, slapping his billy club against the palm of his open hand, and making a whack-whacking sound that had the tempo of a funeral dirge. The pompous ass grinded, showing yellowed crooked teeth and continued his diatribe, "Hey, little girlie, how about

19

you moving them clothes around a little bit so's I can see if this here ol' boy bruised-jah any?"

Randy wanted to leap at his throat, but he knew that was just what the pervert wanted. Any show of resistance and he knew that he would be knocked senseless with the billy club. Then while he was out, the blackguard could have his way with Sherrill. It would be Sherrill's word against this depraved piece of—.

"Well, what's it going to be? I ain't gonna stand here all day."

Randy instinctively knew that this creep would have no trouble convincing whomever he reported to that the couple was trying to frame him, if they brought charges. This had probably happened before and had gone unreported. He started speaking to buy some time, "Look, officer, my girlfriend just told me that she is pregnant and we were overcome with love for each other. There was no one else around to offend, so we thought it would be all right." This statement had a lame ring in Randy's ears, but it was the truth.

The officer, still whacking his billy club sneered, "Nothing like revisitin' the scene of misbehaving; hee-hee-hee—is there?"

Little drops of spittle were starting to form at the edges of his mouth as he continued, "You young'uns should know that there's an ordinance against fornication goin's-on in the park."

Then he piously preached, "What if some little kids should see you? Why, their little minds would be twisted for the rest o' their lives."

Randy wanted to shout, "Is that what happened to you?" But he knew that they were being baited. He had to control himself or lose whatever control he had of the situation.

As the officer was whacking his hand with the club, Randy's conscious thoughts suddenly figured out what his subconscious was hearing. There were the whack-whacks, but also the occasional whack—clinks. He glanced sideways and saw a wedding band on the officer's hand.

He redirected the conversation toward the officer's situation, "We can understand, *Sir*, why you are so concerned, *Sir*. I see that you're married and probably have a lovely family of your own."

Continuing he ventured, "Let me guess—two boys and a girl—right."

Being caught off guard by this turn of conversation, the officer responded just to correct the wrong guess, "No, I got me two girlies and a boy-yo."

Randy quickly inserted, "I'll bet that you're a good daddy and would never let anything happen to your family—right?"

The officer responded, "Right!"

Again, Randy quickly inserted. "That's why you took this job, to protect your family and the public from hardened criminals—right?"

Again, the officer responded, "Right!" He was becoming confused by this turn of conversation, but thought, *by golly, I am a good daddy, and I do protect the public from hardened criminals—so why not say so.*

Randy could visualize the wheels turning in the officer's head and he pressed the advantage. His keen hearing had caught the whine of an automobile getting closer to the crest of the mountain. All he needed was one more minute for the presence of another car to make the scene too public for the officer to revert back to what might have happened moments earlier.

Randy continued, "We now understand, *Sir*, why you were so upset with us. We're truly sorry because we can now understand that you were only protecting your own family from people that flaunt the law and prey upon others."

This struck home with the official because moments before he had been the predator and he was about to break the law by taking advantage of these teenagers.

The car, heard in the distance, finally topped the mountain and instead of parking at the other side of the rim, parked directly behind the official. The lady rolled down the passenger window and called out in a southern twang, "Hi there, Officer, we're from the city and we're gonna visit friends in Frederick. Can you tell us which way to get back on U.S. 62?"

The officer turned around, inadvertently shielding Sherrill and Randy from the passengers in the other car. They quickly got dressed. Randy had a split-second urge to start the car and peel out of there, but he knew that that would be the wrong thing to do. He had to get the officer to let them go.

The officer's arms and hands were gyrating and pointing. The woman made him repeat the instructions over and over again until he was confused and, right now, wasn't sure if he could find his own way down off this mountain.

While he stood there pointing in two different directions, Randy interjected into the conversation, "Hi, Ma'am, my girlfriend and I are going to Frederick and we would be happy to show you the way. We've got friends and relatives there and they probably know the folks that you're going to visit." They started exchanging names of people that they knew in Fredrick and got a couple of matches. Randy didn't want to tell his own name because up to this point the official didn't know who they were.

While the official was standing there like a by-stander, Randy quickly stated, "Sir, you don't mind if we show these fine people the way, do you? They're not familiar with this section of the country. Going through the Refuge can be confusing because so many roads dead end at campgrounds."

The official stammered and stuttered then realized that both kids were dressed. He no longer had the *bare* facts. His control of the situation had ceased to exist and he was smart enough to let these two catfish go. He sternly growled, "You kids go on and show these people the way, now—ya hear. An' I don't wanna catch chew up here again—ya hear?"

With this verbal release in front of witnesses, Randy started the car and led them down off the mountain. The aftermath of the situation caused him to break out in a cold sweat. The traumatic events and the thought of what could have happened had shaken Sherrill; she was slow to compose herself. They were on the road passing the Easter Pageant's "Eternal City" when she finally commented, "Darling, you were marvelous—you should think about becoming a lawyer."

Randy smiled, then retorted, "Look, I don't insult you, so why should you insult me?" They both laughed and she snuggled up next to him. He continued on down the road, one arm around her, and one arm driving.

He remarked, "My dad always said that if you drive with only one hand, you'll either wind up walking down the aisle to ring of wedding bells or wind up being wheeled down the aisle to the knell of dirge bells."

Sherrill looked at him for a moment, "Oh, I get it!" Adding, "You're going to be walking down the aisle to wedding bells—you big handsome lug." He squeezed her tighter with his arm and relaxed for the first time since the traumatic events on top of the mountain.

When they arrived in Snyder, Sherrill asked, "You're not going to take them all the way to Frederick, are you?"

Randy replied, "You bet I am! I'd take them all the way to Dallas for bailing us out of that situation back on the mountain. That park guy's sick and needs some psychiatric help. Things could have turned real ugly if those people hadn't come along."

The small caravan of cars continued to Frederick. Sherrill and Randy waved good-bye then drove to a public park, where children were playing, and had their picnic.

Randy was finishing off a big slice of southern pecan pie, after eating fried chicken, deep fried okra, baked beans, potato salad, fresh baked bread with churned butter, and a Pepsi Cola.

Sherrill was watching the mothers watching their children playing on the slide and swings. She daydreamed; *this could be me with my child in just a few short years.*

The baby wasn't even born yet, but her maternal instincts were being stirred by the excited squeals of the children at play. They vied with each other to get to the top of the slide first then jumped into space and went pell-mell down the slick surface over the bump into the air where their belly buttons felt like butterflies. Landing on their feet, they ran again for the ladder to repeat the cycle over and over again.

She glanced at Randy and became conscious that he had been watching her watching the mothers watching their children. She loved him for many reasons, but most of all because he was usually sensitive to her innermost feelings. He may not fully understand her—sometimes she didn't understand herself—but he seemed to get inside her mind, becoming a part of her without being invasive. This gave her the feeling of being *soul mates* with him. She had never felt this way with anyone before. Probing the depth of her commitment, she resolved that she could never feel this way with anyone else.

She started to ask him—*Randy, what are we going to do?*

But before she could ask, he replied, "I don't know yet, Sweetheart. We're barely past being children ourselves. We still live with our parents, haven't graduated from high school, and I don't have an income to support a family." He concentrated his full attention on the last morsel of pecan pie balanced on the end of his fork, seeking in it a magic talisman that would supply all the answers. After a long pause, and not being provided with the answers he sought, he popped the last bite into his mouth and washed it down with a long swig of Pepsi.

He reached across the picnic table and took Sherrill's hands in his, "Honey, I don't have the answers yet. Seven weeks ago, both of us were virgins; now we are expectant parents. Before then, the big wide world was our oyster—to seek and find the 'pearls of knowledge, wealth, and happiness.'" Pausing with resignation showing in his expression, he summarily stated, "Now our world has shrunk to you and I—and our baby. We've got a tough row to hoe, but I love you and you love me. I'll just have to work it out in my mind."

With that said they packed up the picnic basket and left the park. Their drive home was somber and subdued. They both had deep feelings of love for each other, but the society in which they lived could and would be very judgmental of their situation. Randy could already visualize the gossiping wags counting on their fingers, the months from when they got married and when the baby would be born. The fact that they were still in high school and getting married would immediately cause tongues to wag. He had vowed to protect Sherrill's reputation, now both their reputations would be in shambles.

When they arrived at Sherrill's home, she invited him in. He deferred, "No, I'll have to face your parents soon enough. I want to have a plan of action and discuss it with you before we break the news to our parents that they are going to be grandparents. Your father will probably want to take a horsewhip to me," he interjected, with a trial at humoring the situation. "Maybe, I should wear a leather jacket and football helmet when we tell them."

He kissed her lightly, backed away holding her hand, "Sherrill, I won't be calling you for a couple of days. We can't talk openly on the phone anyway and I need time to think this out. The decisions that we make now will influence the rest of our lives."

A tear started forming in the corner of Sherrill's eye, as she agreed, "I understand."

He stepped forward and kissed her eyelid. Then stepping back again, he squeezed her hand, "Don't worry, Darling, my thoughts will be with you." Then glancing at her stomach, he added, "And, our baby."

He turned quickly and walked away; tears were burning in his own eyes. He didn't want someone inadvertently walking out the door and catching them bawling in each other's arms. That would require an explanation that he was ill prepared to explain. He had a lot of explaining to do to a lot of people. Right now, he just wanted time—time to think—time to make some decisions on his own, instead of life making them for him.

Contemplation

The next day, Randy finished his early morning chores and climbed onto the tractor. He had a quarter section (160 acres) to start plowing. Sometimes the endless circling in the field was almost unbearable for a young man with an active mind and pent-up energy. The right front wheel of the tractor always followed the furrow created by the previous pass, with the plow behind the tractor creating a furrow for the next pass. The cycle was excruciatingly repetitive and boring. He thought back five years ago to when he was twelve.

He had become so bored by the repetitious monotony of plowing that he had rounded off the corners of the square field. After attaching a pair of vice-grip pliers to counterweight the steering wheel, he sat without guiding the tractor and watched the right front wheel, cranked slightly into the bank by the weighted steering wheel. This allowed the tractor to follow the furrow around the field without him having to touch the steering wheel. As he passed the parked pickup, he jumped off the tractor and watched it plow on—without him.

Feeling smug and cocky, he sat in the shade of the pickup, petted his dog, and leisurely drank a long draught of water from the canvas water bag. As the tractor and plow came back around, he mentally patted himself on the back for his ingenuity. The tractor had passed and was going away from him when doubts of *what ifs* clashed through his mind.

What if: the plow hit a rock or stump and jerked sideways, launching the tractor into a different direction? The field was a quarter mile square and if this happened on the far side, he wouldn't be able to run fast enough to reach the tractor in time before it wrecked itself in the flood ditches that bordered the field.

What if: something should break on the plow, detaching itself from the tractor? The tractor would be free of lugging the plow, speed up, jump the furrow, and head off to self-destruction. The end result would be the same—the tractor would be wrecked. His little ass would be grass and his father would be the lawn mower—not a pretty thought.

Motivated by newly found responsibility, but more so reinforced with the dread of getting his little butt kicked, he jumped up and raced after the tractor. He caught up with it at the other end of the field. Stepping onto the tongue of the hitch, he sprang into the seat.

A few short moments had passed, while he was catching his breath, when like divine providence, the plow hit a stump. The steering wheel spun and the attached vice-grips whacked across the back of his left hand, breaking the small bone above his ring finger. The pain had been intense and a quote from one of his minister's sermons had flashed in his mind, *Pride goeth before the fall*. He hadn't known what it meant at the time, but he had surely felt the pain of retribution.

Even though this had happened years ago, the injury had healed badly and he still had an indention of the ring-finger knuckle on his left hand. He still continued to use the vice-grips as a counterbalance on the steering wheel, but now he positioned it out of the way and covered it with a padded glove. If it ever whacked him again, at least there would be some padding to absorb the force of the blow.

His father had asked him why he plowed in circles and he responded that it saved on the brakes. He also reasoned with his dad that doing it the old way packed down the already plowed ground. The corner areas then had to be plowed again so the rain would soak into the ground. His father had agreed that this might be a better way and adopted this new procedure.

Randy had filled the endless hours of repetitive labor by working math problems in his head, reading books and magazines, and singing popular songs. Every Saturday, his sisters pooled part of their allowance and bought the "Hit Parade" magazine of the newest songs. He would borrow older issues and memorize all the songs. Then, like a lothario, he sang to the top of his lungs as he plowed endless hours in the field. The scissor-tailed flycatchers looking for insects and the circling red-tailed hawks looking for field mice were his non-applauding audience.

Today, plowing was still boring, but Randy was far from being bored. He had to figure out what Sherrill and he were going to do. He ran the contingencies through his mind. With each circuit around the field, old ideas were discarded and new ideas were analyzed for their viability. The sun had arched two-thirds of the way across the sky. It was about 2:30 PM and he hadn't stopped to eat the lunch that his mother had packed for him. He was no closer to a plan of action than when he had begun this morning. The problem seemed insurmountable. He was feeling disconsolate and frustrated from the inexperience of solving life crisis problems. Like many young people, he had drifted through his teens with all his basic needs taken care of by his parents. To date, confrontation with the realities of life had been, at worst, superficial.

He recalled losing a ten-dollar bill while playing combat with his friends on and amongst the huge cotton bales lined up in the cotton gin yard. The loss was devastating at the time, since it represented fifteen hours of working for his grandfather in the hay fields.

Now, it seemed insignificant by comparison. Losing the money had only delayed his buying a new baseball mitt. He eventually got the mitt as a birthday present from his grandfather, whom he admired above all men, except for his own father.

He stopped the tractor and sat in the shade of the pickup. Eating the first of his two sandwiches, he washed it down with tepid water from the canvas water bag. His little dog, Knuckles, sat patiently awaiting his share of the sandwich. Randy looked at Knuckles and thought enviously, *you lucky dog.*

The dog lay all day under the shade of the pickup and watched Randy work; then was Johnny-on-the-spot when it was lunchtime. He reached out to pet the dog, but Knuckles shied sideways, his eyes never leaving the sandwich. Randy laughed at the maneuver and remarked, "At least you know your priorities in life—you won't let me pet you until I feed you."

He slowly unwrapped the waxed paper from the second sandwich, and laid it out in front of the little dog. The dog stared with greedy eyes at the feast of a whole sandwich, and then looked back up at Randy for permission. "Go ahead—take it," Randy urged. The little dog grabbed the big sandwich and ran under the pickup to hoard his largess. He devoured it by biting off chunks and gulping them down without chewing. The grateful dog, with tail wagging, came back and started licking Randy's face. Having his priorities straight, he now allowed Randy to pet him. The dog lazily stretched out and a moment later was fast asleep. His body and legs started jerking in reaction to a dream world of chasing mice and rabbits through the field.

Randy didn't want to go back to work. He just wanted to lay down next to his dog in the warm afternoon sun and go to sleep, forgetting about the problems facing him. Instead, he sat staring at a single wheat straw sticking up out of the stubble. Hot tears of frustration and uncertainty filled his eyes. Finally, he blinked the tears away, rose stiffly, and climbed back onto the tractor to continue plowing the endless fields.

He remembered a quotation from Ben Franklin, "If you can define a problem then you're halfway there to solving it." It may not be an exact quotation, but the foundation was there to start putting into perspective the situation that confronted Sherrill and him. In his mind, he reviewed the problem for the umpteenth time: They weren't out of high school yet. They didn't have much money of their own. They were both underage. They would need their parents' consent to get married. *What if—his parents wouldn't give their permission!* No—he couldn't think negative thoughts. That only made the problem more complex.

Sherrill and he each had close to two hundred dollars in savings. This had been saved over a three-year period with her doing babysitting for the neighbors and picking cotton during the school break. His savings were from bucking hay bales for his grandfather and running a thrashing crew during oat harvest.

He had been younger than most of the crew, but competitive school sports had given him the experience of teamwork. He had set a high standard of working himself hard, which motivated his crew. They consistently delivered more wagonloads of oat shocks to the thrashing machine each day than other crews.

Their team effort was rewarded at the end of the week. On Saturday payday, each member of the crew received an extra eight dollars—an extra day's pay at the time. This had resulted in the best men migrating to his crew and the slackers that wouldn't keep up the fast pace migrating to other crews.

Randy, realizing that he was letting his mind go off on tangents of self-congratulating daydreaming, pulled himself back to reality. He needed to focus on succinctly defining the situation. Extraneous hyperbole would only confuse the issues that demanded immediate resolution. He made a mental list:

1) They were underage—needed permission.
2) Not graduated—education was essential, but may have to wait.
3) No money—had to find a job to support a family.
4) No place to sleep with Sherrill at his house—younger brother shared bedroom.
5) No place to sleep with Sherrill at her house—younger sister shared bedroom and bed.

6) No insurance to cover the delivery of their baby—this would take all their savings.

7) No transportation—he used his father's pickup for everything—they would have to live in a city.

8) No job locally—they would have to live in a city because their town had little industry.

9) Loss of reputation—they would have to live in a city to escape the malicious gossip—their families would still be subjected to snide inquiries and innuendoes by gossips.

10) Needed to be alone together as a family—living with either of their families would stifle their relationship. Randy had discovered that Sherrill was a screamer when they had sex and he couldn't bear the thought of her covering her face with a pillow when they made love.

He reviewed the list in his mind and several of the items overlapped each other, but he settled on the ten items. The bottom line was: they would have to move to a city—but where? He had no saleable skills. He was underage, undereducated, and had no job contacts.

He could drive a tractor, but there would be few tractor jobs in a city. He was too young to get a chauffeur's license to drive a truck or a taxicab. He screamed in anguish to the heavens, "God! How could I have been so naive—just two-months ago—to think that I knew everything there was to know about anything."

The continuous circling of the field on a tractor was monotonous, but provided a respite from the decisions that he had to make. As long as he was thinking on the problem, he didn't have to act upon the problem. The problem wasn't going to go away, but at least it didn't demand a decision, today—this week, yes, but not today. He had defined the problem as simplistically as possible and tried to put it out of his head, but it kept creeping back into his conscious thoughts.

To divert his mind, he started singing Tommy Edward's old hit "It's All in the Game," followed by "My Baby Loves Western Movies," then "Purple People Eaters." He threw in some Elvis and Ricky Nelson hits. He was singing "Peace in the Valley" by the Sons of the Pioneers, when his little dog Knuckles ran out from the pickup to greet and remind him that the sun was hanging on the horizon. It was time to do evening chores.

Randy marveled that the little dog couldn't speak, yet knew the routine of farm life. The dog became active and animated when it was time to move on to another scheduled chore. Randy shut down the tractor next to the pickup and refueled it from the propane tank on the trailer. He lubricated the bearings and checked the oil. He did a quick visual check to insure that the tractor and plow would be ready for use early tomorrow morning.

That night, Randy slept a fitful sleep. He woke several times from a dream of falling into a bottomless abyss. His little brother complained several times that he couldn't go to sleep due to Randy's talking in his sleep.

Randy got up and set up a cot on the screened porch. Caressed by the warm summer night breeze, he fell into a deep soul refreshing sleep around three o'clock in the morning. He arose the next morning before the cock's crow. He felt good, even though he didn't have a resolution to *the problem*. Today, he felt that he would find the answer.

Finishing his chores early, he gulped down a glass of milk along with one of his mother's famous cinnamon rolls. He was back in the field before his father had completed his own chores.

Frank quizzed his wife, "What's gotten into Randy—I usually have to shake him outta bed."

Sylvia answered intuitively. "I don't know, but I think that he's got girlfriend problems."

Randy climbed onto the tractor and faced the monotonous task of plowing with renewed vigor. He reviewed the problem, over and over, without coming up with the long sought solution. The sun had climbed through its zenith before he stopped to eat lunch. After gulping down his sandwiches, he went immediately back to plowing.

The friable soil was moist and easy to plow. He thought back to years when the rains had been hard and infrequent, the resulting cracks in the earth were wide and deep enough to snap off the front end of a tractor. Randy reflected on one such incident:

A young minister, fresh out of Oral Roberts Theology College, had taken a summer job to supplement his income. He had very little farming experience, but Randy's grandfather, through his wife's urging, agreed to hire the young man.

Randy's grandfather, an avowed agnostic, had a gruff exterior, but inside had a heart of gold. His main character flaw was that he cussed. Although, it was a damnation type of cursing, it had an almost melodious poetic quality—when directed at someone else; still, it was cussing and could offend, if taken literally.

The preacher was cutting alfalfa, which required watching the mower sickle with one eye and watching where the tractor was going with the other eye. A jackrabbit flushed out of hiding by the mower distracted the preacher's attention.

Almost as if fate were waiting for the moment, the front end of the tractor dropped into a huge crack in the field—snapping off the front end. The tractor pitched to an abrupt stop, almost throwing the preacher over the steering wheel. The sound of the severing metal could be heard a mile away.

Randy, a younger cousin, and his grandfather were vaccinating cattle in the corral. His grandfather looked up and saw his tractor angled at a nosedive into the earth. Instantly, he started cussing, "What the hell—damned college boy—doesn't know his ass from a hole in the ground—hasn't got a damn lick of sense—can't see where he is going—got his head up his ass—," as he strode off to confront the preacher.

This was going to be too good to miss, so Randy and his cousin were right in step with the old man. About fifty yards from the tractor their grandfather stopped cussing, but his stride never slackened and his arms kept pumping.

He strode up to the preacher who had dismounted the tractor and was standing, white-faced and trembling. His grandfather shook his finger in the preacher's face and opened his mouth to let fly a barrage of expletives, but no words would come out....

He shook his finger vigorously again; then forced out, "Well, I'll be *darn*, you broke my *dad-gum* tractor!"

Randy and his cousin had been bowled over by this hilarious reversal of rhetoric. They fell down on the newly mown hay, rolling and twisting in uncontrollable laughter.

As Randy's thoughts returned from the incident, he respected his grandfather even more for being sensitive to the minister's religious beliefs and chosen profession.

Hours passed and he felt depleted. His mind was exhausted from the constant searching for an answer. Even though he wasn't devoutly religious, he decided that a prayer couldn't hurt anything. He lowered his head in humble repose and uttered a prayer, "Lord, I pray that you

31

will help Sherrill and I find the answers that seem to be so far from our grasp." After almost ten minutes of prayer, he murmured, "Amen."

Looking up at the heavens to say, "Thanks anyway, Lord," he noticed the contrail of a jet plane streaking high above the cirrus clouds. The revelation of an answer came to him—he could join the U.S. Air Force. He may not be allowed to pilot one of the airplanes, since he didn't have a college education, but he could learn a skill and work toward a college degree. The military even provided health care for servicemen and their dependants. He wouldn't be making much money as an enlisted man, but it would be a lot more than he was making now.

Sherrill wouldn't be able to be with him immediately, but after boot camp, he would have a permanent base. They could rent a small apartment close to the base and live together as a family. They might even get an airbase close to home, so they could visit their families.

He looked back up at the sky, "Thank you, Lord—forgive me for doubting that you would provide an answer."

Randy felt a new exuberance. He squared his shoulders and shook off the weight of the world. He reviewed how he would discuss the decision with Sherrill. As head of the family, it was he who would make the final decision, but he wanted to include her in the process and have her feel that she had taken part in the decisions. Without her tacit approval, his decisions would be hollow and dictatorial. He wanted to share his life with her—not impose a life of master and slave, as he had observed in a few marriages.

He finished plowing early and rushed through his evening chores. His father asked his wife, "What's got into Randy? He's rushing around here like he has a train to catch."

His mother replied intuitively, "I think he's figured out a solution to his girlfriend problem." However, she didn't have an inkling of what the problem really was and had she known, she wouldn't have been so nonplussed in her reply to her husband's question.

Randy called Sherrill on the phone, "Hi, Honey. I've got to see you right away. Could you meet me at the Dog 'n' Suds?" This was a favorite hamburger drive-in frequented by teenagers as an impromptu meeting place. The drive-in had delicious burgers and frosty root beers.

"Oh, Randy, I've been waiting for your call; my chores are already done. I love you! I'll meet you there in half an hour."

Disregarding the possible eavesdroppers on the line, Randy confirmed, "I love you too, Honey." He terminated the call, "See you there in thirty minutes."

As he rushed past his father, he assumingly asked, "Dad—need to use the pickup tonight—OK?"

Without waiting for an answer, he jumped into the shower. Five minutes later, he was putting on his cowboy boots, while hopping toward the door. He stopped just long enough to kiss his mother on the cheek, "I'm gonna grab a burger at the *Suds* with Sherrill. I won't be too late—bye."

Concurrence

Randy pulled into the Dog 'n' Suds drive-in. His dusty farm truck was in stark contrast to the lowered and chopped hotrods and roadsters painted candy apple red and lime green. Guys that were already out of high school owned most of these cars. They had spent their paychecks fixing up these cars and displayed them like a family coat of arms.

Randy had approached his father about getting a hotrod, but his father had pointed out that the cars were built to attract girls—fast cars and fast women. He counseled Randy by rationalizing, "You already have the nicest, most athletic, best looking girl in the county, Son. So, why would you need one of those fancy cars to attract the wrong kind of girl?"

The logic of his father's statement was hard to argue against, but Randy still felt a twinge of envy when one of those cars roared around his farm truck. The girl's hair flaring in the wind and the boy's cocky *Burt Lancaster* grin pasted across his face as he snobbishly eyed the peon's archaic mode of transportation caused Randy's guts to grind at the injustice.

Randy made a couple of circuits around the drive-in, waving and calling to his friends, "Hey, Jimmy," "Yo, Sonny," "Hi, Bobby." They exchanged toots of the horn and friendly banter. The jukebox's outdoor speakers were blaring out The Beatles' "I Want To Hold Your Hand."

Though Randy didn't have much time to socialize with his friends, he was popular with the drive-in crowd. His contribution as high scorer on the basketball team had helped his team advance to the state finals by winning their division. He had been elected team captain for his senior year and the whole town was talking of winning *state* this year.

He backed his pickup into a parking spot normally used by inside diners. Cindy, one of the carhops, skated over to him, "Hey, bloke, what are you doing over here—stuck up, are ya?" Popping her bubble gum, she added, "Too good for your mates, are ya?"

"Nah, I'm waiting for Sherrill—we'll order when she gets here."

She started to skate away and Randy called after her, "Hey, Cindy, I'm thirsty though. Could you bring me a big frosty mug of root beer?"

"Right, lovey," she acknowledged over her shoulder with an exaggerated Cockney accent that she had picked up from watching British television programs.

Randy didn't have to wait long for Sherrill. She pulled up in her parent's Oldsmobile 88 and backed into a parking space next to Randy. Opening the passenger door of the pickup, she slid in across the seat and gave Randy a long passionate kiss, which was acknowledged by catcalls and whistles from their friends that saw her arrive. The young lovers waved back and the din quieted down as the crowd, having made their pointless point, turned back to their own interest and conversation.

Randy knew that as long as he and Sherrill didn't draw attention to themselves then they would now be virtually invisible to the crowd—in sight, out of mind. Isolated, yet observable by others was a safer place to control their passions, while talking about their future. He was filled with such a yearning for Sherrill that he didn't feel that he could control his passion if they were parked on a remote lover's lane.

What he had to say needed to be said under the bright lights of a public place. He needed to see Sherrill's facial expressions and body language, as well as hear her words, to gauge whether she was accepting or rejecting his summation of their situation. Only after her agreement could he share with her his plan of action. He was convinced that his plan needed her unqualified approval for it to work for them.

Sherrill, sensing his serious thoughts, demurely asked, "May I have a sip of your root beer?"

Randy snapped back from his thoughts, "Sure, Hon, drink as much as you like."

"That's okay," she replied softly, "I just want a sip." Taking the mug, she took a swig, and then provocatively ran the tip of her tongue back and forth across the rim of the frosted mug. Curling the sides of her tongue upward and sucking in gently as she curled the tip of her tongue up to block the airflow, her tongue disappeared into her mouth with a little *sip-pop* sound.

Randy grinned at her lustfully, "You little coquette; you tease me knowing that I can't rip off your clothes in front of our friends and make mad passionate love with you. So, why are you teasing me with that little *sip-pop* thing that you do with your tongue?"

Sherrill countered, "Because I too want to make mad passionate love. But mainly, I'm teasing you just to get your attention away from your thoughts. I want for us to relax and be together for a little while, have a burger; then discuss the situation that both of us have been anguishing over for the last couple of days."

Randy mused at her logic. *She is not just another pretty face; she has a thinking mind to go with her beauty.*

35

Cindy skated up with a tray of burgers, fries, onion rings, and two frosted mugs of root beer. "Okay, Duckies," she twanged as she popped her gum, "I brought out your regular order—way out here. I only do this for special people—so there better be a big tip."

Randy paid for the food and threw in an extra buck. "Blimey!" she exclaimed. "I was only expecting a quarter." She popped her gum and skated off waving the bill in the air to get the attention of the other carhops.

Randy and Sherrill ate their mini-feast of burgers. They talked animatedly about events, both mundane and amusing, that had happened over the last couple of days. Their tension and anxiety slowly dissipated into the air. He gazed at her over his mug of root beer, while counting his blessings that fate had put her here on this earth, so that they could share their lives together. He wished that their present circumstances could have been different. However, he had a feeling that even though he was making the conscious decisions, there seemed to be a greater energy source that was contributing to the direction of their lives.

Randy opened the discussion, "Okay Honey, we've had some time to think of what we need to do. What are your thoughts on the situation?"

Collecting her thoughts, Sherrill focused for a moment on the floating ice crystals in her mug of root beer. She looked around to make sure that no one could overhear the conversation, and then summarized:

"I'm pregnant. We're underage and need our parents' permission to get married. We haven't graduated from high school yet. There are no jobs here to support a family. We can't live with your parents or my parents because there are no extra rooms in the houses. Besides, I've discovered something in myself—I scream when we make love. Lastly, our reputations are shot—we live in the midst of gossips that will crucify us and bluenoses that will ostracize us."

Randy was amazed. This was almost verbatim the list that he had formalized after anguishing over the dilemma for two days and nights. Were their parallel thoughts merely coincidence; or the simple logical conclusion of a common situation; or was this an indication that their psychic karmas were in synchronization and they were of one mind?

Sherrill lowered her eyes and reached out to touch Randy's hands. She breathed out a sigh, "I've thought and thought, but I still don't know for sure what we should do."

Picking up the discussion, Randy expanded on his thoughts, "You've pretty much described the situation as I see it too. We've got to secretly get married—Wichita Falls is the logical place. Texas doesn't require a waiting period. Our parents can give permission and be witnesses to the marriage. It won't be a formal wedding—probably a justice of the peace.

"Next, we'll have to quit school. School starts in two weeks, but I need a job and you'll start showing your pregnancy in a couple of months."

Sherrill broke in, "But Randy, you've got the best chance to be the valedictorian of the senior class at graduation—you've got a solid 4.0 GPA. I can't even match that with a 3.8 average because of the Bs that I got in math. Surely, you could still graduate—what's this going to do to your chances of getting into college?"

Randy replied somberly, "I know, it's not what we had planned, but I can take the GED test and get my high school equivalency certificate. I'll need that anyway to get a job."

Sherrill's eyes widened as she realized verbally, "This means that you can't play basketball—everyone is counting on you to take us to the state finals."

"That can't be helped;" he responded regretfully. "I'm disappointed too, but basketball is just a game. We are now involved in the game of life, which is much more than just a game—it's our future existence."

Tears of realization started forming in Sherrill's eyes. Reaching out, he touched her cheek and tenderly whispered, "Don't cry, *ma chèrie*. I've got a plan—more like a divine inspiration—and I think that it's the answer to what we need to do."

He related the events of the day, concluding with the prayer and the contrail of the jet airplane in the stratosphere. "So you see, Honey," he urged, "I think that the air force is the answer to our dilemma. We will have an income—very small at first. But it should give us enough money to rent a small apartment close to the air base and we'll get free medical care for the baby."

Sherrill interjected, "But, that means that we'll have to be apart while you're in boot camp."

"I know," lamented Randy. "I don't know if I can bear being away from you for three months. I just don't see any other way out of our situation."

Continuing, he rationalized for her, "If we were in a big city, we wouldn't be under constant scrutiny. But here in this small town everyone knows us. Though our families and close friends will support us in any decision that we make, there are many people here who would have a field day with our plight. It's not that they're all mean spirited; it's just the way they look at life—anyone that breaks the rules has to suffer the consequences.

"For example, look at what happened to Gary and Barbara last year when she got pregnant halfway through their senior year. They couldn't even show their faces in town and had to quit school and move back to Illinois with her aunt. People here are still gossiping about them. *His* father lost a couple of business clients that had been with him for years and *her* father lost his seat on the town counsel."

Randy stopped short—he realized that he had been giving a speech—he hated it when he did that. Apologizing, "Sorry, Honey, you know by now that I start stumping like a politician when I get on a subject where I have strong feelings."

"No, don't apologize; I feel the same way. I love the people, but I can't stand some of their attitudes. My parents share some of those same attitudes and they're going to flip-out when we tell them that I'm pregnant."

"I know," sighed Randy. "I just hope that my parents are more understanding. I guess that we'll have to tell them tonight. But first— do you fully agree that I should go into the air force?"

Staring into space, Sherrill mulled over the question in her mind, "Of course, I have doubts.... I don't know what the future holds for us and the air force is a big leap into the unknown.

"This is the only life that I have ever known. This is where my family and friends live; where I grew up and everything is familiar to me; where I know what happened yesterday will probably repeat again today, and where I'm pretty sure of what's going to happen tomorrow. People in general don't like change because it takes control of their lives away from them.

Focusing back to Randy, she smiled, "But, Darling, I do want to share my life with you, to be your wife, to be your lover, to bear your children, to be there for you and to know that you are there for me."

Taking Randy's hands into hers, Sherrill looked deeply into his eyes and vowed, "Regardless of the unknown, I love you with all my life and being."

Quoting from the scriptures, she pledged:

"Intreat me not to leave thee, or to return from following after thee: for whither thou goest, I will go; and where thou lodgest, I will lodge: thy people shall be my people, and thy God my God."

Divulgence

Sherrill and Randy arrived at his house just as "The Dons of Eldorado" starring Laura Blevins was ending. His brother and sister would be going to bed right after their favorite TV program. His parents normally spent an hour reading or talking about events of the day before retiring for the night.

As they walked through the kitchen door, he confided to Sherrill, "This should be a good time to break the news to them—if there is such a thing as a good time!"

They entered the living room and his parents looked up in surprise, chiming in unison, "What are you two doing here?"

Randy replied, "Hi, Mom—Dad. Sherrill and I need to talk with you."

His parents turned to look at each other; each seeking in the other whether he or she knew what this was all about. His dad instructed the younger children, "You kids get to bed—tomorrow comes early."

Randy and Sherrill sat down on the divan, facing his parents. His hands were sweaty; he reached over and held Sherrill's hand; it too was sweaty. He swallowed hard, trying to clear the dryness in his mouth and began, "Sherrill and I love each other and want to get married—right away!"

Darn, he thought, *this definitely is the wrong approach; now I've opened it up for debate.* Continuing, while his parents still registered surprise on their faces, he blurted out, "What I mean is that '*We have to get married.*'"

He squeezed Sherrill's hand for support as he saw the reaction register on his parents' faces. His father's face turned a dark purple as he suppressed his rising rage. In a forced level tone, he asked, "What do you mean, 'you have to get married?'" Then, deciding that he already knew the answer to his own question, he stated, "That can only mean one thing—Sherrill is pregnant!"

The lack of denial on their blanched faces prompted him to go into a tirade. "Boy! Your mother and I raised you better than this! You've heard us talk to your sisters about heavy dating—we don't want any 'bastards' in this family."

Randy was stunned by the term and defensively interjected, "He won't be a 'bastard,' we're going to get married." He realized this was the first time he had referred to their baby in a specific gender. He

40

savored the thought and felt sure now that the baby was going to be a boy. It couldn't be just wishful thinking—could it?

He felt reassured because he had experienced this same strange eerie feeling, before. The other times, he had been right about something that actually happened in the future. He was never one hundred percent right, but when he had this special particular feeling, he was almost always right.

He had prepared himself to talk to his parents by reviewing scenarios of what to say and how to say it, but the actual confrontation left him feeling diminished and ineffective. His tongue was not working like it should; it kept sticking to the roof of his mouth. His mouth felt like it was filled with cotton balls and his lips were involuntarily sucking into a tight circle, as if he had just bitten into a green persimmon.

His mother, seeing his predicament, came to his rescue by picking up the conversation, "Randy—child. What your Dad and I mean is 'we've talked about this before with your sisters during family discussions. The discussions were for your benefit as well as theirs. We may not have talked directly about human sexual contact because you've seen baby animals being born all the time. But you know the social stigmas associated with an unwed girl getting pregnant.'"

Seeing Randy's cheeks starting to relax; some color was coming back into Sherrill's face; the red rage was starting to fade from her husband's face, she continued, "Knowing all you know about consequences, your father and I are shocked and disappointed to hear that Sherrill is pregnant. You two assured us that you were going to wait until you were married before you... just like you were raised." There was an unspoken question in his mother's statement.

Randy knew that they wanted to know what was so weak in his character that he had allowed this to happen. He thought; *How do I shout to the world that I'm a man; that I'm going to be a father; that I feel like I'm on top of the world; that the mother of my child is the most beautiful creature in the world—then be expected to say it in apologetic terms?* It was a conundrum that Randy was ill prepared to answer.

He remembered a quote that he had read, "Maturity—not making excuses for the things you do, and not doing the things for which you have to make excuses." Maturity was coming after the fact; he had already done the thing for which he had to make excuses. At this moment, he didn't want to make excuses, but he felt compelled to explain to the two people that raised him why he was in the circumstances that existed. He realized that the guilt that he felt for his own weakness was also guilt being felt by his parents of their perceived failure in how they had raised him.

Squeezing Sherrill's hand for assurance, he proceeded, "Mom—Dad, Sherrill and I love each other and we love you for being my parents. We know that you are disappointed in our news that we're going to be parents at such a young age and without the formality of a marriage certificate. We don't want you to feel that you failed somehow in raising me. You've both been wonderful parents. When I was born, I didn't get to choose my parents, but if I'd had that choice, I would have chosen you—you're the best parents that a boy could have ever hoped for.

"We hope our child grows up feeling the same way toward Sherrill and me. The only way for that to happen is for us to get married and raise our child. We want your blessings and because we're underage—your permission. We can't undo what has happened—we can only go forward."

Frank recognized a dynamic change in his son. Sitting before him was not a self-centered boy of seventeen, but the beginnings of a man with worry creases across his forehead and a set to his chin that projected responsibility and determination. His eyes were neither the eyes of a slacker nor a zealot, but of someone with a message to the world: *This is my family—they're important to me!*

He felt a rising pride for his son that he had never felt before. *Here was his child—not taking his first steps as a child, but his first steps as a man.* His initial anger having subsided, he addressed the young couple, "Okay, you two have obviously given a great amount of thought to your situation. Now what are you going to do about it?"

Sherrill replied first, "Randy will tell you of our plans, but I think we are going to need some help with my parents. I love them dearly, but I'm their oldest child and they have always cited me as an example to my sister and brother. They are not going to be happy, and definitely not understanding of me being pregnant. I think that my Dad's reaction will be to strike out first, then ask questions later."

Randy's father declared, "If we're there with you, I don't think it will get that far. But if there happens to be a fistfight, I'll not intercede. Randy has always been taught to stand up for himself; he has size and toughness to fight his own battles. Besides, we're certainly not going to jump into a Hatfield and McCoy's type feud with Charles Lindstrom."

Randy considered this for a moment and rationalized his concern, *I am younger and more agile than Mr. Lindstrom is, but he has me by 30 to 40 pounds. If I'm going to hold my own in a fight then I can't let him get in close or pin me down.*

Putting this out of his mind, he addressed the immediate situation by relating their plans, "Sherrill and I want to get married as soon as possible; Wichita Falls is probably the logical place. It is far enough away that word of us getting married will be slow trickling back to our town. It will be old news by the time the gossip mill gets hold of the news."

His eyes glanced back and forth to each parent for support. With the most sincere expression that he could conjure up, he stated, "Here's the part that's going to be the hardest for you to accept. We're not going to live here—I'm going to join the United States Air Force.

His mother's whole body jerked with surprise. She looked like she had just been slapped across the face. She started to respond, "But, but..." thinking of all the inferred negatives of this decision.

Randy interrupted, "I've given this a lot of thought—I've even prayed to the Lord for guidance." He related the revelation of his prayer and of receiving an inspired sign of what to do earlier in the day.

His father dubiously asked, "How can you be so sure that this is God's will?"

Randy retorted, "How can you be sure that it's not? I feel there is a greater power guiding my—." He took Sherrill's hand, pulled it up to his lips, gently kissing it, and then pressed it to his heart. Looking into her eyes, he finished, "—Our lives."

His father, with a sigh of resignation, declared, "Okay, Randy, you seem to have already worked this out in your mind. Tell us the rest of your plan?"

Randy, sensing that his parents were finally coming around, proceeded, "We'll get married and live separately for awhile. As much as we hate to, we know it is the only option at this time. Sherrill will begin school and get a deferment from sports on the pretense of having an inflamed appendix.

"My absence can be explained as getting an ROTC prep-school appointment in Texas. You can explain that I wanted to go to the Air Force Academy in Colorado Springs, which is true. You can justify that this would give me a better chance to get an appointment to the academy. This won't fool our close friends, but it will confuse the gossips for a while.

"Later you can explain my being enlisted in the air force as not getting the academy appointment, and that I decided to complete my military obligation before going back to college. "I know this sounds a little devious, but don't you agree that the end seems to justify the means."

A scowl appeared on Frank Ferris' face, but he said nothing.

Randy continued, "I want to take the high school GED test and get a certificate. I feel that I can pass it, since my counselor at school told me that I'm already at the college level in reading, science, and math. This should qualify me for a technical school in the air force—if my aptitude tests are high enough. I know that I won't be able to be a pilot, but there are other career fields in the air force.

"Once I'm out of basic training, Sherrill and I can rent an apartment close to the air base and she will be entitled to prenatal care. Randy, wanting his parents' blessing, closed by exclaiming, "I might even get a base close to home, so we can stay in touch with everyone!"

The negative frown disappeared from his mother's brow, to be replaced with an expression of concern for her older son. He was taking a giant leap from boyhood to manhood.

His father's expression was somber, but in the back of his eyes was a glint of pride. Pride that his son had thought this out on his own. Pride that he had owned up to his responsibility toward his circumstances and was willing to make sacrifices to do the right thing.

Frank rose from his chair and walked over to the young couple. Taking their hands, he helped them stand. He put his big powerful arms around them and gave them a hug. Randy's mother rushed over with tears in her eyes and joined them in a family hug. The happy tears flowed freely for all of them when Randy's father stated, "Sherrill, welcome to our family."

Confrontation

Randy and Sherrill experienced a sense of release and relief. They were over another hurdle, but now the biggest hurdle faced them—Sherrill's parents. Mavis would support whatever decision Charles made. She, of course, had her opinions and wifely influence, but once Charles made a decision, she staunchly supported him.

Frank stepped back from the family hug and appraised the young couple. They obviously were in love and glowed with an aura that seemed to have an energy source of its own. Pride swelled within him, and yet, at the same time he felt sympathy for their plight. They had chosen, or more so, circumstances had chosen for them a rocky road to travel. His son had made choices, and seemed willing to reap or suffer the consequences of those choices.

He looked at Randy, "Well, son, when do you plan to tell Sherrill's parents?"

"I guess we better do it tonight, Dad. It's not too late and they should still be up when we get there."

"Do you still want your mother and me to come along for moral support?"

Randy looked at Sherrill and she nodded, "I think that would be a good idea. My dad can be a grizzly bear when he becomes angry. With you all there to show support, maybe he will be more receptive to the idea of becoming a grandfather."

Randy's father walked over to the phone, picked up the receiver, "I'll call him to let him know to expect company."

Dialing Charles Lindstrom's number, he recognized the voice on the other end of the line, "Hello, Charles, this is Frank Ferris. Sherrill and Randy have been sharing some plans with Sylvia and me at our house. We would like to drive over and to speak with you and Mavis tonight; that is, if you're going to be up for awhile."

"What's this all about, Frank?"

"It's not something that I'd feel comfortable discussing over a public telephone. We can be out to your place in about twenty minutes, then we can sit down and talk parent to parent—will that time be okay for you and Mavis?"

Surprisingly, Charles responded caustically, "By *damn*—I wish that you were here right now," and then he slammed down the phone.

45

Mavis Lindstrom looked up from her crocheting, "Charles—who was that—why you look so irritated?"

"It was Frank Ferris—he's bringing Sherrill and Randy over to our house to discuss something that can't be talked about over the phone."

He glanced up at the clock on the wall, "You know the hour and the suddenness could only mean one thing!" He walked over to confront Mavis, "That bastard son of Frank's had better not gotten our daughter Sherrill pregnant!"

Mavis' mouth gaped open as she reproached him, "Oh, Charles, that's a terrible thing to say—you know that you like Randy. Besides, we've raised Sherrill better than that." She added, "Randy's a good boy and his parents raised him better than that too."

Charles retorted, "Still, they want to talk about something that they can't talk about over the phone—so you draw your own damn conclusions."

He ordered, "You make sure the kids are in bed, I'm going out into the front yard to wait for them."

Charles opened the garden gate and walked out into the parking area illuminated by a mercury-vapor lamp mounted on a thirty-foot pole. He fitfully paced back and forth, working himself up into a blind rage.

His oldest daughter Sherrill was the pride of his life. In some ways, he loved her more than he loved his own wife. When Sherrill was born, she was perfection in miniature and this perfection had not diminished as she grew up. He loved his other children, but no one could replace that special place in his heart and mind reserved for Sherrill.

As the time passed, his pacing and irritation reached a boiling point. Finally, car lights appeared in the night and the cars turned onto the long dusty gravel lane leading to his house. Frank saw Charles pacing back and forth and stopped his car short. Randy and Sherrill, in her car, pulled up next to him. Frank announced through the open window, "Charles looks like he's worked himself up into a lather. I don't want to get into a shouting match through a car window; everyone out; we'll walk the rest of the way." Randy walked around the car to open the door for Sherrill, he felt the hair standing up on the back of his neck and he felt sure that he was in for a fight with her father.

As the family group approached, Charles ignored Frank's extended hand of greeting; his eyes were riveted on Randy. He brushed past Sylvia and Frank; throwing out a warning, "Stay out of this, Frank."

Pointing toward the house, he yelled, "Sherrill—get yourself into the house—*now*!"

Not waiting for her compliance, he glared at Randy and challenged, "Boy—did you get my daughter pregnant?" Randy had hoped that this could have been settled on civilized terms, but now realized that Charles was way past reasoning. His eyes had the look of someone possessed by a demon and his breathing came in gasps of a man who had just run the 100-yard dash. His words had been shouted out as though he was yelling to someone across the yard, instead of someone standing right in front of him.

"**Boy**—I said, **did you get my daughter pregnant**?"

Under duress, Randy tried to reply in a level voice, "Sir, Sherrill and I are going to have a baby and we want your permission to get married."

"Over my rottin' dead body you will!" roared Charles as he rushed the boy.

Randy sidestepped the charge and shoved him off balance as Charles went bulling past. The enraged man regained his balance and pivoted, turning quicker than Randy had expected.

With his hands raised in peace and showing open palms, Randy backed off a couple of steps and tried again to reason with his adversary, "Sir, I really don't want to fight you—we just need to talk this thing out."

Charles bellowed, "You should have thought of that before you knocked up my daughter." He charged again.

Randy flicked out a left jab and caught Charles square on the nose, breaking it.

Charles stopped dead in his tracks; blood started flowing from his nose. He reached up and touched his tortured proboscis. Glaring at Randy, he lowered his hands to his waist and whipped off his broad heavy leather belt.

He grasped the buckle in his hand, whipped the belt vertically, and brought his wrist down quickly, causing the tip to crack like a bullwhip. He shouted with venom in his voice, "You son-of-a-bitch; you've gone and broke my nose. Now I'm going to horsewhip you within an inch of your life. Boy—you better stand still and take it like a man."

Randy tried to soften the challenge, "Sir, there is no reason to fight; but you need to listen and understand me; I will defend myself."

Charles swung the belt in a huge horizontal arc at Randy's midsection. Randy sucked in his stomach, just enough. The tip of the belt took off a button from his shirt without finding flesh.

Sherrill screamed at her father in disbelief, "Daddy, that's not fair; you can't beat him with your belt!"

Sylvia Ferris grabbed Frank's arm and screamed in horror, "Frank, do something—he's going to whip our son with that big belt!"

Frank started forward, and then checked himself. He turned to Sylvia, preventing her from interceding, "Sylvia, I said before that Randy has to fight his own battle—we're not going to start a blood feud with the Lindstroms."

Charles was oblivious to the other people around him. He focused on this interloper that was trying to take his precious Sherrill away from him. He uttered a minced oath under his breath; "There is no man alive that can do this to me." He swung the belt again in a high overhead loop.

Randy quickly sidestepped to his right, but his reflex to maintain his balance caused his left arm to flare out and the belt caught the tip of his elbow—a patch of cloth and skin the size of a half-dollar sloughed away in the turbulence of the heavy belt.

Charles' arm and body were extended forward and downward after swinging the belt, Randy reacted with a right cross to the mouth. A tooth popped out and dangled by its root over Charles' lip. As Charles was trying to regain his balance, Randy tagged him again with a left hook to his right cheekbone. The sliding blow caught Charles' damaged nose, giving it another painful tweak.

The sting in his elbow had brought tears to Randy's eyes; he blinked quickly to clear them. Charles blinked hate-filled tears from his eyes and blindly attacked again with a looping overhand swing with the belt. As Randy pushed off with his right foot to avoid the arc of the belt, his boot slipped in the gravel and the belt made contact across his right shoulder; four inches of the belt whipped down across his back. He heard his shirt rip and felt the skin pop apart as the belt cracked like a bullwhip. His right arm instantly went numb and he found that he couldn't make a fist with his right hand. Charles, seeing that his opponent had been wounded, came back swinging.

The pain of the blow and the sound of the belt against his flesh galvanized Randy's reflexes. He caught the belt in mid-swing with his left hand and stepped back quickly, pulling with all his weight, as he fell. The unexpected move caught Charles off balance and he went catapulting over Randy. He lost his grip on the belt as he extended his arms and skidded on his hands and knees across the graveled yard.

Randy quickly tossed the belt over the garden fence into the darkness. Dirt and gravel had ground into the open wound on his right shoulder. Just as he was regaining his own balance, Charles sprang back to his feet. Sherrill sobbed in frustrated anguish. She could barely watch the two men she loved fighting each other. She had an impulse to jump in between them and try to stop the fight, but thoughts of her baby's safety prevented her from reacting.

Randy's mother was jerking on Frank's arm, imploring, "Do something—Frank—do something! Can't you see that he is trying to maim or kill our son?"

Frank stood immobile, but his eyes were watching every move of the fight. He reasoned to himself, *the fight is pretty even—Charles looks the worst, but Randy's right arm is wounded.* He saw his son trying to get feeling back into his fingers by shaking his arm and trying to make a fist.

Mavis had stepped back into the shadows, wringing her hands together and not knowing what to do. She liked the Ferrises and she loved Randy like a son, but she had never seen her husband so upset. He was normally a loving husband and a caring father. Nevertheless, this man before her had murder and mayhem in his eyes and he was certainly trying to destroy Randy.

Charles and Randy circled each other with fists doubled, each looking for a weakness in the other. Randy still couldn't make a fist with his right hand, but found that if he extended his fingers in a karate chop position, he could then use his right arm for balancing.

Charles, devoid of his belt, swung and jabbed, but Randy's athletic agility allowed him to easily deflect the blows, while flicking out left jabs that inflicted additional damage to Charles' face. Charles shouted, "Stand still, you slippery bastard," and then charged again.

As Randy jumped backward, his boot heel caught on a curled-up garden hose and he fell backward. He mentally prepared for the momentum to take him into a back roll that would bring him back onto his feet. Unexpectedly, a loop in the garden hose caught the toe of his boot at the same moment Charles' full weight stood on the hose.

Anchored by the hose, Randy threw his hands down to cushion the fall. Just before his hands and butt would have hit the ground, Charles slammed him in the temple with a deadly ham-fisted roundhouse punch. The blow brought instant stars to Randy's eyes and his vision

49

blurred. His body jackknifed sideways into a rolling flip. His head slammed with a sickening thud against the curb that separated the graveled yard from the garden fence. Blood flowing from the new wound quickly matted his hair. Shrouds of darkness started to close around him. He lay defenseless in semi-conscious oblivion, expecting the coup de grâce at any moment.

Randy was unaware that when he had flipped sideways, the garden hose had flipped with him. The coils had snared around Charles' ankles, and his momentum slammed him face down onto the gravel, knocking the wind from his lungs. As Charles slid, he heard the cloth of his shirt rip away and felt sharp shards of gravel dig shallow trenches into his flesh. He tried to rise, but his arms had no strength as he lay gagging and gasping for breath.

The women were immobilized in rigid shock. Each wanted to do something to stop the fight, but their arms and legs wouldn't move. Frank had impulses to end the fight, but each time had checked himself from interfering—the final outcome had *not* been decided. "The contestants," he reasoned, "would have to decide when *enough was enough* or a blood feud might go on for years between the two families."

Charles began untangling the garden hose from around his feet. Randy weakly dragged himself to his hands and knees. He felt sick and dizzy and started to vomit, but by sheer will power he forced back down the rising bile in his throat. He sensed the shadow of doom. Charles was a man possessed and would give him no quarter.

From his own sense of fairness and for Sherrill's sake, Randy had fought her father fairly. He didn't want to resort to kicks to the groin or tripping his opponent or hitting him when he was down, but neither did he want to be beaten up in front of his true love. Right now, he felt defenseless. There was no strength left in his arms and legs, and his head throbbed incessantly. He rose slowly and stumbled sideways before regaining his balance.

They circled each other like gladiators as Randy shook his head trying to clear away the cobwebs. He noticed through the haze in his eyes that without a belt the top of Charles' pants had worked down off his belly and were riding low on his hips. Randy knew that he couldn't survive another massive blow to the head; a vague plan emerged from the misty haze drifting through his mind.

Charles, with his arms spread apart to prevent his victim from sidestepping him, rushed in for the kill. At the last possible moment,

Randy dropped to a squat, while curling his fingers into Charles' pants pockets. Randy's descending weight brought the pants down around his adversary's ankles. Charles had a full head of steam in his charge and he went flying through the air. The momentum of his head was in line with the light pole; he jerked to the side at the last moment to avert a direct hit, but the pole caught his left ear tearing it almost off. It hung loosely; retained only by the meat of the earlobe. His left shoulder received the full impact of the charge and he heard his collarbone snap.

His arms went limp and his face scraped against the rough surface as he slithered down the pole; his naked knees ground painfully into the shards of sharp gravel. He rolled mechanically and rested his backside against the light pole. His trousers were down around his ankles. His injured ear hung comically from the side of his head. Blood was still flowing from his broken nose, requiring him to gasp for air through his mouth. Blood seeped from dozens of gravel wounds on his face, arms, hands, and belly. He reached up and yanked out the tooth that was still hanging over his lip. He stared momentarily at the bloody root in the palm of his hand, and then cast it into the dusty gravel.

Randy rose slowly and reeled drunkenly on his legs. Sherrill ran to him, throwing her arms around him. Kissing and hugging him, she sobbed, "Oh, Randy—Darling, are you hurt badly?" She pulled his head down to her chest, cradling it with her arms, and embraced him. She kissed his hair and said over and over again, "Oh, Darling—oh, Darling," as she rocked back and forth.

The scene was too much for Sherrill's father—his daughter had forsaken him. He bellowed out like an anguished broken bloody beast, "Mavis—git me the gun!"

Mavis moaned, "Oh—oh, what should I do?" She just didn't know what to do. She didn't want any more violence, but in all their marriage, she had never disobeyed her husband.

Charles bellowed again, "Mavis—you heard me; git me the gun!"

Mavis was still in a state of vacillation when one of the children, awakened by the ruckus, ran out of the house dragging an old shotgun.

Charles grabbed the gun in one hand and leveled it at Randy's midsection. "Boy, you and your parents have got two minutes to get off my property."

Sherrill turned and stared disbelievingly at her father. She implored him, "Daddy, what are you saying? I love Randy; we're going to be married—don't you understand—don't you even care?"

51

"Get inside the house, Sherrill," Charles growled bitterly. "I don't want you to ever see this boy again; he doesn't even know how to fight fairly."

"Fight fairly—fight fairly! How can you even say that?" Sherrill rejoined her father in disbelief at his hypocritical statement. "You tried to horsewhip him with your belt! He had no choice, but to defend himself!"

Randy rocked on his heels; raising his head he reiterated, "Sir, I told you that I didn't want to fight you, but you left me no choice." He slurred his words as he continued, "I'm really sorry you got hurt, but you just didn't give me any other choice."

The open wound on his back stung as if fire ants were trying to devour him. He had a splitting headache and his pulse throbbed in his temples. With each heartbeat a gong kept going off in his head and he couldn't seem to hear clearly. The voices around him sounded as if they were coming from an echo chamber submerged in water.

Sherrill entreated her father, "Daddy, please—please listen to me. Randy loves me—we love each other and want to be together the rest of our lives."

Charles threatened bitterly, "Girl, if you love this boy then you'll get inside the house—right now. You keep standing there and you'll see him get gut-shot with this here shotgun."

Sherrill looked beseechingly to Randy for advice. His eyes were bothering him and he had difficulty focusing. He felt like he was in a nether world as resignation and pain played across his face. He forced out the words, "Honey, you had better go inside—can't you—can't you see that your father is out of his head—nobody can reason with him now."

Sherrill slowly pulled away from Randy; futility and frustration masked her face. She did not want to leave Randy, but neither did she want to get him killed. If she stayed then that incredibly might happen. She threw her clinched hands up to the side of her head and screamed at her father, "Daddy, I hate you—you're so mean—so unfair—I—I just hate you!"

She turned and ran crying into the house. Throwing herself onto her bed, her body wrenched with deep sobs of futile desolation. Her world was collapsing around her and she was helpless to prevent it.

Randy conjured up the last remaining ounce of strength and courage left in his body. Stepping toward Charles with his hand extended, he offered, "Sir, let me help you up—to get you to a doctor."

Charles cocked backed both hammers on the shotgun and demanded through clinched teeth, "Boy, I told you that you had two minutes to get off my property—a minute and thirty seconds are already up."

Frank, having steeled himself to be a bystander, stepped forward and wrapped his arm around Randy's waist, supporting him. "Come on, son," he coaxed. "Nothing more can be done here, tonight." Embracing his wife with his other arm, he turned and forced them to walk slowly toward the car. Soothingly he encouraged them, "Walk slowly; I don't want Charles to say that he *ran* us off his property."

In the car, Randy fell across the back seat; he could hardly keep his eyes open. Charles pushed his son's legs onto the seat. He leaned over, "Son, do you need a doctor?"

"I think maybe I'm gonna need some stit-chuuues...," as he collapsed into a coma.

With renewed alarm in his voice, Frank urged his wife, "We've got to get going; this looks very serious." He quickly started the car and beseeched, "God help us—I'm afraid Randy has a concussion." He rammed the car into gear and the tires spun, throwing out rooster tails of gravel. The car cut a half donut in the graveled yard then headed down the lane toward the road as they raced directly toward General Hospital.

The dry dusty farm-to-market road was wash-boarded from vortexes created by passing vehicles. The distance between the peaks and valleys of the washboard was directly proportional to the average speed of the passing vehicles. Frank sought a speed where the car would travel the fastest and still had the smoothest ride. They reached the blacktop-paved road in eight minutes and arrived at the hospital twelve minutes later.

Randy was rushed into the Emergency Room and diagnosed by Doctor Brockton, the ER physician, as having a concussion. Brockton inquired of Randy's father, "This boy is in pretty bad shape; what happened?"

Frank Ferris blinked, thought quickly, and then lied, "I bought a new bull at the sale barn and Randy was unloading him from the trailer. The bull's front foot slipped off the ramp and his head came around and caught Randy, throwing him nearly halfway across the yard."

The doctor hummed, "I see—he's lucky that he wasn't gored."

Frank, thinking of the shotgun, exhaled a sigh of relieve, "Yes, we're thankful that he wasn't gored." He breathed a silent prayer, to thank God for Randy still being alive and asked for forgiveness for feeling compelled to deceive the doctor.

The doctor quickly worked on Randy and wondered, "Why would anyone unload a new bull in a graveled yard, instead of a corral? In addition, why is this young man dressed up like he was going out on a date, instead of wearing regular ranch clothes? The wounds just aren't consistent with an encounter with an animal and what causes a red welt across the shoulder and continues as a long split in the skin down across his back?"

He lifted Randy's left arm and examined the wound with the circular patch of skin missing from the elbow. He saw that the skin had just sloughed off. There was no trauma to the underlying tissue—there was hardly any bleeding. He checked Randy's head. The head wound and resulting concussion were about the only injuries that looked like they might have been caused by a bull.

He continued working on the patient, trying to put these questions out of his mind. Though he wasn't a forensic scientist, it seemed fairly obvious that no crime had been committed. He concluded, "Still, the evidence just doesn't quite add up to an encounter with a bull."

As Randy was being transported to intensive care, Charles arrived at the Emergency Room. Blood had clotted on his severed ear and it had a purplish-black hue. He couldn't breathe through his broken nose and air whistled through the space left by his missing tooth. His collarbone was throbbing as if someone had shoved a red-hot poker into his shoulder. Beads of sweat popped through the dried dirt on his face and hands.

A nurse was cleaning his wounds when the ER doctor returned to the room. He recognized the patient, "Hello, Mr. Lindstrom," he whistled through his lips in exclamation, "You look like you just tangled with a bull!"

Charles looked up in surprise and wheezed, "Uh, yeah, I did." His eyes searched around the room for a moment then he ad-libbed, "I bought this new bull at the sale barn and it reared up when I was unloading it in the yard. Damned animal caught me with the side of his horn and danged near killed me! Hell, he broke my nose, knocked out a tooth, feels like my collarbone is broken, and he tossed me around like a sack-o'-potatoes."

Doctor Brockton made a cursory examination of the wounds and noted what looked and smelled like creosote smears on Charles' shoulder and the collar of shirt. "Lucky you weren't gored," the doctor intoned sympathetically.

"Yeah, you're right. Lucky I wasn't gored," Charles nodded.

"I think that we should keep you overnight for observation," the doctor advised.

Charles impatiently interjected, "Enough of this small talk, Doc—patch me up and get me outta here. I've still got a lot of things that I need to take care of tonight."

The doctor cleaned the loose ear with antiseptic and stitched it back on—this had needed immediate attention to reestablish blood flow. Color was already starting to come back into the severed area. He sent Charles off to x-ray to get pictures of the damaged clavicle.

As Charles was being wheeled away to x-ray, Doctor Brockton thought to himself, "There's been a lot of bull thrown around here tonight. No matter how you look at it, it still sounds and smells like—*Just a lotta BULL."*

Flushed and sweating, Randy awoke in a dimly lit room; there was no daylight outside the window of his hospital room. He could just make out the outline of a girl sitting next to his bed. She was asleep with her head and arms supported on the bed; she was holding his hand. He called out hoarsely, "Sherrill—."

His throat was sore and his mouth was dry. An oxygen tube had been inserted into his nasal passage. When he tried to turn slightly, he felt the tug of the EEG monitor connections attached to his head. A tube ran from a bag of saline solution providing liquid through a needle inserted into a vein in his arm. He swallowed several times to moisten his throat and called out again, "Sherrill—."

The sleeping girl aroused and whispered, "It's Leta, Randy—your sister. Sherrill's not here."

Randy collected his thoughts for a moment. He remembered being in a fight with Sherrill's father, but only had obscure memories of a shotgun being pointed at him after his head had hit the curb. "I must have lost the fight," he thought, "because I'm in a hospital bed with tubes sticking out of me."

He moved slightly and felt a twinge in his back. Reaching up he touched a bandage on the side of his head. He had a low throbbing headache, but his thoughts were clear. He flexed his arms and legs; nothing felt broken.

He looked back at his sister, "Thanks for being here, Sis, but I was hoping that you were Sherrill—where is she?"

"Randy—Sherrill is gone," she whispered to him sympathetically.

Randy scrunched his brow and blinked his eyes, trying to comprehend, "Do you mean that she was here and has gone home?"

"No," Leta replied with finality. "I mean that she has gone away; no one knows where she is. I called her sister yesterday and all that she would tell me was that Sherrill was gone. She said that she couldn't talk about it—that her father was hollering, wanting to know who was on the phone—she hung up on me. When I tried calling back later, her mother answered the phone and said that she couldn't talk and hung up.

"Randy, what's going on...? Mama and Daddy won't even tell us what's going on! They said to wait until you regained consciousness then they will tell us what we needed to know. There are all kinds of stories going around that you and Charles Lindstrom were injured by a new bull, but we don't have a new bull—what are they talking about?"

Randy mused stiffly, "I feel like I've been mauled by a bull, but it wasn't a bull. Sis—I've always shared my secrets with you in the past, but now everything is so jumbled up. I want to tell you what happened, but I'd better not if Dad is being tight lipped about this. You'll just have to wait a little while longer 'til I've talked to Dad."

The night nurse entered the room and cheerfully observed, "Oh, we're finally awake!" She changed the saline solution and checked the EEG monitor graph, interpreting, "Judging from the activity recorded, it looks like you two have had a nice little chat during the last five minutes." Addressing Leta, she grimaced sympathetically, "I'm afraid that I'll have to ask you to leave, Honey—Randy needs his rest. The doctor will be in shortly to examine him."

Leta appealed, "Please, can't I just stay here a little longer with Randy?"

"No, I'm sorry," replied the nurse sympathetically. "We usually let family members stay with a patient while they are in a coma; that's so they won't be so disoriented when they wake up. But now that Randy's awake, you should try to get some sleep yourself—you've been here for two nights now."

"Two nights!" exclaimed Randy with wonderment. "How long have I been here?"

"This is your third night," informed the nurse. "Leta has been sitting with you during the night and other members of your family have been here during the day."

"But—Leta was at home the first night. Who was here the first night?"

"Your father...that man paced the floor the entire night. I even offered to fix a bed for him in the next room, but he just wouldn't hear of it. Your mother wanted to stay too, but she had to go home to be with the younger children."

Leta, feeling confident that Randy was in good hands, leaned over and kissed her brother on the cheek. "I'll be back later, Big Brother. Daddy will be here later after the chores are done. Sleep tight—love ya—bye."

Leta left the room and the nurse checked the dressings on Randy's back and head. "Looks like we're healing all right. Now you just close those big blue eyes and get some sleep. If you need anything, just press the buzzer that's clipped to your pillow."

Randy was left in the semi-darkness of the room with his tormented thoughts, *Sherrill—my angel—my life, where are you? What's become of you? Where have you gone? Why have you gone? Are you okay—do you know why I couldn't be there for you?*

Randy awoke with a start from the cold contact of the stethoscope on his chest. He recalled that his sister Leta had been here at the hospital with him and that he had been half-dreaming and remembering the fight with Sherrill's father.

Doctor Fraiser smiled devilishly and sympathized, "It works every time! People ask us if we keep this instrument in the freezer before we examine them. We tell them 'Yep' because they wouldn't believe us otherwise, but it's actually at room temperature and just feels cold.

"You look to be in pretty good condition, young man, considering that you were mauled by a bull." The doctor raised his eyebrows then winked, expecting some explanation.

However, Randy only intoned, "I don't remember much of what happened; maybe someone else can fill you in."

"Strange thing," maintained the doctor in retrospect. "We had another patient in here the very same night. He had tangled with a bull too. Physically though, he was worse off than you—had a broken collarbone, ear almost torn off, broken nose, missing tooth, and lots of bruises and contusions. That guy was madder than a wet hen—

wouldn't be surprised if he didn't go right back home and shoot that bull."

A shudder went up Randy's spine. He was the *bull* that the doctor was referring to and he remembered the cocked shotgun that had been pointed point-blank at him. *Why did things have to go so wrong—when everything could have gone so right?*

The doctor finished checking him over and reviewed the EEG chart, "You're in pretty good shape for the shape you're in. We thought that you might have suffered a subdural hematoma—that's internal bleeding—but it looks like you just had swelling in the brain that put you to sleep for a while until natural healing took its course. The monitor shows normal brain activity and all your vital signs are good. The pupils of your eyes show normal dilation. Your prognosis is good and I'm going to transfer you to a regular hospital room and keep you under observation for awhile."

"When can I leave the hospital? I feel good enough now."

"Not so fast, young man," cautioned Doctor Fraiser, "you've traumatized your brain. It's a delicate organ and we don't want to move too quickly. If things go well during the next 24-48 hours then we can discuss going home. You are going to have to take it easy for the next couple of weeks—no exertion, and no activities that might cause you to injure yourself again. The brain will take as long to heal as the wounds on your head and back."

"Okay," replied Randy, resigning himself to his circumstances. "When do I move to another room?"

The doctor made a few quick entries on the chart at the end of the bed, and then replied, "I'll have a nurse and orderly move you to another room within the hour. For now, my young Mr. Ferris, you just close your eyes and dream of jousting with the bulls."

Doctor Fraiser, with a twinkle in his eye, philosophized, "*Sometimes you win; sometimes, zee bull—he wins.*" He winked, and then rocking up on his toes made a short pirouette and swung his arm in an arc as though he were holding a cape to let the charging bull pass. Clicking his heels together and shouting in a stage whisper, "Olé!" he left the room.

Twenty minutes later Randy was transferred to a private room where he fell into a deep dreamless slumber.

The sound of boot heels pacing on a tiled floor brought Randy from his deep sleep. Hat in hand, his father's sunburnt face contrasted with the white band across the top of his forehead. Worry lines creased across his brow. He paced back and forth several times then became aware that Randy was awake. Rushing over to the bed, he tenderly grasped Randy's forearm in his big work hardened hand. Mist filled his eyes as he uttered, "Randy—Son, thank God you're okay."

He choked back his emotion and continued, "Your mother and I have been worried sick. I've asked myself a thousand times why I let that fight go as far as it did. I've made a terrible mess of things for Sherrill and you. I want you to know that I'm truly sorry that you got hurt."

Randy was confused as he thought, *If anyone has made a mess of things, it's me.* "I don't know what you're saying, Dad. It was I who screwed up. It started when I let my *little* head do the thinking for my *big* head. But, even after admitting that, I can't say that I would have done things differently. Sherrill and I are going to have a baby. Now that it's happened, I can't make it *unhappen*—nor would I even want to."

Randy's eyes grew bright as he confided, "Dad, she's the most wonderful girl, uh, woman in the world—just the thought of her makes me burst with love. It's almost like I need a zipper on my chest to keep me from exploding into a thousand pieces!"

"I know what you mean, Son," empathized his father. "I felt, uh, feel the same way about your mother." Frank passed up the opportunity to discuss further zippers and anatomy. Randy had made his choices—*even in the blind moments of passion there are choices.*

"What I'm really sorry about, Son, is the way I handled Charles. I can only say that I was caught up in the sudden excitement of becoming a grandfather. I never stopped to think how Charles would feel about the situation. I should have never called ahead on the phone. We should have just gone over to his place and popped the news—just as you did to us.

"We gave Charles way too much time to think the worst and build up a head of steam. I realized *that* the moment we pulled up in his front yard, but it was too late to turn back. However, I swear, Son...never in a thousand years did I expect him to pull down on you with a shotgun. So you see, Son, your old man is not infallible. As I get older, my mistakes may become less frequent, but the consequence seems to turn out more serious when I'm wrong."

Randy lay in his hospital bed, listening to his father's words. They hadn't talked together like this before. Most of their prior discussions had been superficial and esoteric. Here, today, they were talking about feelings—with heartfelt words that conveyed real feelings.

With his free arm, Randy reached across his chest and placed his hand on top of his father's hand. He felt the stitches in his back go taunt, but ignored them. "I love you, Dad," he shared with renewed reverence and conviction. He squeezed his father's hand and felt the mutual love and admiration flow between them.

"I love you too, Son," his father stated with pride in his eyes, but with a whisper of melancholy in his heart, for he knew that he was about to lose his son to a bigger broader world. There was little that he could do or even try to do to reshape his son's destiny.

EXILED INNOCENCE

Sherrill was sleeping an exhausted sleep. She had expended all her tears and hadn't woken to her father's ranting and raving to her mother in the kitchen. The sun had just risen and her mother was gently shaking her awake.

"Sherrill, get up;" her mother urged, "We're going on a trip."

Sherrill wearily opened her eyes. Not comprehending her mother's words, she asked, "Where—what trip?"

"Never mind," her mother stated as she hurriedly helped her daughter into her robe. "Your father will tell you; he's waiting in the kitchen."

Charles was sitting at the kitchen table, red eyed and unshaven. His left arm was taped to his side with a compression splint across his broken collarbone. He hadn't slept and the stale coffee tasted sour in his mouth. He hardly acknowledged the two women as they entered the room and sat down at the table. They each poured a cup of coffee and sat waiting—the silence dragged on for long moments.

Not looking at Sherrill, staring only at the oily film formed on the surface of his coffee, Charles finally spoke, "Do you feel the terrible shame and disgrace that you have brought upon this family?" Not pausing for an answer nor expecting one, he continued, "Your mother and I have striven all our lives to teach you and the other children 'right from wrong.'" Pausing, he reiterated, "What you did was *wrong—wrong for you and wrong for this family!*"

Sucking down a mouthful of cold coffee, he sanctimoniously began again, "I'm a college educated man; I'm past-president of the school board, president of the cattlemen's association, and a respected Deacon in the First Baptist Church. I'm looked up to as a decent God-fearing man and a leader in our community. How'm I gonna be able to hold my head up high, now, with all the gossiping going around that my daughter is no better than an alley cat?"

Sherrill sat in stunned silence. She never thought that her father would ever compare her to an *alley cat*. Alley cats weren't selective in choosing a mate and they didn't get married, they just had litters of kittens. She wanted to marry Randy—her only lover, and have little Randys running around the house. How could her father ever make such a negative comparison of their love for each other? She wanted to cry from shame, but there were no more tears. Pleadingly, she looked to her mother for support, but her mother sat staring vacantly at the handle of a spoon leaning against the rim of her coffee cup.

Her father breathed out deeply and resolved, "Now here's what this family's gonna do. We're taking you down to Mexico to get an abortion. Mother has to come along and drive—since I can't with this bum arm."

His words were incredulous to her as she mechanically rose from the table and stood trembling. An adrenaline rush shot through her and fighting passion flashed across her face. Sherrill shook her head and pounded the table with both fists, screaming, "No, Father—no one on this earth, not even you, is going to kill our baby!"

Her father impassively retorted, "You don't have a choice...you're underage and I'm your father...you'll do whatever I tell you to do."

Sherrill flared back at him with fire in her eyes, "Choice—I most certainly have a choice! Father or no father—you can't force me to have an abortion. I'll fight you or anybody else tooth and nail if you try to force me...Randy and I will run away. We'll live together, even if we're too young to get married without your permission."

Her father sneered with disdain, "Randy—hah! Your boyfriend can't help you—he's in the hospital, flat on his back and in a coma. The nurse in x-ray told me so, last night."

Sherrill's hand came up to her mouth as she exclaimed, "Oh, God—Randy—No!" Then she remembered the sickening sound of Randy's head cracking against the curb and how afterward he had stood like a drunken man. She felt nauseated and choked back the bile rising in her throat. She thought of running from the house and driving away in the car, but her father had the keys.

Charles rose from his chair; Sherrill looked around wildly for something to protect herself. Spying a bread knife on the counter, she reached over and grabbed the handle. She waved the blade defiantly— back and forth—shouting, "Don't you come near me! Don't you even think about laying a hand on me!"

Her father froze in his tracks. He had never expected armed rebellion to his authority. He saw the fire in his daughter's eyes and the determined set of her chin. Holding his hand out, imploring, he begged, "Sherrill, for Christ's sake, I'm your father. We don't intend to hurt you—put the knife down."

"No," screamed Sherrill, "I don't trust you anymore. You say that you don't want to hurt *me*—yet, you want to kill my baby. You—you hypocrite—*my baby is me!*"

Realizing that he had lost yet another fight, Charles sagged back down on the edge of his chair. He had alienated his daughter, even farther. The hate fog slowly faded from his eyes, replaced by futile tears of loss, degradation, frustration, and the physical and psychological pain of last night's disastrous fight with Randy.

His good shoulder hunched forward as he cried the slow hot tears of defeat and devastation. Realization of loss pervaded Charles' mind. Last night, he had lost Sherrill to Randy, but his misguided pride had not allowed him to let go of her. He had thought that if he rid her of the 'bastard seed' inside her then he could win her back. Now he saw the futility of his actions, for he had lost her—probably forever.

The ozone of an electric silence permeating the room slowly dissipated from the charged air; replaced by a questioning silence that strained to be broken. Sherrill laid the knife back down on the counter; temerity forced her to remain standing. She loved her father, but at this moment, she felt only pathetic disgust toward him.

Mavis moved around the table to comfort her husband as best she could. She had ambivalent feelings toward Charles and Sherrill. Both were right—both were wrong. She loved them both and almost hated them both for what they had done to themselves and to each other.

When sides had to be taken, she had always sided with Charles, but Sherrill was her eldest and they had bonded so well when Sherrill was born. Her conflicting thoughts were doing a tug-of-war in her mind as she exclaimed out loud, "I just don't know what I'm going to do with the two of you! You're both so much alike…you're both stubborn and prideful, and there's no middle ground between you!"

Her words brought Charles back to reality. Though his tears had brought a feeling of release and relief, there was also the sense of belittlement at having cried in front of the two women. Still too proud to totally accept lose of face and grudgingly wanting his *pound of flesh*, he presented a compromising proposition, "Okay, Sherrill—you win. I won't force you to have an abortion, but you have to agree to some conditions:

1) You must leave the state to have your baby. I'll call my sister in California. She's got a great big house and no children; I'm sure that you can stay there.

2) No one else in this valley is to know that you are pregnant—that means *no one*.

3) You will leave today—I don't want the Ferrises filling your head with any crazy notions.

4) You will complete your schooling through home study; that should keep your mind busy and out of trouble.

5) There'll be no argument on this one. You will under no circumstance try to contact Randy and let him know where you are, until you are of age—next June.

6) Lastly, you must swear all this on the family Bible and sign a written agreement to these conditions.

Sherrill's mind had been analyzing all the options as the conditions were being dictated. She knew how stubborn her father was, since she had inherited his stubborn streak. She also knew that she could negotiate any of the conditions, except for the one about contacting Randy—her father had included that condition out of spite. The other conditions were less important and got her away from an environment, where she now felt like a stranger in her own home.

She felt disheartened, destitute, and very alone. How she ached for Randy's arms to be around her, protecting her, and loving her. She yearned to be there for him at the hospital. What if he really was hurt badly—he needed her and she needed him. Then she thought of their baby and all sense of self-pity and wistful wishing vanished.

"Okay, Father," she acquiesced. "I agree to your conditions and I won't try to contact Randy. However, you must let Mama send me any news of him. I don't know if he's all right now, since you said that he was in a coma, but the not knowing would drive me crazy. You, also, must let him know that I'm okay; not knowing would drive him crazy."

Her father digested her response with skepticism. Getting Sherrill's agreement had been almost too easy. She hadn't argued with him, as she was prone to do. Yet, she had agreed to the conditions and he had never known her to go back on her word. "Agreed," stated her father. Pulling out the family Bible, a solemn pact was sworn.

Sherrill silently sat in the back seat of the car, lost in her thoughts of events during the last twenty-four hours that had turned her life upside down. She was being driven to the bus terminal at the county seat, instead of the bus terminal in her hometown, because no one there would recognize her getting on the Greyhound Bus bound for California.

Her mother was driving and her father was sitting in the passenger seat. Each bump in the road caused pangs of pain to shoot through Charles' injured shoulder, but he suffered in silence. He wasn't happy with himself and was not happy with the rest of the world. He had tried to protect his family, he told himself, and had lost. He had lost the fight and had lost the one person, except for his wife, that he loved the most in the whole world.

Now his daughter hated him—she had rejected him, her father, and had professed her love for another man, her lover, and the father of her baby. He now realized that he had reacted in a blind rage, but the damage was done. As much as he wanted, he couldn't bring himself to say, "*I'm sorry.*"

Mavis gripped the steering wheel so tightly that her knuckles were white. She drove in silence. Her thoughts were jumbled and she tried to make sense of the situation. Her husband was a proud man, but his pride had caused him to alienate their daughter. She loved Sherrill with the passion of a mother and couldn't bear the thought of her leaving. Last night and this morning she had tried to reason with Charles. She had even asserted herself in Sherrill's defense, but Charles was adamant in his resolve for control and revenge.

Her thoughts drifted to poor young Randy, unconscious in the hospital. She had loved Randy like a son, but that was before he had violated her daughter's chastity. Surely, he must have forced himself upon her. Her daughter was raised to wait until the sanctity of marriage before giving herself to a man.

Then she thought of Sherrill coming to the defense of Randy, only leaving his side when she thought that he might actually be killed if she stayed. She had seen the undying love in her daughter's eyes for this boy. Realizing that she had been holding her breath, she let it out in a long deep silent moan of resignation; finally admitting to herself that Sherrill probably been an equal participant in creating a baby.

Sherrill was just numb. Even though the events played through her mind like a movie reel, she no longer felt like reacting. Her father had forced her to swear on a Bible that she wouldn't contact Randy until she was eighteen and of age. The baby would be several months old when that happened and Randy wouldn't be with her when the baby was born. At least she would know if Randy was all right and she was sure that her mother would let him know when the baby was born.

The car stopped at the curb in front of the bus terminal. Sherrill informed her parents, "Since you are exiling me away from my home and my friends, I would appreciate it if you would just drop me off here and not wait until the bus leaves."

Her mother, hurt by the remark, turned in her seat and with a quivering voice pleaded, "Honey, don't be like that; you know that we love you."

Sherrill retorted, "If this is any indication of your love then you certainly have an odd way of showing it." She opened the door and got out.

Charles held up his hand to end the argument, "That's okay, Mavis. My shoulder is hurting and I want to get back home."

Mavis got out of the car with tears in her eyes and opened the trunk. She helped Sherrill place the two heavy suitcases on the sidewalk. She pressed a twenty-dollar bill into her daughter's hand, "I've been saving this; I want you to have it." She put her arms around her daughter, who was standing rigid, and hugged her.

Sherrill resisted for a moment then threw her arms around her mother, and with a lump in her throat, choked out, "I love you too, Mama—I'm going to miss you—Daddy too. Tell Rosemary and Gary bye for me, and I will write them."

She picked up her suitcases and turned to her mother, "Please be sure and let me know how Randy is doing. I can't bear the thought of being away from him, but I won't go back on my word." She leaned forward and kissed her mother on her cheek then turned and lugged the heavy suitcases into the bus terminal.

Mavis, with tears in her eyes, got back into the car. She looked coldly at her husband, who was vacantly staring straight ahead. Without a word, she started the car and drove back home.

Sherrill purchased her bus ticket and waited in stoic loneliness. The bus pulled in twenty minutes later and she found a seat next to a window. Reaching into her handbag she pulled out a book, "The Scarlet Letter," and empathetically read of another woman—and unrequited love.

She arrived thirty-six hours later in the small city of Merced, California. It was evening and her Aunt Vicki met her at the bus station. Sherrill had not seen her aunt for almost ten years and noted that she hadn't changed much; her hair was a little grayer. Recognizing Sherrill from family photos, Aunt Vicki bubbly remarked, "My, my, child; how you have grown. I think that you were only seven or eight the last time that we saw you." Sherrill was numb from the long bus trip, but her spirits rose from the sincere and enthusiastic reception.

Her aunt had met a boy in college and they were married right after graduation. He had joined the air force and did a tour of duty in Korea. Castle Air Force Base was his last assignment before he left the service and they had decided to remain in Merced. He was in real estate and they had never had children.

Hank Casson had held back until his wife and niece had said their hellos, then he walked up and extended his hand to Sherrill and warmly stated, "Welcome to California, Sherrill. We hope that you will enjoy your stay with us."

Sherrill took his hand; placing her left hand over his, "I really appreciate you and Aunt Vicki letting me stay with you until the baby is born. I'll try not to be too much of a bother."

Her aunt jovially pushed Sherrill's arm with her fingertips, "What are you talking about, Child; you're no bother at all. Now let's get you home and get you all settled."

The house was a large California cottage style home, surrounded by oleander bushes. It was located in a newer part of town within walking distance to the new mall. Sherrill had her own large bedroom on the southwest corner of the house. It had a large picture window and the room was bathed in the warm glow of sunshine during the afternoon.

After a week, she and her aunt had become best friends. Her aunt, not having had children, welcomed the company and companionship of her niece. They walked to the mall each day and Sherrill finally had to insist that her aunt not buy her something every time.

"All right," her aunt finally agreed, "but that doesn't mean that I can't buy something for the baby—oh, by the way, how far along are you?

The subject was always on Sherrill's mind and she answered immediately, "Nine weeks."

Aunt Vicki glanced at Sherrill's slim waistline, remarking, "You aren't even showing. What do you think it's going to be—a boy or girl?"

"Randy thinks that it's going to be a boy; but I don't want you buying something for him every day, either." The mention of Randy's name caused Sherrill to stare off into space and think of him. She had received a phone call from her mother that Randy was out of the hospital and recuperating at home. Oh, how she longed to be with him, to feel the strength of his arms around her and the tenderness of his caresses.

Her aunt, waving her hand in front of Sherrill's eyes, brought her back to reality. She was repeating, "Earth to Sherrill, earth to Sherrill."

Sherrill, slightly flustered, apologized, "Oh, I'm sorry."

"Yeah, I know. You were thinking of Randy—you really love him, don't you?"

"Yes," replied Sherrill dreamily, "I really love him and I don't feel like a whole person without him."

Her aunt pursed her lips, "I just don't know why my brutish brother is putting you two through this."

Then to change the subject, she informed, "While you were in the shower this morning, I called up the school administration office, and the secretary told me that they have a special curriculum available for girls in your circumstances.

"It seems that back in the 40s after they built the new Army Air Corp base close to Merced that a large percent of the high school girls became pregnant. Most of the local young men were off fighting the war and the girls fell in love with the GIs that went through training and shipped out overseas.

"The girls didn't even know that they were pregnant when their boyfriends left. This caused a large dropout rate in the district and the school officials decided to set up a special education course for the girls.

"Like most government programs, it never went away. There are not many students enrolled now, but the secretary said that you could come down and register for classes. The course is home study and tests are given every semester at the school. You will receive an accredited diploma after you complete the required courses."

"Oh, thank you, Aunt Vicki," responded Sherrill. "You and Uncle Hank have really been family to me and I love you for it."

Sherrill signed up for the course and set up a regular schedule to study, while making time to walk to the mall each day with Aunt Vicki and helping her with house chores. She had taken her first bank of tests and had gotten an "A" in every one of them.

She was in her twelfth week of pregnancy. Her tummy was starting to get slightly bigger, but she had gotten over her bouts of morning sickness. At her last check-up, she received a clean bill of health from her obstetrician.

Aunt Vicki pampered her and was always involved with any activity that Sherrill had going on. Sherrill laughed and said, "Aunt Vicki, the way that you carry on about the baby, you would think that you're the grandmother."

"Well, it is my baby. I'm the aunt—aren't I?" They laughed as they hugged each other.

New Horizons

Looking back over the last three weeks at his stay in the hospital and subsequent convalescence at home, Randy marveled at how slowly the time had passed. Yet at this moment, it seemed only a flicker in the space-time continuum. He had quickly recuperated from his injuries, but had not returned to school and the word was that he wouldn't—this kicked off a round of speculation. He stayed at home and never went into town, so no one was able to confront him personally.

He had been unaware of the events controlling Sherrill's life during and after his coma in the hospital. He shuddered at the prospect of having to endure a mundane life at home, not knowing where she was. Sherrill's family had stonewalled all efforts to locate her. They would only say that she was "okay." Unable to communicate with her, he had decided to go through with their plan for him to join the air force. He wanted to prepare for the day when she and the baby could be with him.

During that time, the whole valley had been in a frenzy of gossip about the young couple. Some people asked questions out of concern for the two young people whom they really liked. Others were more self-motivated in their concern of not having their star basketball players, since their absence would adversely affect the school's prospect for a winning season.

Still, others inquired just to get the juicy news of the latest gossip. Their own daily lives having plodded along in a dull drab secular mundaneness, they vicariously received pleasure through the events and excitement of other people's lives. All anyone outside the immediate families could find out was that Sherrill had gone to live with an aunt—no one would say where. The secrecy of Sherrill's whereabouts provided many daily hours of juicy speculation.

The two families stopped socializing with each other. This wasn't apparent to the general public, since each family belonged to a different church and social circle. A few close friends sensed the alienation, but they were discrete in their inquiries, and even more discrete in the dissemination of information to gossipy people. The pervading version of the gossip mill was—Sherrill and Randy had broken up. She was broken hearted and had gone to live with an aunt; Randy was likewise broken hearted and decided to join the air force, rather than face the memories of her in their hometown.

This inaccurate story hurt Randy's sense of propriety, since he wanted to shout to the world, "You're all wrong. I love Sherrill—Sherrill loves me." However, the story provided a smoke screen to the real reason why Sherrill left, so he remained silent.

Randy had taken the high school GED test in Lawton and passed. The guidance counselor had been impressed with his test scores and had advised Randy to enter college and continue his education. Under normal circumstances, Randy would have taken his advice, but this avenue did not provide a place for Sherrill and their baby.

He had taken the air force aptitude test and had been surprised that his highest scores were in electronics, since his closest experience to electricity had been changing a light bulb. He could only surmise that his courses in chemistry, math, and physics had allowed him to get the majority of the test questions right.

He was also surprised that his lowest scores were in mechanical aptitude, since he had grown up on a farm and had overhauled complex farm machinery. One mechanical question that he remembered missing was "What is a Yankee Screwdriver?" He looked it up later and found that it was, "A screwdriver with a spring loaded spiral shaft; the blade turned when downward pressure was applied to the heel of the handle." He had even used this type of screwdriver before, but hadn't known the conventional name for the tool. This tidbit of information was incidental, but it stimulated his desire to learn more of the world around him.

The day finally came when he was to leave for the U.S. Air Force Induction Center. Friends and family had come down to the bus depot to see him off. His best friend David hugged him, "We're going to miss you, Pal—you've been like a brother to me and the town's just not going to be the same without you."

Leta put her arms around him, "I'm not going to say goodbye, Big Brother; I'm just going to cry 'cause I can't stand to see you go." She squeezed him as if this would be the last time that she would ever see him again. Turning, she sought out David, where she wept in his arms.

Parents and grandparents, friends and relatives, all filed by to wish him well. The entire senior class played hooky for the morning, just to say their good-byes. Even the principal and coach, along with some of

71

his old teachers showed up making Randy wonder, "Who's watching the school?"

Although, he felt honored and humbled at this outpouring of feeling from people in the community, he, also, felt a twinge of betrayal that he was abandoning them to sort through their year without his contribution to the basketball team. But, then he thought of Sherrill and their baby and pushed all conflicting thoughts from his mind.

In the back of the crowd, he was surprised to see Charles and Mavis Lindstrom. He wondered, "Are they here to say goodbye or just to make sure that I leave?" The Lindstrom's never approached him to say goodbye, so he could only surmise that they were there to see that he was really leaving.

The bus pulled up and the driver exclaimed, "I don't have enough room for all these people!"

Randy handed him his ticket and explained, "There's just me," and took his seat by a window. The bus pulled away and he waved his final goodbye to the crowd; taking a last look at some of the faces that he would never see again.

The bus bumped along the highway. The expansion strips in the roadway set up a rhythmic thu-thump as the bus sped along. After a couple of miles, the monotony of the beat disappeared from his conscious awareness. Randy pulled out a "Field and Stream" magazine and began reading, but the words just blurred together. He read and reread the same paragraph several times, but each time his thoughts strayed back to the family and friends that he had just left and already he was feeling homesick and heartsick. Strangers surrounded him and his future would be with strangers. Oh, how he yearned for the warm embrace of Sherrill. "If only, were it possible, he could hold her in his arms again, then he would wish for nothing else in the world."

Unable to find out where Sherrill was, he reasoned that Charles' plan was to keep Sherrill from contacting him. Spite was not in Randy's character and it was hard for him to see it in other people. He wanted to scream and lash out at the injustice of the situation, but he knew that it would only be an exercise in futility. He remembered a prayer that his grandmother had recited when she was trying to help him understand why things happened the way they did:

"Lord: Help me change the things I can. Accept the things that I can't change. And Lord, give me the wisdom and insight to know the difference."

He found solace in the prayer and decided that this would be a good motto that could apply to most situations in life.

The bus was not an express and stopped in all of the small towns. People got on and people got off. Some were anxious to share events in their lives, while others were preoccupied with their own world and blankly stared out the window as the bus bumped down the road.

A grandmother on her way to New Orleans for the first time found that Randy showed a genuine interest in her stories about her grandchildren. She proceeded to tell him her life's story and was still talking four hours later when they reached Wichita Falls. As they said their good-byes, she promised to write him and send a picture of "Bourbon Street" from New Orleans.

The induction center was only eight blocks from the bus terminal. Randy walked, occasionally pausing to look into a display window. In one of the windows a female mannequin, dressed in a bridal gown, was on display. In Randy's imagination, the face blurred and reformed into Sherrill's face—she was stunningly beautiful and seemingly alive. A lump formed in his throat; he shook his head and brought himself back to reality. Forcing himself to walk away his pace increased to a brisk walk, which he maintained until he reached the induction center.

The female airman at the reception desk wore a blue air force uniform with two stripes. She handed him a clipboard and mechanically instructed, "Fill out the forms in triplicate and return them to me."

After returning the clipboard, he received a billeting pass to the hotel across the street. She informed "Report back to the center at 0800 tomorrow morning. Until then, you are free to do whatever you want to do."

As Randy stood gazing across the street at the hotel, a young man walked up and introduced himself, "Hey, Bud, my name is Bob Dawson from Paducah. I saw you inside and it looks like we're both taking the patriotic plunge together. Say, let's go out tonight and check out the local chicks?"

"No, that's okay," replied Randy, "I think that I'll just catch a movie."

Bob shrugged his shoulders and replied, "Yeah, I know what you mean. I've got a girl back home, too. Say, mind if I buddy up with you and we'll both go to the movies?"

"Sure, why not," agreed Randy as they crossed the street. "I'll clean up and meet you in the lobby at six. Oh, by the way, my name's not Bud—it's Randy Ferris."

"Yeah, I call everybody, Bud, when I first meet them." They registered at the reception desk and waved as they went to their separate rooms.

That night at the movie, they saw "Tom Jones" starring Albert Finney—an eighteenth century tale of a swashbuckling anti-hero, who had been disowned by his wealthy uncle due to his precociousness and promiscuous antics. However, all ended well when the uncle found out that Tom was not the illegitimate son of a lowly maid discharged because of her indiscretion. Instead, he was, in fact, the illegitimate son of the squire's sister. At the end of the movie, Tom became the heir to a large estate and won the love of his lady fair.

Over a burger and fries, Bob and Randy discussed the movie. Randy's summation was, "Yeah, I wish that real life was that simple and only took two hours to live happily ever after."

The next morning at the induction center, forty men showed up. The group was taken into a large room for a physical examination. The doctor instructed them to take their clothes off and stand in a straight line. Randy glanced down the line and realized that Abraham Lincoln must have been wrong, "All men were definitely *not* created equal"—why there was one recruit who had feet at least 16 inches long."

The doctor instructed the recruits to turn around and spread their cheeks. Everyone broke out laughing when one—the doc moaned as he commented, "There always has to be one!"—hooked his fingers into his mouth and pulled, revealing two rows of shiny white teeth. The recruit blushed beet-red when he discovered that he was spreading the wrong cheeks. He then placed his hands on his gluteus maximus, spreading his butt cheeks.

Next, came the drawing of blood. The stifling smell of isopropyl alcohol permeated the room. Randy was waiting his turn behind a black recruit. Up to this point the examination had been routine. Randy watched as the needle entered the black man's arm and the plunger was pulled out to create a vacuum. Bright red blood spurted into the glass cylinder and Randy's world started spinning. A buzzing sound in his ears grew louder and louder as he staggered over to a window and tried to pry it open for fresh air, but the window had been painted shut.

He placed his arms across the windowsill and rested his forehead against them. His legs felt like rubber sticks, and he had the sensation of sinking into a deep black tar pit. The sergeant beside him was screaming into his ear to get back in line, but Randy couldn't move his legs. The sergeant grabbed hold of his arm, half dragging him across the floor, and plopped him down on a cot.

An orderly came over and sneered, "A big guy like you...you're just faking it. I'm going to draw your blood anyway." He sadistically jabbed the needle in five or six times until he found the vein and took his measure of blood.

Randy laid there mortified for a couple of minutes. He didn't understand his reaction, since—just last month—he had been in the hospital and they had drawn blood several times. He remained prostrate for a couple more minutes; his world was starting to get back to normal. Filled with embarrassment and self-abasement, he vowed over and over, "I'll never allow myself to be this weak again." He forced himself to get back on his feet and took his place in line for the remainder of the examination.

A sergeant called thirty-four names and the group filed into a large classroom where they were instructed to fill out more paperwork in triplicate. Another written exam was given and then they were allowed a break for lunch.

After lunch, thirty-two names were called and they filed back into the classroom, where they were administered the "Oath of Allegiance" by a Lieutenant Colonel Mark Hadley from Sheppard AFB. He ended the swearing in ceremony by stating, "Congratulations airmen, you are now official members of the United States Air Force." He saluted the men as a group, but they had been informed not to return the salute, since they were not yet in uniform.

The recruits were then given a language aptitude test. It consisted of listening through a headset to an audiotape of five different languages and repeating back, what they had heard, into a separate microphone. A sergeant monitored a panel of meters as he watched the audio needle fluctuate and could tell by the rhythm of the needle, who to select to listen in on their responses. He flagged one tape to examine more closely, today; the other tapes could wait until tomorrow.

There were only six test stations, so the rest of the recruits sat patiently without talking or read a magazine. This was Randy's first introduction to "Hurry up and wait," which was endemic to all the military services. The afternoon passed slowly until the last person completed the test.

Around 1730, a local caterer delivered pizzas. Bob grabbed a slice and remarked, "Hey, this is great, I'm going to like this man's air force!" Little did he know that this was the first and last catered pizza that they would ever get from "Uncle Sam."

The recruits processed out and were taken by bus to the train station. There they boarded a train at 1930 for their trip to Lackland AFB in San Antonio, Texas. The train trip started out boisterous and animated, but not wild. Bottles of liquor appeared from stashes in their suitcases. Many of the recruits viewed this as freedom from a stifling dead-end life back home; others were getting away from broken relationships; others had joined the air force to keep from being drafted. Each had his reason and all were ready to celebrate.

There were no uniformed escorts aboard the train, but a recruit named Bart Abbott had been placed in charge, since his name was the first one on the list. He had been instructed, "No alcohol," but he was smart enough to see that it would be an impossibility to enforce. So, he just advised the group to keep it to a low rumble and not to bother any of the other passengers. That wasn't a problem, since they had the entire car all to themselves.

Bob Dawson pulled out a pint of peach schnapps, broke the seal, and took a long slug. He passed the bottle, "Here, Randy, help me kill this thing. It'll be a long time before we get another chance."

Randy took the bottle and wiped the rim with the heel of his hand, "Thanks, Bob." He tipped the bottle and took a long swig. The warm liqueur percolated down his throat and the effervescent vapors backed up through his nose, bringing momentary tears to his eyes. He felt the warmth spread throughout his body and stroke his psychic like the caress of a fur mitten.

After one more quaff of the nectar, Randy switched to a soft drink brought by a porter, and allowed one of the recruits to top it off with a shot of Canadian Club. This would be his last hard drink; he knew from old war stories that boot camp was no picnic and he wanted a clear head for tomorrow.

He joined in on the jokes and antics because he wanted to get acquainted with the men that he was going to be with for the many weeks of training ahead of them. He had learned that he could sit back, observe people, and learn about them. However, there was no substitute for getting into the thick of things to allow others to learn about him. Trust and confidence was a two-way street—sports teamwork at school had taught him that valuable lesson.

His buddy, Bob, chose to sit back and be a spectator, while nursing his peach schnapps. Since the supply of liquor was limited, the partying slowly died down. Most of the men were sleeping in their seats by 0100 hours, just an hour before the train arrived at its destination.

On another train, the Lone Star Limited, Casio Brown stared out the window of the coach filled with new enlistees. Cramped between seats, his long lanky legs jutted up toward his chest, adding to the seething anger reflected in his dark eyes sunk back in high cheekbones. A light sheen of perpetual sweat caused his handsome black face to glow with a healthy vitality that radiated his pent-up energy.

They had been riding on this train from New York City for a night and a day and into their second night. The train was due to arrive at San Antonio the following morning. He was already tired of this trip and ready to get to where there was some street action.

He had his own gang in a black section of Brooklyn and would still be there had it not been strongly suggested by a judge for him to join the military services. His other option was to go to jail for six months.

Sure, he had cracked a few heads and shaken down a couple of old ladies out of their rent money, but that was life in Brooklyn. He had spent some time in juvenile hall and several nights in jail, but his old man had always bailed him out. They had an agreement—Casio would complete high school in exchange for his father helping him get out of an occasional scrape.

This had worked out okay, but graduation had been last June and the long hot summer grew boring. He and a couple of members from his gang had stolen a car and had gone for a joy ride. They would have ditched the car after a couple of hours and no one would have been the wiser. That was the plan until Cedric had thrown a beer bottle out of the car, right in front of an NYPD patrol car. They might even have gotten away if it hadn't been for that white bitch with a baby carriage crossing the street. He had swerved to avoid hitting her and the car and his gang had ended up in the East River.

Now he was on his way to play flyboy for four years. Well, he would soon kick some serious ass there too, and show everybody who was top dog. It wouldn't be so bad; the air force provided a place to stay and three square meals a day—they even gave ya some spending money for partying. It had to be better than pacing up and down inside a jail cell for six months.

Boot Camp

Captain O'Brian at Lackland AFB picked up his phone at TAO (training administration office), locally known as the "Green Monster" due to its size, color, and function. Located in the labyrinth sections of this building were the nerve centers of personnel who decided the advanced training and destination for all the air force boot camp trainees. "Captain O'Brian," he announced into the phone.

"Captain O'Brian—Lieutenant Colonel Hadley at Sheppard. I swore in a batch of new recruits today and Sergeant Sellars, down at the induction center, flagged a file on one of the recruits. His name is Randall T. Ferris and it seems that he aced the preliminary language test, a first for the center.

"I've looked over his paperwork and he's an interesting kid. His high school transcript shows a perfect 4.0 GPA. He hasn't graduated from high school, but he passed the high school GED. He's lettered three years in basketball and is 6'2." His aptitude test also shows high scores in both the electronics and general administration categories. I'd like you to run a 'Top Secret' clearance on him, ASAP, and monitor his progress in basic training. If you can, have his DI start him off as 'Barracks Chief.' We want to see if he has potential leadership skills.

"We can do that," confirmed O'Brian.

"I'd really appreciate it if you would keep me posted. Viet Nam is starting to heat up and we've got some slots to fill on Special Forces. I know that he's young, but like I said before, he looks promising."

Captain O'Brian, always the team player, responded, "Yes, sir, Colonel Hadley, I'll start the ball rolling from this end. I'll keep you posted."

O'Brian hung up the phone and thought; *this must be a promising recruit.* Most priority flags for enlisted personnel were handled at the senior NCO level and weren't even reviewed until the 3rd or 4th week of basis training. He pulled out a form, made some entries, and then stamped it "PRIORITY" and checked the box—*weekly progress report.* Then he passed it to his adjutant, who passed it to a senior NCO, who passed it to a junior NCO, who passed it to an airman clerk for implementation.

Randy's train pulled in at 0200 (2:00 AM). The recruits were directed to a blue air force bus for the short ride to Lackland AFB, a large basic training base for all air force enlisted personnel located on the outskirts of San Antonio. The recruits were groggy from the booze and lack of sleep. They were looking forward to crashing on their bunks after they got to their destination.

An ill-mannered ill-tempered Staff Sergeant Stark met the bus at company supply. Stark had been in the air force for six years and had been promoted to E5 only a month ago. He had been in the Air Training Command his entire career and had been stuck at Lackland, except for a two-month TDY assignment during the Cuban missile crisis.

Promotions in his career field had been frozen for years due to the upper enlisted ranks being saturated by men who had been in the Korean War over a decade ago. He was married to a local girl Maria and had two children—Steven, four and Judy, two.

He had found his comfort level in married life, but due to his job he was required to live in the barracks for the first two weeks of each training cycle with the new recruits. An assistant DI (drill instructor) filled in on weekends so that he could spend some time with his family. After the initial two weeks, he and his assistant would rotate being in the barracks with the recruits.

Nevertheless, like any repetitive job, he had grown tired of babysitting a new batch of snot-nosed kids that had been babied and pampered all their lives by their ever-loving mamas. He didn't like being here at 0200 and was further ticked because he had been sent a dispatch from the Green Monster. They were telling him for the first time in his career whom to pick as a barracks chief. They were also requiring him to do extra paperwork just to tell the paper-pushers how one of his *dregs* was doing. *Must be a senator or a congressman's son*, he reasoned.

He entered the bus and had the driver flip on the interior lights. In a raucously booming voice he announced, "All right you listless bunch of maggots, get your lazy asses off this bus and form a straight line. I want it done **'right now!'**" He stepped off the bus and the recruits started scrambling out, hurried along by his pounding the flat of his hand against the side of the bus and shouting a diatribe of demeaning expletives.

A semblance of a line formed and the DI paced up and down the line, ranting in an invective voice, "I've never seen such a sorry bunch of recruits in my life! Where do they dig up so many lowlifes— bumfuck Egypt? I just don't know what this man's air force is coming to. They expect me to make airmen out of you! If I had my choice, I'd

80

load the whole bunch of you back on the bus and send you over to the army; they always need more ground pounding tater-peeling cannon fodder over there."

He stopped short and faced the recruits, "You sheep dips have been drinking—I can smell it. Who's in charge here?"

Abbott tentatively raised his hand halfway and responded, "You are, sir." Everyone laughed at the patronizing comment.

The DI's face turned a deep purple, he screamed, "Oh, I've got a bunch of funny people from the funny farm that thinks everything is funny. Okay, everyone down on the ground and give me twenty-five pushups—now!"

Exhorted on by the group the last one finally completed his twenty-fifth pushup. The DI resumed his pacing back and forth. He stopped again and slowly turned to face the recruits, "OK, now funny people—who was assigned to be in charge of this group of flea-bitten reprobates at your induction center?"

Again, Abbott tentatively raised his arm, "I was sir, Abbott, sir."

The NCO turned on him and shouted, "Abbott—do you see any bars on my shoulder? I'm a sergeant—an NCO," patting the stripes on his arm to make the point. "For you uninitiated imbeciles that means *non-commissioned officer*. Officers are addressed as '*Sir*' because they are deemed '*gentlemen*' by congressional decree and deserve to be shown the respect associated with the rank. You will address me as 'Sergeant' or 'DI' or 'Sergeant Stark.' However, you will add '*Sir*' at the end of your reply because I not only expect your respect; I damn well demand your respect. Now, does anyone have any questions as to that point?"

He paused, daring a response. Having received none, he continued, "Okay, Abbott, you were told 'No drinking' and you violated those instructions—therefore, as of this moment, you are fired. When we get to the barracks, you are on latrine duty until further notice."

The DI continued his pacing back and forth, berating the longhaired hippies, and denouncing the heritage of all the recruits. Again, he stopped suddenly and demanded, "Okay, who's Ferris?"

Randy was caught off guard. He had been following the monologue and thinking that it reminded him of his basketball coach as he lectured the incoming freshmen's basketball team. His coach's style had not been nearly as coarse and vulgar but the intimidation factor had been just as effective. All the freshmen had given the coach their immediate undivided attention.

Responding to the DI, Randy reactively fell back on old war movies that he had seen and stepped forward. He clicked his heels together and came to attention (stomach in, chest out, and chin up). He was taller than the DI and looked him straight in the eye to display confidence, "I am, DI, sir; Randall T. Ferris, DI, sir."

The DI swaggered over. Randy's eyes followed him all the way and he thought, what *the heck did I do to get singled out—how does he know my name*?

"Okay, Airman Randall T. Ferris. When you are at attention, your eyes will be looking straight forward. Only when you are 'at ease' will you be allowed to look around. Is that clear, Airman Randall T. Ferris?"

Randy remembered that the DI had only instructed them to form a straight line and had not called them to attention. However, to remind the DI of this at this particular moment would be a moot point that would appear adversarial and encourage the wrath of the raving man, so he simply responded, "Yes, DI, sir."

The DI had been instructed to make Randall T. Ferris the "Barracks Chief." Normally he wasn't interfered with in making his own choices. He wondered, "What pull does this airman have to be granted this special responsibility?"

He had spotted Randy as the likely person when they filed off the bus, but had to get the preliminary bullshit over with before he addressed this issue. *Randy seemed younger than the rest*, he thought, *but he looked sharp and knew how to respond to a question. Let's see how well he executes orders.*

"Okay, Airman Ferris, a marching unit smaller than a company in the air force is called a 'flight.' You have a flight to oversee; I am making you 'Barracks Chief.' Now let's see you get this flight to the supply room and check out their bedding.

Randy gulped. He was just not prepared for this new responsibility. He came here expecting to learn how to be an airman—now he was suddenly thrown into a position of leadership and expected to do what he had to do before he even knew how to properly do it.

Oh well, he thought, *they can only fire me*—not that he wanted that, so all he could do was try his best. He wished now that he had paid more attention to detail when he had watched the war movies. Jutting out his jaw, he commanded, "Flight—attention!" The men in the line straightened their shoulders a bit but still looked sloppy.

Sergeant Stark jumped into his face and screamed, "You call that a command. If you want their attention, you've got to put your gut into it when you say 'Aten-hup.'"

Randy didn't want to alienate newly formed friendships, but neither did he want to be the target of the DI's wrath. He knew that the flight did not pass even his civilian criteria as a team, so with more rage and force in his voice, he lambasted, "You men want to get to bed tonight; I want to hear your heels click when I call attention. I want to see your heads up; stomachs in, chests out; chins up; shoulders back. Just so that we understand each other when I shout, 'Is that clear?' I want you to shout back, 'Yes, Barracks Chief.'" Randy wasn't sure that was the proper title, but the DI had appointed him barracks chief, so he thought—always *go with the gut feel.*

"Is that clear," he shouted

"Yes, Barracks Chief." The reply was chorused, but mumbled.

Randy cupped his hand to his ear and shouted demandingly, "I can't hear you!"

The flight shouted in unison with more enthusiasm, "Yes, Barracks Chief."

"Okay, let's try this again. At ease." Looking up and down the line a moment for effect, he shouted, "Flight! Aten-hup!"

The men came to attention in a ripple, but it was a big improvement. Randy could see through the open sliding door where two sleepy supply clerks were waiting to hand out bedding. He addressed the flight, "Okay that's better. We're here for training and you have just had your first taste of it.

"Now when I say 'at ease,' I want you to form two lines behind me and get your bedding. Then I want you to get your suitcases and form two lines behind me for the march to the barracks. **Is that clear**!

"Yes, Barracks Chief," they chimed in unison.

Randy reasoned that everyone would scramble over each other unless they were in a long line to begin with, so he shouted the command, "Left face."

Most of the men turned to face their left, but there were a few recruits that faced to their right—staring at the person that should have been behind them. Snickers rippled through the formation and the embarrassed red-faced airmen quickly spun around and faced the correct direction.

Randy said almost softly, "At ease," then walked to the counter and drew his bedding.

Bob Dawson was right behind him while they were removing their suitcases from the bus and remarked, "Ooyoo, I didn't know that I was sharing my schnapps last night with Mister Ogre."

Randy snapped back, "Knock it off—Bob. It's just teamwork; except here they have *designated dictators* instead of team captains."

While the flight was getting their bedding, the DI reviewed in his mind. Airman Ferris was impressive for a new recruit. He obviously hadn't had previous training because his eyes had followed him while he was at attention. He seemed to have good instincts and he was winging it pretty well—maybe the brass did know something after all. He would keep an eye on this recruit and see how much metal he had in him. A barracks chief was just above a drill sergeant in the popularity poll—or maybe it should be called a non-popularity poll.

When the last straggler was in line behind him, Randy called, "Flight, Aten-hup!" He then turned to the DI and announced, "Flight ready to march to the barracks, DI, sir."

The DI said, "Very good, Barracks Chief," and took over command. "Okay, you bunch of misfits; we're going to walk to the barracks instead of marching. Enjoy your walk because tomorrow and all the other tomorrows you are going to learn how to march." He knew that even if they could march, it would be difficult to stay in step while lugging suitcases—the military always wanted to look sharp when they were marching. He commanded, "At a walk, forward harch."

The two supply clerks ran forward with red-ringed flashlights to act as road guards to stop any early morning traffic as the flight went through the roadway intersections. They reached the barracks about 0300 in the morning and the men sloppily threw their sheets on their beds and fell into their bunks. All bunks were doubled except for the barracks chief and the two area chiefs, who would be assigned to oversee the row of bunks on their side of the aisle. The only other perk of being a chief was a placard with their functional title attached to their wall locker.

Randy lay on his back in his bunk for a moment, staring at the ceiling that was dimly illuminated by the exit sign over the doorway. Snoring already echoed off the walls of the open bay barracks, sounding much like a chorus of frogs sitting on the banks of a pond on a warm summer night.

An apparition of Sherrill's face formed in his mind and she spoke softly to him in his semi-dream world, "Darling, I'm okay. I love you."

A feeling of warmth and contentment flowed over him. He rolled over on his right side and fell into a deep sleep.

Sherrill had been with her aunt about six weeks when she received a call from her mother. She was told that Randy was fine and that they had seen him board the bus that would take him to the air force. She had mentioned that half the town was there to say good-bye to him.

Sherrill had to ask her mom to hold on for a minute. She grabbed a Kleenex and wiped the tears from her eyes and blew her nose. She knew that she should have been there to see him off. She was unsure which would have been more heart wrenching—being there and having to say goodbye or not being able to say goodbye because she couldn't be there.

That had been two days ago, now she was suddenly awake and sat up and looked at the clock—it was 1:10 AM, California time, (3:10 AM, Texas Time). She had been dreaming of Randy and the dream was so real that it seemed that he was in the room with her. She spoke out loud to her dream apparition, "Darling, I'm okay. I love you."

A feeling of warmth and contentment flowed over her. She rolled over on her left side and fell into a deep sleep.

Randy felt like he had just closed his eyes when the barracks' lights came back on. His wristwatch showed 4 o'clock—it couldn't be four in the afternoon and they had just gotten to the barracks at 3 o'clock in the morning. He shook his head and muttered ruefully, "This is definitely not going to be a fun day."

The DI was pacing down the center of the barracks and exhorting the men, "Get your lazy asses out of bed, what do you think this is— Boy Scout camp? Everybody gits up—everybody gits shaved— everybody gits showered—everybody takes a shit—everybody's bunk gits made up—roll-call formation in ten minutes!" Having laid down the rules, he walked out the door and waited for assembly.

Randy's bunk was closest to the door labeled "Latrine." He opened the door slowly, just to make sure that the sign indicated the military version of a bathroom. He jumped into the shower for thirty seconds and whipped out his razor. This would be easy—his beard was light. He brushed his teeth and took another minute to handle nature's calling.

He threw his civilian clothes on and let them finish drying his body. "Almost like at home," he noted, when he was in a hurry to go see Sherrill. The thought of her brought a pang to his chest and he forced himself not think of a *what could have been scenario*—it would only distract him and there was not time at the moment to be introspective.

Randy looked at his bunk and wondered what "made up" meant. He knew the military was fastidious, from tales told by his three uncles that had been in the Army—two majors and the youngest had been a corporal. Randy folded the corners of his sheets, as he remembered seeing the nurse in the hospital making beds with 45-degree corners. He remembered asking her why she made them like that and she had replied that it made them look neat. Therefore, he tried to duplicate from memory what he had seen.

Several of the men were already walking out the door, so he quickly looked around that nothing was lying out and followed them out the door. He jogged ahead of them and took his place, heading up the line that was slowly forming. Three stragglers came out after the ten minutes had expired and the DI forced them to do twenty pushups before they fell in line in the formation.

"All right, you poor excuses for civilized humanity," the DI harangued, "Your mamas were probably ashamed of you and sent you here for me to whip into shape. Well, that's what Uncle Sam pays me for and you can be damned sure that you will be in shape when you leave here. I'm going to teach you to be airmen. Here, there is no day and there is no night—just time—my time.

"Some of you will be here for five weeks. If you qualify for a technical school and you haven't screwed up in basic training then you will be sent to another base and complete your advanced basic while going to school.

"The rest of you will get to be with me for an additional month and I can guarantee that you will **not** enjoy the experience. After you have finished basic training, the air force will find a place for you—probably guarding some airplane in the desert or, if you're real lucky, on some blizzard swept flight line on Ice Station Zebra in Alaska, where the temperature never gets higher than your age.

"For those of you that really screw up and are dumber than dirt then you will be washed back two weeks and get to repeat the two weeks again. I can tell you right now that DIs don't like wash backs and you'll be put on every shit detail that comes along." The DI paced up and down the line looking at the airmen and making each one of them feel that he was personally being singled out for further scurrility. He turned on them and shouted, "Is that clear!"

They all shouted in unison, "Yes, DI, sir."

86

The DI thought, *well, that was a decent response.* Then he remembered that Randy, not two hours ago, had exhorted the proper response from them. "OK, now listen up. The barracks is not full yet. There will be an additional twenty-eight people in today from the New York City area. They had farther to travel than you did. We usually get some badasses with a real smart mouth attitude from that area. But, they are going to find out that I'm the worst badass nightmare with an attitude that they've ever seen. So—if you think that I'm going to go easy on any of you reprobates, then you've stopped thinking and started hoping.

"Now I'm going to show you some basic formations. Form four lines—now! They broke ranks and got into four lines facing the sergeant.

The DI shouted, "Right face." Everyone turned to face the right. "Now if you are taller than the man in front of you, tap him on the shoulder and take his position." The lines rippled as the tallest men moved to the head of the lines. "Left face. Now if you are taller than the man in front of you, tap him on the shoulder and take his position." The lines rippled again and the flight was properly sorted according to height.

The DI noted that Randy was the tallest and in his proper position, but there would be more people getting in later, so he explained, "Okay, now you are in proper flight formation. There will be one exception. The barracks chief will always be in the left front position. Are there any questions?

An airman from Waco raised his hand, "Yes, DI, sir. The barracks chief is now in the right front." There were a few snickers in the group.

The DI glared at the airman, "You dumb shit—this is a roll-call formation. After we do a right face, you will be in a marching formation. That places him in the left front."

The Airman from Waco gulped, feeling arbitrarily chastised. He thought, "How in the hell was I supposed to know that we're in a roll-call formation...I just asked a question." He shrank his shoulders down, wishing to disappear.

The DI shouted, "Now, are there any more funny people with funny questions?"

The flight responded, "No, DI, sir."

"Okay, now we're going to dress right. Put your left fist on your left hip. Extend your right arm out and move to your left until you can just touch the shoulder to the person on your right. Then make your final

87

position directly behind the person in front of you and come back to attention." He thought to himself, this is going to be interesting. He shouted, "Dress right!" There was a lot of shuffling, but the slower comprehending recruits looked around and copied what the others were doing. Finally, everyone was spaced properly.

The DI stated, "OK, now I'll demonstrate an about face." He proceeded to place his right toe behind and to the left of his left heel and pivoted, facing his rear. Then he shouted, "About face." Paused. "About face." Paused—repeating the command a half dozen times.

"Okay, now you are going to do some calisthenics. You need space to do this. When I command exercise position, I want you to extend both arms out and space from the barracks chief until your fingers can't touch. "Exercise position, harch. Everyone spaced out. "Right face, harch." Everyone rotated 90 degrees and faced right. "Exercise position, harch." Everyone spread allowing clearance for exercising. "Left face, harch. Okay, you're gonna do twenty-five pushups—on your bellies. "Hup down, hup down," counting twenty-five pushups."

"Okay, we're going to do twenty-five jumping jacks. Hup down, hup down."

"Okay, we're going to do twenty-five sit ups. On your butts—hup down, hup down," counting out the twenty-five.

"Okay, I love pushups and you're going to love them too. On your bellies—hup down, hup down," counting another twenty-five. Even though Randy was in good shape, he worked up a sweat and an appetite.

The DI called attention and announced, "Okay, fall into marching formation. Everyone lined up keying on Airman Ferris. We're going to march to the chow hall. When I command 'column left' the front row will turn left; the rest of you just follow them. When I command 'column right,' the front row will turn right and the rest of you follow them. Now do you dunderheads think that you can do that?"

The flight responded, "Yes, DI, sir."

"When you start marching, always start out with your left foot. If you find that you are out of step then skip-step once and that will put you back in step with the rest of the flight.

"Okay, we need road guards. Right face. You four people in the rear run forward and stop traffic at the intersections. You won't be told where we are going, so if we turn then you will run forward to the next intersection in front of the flight. Is that clear?"

The four airmen shouted, "Yes, DI, sir," feeling good that they wouldn't have to march. *Well, what do you know*, they thought to themselves, *there are some privileges for shorter people after all*. Later they would find that this was a rotating privilege, as all airmen must learn to march.

Since barracks guards had not been posted, Sergeant Stark walked over to the barracks and locked the door. He walked back to the flight; they were still at attention, and looking bedraggled with their long hair and civilian clothes. He looked up and down the ranks and thought to himself, *a pretty sad looking bunch, but I've seen worse*. After a little food in their bellies and haircuts, they would improve—just like the many recruits that he had trained in the past.

He cupped one hand to his mouth to direct the sound and commanded, "Forward—harch." They approached an intersection and he commanded, "Column left—harch." The flight flowed around the corner and they proceeded to the chow hall.

Randy was first in line for breakfast and found a table. Each individual of the flight glanced in his direction then found another table to sit. He smiled when Bob Dawson approached, but even Bob sat at another table. Randy thought to himself, *did I forget to put on my Right Guard deodorant this morning?* He was even tempted to lift his arm and check if he had a peculiar odor, but suppressed the reflex.

A tall lanky airman in fatigues came over with his tray, "You must be the new recruit barracks chief; mind if I sit with you?"

"Not at all; please have a seat." Randy watched him place his tray on the table and pull up a chair. He curiously asked, "How did you know that I'm the new barracks chief?"

"It was obvious; you're still in civvies. You're a nice enough looking guy, but none of your flight will sit with you because you're quote-unquote, 'One of them—not one of us.' But don't let it worry you. Same thing happened to me. I made friends on the trip down to the base, but when I got selected for barracks chief—poof, my friendships evaporated into thin air."

Randy countered, "But I didn't ask to be barracks chief."

"Doesn't matter. You'll find that Uncle Sam 'in his great wisdom' makes the decisions. You either go with the flow, or you drop out. No one is allowed to drop out, so you don't have a choice—just make the best of it until you get out of basic training then I hear that they lighten up—a little."

"Thanks for the advice." Proffering his hand, "I'm Randy Ferris."

"Mark Fairchild, from Detroit. By the way, you've only got three more minutes to eat your chow before your DI comes back through, so you better eat fast."

Only then did Randy realize that he hadn't touched his food yet. With that encouragement, he quickly gulped down what was on his plate and only had a half a cup of coffee drank when the DI reappeared and ordered everyone to put their trays on the conveyer and get into formation.

The flight was marched to the barbershop and run through a similar process of sheep getting sheared. The clippers were set for short and the curly locks fell morosely in clumps to the floor. Huge mirrors on the wall reflected the transition. Heads of hair, the personal pride of the individual, went from crowning glory to a plucked chicken look. Forty-five seconds after sitting down, each airman got out of the chair. Invariably, he reached up and ran his hand across the top of his head, hoping against hope that his eyes were deceiving him.

The flight was then marched to the supply depot and issued clothing. Each received three sets of green fatigues, two sets of dress blues with air force insignia, two pairs of brogans, two pairs of dress shoes, an air force hat, an Ike cap to be worn with an Ike jacket, along with the complement of military under-shorts, tee shirts, handkerchiefs, and black wool socks. All items were stuffed into a duffel bag and lugged back to the barracks.

The DI ordered everyone to gather around Randy's bunk and he took each item and showed the proper military way to roll, fold, and hang the items in the dress cabinet and footlocker. "Now listen up. I want the rest of you to do the same to your personal items. I'll be gone for forty-five minutes to get the rest of the flight to fill the barracks. I'll be back in an hour. I want your bunks made up and I want you in uniform when I get back—there will be an inspection. Anytime that I'm gone and there is no assistant DI present then the barracks chief is in charge. Now get your butts moving." He turned and left the barracks.

Randy felt like crashing on his bunk, but he had learned, "The speed of the leader determines the speed of the crew." So he doggedly unrolled a couple of socks, shorts, and handkerchiefs then rolled them up again to make sure that he could do it without concentrating. Next, he removed the shoestrings and laced them in a different pattern to reflect alternate days of use. The logic behind this was to insure that each person alternated the use of their shoes to keep dampness from fostering fungus infections.

He found a training manual at the barracks guard stand and quickly thumbed through it. His area looked in order, except for his bunk. It did not meet the specifications shown in the book. Someone had penciled in that the blanket should be tight enough to bounce a quarter high enough to be caught in the hand—he assumed quarter meant a coin.

He took a quarter out of his pocket and dropped it on his blanket; it fell and lay there. He ripped the sheets and blanket from his bed and remade it. Then he tried the quarter again and it bounced up and he was able to catch it in midair on the rebound.

Randy glanced at his wristwatch. They had fifteen minutes before the DI was due to return. He put on his fatigues and checked them against the manual...looked okay. He walked down the rows of bunks and mentally noted who was prepared and who was not. He had an urge to help some of the people that were behind, but reconsidered. He figured that they would get their butts chewed by the DI, but that had to happen before he could step in and try coordinating his barracks into a team.

So, he merely walked back to the front of the barracks and clapped his hands together to get their attention, "Ten minutes before inspection—get dressed." There was a lot of scrambling, but everyone was dressed by the time the DI arrived with the additional recruits.

When Randy saw the DI outside the door, he stood beside his locker and bellowed out, "Barracks—Tench-hut!" People got off their bunks and looked around curiously. They saw Randy standing at attention, next to his footlocker. The men closest to him had also spied the DI at the door and were following Randy's lead. The others just looked at each other and shrugged their shoulders; then the barracks' door opened and the DI stepped in. The rest jumped to their spot and came to attention.

The DI walked down to the last man and turned around and came back. He usually picked this time to do some serious ass chewing, but the fact that the recruits were standing at attention, without him calling for attention, impressed him. Everyone was dressed in fatigues. They had their stuff put away—only the bunks were in disarray, except for Randy's and a couple of people around him.

He was sure that Randy had no previous military training, since his eyes had followed him when they got off the bus, but he had better check. "Airman Ferris."

"Yes, DI, sir."

"Where did you learn to make up a bunk?"

"From the manual, DI, sir."

"What manual, Airman Ferris?

"The manual at the barracks guard stand, DI, sir."

The DI swiped his brow with the back of his hand and cynically lamented, "Oh, my God, they sent me someone who can read! What's this man's air force going to do to me next?"

He walked over to the bunk and dropped a quarter and it bounced back into his hand. He walked past Randy and muttered, "I'm impressed."

He continued walking until he came to the airman with the worst made bunk. "Airman, where did you learn to make a bunk?"

"No where, DI, sir."

"That's obvious," the DI growled, "I want you to drop down and give me twenty pushups—now!"

The airman dropped to the floor and pumped out twenty pushups.

The DI announced, "I'm going to show everyone how to make a proper bunk. But first, I'm going to bring in the rest of the recruits. You can stand at ease by your footlockers. I want you to look over the new people as they come in because you're going to be spending a lot of time with them in the next five weeks. 'At ease.'" He walked out the door.

The new recruits were standing at attention in the hot October sun. They had already gotten their haircuts and clothing issue after getting off the bus. Sweat was running down their faces and soaking their civilian clothes. The DI had been in the barracks only twenty minutes, but many were feeling faint from the effects of too much alcohol consumed on the train trip and were rocking back and forth on their heels and toes.

The DI walked up berating them, "What a bunch of pantywaist. You've stood in the sun for a couple of minutes and already look like you're going to pass out. Well, get used to it; you're going to be standing at attention a lot and the temperature in this part of Texas will still be around a hundred degrees for the next month. When I command 'fall out,' I want you to pick up your duffel bag and find yourself a bunk. Then I'm going to show everyone how to make a bunk. Fall out."

The flight filed into the barracks. Casio Brown's eyes locked immediately onto Randy's and an unspoken challenge passed between them. Randy quickly studied each face as they passed by him. This would be his team and he would have to pick out the leaders and followers without knowing their background.

He thought to himself, *I'm glad I had sports in high school; it taught me to evaluate my opponent's strengths and weaknesses, as well as, how to function as a team.* He would be applying this knowledge many times in the months to come.

The DI bellowed, "Listen up. I want you new people to get into your fatigues and pack your civvies in your suitcases or wrap them in brown paper bundles. They will be shipped back to your home—you won't need them here. Do not, I repeat, do not keep any civilian items except for your wristwatch, money, and toiletry items.

"You may keep writing paper, envelopes, and postage stamps because you will write to your mamas tonight and every third night. I will read every letter before it is sent. We don't want you whining to your mamas about how tough you're being treated.

"You will not be allowed to keep knives or weapons of any kind. This is not the army—you don't sleep with your rifle and bayonet. When you need a weapon for training, you will be issued a weapon. When you're done with that weapon, it will be turned back into supply. Your person, your living area, and this entire barracks are subject to inspection twenty-four hours a day and if I find any unauthorized items, you will be summarily dealt with.

"I know you guys from the New York City area have a reputation for being badasses. Well, I want to introduce myself as 'King Kong of the Badasses'—that goes for you Texas cowboys, as well. There will be no fighting, no blanket and brogan parties, and no grab-assing in the shower.

"I had a recruit about four months ago from Philly, who thought he was a real badass. After the doctors set his broken arm and wired together his broken jaw, the AP's stuck him in the brig. He should be getting out around Christmas to start his basic training all over again. So if there are any of you that wants a piece of me—step forward now." He paused, waiting to see if there were any takers—there were none.

"Okay, that's settled. Next, when people exist in close proximately to each other then there are going to be frictions and disagreements. I strongly recommend that you work them out between you.

"If it's minor, then go with the advice of your area chiefs. If they can't resolve it then the barracks chief will have the final say before it gets to me.

"But let me make myself perfectly clear; if I have to deal with it personally, then no one is going to go unscathed. That means the entire barracks will be punished for the misdeeds of the individuals. I've been doing this job for six years and believe me when I say 'I know a hundred nasty things to do that none of you will like'.

"Now on the other hand, your benevolent Uncle Sam is not heartless. We realize that motivation is a better tool than intimidation, but you can't have one without the other. Your main purpose—my main purpose—for being here is training, training, training, and more training.

"You, as an individual and collectively as a barracks, will be graded on your performance. If you are the outstanding barracks in the company for three of the five weeks that you are here then you will all be issued a weekend pass to go into San Antonio—it's your choice." The DI paused to let it sink in. "Incidentally, my last barracks to achieve that privilege was over two years ago."

The DI looked around and pointed, "You four there are on latrine duty." Spinning around he pointed and repeated, "You four on this side of the aisle are on latrine duty," then added, "Abbott, you're going to be a working supervisor in charge of the latrine crew—I want it to be spotless. You'll find the mops and brushes in the maintenance closet— now get with it.

Addressing the new arrivals, "Now get out of your civvies and get into fatigues. I'll take ten of you at a time and show you how to make a bunk and roll your clothes. The rest of you get your civvies packed and make sure that your area is in shape. There will be a walk through inspection in thirty minutes."

The airmen scrambled to accomplish the instructions. Randy packed away the remnants of his civilian life, including Sherrill's framed 8"x 10" picture. He had seen movies of soldiers with pinups on their locker door, but reasoned that they weren't in basic training. He would take the DI at his word—no civilian items. He took one last look at Sherrill's picture, *Darling; your beauty will always be in my thoughts and my love for you will always be in my heart.* With finality he closed the suitcase and put civilian life behind him.

Thirty minutes later Randy made a walk through inspection with the DI. The DI took Airman Richard Long's footlocker and dumped the entire contents on the floor and told him to redo everything. Airman Dave Arnold's clothes were thrown on the floor and he was told to refold them. Airman Jose Gomez's bunk was ripped apart and he was ordered to remake it immediately. The shoelaces were pulled from his brogans and he was ordered to relace them. The list filled up and Randy made entries next to the names on the clipboard. Each violation was called a flickie and each flickie required an immediate ten pushups. Some airman had to do as many as fifty pushups.

Airman Hector Escondido drew the worst of the DI's wrath. He had a picture of his girlfriend taped to his locker door. She was cute and Hector was obviously proud of her. The DI reached up and tore the picture from the door then sarcastically asked, "Airman Escondido, do you speak English?"

"Sí—Yes, DI, sir."

"Well, you don't seem to hear English. Does this picture look like air force issue, Airman Escondido?"

"No, DI, Sir"

"Do you recall me saying not thirty minutes ago that there will be no civilian items in your footlocker or clothes locker?"

"Yes, DI, sir."

"Well, you obviously chose to disobey my instructions. Down on your face—I want fifty pushups—now."

The sergeant flipped the picture into the air and it fluttered around, descending onto Escondido's back as he was doing pushups. Randy glanced at the face in the picture moving up and down with each pushup. The face seemed to alter for a moment as if she were trying to share her boyfriend's exertion to help him complete the pushups.

They walked into Airman Casio Brown's area. His eyes locked again on Randy's with a smoldering glare. Randy thought, *I'm going to have trouble with this guy.*

The DI found a dirty razor with the blade left in the razor and a button on one of the shirts was not buttoned. He ordered him to do twenty pushups. Airman Brown quickly pumped through twenty pushups and stood up. Randy could feel his eyes burning into the back of his neck as the DI and he walked to the next set of bunks.

After the inspection, the DI announced, "Okay, you know your flickies. If they reoccur on future inspections, you will be required to do double the number of pushups.

"We're going to march to the BX where you will purchase a lock for your footlocker. Your footlockers contain your valuables and it will be locked any time that you're away from your area—even when you're in the latrine. Wear the key on the chain with your dog tags.

"You will also purchase a shoe brush, cotton balls, a shine cloth, and black shoe polish. Tonight you will spit shine your shoes until you can see the reflection of the spacing between your teeth. Now everybody fall out and get into formation."

After returning from the BX and putting away the purchased items, the flight marched to the chow hall. Again, none of the flight sat at Randy's table. Mark Fairchild sat down, "Well, how's your morning going?"

"All right I guess, but it seems like we've been here a week already. I've got one guy from New York that I'm going to have a problem with if I don't do something fast."

"What's his problem?" inquired Mark.

"I'm not sure. Our eyes locked when he walked into the barracks and again during the inspection. He seems to resent me and I've never met the guy before today."

"Well," analyzed Mark, "He probably was the 'Big Kahona' where he came from and here you're the top dog. He resents you for not who you are, but what you represent and that's *authority*."

"You're probably right. But I'm not sure that I know the proper way to handle it. I think that he wants to force a fight between us. I could probably whip him, but I don't think that's the answer. The last fight that I was in turned my life upside down."

"Definitely, no fight," Mark cautioned. "You will both wind up in the brig—it doesn't matter who started it. The air force wants people who are team players. If you want to fight then go join the army or marines."

Mark thought a minute, and then suggested, "If you haven't selected area chiefs yet then why don't you make him one of your area chiefs. He can focus his aggressive energies on a group of men instead of focusing all of it on you. It will give him a certain amount of status that his ego needs and maybe he can motivate his side of the barracks to try doing things better than the other side of the barracks. If that doesn't work out, you can always demote him and put someone else in his position."

The idea of promoting and demoting people was not new to Randy. His old basketball coach had used it all the time. Every player wanted to be a starter; no one wanted to sit on the bench. The difference was that basketball coaches made all the decisions, here Randy would be included in the decision making process. He didn't realize until now that he had that option. He assumed that the DI would make the selections and he would have to live with them.

He reached out and shook Mark's hand, "Thanks, Mark; you've been a great help."

Mark smiled, "No sweat; I've been here two weeks and it seems like two months."

Time was growing short and the DI would appear any moment to call formation; they quickly devoured their food. The DI appeared right on schedule and the slow eaters were forced to put their unfinished trays on the garbage conveyer and fall into formation.

Having called the flight to attention, the DI paced up and down in front of the flight. "Okay," he patronized, "you all have got your bellies full and now you probably need a little nap."

He bellowed, "Well, there are no siestas here; you're north of the border and this ain't kindergarten. You're going to learn to march, and then you're going to police the area for cigarette butts and other trash that blows into the area, then you're going to march some more. Before you get done here, you're going to be marching in your sleep.

"All right now, let's wear some fat off your asses. Flight, Tench-hut!' 'Forward harch.' 'Column left harch.'" They marched to the parade ground and marched in the hot sun for three hours. He would have kept them marching except for a red flag that appeared over the Company Headquarters that indicated the heat index had reached one hundred and twenty degrees. He marched them back to the barracks and ordered everyone to spit shine their shoes.

The flight was in the barracks for only fifteen minutes when the DI called Randy into his living quarters, a small room with a bunk and a desk—little else. "At ease, Ferris—close the door."

Randy complied with the request and remained standing. The sergeant pushed back from his desk and crossed his legs, projecting a relaxed posture. Randy forced his shoulders to loosen a little, but he stayed alert. He didn't know this man, but knew enough of him to realize that he might flare up at any moment—like a wild fire, burning those around him.

The DI studied the man in front of him for a moment. Looking into his eyes for character flaws and finding none, he observed his posture and body language, specifically noting his hands and fingers; they were steady. His posture was tense, but not rigid. He looked athletic and his records indicated that he was 6' 2" and weighed 185.

The DI asked casually, "Ferris, why are you here?"

Randy replied truthfully, "To learn a technical skill, DI, sir."

"Relax Ferris, when the door is closed and you are not at attention then we dispense with most of the military formalities. Now, why are you here?"

Randy didn't know where this conversation was going, but he had spoken the truth before and he had learned at an early age that truth needed no excuses. Therefore, he replied the same, "To learn a technical skill."

The DI studied his face and eyes for evasive inflections—there were none. "Okay," continued the DI, "I've looked over your records and you are college material. With a college degree, you would be taking officer's training, instead of enlisted training. Now why did you not go to college instead of enlisting in the air force?"

Sherrill's face flashed across his mind's eye for a split second then Randy replied, "It's personal, Sergeant Stark."

Stark noted the flicker of the eyelids and the slight twist of the right thumb and forefinger. These reactions, instead of negating the response, validated the sincerity of the response. During his career, Stark had interviewed many young recruits. He knew the difference between honesty and bullshit—it even had a smell about it. There was no smell here except from exercise in the hot sun and even that smell had honesty about it.

"Okay," he replied. "I'll respect your privacy as long as it doesn't interfere with your training or the training of the rest of the men in this barracks."

"It will not interfere; I can promise you," replied Randy.

"Well, let's get down to business. We don't have area chiefs appointed; I'm going to let you do the selection. Do you have anyone in mind?"

"Yes, I have. But I want to interview them before I make the selection."

The DI raised one eyebrow and asked, "Why do you think that you need to interview them—area chief is just above a grunt position without additional rank or pay."

"I want to see if they are committed to being a team player. I don't want to be going in one direction and them going in another direction."

The DI replied, "That sounds reasonable. Where do you plan to do the interview?"

"I would appreciate using your quarters; it shouldn't take long."

"Okay, I'm going out for a short time. Who do you want to interview?"

"I would like to interview Airman Casio Brown first and I'd really appreciate it, if you would tell him that I want to speak with him."

"I like your style, kid. You want to have the hammer and you want to start out on an even playing field. OK, I'll send him in."

This was one of the few times that Sergeant Stark had allowed himself to pay a compliment. He normally sought to keep the recruits off-balance with aloofness—there were fewer problems that way. This new barracks chief seemed to be a straight shooter and he would shoot straight with him as long as it continued.

The DI left the room and Randy walked over to the window. He could see the shimmer of heat rising off the parade grounds. The company grounds were free of pedestrian traffic; only a few cars moved slowly along the streets—limited by the 15-mph speed limit signs.

The door opened and Airman Brown with a surly look, demanded, "Yeah, what-da you want, white-boy?"

Randy turned away from the window and stated politely, "Please close the door." He studied Brown for a moment, noting that there was a smoldering rage in his eyes. He was taller by a full inch, but thinner—probably topped 165. If there were to be a fight between them, Randy felt confident that he could take him—as long as the fight was fair, but fights weren't always fair. He resisted letting his mind lock onto the fight with Sherrill's father.

Randy thought of optional ways to start the conversation and settled on the direct approach that laid the cards on the table. "Brown, I want to know what your problem is."

Casio's eyes flashed. He glared at Randy and rabidly spouted, "I ain't got no problems. You're the one with the problems, 'cause I'm going to kick your white ass all over this air force base." He caught himself and glanced around furtively, "What'd you been doing in here anyway—whining to the DI about me?"

Randy saw that Brown's fists were clinched and that he had shifted his balance to better initiate an attack or defend himself. Randy's posture remained neutral and he didn't reply immediately. He could see that Casio's reaction was waiting on his response to the accusation.

"No," replied Randy evenly, "We were only talking about me." A slight tension went out of Casio's stance, but he kept his fist clinched. Randy continued, "If you want to fight, well, we can fight; then we can become friends in the brig together, while the rest of the barracks finishes their training and ships out of this hellhole.

He paused just long enough for the words to sink in, but not long enough for a reply. "But first I want to warn you that the last man that I fought is recovering from a broken collarbone, talks funny through missing teeth, and has an ear that had to be sewed back on."

Randy paused again, reflecting that he neglected to say that the light pole in Charles Lindstrom's yard had done the majority of the damage. He saw Casio's eyes shift from outrage to indecision. Then he proffered, "What I'd like to be is your friend, but if we can't be friends then I would like your support."

"I ain't gonna be no friend to no whitey, but what do you mean by support?" Casio asked cautiously.

Randy measured the situation and stated, "I'm barracks chief. I didn't ask for the position, but I've got it anyway. We both have to get through basic training and we can do it the harder way...or we can just do it the hard way. From what I've seen, there is no easy way. The harder way is for us to be adversaries. The hard way is for us to work together as a team going in the same direction. The bottom line is: 'I want you as my area chief on the right side of the barracks.'"

Casio was suspicious of the offer. He had never gotten an even break from a whitey. More truthfully, he had always insulated himself by having black people around him, so whitey never got a chance to ever give him an even break. He asked, "Why you wanna do this for me; what's in it for you?"

Randy thought for a moment. *I can't bullshit this guy; he's street smart and would see through me in a second. I can't tell him that I like him because I don't. I'm not predisposed to prejudice, but I don't like this guy's attitude. However, he does have strengths. I watched him march and he catches on fast.*

He looked Casio straight in the eyes, "I'll level with you. I want to win the weekend pass for the best barracks in the company. I want to win it for four weeks in a row, not just three out of the five weeks. We won't have a chance the first week because there are too many things that we don't know yet, but there is no reason why we can't win it the next four weeks.

"We've got to go through the training and put up with the bullshit anyway, so why not get recognition for our efforts?" Randy paused for a moment then added, "I think that you're one of the key people that can help achieve that goal."

Casio let his gaze drop away from Randy. *This guy wasn't bullshitting him—he could detect bullshit a mile away. So he is barracks chief and I would be under him, but I would have my own group and that wouldn't be too bad. Besides, this guy would have to be directly under the thumb of the DI and this would take some heat off me.*

He glanced back at Randy and consented, "OK, but I want all the guys from New York on my side of the barracks."

Randy was afraid that this would be his demand, but he couldn't let that happen. "No can do," he asserted. "This is not the streets of New York City. Here, we not only live on the same street, but in the same house. I don't want this to turn into '*Us and Them,*' I want it to be '*We,*' as a team. We both need to learn how to work with people from different environments and different cultures because we still have another four years to go after this training."

Casio was surprised. He figured that whitey would cave-in to his demands, but here was a whitey that knew where he wanted to go and he was speaking to him as an equal. "OK," he replied, "but I'm not going to take any shit off you."

Randy replied, "I don't generate shit; I just pass it down from the DI. If I get on your case, it's because you aren't putting your maximum effort into the team. I think that you're smart enough to tell the difference." He extended his hand and they shook hands as an understanding passed between them—it was a beginning. He dismissed him by saying, "Okay, move your gear up to the area chief's bunk."

Randy walked into the latrine to relieve himself. Airman Abbott was diligently scrubbing down the walls of the shower. He washed his hands and called, "Abbott, come into the DI's quarters, I've got another job for you."

Abbott dropped the brush into the pail and followed Randy. He thought to himself, *what does he mean another job?*

After they walked into the room, he motioned to the DI's chair, "Have a seat; you look a little dragged out."

Abbott replied, "Yeah, we've been here almost a day, and I feel like we've been up for a week."

Randy sympathized, "I know what you mean. I think we all wished that we had slept last night on the train, instead of partying."

He continued, "Abbott, I liked what you did for the guys last night. You were put in charge of a bunch of civilians, but you had the good

101

sense to tell us to 'just keep it to a dull roar.' You paid the dues for all of us when we got here and you haven't complained.

"The DI put you on permanent latrine duty, but I'm going to offer you a different job—maybe even tougher." Then he went on and explained the goals that he had shared with Casio.

Abbott listened intently then asked. "I'm all for it, but where do I come in?"

Randy replied, "I want you to be area chief on my side of the barracks—Casio Brown from New York has the other side."

Abbott thought for a minute, "Does that mean that I'll still have to be on latrine duty?"

"No, it means just the opposite. You'll be in charge of the men in your area.

"I'm calling Casio's area 'A' flight and your area as 'B' flight. I don't know if that term is used in the air force for barracks' areas, but we will use it until we learn differently.

"We are going to have to generate some friendly competition inside the barracks to win the weekend pass. I want you and Casio to set it up so that the men in one set of bunks inspect the bunks next to them. I want the flickies caught before the DI or someone else inspects them.

"We're going to practice marching more than the other barracks and we're going to do everything better than the other barracks. You're going to get some grumbling, but I think that we can do it. Now, are you in or out?"

Abbott grabbed Randy's hand and shook it hard, "I'm in! I would do just about anything to get out of the latrine duty, but I also like your idea of being the best—since we have to do the job anyway."

Randy walked out with Abbott, "Get your gear, and move it up to the area chief's bunk."

He then entered the latrine, picked up the bucket and brush, and finished cleaning the shower walls. Several people used the latrine during that time and noted that the barracks chief was pulling latrine duty.

Casio appeared at the door, "Hey, I hope you don't expect me to do that too."

Randy paused for a moment and stated, "No, I'm just finishing up the job for another guy that now has a more important job—the same as yours.

"I asked Abbott to pair the bunks and have the men do a pre-inspection on their neighbor, and then you area chiefs do a random

102

inspection to see that they are doing it right. Now get back to your area and make sure that it's in shape."

With that said, Casio's head disappeared from the doorway and Randy completed his task.

He had just stowed the cleaning items and was doing a final quick inspection when the DI walked into the latrine. He looked around and was visibly impressed. "Where's Abbott, he's supposed to be on latrine duty."

"Not anymore," informed Randy. "He's now got a more important job."

"What do you mean?" Slight confusion showed on the DI's face.

"You put him on latrine duty until further notice, and he has paid his dues. He's learned his lesson and I just gave him notice. He's now area chief for the left side of the barracks—Airman Brown's area chief for the other side."

The DI started to raise his finger to stress a point that he was going to state, but Randy quickly interjected, "Abbott's solid, I need him to balance out Brown's sometimes volatile personality. Brown's a mover shaker and he'll get things done, but he needs an anchor—Abbott's the anchor."

The DI still had his finger raised and he shook it at Randy and asked half-seriously, "Are you sure that you've never had military training before?"

"No," replied Randy, shaking his head. "I learned about teamwork through three years of high school varsity basketball. Personalities among a group of men are pretty much the same, just the faces and uniforms change." Then he added, "Coach Martin was a great basketball coach."

That evening at the mess hall, Abbott and Brown came to Randy's table to sit with him. "I appreciate your offer of company while I eat, but I want you two to be the eyes and ears of the team. Sit with people in your flight and find out their strengths and weaknesses. We'll use the strengths to correct the weaknesses—'a chain is only as strong as its weakest link.'"

"No problem, BC," they responded; then found tables with their respective flights.

"Hey, Casio," Julius asked as Casio set his tray down on their table. What do ya think of the BC?"

Casio replied matter-of-factly, "He's good," then added with a little awe in his voice, "I ain't never seen no whitey like him before!" Their conversation migrated from training, to home, to girls, and back to training.

Abbott was asked similar questions when he sat with a group of airmen in his flight. He responded, "He's got a good head on his shoulders and he's focused on our being the best of the boots. Besides, you're lucky—you could have gotten me as BC."

"What'd ya mean, lucky," retorted Bob. "We got you anyway—as area chief." Everyone at the table laughed. Then their conversation migrated from training, to home, to girls, and back to training.

Mark Fairchild dropped by Randy's table, "Hey, Pardner, how's it going?"

"Much better," replied Randy. "Things are starting to come together. I think that we may even survive the next five weeks.

"Oh, and thanks for your suggestion. Casio is now an area chief and I think he'll do well because now he has some direction to vent his aggressive energy. He'll try to do better than Abbott, which will instill some internal competition among all the men in the barracks and should cause them to all try harder to do their best.

Focus

That evening, the DI made a quick walk-through inspection. He was impressed with the results. This was still the first day of basic and he had already seen a tremendous improvement from this morning. Prior groups had required three or four days to get to this level.

He gave Randy an open list for latrine duty and barracks guard. The barracks would have a guard posted on duty twenty-four hours a day, on four-hour shifts. Their function would be fire and security inspectors and to prevent unidentified personnel from entering the barracks—this included the "General of the base" if he didn't show proper identification.

Randy called his area chiefs together and they helped him handpick the guards. *The barracks guards were very important,* he reasoned because *they would represent the barracks during a surprise inspection while the rest of the flight was training.* He selected six guards for permanent duty and two alternates to fill in if anyone had an appointment that conflicted with his guard duty time slot.

He had a functional duties manual for each guard and would ask them to memorize it. He gave the two area chiefs a manual and asked them to become intimately familiar with it and then randomly check the guards to make sure that they knew the procedure for any contingency without having to look in the book; he kept one for himself.

He passed the latrine duty list to the area chiefs, "I want you area chiefs to rotate the duty between 'A' & 'B' flights and rotate the men used each time. The duty period will be for one 24-hour day or passing inspection—which ever comes first. More than two flickies found and I want the same team to repeat latrine duty until it passes.

"I prefer that latrine duty not be used as punishment for other flickies found in the living area. Instead, have them memorize a chapter in the barracks guard manual and test them. This should improve their knowledge of military protocol and also their morale, since they won't be shoved into the shitter as many of the other barracks do. If they don't pass the oral test on the chapter then you can use other means, within reason, to motivate them.

"Now get with your men and implement the scheduling. Make a couple of spot checks to see that your area will pass inspection. Oh, by the way, the barracks guards are off the latrine roster—it's their reward for pulling guard duty. Now are there any questions?"

"No, BC," Casio and Abbott chorused.

"Okay, get with it, the DI should be back from company headquarters soon."

The area chiefs left to carry out their instructions. Randy mused, *BC, instead of barracks chief, I wonder if they secretly have a different meaning for the initials?* He couldn't think of any, so he put it out of his mind and called the barracks guards together for a short meeting. He gave them the manuals and explained their duties.

The DI returned from headquarters and noted that everyone was busy doing something. He made another quick walk-through inspection and his sharp eyes didn't detect any blatant infractions.

"Okay, everybody listen up. You've had a long day and lights out at twenty-one hundred hours; it's now twenty hundred hours. I want you to write your mother, and then you can hit the sack when you're done. I'm going to tell you exactly what to write, so grab your paper and pencil."

Everyone grabbed their stationery and was ready in thirty seconds.

"Okay, write 'Dear Mom.' He paused, and then added, "Everyone with me so far?"

He heard a chorus, "Yes, DI, sir." He noticed a few rolled eyes at the jibe, but chose to ignore them.

"Now write, 'Arrived at my training base okay. I've got a bunk and eat three square meals a day. We do a lot of marching. I'll write you later. Love,' now sign it. That's it, nothing else. Put the letter in an addressed envelope, but don't seal it. Now bring your letters to me; I will read each one of them and if there is anything added then you personally will hear from me."

The airmen quickly complied and then crashed in their bunks. There were snores coming from some of them before the last letter was handed to the DI.

Randy was super tired from little sleep and the long day's activities, but he forced himself to open the guard manual and read until lights out.

The next three days were spent marching. Randy quickly learned that one of the most difficult maneuvers and the most obvious when someone screwed up was 'Double to the rear to the rear—harch maneuver.' This command reversed the direction of the flight; they would take one step then reversed direction again, and continued in the direction that they were going before the command. When it was

106

executed for the first time, half the men banged into the other half and there was mass confusion. Randy knew that if the flight got this maneuver down pat then any of the other marching maneuvers would become easier.

The DI had to go to an appointment and left Randy in charge of the flight. Randy gave the men a five-minute break, and then had them reform as separate flights, A & B. He had Casio and Abbott drill their flights until the maneuver 'double to the rear to the rear—harch' was smooth.

Then he combined the flights and drilled them until their movements were as one body. He had Casio and Abbott take turns commanding the marching maneuvers so that he could get some practice marching in formation and the men would become accustomed to the voice and cadence of different commanders.

The DI came back after two hours and Randy had just given the flight a smoke break. The DI came up ranting as he flashed a jaundiced glare at Randy and addressed the flight, "What are you hammerheads doing standing around with your finger up your butts. You're supposed to be learning how to march. 'Fall-in!'"

To make his point, he started them marching, and then gave the command 'Double to the rear to the rear—harch' five times in a row. The whole flight executed it flawlessly. The DI stood staring in disbelief; then uttered "Oh!"

He halted the flight and ordered, "Barracks chief, front and center."

Randy fell out and came to attention in front of the DI. The DI remarked, "Damn good job. Take 'em to chow." He threw a—highly unusual—quick salute to Randy and the flight then turned and left the parade grounds. Stark's destination was the 'Green Monster' to file his special report on his new barracks chief.

Randy called the flight to order and marched them off to chow. Their marching had a new snap of pride, for each man realized that the DI's salute had been a special stamp of approval of their progress. At the chow hall, the men sat with their usual group, but as each man passed Randy's table, he caught their eye, and they smiled back—he knew then that he had received tacit approval as their team leader.

Their enthusiasm carried over to the barracks that evening. Without being told, each man got his area in top shape. The DI returned and made an inspection—there were no flickies handed out. He returned to his room and made an entry in his training log, "This is the first time in six years of basic training that a 1st week barracks has passed inspection without demerits."

He walked back into the open bay living area and announced, "Okay, listen up. You will write your mothers tonight, but I am not going to read your letters. You can also write to your wives or sweethearts. The only thing that I ask is that there are no XXX's and OOO's or S.W.A.K's on the envelope, those will be considered as flickies." He didn't share with them that this inane policy was the company adjutant's pet peeve, not his own.

Each recruit wrote his letters and was actually positive in the evaluation of their training, just as the DI trusted that they would. He had sensed their high morale tonight and knew he wouldn't be receiving letters from moms disparaging the treatment of their little boys and questioning his Stark's heritage and ancestry—at least not from the letters written tonight.

The next morning, the flight was issued carbines from company supply. They were drilled in marching with a rifle, and then marched to the firing range. The firing range instructor went over operational rules and safety. He further instructed them on the function of loading and firing an M-1, 30-caliber carbine.

The first group to fire included Randy. He had grown up with guns and had lit kitchen matches with a 22-caliber automatic at twenty paces without breaking the match. He had also practiced shooting hedge apples out of trees by shooting their stems. He felt confident that he could do as well with a carbine.

The instructor had them lay in a prone position then commenced, "Lock and load, ready on the left, ready on the right, ready on the firing line—fire!" Randy was in the act of squeezing the trigger on his gun when his senses were jolted by the thunderous cacophony of thirty high-powered rifles going off at the same time. He jerked the trigger and totally missed the entire target.

Slightly unnerved by the thunderclap of sound, he forced himself to settle down and squeezed off seven more shots through the center of the bull's-eye. The center of the target was so torn up that the scorer assumed that he had put all eight bullets through the center of the target and gave him a perfect score. He repeated the performance in the kneeling and sitting position. His pattern was spread out slightly in the standing position, but all the holes were inside the bull's-eye.

After the scores were tallied, it was obvious that men who had grown up in the southwest were much better shots than the group from New York. There was a lot of joshing and bantering between the groups. Casio remarked, "You cowboys may be better with a gun, but us New Yorkers are much better with a knife."

Roland Glines from Hereford, Texas retorted with a John Wayne drawl, "Yeah, it would be just like a geek from New York City to show up at a gunfight with just a knife." The whole flight burst out laughing at the witticism. Casio laughed with them because he knew that he had just been zinged and it was a good one.

Randy approached the DI, "Are firing range scores included in the barracks' performance evaluation?"

"No," replied the DI, "but they are included in the airman's personnel record. Why do you ask?"

"I haven't seen anything that shows the criteria used to rate the performance of the barracks," responded Randy.

"No problem, I'll get you a copy when we get back to the barracks."

That evening Mark Fairchild sat down at Randy's table, "Well, how did it go at the firing range today?"

Grinning, Randy replied, "Pretty good, I received an 'expert' rating, but on the first shot, I totally missed the target."

"Don't be too smug," cautioned Mark. "Sharpshooters usually wind up guarding airplanes—for obvious reasons."

This revelation jolted Randy. He wanted to learn a trade, not spend four years guarding airplanes, even though it may be an important job as far as the air force was concerned.

"I see what you mean," he agreed. The next time, I think I'll spread my pattern out a little. Thanks for the insight, Mark; you've been a great help. Being that you're two weeks ahead of our barracks in training, what's coming up next in the training schedule?"

"Well," replied Mark, "you'll be doing a lot of marching and part of your barracks will be assigned KP while the rest of you are taking tests at the 'Green Monster.' Then, there will be more marching and the other half of your barracks will be on KP, while the others take tests, and then there will be more marching. Then you will go back to the firing range. Then there is the obstacle course then more marching. You'll have a couple of surprise barracks inspections by the captain and the adjutant. You'll even probably be awakened at two in the morning to mop and wax the barracks."

Randy raised his eyebrows and remarked soberly, "Maybe I shouldn't have asked."

Mark laughed, "Look on the bright side, if you get 'barracks of the week,' then you will probably get some time off to go to a movie on base or do some shopping. By the way, if you buy something, mail it out the same day. If it is found in your area—that's a flickie."

Randy made a mental note of the information to share with his area chiefs. He thought *I'm lucky to have someone like Mark to let me know what's coming down the pike. It makes it easier to plan contingencies.* He had learned to eat while he listened and had just finished when the DI reappeared and called the flight out.

The daily routine had become almost that—*routine*. Reveille sounded at 0500; the recruits formed into a flight formation then exercised for a half-hour. They were allowed to go back to the barracks to wash their hands and insure that their area was in shape, and then they marched to breakfast. There was more marching intermingled with an occasional smoke break; the DI would say, "Smoke 'em if you got 'em."

Randy didn't smoke and he found this time was good to engage in conversation with his men and learn more about them. They seemed less intimidated by his BC position if they had a cigarette in their hand. The men also knew that they wouldn't be accused of sucking-up to the BC if Randy approached them, instead of the other way around.

Their personal interest and attitudes were as varied as their background. Casio had grown up in a housing project with five thousand other people, while Abbott had grown up in the small town of Childress, Texas and had been a calf roper in the rodeo. Escondido had been born in Los Angeles, but moved to Texas to live with an uncle when his parents had been killed in a freeway car crash. Bob Dawson from Waco had tried to play football in high school, but found that he was better at playing the tuba in the band. Each man was an individual and each individual had a story about home.

Many of the recruits had played basketball in high school and Randy suggested that they get a game together when they got some time off from training—if ever that happened. When he suggested taking on Mark Fairchild's barracks in a scrimmage, they were all for it. Randy never bragged about his performance in basketball, except to mention that his school had gone to the state finals last year.

After each smoke break, the flight would scatter out and police the area for loose papers and debris that had blown into the area. Discarded cigarettes were hardly ever found after a smoke break because the men were required to field strip the tobacco and discard it on the ground. They were required to save the paper and filter and discard them into butt cans. The butt cans were emptied into the trash by the barracks guards, only after he was sure that there were no smoldering ashes that might cause a fire.

After policing the area, there was more marching until 1100 when they marched to chow. Because they were coming along so well in their training, the DI had allowed them an extra ten minutes to eat their meals. This did not go unnoticed by the other barracks and was a verbalized source of envy, which made the extra ten minutes just that much more enjoyable.

After lunch, they would do more marching. This included marching in formation with other barracks and learning to pass in revue in front of the VIP grandstand.

The procedure for the revue march was for the right side column to look straight ahead, providing a marching reference, while the rest of the flight had their eyes looking right to pay homage to important people in the stand.

The DI had left for a while and Randy was in charge of the flight. He had given them 'at ease' and was talking to them of the objectives of the barracks to win 'barracks of the week' when a flight of WAFs (Women's Air Force) marched up.

The female DI, wanting to entice the men and play mind games with the women in her flight, ordered them to halt right in front of Randy's formation. She ordered, "Flight, left face." Her flight turned to face Randy's flight. She ordered, "At ease." This allowed the women to smile and return the ogles of the men.

Allowing a moment of indulgence, she then proceeded to lambaste her flight in the most vulgar terms, "You bunch of horny hussies think you're going to get a little tonight—think again. You're going to march and march until the only guy you'll want between your legs is *Ben Gay* to relieve the pain. Now you cunts listen up. When I call attention, I want your heels to snap together so quickly that I can hear your pussies sucking air. 'Flight, tench-hut!'" She turned with a self-satisfied smirk on her face and faced Randy's flight. The women in her flight were stone faced and beet-red with embarrassment.

Randy and his men were aware that they had just observed a serious injustice, possibly even a military protocol infraction. He was powerless to correct it—or was he! He ordered, "Flight aten-hut!" The flight popped to attention with a resonating boom as their heels came together. "Flight—present arms." This would normally be executed with a rifle, but when there are no rifles then the order called for a salute.

The flight held the salute for a full ten seconds. Eyes of airmen at attention weren't supposed to look around, but while holding the salute each man could not help looking into eyes of one of the girls across from him. They saw the embarrassment fade from the girls' faces, replaced by a look of gratitude expressing a restored sense of self-esteem.

Randy commanded, "Order arms." The men dropped the salute and stood at attention. He shouted, "Right face—forward march." As the flight started forward, Randy shouted at the top of his voice, "Three cheers for the Women's Air Force."

The flight in unison hollered at the top of their lungs, "Hip-hip-hurrah, hip-hip-hurrah, hip-hip-hurrah."

The female DI stood seething, and then screamed after them, "I'm going to report you; I'm going to report you." The women in the flight felt like they had just met their Prince Charming in mass. They started feeling good about themselves for the first time since their arrival on the air base.

Later when Sergeant Stark returned to the barracks, Randy knocked on his door. "Come in," the DI announced.

Seeing that it was Randy, he ordered, "At ease," before Randy could come to attention. "What's up?"

"You're probably going to get a complaint from a female DI about the flight today."

"I see," replied the sergeant, thinking of what could possibly have happened. He had found that it was best to get the information from another source when there might be a conflict of interest. He was learning to trust Randy, but didn't like putting his barracks chief on the defensive until all the facts were known. "Okay, I'll get back with you; you're dismissed."

Randy left and the DI called in the barracks guard, who had just come on duty and had been with the flight today.

The barracks guard, feeling uncertain as to why he had been called into the DI's quarters, entered the room, and popped to attention. The DI said, "At ease. Now tell me about the incident on the parade grounds today."

The barracks guard, relieved that it was not about him, enthusiastically stated, "You should have seen our BC today—!" Then he gave a detailed account of the events.

The DI listened intently, "I see. That's it; that's all of it—right?"

The barracks guard replied, "Yes, DI, sir, almost word for word."

Stark stood up, "I'm going out for a bit; go back to your post."

Sergeant Stark entered the company headquarters and the company sergeant looked up in surprise, "We were just going to send for you. There is a very irate Sergeant Gibbons that said that your flight interfered with her flight today. She's in with the captain and the adjutant complaining. Let's go in and get to the bottom of this.

The two sergeants entered the room and Captain Detrich directed, "Have a seat. Do you know what this is about, Sergeant Stark?

"Yes, sir, I do."

"Good. I've just heard Sergeant Gibbons' side of the story, now let's hear yours." Stark related the story told by the barracks guard.

When he finished, the captain turned to Sergeant Gibbons, "Is that pretty much what happened?

"Well, yes," she replied, "but they interfered with the command and control of my flight."

Grimacing at Gibbons, he then turned to Stark, "Sergeant Stark, your flight showed professional restraint under the circumstances. There were no words exchanged between the two flights and your barracks chief showed uncanny good judgment in saluting the WAFs, after an embarrassing diatribe by their DI.

"That was also a nice touch cheering the WAF formation as your flight marched away. Under the circumstances, not many flight leaders would have thought of doing that.... I commend you and your men for the honor that they have contributed to this company.

He then turned to Gibbons, "Sergeant Gibbons, you on the other hand have shown neither professionalism nor good judgment. Your use of vulgar demeaning language might be condoned or at least overlooked if you were in your barracks. However, you intentionally used abusive and vulgar language to embarrass the airmen in Sergeant Stark's flight and the women in your flight. As of now, you are on

113

report and if there is another reoccurrence of your action, I will personally see that you get an 'Article 15.'"

Sergeant Gibbons, trying to continue her case, complained "But now the women in my barracks don't respect me because of them," pointing toward Sergeant Stark.

The captain held up his hand to quash further discussion and philosophically redressed her, "Respect is something that can only be won by you; others can't take it away from you without your permission."

He stood up from his desk and waved his hand outward, "Everyone is dismissed, and I don't want to hear anymore on this subject."

Sergeant Gibbons left the room, mincing between clinched teeth, *"Male chauvinist pigs; just because I'm a woman they ganged up against me."*

As Sergeant Stark walked back toward the barracks, he felt good about himself and his recruits. He entered the barracks and called them to attention. He walked to the middle of the barracks, so all could hear. "There was an incident on the parade grounds today," he began. Every man cringed a little, expecting the worst.

He continued, "This incident has been reviewed by the captain and he feels that the entire barracks acted in a very professional manner. I personally, am very pleased with your conduct in my absence. Tomorrow, between 1300 and 1600, the entire barracks, with the exception of the barracks guard, will have three hours of free time to do what ever you want to do." He added, "As long as you stay on the airbase."

He ordered, "As you were." He walked to the front of the barracks and gave thumbs up to Randy as he passed. He entered his room where he made another entry in the special report on Airman Ferris.

The men were jubilant as they chucked each other on the shoulder and discussed what they would do with their time off. Randy approached the men that had voiced a desire to play basketball and found plenty of volunteers for a game. His popularity with the men had risen several notches due to him directing then in the proper response in correcting an injustice. Getting time off for doing the right thing was a special reward, although at the time, they all had felt that doing the right thing was rewarding in itself.

114

Scrimmage

Taps played at 2100 hours and the lights went out. The DI flipped the lights back on at 0100 shouting, "Okay, everybody up—get your butts out of the rack—you've had it way too easy. We're going to mop and wax the floor then clean every crevice and cranny in this barracks—up and at 'em—that's right—up and at 'em."

The men crawled out of their bunks moaning, "I knew it was too good to last." They cleaned the barracks for the next two hours. They mopped, buffed, and used their blankets to put the final sheen on the floor where they could see the reflection of their faces.

They climbed back in their bunks a little after 0300 and fell directly back to sleep. Reveille woke them at 0500 and the daily routine started over, except today they went back to the rifle range.

When it was Randy's turn to fire, he put the first 4 of 8 shots in the center of the bull's-eye then spaced the next four shots high, low, left, and to the right of the bull's-eye. He did the same for the other firing positions. His score fell considerably, but he still received a marksman's score because all shots had hit the target with four bull's-eyes. The DI personally checked his target pattern and glanced at him with a dubious look, but said nothing.

They marched back to company supply and handed in their rifles then marched to the chow hall for lunch. After lunch, they marched until 1300. The DI halted the flight in front of the barracks, "Okay, everyone is dismissed until 1600, except for the barracks guard and the barracks chief. The men fell out and headed in all different directions to exploit their precious free time.

Randy hollered after Casio, "Get the basketballs and lineup the scrimmage. I'll try to catch up with you later."

Casio flashed back the 'high sign' to acknowledge that he understood. He and Leubrecht headed toward the recreation supply building, while the rest of the players headed for the outdoor basketball court behind the company headquarters building.

The DI motioned to Randy, "Come with me, I want to do a thorough inspection of the barracks before the captain makes his inspection."

They entered the barracks and the DI meticulously inspected every item on an extended checklist. He even used a white glove to check for dust on the windowsills and the tops of clothes lockers. When they had finished, there was not a single check mark beside any of the items.

The DI led Randy back to his quarters and motioned to a chair, "Have a seat." He found a couple of glasses and returned from the water cooler, handing a cool crisp glass of water to Randy.

He sat down behind his desk and took a long draught that emptied the glass. Randy sipped slowly, savoring the cool liquid with each swallow. The DI set his glass down and asked remotely, "Okay, Airman Ferris, what gives at the rifle range this morning?"

Randy, unsure of what he was asking, but suspecting that he already knew, asked, "What specifically are you referring to, Sergeant Stark?"

The DI pursed his lips and jabbed the top of the desk with his finger to make the point, "What I'm specifically referring to is that on your very first time at the range, you got a perfect score. This time your score fell off drastically.

Randy fidgeted and the tops of his ears turned red. He blurted out almost apologetically, "My scores dropped because I don't want to wind up guarding airplanes—I want to go to tech school and learn a trade."

"I see," replied the DI as he leaned back in his chair. "Apparently you've been advised by someone from another barracks ahead of ours." Randy's silence was a tacit confirmation of the fact.

"Well, you almost outsmarted yourself," the DI continued, "I took a grease pencil and drew a vertical and a horizontal line connecting the holes in the target. The intersecting lines made an almost perfect plus mark on each of the four targets. It takes a crack shot to purposely shoot that type of pattern."

Randy gulped with embarrassment at having been confronted with his little ruse. He had subconsciously shot his best, even as he spread out the pattern. Feeling that he needed to make some reply, he looked the DI straight in the eye and stated, "I have no excuse, sir; just the reason that I stated."

The DI seemed to ignore his statement and went on to another subject. "We just inspected the barracks and there were no flickies. This is the first barracks in my six years of being a DI that had passed an inspection without flickies during their first week. This is the end of your second week and I would be surprised if we don't get barracks of the week after the captain's inspection—what do you attribute that to?"

"We have a very good group of men in our barracks," Randy replied with sincerity.

"As a group, I've had better and I've had worse," stated the DI matter-of-factly. But this group seems to click together better than the other ones. Why do you think that is possible?"

Randy shrugged his shoulders,

"I don't know—chemistry...teamwork—."

"Okay, I'll buy that. But both chemistry and teamwork need a catalyst to work well. Personally, I'd like to take full credit for this accomplishment, but I think that catalyst—is you, Airman Ferris."

This unexpected compliment caused Randy's face to flush and he stammered, "Uh—oh—uh—thank you, sir," as a half smile crept across his face.

The DI snapped sternly, "If you deserve it, never be embarrassed by a compliment. It makes the giver uncertain that they should have given you the compliment in the first place."

Randy's smile disappeared and he straightened in his chair as he responded, "Yes, DI, sir."

The sergeant digressed, "I don't select who does or does not leave here and goes on to a tech school. That decision is made over at the 'Green Monster' and factors in many considerations—test scores, physical capabilities, manning requirements...even personal whims."

He then confided as a mentor, "My advice to you, Airman Ferris, is to do the best at whatever you are called upon to do. Give the evaluators and schedulers a chance to act toward your best interest and that of the United States Air Force—only then can it become a win-win situation. Now is there anything that I can personally do for you?"

Randy considered the validity of the advice, and then answered the question "Yes, there is. Our barracks would like to challenge Airman Mark Fairchild's barracks to a basketball scrimmage."

The DI mentally noted that Randy had not asked for a favor for himself, but for the barracks as a group. He replied, "I'll talk to his DI and see if we can set up a game. I've noticed that they have been practicing during their free time—do you think that our team can beat them?"

"Yes," replied Randy. Normally he would have hedged his statement and said that the results of the game would speak for itself. But after the discussion with the DI, he could see that the appropriate response was simply a definitive 'Yes.'"

The DI removed the lanyard holding his whistle from around his neck. He disappeared for a moment and returned shaking the excess water from the whistle. Handing the whistle and a clipboard to Randy,

117

he encouragingly stated, "Okay, now get out there and practice with your team. I'll talk with the captain; maybe we can make this a company spectacle and invite the other barracks to watch."

As Randy approached the basketball court, he saw that Casio had already started the group with warm-up shots. He stood and evaluated each of the players before interrupting their practice. They wore brogans, which made their movements stilted and clumsy. But this limitation didn't mask their ability to shoot and he quickly saw a difference between who had played the game merely for recreation and who had played the game in organized sports competition.

He discarded the urge to get a game going immediately. They would have to choose sides and there would be those that would feel slighted if they were asked to be substitutes. The prudent tactic would be to let each player compare his own talent in a 'one on one' scrimmage. This would sort out who was good and who was better. Then the players would know that the selections were made on ability and not on personality.

Casio came over and jived with a supercilious grin on his face, "Ready for a game, white boy?"

"Later," replied Randy. "But first I'd like to see some 'one on one'—you and I will go last."

"Fine with me—that'll give me a chance to kick your butt—just like I said I would." He walked back to the group and halted their practice.

Randy walked up, picked up one of the balls, and flicked it toward the basket. It was a forty foot shot and had little chance of going in, but the ball hit the back of the rim, danced around the edge and finally fell through the net. He knew that he had been lucky and saw the surprised admiration in the men's eyes.

Seizing on the moment, he remarked, "That was just to get your attention. I just had a talk with the DI and he is going to try and get a game going with another barracks. Are you guys up to it?"

"Yeah," they chorused in unison, a few iterating, "We'll kick their butts!"

"I'm sure we can," assured Randy. "But it is going to take special effort and teamwork. Some of you may be very good, but we can't win a game with a couple of hot 'loose cannons.' The other team is going to have some talented players on their team and they have already been practicing together. We don't know how good they are, so our best chance is to play as a synchronized unit and play our talent.

"Some of you may be better at shooting and some of you will be better at defense. The game changes ends of the court quickly and we've only got a short time to sort out your abilities. So, we're going to have some 'one on one' before we start a game.

"We've got a little over an hour and thirty minutes to play ball. We're going to quit twenty-five minutes ahead of time for a shower and boot polishing because your brogans are going to get scuffed and we don't' want flickies during a surprise inspection.

"Okay, when I call out pairs of names, I want you to form two lines. Doesn't matter which line you're in as long as you are opposite each other. I want you to alternate offense and defense; flip a coin between you to see who gets the ball first. The first player to make three baskets wins that round. Winners form a line there; extend it to the right." He pointed to the center of the court. "Others form a line to the left." He had chosen this arrangement so that each man would have full view of the play action.

Sixteen men had shown up for the scrimmage. This was good because he knew that there would be dropouts after an individual realized that he didn't measure up to the other talent on the team. The fact that they needed the best talent to beat the other barracks would soften the disappointment of an individual not making the starting team.

Due to time constraints, Randy wanted a quick selection, so he paired a good shooter with a poorer shooter. The poorer shot would have to make the team on defense or prove that the couple of shots that Randy had observed were just fluke misses and the player really was a better shot than first impression.

He blew the whistle and flipped the ball to the first pair. The rest of the group quickly picked their favorite and shouted words of advice and encouragement. The first winner was clearly the better of the two. The next pair was much closer with a 3 to 2 score. After seven pairs, it was Randy and Casio's turn.

Casio walked up, flipping a quarter over and over, "Okay, Mr. Hoopster—call it."

"That's OK," replied Randy, "You shoot first."

Casio's face registered surprise, "You really do want to get your butt kicked—don't you?"

119

Randy flipped him the ball and backed off in a defensive posture. Casio started a slow dribble, looking for a weakness in Randy's defense. He made a feign dribble to the right then to the left and saw that Randy always placed himself between the basket and his opponent. Casio slowly dribbled toward Randy. As they reached the free-throw line, Casio suddenly stopped, jumped, and shot. Randy was in the middle of moving his left foot backward and was late in jumping to block the shot. The ball swished through 'nothing but net.' The other players cheered.

Randy took the ball; he mentally noted that Casio had looked down, then up, then jumped. He complimented, "Good shot."

Casio retorted, "Yeah, white boys can't jump."

Randy started dribbling rapidly toward Casio, backing him up. He cut quickly to the right, stopped, and took a hook shot. The ball arced high over Casio's head and swished through the basket 'nothing but net.' The onlookers jumped up and down and cheered.

Randy flicked the ball to a chastened Casio and razzed, "White boys don't need to jump."

Casio took the ball and started dribbling rapidly toward Randy. Randy backed away quickly in a defensive posture. Casio slowed suddenly and Randy moved toward him. Casio jutted his chin to the left and rolled his eyes. Randy had seen this ploy before. Most right-handed players cut to their right and Randy moved to cut him off, but Casio cut to his left. Randy tried to correct his direction, but his brogans slid on the concrete court. Casio drove past him and effortlessly laid up a shot on the backboard. The ball fell freely through the net.

Randy could see that Casio was street smart and executed the moves well.

The other players cheered as though they were watching a real game.

Randy took the ball and started dribbling directly toward Casio. Casio backed off, waiting for the moment for Randy's cut, but Randy kept driving. They came to the point where Randy would have to take a shot or go out of bounds. Casio jumped a split second before Randy jumped. Randy could see that Casio was going to block the shot, so in midair, he switched the ball from his right hand to his left and laid the shot around Casio's extended arm. It slid across the backboard and fell through the net. The team was beside themselves. They were cheering and pumping their fists in the air.

Casio was silent and slightly stunned that he had been finessed. The BC was much better than he had anticipated, but the rule was the first one to make three baskets—wins. He had the ball and he would get this over quickly. He drove directly toward Randy, slowed, and looked down, then up as his toes pushed against the concrete. To his absolute surprise, Randy was already in the air, but Casio had already committed himself and forced the shot. Randy seemed to rise a head above him and easily blocked the shot.

"Motha-fucker," Casio minced, "white boys can jump."

Randy's momentum to block the shot took him past Casio. The blocked ball had a backspin and came back just within Randy's reach as he landed. Casio quickly recovered. Randy had the ball, but had his back toward his opponent. Casio's lanky arms and legs were spread out making it next to impossible to spin and dribble around him. Randy faked left then right, and then rolled the ball between their legs.

Casio was too close and concentrating on Randy's body movements to see the ball leisurely rolling toward the basket. Randy spun quickly and clapped his hands together over his head.

Casio froze momentarily thinking, *where's the fuckin' ball?* Before he could react, Randy stepped around him, scooped up the ball, dribbled twice, and dunked the ball through the net. The team stood in shocked silence; then broke running toward the two players. They ran up and pounded both players on the back; congratulating them for the best 'one on one' play that they had ever witnessed.

It was clear to the rest of the team that Randy and Casio were the best players. Randy blew his whistle and said, "Thanks, but it is going to be teamwork that beats the other barracks. Get back in line and let's have a couple more 'one on ones.' Casio and I will sit out and evaluate the play."

As the next pair played, Casio walked up, "That was quite a move you put on me. Where did you learn it?"

Randy replied, "I watched the Harlem Globetrotters play against the Washington Generals." It was one of their razzle-dazzle plays. I tried it on my buddy, David, back home, but found that it only works one time. You're very good—sorry that I had to resort to it."

Casio, ignoring the compliment, refuted, "I knew that you had to learn it from a black man—but you're right, it'll only work one time."

Randy chucked him on the shoulder, "Don't be too ticked. Basketball was a big part of my life before I came here."

"Then how did you know when to block my jump shot?"

"You telescoped your intentions. You charged with your dribble, slowed, looked down, then looked up, and jumped. You caught me moving the first time, but like you said—it only happens once."

Casio half-grinned and slapped Randy on the back, "You are one surprisin' motha-fuckin' white dude!"

Randy smiled back, "I guess that I should take that as a compliment—so I will."

They turned their attention to the play and discussed the pros and cons of each individual's capabilities. By the third round of 'one on one,' they had their starting team.

He started the scrimmage with their best shooters and had them practice the quick break, but their brogans limited their maneuvering. He had the players concentrate on passing the ball longer distances, while giving key players the additional time they needed to get into position for a higher percentage scoring shot.

Randy substituted himself a couple of times to feel the rhythm of the team, but allowed the other members to play most of the time, since he wanted to concentrate on evaluating their instincts of the game. He had learned from his high school coach that basketball was a game of doing what had to be done without consciously thinking. If you had to stop to think then your opponent was already counteracting your next move.

Randy whistled and stopped the play. "Okay, guys, you're looking good. It's 1535; we have to return the balls and be outside the barracks for formation by 1600. Our brogans have taken a lot of scuffing; make sure they're in shape for inspection.

That night in the barracks, the airmen chatted about their experiences during their time off. However, most of the talk was about the 'one on one' between Randy and Casio and the upcoming game with the other barracks. Randy dropped off to sleep, thinking of Sherrill and feeling that they had been apart for a year instead of two months. He felt good about today's activities, but missed her to the point of tears forming in the corners of his eyes. He had a tight feeling in his chest, as though a part of his heart had stopped beating in her absence.

Cameo

Sherrill's life had developed into an insouciant routine, but her Aunt Vicki's hustle and bustle had insured that it was never boring. After the housekeeping chores and the morning home study session were completed, they would have lunch somewhere interesting. It usually involved walking to the mall for exercise, but Vicki had her own car and they sometimes drove to surrounding towns to visit the shops or to Lake Merced for a picnic, where they would lounge on a blanket and watch the water skiers cavort across the choppy waves and wakes left by the speeding boats.

Vicki seemed to know almost everyone in town and often included other friends to join their outings. The weather in the San Joaquin Valley was ideal for irrigated truck gardens, vineyards, and orchards. Aunt Vicki and a few of her friends often traveled to a regional winery and sampled the vintage vino. Sherrill deferred imbibing the fermented wines due to her age and consideration of how it would affect her baby. She did however enjoy the fresh fruits and produce. Cheeses from the Sierra Nevada Mountain region were excellent and were an epicurean's delight when sampled with the sweet non-alcoholic wines produced by the wineries.

Lunches often lasted longer than two hours and the conversations were intermixed with local folklore and current events. She learned of the gold strike in 1848 at Sutter's Mill and the subsequent explosive immigration in 1849, as gold seekers sought to make their fortune. Many of the fortune seekers discovered instead a more permanent wealth in developing the land and raising a family in the "Big Valley."

On one such excursion they stopped at a filming site where the TV series "The Dons of Eldorado" was filming action scenes against the backdrop of a historical locale—(**Don** - a courtesy title used before the name of a man in a Spanish-speaking area). With this group was the beautiful young actress, Laura Blevins. The series derived its name from three male cousins; all named "Don" after their paternal grandfather, Don Broderick.

Shortly after the American Civil War, the cousins' families had been traveling to California in a wagon train decimated by a smallpox outbreak, renegade Indian attacks, and a flash flood. The three boys were the only survivors of the extended family and were adopted by an aunt and uncle that had earlier established a large cattle ranch in the big

123

valley. Their far-reaching wealth included orchards and vineyards, but their main source of wealth came from gold mines located in the Sierra Nevada Mountains. Bandits had bushwhacked the uncle and stolen the mines' payroll. The widowed mother then became the matriarch of the Broderick family, which included Don Matthew, Don Mark, Don Luke, and her beautiful daughter—Belinda.

Sherrill watched in awe at actually seeing the beautiful actress Laura Blevins playing the part of Belinda Broderick in the television series. She had hoped to meet her, but the filming area was roped off and security personnel were ever present to prevent the public from interfering with the scripted action. Aunt Vicki casually watched the filming with her and chatted about highlights from previous episodes.

The director glanced over at Sherrill standing in the radiant sunlight. Her pale pink sleeveless blouse with embroidered tea roses hugged the curved lines of her slender waist. Her curvaceous hips were clad in a pair of white shorts complimenting her long slender legs. The collar of her blouse was turned up in the back and the wings arched downward in front, accenting her long slender neck and exposing a hint of full supple breast. She wore white open-toed sandals that completed the illusion of her being a modern day Greek goddess.

During a break the director approached her, "Excuse me, Miss, but I couldn't help noticing how beautiful you are with the sun on your face and the wind blowing through your golden hair. Come with me to Hollywood and I will make you famous."

Sherrill didn't know whether he was serious or just trying to hit on her. The statement caused her to blush and she demurely replied, "Thank you, sir, but my aunt and I have only come to watch the filming."

The director apologized, "Ah, I hope that I have not offended you. You see—I noticed my camera crews were not paying attention to the scene, but were looking at you instead. It was then that I noticed that you have a radiant beauty about you, much like our beautiful star, Laura Blevins."

Another blush flushed across Sherrill's face and she had to control the tremor in her voice to the point of sounding husky, "You are very glib with your compliments and I thank you, if they are sincere. But I have no desire to go to Hollywood. I would, however, like to meet Miss Blevins, if that could be possible."

"It is possible," replied the director, "but, first, you must grant me one request. I have a small non-speaking part that requires a beautiful girl such as you. We were going to film it on a studio set, but we can film it here just as easily. I must get you on film and I will introduce you to Miss Blevins and pay you five hundred dollars, if you agree to do this for me."

Sherrill turned to her Aunt Vicki and asked with disbelief, "Am I naive, or is this guy for real?"

Her aunt replied, "Yes, you are naive and we'll find out if this guy is for real."

She turned to the director, "I am this young lady's guardian aunt. If you are sincere with your offer, I'm sure that you have a standard contract that you can sign that will insure that you put your money where your mouth is."

The director replied, "I will be happy to sign a contract and I will even pay you in cash up front."

He motioned to an assistant producer and instructed, "Please pay this young lady five hundred dollars. We are going to shoot a small scene with her as Annabelle Lee; you know the part that I am referring to, but I will explain it to her.

"It is a part where Don Luke is being lectured by his adopted mother that he can't keep his mind on the family's ranch business without being distracted by a beautiful face. Then Annabelle rides by in a carriage. Luke's eyes follow Annabelle as she disappears out of view.

"He turns back to his mother and says, 'Sorry mother, what were you saying?' The director added, "Shooting the scene shouldn't take more than ten minutes and, anyway, the cast needs a short break from the sun."

Aunt Vicki quickly read the contract and signed it. The assistant producer paid her five-hundred dollars in crisp one-hundred dollar bills and the director announced an extended break for everyone. He offered his arm and took Sherrill to meet Laura Blevins, who was about to enter her dressing room inside a trailer house, when the director called after her, "Miss Blevins, please wait up."

The director had noted Sherrill's name on the contract and said, "Miss Laura Blevins, meet Miss Sherrill Lindstrom. She is going to be in a walk-on scene and she has asked to meet you.

The two women curiously eyed each other and then shook hands. Sherrill thought, *she is even more beautiful than on television.*

Laura thought, *what a lovely girl, she has a translucent glow in her face that adds to her beauty.* "I'm pleased to meet you, Miss Lindstrom; but please call me, Laura."

Sherrill responded, "I feel privileged to meet you Laura. Please call me, Sherrill."

The handshake lingered as a mutual respect passed between the two women. Laura suggested, "Please come inside and have a glass of iced tea with me."

A best boy quickly produced two glasses of iced tea and left the trailer. Laura lifted her glass of iced tea and offered a toast, "Here's to Emile Fabio, the director; he has a real eye for beauty. As she took a sip of tea, Laura added, "You have an angelic glow about you; I can see why he was awe struck."

Sherrill felt a touch of heat on her cheeks as she replied in explanation, "Thank you, but the glow is probably because I'm going to have a baby."

"Oh, how wonderful!" congratulated Laura, "But you were introduced as Miss Lindstrom, is that a professional title?"

"No," replied Sherrill, "I'm afraid that it is a fact of fate." She gave a quick summary of her love affair with Randy, including that she was fifteen weeks pregnant, and the reason that she was in California.

When she finished, she stated with astonishment, "I can't believe that I have told this story to a perfect stranger."

Laura replied, with a warm smile, "We're not strangers—remember...we were properly introduced. But what a fantastic story—it's almost like something out of Hollywood."

The costume coordinator knocked on the door, "I need Miss Lindstrom to come with me and dress for the Annabelle Lee scene."

Laura graciously suggested, "Please, let her wear one of my costumes. She's a little taller than I am, but we both have about the same build and the skirts are so long that there shouldn't be a problem. Also, I would like for my personal makeup artist to do her face and hair."

Laura left to finish the filming of her last scene. The director had clued in everyone about the up-coming scene with Sherrill, which would immediately follow. They would do that scene, and then wrap it up for the day.

The male makeup artist looked at Sherrill's face, "I don't want to do anything—. For the human eye, I can't improve upon what God has given you. But for the camera, we'll need a little eyeliner and eye shadow—that is all. He brushed her hair until it glistened, and then added a small amount of his secret cream to cause some strands to wave, while allowing the rest of the hair to flow freely. This gave an illusion that the hair was thicker, while still retaining its natural radiance.

The costume coordinator helped Sherrill dress into one of Laura's costumes. Sherrill looked in the full-length mirror and was amazed. The dress was a soft ribbed tricot fabric of vertical alternating earth tones that complimented Sherrill's skin color, eye color, and hair color. Twin petticoats provided flare at the hem, which drew the eye upward to her narrow waistline. A peach colored riding cape provided upper body protection from the dust and the sun. It was as if she had been transported back to the nineteenth century. She picked up her matching bonnet and started to put it on, but decided to wait until her Aunt Vicki could see her.

As she stepped out of the trailer, the filming crews had finished the last shot and were preparing for the next scene. All eyes turned toward Sherrill and took in her natural beauty. Laura was approaching the trailer and took her by the hand and graciously introduced her to the crew, "Our new starlet, Miss Sherrill Lindstrom!"

Everyone applauded; Laura turned to Sherrill and whispered in her ear, "If I didn't like you so much, I could easily be jealous." She hugged Sherrill, "Good Luck."

The director took Sherrill by the arm and led her to the storyboard, which illustrated each scene, as it should look during filming. He took her quickly through the illustrations, "This is going to be a simple shot. We'll do the scene with the sun behind you and again with the sun shining on your face. The editing room will put the two scenes together as if you were passing in and out of shadows and light; you'll be amazed by the effect. All I want from you Sherrill is to look straight ahead in the moving carriage, glance sideways as if you caught Luke's eye, turn your head to maintain the eye contact, and then look straight ahead again.

Sherrill asked for confirmation, "That's all?"

The director confirmed, "That is all."

Sherrill spread the wings of the bonnet to put it on. The director held up his hand and said, "Don't put it on. Just hold it in your lap. I want the camera to see your face without shadows."

Sherrill stepped into the carriage with a driver that was dressed and aged to be her father. They started approaching several hundred feet from the cameras. To give her a point of orientation, a stand-in for Don Luke was leaning on a hitching rail and talking with a woman. As they approached, Sherrill looked at the young man and pretended in her mind that she was looking at Randy. She executed the shot as instructed. The carriage reversed direction and the filming crew on the other side of the street got the shot with the sun toward her. The carriage swung back around and stopped.

The director assisted Sherrill from the carriage and he remarked, "Perfect, that's a take."

Laura walked up, "You did that very well. I've learned to be critical of a shot and I couldn't have done it any better. Would you like to stay and have dinner with us in town this evening?

Sherrill declined graciously, "You all have been so kind and have made my day very memorable, but I have some lessons that I must complete today." Then she added for conviction because she was very tempted to take them up on their offer, "There is an exam tomorrow that I have to pass."

Laura looked at her and took her hand for a parting goodbye handshake, "You look so lovely in that dress, why don't you keep it as a present from me."

Sherrill moved by her generosity, took a step forward, and kissed her on the cheek. Laura returned the kiss on Sherrill's cheek.

The director stepped up, "I'm sure that Hollywood will be seeing more of you, Sherrill." He shook her hand. A stage grip handed her a bundle that contained her own clothes.

Sherrill waved to the entire crew, blew them a kiss, and spoke as loudly as a lady dared, "Thank you all, you've been great!" She blew them a kiss again and waved goodbye with the presence of a real starlet.

They got into Aunt Vicki's car and drove off. During the drive back home, they relived their fairy tale by discussing every aspect of their adventure. When Uncle Hank arrived home from his office, he got an eye full of Sherrill in her gown and an earful of the afternoon events. He listened attentively, happily sharing their day's adventure.

That evening, the director was with the editing crew reviewing the scene of Sherrill. He was impressed at how well the shot had panned out. He remarked to the senior editor, "I think that we have just discovered another star in the making."

128

At that moment an associate producer approached him, "Do you remember that dust devil that blew through the filming site? Well, we think that it picked up the contract with Miss Lindstrom because we can't find it anywhere."

The director screamed, "You idiots! Don't you realize that we can't use this shot without a contract? Unless someone can locate a Miss Sherrill Lindstrom in the phone book then we'll have to cut this scene. It will be like it never happened."

The associate producer scurried off to see if he could find a way of locating the beautiful actress that had captured the hearts and admiration of both the men and women in the crew.

Rediscovery

The next morning Sherrill rose early and quickly reviewed the subjects on which she would be tested. She had accelerated her home study and only three weeks had passed since her last bank of tests. One of the school counselors, Bill Payson, had offered to come in on a Saturday morning to monitor the test. He was a 24-year-old teacher that had taken a special interest in Sherrill.

When Sherrill arrived at the district administration building, he greeted her as if she were doing him a favor for being there, instead of the other way around. He gave her the test materials, which normally took four hours and sat down at his desk to read the morning paper.

While she was taking the test, several people entered the room and spoke with him in quiet whispered tones. She noticed out of the corner of her eye that they seemed to be gesturing toward her. When she looked up, they quickly glanced away and continued their hushed conversation.

She finished the test in less than three hours and handed in her papers. From out of the blue Mr. Payson asked, "Have they found you yet?"

Puzzled, she stated, "I don't know what you are talking about?"

"Haven't you seen the morning paper?"

"No, it was still outside on the lawn when I left this morning."

"Oh, I see." Holding up the paper, he informed, "Well, your picture is on the front page." Gazing at her, he added, "You're a beautiful young woman—even in 'black and white.'"

Covering his indiscretion, he quickly added, "There is a human-interest story in the 'Life and Entertainment' section of the paper. I read it while you were taking your test." He handed the newspaper to Sherrill.

Her picture, showing her in 19th century dress, was on the front page with the caption, "Missing Starlet" see L&E — pg. 3. Sherrill quickly turned to the article and read:

"Local valley beauty discovered while watching the filming of the popular TV Western series 'The Dons of Eldorado.' According to a spokesperson for the series, the director asked the girl to be in a short scene that is to be aired in five weeks. Her guardian aunt had signed a contract, but a dust devil blew through the filming site and carried the contract away. The spokesperson explained that the scene could not be aired without a legal contract. Anyone knowing the whereabouts of Miss Sherrill Lindstrom should contact their local newspaper."

Sherrill lowered the paper, "This is incredulous; they could have gotten anybody to do that scene. Why would they contact to the newspaper if they knew that I lived in Merced? They could have just came to the school registrar's office and gotten my address?"

As Bill gazed up at Sherrill, he dreamily thought, *she isn't even aware of her own beauty.* Without thinking, he quipped, "Like many others, the director must have been smitten by you."

Sherrill flushed and stammered, "I—I'm not sure what you're trying to infer."

Bill didn't want to explain his statement; instead, he answered her first question. "They don't know that you live in Merced. You were probably aware of the people coming into the room while you were taking your test. They have been talking on the phone with friends from other towns and it seems that your picture is in every local newspaper between Fresno and Sacramento."

Sherrill sat silently, trying to comprehend why anyone would go to such lengths to try to find her. The silence prompted Bill to continue, "To answer your second question, there have been inquiries at the school registrar's office. However, you are on a 'special program' and it is the district's policy to not release any information to the public concerning students in this program."

Sherrill, slightly overwhelmed by these revelations, remained silent. The situation did not demand a response and her mind drifted back to the events of yesterday.

Bill took her first statement and formulated it into a question, "If just anybody could do the part, why have they gone to so much trouble to find you?"

"I don't really know; I was wondering the same thing. The fact is that I don't want to be found. I just want to finish school, have my baby, and marry Randy, my baby's father."

The mention of another man unnerved Bill and he indiscreetly questioned without thinking, "Why isn't the baby's father with you now?"

Sherrill's eyes grew large as she became defensive. "Mr. Payson!" She admonished. "That information is very personal and none of your business as a teacher."

"I'm sorry; I'm sorry," Bill stammered as he held up his hand, imploring Sherrill to understand. "You're right; it's none of my business. It's just that I care for you," quickly adding, "—as a student." Reversing himself, he revealed, "No, that's not entirely true, I became enchanted by you the first day that you walked into school."

Realizing that he was skating on thin ice in a student-teacher relationship, he tried to apologize, "I'm sorry; I know that I shouldn't have said that." In exasperation and trying to justify his statements, he beseeched, "Don't you realize how wonderfully beautiful you are?"

Sherrill, thunderstruck by his superfluity of feelings and emotions, bolted toward the door. Bill rose from his chair and followed her into the hallway. Trembling with mixed emotions he watched as she ran down the hallway and disappeared out the exit. Feeling enervated by his rashness, he thought, *I feel like a schoolboy that has a crush on his teacher...and just told her.*

Sherrill got into her aunt's car and sped away. Her emotions flooded through her like a surging wave carrying her to exhilarating highs, and then backwashing into recriminating lows. She felt stimulated that an older good-looking professional man would confess his feelings for her, but she also felt a betrayal to Randy that she was allowing herself to have these feelings.

She tried to think of anything that she might have done to entice Mr. Payson. As a student counselor, his demeanor had always appeared professional and guileless—until today. She thought back to prior situations and could find no fault in her own actions. She did not dress provocatively, used very little makeup, and never flirted with him or anyone else at school.

When she pulled up into her driveway, her Aunt Vicki came out of the house, locking the door behind her. She got into the passenger side, "Let's go for a drive."

"Where to?"

"Anywhere—uh, better yet, let's drive out to Lake Merced."

Sherrill headed for the lake and her aunt asked, "Have you read today's newspaper?"

"Yes, my counselor showed me the newspaper article about me this morning." Sherrill deferred saying anything about the incident with Mr. Payson, since she had not rationalized her own feelings and didn't feel like sharing them with anyone else until she understood them herself.

Her aunt complained, "Our phone has been ringing off the hook all morning. My friends have been calling me and telling me about the story. I've told them all not to call the paper nor tell anyone where you live. I've even gotten calls from strangers that know someone that knows someone else that knows a mutual friend. I've even been told that your picture is in all the local papers between Sacramento and Fresno."

"I know," responded Sherrill. "I don't know what to make of it. There seems to be an awful lot of fuss over just a small part that took only five minutes to film. Now I'm being listed as a missing celebrity."

"I know," her aunt sympathized. "It's almost like a Cinderella story, except the Prince only has a photograph of you, instead of a glass slipper."

Sherrill blushed at the analogy, "I don't think it's quite like a fairytale."

Her aunt reproached her, "Don't be too naive. This is California and those newspaper people can get into a feeding frenzy that can overtake you like a tidal wave." Sherrill felt that her aunt was exaggerating, but respected her too much to argue with her.

Unexpectedly, her aunt pointed her finger, and then flicked her wrist for emphasis, "Slow down, and pull in there. Let's buy some takeout chicken and have a picnic at the lake."

While they were waiting for their order-up, the two women could not help noticing the whispering at the tables and the discreet pointing in their direction. The manager walked up and took the picnic boxes from the counter clerk. He handed the boxes to Sherrill, "It's on the house, Miss Lindstrom—it's not often that we get a movie star in our establishment."

Sherrill protested, "But I'm not a movie star."

Her aunt cupped Sherrill's elbow in the palm of her hand and guided her toward the door. As they walked outside, Sherrill reiterated, "But I'm not a movie star."

"It doesn't matter," counseled her aunt. "If they think you are a movie star then in their eyes—you are a movie star. It would only burst their bubble if you argued until you proved them wrong."

At the lake, they found a picnic table that was the last table out on a small peninsula extending into the lake. The day was typically warm and a few cirrus clouds painted the blue sky with streaks of white, providing a diffused sun and a mild breeze that wafted soothingly against their cheeks. The picnic lunch tasted delicious and. the two women were lost in conversation, until they noticed a small crowd quietly gathering at the next picnic table and pointing in their direction.

They never approached the two women's table, maintaining a distance of perceived privacy. Their mere presence, however, was quite unnerving. Sherrill and Aunt Vicki quickly finished their lunch. As they left, they had to pass closer to the group, and Aunt Vicki advised, "Just wave as we pass; don't say anything." Sherrill smiled and waved. The people smiled and waved back.

She overheard, "It is her—it really is her!"

Aunt Vicki drove the car back home. Sherrill was not used to all this attention; she felt excited and yet somehow violated. Her rural upbringing had only exposed her to adulation by basketball fans. She knew most of those people on a first name basis. However, in this newfound fame, total strangers perceived that they knew her.

The wire services, noting that many of their affiliates had carried the same story, picked up the story for their Sunday editions. Local TV stations, smelling a bigger story than appeared in the newspapers, contacted the filming crew. No one could or would reveal any more information than was published in the newspaper. They did, however, provide some high-resolution still photos of Sherrill, which the stations carried on their newscast along with a twenty-second sound bite:

"The Dons of Eldorado studio is being mum about their newly discovered 'American Beauty.' All a spokesman would say was that they are trying to locate a Miss Sherrill Lindstrom. She is scheduled to appear in a small part in an episode that is to be aired in five weeks. They merely want another signed contract, so that they can use the film clip."

The camera then panned back to the news reporter, who would stare into the camera and ask the question that varied little from station to station, "This reporter has only one simple question. If almost any actress could do the part at a filming studio then why has the story appeared in so many places at the same time?" Sherrill's photograph flashed back on the screen with an announcement: "Stay tuned to this channel for further late breaking news on this unusual story."

Aunt Vicki, noticing that Sherrill was quiet and thoughtful, said nothing until they were almost home. "Just ignore it, Honey. Like every storm, it will blow over."

She turned the corner to her street and braked suddenly; Sherrill had to throw out her arm to keep from being thrown into the windshield. The street was clogged with a dozen news vans parked in front of their house. Reporters were milling around on the lawn and forming into small groups around cameras that were set up on the driveway and sidewalk.

Aunt Vicki quickly backed around and headed to her husband's real estate office. Uncle Hank saw them pull up and ran out to meet them with a barrage of questions, "Where have you been? Have you seen Sherrill's picture in the paper? I tried to call home and the line has been busy. I drove by the house and there are all kinds of people on our front lawn. Not waiting for answers, he excitedly stated, "Stay right there; I'll be right back." He went back into the office and reappeared a moment later.

He opened the driver's door, explaining, "I asked Ed to close up the office; let's get out of here."

Aunt Vicki slid over next to Sherrill and they headed out of town. Hank admonished, "You two's little excursion yesterday has gotten totally out of control." Then he smoothed the barb by stating, "I know that it's not your fault—the media has no accountability when it comes to digging out a news story."

"Where are we going?" inquired Aunt Vicki.

Hank thought for a minute and decided, "Monterey; we can stay in a motel tonight. No one will be looking for us there."

They drove to Monterey, located on the California coast near Carmel, and stopped at a department store to purchase nightclothes and clothing for the next day. While there, one of the clerks asked, "Aren't you the missing starlet that's on television?"

Aunt Vicki moved between them and answered for Sherrill, "No, she is our niece visiting from back east. She just looks like that girl."

They quickly paid for their purchases and left. Their obvious reluctance to talk and the fact that they were traveling without extra clothes caused the clerk to become suspicious. She followed them to the parking lot and copied down the make, color, and license plate number of the car.

They found a nice motel and Uncle Hank went in alone to register for two connecting rooms. He returned feeling relieved, "No one will find us here. I'll order room service or go out and bring something back to eat. No one knows us here, so now we can relax." The two women said nothing. Feeling overwhelmed by the day's events, they were looking forward to a hot bath and going to bed early.

Reported sightings of Sherrill flowed in from many of the towns in the valley. Reporters were dispatched to follow-up on the leads, but all proved to be a dead-end. Multiple leads started coming in from Merced. Verification quickly confirmed that Sherrill lived in Merced with her aunt and uncle.

Additional reporters were dispatched to get a scoop on the story. They found the residence, but no one was home. Interviews with neighbors and businesses revealed that Sherrill was a senior at the high school. Interviews with various students revealed that some had seen her at the mall or with her aunt, but none of the students had ever met Sherrill or seen her in class.

Reliable sources, who asked to remain anonymous, confirmed that Sherrill was on a 'special education' program with the school district. The school superintendent was contacted and declined a statement, until he was told that there would be a story published with or without his cooperation. After a few quick phone calls to key school board members, he made the following statement.

"Sherrill Lindstrom is a straight "A" student enrolled in a little known 'special education' program set up back in the early '40's for girls who became pregnant and normally quit high school.

The program has a 90% success ratio for girls that graduate. Instead of the girls going onto the welfare rolls, they have continued their education by attending college, going to work at a job that supports their baby, or eventually getting married and leading productive lives. The program is very cost effective, since it only incurs administrative cost for the home study curriculum."

This statement was included in the nightly news throughout the state and included on the front page or in the Life and Entertainment section of the newspapers. Editorials were included that lauded the success of the school program.

State Representative — Neil Blair — appeared on an early morning news interview. Crediting his district with the innovation of this program and asking the question, "Why has this local government program that has proved so successful, not been adopted by every school district in the state?"

The wire services and the TV network's teletypes and microwave systems were burning up with new clues and tidbits of information about Sherrill. No source was identified, but Sherrill's hometown was located and a story revealed that Sherrill's fiancé, Randy Ferris, had battled with her father for Sherrill's hand in marriage.

Randy allegedly had won the fight, but received a concussion and was hospitalized. While Randy was in the hospital, Sherrill's father had exiled his daughter to live with an aunt in California. She was forbidden from contacting Randy until her eighteenth birthday.

This piece of meaty news was a feast for the tabloids and they ground it into *hamburger journalism*, with Sherrill's picture on page 1. It was one of the few times that Elizabeth Taylor's picture was relegated to page 2.

Reporters, trying to find out more about the newly discovered starlet, inundated the public relations office of "The Dons of Eldorado." The official statement was that Sherrill's contract had been signed on location and that the main office knew as little about Sherrill as the reporters.

The producers, however, realized that this story was giving them more free publicity than they had bought since the inception of the series. They instructed their people to find Sherrill and get her under contract—at any price.

Charles Lindstrom was watching the 10 o'clock news and was suddenly confronted with the "missing starlet" saga. He learned along with the rest of the community that Sherrill was missing. Seeing a picture of his daughter flash on the screen brought a lump to his throat. But when the commentator revealed Charles' role in his daughter's exile, he broke out in sobs of self-denial and recrimination. He felt again the pain of his injuries incurred during the fight with Randy, as if they had just happened.

Mavis, numbed by the graphic truth and months of mourning for her exiled child, did not even look at Charles. She stiffly rose from her chair and went to bed. Her inimical feelings toward Charles had caused her to suffer in silence, but as the picture of Sherrill kept flashing through her mind and the words of the commentary kept replaying in her thoughts, a dam of tears broke. She sobbed into her pillow and her body shook, racked with the sorrow that only a mother could feel.

Charles didn't take his family to church the next day. Instead, he read the Sunday paper over and over. Many of the articles were strewn with suppositions and innuendoes. The stories were critical of Charles and presented Randy and Sherrill as a modern day "Romeo and Juliet" caught up in a contemporary tale of unrequited love. The fact that Randy had fought Charles for Sherrill's hand in marriage caused even the most stalwart bluenoses to sympathize with the young couple's plight.

The Baptist Minister, noting the absence of the Lindstrom family, asked the congregation to bow their heads for a moment of silent prayer for Sherrill and her baby. After a prolonged moment, he prayed aloud.

"Lord, forgive Brother Charles for his misguided actions against his daughter Sherrill. He has shown the community in the past that he can be a loving Christian father. Cast Satan from his heart and free his soul from the fires of eternal damnation. Cleanse his spirit so that he may redeem himself in your eyes. And, Lord, let this congregation know the meaning of tolerance. Give them the capacity to feel charity in their hearts and love and forgiveness for their fellow man—Amen."

He then went into his sermon using the theme: "He, who is without sin, cast the first stone."

Randy's parents attended the "First Christian Church." Friends and well-wishers, who asked them about Randy and Sherrill, surrounded them. The newspapers had clarified some of the questions that had been generated by the TV news, but there were many more questions that remained unanswered.

Frank had asked the minister if he could speak to the congregation from the pulpit. After the opening songs and a prayer, the minister asked Frank to address the congregation.

As sweat formed on his brow, Frank's big work hardened hands gripped the podium for support. His hands were accustomed to gripping the steering wheel of a tractor and he had found little opportunity for public speaking. He had forced himself to ask to be allowed to speak because he wanted to set the record straight and felt that only a public statement to the congregation would satisfy the curiosity of his community. He began:

"I want to thank my family and friends for giving us support through these last months of trial and uncertainty. There have been many rumors about Randy and Sherrill. Some have been just wild guesses, while others hit pretty close to the mark; still, they were just rumors. I want to set the record straight—straight, as I can.

"Yes, Randy and Sherrill are going to have a baby." He was stopped by the whispers and murmurs in the audience. After a moment the congregation became quiet, and he continued, "It obviously happened in a moment of passion and weakness. The young couple came to Sylvia and me and asked for our blessing—which we gave. Randy shared with us that he had decided to join the air force to prepare a life for Sherrill and the baby."

He choked up momentarily at the memory of his son and daughter in-law to be and their happiness that night. He composed himself, and then continued. "Sylvia and I accompanied them to see Sherrill's parents, Charles and Mavis Lindstrom, to receive their permission and blessing for the marriage.

"A fight ensued between Charles and Randy; both received terrible injuries that required emergency medical care. As you know, Randy had a concussion and was hospitalized. A couple of Charles' injuries may be permanent.

"The story of an encounter with a bull was what I told the doctor while I was in the emergency room with Randy. I can only say that I was trying to protect the reputation of a fine young couple that love each other and wanted to do the right thing by getting married and providing a stable life for their baby."

Frank paused for a moment. He felt sweat running down his back and fought back tears of recrimination at not having prevented the fight in the first place. The entire congregation was on the edge of their seats, waiting for his next words. He didn't notice a couple of reporters in the back taking down every word.

He struggled on with the explanation, "While Randy was still in the hospital, Charles sent his daughter away to live with her aunt in California. Randy was heart broken; the only word that we could find out from her family was that Sherrill was okay. We just learned last night that Sherrill is living in California with her aunt and uncle, but that they can't be located. They are probably trying to avoid publicity

139

because of Sherrill's 'family condition.' I don't know anything about her becoming a TV starlet, but we all know how beautiful she is, both physically and inside as a person.

"Charles and Mavis are also good people—they couldn't have raised a girl like Sherrill, if they weren't. I don't know why Charles reacted the way he did, but I've learned through experience that 'love and hate' are like emotions on opposite sides of the same coin. The coin flips and the opposite emotion can sometimes land face up.

"Every night Randy and Sherrill are in Sylvia's and my prayers. I ask *you our friends* that they be in your prayers too." He stiffly left the podium, barely able to walk from the emotional strain of the speech. The entire congregation had tears in their eyes. They realized that Frank may not be the greatest speaker, but they had just heard a great speech—it had come directly from the heart.

The minister returned to the podium. "Everyone, please bow your heads for a moment of silent prayer." He then prayed aloud:

"Lord, help us in our time of need. Teach us to love our fellow man and help us realize that they, like we, have their weak moments too. Help us forgive those that trespass against us. Let our hearts open and understand the motives of those that seek to injure us through words and actions. Give us the strength, Lord, to have a strong moral fiber and forgive those of us that may fall short of your expectations. We thank you today, Lord, for Brother Ferris and his inspiring speech, for we know that it came from the heart of a good and decent man. Bless us and keep us through the days of our lives—Amen."

The choir sang "The Old Rugged Cross" and "Bringing in the Sheaves," then the minister delivered a sermon with the theme: "If a man should smite you upon your face then turn the other cheek."

News Conference

Sherrill awoke early Sunday morning. She felt rested after a hot bath and a good night's sleep. The sun was not up yet as she lay in bed lounging in the warmth of the comforter retrieved from the foot of the bed. She stretched arching her back, extending her arms, and pointing her toes toward the foot of the bed. Relaxing, she yawned, not because she was still sleepy but as a reflex to stretching and feeling stimulated.

With the knowledge that her aunt and uncle were in the adjoining room, she felt safe and at ease with the world. This feeling of serenity allowed her thoughts to expand and explore the events of her existence. Yesterday had been hectic and she felt that she had been reacting to outside stimuli. Today, she felt more in control of her world.

Thoughts of Randy permeated and dominated the dreamy-drifter collage of pictures and words flowing through her mind. Remembering his soothing voice and the touch of his lips on her body sent titillating chills and thrills through her. She could almost feel the strength of his hands and the tenderness of his fingertips as they touched and caressed her. She visualized the chiseled edge of his jaw, the sensitivity of his mouth, and the deepness of his azure blue eyes. She tasted the sweetness of his kisses and remembered his words of love whispered into her ears.

Her thoughts paused for a moment, brought to consciousness by her rapid breathing and the tenderness of her nipples against the stiff fabric of her new nightgown. She moaned from longing for her lover, who was physically a thousand miles away, but also inside her; inside her heart and inside the growing child that they had conceived together.

She focused into space, and willed her thoughts to span those thousands of miles and whispered, "Darling, I love you; I will always love you."

Having reconfirmed her love for Randy, she now felt secure in analyzing the feelings evoked by Mr. Payson's revelation of his love for her. Though he may have spoken from his heart, she had reacted from her mind. His affirmation of love had been flattering and even titillating, due to their station and age difference.

Now in the calm of her room she knew that her feelings toward him were strictly limited on a vocational basis. She resolved to meet with him and clear up any illusion that their association might develop beyond a student-teacher relationship.

Her mind drifted off to Laura Blevins. She really liked her as a person and wondered how anyone, who was so generous and gracious, could act out the role of Belinda—a petulant indulgent self-willed daughter of the Broderick clan.

Then she thought of Vivien Leigh in her Oscar winning roles of Scarlett O'Hara in "Gone with the Wind" and, later, as Blanche DuBois in "A Streetcar Named Desire"—two distinctly different acting styles.

Sherrill shivered, not from being cold, but from the realization that even *she* had the capacity to be perceived as a different person to many different people. To Randy—she was his lover and confidant (later she would be his wife and mother to their child). To her parents—she was their eldest daughter. To her brother and sister—she was their sister and role model. To her hometown basketball fans—she was a star and a respected athlete. To her teachers—she was a popular student. To her aunt and uncle—she was their niece and the daughter they never had. Yet to herself—she was still—*just* herself.

Fascinated by this revelation, she visualized the huge rotating mirrorball that had hung from the Blue Grotto ceiling at her junior prom. It was covered by hundreds of tiny mirrors imbedded in its surface, each reflecting a facet of light from many sources.

In her mind she fantasized that the rotating mirrorball represented a person—a movie star. The idolizing gazes of the fans were tiny sources of light that were reflected back by the popularity of the movie star. This phenomenon generated the general illusion that the movie star was the light source of the brilliance and the eyes of the fans were ever drawn to them.

A self-serving question developed in Sherrill's mind, "*Are we, 'who we are' or just the combined reflection of all of the people that influence our lives as we grow up?*"

She modified her own thinking, "*No, it can't be this complicated, nor even this simplistic. 'We are, who we are,' even alone in a room when there is no one else around us. There must be an internal fire within our spiritual and mortal soul that transcends the afterglow of all the people that have influenced our lives.*"

Throwing back the covers, she leapt from her bed and stretched; thinking, "*This is way too complex and problematic...for a Sunday morning.*"

The sun was rising with a diffused glow through the curtains. She heard her aunt and uncle moving about in the adjoining room. After a quick shower, she realized that she had no toothbrush. Taking the courtesy tube of toothpaste, she squished some on her finger and worked it around on the surface of her teeth then swished her mouth clean with the little bottle of complimentary mouthwash.

Dressing in her new clothes, she put the old ones in a plastic laundry bag. Glancing around to make sure that she hadn't forgotten anything, she knocked on the adjoining door and heard her aunt say, "Come on in, Honey. We're just about ready."

Entering the room she saw that her aunt and uncle were in good spirits after a good night's sleep, but she inquired anyway, "Did you have a good sleep?"

"Lordy, yes," replied her aunt. "Even Hank's snoring didn't bother me."

Hank objected, "I don't snore that badly." Then changing the subject, he announced, "How about us going to San Simeon and touring the Hearst Castle?"

"That sounds great," replied Sherrill. Her aunt nodded approval.

"Good," concluded Hank. "Grab your stuff and we're outta here."

He opened the door and was momentarily blinded by a barrage of camera flashes, followed by a babble of questions. His body blocked the door, and as his vision cleared, he stepped outside and called over his shoulder, "Close the door and stay inside."

The parking lot was filled with reporters and camera crews. The mob had started pressing toward him when they had spied Sherrill behind him. He held up his hands and demanded, "What's going on here?"

The mob of reporters stopped and many reporters shouted, "We want to see Sherrill!"

Hank had been an officer in the air force and he knew how to control people. "I don't know what all this hurrah is about, but she is not going to be mobbed by everyone. Select two of you—a man and a woman—no cameras; we'll talk inside."

He turned and let himself in with the room key. As he entered, his eyes were drawn toward the flashing message light on the phone. Aunt Vicki inquired, "What did you say to them?"

Hank held up his hand, "Just a minute, Honey." Dialing the front desk he stated, "Yes, this is Hank Casson in room 122. You have a message for me?"

The manager came on the phone and said, "Yes, Mr. Casson. We didn't want to disturb you by ringing your room, but there are a bunch of reporters in the parking lot in front of your room. They asked for your room number, but it is our policy not to give that information out to anyone. I don't know how they found your room. They must know your car, since it is parked in front of your door."

Hank frowned for a moment then a light bulb lit in his head, *Ah, it must have been the clerk in the department store—she must have gotten our license plate number.* "Thank you, sir, I'll handle the reporters," he spoke into the phone. "I appreciate your discretion—the next time I'm in town, I'll stay here again—goodbye."

There was a knock at the door and he let the two reporters enter—cameras flashed. The reporters smiled at Sherrill and Hank demanded, again, "What's this all about?" He added, "We know that Sherrill's picture was in the paper yesterday, but that was in Merced—this is Monterey."

The woman reporter spoke first, "You don't know that Sherrill's the hottest news story in America today? Photographs of her have been on all the TV networks. News articles about her have appeared in all the newspapers."

Aunt Vicki interjected, "We haven't turned on the TV."

The woman reporter continued, "All of America wants to learn more about the newly discovered starlet. They want to hear about the baby and know more about Randy, and how he bravely fought her father for her hand in marriage."

Sherrill had been quiet, trying to stay in the background, but the mention of the baby and Randy caused her cheeks to pale and her hands felt clammy. Her voice was croaky, as she verified, "You—you mean everyone knows—about us—about Randy and the baby?"

"Everyone that can pick up a newspaper or turn on a TV," confirmed the reporter.

Sherrill's thoughts flashed to her parents, *How they must be suffering from the notoriety;* then to Randy, *I wonder if they allow him access to newspapers and television, during basic training.*

"Please, Miss Lindstrom," the male reporter spoke for the first time, "We just want to get a few photographs and have an interview with you."

Angered by the absurdity of the situation, Hank snapped, "Well, that's just not going to happen,".

"Please, Uncle Hank," Sherrill entreated. "They've already found out everything that we wanted to keep secret. I don't want them to have the wrong idea about Randy and me."

144

"That's right," piped in Aunt Vicki. "If I know these news people, they have already made up stuff to fill in the blanks."

The two reporters opened their mouths to debate the point, thought better of it, and turned their opened-mouth gape into a yawn. The male reporter, thinking quickly, said, "It's been a long night." The female reporter, cupping her hand across her mouth, nodded in agreement.

Hank, still miffed, relinquished, "Okay, but it is going to be structured like a press conference. You can have your photo-shoot. Then, your gang of reporters can ask questions—one at a time. If Sherrill doesn't want to answer the question then that's the end of the question and we'll move on to the next one. I want to remind you that Sherrill is not one of your high-profile political candidates running for office. We can and will end the session at anytime."

Opening the door, he commanded, "Now go out there and explain the ground rules to your news hounds."

The cameras flashed again and the female reporter posed in the doorway, with exaggerated glamour and remarked, "Oh, I didn't know that you all wanted a photograph of little ole me."

The group laughed and someone quipped, "Oh, no! My camera just broke; I'll have to get a another one." The reporters laughed again—even louder. The female reporter scrunched up her nose and made a face in response to the barbed remark, and then walked into their midst to explain the conditions for the interview.

Aunt Vicki grabbed a hairbrush out of her purse and started brushing Sherrill's hair. Sherrill complained, "Oh, I must look a mess."

"Don't worry about it, Honey," Vicki soothed, with cloaked anxiety. "You're beautiful and the press will love you."

There was a knock on the door and Hank growled as he opened it, "We're not ready yet."

"I know," replied a handsome debonair young man. I'm, Brad Thurman, with 'The Dons of Eldorado' studio." He entered the room, dragging a make-up artist by the hand.

He continued, "I heard that there is going to be a photo-shoot and I'd like to offer the services of our make-up artist."

"Fine—fine," agreed Hank as he started to close the door, and then saw it blocked by the foot of a slightly flustered little man, who was just curling his fingers to knock.

"Excuse me, Mr. Casson, I'm the motel manager, and I overheard that there is going to be a photo-shoot. All these reporters are starting to disturb my other guests."

Hank stepped back from the doorway and the manager's eyes brightened as he saw Sherrill. He exclaimed, "Oh, I didn't know that Miss Lindstrom was a guest. Had I known, I would have had a bottle of wine sent to your room."

He smiled at Sherrill with a look of discovery on his face. "Please, Miss Lindstrom, let me offer our swimming pool area for the photo-shoot."

"You are very generous, sir," replied Sherrill.

"I will take care of it," stated the manager. Obviously smitten, he turned and left the room. He started directing the reporters to the pool area as Hank closed the door.

"Hi, I'm Alice," the make up artist introduced herself.

"Hello, I'm Sherrill," she extended her hand.

Alice's first question, "You don't, by chance, have any other clothes?

"No, just shorts and this white blouse," responded Sherrill. Trying to inject a little humor, she added, "You have to travel light when you travel incognito."

Alice smiled. She saw that Sherrill was slightly overwhelmed by all of this attention. "You'll be just fine," she encouraged, as she patted Sherrill on the shoulder.

Alice took a critical account of her charge and noted that she had a beautiful face, supported by a long tapered neck that formed gracefully into her wide, but not too broad, shoulders. Sherrill's hair was her main concern. It was clean and resilient, but not coiffured for a photo-shoot.

"We don't have time to do this properly," she advised, as she quickly combed Sherrill's hair, divided it, pulled it up, and layered it in swirls on top.

She locked the swirls together with a couple of well-placed bobby pins, and then pulled out a tendril of hair on each side of her face. The result accented Sherrill's long neck and framed her face; giving the impression that she had just prepared herself to take a nice hot bath—perfect for a swimming pool shot.

The artist applied eyeliner and eye shadow along with a slight blush of rouge and a small amount of lip-gloss that accented Sherrill's natural coloring. Alice stepped back to observe her work, "Just one more thing."

Reaching into her bag, she pulled out a small rhinestone *tiara* and placed it on Sherrill's head, saying, "There, now you even look like an *official* princess being interviewed by the press."

Sherrill went into the bathroom and looked into the mirror; the transition amazed her. With a renewed confidence, she reentered the room, "Okay, I'm ready."

Hank opened the door, "Okay, let's get this show on the road."

They filed back toward the outdoor swimming pool and entered through an arbor into a garden area at one end of the pool. Cameras had been placed to catch her appearance and there was a collective *sigh* as Sherrill gracefully entered alone through the arbor. The morning sun cast its golden glow on her face and the rhinestones in her tiara sparkled, creating a halo effect. Cameras clicked and the film rolled. Sherrill felt special and wanted to share this special feeling with her audience.

She gazed left, and then right, exposing her long graceful neck to the cameras; the Oleander bushes silhouetted her head. She smiled a broad smile showing her perfect white teeth. She plucked an Oleander flower and lingered a moment, as she breathed in its fragrance. She felt like "Miss America" and wondered what the crowned beauty would do under these circumstances.

Remembering that Miss America always walked the runway for the audience, she glided forward on the path to the pool. Stopping at the edge of the pool, she waved to the cameras and the people gathered behind them. Smiling, her radiance was recorded for posterity and the eagerly awaiting audience of the nightly news.

Off camera, Uncle Hank x'ed his arms in front of his face and pulled his index finger across his throat to indicate "cut." The cameras stopped rolling and the photographers lowered their cameras. Sherrill relaxed for a moment. Alice, the makeup artist, ran up to her, commenting, "You did great; have you had any modeling experience?"

"No," confided Sherrill, "I was just reacting to the cameras and pretending that I was 'Miss America.' I was so nervous that my knees were shaking."

Alice counseled, "Don't ever try to get rid of that feeling; it obviously works for you."

The motel manager had been busy. He had his kitchen crew prepare sandwiches and sweet rolls. Off to one side in the garden, an urn of coffee was set up on a table. Two reporters, who had volunteered to help, lugged a podium from one of the conference rooms. The podium was positioned at a slanted angle to the sun and flowering Bougainvillea in the background to provide contrast. This setup insured that Sherrill would not have to look directly into the early morning sun and minimized shadowing on her face. Microphones were attached to the podium and the sound tested. The cameras were focused and the light measured to insure optimum photography for the news conference.

People were gathered in small groups, chatting about how Sherrill had become such a high profile news story. Many had followed the story from when it broke and were eager to follow-up. The events had assumed a life of its own; inevitably, like a tidal wave breaking across a beach, affecting the lives of all who were touched by it.

More people were arriving by the minute, as the story leaked out that Sherrill had actually been located. Uncle Hank looked around and noted the swelling crowd. He picked up a spoon and rapped its edge against an empty water glass on the table. The shrill ting-ting brought a hush to the crowd.

He raised his voice so all could hear, "Okay, let's get this show on the road. I don't want this news conference to last more than fifteen minutes. Each reporter may ask one question and a follow-up question (if needed). At the end of rotation, I'll allow five minutes of random questions."

The cluster of reporters gathered to one side of the cameras, away from the sun. A master-mixer microphone was handed to the first reporter. Sherrill's mouth was starting to taste like cotton. She took a sip of water and for moral support carried the glass with her to the podium. The cameras started rolling and Sherrill flashed a brilliant smile, remembering to answer to the cameras, not the reporters.

The first reporter began, "Miss Lindstrom—."

Sherrill quickly raised her hand and interjected, "Please, I would prefer that you call me, 'Sherrill.'"

The reporter began again, "Sherrill, having come from a small town background, you must be overwhelmed by all this sudden attention."

Looking into the cameras, she responded, "Yes, I am amazed by all this attention. Yesterday, I was a photograph on the front page of a newspaper; today, I am speaking to people all across America. However, I think that even someone from a big city would be overwhelmed."

She saw heads nod in the crowd and heard murmurs of approval— she was over the big *first* answer.

The microphone was passed to the next reporter. "Sherrill, how did you get the name—Sherrill? It looks and sounds like a Hollywood name."

Sherrill thought to herself, *this is easier than I thought it would be.* Her shoulders relaxed slightly, "My mother wanted to name me Cheryl with a 'C,' but when she wrote it out with my last name Lindstrom, it didn't look right to her; so she phonetically spelled it with an 'S.'"

Next reporter, "Sherrill, what are your plans for the near future?"

Sherrill held onto the edge of the podium and smiled, "My most immediate plan is to get through this interview without revealing how nervous I am." The audience laughed at the paradox of her statement.

Sherrill released her grip from the podium, since the spectators had understood the intended jest in her statement, and continued, "I want to complete the special education program at my high school, and then take some college courses. I love learning about the world I live in and experiencing the wonders that life has to offer.

The same reporter remarked, "That is a very mature statement from someone so young."

Sherrill explained, "The unusual events during the last couple of months have forced me to face the realities of my life. Reality has been a very potent maturing experience." The audience nodded in agreement.

The microphone was passed to the next reporter, "Sherrill, while waiting for this interview, I spoke with several people that represented filming interests in Hollywood. They indicated that they would like to sign you to a filming contract; that is if you haven't already signed with 'The Dons of Eldorado.' My question is: Do you already have an agent to represent you?"

Sherrill thought, *that's a curve.* Then she answered to their surprise, "Yes, I do. My uncle Hank Casson has done a great job this morning with this news conference. He is my legal guardian and has always looked out for my best interest." She glanced at Hank and he beamed with a consenting smile, acknowledging his recent promotion.

Addressing the original contract, she commented, "There is no existing contract with 'The Dons of Eldorado.' It seems that the original contract blew away in the wind. However, I want to add that Laura Blevins and the entire filming crew made me feel special. Their makeup artist even helped me prepare for this interview, so I know that there is interest on their part."

Sherrill paused and took a sip of water while the microphone was passed to the next reporter. "Sherrill, tell us something about Randy."

Her face softened as she gazed past the cameras, willing him to be with her. "I love Randy with all my heart. He is the most special person in the world to me—we are soul mates. He is presently in the air force taking basic training. When he gets a permanent assignment and I turn eighteen then we will be able to get married."

The cameras picked up the glisten of tears in her eyes and the audience had a collective look of sadness at her plight. The reporter steeled herself for the follow-up question that had to be asked, "Sherrill, we learned that Randy fought with your father for your hand in marriage. Did he lose the fight—is that why he is not with you?"

Sherrill knew that some of the questions would be hard to answer; but this was why she had agreed to the interview—to set the record straight. She took a deep breath and replied, "No, Randy did not lose the fight; he was the last man standing. He didn't want to fight my father—for my sake—but he had no choice. During the fight his head hit a concrete slab and he suffered a concussion. Later, on the way to the hospital, he lost consciousness.

"While he was in a coma in the hospital, my father gave me some options. I agreed to live with my aunt and uncle and not try to contact Randy until I turned eighteen."

Sensing the sharks circling, the next reporter grabbed the microphone, "Your father's option sounds like something out of medieval times. Can you tell us what the other options were?"

Reacting, Sherrill snapped back, "I could—but I won't. The other options were not even a consideration. The fact that I'm here should indicate that I took the option that was best for myself and my baby."

Sherrill realized that she had reacted with fire in her eyes and softened the statement by adding with a smile, "At first, I didn't want to come to California, but my Aunt Vicki has been almost like an older sister to me. We have become the best of friends and I appreciate all that she and Uncle Hank have done for me." She glanced in their direction and smiled at the two people whom she had grown to love.

The reporter, slightly chastened, inquired, "Why do you think your father reacted the way he did?"

Sherrill became serious again, without the fire in her eyes and stated, "I do not want to dwell on this subject. I cannot answer for or be responsible for my father's actions.

"I can only presume that he reacted the way he did because of pride, and the feeling of shame and humiliation after losing the fight with Randy. I think that he reacted aggressively toward Randy because he loves me and thought that he was protecting me."

The audience stood in awe at this astute synopsis by the beautiful young girl. A cameraman turned to another cameraman, "This is going to burn-up the six o'clock news. It's the best interview that I've been on in six years."

Hank stepped up and took the microphone from the reporter, "Sherrill, we are going to take some random questions from the audience. They may be a reporter or a fan." Sherrill nodded approval. A woman in the audience held up her hand and was handed the microphone.

"Sherrill, I'm a new fan. What advice do you have for teenagers in America?"

Sherrill smiled and quipped, "I know that you are a new fan because I don't have any old ones." The audience laughed and the uneasiness from the previous questions evaporated.

Feeling on a roll, she quipped again, "You have probably asked the toughest question because teenagers don't take advice." The audience laughed again and their mood turned mellow."

She continued on an informative note, "We teenagers are receptive to information; we learn from everyone and everything around us—we tend to soak it up like a sponge. We are also trying to create our own personal identity and the word *advice* carries the stigma of belonging to someone else—**not us**.

"Therefore, I would like to share my personal observation: 'A few months ago I was looking forward to five more years of youth…my final year of high school and four more years in college. In a moment of passion, I threw away my youthful dreams. I'm now facing the next five years as an adult, having to make adult decisions.'"

"To the young people in America, I can only say—cherish your youth; it is yours and yours alone. Don't let your actions or the actions of others rob you of that youth.

"If parents would only listen, then my advice would be to them, 'Talk to your children about their feelings. *Passion* is a natural emotion; it is a human trait and a wonderful feeling. However, young people lack the experience to put their conflicting desires into perspective. Help them understand these feelings, so that passion works for them, not against them.'"

Sherrill smiled a sage smile, an adult smile; the audience broke into a resounding applause.

Hank, sensing that additional questions would be anticlimactic to the answer just heard, walked over and took the microphone and announced, "Thank you, Sherrill. This news conference is over."

Sherrill smiled and waved to the cameras and the audience, while they applauded. The effect, when it was aired that night to the home viewers, was that she was addressing a huge crowd. In reality she was—the people of America.

Hank x'ed his arms and drew his index finger across his throat. The movie cameras were shut off and the still cameras were lowered. Sherrill walked away from the podium and her knees started shaking. Aunt Vicki rushed up and hugged her, "I'm so proud of you, Honey; I could just cry. I didn't know that we had a budding keynote speaker in our family."

After Sherrill's press conference, representatives from studios wanting Sherrill to sign with them surrounded Hank Casson. He motioned to Vicki and conferred, "Honey, it looks like I'm going to be very busy for awhile. Why don't you and Sherrill take the car and drive down to San Simeon and take a tour through the Hearst Castle."

"That's a good idea," agreed Vicki. "I know that Sherrill could use the break from all this attention. We'll meet you back here tonight— I'm sorry, Honey, that you won't be able come with us."

"That's okay; you and I have been there before, and I think that talking with these people *now* is important." Hank kissed her goodbye, "Have a good time."

He beckoned to Brad Thurman, the representative from "The Dons of Eldorado," and they entered the motel room. Hank poured a half glass of champagne that the motel manager had sent over and offered it to the studio representative.

"Thanks," acknowledged Brad, taking the glass.

"Mr. Thurman," began Hank. "Let's cut to the chase. You can see that I'm going to have to talk to a lot of other studios today and I suspect that others will be contacting me next week. We appreciate your lending the use of your hairdresser for the interview, and we both know that Sherrill adores Laura Blevins—but business is business. Now, I want to hear your best offer."

Brad thought for a moment. His original intention was to offer $10K per episode, but the publicity surrounding Sherrill had made her the hottest unsigned prospect in show business, today. He upped the ante, "Mr. Casson, my studio is willing to sign Sherrill for three episodes at $25K per episode. That's as high as I can go since that equals the same package as Miss Blevins is receiving. Sherrill shows great potential, but she is still an unproven commodity."

"Commodity!" exclaimed Hank, consternation showing in his voice. "I could take umbrage at that statement. You make it sound like we are trading in 'pork bellies' on the stock market. I am Sherrill's uncle. She's not just some chattel to be auctioned off to the highest bidder—she's a person."

"I'm sorry," Brad apologized. "'Commodity' is just a slang term used in the movie industry, whose entire existence is to make money for the stars and for the studios. We are, after all, discussing an offer for her talents and viewer draw. The usage of the term 'commodity' is not used entirely out of context, even though it may not be the appropriate word in describing Sherrill."

"I concede your point," replied Hank. "It's just that all this hullabaloo from the press has me on edge. It has turned our lives into a three-ring circus."

"I understand," sympathized Brad.

"I tell you what," concluded Hank. "Leave your contract and I'll look it over with the rest of the other offers. You've been straight with us, so far. For that, I will call you before we accept a final offer from someone else."

"Fair enough," agreed Brad. "I'll be waiting for your call." He shook Hank's hand and left.

Hank called in the next agent and the negotiation process began anew.

Sherrill and Aunt Vicki walked through the portals of Hearst Castle; she stared in amazement, "I can't believe that people actually lived like this—the view, the Neptune pool, the Roman temple, the baroque statues…it overwhelms the senses."

Aunt Vicki guided her toward the living quarters and exclaimed, "Wait until we get inside!"

Sherrill walked through the tour, awed by the Renaissance and baroque paintings and architecture. To Aunt Vicki she half-jokingly confided, "I must bring Randy here and show him how I want to live after we're married."

They both laughed and Vicki thought, *this is the world of the rich and famous—could my niece find happiness here?* She put the thought out of her mind—only the future would tell.

Sherrill

Sunday afternoon—Sergeant Stark was kicked back in his recliner and watching a football game. Earlier, he had attended church with his family. Now he planned to take life easy because the basic training routine would start again, Monday morning.

This was his first weekend off since he had started the new group of recruits two weeks ago. Yesterday, he had taken care of honey-do errands that always seemed to pile up in his absence. Today, his wife Maria was reading the newspaper, since she didn't share Stark's preoccupation with football.

During one of the commercial breaks, Sherrill's picture flashed on the screen and the announcer hyped, "Missing starlet found. Her news conference will be aired in its entirety during the six o'clock news." Stark stared at her picture and disparagingly remarked, "She's beautiful, but who gives a rat's ass about that Hollywood stuff."

Maria looked up and admonished, "Dwayne, that's not a nice thing to say. You don't even know anything about her. All weekend, they've been flashing her picture on the TV, and I was just starting to read a couple of articles about her in the Arts and Entertainment section of the newspaper."

Stark stared at his wife and callously lectured, "Just a bunch of Hollywood hype bullshit. She wasn't really missing; some studio just wanted everyone to think so. You just watch; next week they'll release a new movie that she's starring in."

Stark went back to watching the football game. Maria continued reading, "Honey, do you know a Randy Ferris at Lackland?"

Stark, concentrating on the game, absently answered, "Yeah, he's my barracks chief."

"Well, he's mentioned in the article," informed Maria.

"What the hell!" His interest piqued, Stark leaped from his recliner, without lowering the footrest, and grabbed the newspaper from Maria's hands. He sat down beside her on the divan and scanned the articles revealing: "Sherrill is going to have a baby; that her fiancé is Randy Ferris, who fought her father for her hand in marriage; that Randy is in basic training in the air force; that she couldn't contact him until her eighteenth birthday."

Staring into space, Stark verbalized, "Well, I'll be damned...that explains it!"

"Explains what—who?"

He turned to face her, "Randy's got a hell of a high I.Q. I asked him why he wasn't in college and he told me that it was personal. This explains it," nodding toward the newspaper.

Stark folded the newspaper and placed it on the coffee table. Rubbing his chin, he inquired, "What do we have in the freezer to barbecue?" A plan was forming in his mind.

"We still have some steaks from that side of beef that you bought at the commissary."

"Good. Pull out an extra one. We're going to have a guest for dinner."

He got up and phoned the base, "Hello, this is Sergeant Stark. Contact Airman Randall Ferris and issue him an off base pass. Instruct him to meet me at HQ in a half-hour.

He hung up the phone and turned to his wife; "I'm going to start the barbecue. Put the steaks off to the side to thaw fast. Make up a salad and bake some potatoes."

He left to start the barbecue and returned five-minutes later, "Where are the kids?"

"Playing with friends."

"Find them and call your sister. See if she can come over and pick them up. We'll go get them, after I take Randy back to the base."

Opening the door, he stopped and added, "Oh—turn off the TV and radio—hide the newspaper; I want the TV press conference to be a total surprise to Randy. I'll be back in less than an hour."

He left and Maria stared at the football game on television. A wide receiver had just run ninety-seven yards for a touchdown and the fans were going crazy. She thought, *I've never seen him leave a ballgame for any reason in the five years that we've been married.*

Stark walked into the day room. Randy was waiting for him—an unspoken question in his eyes. Stark said nothing and signed for the pass. He motioned for Randy to follow him and they got into the car.

No words had been spoken since they left the day room and Randy finally broke the silence. "Thanks for getting me off the base. This is a good break from the routine. Where are we going?"

"To a barbecue at my house," Stark casually informed.

"Oh, is this for getting 'barracks of the week?'" assumed Randy.

"You could say that," Stark cryptically replied.

155

They rode in silence for another five minutes. Randy would have liked more information, but Sergeant Stark seemed almost secretive. Randy distracted himself by observing the houses in the community and the countryside as they sped along the highway.

Stark broke the silence, "How are you getting along with the assistant DI?"

"Fine. He tells us what he wants us to do, then basically leaves us alone until we're finished."

"Good, that's what I told him to do. Do you know what you're going to be doing tomorrow?"

"Yes. There is a list posted on the bulletin board. Half the barracks will test in the morning and the other half will test in the afternoon—except my name wasn't on the list."

"That's because you are going to be taking tests all day," informed Stark.

"Oh," responded Randy, wondering at the revelation.

Stark said nothing more until they pulled up in the driveway, "Come inside and meet my wife—the kids are over at her sister's place.

Randy followed Stark into his home and removed his fatigue cap. Maria entered from the kitchen and Stark introduced them, "Maria, meet Randy Ferris—Randy, this is my wife, Maria."

Randy, noting that the title 'airman' had purposely been dropped during the introduction, smiled, "Pleased to meet you, Maria."

Maria, at a glance, took in his tall athletic body with his smooth handsome face and thought, *I would bet that he is even more handsome with hair—no wonder he's Sherrill's fiancé.* She offered her hand, "Welcome to our home, Randy."

Stark suggested, "Let's go out on the patio." Then added, "Honey, bring us out a couple of cold beers."

They passed the time talking about sports and fishing, while consuming another beer. Stark looked at his watch, "Time to put the steaks on the barbecue."

Maria sat down across from Randy, "You must have a girlfriend back home."

Randy's face brightened then clouded as he thought of Sherrill, and then remembering the circumstances that kept them apart. He replied, "Yes, I do."

"I imagine that she is very pretty," coaxed Maria.

"Yes, she is," confirmed Randy, adding, "but her real beauty is from within her. I can only describe it as having 'a pure heart.'"

"What a nice thing to say," exclaimed Maria, moved by his candid reply. "I don't think that I have ever heard a compliment given quite like that."

Pausing a moment to appreciate his sincerity, she added, "She is a lucky girl to have someone sensitive enough to recognize her real beauty."

Randy unabashedly stated, "If you ever met her, you would recognize it too."

Having put the steaks on, Stark walked up and overheard only part of the conversation. Half-jesting he remarked, "You need to watch out for this guy; he's a pretty smooth talker."

Maria replied, "He's sincere—I believe him."

Stark jokingly confirmed, "That is the worst kind."

Maria said, "Excuse me; I need to check the baked potatoes." She disappeared into the house.

Stark, not wanting to talk shop, searched for a common interest subject. "You're a crack shot. Have you ever been big game hunting?"

"Yes, I went elk hunting with my father and grandfather last year in Colorado. I shot a six-point bull elk south of Steamboat Springs."

Stark, stimulated by visions of past hunts, volunteered, "I go every year with a group of guys from the base. We always go to Black Mountain, north of Durango, Colorado."

"I hear that's a good area," prompted Randy.

"It's a great area," responded Stark, the *call of the wild* in his eyes. "We've filled out our tags every year."

They swapped hunting stories until Maria announced, "The steaks are done." She had noticed that the men were engrossed in conversation, and had taken it upon herself to insure that the steaks didn't burn.

They sat down and devoured the steaks, while discussing previous cookouts that had been memorable. After finishing his meal, Randy leaned back, "That was a great meal. We don't have meals like that on base."

"Thank you," responded Maria. "We're glad that you could be here and share a meal with us."

Stark looked at his watch and suggested, "Let's go in and watch the six o'clock news. You probably feel out of touch with the outside world, since you can't watch TV on the base."

"You're right," responded Randy, "but I miss reading the newspaper, even more."

Stark turned to Maria, "Honey, forget the dishes; watch the news with us." With an impish grin, he winked at her.

They filed into the living room. Stark switched on the TV and selected a network channel. He sat in his recliner, with Maria and Randy sitting on the divan. The lead-in music played and the network logo displayed on the screen.

The reporter looked at his audience and announced, "All of America has become intrigued with the missing starlet from 'The Dons of Eldorado.' She was discovered this morning in Monterey, California and she held a news conference to share with America, who she really is.

"The reasons for her wanting to remain anonymous are vividly revealed in the news conference, which will be aired in its entirety after these commercial messages.

Randy turned to Maria and shared, "'The Dons of Eldorado' was one of the programs that I watched back home. It has a similar format to 'The Big Valley,' except it has some unique twists that makes it different."

"I know; we watch it too," replied Maria.

"I wonder which episode the missing starlet was in?" questioned Randy. "They didn't mention her name."

"She hasn't been on any episodes, yet," informed Maria. "The studio just discovered her and she is supposed to be in an episode that will be aired in five weeks."

Music had been dubbed onto the sound track of the photo-shoot. Soft trumpets played an introduction as the screen showed an arbor of Oleanders. A beautiful girl appeared from the shadows of the arbor. A morning sun bathed her in golden sunshine. She smiled a radiant smile, looking left then right, as she picked a flower and inhaled the essence of its scent. A halo effect from the tiara sparkled above her head as she waved to the world.

Randy had never seen Sherrill with this hairstyle and was slow to recognize her. Suddenly, he sat forward and stared disbelievingly at the screen. "Good God! That's—that's Sherrill." Then thinking that he was the only one that knew of her, excitedly clarified, "My—my fiancée; my—girl—girlfriend from back home."

"We know," revealed Stark and Maria in unison, a conspiratorial sparkle in their eyes and a devious smile on their faces.

Randy wondered. *How did they know?* He couldn't pull his eyes from the TV as he watched Sherrill gracefully approach the cameras, accompanied by background music as she glided down the walkway. A tear of longing formed in his eyes as his heart skipped a couple of beats. Her waving and smiling seemed like she was performing only for him.

Maria commented, "Oh, Randy, she is so beautiful."

Randy's subconscious heard Maria, but his focus was on the image in front of him. The scene faded and switched to Sherrill behind the podium. He was so filled with love and emotion for the girl in front of him that he only heard blurbs and phrases of the interview.

Reporter: "Sherrill; having a small town background, you must be overwhelmed...

Sherrill: "...even someone from a big city...overwhelmed...speaking to people across America."

Maria remarked, "She has such poise in front of the camera. Her answer is so natural." Exposing her own fear, Maria confided, "I would be scared to death in front of the cameras."

Reporter: "...how did you get the name—Sherrill?"

Sherrill: "My mother wanted to name me..."

Reporter: "...what are your plans...?"

Sherrill: "...to get through this interview...."

They heard laughter from the audience. Maria remarked empathetically, "Aah, she is nervous and has a sense of humor—I love her." Randy was mesmerized. He willed that he could be with her.

Sherrill: "...enroll in some college courses. ...learning about the world around me...explore the far corners of the universe."

Reporter: "That is a very mature statement...."

Sherrill: "...unusual events...forced me to recognize the realities of life"

Reporter: "—do you already have an agent?"

(Delayed response with eyes searching)

Sherrill: "Yes, I do. My uncle, Hank Casson...."

Maria observed in awe, "She thinks so quickly. You could see that she didn't have an answer; then suddenly, she has 'the answer.'"

Reporter: "Sherrill; tell us something about Randy."

Sherrill: "I love Randy—we are soul mates."

Randy saw the glisten of tears in her eyes and his own eyes filmed over with tears as he whispered, "I'm with you, Baby; I love you and I'm right here with you."
Maria put her arm around Randy and hugged him with tears in her own eyes, consoling, "You will be, Randy. Just give it time—you will be."
Even Stark interjected, "Damn—Ferris, you are one lucky son-of-a-guy."

Reporter: "...Randy fought.... Did he lose...?"

Sherrill: "No, Randy...last man standing. ...my father gave...options."

Reporter: "sounds...medieval times. ...tell us...options were?"

Sherrill: "I could, but I won't. ...fact that I'm here...option that was best for myself and my baby."

Maria, seeing the fire in Sherrill's eyes, commented, "Ooh, look at her; she has spirit too!"

Sherrill: "At first, I didn't want to come to California...Aunt Vickie...best of friends."

Maria modified her original statement, "She has spirit, but she moderates it with reality."

Reporter: "Why do you think your father reacted…?"

Sherrill: "…pride and the feeling of mortification after losing…reacted aggressively…because he loves me…protecting me."

Maria, "She not only has charity in her heart, but the logic to understand why to forgive."

Hank: "…random questions…reporter or a fan."

Fan: "…new fan…advice …teenagers in America?"

Sherrill: "…you are a *new* fan because I don't have any *old* ones." (Audience laughter)

Sherrill: "…asked the toughest question…because teenagers don't take advice."
(Mellow laughter)

Maria amazed, "With just two statements, she turned around the whole mood of the questions."

Randy shook his shoulders, bringing his mind to focus on what Sherrill was saying.

"We teenagers are receptive to information; we learn from everyone and everything around us—we tend to soak it up like a sponge. We are also trying to create our own personal identity and the word *advice* carries the stigma of belonging to someone else—**not us**.

"Therefore, I would like to share my personal observation: 'A few months ago I was looking forward to five more years of youth…my final year of high school and four more years in college. In a moment of passion, I threw away my youthful dreams. I'm now facing the next five years as an adult, having to make adult decisions.'

"To the young people in America, I can only say—cherish your youth; it is yours and yours alone. Don't let your actions or the actions of others rob you of that youth.

"If parents would only listen, then my advice would be to them, 'Talk to your children about their feelings. *Passion* is a natural emotion; it is a human trait and a wonderful feeling. However, young people lack the experience to put their conflicting desires into perspective. Help them understand these feelings, so that passion works for them, not against them.'"

There was spontaneous applause, followed by more enthusiastic applause as the scene faded with Sherrill smiling and waving. Music had been dubbed into the background and the threesome, Stark, Maria, and Randy, stared at a blank television screen, lost in their personal thoughts of what they had just seen and heard on the television.

After a long five seconds, the news reporter reappeared on the screen and stated, "Ladies and gentlemen, I think you will agree that this has been one of the most moving interviews from such a young starlet that we have ever telecast. Tune in again tonight when it will aired on our ten o'clock news.

Stark shut off the television, chucked Randy on the shoulder, and enthusiastically bragged, "How was that for a Sunday punch!"

Randy, looking dazed, "You could have knocked me over with a popsicle stick. How did you find out about her before the interview?"

Maria handed him the newspaper, "There are several articles in the entertainment section."

Randy took the newspaper and began reading. Maria turned to Stark, "Oh, Dwayne, wasn't that romantic! It was like watching a princess in a fairytale."

Stark, trained to be hard but moved by the interview, observed with a grin, "Yes, it is like a Cinderella story." Dropping his voice to a gravelly sound, he added, "And we've got the charming prince cooling his heels in our living room." His statement set off alarms in his head as he thought, *Randy better not go AWOL to find Sherrill.*

Maria turned and gave a quick hug to Randy, "Yes, he is a prince; such a handsome one too."

Stark felt solid in their marriage, but he suddenly felt a pinprick of jealousy—or was it merely envy? He ribbed his wife, "Maria, I just discovered that *you* have a talent that I wasn't aware of."

"What are you saying?" questioned Maria, confusion showing on her brow.

"Well, during the interview, you gave such a great play-by-play analysis; I thought you might like to start watching football with me, and be my own personal color commentator." He winked teasingly.

Maria stuck her tongue out and made a face, "Oh, Dwayne, you're so funny." They both chuckled. Still smiling, Stark brought his wife's hand up to his lips and gave it a quick kiss.

Randy folded the paper and absently stated, "She lives in Merced, California."

Stark, reacting, blurted out, "Now, don't you go AWOL on me!"

Randy looked up, surprised, "I've promised you before that my feelings would not affect my performance—that still stands."

Stark, relieved, slapped him on the back, "Sorry, Randy, I just had to check. In the military it sometimes happens. I just wanted to be sure that you wouldn't do something rash that would screw up your life."

Maria, sensing a strain in the conversation, changed the subject, "Randy, Sherrill is an angel. When is the baby due?

Randy made a quick calculation in his head, "The week of April 4th."

Maria counted backward on her fingers, "That would make her about four months along." She non-offensively added, "How can you be so sure?"

Randy, blushing, "Because it happened the first time we made love."

Stark, coming to his rescue, "Jesus Christ, Maria. What are you after—the entire story of his sex life?"

"Randy, I didn't mean to offend you. It's just that women like to know about these things. I feel so close to you and Sherrill; like I've known both of you for a long time."

"That's okay," responded Randy. "It's just that I haven't gotten used to the idea that I'm going to be a father. It seems almost like a dream—with Sherrill being in California and seeing her tonight on TV."

"When will she turn eighteen?" asked Maria.

"June 16th," responded Randy.

Maria shook her head, "I just hate her father for putting you two through this."

Randy responded, "Yes, I could hate him too, but seeing her tonight and hearing her explain that her father probably reacted out of love for her, makes me look at the past events in a softer light.

Maria, not convinced, "How could anyone send someone they loved into exile?"

"I don't know," responded Randy. He thought for a moment, and then he asked a rhetorical philosophical question, "Could it be possibly that *self-pride* is a stronger emotion than *love*?"

163

Maria mused for a moment. Glancing toward Stark with a twinkle in her eye, she confessed, "I've thought a lot about *love*, but you'll have to consult with someone else in the family about *self-pride*."

Stark caught the directed remark, which was lost on Randy since he was formulating thoughts in his mind. Staring into space, he thought out loud, "Self-pride is internal and bloats the ego; whereas, love also comes from within, but has to be given freely in order to survive and thrive in the heart."

Stark cut in, "Hey, you two are getting way too *deep*. Christ, next thing you know, you'll be debating whether the sun circles the earth or it's the other way around."

Maria and Randy glanced at each other then laughed because they both realized that Stark was feeling that he had been left out of the conversation.

Randy looked at his watch and stood up, "I guess that I had better be getting back to the base. I have a long letter to write before lights out."

Turning to Maria, "I want to thank you both for making my evening very special."

Maria arose, "Randy, you and Sherrill have made our evening very special too. Please visit us again, if you get the chance." She leaned over and hugged him, and then in the custom of saying goodbye to a younger brother, she kissed him on the cheek.

Stark jested, "Hey—hey, none of that mushy stuff—you just met this guy." He put his arm around Maria and drew her back, shook Randy's hand and remarked, "Sherrill is beautiful. She has added a new dimension to the six o'clock news."

Stark turned and kissed his wife and stated, "I'll be back in less than an hour."

Charles and Mavis Lindstrom had just watched Sherrill's news conference. Oblivious to the picture and sound of the continuing news program, both were lost in their own thoughts.

Charles' emotions had run the gamut as his role in the exile saga had been revealed to the world. He now acknowledged that his actions had been small and spiteful. Moreover, with the revelation to the world that his daughter was going to have a baby, he felt an unbearable burden had been lifted from his shoulders.

Mavis felt that a large part of the void in her heart had been filled. Increasing pride flowed with each insightful answer as she watched her beautiful daughter on television. Sherrill had looked and acted so mature. Only a few months had passed since Sherrill had left; yet it seemed like an eternity. She arose from her chair and went into the kitchen and started paring vegetables for a stew.

Charles walked up behind her and put his arms around her. This was his first show of attention since the day of the fight with Randy. He uttered, "I can't believe that Sherrill got hold of the press and had a news conference; that breaks the *spirit* of our agreement."

Feeling the fear of her secret, Mavis stiffened and remained silent. The ticking of the kitchen clock impatiently tapped in her ears. Finally, she breathed a futile sigh, "Sherrill didn't contact the press—I did."

Charles gently turned her around and stepped back. He reached into his pocket. Taking her hand, he turned her palm up and placed shreds of the *hateful agreement* in her hands. His eyes and tone of his voice begged forgiveness, as he revealed, "I know—."

Mavis stared in disbelief at the shredded *poisoned document* in her hands and questioned that her eyes and ears had deceived her. She thought *how does he know?* Shaking her head, she resolved, *it doesn't matter how he knew—he knows.*

She looked into his eyes that had been vacant of emotion for so long and saw the rekindled love shining through his tears. She embraced him, "Oh, Charles—I did it for us—for Sherrill, for all of us."

He wrapped his arms around her and smothered her against him, saying, "I know, Honey; I know you did for us." They stood clinging to each other and felt—*the antiseptic balm of their mutual love washing clean the sordid wounds of suppressed animosity.*

Aunt Vickie and Sherrill arrived back at the motel at seven o'clock and woke Hank. Enervated by the day's activities, he had napped for two hours. Hungry, since he had only a sandwich for lunch, he suggested, "Let's go to a real restaurant and dine on some of Monterey's famous seafood."

Sherrill and Vicki enthusiastically agreed and Vicki commented, "We picked up some toiletry items on our way back here. Just give us a few minutes to freshen up."

Arriving at the restaurant that Hank had selected from the yellow pages, they noticed a full parking lot and people mingling outside the door. Hank quipped, "This looks like the right place; I always like to see a large crowd; it usually means that the food must be extraordinary."

Hank, followed by Vicki and Sherrill, walked up to the maître d', "A table for three, please."

The maître d' asked, "Did you make a reservation, sir?"

"No, we're tourists and I didn't think to call ahead for reservations."

"I see," said the maître d' as he traced down the reservation times and compared it to the list of available tables.

Looking up, he intoned, "I'm sorry, sir, but it looks like there'll be an hour and twenty—." For the first time, he noticed Sherrill standing slightly behind Hank. His eyes widened and his mouth was slightly ajar when he announced, "Right this way, please." He took them to a plush horseshoe shaped booth large enough for a party of six.

As the small party followed him to their table, a hush flowed over the vocal din in the restaurant. People paused with fork or spoon in mid-air and their eyes followed the party to their table. Many of the patrons had watched the interview on the six o'clock news and others recognized Sherrill from previous new items.

Sherrill, uneasy from the attention, asked, "Why are they staring at us?"

Aunt Vicki patted her on the hand and sagely stated, "You're going to have to get used to it, Honey. You're a celebrity now."

The extended silence suddenly broke into a renewed din as the patrons exchanged tidbits of conversation regarding their knowledge of the newly found 'missing starlet.' The manager approached the table, accompanied by the wine steward, and graciously offered a bottle of champagne "Le Borge — 1955." "Please accept this bottle of champagne and allow us to serve you anything on the menu, 'per gratis.'"

To clarify his generosity, he added, "We get many celebrities in our restaurant, but none quite so beautiful as the princess—Sherrill."

The three diners, feeling out of their realm, simply whispered in reply, "Thank you."

The wine steward popped the cork and handed the cork to Hank, and poured a small amount into Hank's glass.

Hank passed the cork briefly past his nose, breathing in and savoring the aroma of the fruit. He took a sip and swished the effervescent liquid over his tongue. Breathing in slightly through his mouth, he exhaled through his nose. A smile appeared on his face and he nodded approval to the wine steward.

The steward poured a glass of champagne for Sherrill, then Vicki, and then filled Hank's glass. Bowing slightly, he took his leave.

Hank picked up his glass and toasted, "To a beautiful starlet—who just happens to be our beautiful niece."

"Here-here," agreed Aunt Vicki.

Sherrill took a sip; her eyes brightened as she exclaimed, "I love it—the bubbles tickle the tip of my nose." They laughed together, feeling the strain of the whirlwind events slowly draining from their tense muscles and nerves.

Sherrill finished her glass of champagne and picked up a menu. She scanned the entrees, "There are so many choices, and they all look good."

Hank suggested, "Let me suggest the blackened Mahi-Mahi from Hawaii and the King Crab legs from the icy waters of Alaska.

Sherrill and Vicki nodded their approval and Hank concluded, "I think that I will have the same thing." He glanced up and the waiter was instantly at their table to take their order.

During their salad, a photographer appeared and politely asked, "May I take your picture for our 'celebrity collage' in the reception area?"

Aunt Vicki prompted, "Say, 'cheese cake.'" The group smiled, mouthing the suggested phrase.

The photographer's oversized camera flashed and she departed, saying, "Thank you."

The entrée was served and Sherrill hesitated. She had never eaten King Crab legs. Aunt Vicki glanced over, "They are simple to eat, just watch what I do."

She took a leg and broke the shell close to one joint. Picking up the chromed pliers, she cracked the hard shell close to the other joint, and then pulled the sweet firm flesh intact from the shell.

Dipping the exposed delicacy into clarified butter, she popped the morsel into her mouth and closed her teeth. She pulled the translucent flange through her teeth, stripping off the savory delicacy. Her eyes brightened and she hummed, "Uhmm—delicious."

Sherrill mimicked her actions and was rewarded with an explosion of taste sensations. Her aunt and uncle watched the expression of discovery and pleasure flash across her face. They glanced at each other, knowingly acknowledging that a 'steak and potatoes' girl had just been converted to the savory largess of the seas.

The dining experience culminated when the waiter, without asking, brought out Baked Alaska flambé. Sherrill deferred, "I don't think that I could eat another bite."

The flickering flames were mesmerizing and the pungent odor from the heated vapors of the burning sherry recharged her appetite. As the flames on the dessert slowly extinguished themselves, she reversed herself and relinquished, "Okay, just a small portion."

The experienced waiter cut a third of the dessert and placed it on Sherrill's dessert plate. Sherrill protested, "I can't eat all of this."

The waiter urged, "Just try a couple of bites. If you don't like it, I will take it back."

Sherrill slid her dessertspoon from the bottom of the dessert, up to the top. A miniature of the larger portion rested on her spoon. She studied it for a moment, smelled it, and then popped it into her mouth. "Delicious!" she exclaimed.

After a couple more bites, she voiced a revelation, "It's amazing; the more I eat, the less filled I feel."

She paused, scrunched her brow, and giggled "Did what I just said come out right?" She giggled from the effects of the champagne and the rich food, and then she laughed with glee.

Seeing that she was truly enjoying her first haute-cuisine dining experience, her aunt and uncle laughed with her. The manager approached and smiled, "You seem to be enjoying yourselves. Is there anything else that we can provide for you?

Hank answered for all of them, "No, thanks. We really enjoyed the meal—our compliments to your chef."

"You're very welcome," replied the manager. "Now I have but one request of Sherrill. I have photographs for each of you; would you autograph one of them for me?"

Sherrill nodded and took the photographs along with a permanent felt-tip pen. Looking at the photograph, her mind recalled that she had had many new *first experiences* since coming to California. She wrote, "My first autographed photograph—A wonderful dining experience." Then, below the two lines, she signed just her first name: "Sherrill."

The manager took the photograph and read the writing. He smiled knowing that a first autograph of a rising starlet could become a highly sought after collector's item. He shoved mercenary thoughts out of his head and genuinely expressed, "Thank you, Sherrill. I do hope that you will dine with us again."

Sherrill started to hand back the pen, and then reconsidered. "Just a moment...." She autographed a copy for her aunt and uncle, writing, "To my Aunt Vicki and Uncle Hank. Thank you for everything. I love you—Sherrill." She printed the restaurant's name and the date on the back of her copy and handed the pen back to the manager.

Hank stood, "We've had an exciting day; let's get back to the motel." He quickly calculated twenty percent of what the meal would have cost. He pulled out a twenty-dollar bill and placed it next to his plate.

The manager picked up the tip and placed it back into his hand, remarking, "No tip, please. Our waiters are well compensated and I will pay your waiter out of my own pocket."

Then he explained, "I'm the manager; however, I am also the owner."

Sherrill extended her hand and stated graciously, "Thank you, sir. You and your staff have all been wonderful."

Instead of shaking her hand, the manager bowed and kissed her hand, "Please come and see us again—Princess."

Sherrill felt like she was walking on air. The eyes of the other patrons followed her as she floated by them toward the exit.

Having seen the six o'clock news interview, Charles and Mavis Lindstrom allowed their other two children to stay up and watch the ten o'clock news showing the interview. Mavis turned to Charles and proudly commented, "Oh, Charles, isn't she beautiful!"

Charles choked on his reply, saying. "Yes, I can't believe how mean and spiteful I've been toward her."

Gary stared in wonderment and asked, "Wow—Is that really our sister, Sherrill?"

Rosemary, irritated by her little brother's naive question, snidely remarked, "Of course it is, you little dork. Don't you even believe your own eyes?"

When a reporter asked Sherrill why her father fought Randy, Charles stiffened, remembering the pain and degradation. When she answered: *Because he loves me,* he felt a dam break with a flood of love for his daughter. Staring at his daughter's image on the TV, he thought, *She knows—she really knows that I love her—have always loved her.*

Turning to Mavis he reiterated, "I do love her; I love her very much—I've always loved her."

"I know," replied Mavis with tears in her eyes. "We all love her—and miss her terribly."

Charles was moved by Sherrill's advice to parents. After the news went onto local topics, he turned off the TV. Addressing his other two children, he began, "When your mother and I were growing up, our parents didn't talk much to us about feelings and emotions. Because we didn't know any better, we didn't talk about feelings and emotions to Sherrill and now she is paying the price for our ignorance.

"When either of you don't understand your feelings and emotions toward the opposite sex, I want you to come and talk to your mother or me about it."

Rosemary listened raptly, but eleven-year old Gary, responded, "Girls—blah—I'm never going to fall in love."

Charles patiently replied, "You will, Son—you will. When you do, I want you to come and talk to me. I may not always have a ready answer, but we will find the *right* answers together."

Rosemary, secretly in love with her sister's fiancé, abruptly asked, "Will I ever be as beautiful as Sherrill; will I ever find a wonderful boy like Randy?"

Shocked by the unexpected reference, Mavis answered, "Of course you will, Honey. You are beautiful now, but you must give your body and mind a couple of more years to develop. Then, you will be ready to meet your 'Prince Charming.'"

Charles picked up the phone and dialed his sister. The phone rang ten times before he put the receiver back onto its cradle. He thought for a moment and remarked, "They must still be in Monterey."

He turned to his wife, saying, "Honey, write Sherrill and ask her to forgive us. Ask her to come back home. Tell her that we love her and miss her terribly. Tell her that her father knows that he had been an ass, but now sees the errors of his ways."

Mavis surprisingly retorted, "Charles, that's a letter that you need to write. Sherrill needs to know that the words are coming directly from you by seeing your handwriting."

"You're right," acknowledged Charles, and then added, "You are usually right—I just haven't been listening lately."

He pulled stationery from the drawer and emptied his newly restored soul into a letter to his daughter. As he wrote, he felt the healing process of putting one's thoughts into words on paper. After finishing, he realized that everyone was in bed. He slid into bed and wrapped his arms around the woman that had born him three beautiful children. He silently thanked God for being *so blessed.*

The following Sunday, Charles pulled up to the First Baptist Church with his family. Mavis cautioned, "Do you think that it's a good idea for us to go to church after all those hate calls we received this week?"

He replied, "Considering the static on the phone line, most of those calls sounded like they were long distance. I'm a deacon in our church and my actions have alienated a lot of people toward me. I plan to beg the community's forgiveness and the best place to start is in the Lord's house."

The morning following the news conference, Hank, Vickie, and Sherrill drove from Monterey back to Merced. Hank pulled up to his real estate office, noting that the parking lot was filled with cars. Glancing at Vicki and Sherrill, he informed, "I'll just be a minute. I want to see how Ed is getting along."

Before he could open the car door, a frantic Ed excitedly rushed up to the car. He stated, "Hank, am I glad to see you! I've got a dozen people in the office and Betty, the receptionist, has had over fifty calls from people wanting to buy or sell a home. I've called in our part-time sales reps, Bob and Wayne, to help. But we still won't be able to handle all these customers."

Hank turned to Vicki, "You and Sherrill take the car and go on home. I'll call you later."

Vicki and Sherrill arrived home to find reporters and photographers still surrounding their house. Vicki remarked, "They must have camped out here over the weekend."

Vicki honked for people to get out of the way. She pulled into the driveway and clicked the garage door opener, and then drove into the garage. "Go into the house, Sherrill; I'll take care of these news vultures."

"They're not vultures, Aunt Vicki," Sherrill naively defended. "They are just doing their job of reporting."

"They are vultures when they constantly invade our privacy," retorted Aunt Vicki. She walked out to the driveway and several dozen reporters trod toward her, all asking questions at the same time.

She held up her hands for quiet, "I'd like to make a statement." The reporters became quiet, as the soundmen positioned their microphones and the cameras focused.

"I'm sure that you all have seen Sherrill's interview on TV and read the newspapers. You can see that she is a beautiful girl caught up in a media blitz. A little attention is a good thing, but too much attention can be overwhelming.

"At the moment, she doesn't have anything to add to yesterday's interview. I think that I can speak for my husband, her agent, and tell you that she hasn't signed with any studio—yet.

"When and if she does then there will be a press conference and statements will be made at that time. Any future interviews or scheduling of appearances will now have to go through her agent."

Aunt Vicki concluded forcefully, "Those are the ground rules—now clear out of here and give her a life." She turned and entered the house, followed by a babble of questions from the reporters, which she ignored.

Her statement was shown nationally on the news and she was given the title from the lead-in line, "*Queen Victoria, with the iron girdle, makes statement for Sherrill.*"

The newspapers were even less complimentary and headlined, "Iron Fisted Aunt Hammers Reporters." Additional commentaries filled the news space.

The positive effect was that the reporters now gave them space and the photographers shot with telephoto lenses. However, the media blitz remained active. They found second-handed information from interviews with anyone that had ever known or heard of Sherrill.

Hank arrived home late, well after dark. "I tried to call home but the line was busy."

"I know," replied Vicki, "The phone has been ringing constantly since we got home. I finally had to turn off the ringer."

"It's been just as crazy at the office! People have inundated us with listings. We sold seven homes today. Three sold sight unseen because we couldn't free up anyone to show the homes. They bought the homes from the listing description—if the house was big enough and in the right area—they just bought it. We're getting a lot of out of state business from air force people transferring to the air base.

"We also got eleven new listings. I actually hung up from a listing and sold it to the next caller—over the phone. We even got a couple of bids on our house because people had seen it on television newscast."

"On top of that," Hank continued, "I got calls from agents wanting Sherrill to appear on talk-shows and personal appearances. I had to tell Betty to just get their number and I'd call them back later this week."

Vicki mixed a highball for Hank and handed him the drink, "Just try to relax, Honey. It's a storm that we will ride out together."

Hank looked around, "Where is Sherrill?"

"She's in her room reading her fan mail. The postman delivered over five hundred letters today."

"That's amazing!" responded Hank. "The interview was only yesterday."

"I would guess that most of the mail is local," rationalized Vicki. "If that is any indication of the volume to come then she is going to have to hire a couple of secretaries to help her reply to her fan mail."

The next morning the mail carrier dropped off a duffel bag full of mail, followed by two more that afternoon. By Saturday, bags of mail were stacked up against the wall in the garage.

Hank had to hire four additional real estate agents to handle the ballooning business. He devoted most of his time to managing the inquiries regarding Sherrill's future.

Before signing a contract for Sherrill, he contacted Brad Thurman. "Hello, Brad, this is Hank Casson. I've had some real good offers from other studios. Most were offering more money, but they want long-term contracts. Do you have a counteroffer for me?"

Brad thought for a moment, knowing that fame can be fleeting. He responded, "Yes, I have. My original offer for three episodes still stands, but I will throw in an additional 25k for first option to negotiate a new contract after the episodes have been filmed."

Hank thought, *100k for a short-term contract is a better offer than twice that much for a long-term contract because it will give Sherrill a chance to make her own decisions about her life when she becomes of age.*

"Brad that sounds like a fair offer, but I've got a couple of items that we need to address: I've got a ton of fan mail in my garage that I need the studio to handle. I want a release for Sherrill to make personal appearances. She needs a travel allowance for interviews and personal appearances, which includes costumes and make-up. I want the studio to buy her a Corvette as her personal car. Lastly, I want final okay on any press releases put out by the studio."

Brad considered the request. Hank had done his homework and he was asking for *perks* that normally an agent would ask for an established star—not a rising starlet. However, his boss had instructed, "Sign her at any cost."

"Okay, Hank, we agree to your terms. I will issue a press release today while the media is still in a feeding frenzy for news about Sherrill. Do I need you to sign off on that?"

"No," replied Hank. "I think you understand the spirit of my request. I only want to protect Sherrill's personal life. Go ahead and issue the press release about the contract."

Brad queried, "Oh, before we hang up what color do you want for the car?"

Hank pondered for a moment and replied, "Pale yellow with cream tan leather upholstery." *That should accent her hair color*; he visualized, seeing his niece driving with her hair flaring in the wind.

"Consider it done," replied Brad. "By the way, can the three of you fly down here next Wednesday for the official signing and a press conference?"

"Yes, we can do that—we will see you next week—goodbye."

Record Book

Randy sat on his footlocker lost in thought; pen in hand positioned above blank stationery. Visions of Sherrill swirled through his mind's eye as he replayed over and over the press conference that he had viewed with Sergeant Stark and Maria.

Maria had been openhearted and vocal of her impressions of Sherrill. Randy had no doubt that Sherrill's beauty and wit had moved millions of other viewers. Though he was not prone to jealously, he felt more than just a twinge of envy at having to share her with countless, faceless, new fans.

He visualized that a *magic* bubble had surrounded Sherrill and his prior world, insulating and protecting their love from the chaos of the outside influences. But, now it seemed that their bubble had been divided into two bubbles; hers was floating free to mingle with the other bubbles in the world, while his had collided with an invisible barrier that held it firmly.

I love Sherrill, he rationalized, *with all my heart and soul—or do I really? After all, I love my parents, grandparents, siblings, even David my best friend. I love my unborn son. There are many other special people in my life that I love. This love comes from the heart too, so I cannot love Sherrill with all my heart; or, there wouldn't be any heart left to love other special people in my life.*

This introspection caused him to realize that *with all my heart* was only a metaphorical phrase expressing the intensity and depth of his love for Sherrill. Therefore, he reasoned, *giving love to others does not use up the capacity to love. Love simply cannot be finite...love by its own unique nature must be boundless.*

Individual love, therefore, must be compartmentalized to make it special to the giver and receiver. However, that compartment of love doesn't take away from the total capacity to love. Each compartment of love has its own quality, quantity, and intensity to make it unique and special, while adding to the total capacity of love expressed and received by an individual.

Randy felt this revelation of discovery release his jealousy of other people in Sherrill's life. He placed his pen to the stationery and wrote from his heart.... When he finished, he dropped the letter into the pickup box. The letter was simply addressed to:

175

Miss Sherrill Lindstrom
% Hank Casson
Merced, California

Randy awoke the next morning with his bunk in disarray. His top sheet, pillow, and blanket were on the floor; even the sheet that he lay upon was pulled halfway down the mattress. He recalled snippets of his dream of running through a meadow to meet Sherrill in the middle, there to receive her into his arms and swing her around with her feet off the ground. The music of nature's awakening had accompanied their ritual.

The dream had reoccurred over and over. Sometimes, as he reached out to receive her into his arms his embrace wrapped around an apparition that quickly evaporated. He had stood alone, confused and tormented by his inability to move and unable to invoke a vision that would return her to him.

Randy sat upright upon his bed trying to come to terms with his dreams. He recalled that Sherrill had stated during her press conference that they were *soul mates*. He felt an internal shaking of his psychic that she really had visited him during the night and that in fact the dreams were physical and metaphysical experiences that had their own reality.

Though she wasn't physically sitting here next to him, he knew that she was with him in spirit. She was in his thoughts and he was in her thoughts. This bond transcended the thousands of miles of physical separation, making them as one in mind, body, spirit and soul.

The barracks guard walked by then stopped, looking at him. "I don't know what you had for dinner last night, but you talked in your sleep all night and even wrapped your arms around your mattress like you were going to squeeze it to death."

It was then that Randy discovered scrapes and abrasions on his arms from chaffing against the springs and steel slats in his bed frame. He laughed, "Yeah, it was one heck of a dream." He looked at his watch and leaped up from his bunk—five minutes to go before formation.

The assistant DI marched half the barracks to the chow hall to pull KP (kitchen police), while Sergeant Stark marched the other half to the "Green Monster" for testing. The two DIs would switch locations of the flights in the afternoon.

176

Randy, for reasons unknown to him, had been scheduled for testing in both the morning and afternoon sessions. Though he had tossed and turned all last night, he felt alive and invigorated. His mind was functioning as though he was having a continuous adrenaline rush.

During the morning session, he tested on foreign languages. Though his memory was excellent, he didn't have a photographic memory. However, his memory of musical sounds was nearly phonographic. He could hear a song once and was able to sing most of the verses. He could hear a song twice and was able to sing the song on key and hear the musical instruments replay in his mind as he sang the lyrics. This unique talent enabled him to memorize foreign languages in the right hemisphere of his brain. The only drawback was that the words had a singsong effect when he repeated them.

He had discovered as a young boy that when he read the words as he heard them, he was able to memorize and repeat the words without the singsong effect. He didn't know why this was possible, but if it worked for him—why question it?

The afternoon session tested him on psychological profiles. Early into the test, he saw a trend to the questions. This was the military and they wanted people that had leadership capabilities, as well as team player characteristics. This duality of requirements made many of the questions difficult to answer correctly. His home life had taught him to be considerate of others, but sports had taught him to be competitive— to be a leader. So, when he was faced with a choice of being a leader or follower, he chose the leadership answers.

He was given the OCS (Officer's Candidate School) test and the format was similar to the psychological profile tests. His answers were consistent with the earlier testing. The logical and logistical questions were an easy exercise due to his math background and the many hours of working problems in his head while completing the mundane repetitive tasks of rural life.

Since the monitor had a stack of tests from other personnel on his desk, Randy was surprised to see that his test material was graded immediately after he turned in a bank of tests. The results of his test scores were entered onto a form that had a big red stamp "Top Priority." He casually inquired, "How well am I doing?"

Without ever looking up the monitor curtly remarked, "You'll get the results at the proper time."

Late in the afternoon Sergeant Stark interrupted his testing and gave him an on-base pass, stamped "Mess Hall Privileges" and instructed,

"When you're finish with your testing, grab some chow, and then meet me back at the barracks."

Randy walked leisurely toward the chow hall. It was strange not marching, since he had marched in formation ever since arriving on base. The air now seemed to have a different smell and the setting sun lingered on the horizon, as though it was waiting for him to reach his destination.

A warm gentle breeze wafted against his face and arms; reminding him of other wonderful worlds that must be existing outside the confines of this one. He thought of Sherrill and the walks that they had taken together, *hand in hand—alive and in love.*

His thoughts were interrupted as he was jerked back to reality by a jeep stopping next to him. An AP (Air Policeman) sternly demanded, "Let me see your pass, Airman Basic."

Randy handed him the pass, "Is there a problem, sir?"

The AP satisfied with the pass, handed it back and answered, "No…no problem; it's just unusual to see a 'no striper' meandering down the sidewalk like he has no place to go." Motioning with his thumb toward the driver, he explained, "I bet my buddy here a buck that you wouldn't have a valid pass." The driver laughed as he pulled the dollar bill from the AP's hand in the passenger's seat and continued their patrol.

Randy thought, *nothing like a couple of AP's to bring you back to reality.* He briskly completed his walk to the chow hall.

The huge chow hall was almost vacant with just a few sergeants and senior airmen sitting together discussing their day's activities. Airmen from Randy's barracks were busing the tables and mopping the floor. They recognized Randy and waved, but didn't approach him, since a mess sergeant was overseeing their duties.

Abbott appeared at the swinging doors to the kitchen. He looked exhausted. His fatigues were food stained and in disarray. He walked over to Randy's table and collapsed in a chair without saying a word. Randy remarked, "You look like you've been through hell."

"Yeah," moaned Abbott. "Don't ever get put on KP to wash 'pots and pans'; you wouldn't believe how big those pots are in the kitchen—this is my first break today. We have a guy named Yarborough from Ohio on our crew. He's only 5' tall and we stuck him inside a pot to clean it with a mop. We couldn't even see the top of his head as he walked around cleaning the inside of the pot with his mop."

Randy asked, "Have you eaten dinner?"

"No, I'm too tired for food."

Randy got up from the table and filled a tray. He brought it back and instructed, "Eat it, you'll need your strength for the obstacle course tomorrow. Has the rest of your flight eaten?"

"Yeah," responded Abbott as he scooped up a fork full of food, "all except for the guys that were on 'pots and pans' with me. They're out back on a smoke break—too tired to eat."

Randy wolfed down a couple of bites of food, and then headed for the kitchen. He found his men leaning lethargically against the building; some were too tired to even light up.

He ordered, "You guys get in there and get something in your stomachs. I know you're tired, but you need your strength for the obstacle course tomorrow."

As Randy was leading them back to the dining room, a mess sergeant confronted him. "Who in the hell are you? Where are you going with these men?"

Randy flashed his base pass, hoping that it had some significance. "I'm their barracks chief. They are on mess break, aren't they? I ordered them to get something to eat." Then he added, "We don't want any laggards on maneuvers tomorrow."

The mess sergeant thought, *damn, what a hard-ass*. He dismissed them with a motion of his hand, "Yeah, go ahead. I'm done with them anyhow."

When Randy returned to his table, Abbott had signs of life coming back into his body. He had eaten his meal and was sipping on a second cup of coffee. As Randy sat down to finish his meal, Abbott looked at him, "Thanks for filling my food tray for me; you have no idea what that gesture means to me."

"No thanks needed," responded Randy lightly. "You would have done the same for me."

I will from now on, vowed Abbott in his thoughts.

They sat and talked about the progress of Abbott's flight and the upcoming activities for the remainder of the week. The rest of the kitchen crew finished their mopping and busing duties. Bob Dawson approached their table, "Hey, BC, mind if we take a smoke break outside before we go back to the barracks?"

"Sure, go ahead. Make sure that you fieldstrip your cigarettes and put them in a butt can. Abbott and I will be out in five minutes to march back to the barracks."

Randy had them fall into formation and announced, "Look sharp. The AP's are patrolling and we don't want any demerit reports to come back on us. He marched the flight toward to the barracks and passed the two AP's sitting in their jeep. The passenger turned to the driver and remarked, "Isn't that the same guy we stopped earlier?"

"I don't think so," responded the driver. This guy seems to have a destination and is headed there right smartly."

"Yeah, but this flight just came from the chow hall, which means that they were on KP duty. KP guys are always good for a hassle because their asses are dragging. These guys look like they're on their first march of the day."

"I don't know," acknowledged the driver. "But there's nothing happening around here. Let's get on with the patrol." He started the jeep and made a U-turn, not wanting to be stopped at the intersection by the road guards for the marching flight.

Randy dismissed the flight and they filed into the barracks. He knocked on the DI's door and entered, closing the door behind him. "You wanted to see me?"

"Yes," replied Stark. "Have a seat."

He opened a folder and glanced again at his copy of a report that had just been sent over from HQ. "I'm looking at your test scores from today and they are good. As a matter of fact, they are damn good. I'm not at liberty to show them to you, but I can surmise that they will open a couple of doors of opportunity for you. As far as getting you into a tech school, I can't say, since the tests you took aren't standard tech school tests. Just keep up the good work and I'm sure that 'Uncle Sam' will find an assignment to match your talents." He stood up and offered his hand to congratulate Randy.

Randy shook hands and replied, "Thank you, sir."

As he turned to leave, Stark called, "Oh, by the way, Maria was impressed with you and Sherrill. You two were all she would talk about after you left. She even watched Sherrill's interview again on the ten o'clock news. She didn't say much and had tears in her eyes. I don't know why she cried—it was a great interview and I didn't see anything to cry about.

"Also, I want you to understand that I can't be a Randy fan because I'm your DI. But, I can be a Sherrill fan," he added with a wink. "She is one fine looking young lady."

Randy flushed. He noted that Stark had referred to Sherrill as a lady, not as a woman; that, and the wink softened the inference of carnal desire, but he wondered what went through the minds of other men as they had watched Sherrill's interview. He didn't want other men to view her as a love object, but he had no control over their thoughts.

Then he remembered his grandmother's advice: "Having the wisdom to know the difference of what you can change and what you can't change." He put his rising defenses into neutral and replied, "Thank you, sir. I'm sure that Sherrill would feel honored to have you as a fan."

The next day the flight was scheduled to go through the obstacle course. Friendly competition had become established between Flight "A" and Flight "B." Abbott had taken it upon himself to make a list, pairing up airmen from each side of the barracks according to their physical capabilities. He showed it to Randy, "That's a great idea, Abbott. I'll get Sergeant Stark's -stamp of approval.

Casio and Randy had been paired together. The whistle sounded and they sprang from the starting line. Randy had better upper body strength and excelled in the towers, the swings, the monkey bars, and the ropes traversing the water hazards.

Casio was lighter and had slightly longer legs. He made up time on the spare tires, the cross-sticks, the wire hazards, and running. They crossed the finish line in a dead heat.

The timer walked over to Sergeant Stark and remarked with disbelief, "Your two boys just set a new course record by a full five seconds for first-timers through the course."

"I guess that's good," mumbled Stark.

"Good!" responded the timer, his jaw gaping, "That's fantastic—it's like knocking five seconds off the four-minute mile. Do you realize how many recruits have been through this standard course? We've been keeping records since the old army days. The last record was set by Alonzo Smith back in 'fifty-four' and he was a candidate for the Olympic team."

This information impressed Sergeant Stark and he pulled a notepad from his pocket and made an entry for his "special report."

The rest of the flight did well; urged on by competing against a fellow airman from the opposite side of the barracks. However, the next best competitor's score was thirty-three seconds behind Casio and Randy's time.

Casio and Randy were unaware of their accomplishment until that night, when their barracks received a surprise visit from the base commander. In tow was a photographer from "The Air Force Times" and Captain Detrich the company commander. The barracks guard cleared their IDs and shouted, "Barracks, atten-shut—Base Commander in the barracks."

The men in the barracks popped to attention beside their footlockers and Sergeant Stark appeared at his door. Recognizing the general, he saluted, holding the salute until it had been returned. "Welcome to our barracks, General. Your visit is very much a surprise."

"At ease; I like to stay in touch with my men. I want to meet the two airmen that set a new record on the obstacle course today."

Following protocol by rank, Stark introduced Randy first. "This is Airman Randall Ferris, our barracks chief."

The general shook Randy's hand, "Good job, Son. I'm glad that you chose the air force. Otherwise, my army buddies would probably have you on their team."

"Thank you, sir. We hope to do better next time, now that we are familiar with the course."

"I'm sure you will," reassured the general. He turned back to Stark.

Stark motioned across the aisle; "This is Airman Casio Brown, one of our area chiefs."

The general shook his hand and asked, "Where are you from, Son?"

Casio responded, "Brooklyn, sir."

The general asked, "Where did you learn to run so fast in Brooklyn?"

Casio rolled his eyes, obviously embarrassed, and blurted out, "From the cops, sir."

The whole barracks laughed. The general laughed with them and remarked good-naturedly, "Well, Airman Brown, those days are behind you; Sergeant Stark here will see to that."

Casio replied, "Yes, sir."

The general turned to Stark and commented; "Captain Detrich tells me that your barracks got top honors last week. That speaks well of your choice of team leaders."

Stark experienced a sharp pang of conscience before he answered. Ferris had been chosen for him and Ferris had chosen Brown and Abbott.

The general mistook Stark's lack of acknowledgement of the compliment as modesty and continued, "Well, we're here for a picture of these two boys."

The photographer lined them up with the American flag on their right and the U.S. Air Force flag on their left. Randy and Casio were in the center. The general was on one side and the captain and Stark were on the other side. The general turned slightly and shook Randy's hand, while they all smiled into the camera. The photographer reversed Randy and Casio and took another picture with the general shaking Casio's hand.

"I'll give each of you a picture that you can send home to your moms—they always like that," informed the photographer. "The negatives will go to my editor and he'll choose which one goes into the 'Times.'"

Sergeant Stark took the photographer aside and asked, "I'd like a copy for their personnel record and an extra one of Airman Ferris for my wife. She's met Randy and has become somewhat of a fan."

The term *fan* clicked something in the photographer's mind. He repeated, "Ferris, Ferris, Randy Ferris—basic training—Lackland." His eyes widened, "Sherrill's fiancé—Sherrill the starlet—Sherrill on TV. Wow, have I got a hot story for my editor!"

The captain inquired, "Sergeant Stark is your barracks ready for inspection? The general would like to check how we're doing."

"Yes, sir," responded Stark. He turned and bellowed, "Barracks, tench-hut!"

The captain and the general strolled down the aisle way, escorted by the sergeant, who was present to answer any questions. The general randomly checked the living areas—no demerits were detected. They walked back and the general remarked, "Very good, sergeant. I see that you run a proper barracks."

"Thank you, sir," acknowledged Sergeant Stark.

The group started to leave and Sergeant Stark cleared his throat, "Excuse me, General. May I have a moment of your time?" He motioned the general toward his room.

"What's this all about?" asked the general, as he followed Stark.

"I've been ordered to keep a special file on Airman Ferris and I wonder if you would mind signing his obstacle course record?" He pulled a file marked "Top Priority" and opened it.

The general wrote across the document, *Congratulations, John J. Thurman—Brigadier General, USAF*.

The group had left the barracks and was walking back to the Company HQ. The photographer whispered mysteriously, "Guess who Randy Ferris is?" The two officers looked at him as if he had two heads and shouldn't be outside under a full moon. The photographer proffered in a stage whisper, "He's Sherrill's fiancé."

The two officers looked at each other and thought; *this guy has seen too many flashbulbs go off.*

The photographer clarified, "Sherrill—the missing starlet interview on TV."

The captain held up his index finger and expounded, "Oh, the guy that fought Sherrill's father for her hand in marriage—and won."

The general made the connection and said, "No shit. Wait until I tell my golfing buddies that I shook hands with Sherrill's fiancé."

The captain intoned, "Wait until I tell my wife that Sherrill's fiancé is in my company.

The photographer added to the accolades, "Wait until I tell my editor that I have a picture of Sherrill's fiancé."

The three men had more of a bounce in their step as they continued their walk to HQ; each feeling a heightened sense of elation that comes with touching the tantalizing hem of fame and fortune.

Pre-Game

Sergeant Belcher was stretched out on his bunk and blowing smoke rings into the column of smoke rising from the smoldering cigarette between his fingers…he was pissed. His barracks had been challenged to a basketball game and this would normally be good for him and good for the men in his barracks, except that the challenge had come from Sergeant Stark's barracks. Stark was okay, as a DI, but Stark had recently beaten him out of "barracks of the week" competition two weeks in a row.

Belcher had driven his men relentlessly, sometimes ruthlessly, to attain perfection for inspection. However, there always seemed to be several airmen that constantly screwed up. He had summarily dealt out their punishment and even inspected their area a half-dozen times a day, but when the captain or his adjutant inspected, they always found demerits.

The official results for this week were not posted yet, but his inside sources at HQ told him that Stark's barracks had it in the bag; specifically because of the publicity from setting a new record at the obstacle course and the fact that the general had inspected Stark's barracks and found no demerits. Belcher fumed as he thought, *generals can always find demerits, if they want to bad enough.*

Losing the competition also meant that even though his men had already won barracks of the week twice, his men would not get the weekend pass that he had promised them. This was his barracks' last weekend at Lackland. They would be shipping out to tech schools early next week—those left behind would be combined into another barracks under another DI.

Well, we might not get barracks of the week, but we will win the game, vowed Belcher. He walked out to Mark Fairchild and ordered, "Get me the shoe sizes of all the players on our basketball team."

Game time was set for 1000 hours for next Saturday morning. The captain, in unusually good spirits, declared a virtual holiday for the event. He invited all the barracks in his company to watch. And, he even had special services bring over a couple of bleachers for the VIPs that included DIs to generals and their families. He did not expect many outsiders, since this was just a scrimmage game between two barracks.

185

Calls started trickling into HQ inquiring about the game. Most wanted to see the two airmen, who had set a new obstacle course record. When word spread that Sherrill's fiancé would be in the game, the phone started ringing constantly. Reacting to the increasing number of people requesting to attend, the captain assigned the company adjutant to coordinate the activities, including getting outside referees to officiate the game. He ordered more bleachers and made up a battle plan of action with checklists assigned to a half-dozen personnel. A base caterer, seeing an opportunity to make a fast buck, offered to have four canteen vans on-site for refreshments.

Randy and his team were allowed time off to practice on Thursday and Friday afternoon. He had good talent on his team and saw that they accepted him as their *player coach*. He was mildly surprised that they put out maximum effort for him with very little urging. Even Casio did not complain when he was asked to sit out while the abilities of other players were evaluated as substitutes for his center position.

Randy knew from their first practice that moving the ball in brogans was not the same as moving the ball in basketball shoes. They spent most of the practice time passing the ball and developing a fast break. The center court forward was designated to break toward the opposite end of the court the moment that a shot was taken by the opposing team. The other four players would move in for the rebound and quickly pass the ball to the center forward, who should be in position to lay-up a shot or control the ball until the rest of the team arrived down court.

The rest of practice included feeding the ball to the center and concentrating on free throws. Randy explained, "Missing free throws are point opportunities thrown away." His team nodded in agreement and concentrated on finding the range to the net.

Friday's practice period was almost over when two lowboy semi-trailer trucks pulled up three hundred feet from the basketball court and started unloading portable toilets. Randy counted twenty-five on the first truck and the second truck appeared to have about the same number. Casio walked up to him, "Man, what are they doin'? If anybody's got to take a shit, their barracks would be closer than those toilets."

186

Another player walked up, having overheard the conversation, and opined, "Maybe they are just storing them there. That is just a big open area behind HQ that's going to waste."

"I don't think so," replied Randy. "See how they are spacing them out in a line. If they were storing them, they would be stacked close together."

"I got it!" crowed Casio. "I heard that they invited the brass—see, and each one of them is going to have his own personal toilet."

The rest of the team, attracted by the discussion, howled with laughter at his remark.

"What are you all laughing about?" questioned Casio "I'm serious—man; I tell you, I'm fuckin' serious. Them with brass gits a place to set their ass." The deadpan serious expression on Casio's face caused them to laugh even louder.

Two more trucks appeared and unloaded a portable stage with public address sound equipment. One of the bleachers was moved back away from one end of the court to make room for the stage. Portable scoreboards were set up outside the fence at both ends of the court. A crew swept off the court and a paint crew repainted the boundary markers and the free-throw lines. The barracks' numbers for each team were painted in big block letters at opposite ends of the court. The hoops were tightened and new nets were installed. Five more trucks pulled up and twenty-five hundred portable chairs were set up on the grassy knolls at both sides of the court.

Even Casio was sobered by all the preparation. He remarked, "Man, somebody's on LSD. There are enough seats here for a rock concert." He thought pensively, and then added, "Hey, maybe that's it. They got some big hullabaloo planned after the game."

Randy glanced at his watch. "Let's go; our practice session was over five minutes ago."

That night after lights out, Sergeant Belcher grabbed a butt can half filled with sand and sneaked out while the barracks guard was making his fire check at the far end of the barracks. He entered the basketball court that was dimly illuminated by a half moon. He walked the 3-point line, broadcasting a very light coating of sand, just inside the arched line.

Stepping inside the line, he applied pressure on his toes to slide his brogan across the surface. His foot kicked out and he spun halfway around before he regained his balance. *Aahhh! That should do it*, he thought. He sprinkled sand on the lay-up approaches on both sides of the basket. He walked to the other end of the court and completed his devious undertaking.

As he was walking back to his barracks, a jeep slowed down and one of the AP's shined a flashlight on him, and then the jeep continued down the road. The passenger remarked to the driver, "That's strange. That sergeant was carrying a butt can."

The driver retorted, "Well, maybe he was out for a stroll and a smoke. Sergeants do not have to have a reason for being out after lights out. Besides, I know that guy; he's a DI in one of the barracks. His name is Belcher and he's been on this base forever."

The next morning at 0900, the assistant DI halted the flight in front of the barracks. He ordered, "Basketball team—fall out."

He explained to Randy, "I'm going to take the rest of the flight over to the game, so they will have a seat up front. Bring your team over ten minutes before the game. That should give you time to warm up. The DI said not to be too early because you might get stiff just standing around."

Randy entered the barracks and instructed Casio to inspect Abbott's side of the barracks, while he inspected Casio's side. They both inspected the latrine and everything was in order. The men in his barracks had needed very little prompting once they found out what was expected of them. Randy felt lucky that he had such a good group. He had heard stories of people screwing up constantly from other barracks and their DIs had meted out punishment in very debasing ways.

He pulled out his clipboard and made some hieroglyphic notations next to each player's name. It was a shorthand system taught to him by his high school coach. It summarized a player's capabilities and depicted several game plans where that particular player's talents could best be utilized. The added advantage was that a casual observer could view the information, but wouldn't have a clue as to what it meant.

Randy checked his watch; time to leave. He called the flight to attention, and then exchanged positions with Casio, so that Casio could march the flight to the game. He didn't know why Casio derived so much pleasure commanding a flight of marching men, but since he did then there was no harm in letting him do it, when it was just a routine march.

They heard the marching music in the distance and the flight matched their cadence to the music. As they approached HQ, they could tell that the music was coming from the basketball court area. When they rounded the building, the flight fell out of step and halted from surprise.

The entire twenty-five hundred seats were filled and people were still arriving. People were sitting on the roofs of buildings, sitting on the grass, and standing beside the bleachers where television cameras had been set up. As the team filed through the throng, they noticed that many of the people standing near the bleachers were wearing press badges.

Captain Detrich spied Randy and motioned to the band director. The music stopped and the captain walked to the podium on the stage. He looked out across the masses and smiled with a sense of achievement. He tapped on the microphone to make sure that it was on and leaned in to speak. "Ladies and gentlemen, I want to welcome everyone to today's basketball game. This is by far the largest crowd ever to attend a company scrimmage and it is a beautiful day for a game. For your convenience, refreshments can be purchased from one of the canteens in the parking lot and latrines have been set up behind the bleachers at the far end of the court.

"On a training base, we seldom have the opportunity to relax and enjoy such a beautiful day. Most of our personnel, by the nature of our mandate, are transitory. We only have them for a few short weeks, and then they transfer out to other bases to fill positions that are vital to the United States Air Force mission.

"We usually don't have time to get to know them on a personal level. As you have probably heard, we have two young airmen here that have set a new record on the obstacle course. To some of you, this may not seem to be a great accomplishment, until you stop to realize that hundreds of thousands of men and women have been through this same course or courses similar to it. The last record was set back in 1954 by Airman Alonzo Smith, and he was a candidate for the U.S. Olympic team.

"With us, today, to present the U.S. Air Force Athletic Achievement Medal, is our base commander, General John J. Thurman." The captain extended his hand in introduction to the approaching general, "— General Thurman.".

The crowd applauded the captain's speech and continued applauding as the marching band struck up introduction music. General

Thurman took the podium and waited until the applause ended and the band stopped playing. "Thank you all for attending this event. Normally, this would be a great day for being on the golf course, but it is also a fine day for a basketball game.

"We, as Americans, celebrate our sports icons by becoming avid sports fans. Witty sports writers and colorful sports commentators propagate the passion for many sporting events. Though an obstacle course may not be a highly publicized sporting event, it is—nonetheless—just as strenuous and just as competitive as some of the more popular sporting events. Records are kept to measure our achievement against others that have preceded us. To break a record that has endured for over a decade is indeed a special achievement. To have two men break it simultaneously is unique, unto itself.

"Therefore, I call Airman Randall Ferris and Airman Casio Brown to the stage." The crowd broke out in courteous applause as Randy and Casio made their way onto the stage. They stopped at the side of the general and saluted. The general returned their salute and spoke into the microphone.

"When I asked Airman Brown how he learned to run so fast in Brooklyn, he replied, 'From the cops, sir.'" The crowd broke into amused chuckles. "Well," continued the general, "we all can't choose our training ground, but he surely showed us that he could move through an obstacle course in record time."

The general turned and pinned the medal on Casio's fatigue shirt. He shook Casio's hand as cameras clicked. He turned to Randy and pinned a medal onto his shirt. The crowd applauded their accomplishment and the general turned back to the microphone.

Randy and Casio took this as a gesture that the ceremony was over and started walking off the stage. The applause died down as Randy was nearing the edge of the stage, and then he heard the general calling him back, "Airman Ferris, would you return to the podium? We aren't quite finished with you, yet."

Randy returned and stood puzzled, not knowing what was going to happen next. The general, like any good speaker, worked the audience. He paused, a good fifteen seconds, until the last murmur went silent, and then waited another five seconds to heighten the anticipation. During this time, Randy was sweating bullets. He had not even been told that he would receive a medal, let alone receive it at a ceremony. As the tension of anticipation grew in the audience, so did Randy's feeling that he was on public display.

The general finally, mercifully, leaned into the microphone and addressed the audience, "I'm sure that many of you watched the interview of a rising starlet on TV last Sunday. Sherrill's story touched the very heart and soul of millions of viewers. She was beautiful and reminded us of a modern day princess. Her extemporaneous message to parents and teenagers was one of the best that I have ever heard.

"She mentioned a boy, or I should say—a young man that fought her father for her hand in marriage—and won. But fate did not let them walk away into happy oblivion. No! Fate had other plans for their future. Today, fate now places that young man in front of you."

The general paused, turned his head to look at Randy, and spoke sideways into the microphone, "Ladies and gentlemen, I introduce to you Sherrill's fiancé—Randy." The crowd spontaneously rose to their feet and applauded. The general stepped back and motioned Randy to the podium.

Randy stood in front of the microphone—numb. There seemed to be no let up of the applause and cheers. Randy stared out into the audience and thought, *this must be how Sherrill felt at her interview, yet she came across so poised that she appeared to be a pro.* As he thought of Sherrill, calmness came over him. Her voice inside his mind caressed his jagged nerves, *I'm with you darling; I will always be with you—speak your heart; speak what comes into your mind—I love you.*

The applause continued for nearly a minute. People finally sat back down as the applause ceased. Randy did not start to speak at once. He had snippets of thoughts of things he wanted to say, but couldn't seem to zero in on where to begin.

The barracks chief from the WAF flight that Randy had befriended jumped up and yelled, "Three cheers for Randy." Her entire flight stood up with her and screamed at the top of their lungs, "Hip-hip-hurrah; hip-hip-hurrah, hip-hip-hurrah." The crowd, again, broke into spontaneous laughter and applause at the "out of character" display of admiration by the Women's Air Force.

Encouragement from the WAF's broke the ice for Randy and he began, "Thank you—and a special thank you to the members of the Women's Air Force. I guess now I can tell Sherrill that I have a fan club too." The audience laughed.

Randy continued, "I can only guess that they must have been through that same obstacle course that Casio and I went through." The crowd laughed again—not because the line was particularly funny, but because the timing of the remark was appropriate to their jovial mood and the subject of the speech had caught them off guard.

Randy continued in the same vain with feigned surprise, "As I stand here looking over the assembled masses, I am astonished that this huge crowd showed up just to watch a couple of guys—fresh off the obstacle course—play basketball in their brogans."

The crowd laughed and applauded. They realized that he was playing with them, but they didn't care. The humor was infectious and they were having a good time. Randy expounded, "You may have wondered why Airman Brown ran the obstacle course so fast." He paused for them to wonder, and then continued, "At the starting line, I told him that the cops from Brooklyn were after him—." (Laughter)

"Then he told me, 'Oh, yeah—well I told them that you was my **accomplice**.'" The crowd roared and broke into extended applause.

The captain turned to the general and remarked, "This kid is really good."

"Yes, he is," agreed the general, sagely adding, "Timing is everything."

At the end of the applause, Randy didn't continue immediately— not because he was still playing the audience, but because thinking of Sherrill brought a nostalgic wave of emotion over him.

He finally continued, "Seriously though, I know why you are here, today. You want to know more about Sherrill because you watched her on television and fell in love with her…as I fell in love with her.

"I was able to watch the interview on TV through the good graces of my drill instructor, Staff Sergeant Dwayne Stark. On his day off, he came back to the air base and brought me into his home to share a home cooked meal with his family. He and his wife Maria knew what was going to happen—they had mischievously planned the surprise— and I thank them for it.

"I was totally caught off guard when Sherrill's interview was shown on the six o'clock news. I haven't been in contact with her since that dreadful night, when I had a blowout with her father. You know most of the story from the television interview and the newspaper articles. I learned along with you that her father had exiled her to California. Instead of letting this shatter her life, she picked up the pieces and is completing her schooling.

"A Hollywood studio discovered her as she watched the filming of 'The Dons of Eldorado' and they asked her to appear in a small role. There wasn't a problem until the studio lost her contract and contacted

192

the newspapers, trying to find her. She did not want to be found because we are going to have a baby. Television news picked up the story and you know the rest—she became 'the missing starlet.'

"I joined the air force to serve my country and to prepare a stable life for Sherrill and our baby—for the day when we can be together again. The thing that you don't know—is how we really feel about each other. You saw and heard her in the interview say that I was the most special person in her life—that we are 'soul mates.' I feel the same way toward her; she is my earth angel, graced with beauty, intelligence, and a 'pure heart.' I feel weakened and awed in her presence, yet strengthened and invincible in her absence because she is always with me in mind and heart."

Randy paused; tears of love and sincerity were in his eyes. Through his tears, he saw an unusual rainbow pattern reflecting from the sun shining on the basketball court. His eyes scanned the audience and he closed his speech by simply stating, "Thank you, for being here—for Sherrill."

Randy left the stage. The audience was slow to applaud. They were still caught up in the love story that Randy had just shared with them. The applause started slowly then grew into a resounding crescendo as people rose from their seats. People reached out to shake Randy's hand as he stepped off the stage and weaved his way through the crowd to rejoin his team.

In the VIP bleacher, Maria turned to Stark and cried, "Oh, Dwayne. That was such a wonderful speech. I just love Randy."

Stark agreed, "Yeah, he certainly is a heck of a guy."

The captain took the microphone, "That was a very moving speech—Randy. We in the military are sometimes so focused on our mission that we forget that the men and the women in uniform are our greatest asset. They have their lives and loves, and are, above all, human." The crowd applauded. It was refreshing to hear a military man expound family values, instead of the strict standard esprit de corps rhetoric of the military.

The captain closed, "Thank you again for being here to share in our gala events. The referees have to leave right after this game to officiate an afternoon game in San Antonio. So without further ado, '**Let the game begin**.'"

The Game

Sergeant Belcher motioned to two of his airmen standing beside the bleachers. They reached down and picked up two stacks of shoeboxes and carried them to him. He opened the boxes and started handing out basketball shoes to his team. He had purchased the shoes out of his own pocket, but figured the out-of-pocket expense would be a small price to pay when he trounced Stark's team in front of all these people.

The sand that he had sprinkled on the basketball court was added insurance that Stark would lose the game. To brogans, the sand would be like skating on ice. With basketball shoes, his team should hardly notice the sand. There may be a minor feeling of slippage until the particles of sand rolled into the hollow labyrinth pattern in the shoe soles; then the rubber soles should grip the surface of the basketball court.

Stark saw the basketball shoes being put on by the opposing team; he bounded down out of the VIP gallery. Shouting at Sergeant Belcher, he demanded, "You can't have your team wear basketball shoes; that's an unfair advantage. Besides, they will be out of uniform."

Belcher retorted, "Out of uniform, you say. Well, for your information, basketball shoes are recommended footwear on a basketball court. You're just pissed-off because I take care of my boys and you don't."

Stark was enraged. He thought, *Damn, Belcher is right. Basketball shoes are recommended during a game. Brogans are an accepted alternative for airmen shooting baskets for personal entertainment and exercise.* He turned away smoldering at his lack of foresight at not making sure that his team had appropriate footwear. Returning to his seat, he heard murmurs from the crowd, "How come Randy's team doesn't have basketball shoes?"

As he sat down, Maria asked him the same question. Stark replied, "Because this was meant to be just a friendly scrimmage between two barracks. It never occurred to me that it was going to be a televised game with a huge audience." Then he added, "Damn, I could kick myself."

Because there were no uniforms to indicate team colors, a coin was flipped to see which team played without shirts. Belcher's team won the toss and Belcher hollered at his team captain, "Choose Shirts."

As Randy's team peeled off their T-shirts, exposing their strong young muscular torsos, they heard whistles and catcalls from the audience. The rest of the audience laughed at the teasing with jovial participation.

The game began from the center circle. Randy jumped higher than his opponent, and flipped the ball to a guard. The guard threw the ball to the breaking forward. The forward drove in for a lay-up. He planted his foot for the jump and slid down hard on his side, scraping patches of skin from his body. The loose ball rolled out of bounds. The referee whistled and gave the ball to Shirts.

Randy's team rushed to a defensive formation, slipping, at the opposite end. The ball was dribbled and passed back and forth several times until Shirts were in position. The forward in front of Randy received the ball. The forward faked left. Randy wasn't faked, merely widened his stance to better defend in either direction, and did the splits. He twisted quickly to avoid a groin pull and fell down on the concrete court.

Shirts' forward dribbled around him. Casio broke from his center defensive position to intercept the forward; his feet slipped out from under him and he went down. The forward flipped the ball to the center. The center pivoted and flipped the ball to the backboard. The ball fell through the net and the crowd cheered the first two points of the game.

As Randy pushed to get up, he felt the grit of sand under his fingers. He momentarily questioned, "Why is there sand on the court?" since yesterday he had watched them sweep the court before they painted the striping.

He was distracted from reasoning an answer since his two guards were already moving the ball down to the opposite end of the court. He quickly caught up and Skins passed the ball around. One of the guards, over anxious to match the points, shot from the side—missed. The guard on the opposite side of the court rushed over to rebound and fell on his back, getting a bad court burn and jamming both of his elbows.

The other team got the rebound and executed a fast break, making an undefended lay-up. Randy's team got the ball back each time the other team scored, but each time they tried to maneuver for a shot, they went down and Shirts grabbed the ball and scored. Belcher's team had scored 20 unanswered points; the game was a runaway. A disappointed audience yelled boos and catcalls; Belcher sat on the sidelines with a self-satisfied grin pasted across his face.

Randy sent a guard down court and received the throw-in from his other guard. He slowly dribbled down the court and approached the 3-point line. The player guarding him backed away; Randy stopped and shot; the ball swished through the net. The crowd jumped to their feet and cheered—points on the board for Skins.

Shirts inbounded the ball and scored. Randy instructed his guards to feed him the ball. Supported by a cheering crowd, he made three more 3-point shots. However, the opponents scored another basket each time, which cancelled out 2 of his 3 points. At Belcher's screamed instructions, Shirts started double and triple teaming him in a full court press.

The score was 28 to 12. The guards couldn't get the ball to Randy and fed it to Casio. Casio pivoted for a hook shot and fell down hard. He threw out his arm to catch himself and his thumb on his right hand bent backward at an extreme angle. Casio screamed in agony. The other team grabbed the ball and scored. Now the score was 30 to 12.

Randy called time and took Casio over to the bench. Casio was in excruciating pain. Tears were in his eyes and he stifled cries of pain. The majority of Skins' starting team was in pretty bad shape. Everyone, including Randy, had bleeding strawberries on their exposed skin.

Abbott rushed up to Casio and exclaimed, "Let me see that!" Without warning he grabbed Casio's thumb and cranked it back into position.

Casio screamed out in surprise, and then discovered that the extreme pain had suddenly gone away. He flexed his shooting hand to see if he could still have ball control, but observed that his hand had swollen and was still numb.

Randy exclaimed, "Where did you learn that!"

"I worked as an orderly in a hospital last summer."

Stark rushed up and demanded, "What the hell's wrong with your team. They're looking like a bunch of clowns out there."

Randy replied, "There is sand on the court. There shouldn't be because I saw them sweep it, yesterday."

"Then why doesn't the other team have the same problem?

Randy replied without blame, "Because their basketball shoes can handle it; our brogans can't."

Stark grabbed one of the referees, pointed and accused, "There's sand on the court."

The referee slid his shoe across the surface and heard a screech as the rubber firmly gripped, and before he could state his opinion,

Belcher rushed over and slid to a stop. His brogans only moved an inch to prove a point. He mockingly remarked, "You're full o' shit—there is no sand on the court."

Randy grabbed Stark by the arm and led him to the 3-point line, and instructed, "Place your hand down there."

Stark ran his hand across the surface and felt sand. There wasn't a lot of sand, but he could see that it was enough to explain the problems his team was having.

"Damn!" exclaimed Randy, "that explains it!"

"Explains what?" demanded Stark.

Randy explained, "When I was on the stage, I saw a strange rainbow pattern with a couple of spikes at each end of the court. I thought it was due to the tears in my eyes. Now I believe that someone has purposely salted the court with sand."

"Belcher!" intoned Stark. "That son-of-a-bitch!"

He motioned a referee over; Belcher followed.

Stark pointed and adamantly stated, "There is sand on the court."

The referee reached down and swiped his fingers across the surface. With realization, he agreed, "Yeah, you're right."

Belcher interrupted, "So what, this is outdoors—Texas. You've got to expect a little sand on the court. If your team had the proper shoes, they wouldn't have a problem."

Stark demanded, "I want the game stopped until we can sweep the court."

The referee looked at his watch and solemnly stated, "We can't do that. We've got another game to go to right after this game."

The crowd was becoming restless and catcalls were shouted, demanding that the game proceed. Stark continued arguing his point; the referee blew his whistle and called a technical foul, throwing him out of the game.

Randy went back to his team and explained, "There is sand on the court, which is why we have been falling down. It is not everywhere; just inside the three-point line and on the runway for a lay-up on both sides of the basket.

"We can't defend those areas, but I don't think that the other team knows where the sand is located. We can't run on the sand, but we can slide through it and maneuver on the areas that don't have sand.

"Now, listen up; here is the plan. Casio is sitting out; I will play center. Leubrecht takes my place as forward. Feed me the ball while you are outside the three-point line. I'll take a couple of hook shots to pull your guards off you. When they start double-teaming, run, then slide through the sand. I'll feed the ball back to you during your slide. When your foot runs out of sand, take your jump shot.

"Okay, now on defense, we'll press them full court. If they get the ball down court, slide through the sand and defend close-in to the basket. They'll get some shots, but we are not playing against pros. They are going to miss a lot and we'll be in close for the rebound."

He extended his hand into the circle and his team placed their hands on top of each other, shouting in unison, "Let's—go—get—'em!"

Randy looked around for Abbott and couldn't find him. He muttered under his breath as he entered the court, "Damn, where is that guy—we need some brooms."

The other team took the technical foul shots and their score increased by 2.

Stark elbowed his way back toward his seat. He stepped on the stage and walked to where the podium had been set up. He looked at the court and saw the rainbow pattern that Randy had described. He spied the air force photographer that had been to his barracks and tapped him on the shoulder, "Do me a favor and take a couple of shots from center stage of the basketball court. Then send one copy to Captain Detrich and another copy to the air police commander."

"What's up?" asked the curious photographer.

"Just do it," demanded Stark, and added softly, "Thanks."

Stark took his seat next to his wife. She tugged on his shirtsleeve, "What was that all about?"

"I'll tell you later," he replied, cutting her short. Frustrated, he pounded his fists against his knees and uttered, "Damn—damn—damn!"

Randy's team inbounded the ball as he broke for Shirt's end of the court. He slid through the sand and got into position ahead of the Shirts' center guard. He took the pass over his shoulder and slam-dunked the ball. The crowd jumped to their feet cheering.

Randy's team broke to defend their end of the court, running, sliding, running, sliding, until they were in a tight defensive pattern. Their stutter-stepping gait brought laughter from the audience. They looked like they were playing hockey and basketball on the same court.

The Shirts' forward, seeing their tight defense, took an open shot. The ball careened off the rim and the Skins' team got the rebound. The forward dribbled the ball, slid while he dribbled then started running and dribbling. The rest of the team quickly slid, stepped, and ran toward their net. The ball was fed to Randy and he scored a hook shot.

The Skins' full court press confused the Shirts and the Skins took the ball away in mid-court. Randy was in place for a hook shot, but the opposing team reacted by closing in on him. He flipped the ball to a forward sliding through the sand. The forward jumped and shot, just as he slid out of the sand—another 2 points. The crowd cheered encouragement.

A Shirts' guard, rattled by the full court press, stepped out of bounds with the ball.

The Skins took in the ball and fed it to Randy. Randy fed the ball to a sliding guard that popped 2 points. Randy sensed that the crowd was for his underdogs because they were cheering each time his team made a score and moaning when Shirts made a score.

The Shirts took the ball down the court. The Skins were tight around the basket and the Shirts' forward stopped and scored a set shot.

The Skins took the ball and scored.

The Shirts took the ball back to their end of the court. Leubrecht discovered by accident that sliding could have an unexpected advantage. He broke out toward the forward, who had scored the previous set shot. As he hit the slide area, he slid past the forward and flipped the ball out of his opponent's hands.

Running and sliding as he dribbled the ball, he approached the basket head-on and scored. The crowd clapped, cheered, and whistled their approval.

The Shirts took the ball to their end. Leubrecht slid again toward the forward with the ball. However, this time the forward stopped short and Leubrecht slid past him. The forward advanced into the hole and scored.

Randy moved out of the pocket over to the corner guard position. The guard drove toward the basket and flipped the ball to him. Randy popped a 3-point shot from the corner.

The Shirts took the ball down the court and made 2.

The Skins dribbled down the court. A guard took a 3-point shot at the half-time buzzer and missed. The half-time score ended at 38-27.

The marching band struck up half-time intermission music. The crowd dispersed for refreshments and nature's calling.

Abbott appeared with a half dozen men with brooms. Randy shouted, "Abbott, you are a God send."

Abbott breathless from running explained, "We would have been here sooner, but the barracks guards wouldn't give us their push-brooms. We finally convinced them to let us have brooms by letting them keep our 'dog tags' as hostage."

Abbott's crew began their task of sweeping the entire court. They went over the court three times until they were satisfied that they had removed all the loose sand.

A nurse from the dispensary walked up with a first aid kit and observed, "Looks like you guys could use a little TLC." Using alcohol soaked pads; she started cleaning the forward with the missing patches of skin. He gritted his teeth in pain, saying, "If this is TLC then I think that I would prefer being burned at the stake."

The nurse spied three high school girls, raptly watching the procedure—more correctly the airmen. She hollered, "Hey, you wanna help? C'mon in!"

They bounded up, giggling, and entered the court. The nurse instructed, "Just clean the scrapes and abrasions with alcohol and then apply disinfectant ointment."

The girls engrossed in their new task applied alcohol and ointment over the entire torso, from the neck down to the waist.

The wide-eyed girl working on Randy stated, "I can't believe that I'm actually touching Sherrill's fiancé."

Randy grimaced, not as much from the pain as from his loss of identity. "I'm Randy," he corrected.

"I know," the girl tittered, "You were fabulous on the court and I loved your speech."

"Thanks," replied Randy.

The girl looked down at his brogans and asked, "How come your team isn't wearing basketball shoes?"

Randy had the urge to flippantly retort, *because we wanted to give the other team a handicap.* This thought sounded too trite and unsportsmanlike, so he merely replied; "It's a long story."

Abbott came up with broom in hand. Randy looked at the girl and asked, "What is your name?"

"Carol—Carol Schrader," replied the girl.

"Well, Carol, meet the real hero of the game—Bart Abbott, but we all just call him 'Abbott.'"

Abbott and Carol shook hands and despite the ointment on Carol's hands there was an instant attraction.

Randy coaxed, "Hey, Abbott, why don't you escort Carol back to her seat.

"No problem," replied Abbott, throwing his broom aside. They walked away in animated conversation.

Randy sat contemplating the second half of the game. His team should have traction now, but the other team still had superior maneuverability in their basketball shoes.

The second half started. Randy put in five fresh substitutes. His concerns were confirmed. Though his team now had traction and they played their hearts out, they were more prone to foul the other team. The first half had miraculously been foul free, mainly because his team was lying defenseless on the court while the other team shot.

Now both teams were trading fouls. Worse than that, they were trading baskets. There was still an 11-point separation at the end of the third quarter. Score 70-59.

Randy sat realizing that if this trend continued then they would lose the game. His team was already playing their best—*what would Coach Martin, his high school coach, do in this situation?"* He searched his memory and couldn't come up with a good answer.

He demanded of himself, "Okay, Mr. Ferris, what are you going to do about the situation?"

A plan formed in his mind. He turned to Casio and asked, "Can you play?"

Casio replied tentatively, "Well, yeah, but my shooting hand is still numb. I've only got a little feeling in my fingers."

"Can you slam-dunk a ball?" asked Randy.

Casio responded, "Yeah, I could slam-dunk a basketball with my arm in a sling."

His team gathered around him and Randy explained his strategy, "Okay, here is what we're going to do. Our starting team goes back in. Casio, I want you to stand in front of our net. We'll implement the fast break every time the other team shoots then pass the ball to you. You will dunk the ball.

"The other team isn't stupid and they will put a man on Casio. He can handle a one-on-one; then they will double-team him. This will give us a defensive advantage on their end of the court to take away the ball without them scoring. We fast break the ball down the court. If Casio is still covered then we take our best shot. Okay, let's go out and win this game. Together now, 'Hooah.'"

The team gutturally grunted, "Hooah," in unison and took their position on the court. The Shirts took the ball in. They didn't even notice that Casio had trotted to the other end of the court. The Shirts' forward dribbled the ball, and then noticed that someone was missing. He looked over his shoulder and lost the ball. It was picked up by a Skins' guard and passed to Casio, who leisurely dunked the ball.

The Shirts threw in the ball and left a man to guard Casio. The Skins put on a full court press and took the ball away. They fed the ball to Casio. He faked a jump—then jumped. As the guard was on the way down, Casio was on his way up and dunked the ball.

Two guards were put on Casio. As the Shirts dribbled the ball, Randy hung back slightly. A guard passed to a forward, who passed to the other forward. Randy stepped in and received the ball. The forward, angry that the ball had been stolen, immediately fouled Randy.

Randy was entitled to 1-1 (make the first shot; get a 2nd). He dropped both shots through the net. Score 70-65.

Belcher screamed, "Call time—call time."

He started ranting and cussing at his team. "You stupid fuckin' morons look like a bunch of pussies out there." He used every expletive that he had ever heard and made up a few new ones.

People setting up front overheard his diatribe and turned their heads away in embarrassment.

He closed, threatening them, "If you guys lose this fuckin' game, you'll be mopping fuckin' floors and cleaning fuckin' latrines until you ship out from this fuckin' base. Now every time the other team gets the ball—foul them. Do I make myself perfectly fuckin' clear?"

They replied in unison, "Yes, DI, sir!"

Shirts started playing with intimidated demonic vigor. They knew that their DI was a man of his word. They placed a single guard on Casio—if he got the ball then foul him.

Shirts inbounded the ball and swiftly made 2 points.

The Skins' other forward got the ball and was immediately fouled. He made both shots.

Shirts took the ball down court. A forward cut sharply and ran into a moving guard. The referee called a foul on the Skins' player. The Shirts' forward made the first shot, but missed the second.

The Skins threw in the ball and the guard was immediately fouled.

The Skins' guard shot and made the first free throw, but missed the second.

Shirts got the rebound, initiated a fast break down the court, and scored.

Randy received the throw-in. He was clear for a split-second and threw the ball all the way down court to Casio. Casio was immediately fouled. Casio stepped up to the free-throw line. His hand was numb and he missed the basket entirely, forfeiting his 2nd shot.

Shirts responded with 2 points.

Randy saw that Shirts were now fouling every time that the ball was thrown in. He informed his guards to immediately get the ball to him. Randy was fouled and made both free throws.

The Skins countered with 2 points. The score climbed evenly to 91-79, but precious minutes had ticked off the clock. The good news was that the Shirts' starting team was fouling out with five fouls. Three of their key players were now sitting on the bench. The bad news was that Randy's team was still behind 12 points.

Randy called time and took his team into a huddle. "Okay, guys, the situation is bad, but not lost. I want three substitutes without fouls. Two can play the same game and I want you to foul the other team as soon as they get the ball.

"Casio and I will stay in. Casio, I want you to line up on the right side of the basket during my free throws. I will make the first basket and I'll aim for my second shot to hit between the right side of the rim and the backboard. The ball should fall into your hands. I want you in the air on my second shot to dunk the rebound." Casio dubiously rolled his eyes, "I can do *dat*—can you?"

Randy exhaled, "I can only try."

Randy took the throw-in and was fouled. The teams walked to the other end. Randy made the first shot then shot his second shot. It hit between the rim and backboard. Casio took the rebound on his way up and dunked the ball. Score 91-82.

Shirts threw in the ball and the guard was immediately fouled.

The Shirts' first shot hit the rim. A Skins' substitute, rather than receiving the ball, tipped it to Randy, who was immediately fouled.

The Skins walked to the other end of the court and using their strategy, racked up 3 more points. Score 91-85.

Shirts threw in and were fouled. They made the first shot, but missed the second.

The rebound was again tipped to Randy. He was fouled and the Skins racked up 3 more points.

The play sequence repeated itself. Score 93-91.

Belcher panicked and called time. He made the mistake of yelling out to his team, as they approached, "No more fouls—no more fouls."

Leubrecht overheard this information and he passed it on to his teammates, as they huddled in a circle.

Randy explained his strategy, "Okay guys, this is win or lose. We've only got twenty seconds left in the game and Shirts have the ball. Foul them immediately—make then shoot a free throw.

"If they aren't going to foul us then we can move the ball down the court, but we're only going to have time for one, maybe two shots—make it count.

Belcher had fire in his eyes and berated his team, "You fuckin' idiots are blowin' a 12 point lead. If one more shit-head screws up then all of you are going to pull KP every day on 'pots and pans'—in addition to latrine duty. Is that perfectly fuckin' clear?"

The Shirts were subdued in energy and spirit. They each had played their best, and not even that was appreciated. Returning to the court, Shirts received the ball and were fouled.

The guard made his first shot. Score 94-91. Sweating from exertion and tension, he remembered Belcher's words. With tense muscles, he shot and the ball hit the rim. Skins got the rebound and initiated a fast break down the court, passing to Casio. Casio had to step out of position to receive the ball. He knew that he couldn't shoot and fed the ball back to his forward, who scored against the center guard, who had been pulled out of position to defend against Casio. 10 seconds had elapsed; 10 seconds left in the game. Score 94-93.

The Shirts were fouled again on the throw-in and lined up for the foul shot at the far end. The Shirts' player was trembling, as he tried his first free throw. The tension was too much and the ball missed the backboard and went out of bounds.

Shirts rushed to a defensive position. Randy ran down to mid-court and took the passed ball. Shirts moved out to defend and Randy passed to the other forward. The forward dribbled the ball, looking for an opening. Seeing none, he passed to a corner guard. Seconds were ticking off the clock. The guard, not finding a shot and seeing that the forwards were tied up, threw a low pass to the guard on the opposite side of the court.

Casio thinking that the ball was a tip-in pass—jumped. The ball was thrown too hot for his numb fingers and he only diverted it in the air. The ball fell short and hit the defensive guard on the back of his leg. The ball rolled toward the free shot line and Casio rushed forward and retrieved it. He hesitated with uncertainty. He was away from the net and he couldn't shoot the ball.

His opponent had moved up behind him—arms and legs spread in a defensive stance. Casio could dribble with his left hand, but he couldn't shoot with his left or right hand. The Shirts were playing his team man-to-man and the clock was ticking down with 3-seconds to go.

Randy and his other players had desperately been trying to get open, but their opponents were on them like glue. He glanced at the clock and saw that the score was 94-93 with 3 seconds to go. Randy stopped and cupped his hands to his mouth and yelled, "Casio—Globetrotters—only happens once."

Comprehension flashed across Casio's face. He rolled the ball between his legs, turned, and clapped his hands above his head. The center guard froze, wondering where the ball had gone. Casio stepped around him, picked up the rolling ball, and dunked it as the buzzer sounded to end the game. **Final Score 95-94—Skins win!**

The crowd went wild! They stood cheering and applauding for more than 5 minutes. Even the referees applauded what they had considered at the start of the game as an impossible feat. They went to each battered and bruised Skins' player and personally congratulated him as the band played "The Notre Dame Fight Song."

Captain Detrich had the podium set back up. When the cheering and applause died down, he announced, "I would like to have Sergeant Stark and his entire team come up to the stage. Leave your shirts off; I want the crowd to see and appreciate your heroic battle wounds.

The crowd began applauding again. Randy's team moved single file to the stage. People in the crowd reached out; satisfied with just touching the players, since they could see that a slap on the back would only bring undeserved pain to their battered torsos.

Stark and his team lined up behind the captain. The applause started to die down. As he stood next to his bare-chested men, Stark, feeling conspicuous in his civilian clothes, impulsively removed his shirt and tossed it to the edge of the stage. The crowd was hushed by the action. Maria stood and gave him a lone 'wolf whistle' that could be heard throughout the area.

The crowd, pumped up by the excitement of the game and feeling festive, burst into laughter and applauded. Stark's complexion changed three shades of red.

Captain Detrich waited for the applause to end. "Thank you again for attending the game. I do not think that I am being presumptuous when I say that it was one of the most unusual and exciting games that I have ever watched. I think you will agree that when the score was 20 to zip that not even Las Vegas would have given odds for Sergeant Stark's team to come back and win.

"You were probably surprised along with me when you saw his team slipping and sliding around during the 1st half. We had the basketball court swept yesterday, but apparently sand or something else was on it and almost caused them a catastrophic loss. The slipping problem seemed to go away after the court was swept.

"I want to pay tribute to Randy and his team for overcoming a very difficult handicap. They not only were playing in brogans on a slippery surface, but as you can see when they fell, they lost several layers of skin. Their innovative and versatile strategy of adapting to the playing conditions was the turning point of the game. We are very proud to have men like them in the United States Air Force.

"Airman Randy Ferris and Airman Casio Brown have proved once again by their outstanding performances that they were worthy of the United States Air Force Athletic Achievement Medal, which you saw them receive earlier in these ceremonies. Again, I ask for your participation in paying homage to these valiant athletes."

Captain Detrich turned and applauded the airmen. The crowd indeed feeling that they had seen an outstanding feat, applauded with enthusiasm. Stark, in a stage whisper, instructed, "Bow, don't salute." His men followed his lead and bowed. Turning, they bowed to the VIPs in the bleachers. Turning again, they bowed to the general audience. Waving to their fans, they followed Stark off the stage.

At the end of the applause, Captain Detrich announced, "I declare this game and these ceremonies concluded." The band struck up with, "When the Saints Go Marching In."

Maria rushed down out of the bleachers and grabbed Randy's hand, pulling him out of the line. Her arms were open to give him a hug. "Oh, Randy, you guys were wonderful." Noting that Randy held back from a hug, she observed up-close his bruises and abrasions. She reached up and pulled his face to her lips. She kissed him on the cheek and said, "I love you like a brother."

Returning the kiss on her cheek, Randy whispered, "I love you like a sister."

Stark, putting his shirt back on, overheard the whispered words. Maria turned to him and kissed him full on the mouth. She whispered in a husky voice, "And—I love you like a husband—you big stallion."

Stark laughed, "Okay, let's get the Hades out of here."

Randy started to rejoin his team and found himself surrounded by Sherrill's fans wanting his autograph. He took whatever material they presented to him and signed, without delusion: *Best wishes—Sherrill's fiancé—Randy Ferris.*

Culmination

Stark's eyes scanned the exiting crowd—.

Maria caught up with him, "Now tell me; what made you so upset?"

"Later, Honey. First, I need to find Captain Detrich. Espying the captain, he touched Maria on the arm, "I'll meet you back at the car—I'll just be a little while."

"Okay, but I still want to know." Turning, she saw Sergeant Henderson's wife and struck up a conversation with her as they walked toward the parking lot.

Stark approached the captain, "Excuse me, Captain Detrich. May I speak with you for a moment, sir?

"Certainly, Sergeant Stark, I'm glad that we ran into each other. I wanted to personally congratulate you on the exciting basketball that your team provided today. I'm still amazed that they came back and won the game."

"I was surprised too, sir—under the strange circumstances…"

"What do you mean—strange circumstances, Sergeant?"

"Well, sir, it appears that someone salted the basketball court with sand."

"That is a very serious allegation, Sergeant. Who do you think would do something so underhanded?"

"I'd rather not say who, sir, but I did ask Bob, the Times photographer, to take a couple of photos. He will send one to you and the AP's will get a copy."

"You really think that the AP's should get involved, Sergeant?"

"I don't really know, sir—that's your call. I only know that my team members suffered injuries due to sand being on the court. We were lucky that no bones were broken. You, sir, stated that the court was swept yesterday and we haven't had any dust storms since then. I don't know for sure who did it; but I do know that someone was unethical and certainly demonstrated poor sportsmanship."

The captain patted Stark on the back, "I agree with you, Sergeant—I'll look into it. Now, you and Maria enjoy the rest of your weekend off."

Stark found Maria at the car and they drove off the base. Halfway home, they stopped at a roadside tavern. Finding an isolated booth, Stark ordered a beer and Maria ordered a Coke. Stark took a couple of swigs to relax, and then summarized for Maria:

"You saw how much trouble our basketball team had maintaining their balance. They looked like they were playing on ice instead of on concrete. I think that Sergeant Belcher put sand on the court."

"Why, that rotten bastard!" minced Maria. "Randy could have been badly hurt!"

"All of them could have been badly hurt, not just Randy," corrected Stark.

"You're right. It's just that I know Randy—I don't know the rest of your team. What are you going to do about Belcher?"

"It's out of my hands now. I explained it to the captain and he indicated that he would look into it."

"Well, I hope they hang Belcher by his *proverbials*—" interjected Maria.

Stark unconsciously cupped his hand over his crotch. "I didn't tell the captain that I thought it was Belcher—that's just between you and me—okay?"

They clicked their glasses together in understanding. Stark ordered another round and they spent a leisurely half-hour together, recapping the events of the day before picking the kids up and going home.

Stark walked into his home and picked up the phone. He called Sergeant Scott at Castle AFB, outside Merced, California. "Scotty! This is Dwayne Stark from Lackland."

"Hey, Starkey! We haven't talked in over a year. How're Maria and the kids?

"Fine—fine. Listen, Scotty, I want you to do me a favor. I want you to contact a Hank Casson in Merced. I think I remember the papers stating that he was in real estate."

"I know him," replied Scott, "We bought our house from him. I've got his card here some place—. What do you want me to tell him?"

"Tell him to have Sherrill watch the six o'clock news. I think that she will see something interesting," informed Stark.

"Sherrill! You mean the starlet, Sherrill. How do you know her, Starkey?"

"Her fiancé is my barracks chief," informed Stark.

"No kidding—you mean, Randy?"

"Yeah," replied Stark, "but how do you know about Randy?"

"I don't know about your neck of the woods, but Sherrill's put Merced back on the map. There are lots of articles about her and anyone else connected with her in the newspaper and news clips on TV every day. She just signed for three episodes with "The Dons of

Eldorado" and a retainer for future episodes. She got a cool $100k out of the deal—that's more than you and I will earn in the next ten years."

"Yeah, that's a lot of moolah," agreed Stark

Scott added, "The last movie star from here was Janet Leigh—you know—the star in 'Psycho.'"

"Yeah, I remember. It was probably Hitchcock's best film. Maria still has an occasional nightmare about it."

"Anyway," concluded Stark, "Would you contact Mr. Casson for me?"

"No problem, buddy. Hey, when are you going to get out our way?"

"I don't know. I think that I'm a lifer—here at Lackland."

"Well, if you do, you know your old buddy, Scotty, has a place for you."

"Thanks, Scotty. The same goes if you get back this way." Stark hung up and whistled, "$100k—whew, that's a bankroll!"

After signing autographs for over an hour, Randy walked into the barracks and was met with cheers. His barracks mates surrounded him and hoisted him on their shoulders. They paraded him up and down the aisle—cheering and yelling. Embarrassed by this outpouring of admiration, he tried to get down, "Hey, guys, it was a team effort—let me down." They ignored his pleas and continued the revelry.

The assistant DI walked in and they dropped Randy on his feet in front of the DI. The DI reached out, shaking Randy's hand, "I just got back from HQ, and the captain has issued day passes for the entire barracks. You are all free to do whatever you want until 1700, and then we'll assemble for the march to the chow hall. I'll relieve the barracks guard until you get back."

The barracks cheered their good fortunate. Randy held up both hands for quiet and announced, "Make sure that your area is ready for inspection, and then you're free to leave—except for the basketball team and Abbott."

Randy took a quick shower and dressed as the last man left. He called the team together, "The reason that I wanted you to stay is that I want to take all of you over to the Airmen's Club and treat you to real hamburgers—the works."

Casio interrupted, "No, Mr. Randall T., the treat is on me. If you hadn't hollered *Globetrotters*, I would never have remembered that play—we would have lost the game."

The team hollered, "Hooah," in agreement."

Randy shrugged his shoulders in resignation and they walked laughing and joking to the Airmen's Club to celebrate their hard fought win.

Sherrill felt overwhelmed by all the fan mail. She would complete her school lessons in the morning, but spent the rest of the day and into the night responding to fan mail. She unburdened to Aunt Vicki, "I didn't know that being popular was going to take so much of my time. For every letter I write a response to, I get a hundred more."

"I can see that," her aunt sympathized. "I just pulled out one of the bags from the stack and found our utility bill inside it. I don't have a clue where the other bills might be. I'll have to talk to Hank about that, maybe he has some ideas."

Hank walked in with a pizza. Vicki remarked, "You're early, it is only six—how did you get away from the office?"

"I own the office—remember. I still have a pile of contracts on my desk and I just clicked off the lights and walked out," adding, "I'll probably have to go in tomorrow."

Sherrill squealed, "Oh, you brought pizza—what kind?"

"The works," informed Hank. "We all could use a break—let's flip on the news and enjoy a pizza."

"What's the weather doing on already," noted Vicki, looking at her watch. "They always show that after the news."

A toothpaste commercial came on as the trio munched on their pizza. The announcer came back on, "We have a treat for Sherrill's fans. Our sports coverage has been expanded tonight to bring this special program to you."

"Sports coverage! What are they going to do—show some of Sherrill's old basketball films?" Vicki sarcastically declared.

Hank just sat back with a passive look on his face and didn't comment. Sherrill sat with a bemused look on her face. *The only filmed games were the divisional playoffs*—she thought.

The sports special opened showing an air force general making a speech. "Thank you all for attending this event—.

When he summoned Randy to the podium, Sherrill's world became the event that she was watching on TV. The achievement medal was pinned on Randy and the two airmen left. Sherrill, feeling slighted for Randy, observed, "The general didn't even shake his hand like he did with the other guy."

The general was instantly forgiven when he called Randy back to the podium. He made a preliminary speech then introduced Randy to the audience as Sherrill's fiancé. She saw and heard the crowd go wild; her skin flushed with joy at seeing her man. She had an eerie compunction, a feeling of wanting to stand and applaud with them.

The next scene showed nearly a hundred women in uniform standing and cheering Randy. Sherrill suddenly felt a ripple of jealousy flow up her spine that caused gooseflesh on her arms.

Randy's opening statement further heightened her discomfort. "Thank you—and a special thank you to the members of the Women's Air Force. I guess that I can now tell Sherrill that I have a fan club too." She heard the audience laugh, but didn't know why they would laugh at something that made her feel so—so left out.

His joke about the cops chasing them through the obstacle course was lost on her. She was close to tears when he stated, "Seriously though, I know why you are really here. You want to know more about Sherrill. You watched her on television and fell in love with her as I fell in love with her."

His profession of love for her in front of the entire world melted her heart. She felt so ashamed for having feelings of jealousy and suppressed a quiet sob.

She watched Randy speak of her and her strength to endure, but at the moment, she had never felt so weak and fragile. She saw and heard him speak of their relationship, "—that we are 'soul mates.' I feel the same way toward her."

Tears completely obliterated her vision. Stumbling blindly toward her bedroom, she only heard his closing statement, "Thank you for being here—for Sherrill."

The network broke for a commercial, announcing that highlights of the basketball game would immediately follow. Hank and Vicki glanced at each other; both had been moved by the speech. He asked, "Do you think that you should go and comfort Sherrill?"

Vicki responded wisely, "No. Sometimes a good cry can be a girl's best friend—I'll talk with her later."

The sports announcer came back on the screen. "Seldom have we viewed a more unusual game. During the first half, Randy's team had trouble maneuvering on the court. The court was swept during halftime and the second half was a whole new ballgame.

"For you college coaches—eat your hearts out. The air force has a bright young athlete that I think every coach would wade through alligators to have on his team. For you college recruiters, note that he misses his second free throws on purpose, so that his teammate can slam dunk two extra points."

The edited version of the game was condensed into seven minutes. Most of the action showed Randy shooting and making baskets. His three-point shots and free throws were grouped together, which made him appear as a one-man basketball game. The game ended with Casio's razzle-dazzle Globetrotters' play. Final score - 95-94, Randy's team wins. The audio volume was increased to emphasize the audience's response.

The program switched to a commercial and Vicki exclaimed, "My Lord, Randy sure looked good—I didn't know that anyone could really be that good?"

"Yes, Randy was good," replied Hank. "However, you need to realize that all that action was condensed from sixty minutes play time to a little over seven minutes show time. Still, Randy was damn good; he surely deserved MVP for the game."

The following Monday, Sergeant Belcher was standing in front of Captain Detrich. Sergeant Major Hanson and Sergeant Stark were sitting in attendance, along with the adjutant from the air police squadron. The captain addressed Belcher, "Sergeant Belcher—we have uncovered evidence that someone salted the basketball court with sand before the game last Saturday. Do you have anything to say about that incident?"

Belcher broke attention and turned on Stark, "Stark's a liar. He always disliked me and wants to ruin my career. The sand probably just blew in and Stark wants to put me down and smear my good name."

The captain continued, "I'm not so sure that you have a good name to smear, Sergeant Belcher. We received many complaints from the audience that you used the foulest possible language in berating your own team. I also have duty rosters showing that you scheduled your entire basketball team for 'pots and pans' and have them pulling KP every day until they ship out.

"I watched your team play and they played their hearts out—they were just beaten by a better team."

Belcher, still feeling stung by the loss, iterated, "I told those slackers what would happen if they lost—the punishment fit the crime."

"The only crime that I see here was committed by you Sergeant. Your deliberate actions resulted in the damage to government property, namely Sergeant Stark's team members. Some had to go to the infirmary and all received cuts and abrasions."

"It's Stark's fault. He didn't give his team basketball shoes," yelled Belcher. "If he had of—then I wouldn't be in front of you now."

The captain stared at Belcher and wondered how a man like this had lasted so long training men in his company. He could only surmise that Belcher had used intimidation and that none of his people had complained. He made a mental note to be more observant of his DI's tactics in the future.

He continued redressing Belcher, "I'm sure that Sergeant Stark was unaware that you purchased basketball shoes for your team. Most recruits' basketball games are played in their brogans. They would not have had a problem with balance if there hadn't been sand on the courts.

"Now that gets us back to the reason that you are standing in front of me, Sergeant Belcher. Lieutenant Stuart has investigated this incident and we will hear his report—Lieutenant Stuart."

"Thank you, Captain. We received two photographs of the basketball court—one before sweeping and another after the court was swept."

Passing the photo around, he continued, "The first photo shows a reflective pattern on the court. As you can see from the second photo, the reflection is gone. Suspecting that sand had been salted on the court because Sergeant Stark's team was unable to maintain their footing, we took samples of the sand that had been swept to the side.

"The sand was not the normal dirt blown in by the wind. It matched sand used in butt cans for extinguishing cigarettes. Because Sergeant Belcher had the most to gain, we checked his barracks first and found one butt can that had less sand than the others. That was the only butt can that had Sergeant Belcher's fingerprints on it.

"Our investigation also revealed that Sergeant Belcher was seen the night before the game walking back from the direction of the basketball court. He was observed carrying a butt can of the type that had his fingerprints.

Additionally, the barracks guard did not see Sergeant Belcher leave, but did see him reenter the barracks carrying the butt can.

"To be fair and thorough, we investigated Sergeant Stark's barracks and found nothing amiss. The evidence points out that Sergeant Belcher

214

did in fact perpetrate a crime—motive, opportunity, and physical evidence."

"Thank you, Lieutenant Stuart," acknowledged the captain. Swiveling his chair to face Belcher, he commanded, "Stand at attention, Sergeant Belcher.

"Under the rules of the Uniform Code of Military Justice, I am issuing you an Article 15. You are relieved of all duties on this base. You will be fined 15 days of leave time and 15 days' pay. You will be transferred to another base.

"This action will be recorded in your personnel file with the recommendation that you never again be allowed to train men. Is that clear, Sergeant Belcher?"

"Yes, sir," gritted Belcher.

"Furthermore, Sergeant, if you decide to challenge this punishment, which is your right; I will see that a court martial reduces you in rank and provides brig time.

"If you think that this threat is intimidation, just remind yourself of all the times and hundreds of men that you have bullied and intimidated while you were supposed to be their leader and set a good example for them to follow. I have nothing further to say to you. Now get out of my office and out of my sight!"

The sergeant saluted and left. The captain turned to his sergeant major and said, "Relieve all of Belcher's men from KP; give them a day pass for San Antonio. They deserve it after having to put up with that son-of-a-bitch."

He turned to Stuart, "Thanks for coming over lieutenant—that was a fine report."

"You're welcome, Captain Detrich," the lieutenant remarked as he left.

"Well, that just leaves you and me, Sergeant Stark. I saw the sports special on TV and I was even more impressed by your barracks' performance—tell me more about Randy—."

Hollywood

Sherrill commented as she entered Bill Payson's office, "Thank you for seeing me on such short notice, Mr. Payson. I am leaving for Hollywood tomorrow and I felt that we should talk before I leave."

Bill arose from his chair and shut the door, smiling as he offered, "Please have a seat, Sherrill. I wanted to talk with you too." Looking into her eyes, he sincerely stated, "I want to apologize for my unprofessional demeanor."

Sherrill's shoulders relaxed with relief at his having initiated the topic. She started to accept the apology—.

Bill held up his hand, cutting her off. "I admit that I was and still am attracted to you, but *c'est la vie*—that is life. I saw you on TV at your press conference and looked upon you as a very beautiful woman.

"Then, I saw Randy and heard him speak at his awards ceremony. He is good looking and athletic. He also comes across as a talented speaker—despite his youth. When he professed his love for you in front of the world, I saw that same look in his eyes as I saw in yours. I realized then and there that I didn't have a chance of being more than just a friend to you."

"Thank you, Mr. Payson, for being open and understanding. I respect you very much and I appreciate the time that you have devoted to helping me with my courses."

"I felt it a privilege, Sherrill. I want to be more to you than just a counselor. I want to be your true friend—a proper friend. If there is anything that I can ever do for you, just call me—I'll be there for you."

Sherrill arose to leave and Bill remembered, "Oh, I nearly forgot. The superintendent told the staff that he had received over a thousand inquiries from all over the United States about the special education program we have for girls. He has the school board's blessing to expand the program. It will now be offered to all former students that haven't received their high school diplomas.

"He also stated that you have proven to be a very good ambassador for this school district. He asked me to see if you would speak at the commencement ceremonies for this year's graduating seniors."

"That's a long way off," replied Sherrill, mulling the thought over and feeling honored, yet feeling the instant moisture on the palms of her hands at the thought of speaking directly to her peers. She forced

216

back her feelings of trepidation and indecision, "If I'm still in Merced, tell Dr. Rawlings that I will do it."

"Thank you, Sherrill," Bill said as he extended his hand. "You have a good trip to Hollywood. We'll all be rooting for you."

"Goodbye, Mr. Payson."

Before their shopping spree, Sherrill met Aunt Vicki for lunch. So many people seemed to know her now by sight. They waved and called out, "Hi, Sherrill!" as if they had been good friends and known her for a long time.

Sherrill, feeling strange at this one-sided phenomenon, either waved back or responded with a simple, "Hi!" or "Hi—how are you?"

Mark Fairchild sat down at Randy's table and extended his hand, "Congratulations! You guys played one hell of a game!"

"Thanks Mark; your team was good too. There was only one point difference in the final score."

"Yeah," agreed Mark. "But we had an unfair advantage and I don't mean just the basketball shoes. Belcher sprinkled sand on the basketball court."

"I suspected as much," responded Randy. "How did they prove it was him?"

"I don't know," replied Mark, "but they shipped his ass out of here. Our assistant DI is now in charge of our barracks." He added, "No big deal, since most of us are shipping out tomorrow for tech schools."

"I'm sorry that your barracks didn't win the weekend pass to San Antonio." Realizing that this sounded trite and condescending, since Randy's barracks had beaten them out of the prize, Randy explained, "I guess what I'm trying to say is that I wish that you could've competed and won against someone else, instead of us."

"No hard feelings," reassured Mark. "Your barracks deserved to win. Besides, the CO gave us a day pass to town for having to put up with that bastard Belcher. I've never met more of a genuine asshole than him."

Mark continued, "I don't mind most people that are hard, as long as they are fair. Belcher handed out arbitrary punishment for the least little infraction. The morale of my barracks was in the shitter most of the time."

Randy empathetically shared, "I thought Sergeant Stark was a bastard when we first arrived on base, but now we're friends. He's got a

217

real nice wife, but I didn't get to meet the rest of his family. I'm actually going to miss them when I ship out."

Mark stood and extended his hand. "I'm glad that I met you, Randy. I guess this is good-bye, since the only time that we ever see each other is in the chow hall."

"You take care of yourself, Mark. Maybe our paths will cross again in the next four years." Mark left and Randy reminisced, *I wish that I had had a chance to know him better—nice guy.*

Randy glanced down at his on-base pass. He had been scheduled for another all day testing session at the Green Monster, while the rest of his barracks was drilling. He momentarily wondered why he had been singled out for testing then put it out of his mind, rationalizing, *the air force has its own agenda and few people are privy to the full reason for any decision.*

Randy opened his test booklet. The format was similar to the test that he had taken for his high school GED, except the subject matter was more complex. He was surprised when he finished the test that it didn't have a section on math. Although the test covered many of the sciences, it mainly consisted of reading comprehension and he felt sure that he would score high.

When he asked the monitor how he did, the monitor gave him the, "You'll find out at the appropriate time."

During his lunch break, Randy found a pay phone and asked the operator to put a call to the residence of Hank Casson in Merced, California. The phone rang ten times and the operator informed him that no one answered. He told her, "Thank you, I'll try later."

The afternoon test session was on more languages, followed by a bank of logic problems, which he whipped thru. He sat back feeling confident, thinking, *I guess all that time I spent working through problems in my head, while driving a tractor, has finally paid off.*

On his way back to the barracks, he tried another long distance call to the Casson's residence and heard the operator say, "I'm sorry, sir, no one answers."

He entered the barracks and went directly to his living area. He picked up a brogan and started polishing it, lost in thought.

Finally Abbott looked over and asked, "What's the matter, man? You haven't said a word to anybody since you got in."

Randy shook his head and snapped back to reality. He had promised Sergeant Stark that his problem would not affect the barracks. "It's nothing, Abbott; I was just thinking of Sherrill. Then in a different tone, he inquired, "Is the barracks ready for inspection?"

"No problema," responded Abbott. "Everyone in our barracks knows what is expected of them and they just do it without being told. They can't wait to ship out for tech training. I hear that they are going to post the list of assignments this week."

"I heard that too," replied Randy, wondering where he would be sent. He picked up a sheet of stationery and wrote to his parents. All through the letter he was distracted with thoughts of Sherrill and found it difficult to stay focused on his writing.

The next day the flight went through survival exercises. Small groups wearing gas masks entered a windowless building. Tear gas was released and they were ordered to take off their masks.

Most of the men suddenly breathed in from the shock of the tear gas burning their eyes. After a minute of exposure, the door was opened and they exited coughing and crying.

Sergeant Stark addressed the flight, "Okay, you bozos, now you can appreciate the need of a good gas mask—don't forget it—it may save your life."

He marched them to a classroom where the lecturer showed them film footage of actual atomic bomb tests. The lecturer explained the meaning of the different siren sequences that warned of a nuclear attack, and then gave a short test to check their comprehension.

He closed the lecture by explaining, "In case of an 'imminent nuclear attack' in your area, sit under a sturdy table or desk. Place your head between your legs and 'kiss your ass—goodbye.'" He was the only one to find humor in his hackneyed joke.

That evening, Randy tried to call Sherrill. Again, he heard, "I'm sorry, sir. Your party doesn't answer." He went back to his barracks and wrote another letter to her.

He hadn't heard back from her on the first letter and wondered if she had even received it. Must not have, he reasoned, otherwise, she would have written. However, he hadn't received his letter back 'Return to Sender — Address Unknown,' so the post office must have delivered it. He anguished, "*What gives...?*"

Sherrill boarded the twin turbo-prop commuter plane with her aunt and uncle. Uncle Hank suggested, "Sherrill, sit next to the window. We won't get too high on this puddle jumper and you can see some sights along the way."

The airplane stopped in Fresno and Bakersfield before arriving at LAX. Sherrill saw the grapevine (U.S.-99) snaking through the mountains north of Los Angeles. She commented to Aunt Vicki, "The cars and trucks look like pearls strung on a necklace. I wonder why they are stopped."

Her aunt replied, "This is California. No one knows why the traffic stops. Sometimes the roads here become the world's largest parking lots. Then the traffic mysteriously clears and everyone drives like hopped-up teenagers until the next traffic jam shuts them down."

Sherrill had heard her aunt several times explain the unexplainable by simply stating, "This is California." *Can it really be so unique from other states?*" she wondered.

Brad Thurman met Sherrill and her guardians at LAX with a chauffeured limousine and whisked them off toward the Beverly Hill's Hilton. Sherrill noticed a street sign and just for polite conversation asked, "What does Sepulveda mean in Spanish?"

"I'm not sure", responded Brad, "but I think that it means 'Green Garden' or 'Flower Garden' or something like that."

"It is certainly beautiful here," responded Sherrill in awe. "There are so many flowers and fruit trees. Does the temperature ever get below freezing?"

Brad, assuming the duties of tour guide, explained, "The temperature seldom gets below freezing, and then only for a very short while. We don't get hard freezes. That is one reason that so many people have immigrated to LA from the colder climates of the world. The Pacific Ocean moderates the LA basin weather. But just over the mountains to the north and east, snow falls several times a year."

"The homes here are neat and clean," observed Sherrill, "but I was expecting everyone to have mansions and swimming pools."

Brad laughed, "That is a common misconception. You will see plenty of mansions and swimming pools in the Hollywood area, but like every metropolis, the worker bees have to live somewhere too. We are now driving through a typical working community. Although many of these people work in the movie industry, they work for scale wages and lead modest lives when compared to the superstars and movie moguls."

Arriving at the Beverly Hilton, they were escorted to their rooms. Sherrill noted "The Princess Room" on the door opened by the bellhop. As she entered the room, her breath caught in her throat.

The room was decorated in pink marble and trimmed in gold. Mirrors were strategically located to brighten and widen the rooms. The suite opened onto a lanai balcony, tastefully decorated with tropical flowers and vines. The view was unobstructed and a morning shower had cleared the air. In the far distance, Sherrill could barely discern the Pacific Ocean as a thin line dividing the colorful rooftops and the silver streaked blue sky.

Breathing in the fragrant air, she remarked to Aunt Vicki, specifically, and to the rest of the group, generally, "This is so beautiful; I feel like I'm in wonderland."

Aunt Vicki, awed by the ambiance, remained silent. Brad picked up on the remark, "We knew that you would like it, Sherrill. Your aunt and uncle have an adjoining suite and tomorrow you can have breakfast on the lanai."

He caught the eye of the bellhop and nodded toward the dining table on the lanai, "Let's have a glass of fresh lemonade."

The foursome sat while the bellhop poured the tall glasses of lemonade. Brad raised his glass to toast, "Welcome to Hollywood—Sherrill."

They took a long draught of the cool tart liquid. Brad, Vicki, and Hank engaged in small talk about the early morning flight, while Sherrill stared into the distance. Her eyes took in the scenery as her mind drifted with thoughts of Randy. She thought, *this would be perfect if Randy were here.* Sherrill was brought back to reality when she heard her Aunt Vicki remark, "Oh, we've lost her. She's got that *Randy look* in her eyes."

They all laughed as a slightly flustered Sherrill regained her composure after being yanked back from her daydream world. Brad inquired, "Sherrill, how do you feel after the flight? Do you feel up to going shopping for the photo-shoot tomorrow?"

Sherrill replied, "I feel great."

Aunt Vicki interjected, "Brad, you know women. We are always ready to go shopping, but we did some shopping before the trip. We bought traveling clothes and clothes for dining and entertainment."

"That's fine," replied Brad, "but we need some era clothing for the photo-shoot. I'll have a costume coordinator available this afternoon and she will take you to the shops on Rodeo Drive. Sherrill will be outfitted for the photo-shoot and we also want some ensembles for a publicity collage for her fans."

Turning to Sherrill, he revealed, "Your uncle and I have a surprise for you—we think that you will really like it."

Sherrill turned and looked at her uncle. He had a twinkle in his eye and she was sure that he wouldn't divulge the surprise, but she asked anyway, "What kind of surprise, Uncle Hank?"

True to his nature, he deferred, "As Brad pointed out, it's a surprise."

Sherrill turned to Aunt Vicki for some hint, but she also deferred, "Don't look at me. I know about the surprise, but I promised that I wouldn't tell."

"You are all mean and spiteful to keep secrets from me," chided Sherrill. A pout started to form on her lips, but she couldn't hold back a smile of anticipation. She felt a new exuberance and put thoughts of Randy out of her mind. "Okay, as Uncle Hank says, 'let's get this show on the road.'"

Brad picked up the phone and spoke into it for a moment. Hanging up, he informed, "Carol will be here at 1:00 to take the ladies shopping. Meanwhile, Hank and I have some business to wrap up.

"We'll meet you in the restaurant lobby at eight o'clock tonight for dinner at Marco Polo's. You'll like it; it's a fine Italian restaurant off the beaten track, and we won't have a problem with the press."

Carol Whiting was punctual and very professional. She brought with her a list of shops and story-line drawings of the costumes that would be required for the filming of Sherrill's first episode of "The Dons of Eldorado." She also had suggestions for evening dresses for the required round of "see and be seen" publicity events to launch Sherrill into the Hollywood mainstream of stars. Sherrill noted that Carol's selections were much more svelte and risqué than the ones that Aunt Vicki and she had purchased in Merced.

Although Sherrill's 20" waist had expanded to 22" to accommodate the baby, the clothes and accessories that Carol had suggested, plus Sherrill's 5' 10" height gave the illusion that she was not pregnant and even enhanced the appeal of her figure.

At eight, the shopping trio met Brad and Uncle Hank at Marco Polo's Restaurant. They were immediately seated and Brad ordered *calamari* as an appetizer. Everyone watched Sherrill as she took her first bite of the delicacy. Brad smiled, "How do you like it, Sherrill?"

"It's delicious. What is it?"

"Actually, it's squid."

Sherrill paused and felt a lemony taste tingle at the base of her jaw at the thought of eating squid, and then decided, "It's delicious, so it can't be so bad. I never thought that I would be eating squid."

Brad, encouraged by her receptive remarks, decided to press the point, "If you are going to immerse yourself in Hollywood cuisine then you have to go all the way. I am going to order for you *calamari seafood chowder* and *calamari steaks* as a main entrée. The secret is to eat small portions at first because it is very rich in protein and flavor."

As the meal progressed, the conversation drifted into small talk about their shopping spree. The group vicariously enjoyed the experience as Sherrill animatedly related her impressions of her first Hollywood exposure.

Brad asked, "Did the people that you met in the shops recognize you?"

"Many of them did," replied Sherrill. Then, collecting a general impression in her thoughts, she remarked, "They recognized me, but their reaction was completely different than I expected. They were cordial and helpful, but almost blasé in their reaction.

"In Merced and Monterey everyone that recognized me responded with awe and adulation. Here in Hollywood, they addressed me as 'Sherrill' before we were even introduced, but their demeanor was 'business as usual.' I found that refreshing, but also a little bit disconcerting."

Brad smiled, "That's Hollywood for you—there is no other place on earth like it. People have become so accustomed to seeing stars and superstars that a new one on the horizon doesn't even faze them. But you can be sure that, tonight, they will tell their children and friends that they have met or seen you.

"Our marketing research shows that you are one of the most readily recognizable faces in America today and that the general populace knows you only by your first name, 'Sherrill.'" Brad paused for a moment and Sherrill stared into space, contemplating the revelation.

"I feel comfortable with that," she responded, "Everyone back home always referred to me by my first name and it doesn't seem strange now."

Brad continued, "Only a few Hollywood superstars are known by a single name and our publicity department is going to run with it. All our press releases will refer to you as 'Sherrill.'" He picked up his wineglass and offered a toast, "Here's to Sherrill! Take notice, Hollywood, 'A Star Is Born.'"

Sherrill took a sip of wine and resolved that it would be her only sip. She could already feel the baby responding to the rich food as she felt a twinge in her abdomen. A feeling of contentment came over her as she listened to Brad relate the filming sequence for the weeks to come.

"Due to your pregnancy, we are going to film all the scenes of your first full length appearance, which will air in four weeks. Then we will have a special filming crew do all the scenes that require showing your full figure. You will have a break over the Christmas and New Year's holidays and then we will film the scenes that are distant profiles and close-up shots after the first of the year. We will be on a tight schedule and some of the days are going to be long.

"Most of the filming will be on studio sets, but there will be location shots that will require some travel and living in a travel trailer or a motel room. So, Sherrill, do you feel up to this rather rigorous schedule?"

"I feel fine," responded Sherrill. "So far, the pregnancy has been easy. I've only felt morning sickness a couple of times, but it has passed quickly."

"I'm going to be with her the entire time," interjected Aunt Vicki as she turned to Hank for tacit approval.

Hank nodded approval and lamented, "I'll be lonely without my girls, but the show must go on. Besides, my real estate business has increased so much that I won't have much spare time for home life endeavors. At least, until I get my new staff trained and self supporting."

"Great!" exclaimed Brad, "This has worked out better than I had hoped. I'll have a limo pick you up at 9:00 AM tomorrow. We'll have a kick-off promotion at the studio with a press conference. Sherrill, you won't be required to directly address the reporters. Our publicity department already has a press release and our publicity commentator, Myra McDonald, has a promotional sequence on film which will be integrated with film clips of you basically reacting to the scenes staged tomorrow.

"Judging from the tremendous influx of fan mail—they want more of you. The promos are designed to promote the upcoming episodes dedicated to the 'Annabelle Lee' character that you will be playing. Your Uncle Hank and I will field any questions the reporters have regarding your past, present, and future."

Sherrill, momentarily distracted by the name "Annabelle Lee," missed Brad's last statement. She had almost forgotten that this was the name of the character which she had assumed in the carriage scene only a few short weeks ago. Now it seemed like months—no—years ago, since so much had happened to her in the interim. At first she felt isolation, and then a strange bonding with the character as she recalled the emotions of the events that day.

Brad, noting that her attention was in another orbit, paused. After a few moments, Sherrill blinked and stammered, "Oh, sorry—sorry, my mind was elsewhere. What did you just say?"

Brad arose from his chair and walked around behind Sherrill. He gently squeezed her shoulders and placed his cheek next to hers, giving her a hug. "I said—don't worry. Your Uncle Hank and I will take care of everything."

Corvette

All the flights on the training base were passing in review in front of the base commander, General Thurman, and his staff. As they approached the VIP stand, Sergeant Stark ordered, "Eyes right." The rightmost column looked straight ahead, providing an alignment reference, while the rest of the flight turned their heads to the right in the direction of the general.

Sergeant Stark barked the command, "Double to the rear to the rear—harch." The flight executed the double reverse maneuver and then continued marching in review. Twenty paces further, the DI barked the same command. Again, the flight flawlessly executed the complex direction change and continued marching in review.

The general turned to his protocol aide and inquired, "With their *eyes right* that was a very risky maneuver by a training flight to execute in front of their general. They did it twice in succession; whose flight is that?"

Major Wooten glanced down at his review list, "That is Sergeant Stark's flight, sir. They are completing their fourth week of training."

"Stark—Stark, that is Randy's DI, isn't it?" asked the general.

"Yes, sir," confirmed the major.

"Well, I'll have to give him credit for having kahunas. None of the other drill instructors would have tried that maneuver in front of me until nine weeks of training and even then, most of them screwed it up.

To show his efficiency, the major added, "Sergeant Stark's reports indicate that this flight is the best that he has instructed in his six years on this base."

The general, remembering his own comments after Randy's speech, ruminated, *'Chemistry and Timing'—is everything. Some people seem blessed with it, while others spend a lifetime stumbling and groping toward it.*

After the review ceremonies, the flight halted next to the company bulletin board. Sergeant Stark announced, "Our barracks has won 'Barracks of the Week' three weeks in a row. All of you will be given a weekend pass to San Antonio. You can come back to the barracks at night or stay in town at a motel. The barracks will be locked from lights out until reveille. This will enable the barracks guards to have the time off too. If you come back to the barracks, you will be responsible for your own latrine duty and area cleanup.

"Normally the weekend pass doesn't start until 0600 tomorrow morning, but the captain has issued a special pass that will give you two nights in San Antonio. Your pass will be effective immediately after this formation breaks up and will terminate at lights out Sunday night."

The flight forgetting that they were still at attention—cheered!

The DI growled, "As you were; I'm not finished."

The flight quickly composed itself and the sergeant continued, "Also, the tech school listings have been posted. You can now see where you will be sent for advanced training. Flight—fall out!"

The men raced eagerly toward the bulletin board and strained to see their name and destination. Randy held back, listening to the elated shouts of: 'Lowry,' 'Chenault,' 'Sheppard,' 'Keesler,' 'Maxwell,' 'Gunter.'

He watched for the slumped shoulders that would indicate who would stay at Lackland for four more weeks of training. Casio slowly trogged away, his eyes downcast, and his shoulders stooped. Six more dejected airmen caught up with him. They trudged together toward the barracks. Talking animatedly, with their arms gesticulating in the air, their body language telescoped their futile frustration at not getting an assignment on another air base.

Peering over the shoulders of the remaining men, Randy scanned the list for his own name. Not finding it, he scanned it twice more. His brow wrinkled and his shoulders sagged slightly as he questioned the omission. *Does this mean that I also have to stay at Lackland? Maybe it is just a clerical error—that happens sometimes.*

He plodded toward the barracks thinking. *Nothing seems to be working out as I had hoped. I haven't heard from Sherrill. I don't know if or why I'm staying at Lackland. I don't know why I was selected to take extra banks of tests. Sergeant Stark hasn't given me any clues; all he said was "Do your best"—but for what? I feel like I'm suspended in purgatory.*

Moisture glazed across his eyes as he fought back the frustration of not knowing which direction his future was headed. After all, his future was not only *his* future, but also that of Sherrill and their baby. He cursed his youth and inexperience for limiting his ability to put his life into perspective.

He had persevered and survived the last four weeks out of sheer will, bolstered by his love for Sherrill and the knowledge that no matter where he was or what he was doing—Sherrill loved him—*didn't she—surely she did?*

As he walked up the steps to the barracks' entrance, he jutted out his jaw and resolved. *To hell with uncertainty—there are no guarantees in life—there never has been. I've got a weekend pass and a whole weekend to sort things out. Decisions can only be made if there are options. At the moment, my environment—basic training—severely limits my options.*

The feeling of restriction dogged him as he entered the barracks. Walking directly to his dress cabinet, he grabbed a towel and quickly undressed. Ignoring the jubilant comments of his barracks mates, he headed to the showers and felt the hot spray cleanse his body and elevate his spirits.

Walking back to his bunk, he glanced over at Casio lying on his bunk and staring at the ceiling. He kicked the bunk with the heel of his bare foot. "Get your ass off your bunk, Bro; we're going to town."

"Leave me be," groaned Casio. "I ain't going to no town."

"Yes, you are," asserted Randy. "I don't know where they are sending me either. We'll get a motel room and have Abbott smuggle in a case of beer. After a couple of cold long necks, we won't care if they keep us at Lackland for the next four years."

Casio stirred to life and raised himself to his elbows, "You really don't know where they are sending you either?"

"No," replied Randy. "My name wasn't even on the list. It may just be a typo, but I'm not going to let it ruin my weekend."

"Look on the bright side, you'll get your first stripe in four weeks. The other guys have to finish their basic while going through tech school. That means that you'll get promoted first."

Casio swung his long legs to the floor. "Yeah," he iterated. "I'll outrank all those other motha-fuckers." He grabbed his towel and headed toward the showers.

Randy turned and saw Abbott staring at him, smiling, "You sure know how to pull Casio's string, don't you."

Randy shrugged, "He just needs a little direction once in awhile. He still makes his own decisions—that's important to him."

"I know," Abbott replied wisely. "It's still interesting to see how easily his final decision falls in line with a decision that you have already made."

Randy pondered on Abbott's statement for a moment. *Was Abbott being cynical or merely stating a fact? Wasn't motivation, to get one's way, more expedient than ordering someone around?*

He thought of his experiences in sports and his limited experiences in the military then decided, *There is a time and place for either motivation or intimidation—circumstances dictate which is applicable.*

He put the thought aside and turned back to Abbott, "Is your latrine crew aware that they have to complete their duties before they leave the barracks?"

"I'm sure they are," assured Abbott. "But just to make sure, I'll remind them now."

Randy put on his 'Class A uniform' and placed his shaving kit and extra clothes in his flight bag. He had just finished checking that his bunk area was in shape when Sergeant Stark entered the barracks with a handful of passes.

He handed the passes to Randy, instructing, "Hand these out and remind each person that their area must be in inspection order before they leave." He paused, watching Randy and waiting for the inevitable question of why his name wasn't on the training list.

Randy simply replied, "Yes, DI, sir. Are their any other instructions?"

"No," replied Stark, "you guys have a good time and don't get into too much trouble."

"Thank you, DI, sir," Randy replied flatly.

Stark, not knowing why, had received a memo ordering him not to reveal information to Randy regarding additional training. He hesitated for a moment longer, half-expecting 'the question,' then headed to his own quarters. Pulling out his special report, he made a couple of entries. Staring out the window, he thought, *at his age and experience Airman Ferris is certainly a cool character. If I were him, I would have demanded to know why my name wasn't on the tech school list.*

Randy, Casio, and Abbott exited the bus at the Alamo National Monument. Bob Dawson approached them, "You guys possibly looking for a tour guide?"

"Oh, you've been here before, Bob?" inquired Randy.

"Yeah…once. My family came here to the Alamo when I was fifteen. We stayed at the hotel across the street—not bad and it's centrally located. We can get to the 'River Walk' from here or catch a carriage downtown to the shops and cantinas."

"Convinced me," voted Abbott.

"Yeah, me too," agreed Casio. "A room split four ways is cheaper than three."

"I guess that makes it unanimous, Bob," concluded Randy. "You're designated to be our official tour guide. The first thing on the agenda is to get situated; let's check out the hotel across the street."

The foursome approached the "Registration Desk." Carrie, a cute young blonde, beamed a smile, "You gentlemen need a room?"

"Yes," replied Randy. We're looking for a room with four beds and a 'fridge'—got such a place?"

"Yes, we do," replied Carrie, blinking her large blue eyes at Randy. "We get a lot of business from air bases around here and the accommodation you requested is our most popular. We're also between seasons and with your military discount, we can let you have the room for half price."

"Sounds like the second best deal we've had today—we'll take it," remarked Randy.

As he was filling out the registration card, Carrie couldn't help asking, "What was your best deal, today?"

"Getting our weekend pass a night early," smiled Randy. "Know any girls as cute as you that would like to meet my buddies?"

Carrie surveyed the other three men for the first time. "Yes, I know a lot of single girls. We sometimes go downtown to the USO and dance with the airmen. I don't have any colored girlfriends, but I've talked to a few at the club."

She glanced back and studied Randy's face. "You look familiar," she reflected. "Have you stayed here before?"

"No—first time," informed Randy. "This is our first time off the base—basic training, you know."

Carrie read the registration card; recognition flashed across her face. "You're—you're that Randy," tripped across her tongue.

"Yes, that's what my friends call me," responded Randy. "Randall T. is me."

"No," corrected Carrie. "I mean that you're *Sherrill's* Randy. I saw you on television when you talked about Sherrill at your basketball game—most of my girlfriends were goggle-eyed over you."

At hearing Sherrill's name, Randy's interest sparked, "We've been cooped up on the base for a month and haven't even had a newspaper to read. Is Sherrill really that well known?"

Carrie looked at Randy in amazement. "She's been on the TV news almost every night for the last three weeks. She's just signed an acting contract with "The Dons of Eldorado" for a hundred thousand dollars."

Randy's knees felt rubbery as he tried to contemplate a hundred thousand dollars. The Dons of Eldorado was one of his favorite TV programs and Sherrill would be a part of it—*was this why Sherrill hasn't answered my letters?* He thought of his two hundred dollars savings in the bank; the contrast made his paltry sum seem insignificant...which made him feel insignificant.

Flushed, he demanded, "We'll need four keys, please. Then as an afterthought, added, "Is there a library around here?"

Glancing at her watch, Carrie informed. "It is downtown and closes in thirty minutes, but it will be open tomorrow from nine to two."

"Thanks," Randy replied mechanically. He picked up his key and left to find his room. His three companions, seeing the transition in him, picked up their keys and silently followed him.

Randy opened the door and surveyed the room. Four twin beds had been cramped into the room designed for two regular beds. A TV was in one corner. In the other corner, a small refrigerator sat next to a sink above a small cupboard. A clothes closet filled the space in-between. The room was austere, but functional.

He threw his flight bag onto the closest bed, grabbed a couple of hangers from the closet, and headed toward the bathroom. He had showered before leaving the base, but now felt the immediate need for another shower.

Hanging his uniform on the towel rack, he entered the shower and turned on the hot water to steaming. He felt the hot water surge across his body. The sting was almost unbearable, but deadened the pain of uncertainty that possessed him.

Two lines of a song, he was composing in his head, repeatedly ran through his mind:

Seeking love from the day we're born
Sans l'amour leaves us lonely and forlorn.

As he toweled off, he observed his diffused profile in the fogged up mirror. His reflection looked back at him like a misty apparition free-floating in the room. He thought, *I look exactly as I feel at the moment—a thinly veiled enigma surrounded by a fog of uncertainty enveloped in a cloud of doubt.*

231

Exiting the bathroom, the warm outflow of mist followed him. Abbott shoved a cold wet "Lone Star" in his hand. Tipping the neck of his own beer in silent salute, Abbott took a long draught, indicating that the elixir was the short answer to any immediate problem.

"Thanks," replied Randy. He upended the bottle of beer and felt the cold wet bitter liquid drain down his throat. Chucking the empty bottle into the trash basket, he opened the fridge and retrieved another. As he sat down on his bed, he took a couple more deep draughts and felt the alcohol rush to his head. A mellow feeling crept through his body as he stared, starved for news about the world around him, at the TV with his roommates.

A game show had just ended. The commentator was announcing network promos—"Sherrill's debut in Hollywood; stay tuned for highlights during the six o'clock news."

Randy jumped off the bed, staring at the TV, shouting, "That's my girl."

At the same moment, Abbott turned toward him, "Are they talking about YOUR Sherrill?"

Casio intoned, "Cool—we get to see Randy's ol' lady. She's in Hollywood knocking out the guys and he's bunking in Texas with three ugly dudes—. Make that *two* ugly dudes," he chuckled.

"Is this the girl you said was back home?" inquired Bob.

"Yes-yes-and yes!" replied Randy enthusiastically. "God—how I miss her! She lives in California now. She's the reason that I'm in the air force."

"Tell us about her," coaxed Abbott.

"Yeah," urged the other two roommates in unison.

Randy began, "Well, I've known her since 1st grade—." He continued the story, omitting the intimate details, up to the day he left for the air force induction center. He concluded, "I didn't know where she was until I saw her on television at Sergeant Stark's place."

During the story, Abbott had catered beer to the group. Randy was surprised to see three more empty bottles on the end table next to his bed. The TV was now showing commercials between programs. Randy glanced down at his watch and realized that thirty minutes had passed since he had started the story. He felt a buzz from the beer; but more importantly, he felt a great weight lifted off his shoulders after having shared a summary of his life story with three friends. The months of pent-up emotions dispersed into the background of his mind.

"That was a great story," Abbott sympathized, "it's made me realize how much I miss home and family."

Bob nodded, "Yeah, me too."

"So her ol' man was the guy that you thumped on?" Casio interjected.

"Well, I got in a few good punches, but the light pole did most of the damage," conceded Randy.

"Still, you put him into the light pole," argued Casio. "No wonder he was so pissed-off and sent your woman to live in California."

Randy thought for a moment about how Charles felt—. The news commentator headlining the top stories interrupted his thoughts. The group's attention focused on the television. They suffered through local news, weather, and sports, and finally came the announcement: "Stay tuned for our top story of the hour after these commercial messages."

Randy beat Casio to the bathroom, while Abbott retrieved another round of beers. Standing over the toilet-bowl, rocking back on his heels from the effects of the beer, he stared down at the head of his penis and detachedly observed, "If it wasn't for *you*, I wouldn't be stuck here in "Hellhole, Texas." I could be living my life with Sherrill, instead of waiting to watch her on television—surrounded by California dudes." Realizing how crass and irresponsible his thoughts sounded, he gave *it* a couple of flicks, shoved it back into his shorts, and zipped up.

Reentering the room, he swung the foot of his bed around and gestured to his three friends to sit closer to the TV. The foursome sat lined up in a row, beer in hand, and listened as the commentator recapped Sherrill's meteoric rise to fame.

Concluding, she prefaced, "This is Sherrill's first day at the television studios of 'The Dons of Eldorado.'" The picture faded and switched to a press release.

"Hello, I'm Myra McDonald. 'The Dons of Eldorado' recently signed Sherrill to a three-episode contract. Next Tuesday, you will have your first chance to see her as an actress in a bit part filmed the day that director 'Emile Fabio' discovered her. On location, her original contract was whisked away by a 'dust devil' and the studio contacted the press to find her.

"This fortuitous little 'dust devil' caused a whirlwind of press coverage that focused national attention on finding Sherrill. Overnight, she became 'the missing starlet.' Thanks to the enormous press coverage, we rediscovered her in Monterey, California.

The picture switched to Sherrill's 'walk to fame' at the press interview in Monterey. Bob Dawson reacted, "Hubba-Hubba!"

Casio intoned, "Man is she stacked—she's Uptown-Downtown My-Way-Broadway."

Abbott added to the comments, "She's a 'Rodeo Queen'—with a rocking 'R' in 'Rodeo.'" None of the others understood his idiom, but the rapt expression on his face explained everything.

Randy, remembering his impression at Stark's home, reiterated, "She's my 'Earth Angel—my Baby.'"

The scene switched to a statement by the director, Emile Fabio. "I discovered Sherrill while shooting scenes on location. She was in a group of spectators watching the filming and I noticed that my camera crews were looking at her instead of concentrating on the next scene that we were going to shoot. One look at her and I knew that I must have her on film—she was Aphrodite incarnate."

Laura Blevins appeared on the screen, stating, "When I was introduced to Sherrill, she had a pervading presence and beauty that made you want to look at her. She has beauty and poise, but also an aura radiated from her that appeared mystical and naive, yet wholesome and refreshing.

"I remember having had that feeling once before when we were filming in Yosemite National Park. I had extended my hands into the cascading waters of Bridal Veil Falls and felt the exhilaration of reaching out and touching nature in its truest form.

"I don't know why Sherrill had that initial effect upon me, but she did. I probably should be jealous of her, but I can't. I'm looking forward to working with her—we are best of friends."

Myra McDonald panned to a couple of staged scenes filmed at the studio. The first scene showed an excerpt of Sherrill and the cast at a square dance. Don Luke was obviously her beau and the fiddler's music added reality to the scene.

Randy felt a twinge of envy that bridled on the cusp of jealousy. He glanced sideways at his roommates. They were raptly staring at the television.

The next scene showed Sherrill and Don Luke at a picnic next to a deep green pool formed by a waterfall. They were just sitting together with Don Luke chucking pebbles into the pool. Sherrill had her bonnet off and the light radiated through her blond hair with soft red streaks.

234

The scene jolted Randy's memory back to when he had picked her up at her church before they had driven to Mt. Scott—the day he had found out that she was carrying his baby.

The final scene showed Don Luke walking her up to her door and tenderly kissing her hand as they said goodnight. Randy felt a personal sense of violation, and then suppressed the feeling with the realization that this was just a Hollywood scene—not reality.

The picture switched back to Myra McDonald prefacing the signing of the contract by Brad Thurman and Hank Casson.

Brad stood up and faced into the camera, "Sherrill's Uncle, Hank Casson, is a tough negotiator. We consummated the deal with a surprise for Sherrill." He dangled a set of keys from his hand and placed them into Sherrill's hand.

An astonished Sherrill stared at the keys as a curtain opened revealing a shiny new Corvette, pale yellow with a cream tan leather interior. Sherrill, immobilized by the surprise, finally blurted, "This is for me—really for me!"

The four airmen, caught up in the surprise, exclaimed a collective, "Wow!"

Sherrill, dressed in casual ware—shorts, tank top, and athletic shoes—walked on stilted legs toward the car. The realization sank in as her pace picked up; she finished the last couple of steps running on her toes. She hand vaulted the door, stabilized herself by grabbing onto the top of the windshield, and unceremoniously, but gracefully, settled into the driver's seat. Grabbing the steering wheel with both hands, she turned and beamed an undisguised smile of glee to a laughing applauding audience sharing her feelings.

She stuck the key into the ignition and started the car. Off stage, huge fans powered up as a background travel scene appeared on a huge screen. She glanced at the scene and reacted as if she were actually driving.

The on-rush of air angled toward the car so that most of her hair trailed backward, but small eddy currents from the backwash blew wisps of hair forwarded across her face. She reached up with one hand and unconsciously drew the strands back across her ear.

The graceful motion enhanced her femininity and reminded Randy of when they were on the Ferris wheel at Craterville as gossamer strands of silk enveloped them in a cocoon of ecstasy. The feeling was so intense that he had to shake himself back to reality.

The travelogue scene, accompanied by the music of *The Beach Boys'* "California Girls," continued for a minute, and then the picture switched back to Myra McDonald. "Sherrill's first episode in 'The Dons of Eldorado' will be aired in four weeks. You can write to Sherrill at the address shown at the bottom of your screen."

Randy repeated the address several times to himself.

The local news commentator reappeared on the screen, "I know that was a great treat for you Sherrill fans—it was for me. I felt like I was riding in the car with Sherrill and I can't wait to see her first episode in 'The Dons of Eldorado.' We'll close with Sherrill leaving the studio."

Sherrill was being escorted to her limo and the reporters were throwing out questions, trying to get additional tidbits of personal information. "Sherrill—where are you staying?" "Sherrill—what are you going to be doing while in Hollywood?" "Sherrill—have you heard from your family?" "Sherrill—what are your plans for the future after 'The Dons of Eldorado?'"

Brad and Hank waved off the questions until Sherrill was about to enter the limo. One reporter hollered over the din of questions, "Sherrill—what about Randy?"

Sherrill turned and faced the onslaught of reporters. Quietness fell over the crowd as Sherrill's smile transformed into an expression of undisguised sincerity. Looking directly into the cameras and waving her hand in a wide arc, she stated, "I would trade all of this just to be Mrs. Randall Ferris—to share every day with Randy." Fighting back tears, she turned and entered the limo.

Randy felt a sledgehammer hit his chest. He could hardly breathe and felt totally humbled by the statement. Tears streamed down his cheeks as he lamented his thoughts, *Sherrill, darling, how could I have ever doubted your love—your motives—your fidelity!*

His three companions turned to stare at him. Here was their indomitable leader with tears streaming down his cheeks in front of

236

them. The tenderness of the moment brought tears of empathy to their own eyes. One by one as they passed him, they patted him on the back and voiced words of encouragement and support.

The three roommates exited out the door, leaving Randy to his thoughts. He stretched out on his bed staring at the ceiling. Thoughts of Sherrill swirled and twisted through his mind. He could smell her perfume and the natural scent of her body. In his mind, he could hear the pealing ring of her laughter and recalled special moments that they had shared together.

Remembering back to an all-night date on an Easter week-end, he could feel the heat of her thigh against his as they lay staring at the stars. They were one couple among a throng of thousands waiting for the special Easter Sunrise Service conducted each Easter morning at the "Eternal City."

His sister Leta and her boyfriend, David, lay on a blanket next to them, but to Randy, they could have been a thousand miles away. He remembered his big manly hand holding Sherrill's long tapered fingers and feeling the electricity of life and love pulsating back and forth in their touch.

Flashing to the memory of the first time that they had made love, as an aftermath of the devastating hailstorm, was as real and intense as if it had happened yesterday. The vision of her beauty was burned into his memory and he became aroused by the feeling of remembered realism and passion.

This rigid tenseness brought his mind close to the level of awareness of the room around him. He gazed myopically at the ceiling. Through the mist of his thoughts he visualized railroad tracks, parallel lines seemingly converging in the distance but never quite touching.

Sherrill and he were leading *parallel lives*, heading in the same direction but with separate agendas. They had begun the journey from the same location, but would fate allow them to arrive at the same destination? Would they ever find each other again among the masses, hampered by the twisting and turning of events that seemed to dominate their lives?

Then he remembered Sherrill's last statement in Hollywood; "I would trade all of this to be Mrs. Randall Ferris—just to be with Randy." With the demons of uncertainty abated, smiling and feeling blessed with her love—he dozed off.

The smell of pizza permeated his senses. It was so real that he came awake with a start. Abbott was bent over waving a slice of pepperoni and cheese under his nose and laughing at his disoriented expression. "Thanks," mumbled Randy, as he sat up and took the proffered slice. Abbott placed an opened bottle of Pepsi on the nightstand, and then dug into the pizza, himself.

Casio whined, "You knock back for a few zzz's and Abbott takes over. He's got us drinking soda pop—instead of beer."

"Abbott's a solid guy," commended Randy between chews. "Those couple of beers was just for cooling off our overheated frustrations. All I can say is that I don't want to spend the rest of my free weekend in a drunken stupor."

USO

The four airmen entered the large smoke filled room of the USO (United Service Organizations). A western band was playing at one end of the room. Tables and chairs were located at the other end, with a large dance floor filling the space in between. A long bar ran in front of one wall with mirrors giving the illusion that the room was much wider. Taped to the mirrors were placards indicating 'No Alcohol'. Behind the bar was a large grill area next to a walk-in cooler that extended to the edge of the dance floor.

Casio spotted a trio of colored girls sitting together and left the group with a simple, "Catch up wit' cha later."

Abbott noticed two cute girls sitting at a table for four. They glanced his way and giggled. Averting their eyes to each other, they secretly whispered while glancing back at the airmen. He tapped Bob on the arm, "Hey, Bob, let's try our luck over there."

Randy stood alone for a moment surveying the layout of the room, then strolled to the bar and ordered a Coke. He casually leaned against the bar, while sipping his drink and watched the dancers boot-scootin' to the rhythm of the music. An alluring young brunette, wearing a black sheath dress split up the left side to mid-thigh, approached him and commented, "We don't get many air force officers in this club."

The girl's sensual smile and twinkling eyes caught Randy off-guard. He eyed her, noticing her seductive breasts under a bodice cut for maximum exposure, while still maintaining a suggestive air of naive modesty. She was tall and wore black flats to de-emphasize her height. He asked, "What do you mean?"

The girl brushed her palm across his sleeve as she explained, "You don't have any stripes, so you must be out of uniform because I don't see any bars on your uniform either."

Randy smiled. She was obviously schmoozing him, "I used to be a captain," he quipped. "But on my way to work last week I misplaced my jet plane and they took my bars away."

The girl's eyes twinkled brighter and a broad smile broke across her lips, "You are too young to be a captain, but I like a quick witty answer. It shows that you have intelligence and a sense of humor. Most other airmen would have just blurted out that they weren't officers." She smiled a disarming smile and extended her hand, stating, "My name is Suzette, but you can call me Suzy."

239

Randy grasped her hand and responded, "My name is Randall, but you can call me, Randy."

Suzy studied his face for a moment, "You look familiar; have you been here before?"

"No, my first time. I came here with three of my buddies. They spotted a couple of girls and deserted me."

"That happens, you know," Suzy sympathized. "But you don't look like you would have any trouble finding girls to keep you company."

"I've got a girl back home. My buddies and I just came here for a little excitement. We've been stuck on the air base for the last month and getting our off-base passes was like drawing a 'Get out of jail free card.'"

"Well, you know that card also allows you to dance. Would you care to dance with me?" offered Suzy.

Randy looked around. It was a public place and the band had a good beat. Shrugging his shoulders, he extended his hand, "Sure, why not."

Suzy took his hand and led him onto the dance floor. The band was playing a Texas two-step. Randy felt rusty and out of practice, but after a few moments he relaxed and was caught up in the rhythm of the music.

As they danced, Randy noted that she had deep-blue almond shaped eyes—almost a royal violet. Her face had an unblemished light tan with a healthy glow that radiated her natural beauty. She wore pierced earrings with a small pendant cross of blue sapphire and a chain necklace of platinum supporting a silver cross that dangled above the crevasse formed by a well-endowed chest.

"You dance well," remarked Suzy.

"You follow well," observed Randy, returning the compliment.

"I know the band members—do you play a musical instrument?" Suzy asked, trying to find a commonality.

"Yeah, I sometimes play the guitar, but I've never played in a band. I like to sing, but also I've never sung in a group. I guess my forte would have to be basketball."

Suzy stopped dancing and stepped back to look at his 6'2" height. The word 'basketball' had clicked something in her mind. She stared at the nameplate "Ferris" on his uniform.

A click of recognition flashed across her eyes. "You're—you are 'Sherrill's Randy—aren't you! I remember now, seeing you play basketball at Lackland—we were at the game—my father is a colonel at Randolph—we sat in the VIP section and watched you play—what a *butch* game!—I cried during your speech—it was so romantic and sincere."

Randy stoically listened to the salvo of enthusiastic statements. Suzy, instead of being intimidated, moved closer to him and they completed the dance in silence.

Walking back toward the bar, Randy caught the eye of Abbott and suggested, "Come on over and meet two of my buddies. As they approached the table, the two airmen stood up. "Suzy, this is Abbott and—Bob."

Suzy laughed, "I thought you were going to say, "Abbott and—Costello." Then she countered by saying, "I know, bad joke—right." She shook their hands, saying, "Hi, Abbott; hi, Bob—I'm Suzy."

Abbott gestured toward the two girls sitting at the table, "Karen and Mary Jo...."

Bob reached around and pulled up another table to butt up against theirs. "Have a seat," he offered.

Abbott volunteered, "Karen and Mary Jo work for an insurance company. What do you do, Suzy?"

Suzy responded, "I'm an air force brat. I'm attending Trinity University and am majoring in drama."

She looked at their uniforms and observed, "None of you guys have stripes, either. How did you work it to get off the funny farm?"

Randy jested, "We three are the general's personal boot polishers."

The entire group laughed, except for Mary Jo. She queried, "Why would it take three guys to polish two boots?"

The group laughed again. Abbott quipped, "Because I specialize in heels and toes—Randy does the uppers—Bob scrapes the soles." The group was holding their sides from laughing, while Mary Jo sat with a quizzical look on her face.

Bob came to her rescue, "Nah, Mary Jo, we've just been teasing with you. We earned our pass for winning 'Barracks of the Week' for three weeks in a row.

Mary Jo, embarrassed by the ruse, could only say, "Oh. I don't know anything about the air force. I've only been here for three weeks, since I moved from Plano, Texas."

Abbott, still caught up in the jesting, quipped, "You're from *plain ol'* Texas; well, I'm from *unique* Texas."

Mary Jo looked at him incredulously, "I don't know where Unique—," then she burst out laughing, "Oh, I get it. You're still joking with me."

Suzy rolled her eyes in wonderment, "Excuse me, the band just went on break. I want to talk to Jerry for a minute."

Casio strolled over with a girl in tow. "Hey, guys. I want youse to meet Gloria. She's here with a couple of her girlfriends, but I snagged her away to meet my buddies."

"Have a seat," offered Randy. "We were just getting acquainted, ourselves." He introduced Casio and Gloria to the rest of the group.

Casio raised his eyebrows and rolled his eyes, "Who was that foxy looking momma that just glided away from here?"

Randy smiled at Casio's idiomatic colloquialism. His friend from New York never seemed *just* impressed...he was either *under* impressed or *overly* impressed—this contrasting trait in his personality gave him a charismatic appeal, which made him interesting company. "That was Suzy. She just went to talk to the band for a minute—she'll be back."

Casio patted his stomach, "Man that pizza's startin' to wear thin. Who else would like to order a burger?"

All agreed and placed their orders. Suzy came back and introductions were made again. Randy leaned over to Suzy, "We just ordered burgers, would you like one too?"

"No, thanks. I'll just share one with you, if that's okay."

The break for the band was over and Jerry announced, "Ladies and gentlemen, we have a surprise celebrity in the house tonight. He sings and plays the guitar. Let's see if we can get him up here on stage to share a little of that talent with you."

The crowd glanced around for a famous face. There was a lot of murmuring speculation, and then Jerry announced, "Ladies and gentlemen, let's give a big Texas welcome to Sherrill's fiancé—Randy."

The crowd clapped wildly. Randy looked at Suzy, "You didn't—."

Suzy gleamed back, "I did—."

Randy rose slowly and walked reluctantly to the stage amid increasing applause. He shook hands with Jerry, "Hi. I've never played with a band."

Jerry nodded, "I know; that's what Suzy told me, but you can play a guitar—right?"

"Well, yes. But I don't play lead."

"Okay," responded Jerry. "Here is a rhythm guitar. You only have to play a few basic chords. Suzy said that you sing. What songs do you know?"

"I know a lot of songs," confirmed Randy, "but I've never sung with a group."

"No problem, we'll just harmonize with you and back you up on the chorus."

Randy felt penned in. He muttered to himself, "I'm going to strangle that Suzy-girl."

Jerry led off with a song, allowing Randy to pick up the rhythm. Randy blended well, with only a few minor variations, and he got better as they progressed.

At the end of the song, Jerry turned to him, "Hey, you did good. What song would you like to sing?"

Randy thought for a moment, "Well, my father's favorite song is 'Peace in the Valley,' by the Sons of the Pioneers."

"Good," responded Jerry. "You're on!"

Randy sang the lead while Jerry's group harmonized. The crowd warmed to the crooning melody and enthusiastically applauded their approval.

He felt daring and suggested, "El Paso" by Marty Robbins. He started out, "Out in the West Texas town of El Paso, I fell in love with a Mexican girl...."

Marty Robbins might have thought that he was listening to himself. This was a song that Randy had sung many times in the fields back home and he had perfected every nuance of the tune. Everyone on the dance floor had stopped to listen to the singing. At the end of the song the crowd applauded wildly and yelled for more.

Randy was caught up by the exhilaration of performing on stage and agreed to continue. The next song was "I'd Walk the Line"; then "Tumbleweed"; followed by "King of the Road" by Roger Miller; and then "Detroit City" by Johnny Cash.

He discovered that Jerry's band could also play *rock and roll*, so he sang, "Love Me Tender" by Elvis Presley and "Lonesome Town" by Ricky Nelson. He played with the band until their next break and left the stage to a standing ovation of cheers and whistles.

His buddies pounded him on his back as he sat back down. Casio quipped, "Man, I never even liked country and western music until I heard you sing it."

Abbott paid him the ultimate compliment, "Damn, you're good! There ought to be a law in these United States against *one man* having so much talent."

Suzy looped her arms around his and squeezed, pulling his arm against her chest, "I had no idea that you were so good."

Randy, exhilarated by all the attention, replied excitedly, "I didn't either. That was my first time on stage!"

Sobering, he turned to Suzy and shook his finger, "Young lady, I owe you a stranglin' for getting me up there."

Suzy brazenly lifted her chin, baring her throat to him, "Go ahead; I probably deserve it."

Randy placed his hand to her throat, but only applied light pressure. Pausing, he looked into her trusting eyes as his fingertips slid up under her jaw. His index finger curled supporting her chin and he felt a strange tingling run through his arm into his chest. He shrugged, "No, I guess that I should really thank you. I didn't know what a thrill it would be to perform on stage in front of a live audience."

He pulled his hand away and Suzy had a twinge of disappointment. *His hand felt good on me,* she thought.

Randy looked down at a lone slice of onion left on the plate. He looked at Suzy and she confessed, "I ate your hamburger...listening to you sing made me hungry."

"That's okay," he assured, "but I am thirsty—want another Coke?"

"Sure," replied Suzy, "but let me get it for you—for eating your burger." She left to go to the service counter at the bar.

Randy pulled out a chair and took a seat. Abbott leaned over and cautioned, "You'd better watch yourself, Randy. That little filly is starting to get the HOTS for you."

"What are you talking about?" responded Randy with surprised exasperation. "I've only just met her—we haven't even talked that much."

Abbott sagely advised, "You were *talking* and *stroking* the entire time that you were on stage—*singing.*"

Randy glanced around the table. His buddies and the girls at his table nodded their heads, up and down, in agreement.

He pushed back from the table and sat pensively, considering if he had done anything inappropriate to lead Suzy on. They had just met and he was here to unwind with his friends. He did not want a replacement relationship. Sherrill was the only woman in the world for him. Did fidelity mean isolating himself like a monk and not enjoying other people—as just people?

His friends had indicated that he was standing on the edge of an abyss—one false step and he was gone. Nevertheless, he didn't feel that way. He felt secure in Sherrill's love. Had there been a big misunderstanding of his attention toward Suzy? If there was then he had to nip it in the bud.

Suzy set his Coke down on the table and quipped, "Here's your Coke, Cowboy."

"Thanks," replied Randy. He rose from his chair and asked, "Is there someplace that we can talk privately?"

"Sure," replied Suzy. "Let's go outside for a walk."

They strolled for a couple of blocks without conversation. Randy stopped under a streetlight and stared into Suzy's dazzling eyes.

"Suzy," he began, "you are a very lovely girl and I'm sure that you have many boyfriends.

"My friends, however, think that something is happening between us. I told them that I had just met you and that was impossible.

"You even had Jerry introduce me as Sherrill's fiancé, so you know that I'm deeply involved with her. We are going to have a baby together and she is the only woman that I love. I just don't want you to think that I'm leading you on in any way."

Suzy flushed and irritably flipped the ends of her hair back with the tips of her fingers. She replied louder than needed. "MEN—you're all so smug and egotistical. You think that every girl that asks you to dance is really asking you to go to bed with her.

"Yeah, I admit that you are attractive and fun to be with, but Jerry, the band leader, and I have a thing going. I'm just hanging out until he gets off his gig. You were handy and I used you for company—is that a crime? You looked lonely too, so where's the harm?"

"I—I'm sorry, Suzy," stammered Randy, feeling that he had totally overreacted. "It's just that I have been stuck in basic training and Sherrill is surrounded by the bright lights, glamour, and excitement of Hollywood.

"I've been totally miserable and I guess I just overreacted to a little attention." He reached out and took her hand, "I apologize for reading more into your friendliness than was there. We can still be friends—can't we?"

"Sure," smiled Suzy, giving him a hug. Randy returned the hug and they walked back to the club.

As they approached the table, their friends looked up in anticipation. Randy smiled, while giving the thumbs up to quell their concern. He reassured them, "No problem."

To further diffuse their concerns, Randy grabbed Casio's girlfriend by the hand, "Come on, Gloria, let's dance," adding, "Casio doesn't like country and western, anyway."

As they wound their way toward the dance floor, Casio called after them, "Yeah, but I likes *my western women!* You've got just one dance—Mister *Tune Crooner.*"

Suzy turned to the group. Beaming a smile, she offered, "Hey, look, my parents own a horse ranch and they stable a lot of horses. Why don't all of you come out to the ranch tomorrow afternoon for a barbecue? We can ride horses and there are lots of other things to do. I'll guarantee that you'll have a fun time."

Casio laughed, "I ain't never rode no horse before. Maybe we can play 'Cowboys and Indians'. I'll even be one of them Indians."

"Just what kind of Indian would you make?" asked Bob, with a touch of sarcasm.

Pausing, Casio lifted his leg above the table and pulled up his trouser leg. "I be a bona fide *Blackfoot,*" he replied with a deadpan look on his face.

The group burst into laughter. Their jovial mood took away any thoughts of excuses and they all agreed to the barbecue.

Gloria and Randy walked back from the dance floor. Casio announced, "Hey, man, I gets to ride me a horse. Suzy has invited all of us to a barbecue, tomorrow at her place."

"That sounds like it may be a lot fun, but I've already planned to go to the library," replied Randy.

"Library," Casio chortled, "that sounds more boring than a drunken stupor weekend—remember a certain BC chiding me about that earlier?"

"Yeah, I did," confessed Randy. "But I want to check the newspapers for articles about Sherrill."

"You can read them at the ranch," volunteered Suzy. "My father keeps all the old newspapers in bundles until we have enough for a bonfire."

Randy hesitated, thinking of the apparent pairing of *guy—girl.*

Suzy sensed his reticence and interjected, "Jerry should be there too...you like him, don't you?"

"Well, yes, I do," agreed Randy. Relinquishing, he added, "Okay, how do we get to your place?"

Gloria volunteered, "I'll bring Casio. He's already promised to buy me breakfast."

Karen interjected, "I've got a car. Mary Jo and I will pick you-all up at noon in front of the Alamo."

Suzy grabbed a couple of napkins and drew out directions. She wrote her phone number, and then handed them to Karen and Gloria. She pulled out a matchbook and wrote her name and phone number on the inside cover; this she handed to Randy.

Randy stood up and announced, "I'm going back to the hotel. You-all stay and have fun."

Suzy cautioned, "You don't want to be walking alone in uniform. There are some pretty mean cowboys around here that are jealous of the airmen stealing their girlfriends. And, you don't need to pay for a taxi—I'll drive you."

Randy thought for a second, and then accepted, "Thanks, I don't want to impose on your hospitality, but I accept your offer anyway."

They waved goodbye to their friends and walked to the parking lot, where Suzy unlocked the door of a '56 Thunderbird convertible, pink with white leather interior.

"Nice car," Randy whistled as he got into the passenger side.

"Yeah," agreed Suzy, "but it can't compete with Sherrill's pale yellow Corvette—can it?"

"Touché," responded Randy.

They drove to the hotel in silence. Suzy pulled up in front of the office, leaving the motor running. She reached over and touched Randy's hand. "I'll see you tomorrow—goodnight."

Randy replied, "Goodnight—mañana." He got out of the car and Suzy drove off.

She didn't drive back to the USO club. Instead, she drove straight home. Her parents were still up and her mother noted with surprise, "You're home early, Honey; is there anything wrong?"

"No," replied Suzy. "Mom, I've invited some friends over for a barbecue tomorrow. Is that okay?"

"Sure, Honey. You know that we encourage you to have friends over. How many are you expecting?"

"Seven," responded Suzy. "I'm going to bed now." She kissed her mother and father on the cheek and went to her bedroom.

She lay in her bed with her arms wrapped across her breast. Remembering the rapturous warmth of Randy's hug on the street corner, she fell into a dreamy blissful sleep.

Paseo Del Rio

Randy awoke at 0500. His body had been conditioned to a regimen dictated by the strict basic training routine. He felt alert and restless, but this was his first weekend off and he tried to go back to sleep. Ten minutes of rolling and tossing passed before he realized the futility of fighting his circadian rhythm.

The sun was not up yet, but light from the street dimly illuminated the room. He looked around and noticed Casio's empty bed. Smiling, he thought; *Casio is a character; meets a girl for the first time and then spends the night with her.*

Randy searched his own conscience and found it hard to comprehend how someone could treat romance so lightly, but he would not impose his ethics on Casio. *I'm not my brother's keeper,* he admonished himself.

He moved the two empty beds further apart and completed a hundred pushups. Then threw his blanket on the floor and worked through two hundred sit-ups. Tossing his blanket back on the bed, he bounced through two hundred jumping jacks. He finished off his exercise regimen by running in place for five minutes. By this time, he had worked up a good sweat and headed into the bathroom for a shower.

Abbott and Bob hadn't stirred, so he decided to let them sleep and stepped outside. A tinge of pink showed in the east announcing dawn. The street was lit, but across the street in the shadows loomed the Alamo Shrine. It consisted of low-lying adobe buildings with the entrance through an arched wall. An early morning fog gave the structures an eerie ethereal quality as though ghost of the past still lingered there.

Randy paused and thought of the 187 men that had made the ultimate sacrifice by giving their lives for Texas' independence. 4000 Mexican soldiers had besieged the Spanish mission. Randy shuddered at the fate of Colonel Travis, Jim Bowie, Davy Crockett, and the others as they were forced to listen, day and night, to the music of the Mexican funeral dirge preceding the final fatal attack.

Texans had been fighting to become an independent republic. From his history class, he remembered a quotation from Davy Crockett, "*Republic,* I like the sound of the *word.*"

He walked a couple of blocks and found an open café. He ordered the "Steer Roper" breakfast from the menu and was served steak and eggs, with biscuits and country gravy. After that and two cups of strong coffee, he felt invigorated and ready to explore the city.

Continuing down the street, he came to a Catholic church. He had never attended a Catholic Mass, so he found a seat in the back to observe the ritual ceremony. He was surprised that the Mass was in Latin. Furthermore, he was mildly surprised that he understood some of the words, since his only exposure to Latin was from the language testing at Lackland.

He left the church and his wandering eventually took him down to the Paseo del Rio, "River Walk." Here, there were many bridges over the canals that branched off the San Antonio River. Along the banks were rows and tiers of shops and restaurants. The sun was up, but it was still too early for Saturday morning crowds and most of the shops were not yet open.

Large motorized gondolas were tied up at docks along the canal. They looked interesting and he made a mental note to take a tour on one before he returned to the airbase.

Climbing the wide concrete steps to a bridge that spanned the canal, he heard terrified screams. Peering around a tall decorative pillar at the end of the bridge, he saw a woman lying on the sidewalk. Two muggers were running away from her and toward him. The first had a purse in his grasp and the second brandished a knife.

Randy ducked back behind the pillar and the first man turned the corner to run down the steps. Randy leg-whipped the surprised man across the thighs, causing his feet to flip out from under him. His heavy torso plunge forward and he tumbled down the stairs, breaking an arm and a leg as he fell.

His screams caused the second man to stop cold as he rounded the corner at the top of the stairs. Randy caught him with a right cross to the jaw. The man's legs melted beneath him. The knife fell to the concrete and the man slithered—face first down the steps.

Grabbing the knife so they couldn't use it against him, Randy ran to the woman, who was screaming hysterically. She cowered, screaming, "Don't hurt me! Don't hurt me!"

He tried calming her by saying, "It's okay; it's okay," then realized that she was afraid of the knife. He flipped the knife around and placed the handle in her hand. He soothingly repeated, "It's okay; I'm here to help you—it's okay."

Drawing courage from the knife in her hand, the woman calmed down and lamented, "They stole my purse—they stole my purse."

A young couple stopped to see what the commotion was about. Randy informed them, "Two men robbed this woman; call an ambulance and the police."

The man ran for a phone, while the woman comforted the victim. Randy left them by explaining, "I need to make sure that the robbers don't get away."

He quickly descended to the bottom of the stairs. The man that he had hit was still out cold, face down on the concrete with his legs extending up the steps.

The man with the broken bones was trying to crawl away. He was still clutching the strap of the purse. Randy was fuming with emotion. He hated leaches that preyed on weaker people. He told the man trying to crawl away, "Don't move another inch, or I'll break your other leg." The whimpering man stopped moving and lay trembling in pain and fear.

More people started gathering around, asking what happened. Randy explained, "These two men robbed and assaulted a woman on the bridge. I stopped them from getting away."

An older woman in the crowd walked up and started kicking the man with the broken leg. Randy had to pull her off him.

He shouted to the crowd, "Help me maintain control until the police get here." Two men stepped forward and restrained the woman.

Randy left the crowd, saying, "I want to check on the injured woman."

He climbed the steps to find another crowd gathered around the woman. He pushed his way through the crowd, kneeled, and asked, "Are you okay, Ma'am?"

The woman reached for Randy and said to the crowd, "This is the boy that saved me. Still brandishing the knife, she added, "He even took their knife away from them." She reached up, pulling Randy's face to her, and hugged and kissed him. People stepped in and patted him on the back, praising how brave he was.

Three police cars and an ambulance arrived within minutes. The medics examined the woman and found only bruises and mild scrapes caused by her fall to the concrete. The two robbers would require hospitalization. They were loaded onto stretchers and taken by police escort to a local hospital.

Gathering names of the witnesses, the police proceeded with a preliminary investigation. One of the policeman approached Randy, "I'm sorry, but you'll have to come down to the station to make a statement. The woman was carrying over a hundred dollars in her purse and suffered minor injuries. Being that there was a knife involved; we're charging these two men with felonious assault and robbery."

While a photographer strolled through the scene snapping pictures, a reporter was taking a statement from the assaulted woman. A murmur went through the crowd when someone recognized Randy from his speech on television. A larger crowd gathered as word spread that Sherrill's fiancé had rescued the woman from a knife assault.

Many of Sherrill's fans tried to get close to Randy, just to say that they had touched him. The police finally had to form a protective ring around Randy as they led him and the assaulted woman to the police cruiser for the ride to the police station.

When they arrived at the police station, Randy was surprised to see cameras and reporters already lined up. He wondered to himself, *where do they all come from? How does word spread so fast? Only thirty minutes have passed since the incident happened.*

The police formed another protective circle around Randy and escorted him inside the police station. A man in plain clothes introduced himself, "Hello, I'm Detective Fred Dupree. I'll need a statement from you as to what happened during the assault."

Randy spent the next hour explaining something that had only taken two minutes to happen. He had just completed signing the statement when two air policemen entered the room. Detective Dupree explained, "Whenever an incident involves military personnel then we have to call the military police. They review the incident and determine if further action is required.

The AP in charge read Randy's statement, "I'm sorry, Airman Ferris, but anytime that a person in basic training is involved in an incident, we must take him back to the air base."

Randy felt the injustice of the situation and looked at him incredulously, "You mean for helping this lady, you are canceling my first and only weekend pass!"

"We don't make the rules; we just carry them out," sympathized the air policeman.

Randy lamented at the irony of the situation, "That's just not fair! I'm in town with buddies from the base and we're expected at a barbecue this afternoon."

The air policeman interjected, "If you know an air force officer that I could release you to then I won't have to take you back to the base. But seeing that you're in basic training, I doubt that you know any officers."

Randy felt in his pocket and found the matchbook. He turned to Dupree and asked, "May I use your phone?"

"Sure, go ahead," replied the detective.

Randy called Suzette's number and her mother answered. "Hello, Mrs. Sommers, this is Randy Ferris, I was supposed to be at a barbecue at your home this afternoon. May I speak with Suzy?"

Suzy's mother cupped her hand over the mouthpiece and called to Suzy, "Suzy, there is a Randy Ferris on the phone and it sounds like he is canceling out on the barbecue."

Suzy's heart leaped, and then sank as she took the phone, "Randy, please don't tell me that you're not coming to the barbeque."

"No. I want to be there, but I'm down at the police station." He then went on to explain the circumstances.

Suzy interrupted, "Randy, wait a minute." It was a good five minutes before she came back on the line. "Randy, here is my dad."

"Hello, Randy, this is Colonel Sommers. You say that there is an AP there that will release you to my custody?"

"Yes, sir," replied Randy.

"Then let me speak with him," instructed the colonel.

The air policeman took the phone and listened. Randy could only hear one side of the conversation, which was mostly an occasional, "Yes, sir."

Then he heard the AP giving the address of the police station. Hanging up, he turned to Randy, "Well, I guess that you do know an officer. He was very persuasive and said that he will be down here in thirty minutes.

Randy pulled out his hotel receipt and found the phone number. He called and had the operator ring his room, but there was no answer. He left a message with the front desk for his roommates.

A police sergeant appeared at the door and announced, "Hey, Dupree, there are a bunch of reporters outside the station that want to interview Sherrill's fiancé." Recognition suddenly flashed across the detective's and the AP's faces.

Randy said, "I really don't want to talk to them. I think that this whole thing has been blown out of proportion and I don't really have anything to say to them."

The detective replied, "No problem," and waved off the police sergeant. Then he added, "You've got thirty minutes before your ride gets here. How about sharing with us a little inside information about Sherrill." Randy spent the next thirty minutes talking about his favorite subject—Sherrill.

Suzette burst through the door with her father in tow. The detective explained the incident to them and Randy's role in apprehending the assailants.

Colonel Sommers smiled, "Well, it looks like our boy is a hero—doesn't it."

He signed a release form for the air police and turned to the detective, "There are a lot of reporters outside. Is there any way to leave without them knowing?"

"Sure," replied the detective, "pull your car around back. I'll have someone let Randy out the rear door."

As the group left, Suzy looped her arm through Randy's. The two AP's got into their jeep parked in front of the police station and the passenger commented, "Did you notice how that girl reacted to Airman Ferris? I wonder how many fiancées he's really got."

"I don't know," replied the driver. "Some guys are just lucky with women." Then he corrected himself and observed, "Maybe I should say—'unlucky with women.'" They both chuckled at the irony of the statement as they drove off.

Driving out to the ranch, Randy opened the conversation, "Thanks for rescuing me. I sure didn't want to spend the rest of my weekend pass back on the base."

The colonel replied, "Well, Suzy can be very persuasive. She argued that the barbecue would be a bust without you. By the way, you are our weekend guest; that was the only way that I could sign for you. We've got plenty of room; you can stay in Steve's room. He's in his second year as a cadet at the Air Force Academy."

"Thanks," replied Randy. This was a new twist that he hadn't planned on.

"Don't mention it," responded the colonel. "You did a brave deed in helping that lady against those two thugs."

"He's my hero," intoned Suzy.

Her words gave Randy an odd feeling. The whole situation made him feel uncomfortable. He was caught up in circumstances where his life was being guided by events, instead of his conscious decisions. He again remembered his grandmother's words and decided to make the best of his circumstances.

"My flight bag is back in my hotel room," Randy informed.

"No problem," replied the colonel. "You two can drive in later and pick it up."

Sommers' Arabian Farms

They pulled through a gate with a large sign, "Sommers' Arabian & Thoroughbred Horses. In smaller letters 'horses boarded.'"

"How long have you raised Arabians?" asked Randy.

"All my life," replied the colonel. "My father raised them back in Virginia. I continued the business after I went into the air force. Since I've been assigned to different bases, we've had Arabian Farms in five different states. This one is my favorite."

White wooden fences defined the ranch's borders. Similar fences separated the pastures. Setting back several hundred yards from the road was a large modern ranch house built of tan brick and a low adobe fence forming a courtyard shaded by Lombardy poplars interspersed with Live Oaks.

Off to one side and to the rear of the house were a dozen horse barns and utility sheds. Several sheds were filled with alfalfa and timothy hay, while other sheds housed modern farm equipment, workshops, and a blacksmith forge.

Impressed, Randy whistled, "Whew, this is really a nice spread. This is something that I have always dreamed of having someday."

"It is the fulfillment of my dream too," offered the colonel. "I'll probably retire here, even if I'm reassigned to another base before I retire."

They pulled up in front of the ranch house and Suzy's mother came out to meet them. She looked approvingly at Randy and offered her hand, "Hello Randy; I'm Suzette's mother Anne. It sounds like you've had a lot of excitement this morning. Welcome to our home."

"Pleased to meet you, Ma'am. You have a lovely place here."

Suzy grabbed Randy's hand and urged, "Come on, I'll show you the horses." She led him off toward the horse barns.

Anne turned to her husband, "What a nice looking boy. I wonder where Suzy met him."

"Probably at the USO," her husband offered. "That's where a lot of the airmen go when they get their first weekend pass."

Suzy led Randy through the paddock. Basking in the warmth of the sun, several horses had their heads extended out the top of the Dutch doors. They whinnied in recognition, as other heads appeared to see what was happening.

Suzy walked over to a box attached to a wall of the stables. She extracted a handful of sugar cubes and handed them to Randy. Taking another handful, she walked down the row and treated each horse to a sugar cube. Randy followed behind her, offering each a cube and stroking their soft silky muzzles.

She named each horse and recited a short history of their pedigree. Finally, she came to an exquisite mare that Randy mistook as an Arabian. "This is 'Majeen' and she is a Thoroughbred. She is ready to foal at any time. The sire is 'Rajah' and my dad hopes to race their offspring in the Kentucky Derby.

Randy petted the horse and handed her a sugar cube. The horse nuzzled Randy's chest and whinnied. "She likes you," remarked Suzy. "That is a great compliment because she's very particular who she lets around her, since she is so near to foaling."

Randy stroked the side of her cheek and observed, "She is a very beautiful horse." Majeen whinnied again, as if acknowledging the compliment.

When they walked away, Majeen whinnied after them. They roamed over the property. Their wandering took them to a large grove of cottonwood trees surrounding a very large, very deep pool bubbling out of the ground. Suzy offered, "This is a spring from the Edwards Aquifer. It is the main water source for San Pedro Creek. Dad says that it triples the value of our ranch."

The pool was deep, but the water was crystal clear. Randy could see trout and bass lazily swimming around in the water. He remarked, "I'm surprised to see trout this far south."

Suzy explained, "The water coming out of the spring is a constant forty-two degrees and the cottonwoods and willows shade the pool in the summer."

"It's a little piece of paradise," Randy observed. "I just feel so out of place, sitting here on a log in my air force uniform."

"Maybe you could wear some of my brother's clothes," offered Suzy, pulling him up off the log.

Randy stripped off his uniform and tried on the clothes laid out on the bed. Suzy opened the door without knocking, explaining, "I figured that I gave you enough time to get dressed."

Randy stood in his stocking feet. The blue jeans were a good three inches too short and fit skintight. He couldn't button the top two buttons on the shirt and the hair on his chest sprang from the gap.

Suzy had a catch in her breath as she huskily said, "Turn around."

Randy did as she suggested. Suzy observed aloud, "Nice butt."

Randy blushed and shook his head, "This just isn't going to work. I'll split out the seams if I try to walk or sit down."

"You're right," agreed Suzy as she picked up one of his shoes and noted the size. She picked up his Ike cap from the bed and placed it on her head. She stuck three fingers inside and jiggled the cap. Tossing the cap back on the bed, "OK, get dressed," and left the room.

Randy dressed in his uniform, wondering, *"What was that little ceremony all about?"*

He found Suzy's mother in the kitchen, "Have you seen Suzy?"

Anne replied, "She told me that she had to run to the store for a couple of items for the barbecue. I don't know what she is getting; we have most everything here that we need."

Randy looked around for a newspaper, "Suzy mentioned that you save the newspapers. Do you mind if I read them?"

"They are stacked in bundles in the shed at the end of the patio. The latest editions are on top of the stack. Why don't you relax on the patio while you read them? I'll bring a glass of lemonade out to you."

Randy pulled a bundle off the top and reclined in a chaise lounge. He paged through the paper and read each article twice. Anne brought him a glass of lemonade, sweetened just enough to kill the acid taste while retaining the tingling tart flavor.

As he read the articles in reverse chronological order, he was amazed at how much personal information had been revealed about his family and friends. He discovered that he had second and third cousins that he had never met.

The press had microscopically examined the lives of Sherrill and her family. Her grades for all her years in school had been listed. All her former teachers had been interviewed and each one had a special anecdote to share with the interviewers.

Randy found it odd that Sherrill's pregnancy was hardly mentioned. The only references had come from her initial press conference, his father's speech, and his own speech at the air base. It was as if the world understood and had forgiven their indiscretion because they were young and in love. Randy felt a lump in his throat at the generosity of the reporters' tolerance and understanding.

Charles, on the other hand, had been damned and persecuted by the press. However, even that had turned mellow after he had publicly apologized to the congregation in his church.

Randy read a verbatim report of his father's speech in front of his own church congregation. He felt proud because he knew how tough the speech would have been for his father.

Leta had been interviewed and her love for her brother was vividly revealed. She had championed her brother as a knight in shining armor. Randy felt undeserving of such adulation, but he felt the same love and respect for his sister.

He laid on the lounge, daydreaming, almost dropping off to sleep, when Suzy popped her head out the door and beckoned, "Come inside. I've got something for you."

She led him back to her brother's room, "Try these on for size."

A Stetson hat was on top of a large bundle. Randy tried on the hat and was surprised that it fit perfectly. He untied the bundle and found two western shirts, two pairs of jeans, a belt, and a pair of Tony Lama cowboy boots. He tried the clothes on and found that they fit, as if he had purchased them himself.

Suzy opened the door without knocking, "I took a chance that you were dressed. How do you like them?"

"They fit great. How did you do it?"

"Well, I know my brother's sizes. I saw how his clothes fit you, so I just made some adjustments in my head. I cheated a little when I looked at your shoe size and you know how I measured for your hat."

"They are just wonderful!" exclaimed Randy. "How much do I owe you?"

"Nothing," replied Suzy. "Consider them a present. When is your birthday?"

Surprised realization flashed across Randy's face. "Why, it's today! It's November the 21st, isn't it? I had completely forgotten about it."

"Well, there you go—'Happy Birthday.'" She reached up on her tiptoes and kissed him fully on his lips, lingering longer than a normal breath. Then she flippantly stated, "That's just a 'Happy Birthday' kiss."

Randy reeled slightly from the passion of the kiss, "If that was just a birthday kiss, I can only imagine what an 'I like you a lot, kiss' would be."

Suzie said nothing as she wrapped her arms around him and gave him a long lingering hug. Then she broke away and grabbed his hand, "Come on, let's go show Mom and Dad."

Gordon Sommers had just returned to the house for a noon snack. He had been exercising some of his boarded horses with two of his employees.

Suzy showed off Randy in his new duds. When Gordon found out that his daughter had bought the outfit for Randy's birthday, he remarked, "Suzy can be spoiled and petulant and we still love her. But she can also be gracious and giving to a fault and we like her even more."

Anne observed, "Why, Randy, you look just like a real cowboy—except, without hair."

They laughed at her little joke, and then she offered, "I've made up some sandwiches; are you all hungry?"

Randy started to defer, but Suzy interjected, "Let's have a picnic at the spring." Without waiting for his answer, she grabbed a picnic basket and quickly filled it with a tablecloth, sandwiches, fruit, and bottles of Coke.

Grabbing Randy by the hand, she called over her shoulder as they went out the door, "Send our friends down to the spring. We'll see you later."

The Sommers still hadn't made the connection that Randy was Sherrill's fiancé. Anne turned to her husband, "She seems quite taken by this boy. Oh, I hope that he doesn't break her heart."

The colonel replied, "He may not have a choice. He's probably going to be shipping out to another airbase in a week or so."

Randy leaned back, bracing his broad shoulders against a cottonwood log as he gazed across the bubbling pool. A warm November sun cast shadows of the swimming fish onto the shallow bottom at the edge of the pool. He could only see bass and crappie, since the trout had migrated below the thermocline into the deeper cooler areas of the pool. A lone buzzard circled on the warm air currents. Birds chirping in the trees provided a musical link with nature and an occasional horse neighing in the distance softly strummed his feeling of peace and contentment.

Suzy was sitting in a lotus position at the edge of the tablecloth. She was half-turned toward him and staring in the distance in meditation. Randy glanced at her and for the first time realized how really beautiful she was. Alarm bells should have gone off in his head, but his full stomach and the serene surroundings dulled his sagacity. He simply gazed upon her face and felt a warm kinship attraction toward her.

Her eyelids fluttered, as she became aware that Randy was staring at her. Turning her head to look at him, a tear formed in the corner of her eye and she confessed, "Randy, I love you. I've loved you since the first day that I saw you, but I never expected to see you again. Then when fate crossed our paths again at the USO, I fell even farther in love. Now that you're here with me, I feel like I'm going to die with love."

Instead of being shocked and reproachful, Randy responded, "I love you too, Suzy.

He paused to gather his thoughts then qualified his profession of love by explaining, "Being here with you, I've been trying to think through the 'meaning of life,' and I've discovered the revelation that we, *humans,* have an infinite capacity for love. We also are capable of experiencing different levels of love. To deny that would be like denying our very own existence."

Suzy listened intently in silence as he continued, "At first, I didn't think that I could ever love another woman without violating my love for Sherrill. However, being here with you, I now know that I was naive. It doesn't mean that I will be unfaithful to Sherrill and have an affair with you; it just means that I can feel genuine love for you too."

A dreamlike serenity radiated from Suzy's face as she accepted the deep wisdom of Randy's statement. She felt a euphoria that transcended physical love. She had harbored the idea of demanding that Randy choose between Sherrill and her, but Randy's explanation had freed her of that possessive impulse.

Now she felt something even more precious. Unrequited love—yes, but a love that was neither destructive nor compromising. Here was a man who loved her for herself. He demanded neither sex nor exclusive love, but offered his love as one human being to another. It was a love that she would use as a standard for the rest of her life.

She crawled over and nudged his knees apart. Leaning back in his arms, she murmured, "Just hold me." Randy wrapped his arms around her. Both feeling at harmony with themselves and nature, they slowly drifted off to sleep together.

They awoke to the giggles of Karen and Mary Jo. Their four friends were standing over them with looks of judgment on their faces. Randy thought of explaining, but saw that they had already prejudged the circumstances. Instead, he waved with a smile, "Hi, glad to see that you all made it okay. Where are Casio and Gloria?"

Abbott answered, "We haven't seen them." Then he looked up and saw them coming through the cottonwoods. "Oh, they're here now."

Randy diverted their attention, "Look at all the fish in the pool."

The group turned and spied the fish. Mary Jo squealed, "Oh, can we go fishing?"

"Sure," affirmed Suzy, "but they don't start biting until around sundown. In the meantime, why don't you-all try your hand at archery?"

"Sounds like my kind of sport," interjected Casio. "I gets to practice being an Indian."

She led them to a cordoned off area behind a shed where three archery ranges had been set up. She retrieved a half dozen bows and quivers full of arrows and handed them to the group. "The bows are of different strengths," she explained. "Try them out and find one that suits you. I'm going to help my mother and I'll be back later."

Suzy walked into the kitchen and her mother instantly noticed a change in her daughter. She surmised, "Suzy, you are in love, aren't you?"

Suzy smiled with a virtuous look on her face, "Yes, but it's not what you think. Randy is Sherrill's fiancé—you know the movie star that's been in all the newspapers. I know that I can't have him, even as a lover, but I have found someone that I can call a *love-friend* for life."

The double revelation caused Anne's knees to buckle. She caught herself by holding onto the counter. She called out, "Gordon, come here."

Gordon entered the room with the newspaper in his hand. Anne related the conversation to him. Shock appeared on Gordon's face. They both looked at Suzy, trying to detect any deception in her expression. Instead they both noted a look of serenity and even an aura of maturity that hadn't existed before Suzy had gone on the picnic.

Her father counseled, "You know that Randy will probably be shipping out soon."

Suzy replied, "It doesn't matter. I've met him, I love him, and I know that we will always be special friends.

"Someday I may fall in love and get married. I will probably even have babies, but I will always cherish this day as a turning point in my life."

To emphasize the point, she announced, "I'm going to change my major in college from drama to journalism. I want to live and feel life, as it exists, not acting out someone else's illusions. I want to relate that feeling to others through writing—maybe even television reporting. I feel so alive right now; it's like I've never lived before!"

Both parents stared at her with their mouths ajar. They had never heard their indulgent petulant daughter display such a joyous mature attitude toward life. Instead of a broken heart, she had found her true heart. Moreover, it was a heart turned outward to others, instead of inward to self.

Her mother rushed forward and hugged her. Her father put his arms around both of them, "We're so proud of you, Honey. All we can say is that we love you and support you in whatever you decide to do with your life."

Suzy paused to think of what she had just said. She had never consciously considered journalism. Then she realized that it must have been from her subconscious dreams while she was enfolded in Randy's arms. It was as if a part of him had transferred to her and filled the empty recesses of her being; she loved him even more.

Suzy, outfitted in English riding clothes: Black suede breeches, white ruffled blouse with a fuchsia scarf, and black silk jacket, complete with calf-length black leather boots, cap, and riding crop, rode up to the archery range on a steel gray mare. She sat easily on the English riding saddle. Her hair was pulled back into a ponytail, exposing her pixie-shaped ears, which enhanced her radiant smile and the natural impish gleam in her violet eyes.

Her friends turned to her and Bob observed, "That's a beautiful horse; what do you call her?"

Casio nudged Randy in the ribs and whispered, "Who be looking at the horse?"

Randy realized that his eyes had been locked on Suzy; the tips of his ears reddened as he quickly averted his gaze to the horse.

"Her nickname is 'Musket,'" informed Suzy. "Are you all ready to go for a ride?"

"Sure," they agreed in unison. She led them off to the stable where the groom Manuel Gonzales had saddled seven horses.

"I've tried to pick horses that I think you will like and hope that they will like you," announced Suzy. Manuel led out each horse and Suzy pointed to the designated rider. He adjusted the stirrup length and rechecked the cinch.

Suzy rode over and untied a beautiful Appaloosa gelding. She led the horse back to Randy. "This is 'Chief Joseph.'" Randy stroked and petted the horse for a minute so that the horse would get his smell.

He climbed up into the saddle and found that the stirrups had already been adjusted to the correct length. He turned to her, "How did you—?"

She interrupted his question, "I know your inseam—remember."

He looked down at his new jeans and exclaimed, "Of course."

Manuel led out a black and white piebald Pinto. Suzy pointed toward Casio. Casio complained, "How come I gets the shortest horse?"

Suzy explained, "His name is 'Geronimo' and he may do a little pitchin' at first because he hasn't been ridden for awhile."

"Pitchin'—what's pitchin'?" asked Casio.

Suzy explained, "They call it buckin' in other states. Most Texans around here call it pitchin'."

"Well, Bitchin'—I like pitchin'!" exclaimed Casio. "Now I gets me to be a bronco buster."

Manuel had "Geronimo" tied to a hitching rail while he adjusted the stirrups. The horse was docile enough until Casio was handed the reins. The horse gave three quick pitches and Casio with arms and legs akimbo came out of the saddle and landed on his hands and knees. He got up and dusted off his uniform.

Suzy offered, "I'll get you another horse, if you want."

Casio obviously embarrassed, sternly replied, "No, thanks, I'll ride this cussin' Cayuse."

Suzy suggested, "Hold on with your legs and lean back when he pitches."

Casio climbed back onto the saddle. The horse pitched three times, twisted sideways, and pitched three more times. His friends called words of encouragement, "Ride-em, Casio!"

The horse slowly settled down and Casio sat nervously in the saddle, remarking, "Hah—I gots your number—you ol' nag-bag."

He kicked the horse in the ribs and the horse bolted, almost throwing him off backwards. The horse raced away and Casio yelled, "Whoa, you son-of-a-bitch, whoa." The horse planted his feet and stopped suddenly, throwing Casio up onto its neck. He held on tightly with his long arms wrapped around Geronimo's neck. Randy rode up laughing with tears in his eyes. "You okay?"

"Yeah, but I don't think 'ol' Geronimo' likes me—even after I gave him a big hug," opined Casio.

"Sure he does," reassured Randy. "But you have to talk to him with body language. When you want to go, give him a little rein and only light pressure with your heels.

"When you want to stop, brace yourself in the stirrups and say 'whoa' while pulling back gently on the reins—try it."

Casio followed Randy's instructions and found that the horse responded to his commands. He asked, "How come you know so much shit about everything and horses?"

Randy responded, "I grew up on a ranch. We raised Quarter horses."

Casio looked at him dubiously, "How can you raise *parts* of horses?"

Randy laughed, "It's a breed of horse. They are used for rounding up cattle, competition in rodeos, and short races."

"Oh—yeah," Casio sheepishly replied, "I knew that."

Together, they rode back to rejoin their friends. Manuel completed his saddle adjustments and the group rode off at a trot.

An hour later they headed back to the stables. They were a quarter of a mile away when Suzy challenged, "Race you back." She made a couple of clicking sounds in her cheek and put her heels into the sides of her horse; the horse bolted ahead.

Randy chased after her; his Appaloosa was fast, but the Arabian was faster. Suzy arrived at the stables several lengths ahead of him. The rest of the riders arrived at a gallop close behind him. They jumped off their horses, laughing and squealing from the exhilaration of riding like the wind.

Suzy announced, "We need to walk them around until they cool down." She led them off down the paddock. Leading Chief Joseph, Randy caught up with her and the other riders paired off.

Casio rubbed his hip and remarked to Gloria, "My butt's sore."

Gloria looked at him and coyly suggested, "From gettin' bucked off your horse or from last night?"

Casio glanced at her, grinning, "There be a difference, woman?" He laughed out loud at his own joke.

Gloria swelled up and retorted, "Well, if you can't tell the difference, 'Mr. Bedtime Man,' then you can just get back up on your horse and ride on outta here."

Casio quickly sobered, "Just jiving—just jiving. Don't go funnin' about the lovin'."

Randy passed by Manuel, "Manuel, would you find me a brush and a currycomb? Gracias."

They walked the horses for ten minutes and returned to the stables. Randy tied his horse to a hitching rail and removed the saddle. Manuel handed him the brush and currycomb then Randy started grooming his horse.

Casio walked up and inquired, "What are you doing?"

Randy explained, "I'm brushing down the horse after the ride."

Casio inferred, "Is that kind of like stroking your ol' lady after making love?"

Randy looked up in surprise, "Well, that is one analogy, but probably not one that I would have thought to use."

Suzy walked up and started brushing the other side of Chief Joseph. The rest of the riders paired off and began grooming one of their horses. They exchanged playful banter and soon the chore was completed.

Manuel went to each of them, nodding his head in approval of the work they were doing, "Gracias—gracias. You have saved me mucho work—muchas gracias."

The tenderfoot cowboys stiffly walked back to the patio and Anne produced a two gallon jug of pink lemonade. They sat around discussing their joy of the ride and learning more about each other. John Gomez was overseeing the cooking of the barbecue while his wife Rosalie was helping Anne prepare the side dishes.

Abbott spied a croquet course set up at one end of the large courtyard, "I'm going to play croquet—any challengers?"

Suzy, knowing that the game only had six mallets, deferred, "I'm going to change clothes and then help mother and Rosalie with the barbeque preparations. Y'all go ahead and enjoy yourselves."

Randy, noting that there were six other people, also deferred, "I'm going to check on Majeen, she should be about ready to foal." The remaining six players ambled off to select their favorite colored ball.

Suzy returned from her bedroom and her mother remarked, "It looks like your friends are having a good time."

"They are, Mother, and this is the best weekend I've ever had." Suzy smiled with newly found purpose as she picked up a paring knife and started cutting up vegetables.

Anne looked at her daughter helping out and thought *I really do like this new Suzy.*

Randy entered Majeen's stall and stroked her neck. She was lying down and he detected an infrequent contraction. He moved her tail aside and noted a profuse puffiness, but no exterior dilation of the birth canal. He stayed with her for a half-hour longer, stroking and soothing her. He went back to the barbecue and announced, "Your horse population is going to be increased by one more before the night is out."

Suzy reassured, "Manuel will keep an eye on her until she foals."

John Gomez announced that the meat was ready. Randy washed his hands and sat next to Suzy. The food was served to the family and guests, and then John and Rosalie seated themselves and shared in the feast.

Randy ate a couple of baby-back ribs and remarked, "Uhmm, this is the best barbecue sauce that I have ever tasted."

Anne acknowledged the compliment, "John buys a local brand of barbeque sauce, and then adds a little of Justin Wilson's Louisiana Cajun Sauce to it. That's the zesty flavor you taste. I've told him that he should start selling his own value-added brand, but he just laughs and says, 'Maybe I gonna someday.'"

Randy called across and gave a thumbs up, "John, great sauce."

John beamed with a smile, "Tanks you, Señor. You try the brisket and pork. I baste them with sauce too."

Randy tried everything and commented, "I can't remember when I've had a better meal. Mom's a great cook, but she cooks with different spices and flavorings."

The conversations rotated and crisscrossed among the diners. Casio's antics and Abbott's dry humor entertained them. Randy contributed tidbits of trivia and anecdotes. Mary Jo added to the humor by asking questions that had obvious answers or no answer at all, since the statements had been made in jest to get her to react. Karen, Gloria, and Bob were mostly quiet as they listened and laughed to the flow of the conversations.

Suzy, who normally would have tried to monopolize the conversation, was content to sit next to her newfound love-friend. She listened to a conversation for the first time with the ear of a journalist and discovered that a whole new world was awakening in her.

After the meal, the guests offered to help with the dishes, but Anne declined, "Rosalie and I can handle the dishes. You all just relax and enjoy yourselves."

Suzy suggested, "Let's make a bonfire down by the pool."

She opened the shed door and handed each of the guests a bundle of newspapers. They filed down to the pool and found a large open area, where they piled the newspapers. Then they spread out and brought back a large supply of broken dried limbs from the cottonwoods. A stack of limbs was placed on the newspapers and ignited. Abbott and Bob rolled a couple of cottonwood stumps onto the pile and within minutes a huge bonfire was burning.

Larger cottonwood logs were rolled up to encircle the fire. The logs provided a place to sit or a place to lean back against. Suzy retrieved a battery-operated radio from her room and tuned it to a rock and roll station. The campfire cadre settled down to stare at the mesmerizing flames. The heat and the music added to the contentment from their meal and soon everyone was nodding off.

Randy stirred in his dream as he breathed in the fresh smells of outdoors mingling with the provocative scent and perfume of a woman. He felt the heat of her body where she leaned against him and was aware of the soft curves of her body. Wisp of her hair wafted against his cheek and tickled his nose.

His eyes came open and he realized that the dream was reality. He shifted his shoulders against the log and scooted his hip back slightly to accommodate the arousal in his jeans. Suzy felt him move and woke up. She leaned hard against him as she stretched and yawned, her hips slid back against his crotch and she suddenly stopped stretching in mid-motion.

Randy stood up quickly, scraping his back against the log as he lifted her with him. He glanced at his watch and whispered urgently, "I need to go get my flight bag." He grabbed Suzy by the hand and they crept away from their dozing friends.

Suzy stopped beside her mother on the patio, "Mom, we have to get Randy's flight bag from his hotel. Is there anything you need from the store?"

Her mother thought for a moment, and then replied, "Yes, why don't you pick up some vanilla ice-cream. We'll make your father's famous 'rum n' black-strap molasses milkshakes."

Anne started to get some money and Randy intervened, "We don't need any money, Mrs. Sommers; we'll get it."

Suzy picked up her purse and handed the car keys to Randy, "You drive—I'll navigate."

They arrived at the hotel and Suzy followed him in. "I just want to see what your room looks like."

Randy retrieved his flight bag and shrugged his shoulders, "Well, this was home for one night. It ain't much, but we didn't plan to spend much time here, anyway"

Suzy sat down on the bed and bounced a couple of times. She stood up, "You'll like my brother's bed better."

They left, and then stopped at an HEB grocery store. Suzy picked up two gallons of *Blue Bunny* vanilla, saying, "This brand makes the best shakes." Randy paid for the ice cream and they drove back home.

Suzy put the ice cream in the freezer, and asked, "Didn't Mary Jo say that she would like to go fishing?"

"Yes, she did," replied Randy. "Probably everyone would like to try their hand at it."

Suzy rummaged through the pantry, "The fish go crazy over miniature marshmallows soaked in Louisiana Crawdad Sauce." She retrieved a jar and poured half of it into a bowl. She dumped a bag of marshmallows into a bowl and started stabbing them with a fork.

"What in the world are you doing?" asked a bemused Randy.

"Stabbing marshmallows," replied Suzy matter-of-factly. "It allows the sauce to soak into the holes and oozes out slowly in the water. Sometimes, you can catch four or five fish with a single little marshmallow."

Randy drawled, "Well, I've been to two church socials and a hog calling contest and I ain't never heard of no such a thing...."

Suzy laughed at his idiom and made up one of her own, with a drawl, "Well, I've been to two high school dance proms and a snipe hunt and I tell you it really works." They both laughed at the silliness of their inane statements.

"There is a bundle of cane poles with barbless hooks in the patio shed," informed Suzy.

Randy retrieved the poles from a shed and they strolled back down to the fishing pool.

Abbott, with his left eyebrow raised, inquired, "What kind of hanky-panky have you two been up to?"

"We had to drive to the hotel to get my flight bag," informed Randy.

Eyebrows were raised as the group collectively stared at the couple in anticipation of a juicy explanation. "It's not what you think," replied Randy. "The AP's signed me over to the custody of Colonel Sommers, so I have to stay here for the rest of the weekend.

Curiosity flashed across their faces and Abbott asked, "AP's—what AP's? What happened?"

"It was nothing," assured Randy. "I'll tell you about it later."

His friends were overcome with curiosity. Gloria demanded, "Does Suzy know?"

"Well, yes," replied Randy.

Gloria grabbed Suzy by the arm and ordered, "Come with me, girl." She dragged Suzy off into the cottonwoods, demanding, "OK, Girl, spill it,"

Suzy was reticent; "Randy said that he would tell you later."

"No, he didn't; he will tell his buddies. I probably won't see Casio again, so you needs to tell me now."

"Okay," Suzy reluctantly conceded. She told the story of the assaulted woman on the bridge and the criminals being sent to the hospital.

Gloria returned to the bonfire and whispered for a few minutes in Casio's ear. Casio whispered in Abbott's ear, Abbott whispered in Karen's ear and the story passed around the bonfire. Mary Jo leaned over toward Randy, and then caught herself, "Oh! You already know about you." Everyone roared with laughter as a scarlet blush appeared on Mary Jo's face.

They finally stopped laughing and turned to Randy with admiration in their eyes. Randy, embarrassed by the adulation, "Hey, I told you that it wasn't anything." Looking for something to change the subject, he picked up a cane pole and handed it to Mary Jo, "Here, have Suzy show you how to bait it." He passed out cane poles to the rest of the group.

Suzy clapped her hands to get their attention, "Okay, now listen up. We are using barbless hooks on the lines so that we can release the fish. The fish really go crazy over the marshmallows, so the rule of the day is 'catch and release.' Otherwise, you will wind up with a ton of fish."

Casio looked at her disbelievingly and stated, "I ain't never caught no fish before." He tossed his line into the water. The red and white bubble cork bobbed a couple of times, and then disappeared. He pulled back on the pole. The pole flexed for a moment, and then a large

270

crappie seemingly launched itself out of the water, soared through the air, and with its tail smacked Casio across the face.

Casio stepped back in astonishment, then bent over and picked up the flopping fish, staring at it with disbelief. He held it up with one hand for everyone to see and wiped his face with the back of his other hand. "I been smacked in the face for misbelievin'." His friends burst out laughing.

Abbott quipped, "Casio that is probably a girl fish. You got slapped for getting too fresh with a fresh fish." The group chuckled at his dry tongue-twisting humor. Then, one by one, they cast their lines into the water, and got instant action.

After thirty minutes of hauling fish out of the water. Casio held one up, "Hey, I know I caught this same fish three times—I never forget a face."

Randy laughed with the rest of then and resigned, "Casio, you're too much for me. I'm going to quit fishing and go sit on a log. I can't take any more of your fishy humor.

He threw a couple of large limbs on the fire and sat down on the log. Suzy joined him. They sat staring at the flames, each lost in their own thoughts, and feeling peacefulness in their friendship.

Mary Jo was the last to quit. She walked toward the fire and the center of her blouse sparkled in the firelight like sequins sewn into the fabric. Abbott pointed, "Hey, Mary Jo. Why do your breasts sparkle?"

Mary Jo looked down and brushed the fish scales from the front of her blouse. She answered, "Because the fish were slippery and I had to trap them against me to get the hook out." Everyone laughed. It seemed like everything that came out of her mouth was so naive that it was funny.

Bob, caught up in the humor, made a fish face with his lips and said, "Well, Mary Jo, I'm hooked; come over here and trap me." Mary Jo walked over to Bob and slapped him on the arm for the remark, but she sat down next to him, anyway.

Abbott quipped, "What did the baby minnow ask his 'Northern Pike' father and his 'crappie' mother?"

They shook their heads and Abbott grinned, "When I grow up, am I going to 'turnpike' and wind up with a 'crappie attitude?'" The group moaned, but his joke started a round of fish jokes. Everyone was laughing and enjoying even the most inane jokes.

The joking ceased when Casio quipped, "What is the definition of 'mass confusion?'"

Each shook his or her head. Casio delivered the bomb, "Twenty blind lesbians wandering around inside a fish market—get it?"

The guys snickered, but the girls sat wide-eyed and embarrassed with their hand across their open mouth.

Finally, Suzy stood up, "Come on, girls; let's go inside and have milkshakes." They walked away without saying another word to the guys.

Randy looked across at Casio and scolded, "Hey, man, I think that you just crossed the line."

Casio looked around and held up his hands, "Hey, wha'd I say? It was just a joke—right. The guys in my gang back home thought that it was hilarious. What's the problem?"

Abbott interjected, "I think that the *keyword* here is 'guys liked it.'"

The four men sat alone, staring at the fire. Finally, Randy shrugged his shoulders and resigned, "Come on, let's go make up with them. Maybe they'll still share a milkshake with us anyway."

They entered the kitchen to stone cold silence. The girls were finishing up their shakes and looked at each other, but wouldn't look at the men. Abbott sidled up to Karen, "How come you are mad at me? I didn't tell the joke."

Karen stared straight ahead and replied, "Yes, but you laughed at it—didn't you."

Abbott admitted, "Yes, but no one ever accused us guys of having good taste in jokes."

He leaned over and sniffed the milkshake that she was holding. "Pardon me, but doesn't that milkshake smell a little like fish?"

Karen's eyes widened and she exclaimed, "No! That's the smell of fish on my hands." Everyone laughed and the ice was broken.

The girls forgave them and Suzy made milkshakes with a commercial style malted mixer. Randy was the last to be served. He took a sip and exclaimed, "This is awesome! What's in it?"

Suzy explained, "Vanilla ice cream with a shot of dark rum and a tablespoon of black-strap molasses. It's my dad's discovery when he was stationed in the Caribbean. My mom was pregnant with my brother and craved something sweet to eat at two o'clock in the morning.

"Dad offered her regular ice cream, but she wouldn't have it. Out of desperation, he searched through the cupboard and found rum and molasses. He whipped up the concoction and she loved it. We've been drinking them ever since."

272

The group stood around talking while they finished their milkshakes. Gloria had goose bumps on her arms from ingesting so much cold liquid. She, along with the rest of them, had indulged in a second shake. "I'm cold," she complained. "Let's go back down to the bonfire."

Karen chimed in, "Maybe we can convince Randy to sing for us."

"That's a great idea," exclaimed Suzy, "I want Mom and Dad to hear him too." She disappeared for a couple of minutes, and then returned carrying her brother's guitar and leading her parents.

She handed the guitar to Randy. He shrugged his shoulders with resignation, "Don't I have anything to say about this?"

His friends all chorused, "Nope—you're outnumbered."

Suzy grinned, "I guess that means that you'll have to sing for your supper."

As they walked down to the bonfire, Randy plunked on the guitar to get it in tune. Arriving at the pool, he placed one foot upon a cottonwood log and chided, "Okay, if I'm going to sing then all of you have to sing too."

He led off, "Oh, bury me not on the lone prairie, where the coyotes howl and the wind blows free..." The rest of the ensemble slowly joined in and became caught up in the thrill and camaraderie of group participation. To enable Casio and the others to learn the words, he played several songs two or three times.

More than an hour had passed and Randy was finishing up a requested solo, "El Paso." He crooned, "—one little kiss and Felina—goooodbye."

The audience was clapping when Manuel ran up and interrupted, "Señor Sommers—come quickly! Majeen is foaling; the foal—it is stuck."

Gordon turned to his wife and instructed, "Call the vet—tell him that it is an emergency." He raced to the stables and everyone followed him. Gordon went inside the stable with the mare, while the rest of them craned their necks through the Dutch doors to see what was happening.

The foal's head and neck along with one leg partially extended out of the mare. A thick gray cord was wrapped around the foal's neck and the foal's tongue dangled from its mouth. Mary Jo screamed, "Oh, it's dead," and turned away. Karen took her place, stared for a moment then turned away crying.

The mare was thrashing about from contractions; the foal weakly moved its head. Anne ran up and announced, "The vet's at a convention in St. Louis. His assistant is out on a call and won't be able to come here for another hour."

Randy interjected, with alarm, "The foal doesn't have an hour—it has only got about ten minutes." He turned to Suzy, "Bring me some mineral oil and some towels." He turned to Manuel, "Get me a bucket of hot water and some strong soap."

He opened the door and took a closer look at the foal. The foal couldn't breathe against the contractions of the mare, but he detected a slight pulsation in the umbilical cord, which meant that the foal was still getting a small amount of oxygen.

Manuel reappeared with a bucket of hot water and a bar of soap. Randy stripped off his shirt and quickly washed his hands and arms. Suzy rushed in with mineral oil and towels. Randy dried his arms and hands, and then doused his left arm with mineral oil. He worked the mineral oil over his arm and hand, and then knelt down in front of the foal.

He tugged lightly on the umbilical cord; it was as taut as a banjo string. He reached through the opening and found the foal's shoulder. He pushed, but the mare's thrashing and contractions prevented him from moving the foal. He hollered over his shoulder, "Suzy! Calm Majeen down."

Suzy knelt down and stroked the mare's neck and spoke to her soothingly, "It's okay, girl, it's okay. You're going to be okay. It's okay, girl."

After a couple of minutes the mare relaxed. Randy was fighting against the clock. Precious moments had elapsed and he could see that the foal was in dire distress.

He pushed against the shoulder again and the foal slid back in an inch. He braced one foot against the wall and pushed with all his strength. The mare flinched, but the foal slid back in, except for its head. The umbilical cord now hung loosely in a loop.

Randy worked the umbilical cord around the foal's nose and with his left hand slowly pulled the cord back into the uterus. He felt around and found the right leg that was doubled back. Pushing his arm further into the mare, he grabbed the leg and worked it toward him.

The foal was becoming more active, which indicated that it had a restored oxygen supply. Randy pulled the leg as far as it could come, and then found the other leg and pulled on it. He said to Suzy's father,

"Use the flat of your hand and rap two quick times on her side, like you're wanting her to gallop." Gordon followed his instructions and the mare kicked out and started contracting.

Randy pulled alternately on the feet and more of the neck started to appear, followed by the legs. He grasped the feet with both hands and pulled; the foal's shoulders appeared. Two more contractions and the foal came out all the way. Randy cleared the mucus from its nostrils and reached into its mouth and removed the mucus from around its tongue. The foal shuttered, and then started breathing on its own. The onlookers gave a collective sigh of relief.

Randy looked around and everyone had tears in their eyes, including the colonel and Manuel. He felt hot tears in his own eyes from the aftermath of the drama.

Colonel Sommers patted him on the shoulder, "Son—this is the most fantastic thing that I have ever seen. How did you know what to do?"

Randy replied, "I watched a vet do it for one of our cows. The umbilical cord wasn't wrapped around the calf's neck, so he had time to use drugs to relax the cow. He got the legs straightened out first, and then used more drugs to induce labor."

The colonel looked at the reincarnation of the new foal, "You just saved a very valuable foal from certain death. I won't ever forget this."

Randy stood up to stretch his cramped muscles. His jeans were soaked with amniotic fluid. He grabbed a towel and started cleaning himself off. Suzy arose and walked over to him. She wrapped her arms around him and buried the side of her face into the hair on his chest. She held him tightly and spoke softly, "You were wonderful."

To Randy's surprise, everyone spontaneously broke into applause as if the curtain had just come down after a scene from a melodrama. Her embrace became embarrassingly long. Randy whispered, "Suzy, I need to move the foal so that Majeen can smell it."

He reached down and helped the foal to its feet. The foal stood shakily on trembling stalks. It took a couple of steps and Randy guided it over to Majeen's head.

The mare raised her head and snuffled several times, taking in the foal's scent. Then she struggled to her feet and started licking the foal. The foal smelled her and started nuzzling along her side. Randy guided the foal back until it found a teat and started nursing.

A cheer went up from the onlookers. Everyone was smiling and acting as if they were surrogate aunts and uncles. Randy thought, *Birth is such a wonderful thing to behold.* Then he thought of his own son, who would be born next year and a smile came to his own face.

The vet appeared at the door and stated urgently, "I came as quickly as I could." He looked around and saw the newborn foal nursing. Then he saw Randy's soaked jeans and bare torso. "I guess that you found another vet—that's good because a wrapped umbilical cord is almost always certain death."

The colonel beamed with pride, "No, Randy is our houseguest. He's a good man to have around in an emergency."

The vet gave both horses an examination. He tied off and cut the umbilical cord. Then he pronounced, "Looks like everything is fine here. The mare should slough off the afterbirth in a couple of hours. After that, I don't expect any problems."

The vet filled out a birthing form to authenticate the birth for the 'Registry' and Gordon signed for the charges, "Thanks for coming out, Doc."

Randy looked at himself, "Looks like I need a shower and a change of clothes."

Suzy beamed, "Come with me, *Doctor Vet*. I'll take care of you."

The rest of the group headed back to the bonfire. Casio humbly testified with admiration, "Randy's the coolest dude *black or white* that I've ever met. I would have passed out doing what he just did—I almost did—just watchin'." The statement brought empathy and laughter from the rest of his friends.

Suzy showed Randy the shower and where the towels were located. She went into his room and removed the tags from his other set of clothes. She hung the clothes on a hanger and put a pair of shorts and socks in a bag. These she hung on the bathroom doorknob then rejoined her friends at the bonfire.

When she approached the fire, they were voicing their own feelings of the birthing experience. She overheard Mary Jo say, "If I ever have a baby, I want Randy to deliver it."

Everyone laughed and Bob said, "Mary Jo, after we ship out, I won't have anyone to make me laugh anymore."

"When is that going to happen?" asked Suzy, suddenly aware that they were also referring to Randy leaving.

"In about a week," answered Bob. He was also saddened that he had just met these wonderful people; now he would be going away too.

A cloud of gloom gathered over the young people as they gazed quietly at the fire.

Randy walked up, "Why is everyone so serious?"

Suzy replied, "Because Bob just told us that you-all are leaving in a week."

Casio piped up, "Not me, no siree. I'm bummed-out cause I have to stay here for another five weeks to complete basic training."

Randy tried to disguise his feelings on the subject, "I don't know when I'm leaving. The tech school scheduling list didn't have my name on it."

Suzy suddenly took heart, "What does that mean? Does that mean that you are going to stay here?"

"I just don't know," answered Randy. "I've had to take some special tests, but no one will give me a clue as to why—."

Mary Jo stood up and announced, "I'm starting to feel funky—let's go, Karen."

That was the catalyst that ended the party. Everyone agreed that it had been a fun day filled with excitement, good food, good friends, and a birthing. Each person exchanged a hug or a handshake or both. Randy and Suzy walked with them back up to the house. Each one said their good-byes to Suzy's parents.

They walked out the front entrance and Randy informed them, "I'll see you guys back at the barracks tomorrow night before lights out." Suzy and he waved as their friends got into their cars and drove away.

They walked back into the house and Randy said, "I'm going to throw water on the fire so there is no chance that it spreads."

Suzy agreed, "I'll pick up the fishing poles and make sure that nothing is left outside."

Suzy found a three-gallon bucket in the shed and handed it to Randy. They walked back to the bonfire and stood for a moment feeling the heat. Suzy placed an arm around Randy's waist and Randy put his arm around her shoulders. Suzy stared at the fire and unexpectedly asked, "Randy, will I ever meet someone special like you and get married?"

Randy didn't quite know how to answer the question. He stared into the flames and thought for a long time. Finally, he turned and faced toward her, "Isn't your brother Steve, special—the man that you use to judge all other men?"

"Yes, but how did you know?" asked Suzy.

"Because, my sister Leta feels the same about me." He continued, "I'm not really special. So far, I've only been able to react to events in my life...instead of being able to take the initiative to make decisions that will affect my future.

"Someday, you will meet a man—a special man, who has it all together. He will be the one with whom you will want to spend the rest of your life."

Suzy turned and placed her arms around him. She clung to him for a long time, digesting and evaluating all he had said to her. She reluctantly pulled away, "OK, I guess it's cleanup time."

Randy dumped several buckets of water on the fire. Each time he filled the bucket, he would see the fish swirl and jump in the moonlight. They walked back to the house and Randy stopped on the patio, "You go ahead in, I'm going to check on Majeen."

He entered the stall and saw that the foal was asleep, snuggled up to the mare. The mare's afterbirth had not yet come out. Randy sat on some bales of hay and he leaned back against the wall.

He closed his eyes and his brain started reviewing the day. So much had happened since he had eaten steak and eggs early this morning. It was almost incredulous that so much could happen in one day. He thought of his longest day in basic training, but in perspective, it felt weeks shorter than today.

He didn't hear Suzy enter the stall, but he felt her wrap a blanket across his shoulders then sit next to him, wrapping the other end of the blanket around her shoulders. She leaned into him and they fell asleep.

They were awakened around two o'clock when her father entered the stall. "You two go on up to the house and go to bed. Manuel and I will keep an eye on Majeen. Randy looked over and the mare had sloughed the afterbirth. He put an arm around a sleepy Suzy and guided her to the house.

Rajah Ty-Ron Majeen Sommers

Randy didn't remember going to sleep; the smell of bacon frying brought him out of bed. He checked his watch and saw that it was after seven. He hadn't slept this late for over a month.

Anne knocked and announced through the door, "Breakfast is about ready, Randy; dress for church."

Randy slipped on his jeans and headed for the shower. He may have slept late, but he couldn't forgo his morning shower. Five minutes later he was showered, shaved, and dressing in his Class "A" uniform. He walked into the kitchen. A still sleepy Suzy, wearing a blue-violet silk chiffon robe, was sitting at the table with one leg crossed under her.

Anne served ham, bacon, and sausage with eggs and home fries covered with white sausage gravy, along with fresh squeezed orange juice and coffee. During the course of conversation, Randy asked, "How are Majeen and the foal?"

"They are just fine," informed Gordon. "We are a happier family today because of your quick action, Randy."

With a serious look, he continued, "Anne and I have talked it over and we want you to have a quarter interest in the foal's future. If it weren't for your taking command of the situation, then there wouldn't be a live foal, today."

Randy was taken back by this generous offer. "I really can't—"

"No arguments; no denials," commanded Colonel Sommers. "I outrank you and our decision is final."

Suzy interjected, "Okay, now that's settled, and since Randy is part owner, and the foal was born on his birthday then he should be allowed to pick one of the registered names."

Randy was still numb from the news. Thoroughbreds sold for up to a million dollars. This horse was a Thoroughbred and could run in the Kentucky Derby—Suzy had said so, herself.

These folks, whom he had just met yesterday, were offering—no—demanding that he take a potential quarter of a million dollars gift. Randy stammered, "Right now, I—I can't even afford to pay for my part of the vet bill."

"No problem," assured the colonel. "We won't charge you anything until the horse wins a purse, or we auction it off."

Suzy pounded on the table for attention, "We still haven't named it. Randy, what is your middle name?"

"Ty-Ron, with a hyphen and a capital 'R,' stated Randy. My mother wanted to name me Tyrone, but my father wanted a special name for his oldest son, so he compromised by choosing the spelling and enunciation."

Suzy raised her head and stuck out her chin. "Good—then Ty-Ron it is. If the name is good enough for one Thoroughbred then it's good enough for another."

Randy blushed at the compliment. Then he remembered Sergeant Stark's statement about accepting compliments. He capitulated, "OK, I accept your generous offer and the name. I can't fight all of you."

Gordon finalized, "Great! Then it's official. The new foal's registered name will be 'Rajah Ty-Ron Majeen Sommers.' We'll call him, 'Rajah Ty-Ron.'"

Suzy jumped up from her chair; she had a look of glee and accomplishment. Her robe gaped open, revealing more than Randy was expecting to see. With only a slight tinge of embarrassment on her cheeks, she glanced at the kitchen clock and announced, "Oh, I need to get dressed for church."

The Sommers and Randy entered the Hillshire Presbyterian Church and found a pew in the middle. Some of the parishioners turned and stared, and then whispered to the person next to them.

After a few minutes many people turned and looked toward Randy and the Sommers. Randy felt uncomfortable. He had taken his Ike cap off when he had entered the church and he wasn't the only person wearing a military uniform. He glanced over his shoulder and saw more people actively discussing something.

He leaned over to Suzy and asked, "What are they staring at? Do I have a bird or something sitting on my head?"

Suzy looked up, and then giggled, "Of course not. I don't even know why I looked." She asked her mother, who then asked her husband. Both of them shrugged their shoulders and shook their heads.

Randy looked over at the choir and noticed that even they were motioning and whispering. He had never been subjected to such scrutiny and didn't know why. He picked up a hymnal and started paging through the songs to divert his attention. Ten long minutes passed before the service commenced.

The choir sang two songs, and then the lay-minister made several announcements pertinent to the church congregation. Finally, he announced, "We are fortunate to have a true hero in attendance this morning. I'm sure that everyone saw his picture on the front page of this morning's paper and recognized him sitting with the Sommers family. Randy Ferris, would you please stand up and let the congregation acknowledge the young man that rescued a woman being assaulted by two armed men on the 'River Walk.'"

Randy was totally surprised. He felt himself blush, in spite of his desire not to. He stood up and the lay-minister continued, "Randy was already known of us before his heroic deed yesterday. Many of you heard his speech at a televised basketball game played at Lackland AFB. It was there that he was introduced as the fiancé of the now famous 'Sherrill.'"

The congregation uncharacteristically stood and applauded Randy. He felt himself blush again. He could only raise his hand and wave acknowledgment. He turned to acknowledge everyone who was clapping. He stood a moment longer and then took his seat as the applause died down.

Suzy sat back down and squeezed his hand in admiration. She leaned over and said, "Well, at least now we know why they were staring and whispering."

As Randy contemplated his newly found fame and fortune, a verse formed in his mind:

> Fame and fortune—kith and kin
> Touching our lives as fickle friends.

Remembering that he was in church and that all things come from God, he added:

> For those of us inclined to pray,
> We count our blessings day by day.

Sergeant Stark retrieved the newspaper from the front yard. He racked back in his recliner, and then pulled out the 'Parade Magazine' and handed it to Maria. Per his routine, he glanced at the front page before going to the sports page. "Well, I'll be a 'Son of a bitch!'"

"What's wrong?" inquired Maria

"Randy's picture is on the front page"

"Why?"

Stark held up his hand. "Wait a minute; I don't know yet—I'm reading about it now."

After he finished, he breathed out, "Poor bastard." He handed the article to Maria.

Maria read the article and commented, "It says here that Randy is a hero. Why did you say, 'Poor bastard?'"

Stark explained, "Because, when an airman in basic training is involved in an incident then the air police pick him up and transport him back to the base. Randy finally got a pass and had it cancelled because he was some kind of a hero."

Maria gaped at him, "But that's so unfair."

"I know-I know, but that's the rules." He reached for the phone and called the company headquarters, "Hello, this is Sergeant Stark. What time did Airman Ferris sign back in?"

The NCOIC (non-commissioned officer in charge) informed him, "Airman Ferris has not signed in."

That's odd, thought Stark. He called the Air Police Headquarters. "Hello, this is Sergeant Stark. Did you have a pickup order for Airman Randall Ferris?

The NCOIC reported, "We had a pickup order on Saturday morning, but a Colonel Gordon Sommers had signed for Airman Ferris."

Stark hung up, "I don't know any Colonel Sommers at Lackland."

Maria prompted, "Dwayne, what are you talking about?"

Stark thought for a minute then explained, "Randy didn't have to go back to the base. He got a Colonel Sommers to sign for him," adding, "resourceful bastard!"

He glanced at Maria, who was scowling at him. He clarified, "Don't gimme that look. I meant '*resourceful bastard*' as a genuine compliment."

Doctor Bill Johnson read the front-page article and recognized Colonel Sommers' houseguest. He picked up the phone and called the city desk. "Hello, this is Doctor Bill Johnson. I have a human-interest story about Randy Ferris that you might be interested in—."

After church, Randy opened the car door and sat next to Suzy. He flexed his fingers that were sore from shaking hands with the entire congregation after the church service. He knew that they simply wanted to congratulate him, but their enthusiasm intensified the pressure of their handshake. After over seven hundred handshakes, he now knew how politicians must feel after returning from the campaign trail.

Gordon looked at his watch and stated, "It's too early for lunch. Is there anything special that anyone would like to do?"

Randy suggested, "I had planned to take a gondola ride at the 'River Walk.' Does that interest anyone else?"

Anne nodded in agreement, "Sure, we haven't been there for a long time." Suzy and her father nodded their assent.

The gondolas were more like small-motorized barges than the colorful narrow oar-powered gondolas, seen in *National Geographic*, on 'The Grand Canal' in Venice. Nevertheless, the cruise was enjoyable. There were frequent stops where passengers could get on or off, go shopping, dine at one of the many riverside theme restaurants, or stroll along the river and then catch another gondola to continue their trip.

At one of the shops, Randy bought a small exquisitely carved mahogany Thoroughbred horse with the coloration of the new foal. He took it to a jewelry store and had them attach a nameplate: "Rajah Ty-Ron Majeen Sommers." On the bottom of the base, he had them attach another plate: "Suzette Sommers, With Love, Randall Ferris.

He handed the gift to Suzy and said, "I want you to have this—it has been a very special weekend being with you and your family."

She read the inscriptions; then held the gift to her chest, "Oh, Randy, this is the most precious gift that I have ever received. I will always cherish it." She had tears in her eyes as she kissed him on his cheek in front of her parents.

They boarded another gondola and finished the tour. Walking to the car, Gordon suggested, "Let's go out to the San Pedro Creek Country Club and have lunch."

The country club was named after the creek that meandered through it, the same creek whose headwaters were located on the Sommers' farms.

Suzy elucidated, "During the summer, before Steve went away to the academy, we would canoe from the pool at home to the country club dock. There were a few small falls that we had to portage, but the trip was always a lot of fun."

Randy visualized the trip in his mind and felt almost envious that he hadn't been a part of the gala outings. He pictured in his mind paddling downstream through the calm clear waters, shooting the rapids, portaging the falls, and then gliding up to the dock and handing his golf clubs to a caddy.

After playing eighteen holes, he would have a couple of cocktails with his friends; then sit down to a crown roast dinner with champagne. Afterwards, he would fire up a Cuban cigar and discuss the Dow Jones Averages with his stockbroker seated at the table.

There was something wrong...he felt a void in his daydream—there was no Sherrill in this scenario and he felt a sadness spreading through him. He blinked rapidly a couple of times then came back to a conscious level. He turned and looked at Suzy, not recognizing her for a split-second. She was staring at him with concern on her face.

He apologized, "I'm sorry. When I go down under several levels in deep thought, I'm not even aware of my surroundings."

"I know," replied Suzy. "I waved my hand in front of your eyes and you didn't even blink."

"I was just daydreaming of taking a canoe trip down San Pedro Creek," he stated lightly.

"Well, the canoe must have capsized because you had a look on your face like you were a drowning man," she observed resolutely.

Randy smiled at the analogy; then sobered because it probably was a fairly accurate observation.

Gordon pulled up to the entrance of the clubhouse. A valet handed him a parking stub and they walked into a commons area the size of a ballroom. The room was filled with expensive leather furniture arranged to provide a nuance of discrete semi-privacy for small groups. Potted plants and moveable floral arrangements provided a Caribbean atmosphere.

The maître d' greeted them, "Good afternoon, Colonel and Mrs. Sommers. I see that you have your daughter, Suzette, and a guest for lunch today. He handed menus to a server that seated them next to a window overlooking the eighteenth hole of one of the golf courses.

The wine steward appeared carrying two glasses of red wine and a Shirley Temple. "And, what would the young gentleman like to drink?"

Randy looked at the drink in front of Suzy, "I'd like to have what ever she is drinking."

"That is a Shirley Temple," informed the waiter.

"Well, do you have such a thing as a John Wayne Temple—Pilgrim?" voiced Randy with obvious chauvinist inference.

His dining companions laughed at his attempt to imitate John Wayne.

The wine steward clicked his heels, "I'll see what I can do, sir," and then left.

Gordon glanced out the window as a foursome was finishing their play, "Randy, do you golf?"

"No, basketball has always been my game, but I would like to learn golf."

"Then you should," confided the colonel. "The game is not only relaxing and good exercise, but more contacts and contracts have probably been formalized on golf courses than in all the boardrooms of Corporate America."

"Why is that?" asked Randy, suddenly interested.

The colonel enlightened, "In a stuffy formalized boardroom, you only have about ten minutes to present your case. On a golf course, you are in an informal relaxed environment with a couple of hours to influence a captivated audience of 'movers and shakers.' At 'hole nineteen,' you can finalize the deal."

Randy looked out at the golf course and saw the foursome finishing their game. Judging from their pantomimed body language they looked relaxed and were obviously enjoying themselves,. Randy considered the colonel's explanation and found it valid. He asked, "Where is the nineteenth hole located?"

Anne interrupted and explained with light sarcasm, "It's the lounge…that is why it takes them four hours to play a two an a half hour game." She and Suzy knowingly laughed.

The colonel defended himself, "All I can say is that I wouldn't have made so many good deals, buying and selling horses; or gotten so many plum assignments in the air force, if it hadn't been for the game of golf."

Randy smiled at this ruffled exchange. He could see that the subject of golf had been broached in previous discussions between husband and wife.

The wine steward reappeared and placed a large frosted mug with a curved spur handle in front of Randy. The drink was garnished with a sprig of Tumbleweed. Randy took a sip and drawled, "Well, that's more like it—Pilgrim."

The waiter appeared, "Are you ready to order, sir?"

Gordon looked at Randy, "Why don't you order."

Without looking at the menu, Randy shared, "While we were driving out here, I developed a craving for crown-rib roast.

Gordon and Suzy nodded their approval. Anne remarked, "Well, this is lunch and I usually have something light, but the roast does sound delicious—OK, I'll have it too."

They finished their meal and the colonel sat back and lit up a cigar. He offered one to Randy, but he declined. Randy saw an airplane in the distance, "Have you ever flown, sir?"

"Yes, I flew jets in Korea, but I've got a desk job now. We leave the military flying to the younger jet-jockeys. Our son Steve wants to be a pilot after he graduates from the Air Force Academy.

"I—we (indicating his family)—do co-own a D18S Twin Beech with three other officers. When we do not need it, we charter it out for trips to Cancun and Belize."

Seeing Randy's sudden interest, Gordon suggested, "Say, how would you like to go up for a Sunday afternoon flight?"

Excitement showed across Randy's face, "Yes, very much!"

Anne looked at Gordon, "I don't know. We've just had a big meal."

"I'll be good and not pretend that I am still a fighter pilot," coaxed the colonel. "Besides, our meal will be settled by the time we take-off." He excused himself to go call to see if the aircraft was available.

Randy turned to Suzy, "Is that alright with you?"

"Daddy knows that he doesn't even have to ask. I'm ready to fly anytime."

Gordon returned, "We're in luck—the plane's available."

As they were leaving, Randy noticed for the first time that people were staring at him. At the table he had been seated looking out the window, and had been absorbed by the good food, good friends, and the ambiance of the view. As he passed their tables, the diners nodded in recognition and approval of what they had read in the newspaper about him. Randy smiled, nodding back to acknowledge their interest in him.

The colonel finished his preflight check of the aircraft, and then climbed in and sat next to Randy. He started the left engine, and then the right engine. He waited, watching the gauges climb to normal, and then picked up the microphone and spoke into it, "San Pedro tower, this is Beech, Tango Baker Zebra one-niner-four, requesting permission to taxi."

Randy heard from the speakers, "Roger, Beech, Tango Baker Zebra one-niner-four, proceed to runway three one.

Gordon taxied to the runway. He requested and received permission from the tower to take off. Pulling onto the runway, he set the brake and revved up the engines. He made a last minute check of the gauges, and then released the brakes. The plane launched forward and was airborne before it was a third of the way down the runway.

The exhilaration of flying was new to Randy. He watched as the fields below him slowly receded into the size of postage stamps. Gordon turned the aircraft and flew over the hills north of the city. He leveled out and turned to Randy, "OK, Son, the yoke is yours."

Randy grabbed the controls and gripped them with a death lock, not daring to move. He had watched Gordon take off and maneuver the plane. The procedure had appeared so simple. Now that he was in control, it seemed next to impossible.

Gordon soothingly explained, "Relax; flying an airplane is like riding a well trained horse. It responds to the nuances of body movement." He explained the function of the controls.

Randy relaxed and experimented. He dropped the left wing—then overcorrected and the right wing dropped. He brought the aircraft back to level and flew straight for a moment, and then experimented with the controls until the airplane and he were starting to feel as one. With each maneuver, his confidence rose and soon he was initiating slow circles and shallow dives.

Gordon complimented, "You have a nice touch. Have you ever thought of becoming a pilot?"

"Yes, I wanted to go to college and then go into the air force to become a pilot, but—." He paused, trying to think how to explain his circumstances, and then he said straight-from-the-shoulder, "But Sherrill and I made a baby, and they've become more important to me."

"I understand," the colonel sympathized. "I don't condone premarital sex, but I do admire your acknowledgement of your responsibility."

Randy piloted for an hour, exchanging anecdotes with the passengers. He flew by Lackland AFB and the colonel directed his attention. "Below is where you are based."

Randy looked down. The base looked so small and insignificant in contrast to when he was in his barracks, which had been his whole world for the last month.

The colonel instructed, "Take her down to three thousand, and I'll take over."

Randy dropped the left wing and nose. He watched the altimeter decrement to three thousand feet, and then smoothly leveled out.

Gordon took the controls and remarked approvingly, "Well done."

Suzy leaned forward and patted Randy's shoulder, whimsically stating, "You can fly me anytime."

Randy, hearing the words, wondered, "Is she making a double-entendre?"

Choosing not to dwell on her statement, he gazed at the terrain below him and reviewed all that had recently happened to him. His weekend had been filled with so many interesting activities that he found it hard to completely comprehend all that had happened.

He was the guest of a very gracious and generous family. They had wealth, but it didn't corrupt them. He remembered listening to many sermons of "Money Corrupts," but this family was no different from his own family. They had love and respect for each other and charity in their hearts toward their fellow man.

Randy formalized an understanding in his mind. *Wealth, as a singular goal is corrosive and self-indulgent and can short-circuit other important values.* That kind of money, he surmised, was probably the gist of the sermons that he had heard. However, *Wealth, accumulated through honest endeavor, while retaining integrity and personal values, was what the "Great American Dream" was all about.*

Randy revolved these thoughts through his mind and concluded; *being in the right place at the right time didn't harm the process.*

Then he remembered a quote; "Opportunity comes to those who prepare themselves." At the present, he was unprepared for opportunity. He had neither education nor training nor maturity.

Because of his obligations to Sherrill, the air force, and himself, he was on a fast track toward maturity. However, education and training were lacking. He vowed to correct that, and soon!

The touch of the wheels landing brought him out of his thoughts. Gordon taxied the plane toward the hanger and remarked, "You seemed pretty deep in thought."

Suzy interjected, "Yeah, it seems to be his favorite form of entertainment." Then, to soften the jibe, she good-naturedly pushed him on his shoulder.

Randy explained, "I was just thinking how lucky I am. Fate has smiled upon me by allowing your family to touch my life."

Gordon laid his hand on Randy's shoulder, "We feel the same way, Son; we feel exactly the same toward you." Suzy and Anne reached forward and laid their hands on top of Gordon's to show their support for his statement.

Arriving back home, Suzy and Randy rushed to the stables to see Majeen and Rajah Ty-Ron. Filled with life, the little foal was nursing and whisking his tail back and forth. Seeing that everything was okay, they walked hand in hand to the pool.

Randy sat on one of the logs and Suzy leaned back into him. He supported her by squeezing his legs against her and wrapping his arms around her. They both could feel the intense exchange of body heat. Together they watched the sun sink below the horizon.

Suzy asked, "Randy, where do I fit into *your* definition of love?"

Randy thought for a long time, "You know that I am dedicated, heart and soul, to Sherrill." He felt Suzy stiffen and shudder. "I guess that in the greater scheme of life and love that I am more than a brother to you, but less than a lover. I'm a man that loves you as one human being for another—for whom you are and what you are."

Suzy asked, "If I were a man, would I be your best friend?"

Randy didn't have to think, he simply replied, "You are not a man and I would never wish that you were—."

Suzy stood up and said, "I accept that." She took his hand and helped him up. They walked back to the house, hand in hand.

Anne suggested, "Why don't you two watch some television, while I fix something to eat?

"Thank you, Mrs. Sommers, but I should be getting back to the base."

Suzy interjected, "We'll grab a burger on the way."

Randy walked over and hugged Anne. Anne had tears in her eyes. She knew how much Randy meant to her daughter, but she had also developed a motherly kinship for this boy. "Randy, you will always be welcome in our home."

Randy replied, "Thank you, Ma'am." Then he hugged her again.

He walked into the living room, where Gordon was watching the news. He arose from his chair when Randy entered. They shook hands and a silent understanding of mutual admiration passed between them. Randy simply said, "Goodbye, sir."

Randy entered Steve's room and packed his loose items in his flight bag. He returned to the kitchen, "I'll have to leave my civvies here, since I can't store them in my locker at the airbase.

Anne replied, "We'll pack them away and they will be here for you when you come back." Her words gave heart and hope to her daughter's loss.

Suzy and Randy stopped by the Jet Drive-in and shared a meal. Then they drove to Lackland. She drove her Thunderbird up to the gate and the AP waved them through. Randy asked, "Why didn't they stop you and ask for your ID?

Suzy informed, "Because I have an officer's sticker from Randolph on my front bumper—VIP, you know."

She dropped Randy off in front of the company HQ. They parted with a simple handshake that had to suffice for all the words they yearned to say to each other. She drove away with tears in her eyes.

Randy blinked the mist of tears from his eyes before he entered the building and relinquished his pass to the NCOIC. Then he walked to his barracks. Upon entering and being recognized, the barracks guard uttered, "Welcome back, *Doctor Vet*."

Randy curiously looked at him, not comprehending his greeting. He walked back and threw his flight bag on top of his footlocker. Many of his barracks mates came up and greeted him with the title "Doctor Vet."

He looked over at Abbott, who had a smile on his face and a gleam in his eye. Abbott chimed, "Welcome back, Doctor Vet."

Randy acknowledged the greeting with a simple, "Hi ya," not realizing that he would be stuck with the "Doctor Vet" moniker for the rest of his air force career.

Decisions

As he flipped open the morning paper, Sergeant Stark reached for his cup of coffee. He exclaimed, "Jesus!" dropping the cup back into the saucer and spilling half its contents.

Maria was frying bacon and a couple of eggs for him. She looked over and saw the surprised look on her husband's face. "What now?"

Stark silently read the article, and then replied, "Randy's on the front page again. Remember that colonel that signed for him at the police station? Well, he owns a jillion dollar horse. According to a Doctor Johnson, Randy performed some complex veterinary procedure to save its foal. The doctor stated that the procedure normally requires the administration of drugs to relax the mare.

"The foal had one of its legs doubled back and the umbilical cord wrapped around its neck. It only had a few minutes to live and Randy saved it. The doctor stated that without Randy's quick action, the foal would surely have died."

Maria flipped the bacon and eggs onto Stark's plate then pulled the newspaper out of his hand and ordered, "Eat—I'll read."

She leaned back against the counter and read the article. The article began, "While Sherrill has became famous in Hollywood, her fiancé, Randy Ferris, has been making a name for himself in San Antonio." The article recapped the story of Randy saving the assaulted woman then went into the current story.

She looked up and stated, "But Randy is so young. How could he possibly know what to do? It must takes years of training to become a veterinarian?"

"I don't know," replied Stark. "But what I got from the article was that the doctor was awe-struck that anyone could do the procedure without proper training and the application of specific drugs."

Maria smiled with pride, "I've always told you that Randy is special."

"I know," agreed Stark. "I've got a thick dossier on him that confirms your opinion."

He glanced at his watch, "I've got to go. I have to be at the base before 0700." He kissed Maria, and then picked up the newspaper, "I'll call you later."

Colonel Sommers called General Thurman, "Hello, John, this is Gordon Sommers at Randolph. How's your golf game?"

"Not as good as yours," conceded the general.

"Well, John, the reason that I called you is that I had an Airman Randall Ferris as a houseguest over the weekend. He's in basic training at your base and I just want to say how impressed I am with the young man."

The general broke in—, "It's odd that you should call at this moment Gordon because I have in my office a Lieutenant Colonel Mark Hadley from Sheppard. We were just discussing, Randy.

The informal use of Airman Ferris' first name clued the colonel that the general was more than familiar with Randy. The colonel said, "Well, John, then I won't keep you on the phone, but if you ever need a character reference for Randy then let me add my two-cents worth."

"You just did," acknowledged the general. "Now, how about a foursome round of golf at the country club this Saturday?

"Sounds good, John. You bring a guest and I'll bring Charlie; we'll play for drinks afterward at the clubhouse."

"You're on," replied the general. "I'll call you with a tee-time. Say hello to Anne for me—goodbye."

The general looked at Colonel Hadley, "If Randy keeps going around impressing staff officers then we'll have to make him one of us."

"That's one of the items that I wanted to discuss with you about Airman Ferris. His DI has been keeping a special file on him. That, along with the newspaper articles that you showed me, makes a very impressive portfolio.

"I want him in my 'Special Forces' and I have planned out a career path for him."

The colonel went on to detail his plans to the general—. "In conclusion, I know that Sherrill is his fiancée and he will be tempted to pass up this career opportunity because it will require that they be apart for a long time. I can't give him a field promotion to O-1. However, as his commanding general, General Thurman—*you can.*

The general thought for a long time before answering, "What you're asking is highly irregular during peacetime and sets a precedent."

"I know," replied the colonel. "But Viet Nam is not going away. The President and the Secretary of Defense are bent on escalating the war. They have authorized the creation of a multi-force 'Special

Intelligence Group.' I am what you might call the 'Pentagon's legman' for the USAF Mission in this group.

The men in the SIG (Special Intelligence Group) are going to be called upon to covertly operate far behind enemy lines and even in countries where we're not even supposed to be.

"They will be required to gather intelligence and function autonomously under very dangerous situations. This is why we need men with Airman Ferris' qualities.

"I've already selected outstanding junior officers from all the commands in the air force. Randy has all the qualities of these officers, plus his uncanny grasp of languages."

"You've argued your case well, Colonel, and I agree with you," acknowledged the general. "When will his special training start?"

The colonel sighed, "Well, we are on a tight timeline. The rest of his group starts their 'Special Forces' training at Fort Bragg, North Carolina on Saturday. He'll have to transfer out from Lackland, fly to Fort Bragg and transfer onto that army base.

The general looked at the colonel with disbelief. He stated with exasperation, "Before you came into my office, I received a call from the Mayor of San Antonio. He wants to give Randy a "Certificate for Bravery and Meritorious Service" and a "Token Key to the City." I wanted to present these at a parade in his honor next Saturday. When you suggested a field promotion, I was planning on performing that ceremony at the parade."

The colonel hesitated for a moment then confided, "I'm afraid that the keyword here is 'covert.' Randy is going to disappear into a virtual 'black-hole' after he leaves this base. I will allow people to see his promotion, which will explain why he is moving out of his barracks before his training is completed. However, any other honors will just have to be slipped into his personnel record."

The general was fuming; he was not accustomed to a subordinate officer practically dictating his options. He looked at the colonel and asked again, even though he already knew the answer, "How far up the chain of command did you say your authority goes?

"From the 'Commander-in-Chief,' sir'" replied the colonel.

The general sighed in resignation, "Well, we'd better get the ball rolling. I'll have Airman Ferris report to you, immediately."

"He's already here outside your office, waiting. I cleared it with your adjutant to summon him, sir."

The general expounded, "I'll certainly credit you an "E" for *efficiency*, Colonel; and, I'll even throw in a "B" for *balls*."

"Thank you, sir," the colonel replied simply.

The general pressed the intercom button to his secretary, "Send Airman Ferris into my office."

Randy was sitting in a chair in the reception area across from the general's secretary. He had been marching when a runner from company HQ intercepted his flight and handed him a summons to the Base Commander's office. The summons was accompanied with a base pass.

He had turned over the flight to Casio and walked the fifteen blocks to base HQ. While waiting, he had made several trips to the water fountain and a trip to the latrine to relieve the nervous pressure in his bladder caused by the summons. After waiting for over forty-five minutes the secretary approached him, "Airman Ferris, you can see General Thurman now."

Opening the door, he recognized the colonel from Sheppard AFB that had sworn in his group of recruits. He walked to the general's desk, stood at attention, and saluted, "Airman Ferris reporting to General Thurman, as requested, sir."

The general returned his salute, "At ease, Airman Ferris. This is Lieutenant Colonel Mark Hadley from Sheppard AFB."

"Yes, sir, I recognize Colonel Hadley. He was the officer that swore in my group at the induction center."

The general rose from his chair, "Well, he wants to speak with you. I'm going to take care of some personal business and you can use my office." He added, "Feel free to use my phone for long distance calls. Just dial '0' for the base operator and have them place your call. I'll be back within the hour."

The general left and the colonel stood up and shook Randy's hand. "I've heard a lot about you Randy, and I want you to know that it's a pleasure to finally meet you."

The colonel sat back down and motioned to a second chair in front of the general's desk, "Please be seated."

Randy squared his chair to face the colonel and sat down. He noted that the colonel was being extremely informal.

The colonel began to explain, "Ever since you left the induction center, we have been keeping a special file on you to monitor your progress. I must say that the file has been very complimentary. There have been several surprises, even though we started with high expectations.

"Just a couple of those surprises were your breaking the obstacle course record and winning a seemingly impossible basketball game that was rigged against your team. I am well informed regarding your background. I was thoroughly moved, from laughter to empathy, by your speech at your award ceremony.

"Now, as to why I'm here. I am presently in charge of forming a 'Special Forces' group. We are looking for gifted individuals that demonstrate these characteristic traits: intelligence, leadership, innovation, marksmanship, honesty, integrity, and someone, who is a 'Team Player.'

"I feel after reviewing your record that you are such an individual. Therefore, I am prepared to make you a career advancement offer. However, I must first add that it is not an offer void of danger, isolation, and personal sacrifice.

"The offer is: 'If you agree to complete the following training - Special Forces, language, crypto-radio, and survival then we will give you a brevet promotion to second lieutenant, with pay—today.'

"Upon successful completion of the training, you will be sent to Officers Training School, instead of Officers Candidate School and will become fully commissioned as a second lieutenant in the United States Air Force."

Randy had sat listening attentively to each word, but his mind had been racing in-between words. He now understood why he had been selected as barracks chief when he got off the bus. He understood the significance of Sergeant Stark's special report and all the extra testing at the Green Monster.

He *now* understood Sergeant Stark's advice for him to do his best at marksmanship and anything else he was called upon to do, to give the air force planners the opportunity to place him where his talents would best serve the air force mission.

This colonel in front of him had offered him a commission, which Randy had previously thought would be unattainable for a long time. Nevertheless, the offer had not been made without strings attached. He had even implied danger, isolation, and sacrifice by couching the term "not void of."

Randy answered almost immediately after the colonel completed his long statement. He stated, "I know that the term 'brevet' means temporary or conditional. In what context are you using the word?"

The colonel was further impressed. Randy had apparently quickly understood his lengthy offer. He had **not** asked, "What if I fail or what if I quit." But, instead he had simply asked for clarification of the little used term, 'brevet'—he even knew the definition."

The colonel replied, "It means that if you don't complete your contract then you will lose your officer rank and will be required to fulfill the rest of your military obligation as an enlisted airman."

Randy acknowledged, "It is a very good offer, considering that I am just beginning my military career. However, I must try to contact my fiancée Sherrill. This affects her life too. How much time do I have to decide?"

The colonel looked at his watch, "You have thirty minutes—training starts Saturday. If you speak with anyone, you can mention your promotion and that you are getting special training. Don't get any more specific. He stood up and placed his hand on Randy's shoulder, "I want you on my team, Son." Then he turned and walked out the door.

Randy didn't move for a minute. It was the moment of decision. He had already seen the advantage of taking the offer from a career standpoint, but to make the final decision without trying to contact Sherrill would violate the trust between them.

He moved around the desk and sat in the general's chair. The world took on a different perspective from here than on the other side of the desk. He picked up the phone and dialed '0' for the base operator.

The base operator noting that it was the general's private line asked, "Where may I place your call, sir."

Randy tried to make his voice deeper, "I want to speak with the receptionist at "The Dons of Eldorado" studio in Hollywood. The operator forwarded the call to another air base, which confirmed the number and placed the call.

Randy heard on the line, "The Dons of Eldorado, where may I direct your call?"

Randy began, "Hello, this is Sherrill Lindstrom's fiancé, Randy Ferris. It is very important that I speak with her."

The receptionist responded, "I'm sorry, sir, but Sherrill is unavailable for calls."

Randy felt desperate, "Please, this is an emergency; I must speak with her."

The receptionist responded in the same tone, "I'm sorry, sir, but Sherrill is unavailable for calls."

Randy implored, "If you can't put my call through, would you please tell me where she is staying."

The receptionist replied, "I'm sorry, sir, but we do not release that information." Then she hung up.

Frustrated, Randy slammed the handset down in the receiver. He picked up the phone again and dialed the operator.

The base operator asked, "Where may I place your call, sir?"

"I want to call Frank Ferris at Taylor 6-9639."

His mother answered and Randy said, "Hi, Mom, this is Randy. I want to talk with you, but is Dad there?"

Sylvia said excitedly, "He just walked out the door to get into the truck. Just a minute, I'll be right back."

He heard in the background his mother calling after his father. She came back on the line, "I caught him just in time; he'll be here in a minute. Oh, Randy, how have you been? We really miss you here, Honey."

"I miss you too, Mom. It seems like I've been gone a year, instead of a month. So much has happened and I need Dad's advice. How's everybody else?

"Oh, Randy, your voice sounds so good. Everybody else is fine. We saw your basketball game on television and we were so proud of you. People around here are still talking about your speech. Your dad's here now. I love you, Honey—bye."

"Bye, Mom—I love you." Randy had a lump in his throat when his father came on the line."

"Hello, Son. How've you been?"

"Fine, Dad" responded Randy. "I haven't been able to contact Sherrill. Do you know of any way that I can reach her?"

"Well, we know that she is in Hollywood; her parents are out there visiting her, but we don't have a number. Have you tried the studio?"

"Yes, I just got the runaround from them." Randy remembered the time limit on their line. "Listen, Dad, the air force has offered to promote me to a second lieutenant and send me to some special training, but I won't be able to see Sherrill for a long time. What do you think that I should do?"

His father advised, "Well, Son, you are the head of your family now. I can't tell you what to do. You'll just have to do what's best for you. In the long run that is usually what's best for your family."

Randy heard a click and the line went to half volume. He hollered into the phone. "Thanks, Dad, I love you—bye." He hung up the phone and sat there, feeling numb. Hearing his mother and father's voices made him feel very homesick. At the moment, he just wanted to go back home and be back in high school with all his friends.

Then he remembered the reason that he was sitting here—to prepare a life for Sherrill and the baby. He could do it as an airman and probably be with Sherrill in a couple of months or he could do it as an officer and be with Sherrill in a year.

As an airman, he had no idea of the technical training that he might receive. As an officer, he had been promised language training. In addition, an officer's pay would allow him to provide some of life's amenities that he would be hard pressed to provide on an airman's pay. As an officer, he might be able to eventually fly jets. As an airman his only option would be flying as a passenger.

He remembered Suzy's statement, when she had been waved through the gate onto the base—"VIP—you know." It was obvious that officers were afforded many privileges and perks that were not available to an enlisted person.

He was looking at an additional ten months separation from Sherrill to attain a lifetime of living at a higher social and economic level with her. The decision was obvious—he would take the colonel's offer. With the decision out of the way, Randy felt a huge weight lift from his shoulders. He picked up the phone and dialed the operator.

The base operator asked, "Where may I place your call, sir."

"Casson's Realty in Merced California." Randy heard several interchanges, and then finally a ring.

"Casson's Realty; Betty speaking."

Randy was elated that he finally had gotten through to a person in California, "Hello, Betty, this is Sherrill's fiancé, Randy Ferris. I'm calling from Lackland AFB. May I speak with Sherrill's Uncle Hank?

He waited on the line for a couple of minutes, and then finally heard, "Hello, Randy, this is Hank Casson. I'm sorry, but I was on another line with a client. Business has been crazy since Sherrill became a television star. We haven't met, but after listening to Sherrill, I feel that I know you. How have you been?"

Randy wondered if everyone in California talked that much and that fast in one breath when they said hello. "Please tell Sherrill that I have written to her and have tried to call her, but I haven't heard from her except for television and newspapers.

"Tell her that the air force is promoting me to a second lieutenant and is sending me to special training. I won't be able to contact her for a long time, but I think of her constantly."

Hank paused before he answered. He had been an officer in the air force and had never heard of anyone becoming an officer after four weeks of basic training. He tried to think of something that only Randy would know. Then he remembered Sherrill telling Vicki the date that she had conceived.

He cautiously asked, "Randy, I apologize for asking you this, but we get so many kooky calls. What date did Sherrill get pregnant?"

Randy was taken back by the question, but he promptly replied, "July 4th."

Hank replied, "Okay, Randy, I know that it is really you on the other end of the line. How is it that the air force is making you an officer, so quickly?"

"Uncle Hank, I can't say anything more, except that it was a package deal. I wanted to discuss it with Sherrill, but what I told you is all that I would be allowed to tell her."

This set off danger alarms for Hank, but he didn't let Randy know. Randy had obviously thought out the situation and had made his own decision.

"Randy, good luck in your career decisions. I'm sure that everything will eventually work out okay, for the three of you.

"Oh, before I forget it, the reason that Sherrill hasn't responded to your letter is that she gets tons of fan mail and your letters must have been lost in them along with our utility bills. The studio is sorting through them, but even *they* are having trouble trying to keep up with the volume—."

Randy broke in, "How is Sherrill and the baby?"

"Oh, they are doing just fine. Her Aunt Vicki is with her and Sherrill's parents came down to take Sherrill back home—she and her father have made up.

"Sherrill wants to stay in California. She told her parents that her contract requires her being here and that home just wouldn't be the same without you. She is financially independent for now. She invested most of the money for the baby's education.

Randy said, "I want you and Aunt Vicki to know how much I appreciate your being there for Sherrill and the baby. Tell her that I love her very much—and one day, we will be together as a family."

"I will tell her, Randy. Good luck and we hope to meet you someday."

They said their good-byes and both men paused and reviewed their conversation. Both thought, *I want to meet that man; he sounds interesting.*

The general's secretary looked up at the colonel, "The telephone light on the general's line has been off for awhile, so I think that Airman Ferris is through using the phone. The colonel opened the door and walked into the room. Randy was reviewing all that had happened this morning. Seeing the colonel, he jumped up.

"Sitting in the general's chair feels pretty good, doesn't it?"

"Yes, sir, the world looks different from this side of the desk."

"That's because it is a different world. However, it's a world not without its own cross to bear. With the privilege of power comes the obligation of responsibility. The general's decisions affect thousands of other people and a wrong decision can have a devastating effect on the masses. A right decision is just considered as part of his job. Remember that—as you go through life."

"Yes, sir," replied Randy.

The colonel asked, "Have you made your decision?"

"Yes sir. I did have a conversation with my father." He said, "As head of a family, make the decision that is best for you. That decision will usually be best for your family in the long run.'"

"Your father sounds like a wise man," observed the colonel.

"He is, sir. He has taught me the value of *honor and integrity*. He says that *those qualities are the foundation of all that you can be and all that you will become.*"

The colonel raised his eyebrow and thought on the statement. He saw in Randy a living example of those words. He committed the words to memory and planned use them to motivate men in the future to excel to their own personal potential.

The colonel surmised, "Judging from that statement, I assume that you have decided to accept my offer."

"Yes sir. I step up to the challenge. I will not disappoint your expectations or those of my own."

The colonel reached across the desk and shook Randy's hand, saying with probity, "Welcome to the 'Special Intelligence Group,' Lieutenant Ferris."

"Thank you, sir. I'm sure that you will brief me on the training requirements and provide documents for travel. However, I'm uncertain on one subject. I know the protocol for enlisted personnel, but I don't know the protocol for being an officer."

The colonel replied, "The base library has all the books on rules and regulations. You have two days to transfer out, one day of travel and two days to transfer in at Fort Bragg. I would suggest that you make good use of your free time to study up.

"There is an Officers Training Manual that you would normally learn by heart before you get your commission. However, seeing that we've done things in reverse order, I suggest that you get a copy.

"It's going on lunchtime. I'll take you to the Officers Club and we'll discuss your training there. The Club will give you a feel of how officers interact with each other."

Randy had just walked around the desk when the general entered, followed by his adjutant, Colonel Cox. Colonel Hadley stood at attention and Randy followed his lead. The general said, "At ease." He had noticed the smiles when he entered; those smiles had disappeared when the men popped to attention.

The general observed, "Judging from your smiles, I assume that you two came to a positive decision."

"Yes, sir," responded the two men.

"I've asked Colonel Cox to witness Randy's commission ceremony."

He began: "By the power invested in me by the Congress and President of the United States, I hereby commission Airman Randall T. Ferris to the rank of Second Lieutenant, brevet—."

The general administered the "Oath of Allegiance" and extended his hand, "Congratulations, Second Lieutenant Ferris, I'm sure that you will serve your country well."

The general turned to the adjutant and was handed a pair of gold bars. These he placed on the collar of Randy's fatigue uniform. "I bought you a set of insignias and emblems for your fatigue cap and your class "A" uniform. You will have to go to the BX *Base Exchange* for additional items."

The general stepped back and smiled. This had been only his third field promotion ceremony during his career. He felt confident that this young man's potential merited it. "Well, Lieutenant, is there anything else that I can do for you?"

"Yes, sir. Colonel Hadley and I are going to lunch, but after that, I would like to say goodbye to my friends in the barracks. They are probably out marching and won't be back in the barracks until after I have moved out."

"That won't be a problem, Lieutenant. You are temporarily assigned to my staff until you transfer out. I'll contact your company HQ and tell them that one of the officers on my staff will be down at 1300 hours to conduct an inspection of the barracks' personnel. I will clue them in, 'not to have anyone else from company HQ there.'"

The general paused, "Oh, I have one other item for you." The adjutant handed Randy a copy of the "Officers Training Manual."

Randy flipped open the cover and found that the general had personally autographed it. "Thank you, sir; I will always remember this day as a major turning point in my life."

Colonel Hadley said, "By your leave, sir." He and Randy saluted the general, and then left the room.

The general turned to his adjutant and said, "Well, Paul, we may not have made history here today, but I feel that we may have tweaked the future—just a little."

The general's secretary stopped Randy, "Lieutenant Ferris, I'll have a packet of information for you after you return from lunch."

She handed him a temporary ID card, "Lieutenant Marla Ledderman will be your contact until you leave the base. Coordinate any questions or plans through her. The general's driver will be at your disposal until you get moved into the BOQ (Bachelor Officers' Quarters). The general said to tell you that you are free to do whatever you choose until 0700 hours tomorrow, when you start out-processing."

Randy placed the ID into his wallet. Having noticed her nameplate earlier, he said, "Thank you, Mrs. Feingold. I'll see you after lunch."

Randy and Colonel Hadley rode in the general's car to the Officers Club. They both ordered a Cobb salad and a soda.

Randy noticed immediately the relaxed atmosphere. People in uniform were actually enjoying themselves. Their mannerisms were animated and loud laughter pealed from a small group of staff officers.

Off duty Officers were in the lounge having cocktails and solving all the current world problems through lively conversations. The club had civilian waitresses that looked more like models recruited for their epicurean sensuousness than employees of the culinary profession.

302

Colonel Hadley pressed, "I like to know my men and those who are dear to them. Tell me a little about Sherrill."

Randy began, "Well, there has been a lot of information printed in the newspaper. I finally got to read about her at Colonel Sommers' home this last weekend. The newspapers only report the physical facts as they see them.

"Sherrill is a much more complex person than any media could ever record—." Randy spent the next thirty minutes discussing his perception of Sherrill.

Having listened to Randy's usage of the English language, the colonel understood why Randy had scored so high in languages—it was a gift.

When Randy finished, Colonel Hadley noted, "It looks like you two are a match made in heaven."

"We thought so too, but some of the events suggested that there may have been other forces at work."

The Colonel laughed, "Yes, I read about your fight with her father. Have they made up yet?"

"Yes, I spoke with her uncle today and he said that her parents were visiting her in Hollywood, where she is shooting her first full-length episode for television. He said that Sherrill and her father had reconciled their differences."

"Oh, then you didn't talk with Sherrill," confirmed the colonel. He didn't tell Randy that his language school would be located in California because he wanted Randy to focus on his training at Fort Bragg.

Randy replied, "No. I got in touch with the studio, but they gave me the proverbial runaround. They said that she was unavailable for calls."

"I'm sure that they were just trying to protect her privacy," the colonel sympathized. "She is after all, a very high profile television celebrity."

The colonel changed subjects, "What's your opinion of Staff Sergeant Stark?"

Randy thought, then stated, "Sergeant Stark is a professional airman, but something of a paradox. As a DI, he is focused and sometimes seems to be very hard.

"When I first met him at two o'clock in the morning, I thought that he had a sadistic personality, but as I got to know him, I saw that he was just trying to train us in the shortest possible time.

"He and I have formed a mutual trust and admiration for each other. He even drove out to the base and brought me into his home to watch Sherrill's press conference. I met his wife Maria, and love her like a sister. The short of it is—I have the highest regard for Sergeant Stark."

The colonel looked at his watch, "You've got a walk-through inspection at 1300 hours...we'd best be leaving."

During the ride back to headquarters, Colonel Hadley qualified with a gleam in his eye, "You said that you and Sergeant Stark have a solid relationship, right?"

"Yes—why?" asked Randy, since this had already been established.

"Well, he is going to wonder why you got a field commission and why you are making a barracks inspection. You could pretend that you are an undercover plant from the IG's (Inspector General's) office."

Randy replied, "Brrr, that sounds pretty cold blooded."

The colonel chuckled, "I know. During the Korean War, identical twin brothers were assigned to the same base; one of them was an officer. The enlisted man's Sergeant tried to throw the officer in the brig for impersonating an officer. Don't you see, Randy, you could be your own twin."

Randy laughed in agreement, "I like your idea. I owe him at least one mild heart attack for the first day of basic. I just hope that I can pull it off."

Sergeant Stark paced the floor in his quarters. He kept looking at his watch—ten minutes until inspection. He kept wondering: "Where is Randy? Why had a runner from HQ picked up his file? Why had Randy been summoned from the flight to the Base General's Office? Why wouldn't anyone tell him why Randy's name wasn't on the training list?" The "whys" kept piling up and repeating themselves in his head, as he restlessly paced the floor.

The colonel and Randy arrived at headquarters. Randy retrieved his packet from the general's secretary. Colonel Hadley shook Randy's hand and said, "I'm flying to Fort Bragg this afternoon. I'll see you there on Saturday."

Randy replied, "Thank you, sir; I'll be there."

Randy found Lieutenant Marla Ledderman and identified himself. She explained that everything he needed for the moment was in the packet, including her extension phone number. He left headquarters and rode to his barracks.

Randy opened the door to his barracks. The barracks guard recognized him, and then saw the gold bars on his collar. He popped to attention and shouted, "'Atten shup.' Officer in the barracks."

Sergeant Stark came out of his quarters and glanced at Randy before coming to attention. He stood at attention with his mouth agape and his eyes wide and unblinking. He wanted to cough because he felt that he had actually started to swallow his tongue.

Randy walked up to Stark and asked, "Is your barracks ready for inspection, Sergeant?"

Stark was a seasoned NCO, but the shock had been total. He stammered as he replied, "Ye-Yu-Yes, sir. The barracks is-is ready for inspection, sir."

Randy leaned up close to Stark and whispered just loud enough for him to hear, "Before we perform the inspection, Sergeant Stark, I want to inform you that for the last month your barracks has been under scrutiny by the IG's office for corruption and abusive use of power. Now get your clipboard and let us proceed."

Stark's knees were actually knocking together as he retrieved his clipboard with the inspection checklist.

Randy walked through the latrine and found it spotless. He accused, "Your latrine is too clean, Sergeant. You must drive your men mercilessly."

Stark, by now almost in a state of apoplexy, replied, "No, sir. You, yourself, had the area chiefs set up the latrine schedule."

Randy ordered, "Put it in the comments section—'Latrine Too Clean.'"

He walked out to his own area and opened his lockers. It was neat and clean. He unbuttoned a pocket on his Class "A" uniform and retrieved the book of matches with Suzette's phone number.

He stated, "Unauthorized item in clothes locker—one demerit. Pocket unbuttoned—another demerit."

He by-passed Abbott, who had a stone look on his face, but his eyelids fluttered, as if he were trying to clear his vision.

Randy knew his men's strengths and weaknesses. He headed to the bunks of the men most inclined to be sloppy. He dropped, not bounced, a quarter on one of the bunks. He had to pick up the quarter. "Improperly made bunk—one demerit. Shoe heel scuffed—another demerit. Magazine hidden under shorts in the locker—one more demerit."

Stark's mind had finally started to partially function and he rationalized incorrectly, "**Now that explains it!** When Randy had first gotten off the bus, his eyes had followed me, not because he was a civilian, but because he was an undercover IG officer.

"No wonder he had been selected as barracks chief by someone else. No wonder he picked up on marching so quickly; he already knew how. No wonder he was so good with a carbine; no wonder he could speak so well; no wonder he knew a Colonel Sommers and didn't have to return to the base when he was in San Antonio." In his mind, the *no wonder* list grew longer and longer.

Randy brought him back from his thoughts by asking, "Did you record that last demerit, Sergeant?"

Stark replied honestly, "No, sir. I was lost in thought, sir."

Randy said, with a deadpan tone and expression, "DI lost in thought—two demerits."

They walked back up the other side of the barracks, recording demerits. Randy stopped inspecting at Casio's bunk and took the clipboard out of Stark's hand. He counted the demerits and stated, "Sixteen demerits, Sergeant. I've seen first week barracks with a better score."

Stark's eyes turned cold and he replied, flatly, "No excuses, sir."

Nevertheless, his mind still struggled with his eyes and ears. He thought, *I am a good judge of character. Randy has been in my home, eaten my food, and had tears in his eyes when he watched Sherrill on television. Maria loves him like a brother. Randy has the respect and admiration of all the men in the barracks, including my own. How could I have been so wrong about this man?*"

Randy sensed that the ruse had gone far enough. The men were fidgeting and formulating opinions in their own minds. He peeled off the inspection form and threw the clipboard onto Casio's bunk. He unceremoniously tore up the inspection form and tossed the pieces into the air.

Stepping forward, he lifted Stark off his feet, and swung him around in a wide circle before setting him back down. Grinning broadly, he yelled, "Got-cha!"

Stark was stunned. He staggered backward and plopped down on the sharp edge of the clipboard.

Pointing to the bars on his collar, Randy exclaimed, "I just got a field commission to second lieutenant!"

The whole barracks was in shock. For the last month they had been so regimented that reality was hard to comprehend.

Finally, Abbott rushed forward and shook Randy's hand and hugged him, saying, "Congratulations! I knew that you had the *right stuff.*"

Then the whole barracks rushed forward to congratulate Randy. They finally backed away and opened an area to their DI, anticipating—something—?

Stark stared with glazed eyes and muttered, "Lieutenant Ferris—you owe me for ten years of my life," then he added—"Sir." The men burst out laughing.

Randy reached his hand out and helped Stark to his feet. He turned and said, "Casio, take the men outside and give them a fifteen minute smoke break, while I talk to Sergeant Stark."

The men closed their lockers and filed outside. Many stooped down and picked up a piece of the inspection form as a memento of Randy's farewell. They would tell this story to their buddies on other bases for years to come.

Stark and Randy went into Stark's quarters. Abbott, instead of going directly outside, went to Randy's open lockers. He pulled out Randy's duffel bag and carefully packed all his belongings, and then went outside.

Grinning, Randy apologized, "Sorry about the ruse, but Colonel Hadley thought it might be funny."

Stark replied, "Yeah, funny as a heart attack—you almost gave me one, ya know."

Randy laughed, "You did look shocked."

"Shocked!" exclaimed Stark. "A bolt of lightning wouldn't have fried me more. By the way, who is this Colonel Hadley?"

"I can't tell you who he is, but he is the one who has been receiving your reports on me. He only suggested the ruse when he learned that you and I have a mutual admiration for each other."

Stark was moved by Randy's words, "You really do consider me as a special friend, even though I am—was—your DI?

"You were more than just a DI to me. You and Maria are my friends, who brought me into your home and made me feel welcome and a part of a happy loving family.

"Your instructions and drilling have been hard, but fair. I realized that you had to resort, at times, to intimidation instead of motivation. That's because you only had us for a short time; to teach us what we needed to know for our next phase of training.

"I also know that you must have turned in excellent reports on me—else I wouldn't be wearing second lieutenant bars right now."

Stark's face flashed many convoluted expressions, and then with a duped expression, he stated, "When you and Sherrill get married, consider yourselves as a *family of actors*. You had me totally and undeniably convinced that you were an undercover plant from the IG's office."

"I know," laughed Randy. "I'd give a month's pay for a movie of the looks on your face during the inspection."

Stark turned serious, "Okay, explain to me how you got a field commission. We are in peacetime and what has just happened to you is something that I've never heard of before—especially for someone so young."

"I wish that I could tell you. All that I can say is that I'm being assigned to a special training program. The commission was part of the package."

Stark shook his head, still not comprehending the reality that an Airman Basic, during basic training, could get a field commission. He stated, "I thought that I had seen it all during my six years in the air force. Now you come along and totally blow my mind."

Randy looked at his watch, "I've got to pack my clothes, and you, Sir, have a barracks to train."

He opened the door and saw out of the corner of his eye the barracks guard motioning to someone through the glass in the door. He walked over to his bunk and was surprised to see that his duffel bag was already packed. —*Abbott*, he thought.

He picked up the bag, and then noticed the clipboard on Casio's bed. He dropped the bag and retrieved the clipboard. He wrote on the form and handed it to Stark, "Here, this will get you started on winning 'Barracks of the week' for your fourth week in a row."

Stark looked at the form and saw that there were no demerits. Written in the comments section was: "Top Notch Barracks," 2nd Lt. Randall T. Ferris — General Thurman's staff."

Stark looked up and sincerely stated, "Thank you, Randy. You really didn't have to do that—so thank you very much."

Randy picked up his duffel bag and they walked out the door. The flight was in formation, but at ease. Casio ordered, "Flight — ten shut!" The flight smartly popped to attention. Then Casio yelled, "Three cheers for Lieutenant Ferris."

Randy heard each man's voice cheer at the top of his lungs, "Hip-Hip-Hurrah, Hip-Hip-Hurrah, Hip-Hip-Hurrah."

Casio ordered, "At ease."

Randy waved and the entire flight waved back. He got into the general's car and instructed the driver, "BOQ, please." Thus, closing another chapter in his life.

Parting Is Such Sweet Sorrow

Randy thanked the general's driver and entered the BOQ. He identified himself, showing his out-processing papers and billet authorization from the packet.

The airman first-class looked at his list of available units. "It looks like all the quarters for junior grade officers have been filled."

Randy asked, "What does that mean?"

"Well, sir, seeing that you are only going to be on base for two nights, I'm going to have to put you up in field-grade officers' quarters."

Randy smiled as he received the key and responded to the intended irony of the statement, saying, "Thank you, Airman. I guess that I'll have to suffer through it, seeing that it's only for two nights."

Randy opened the door to his new quarters and saw that it was a suite of rooms. He entered and discovered that he had two television sets, one in the living room and one in the bedroom; three phones, one was in the bathroom; and a kitchen, with laundry facilities.

He opened the curtains, cynically half-expecting a helicopter pad, and to his surprise, there was one. He unpacked his clothes and placed them in the closet and dresser.

He sat at the desk and reviewed the contents of the information packet. It contained a meal pass to the Officers' Mess, a facilities map of the base, an itinerary for out-processing, a copy of his commission, a copy of his temporary assignment to the general's staff, and a copy of the orders transferring him to Fort Bragg, North Carolina. The last two items were *checks* for an initial uniform allowance and a travel allowance. Randy sighed, "Thank goodness," for he was down to his last ten dollars.

He opened the "Officer Training Manual" and quickly thumbed through it, noting the insignia and clothing required. He turned to the military protocol section and read the chapter.

Leaving the BOQ, he cashed his checks at the on-base bank and walked to the BX. There he purchased an attaché case and a medium-sized travel trunk, several sets of insignia, nametags, second lieutenant bars, and an officer's dress uniform, plus some snacks, a six-pack of Pepsi, and a travel alarm clock.

He called a taxi and returned with his items to his quarters. The quietness in the room was unnatural, so he switched on both televisions to the same channel and reclined in a Lazy-Boy chair to leisurely watch a soap opera for the first time in his life.

While watching the program, the thought occurred, "Why don't they have soap operas about the military—the plots and action would certainly be a lot better?"

He picked up the phone and read the instructions on a sticker for dialing off base. He dialed the Sommers' residence and Anne answered, "Hello, this is Anne Sommers."

"Hello, Mrs. Sommers, this is Randy. Is Suzy back from classes yet?"

"I expect her in about thirty-minutes," replied Anne.

"Well, would you tell her that I would like to buy her dinner at the Officers Club? Tell her that I'll meet her in the club lounge at 1800 hours. My base extension number is 8086, but don't give it to her, unless she can't make it."

"I'll tell her, Randy," replied Anne. "Goodbye."

"Thank you, Mrs. Sommers—goodbye." Randy hung up and felt a warm flush in his chest with the anticipation of seeing Suzy again. So much had happened to him that he just had to share it with someone...she would be surprised!

Suzy bounded through the door and excitedly informed her mother, "I changed my major to journalism at college today. My drama class friends just couldn't believe that I had switched.

"They even melodramatically got down on one knee and begged me to reconsider. When I told them that they needed to have someone write about them, they got up off their knee and agreed, 'Hey, yeah, you're right.'"

Her mother laughed with her at their fickleness, and then changed the subject, "Guess who called for you today?"

Suzy thought for a moment, "I don't have a clue—Who?"

Her mother answered with a gleam in her eye, "Randy requested your presence to dine with him at the Officers Club at 1800 hours."

Suzy got a quizzical look on her face, "How is that possible? Are you sure that he actually said 'Officers Club?'"

"Those were his words," assured her mother.

"But—but?" questioned Suzy.

Anne interjected, "I know it sounds crazy. But knowing Randy, I'm sure that he has a good logical explanation."

Suzy entered the Officers Club lounge, half-expecting not to find Randy. She caught his eye and stopped cold. He was wearing an officer's dress uniform with second lieutenant bars on his epaulets."

Randy, seeing the stunned look on her face, got up and escorted her to his table.

Suzy sat, staring for a full minute, "I just don't understand—."

Randy smiled, toying with her, "I found my airplane, so—they let me start all over again."

Suzy, remembering his quipped statement at the USO Club, admonished, "There never was an airplane. Now, tell me what really did happen."

Randy ordered her a Coke and spent the next twenty minutes explaining all that had happened to him, even the barracks inspection ruse.

Suzy laughed, "I bet that your DI was ready to strangle you."

Randy grinned and mused, "I'm sure that he wanted to, but he was too close to fainting."

They both laughed, Suzy picturing in her mind the shaken Sergeant Stark's quandary.

The hostess approached them, "Lieutenant Ferris, your table is ready."

Randy pulled out Suzy's chair and seated her. He took his seat and the waitress was immediately there. "May I serve you a glass of wine?"

"No, thank you," Randy deferred. "We are ready to order."

The waitress smiled, "I can take your order now; what would you like?"

"We would like two shrimp cocktails; for the entrée, 'Steak Diane, flambé;' a dinner salad with creamy Italian dressing on the side; and baked Alaska for dessert."

Holding up two fingers, he added, "Oh, and two Cokes."

"Thank you, sir. I'll be right back with your appetizers and drinks."

Suzy's big eyes stared at Randy with wonderment. He looked back at her with a twinkle in his eyes and a knowing smile. He had neglected to tell her that he had asked the hostess for suggestions, for a special farewell dinner for a special girl. He already knew, from the barbecue at her home that she liked creamy Italian dressing on the side.

Seeing that the couple had finished their appetizer and salad, the waitress rolled up a portable propane grill. She lit the burners and made preliminary preparations. Then she turned to Suzy, "How would you like your steak prepared, Miss?

"Medium rare, please." The waitress seared both sides of the steak, and then doused it with cooking sherry. She swished the sherry around to evenly distribute the liquid, and then tilted the pan to ignite the sherry. Four minutes later, she served the steak still in the sizzling metal dish with sautéed mushrooms, petite new potatoes, and snow peas.

The waitress looked at Randy, "And you, sir?"

"Exactly the same way." He looked at Suzy waiting for him, "Go ahead and start. I've been conditioned to eat fast."

Suzy sampled each item and said with obvious pleasure, "Perfect!"

Five minutes later, Randy agreed with her. They dined in animated conversation and soon the main course was finished.

The waitress served the flaming dessert. Randy and Suzy had a lull in their conversation and couldn't help overhearing the two captains at the next table.

One of the captains was relating the story of a first lieutenant inspecting one of the basic training barracks. The story had already metamorphosed into Randy being a first lieutenant and having a twin brother who was away from the barracks during the inspection.

Randy was humorously amazed that the story was already in circulation. When the captain finished the story, he and his companion laughed. Randy and Suzy laughed for a different reason.

The captain turned to them and said, "Great story, wasn't it?"

Randy grinned, "Yes, that was a hilarious story." Then both he and Suzy laughed again. The two officers laughed with them, and then continued their table conversation.

Randy and Suzy looked at each other and had to stifle another round of laughter. Randy leaned closer and whispered, "Now I see why they say, 'don't listen to scuttlebutt.'"

Randy looked at Suzy, "Did you enjoy your meal?"

Suzy smiled, "You know I did; it was excellent. How did you know exactly what to order?"

He replied casually, "Girls have moments of intuition. Guys have moments of *inspiration*—or should that be *aspiration*?"

With one eyebrow raised, Suzy smiled, "My *intuition* tells me that guys should be honest and call it what it actually is—a lot of **BS**."

Frowning, Randy feigned being slighted, and then relinquished with a smile, "Your intuition is probably right."

They laughed together and he asked, "Do you have to be home early?"

"No, so which movie do you want me to see?"

It was Randy's turn to raise his eyebrow and wonder. "When I was riding in the general's car to the BOQ, I noticed that 'Tom Jones,' starring Albert Finney is playing at one of the base theaters.

"It is a ribald comedy depicting life during eighteenth century England. Bob Dawson and I saw it in Wichita Falls, but it is funny enough to go see a second time."

Suzy replied, "Well, if it's worth seeing twice then it's worth seeing once—let's go."

Randy drove Suzy's car to the theater and bought tickets. Suzy remarked, "You have good timing, we'll only have to wait ten minutes."

As she watched the scenes in the movie, she kept glancing at Randy out of the corner of her eye—longing to be alone with him. She could tell when a funny scene was going to happen because Randy's facial expression changed in anticipation of the scene.

They walked out of the theater feeling entertained and giggled as they discussed some of the more ribald scenes. Randy remarked, "I'll have to admit that I enjoyed the movie with you much more than I enjoyed it with Bob." Suzy looped her arm through his and they walked to the car.

Arriving at the BOQ, Randy turned and kissed her on both cheeks, saying, "I want to tell you how much I enjoyed having you as a friend to share my first night as an officer. I'd invite you in, but—."

Suzy opened the car door, "No buts. You are an officer now and you can have guests in your quarters. I want to see how a bachelor officer lives."

Randy followed her, thinking, *that's not what I meant.*

He opened the door and Suzy walked through inspecting the quarters. She quipped, "Not bad for a 2nd Louie."

Randy corrected her, "They didn't have regular BOQs available, so they gave me a field officer's quarters."

Suzy opined, "Sure beats sleeping with sixty snoring guys, doesn't it?"

Randy replied, "You do make a valid point."

He turned on the television in the living room and Suzy asked with a devilish twinkle in her eyes, "What's wrong with the TV in the bedroom?"

Randy handed her a glass of ice and a Pepsi, and cautioned, "Let's not even go there..."

Suzy took a sip of her drink, "—I agree. But, would you sit on the carpet and lean back against sofa; then I could sit between your legs and lean back against you, like we did after the barbeque?"

Randy hesitated, thinking, "I think that I trust her, but I'm not sure that I trust myself."

Her pleading eyes, filled with an innocent demure, convinced him that the arrangement was not a compromise. In addition, he felt the need for her closeness, since he had no one else to share his anticipation and apprehension of venturing into the great unknown of Ranger training in North Carolina.

"I'll be back in a moment." Entering the bedroom, he took off his uniform and put on a pair of fatigue pants and an air force tee shirt. Barefooted, he returned to the living room and slid down beside her legs as he leaned back against the sofa.

Suzy glanced at him, rose from the sofa, "I feel overdressed," and then disappeared into the bedroom. She returned five minutes later clad in a robe that she had found in the closet. "These officer's quarters have nice amenities," she remarked, as she settled between his legs and faced the television.

Randy felt the instant heat of her body through the thin satin material and he shifted his position on the floor to allow room for her firm rounded hips. He brought up his knees to support her and to provide a place for her to rest her arms. She leaned her head back against his cheek and his senses were filled with the faint scent of her perfume mingling with the alluring female scent of her body. He breathed deeply several times, hoping that the additional air would clear the heady feeling of her closeness, but he felt himself becoming intoxicated.

He wrapped his arms around her and squeezed. The tips of his fingers came in contact with the softness of her breast as the edge of the robe slipped away. He gazed down past her cheek and saw the roundness of her exposed breast and he saw her nipple extend as she gasped, "Oh, Randy."

Rolling in his arms, the other breast became exposed as she reached up and pulled his head to her. Their lips met softly, brushed across each other, and then came together with an ageless hunger driven by sensation and sensual stimulation. Their breathing increased into short gasps, as they were lost in the intensity of arousal.

Randy slid sideways against the sofa as he laid on the carpet with his arm providing a pillow for Suzy. She reclined on the carpet and the robe slipped away exposing her full nudity. Randy's vision blurred with passion as he wrapped his arm around her waist and pulled her against him. She lifted her knee and rested it against his thigh. The back of his fingers stroked down across her abs and the side of his hand found the pubic vee between her thighs. Her hair had a thick soft cashmere feel as his finger stroked between the hot puffy wet lips of her femininity. He felt her hips move into the pressure of his hand as she moaned with rising desire and kissed him passionately.

Suzy touched the bulge in his fatigues. She popped open the top button and worked her hand down inside the front of his fatigues where she grasped the fullness of his manhood. Randy moaned and buried his face into her hair. He moaned as he whispered, "Sherrill—Sherrill, oh, Baby, I want you."

Suzy stiffened; retracting her grip from inside his fatigues, she pulled the edge of the robe across her body. Randy sensed her stiffness and pulled away. His vision focused and he drew back, "Oh, Suzy, I'm sorry; I'm so sorry. He sat upright and Suzy sat up, pulling the robe tighter around her.

She leaned her forehead against her knees and began crying. She sobbed, "Oh, Randy, I feel so shamed. I've never been with a man, but here with you…I was willing to give you my all. I wanted to feel you inside me like Sherrill felt you. I love you so much and I was willing to do anything to show you my love. I knew that you loved Sherrill, but I hoped that you could love me too." Her shoulders shuddered; she sobbed deeply once, and then she cried quietly. Randy came to his knees and wrapped his arms around her. With a lump in his throat, hot tears filled his eyes as he felt her sobbing softly in his arms.

He loved Sherrill with an intensity that could only be described as soul mates. Nevertheless, he also felt a kinship toward Suzy that transcended friendship. Last night he had almost casually told Suzy that she was more than a sister to him, but less than a lover. Now that description had a hollow ambiguity about it. Common sense told him that other men throughout history must have felt as he was feeling now.

He thought of literary star-crossed lovers: *Tristan* and *Isolde, Lancelot* and *Guinevere, Romeo* and *Juliet*…. However, none of his exposure to great works described the feeling that he now felt for Suzy. His mind scrambled a piecemeal definition. He thought of stellar (star), dys- (bad or not), and rhythm. The word meanings combined into the phrase—"*Stellar-Dysrhythmia*"—to describe their **star-crossed love** that lingered at the outside edge of the moral rhythm of society.

In his anguish he realized that their mutual love and desire, no matter how intense, could never be expressed in a physical love affair—society would destroy it. His own guilt would then surely destroy this beautiful love that existed with Sherrill. Therefore, Suzy's and his love could only survive; even thrive, in the intimate secret recesses of their own hearts and minds, there to remain insulated and sheltered away from the moralist and naysayers, who would surely seek to destroy even that—.

As he lingered thinking, he gently stroked her hair. She raised her head and looked at him through tear-filled eyes. He tilted her chin and kissed her on the mouth; releasing her lips only after he felt the renewed rising passion within his body. He tenderly whispered, "I love you, Suzette."

Suzy clung to him, her body shuddering with longing. She throatily whispered, "Please, Randy! Take me to your bed—I want to be with you tonight; we may never see each other…!"

Choking back his emotions, he released her and stated huskily, with finality, "No, I can't; I won't—it wouldn't be fair to you, even though *right now* I want you as much as you want me." With his heart pounding white-hot lead in his temples, he rose and stoically pulled her to a standing position. He grasped her shoulders and looked deeply into her eyes, willing her to understand.

She reached up with her fingertips and brushed his cheek. Shrugging her shoulders and smiling a quick crooked little smile, she turned and disappeared into the bedroom—Randy stood transfixed. He heard the sound of running water, then the soft swish of clothes being donned and the rasping sound of a zipper. Suzy reappeared at the door and smiled across the room at Randy. "I'd better go to my car alone," she informed.

Randy nodded, fully understanding her need to leave without further contact. He knew in himself, that if he held Suzy one more time then he might not be able to pull away. With the sincere glisten of tears in her eyes, she whispered across the distance, "I really had a wonderful time being with you tonight, Randy. I just want you to know that wherever you might be, whatever situations you might face, whenever you feel black despair or feel like giving up, just remember that there are **two** women who love you and want you to come home safely."

She turned, opening the door, and left without closing it. Randy moved over and leaned against the doorjamb, staring at the diminishing apparition in the low street light. Suzy opened her car door and collapsed into the driver's seat. She tightly gripped the steering wheel and found that she had no more tears, but knew that there would be more—later. Slowly, a calming transition crept over her. She rationalized, *I've met him; I love him; he loves me. Before he came, my heart was void of love—now it is filled. I will always have a part of him in my thoughts and memories.*

She started the car and drove away—to seek fulfillment of her own destiny. Randy slowly closed the door and felt a sadness that physically drained the strength from his body and the vitality from his soul, leaving him feeling stiff and weakened.

First Episode: Act-1; Scene-1—Action

Sherrill leaned back, feeling the pulsating jets of the Jacuzzi soothe her tense muscles. She had just returned to her hotel after her first day at the studio. As she thought back on the events of the day, she still couldn't believe all that had happened—culminating with receiving the keys to a beautiful brand new Corvette.

She closed her eyes and daydreamed of cruising the highways and byways with Randy, walking along the beach, frolicking through Disneyland, or just exploring the sights of the city together. Her daydreams drifted into night dreams as she dozed off.

The timer on the Jacuzzi shut off and she awoke realizing that she was totally relaxed, but needed to hurry. Grabbing a washcloth, she bathed herself and stepped out of the tub. Her day was not yet over.

Brad Thurman and her agent, Uncle Hank, seeing the value of maximizing her exposure to the Hollywood press, had scheduled an escorted night on the town with Gary Binger, who played the character of Don Luke. The five of them, including Aunt Vicki, would be dining, visiting a comedy club, and dancing at one of the nightclubs. Brad had picked places where stars went to be seen and the newspeople naturally followed.

Sherrill, in the meantime, had to learn her lines for tomorrow's scenes in her first full-length episode. She walked out onto the lanai to have a quick peek at the city and discovered that radiant heaters had been turned on to take the chill off the light breeze blowing in from the ocean. She leaned back in a chaise lounge and opened her script. As she read, she wished that she had observed the characters more closely in prior episodes.

Memorization of the lines came easy; her concern was delivering the lines while acting. The uncertainty caused her stomach to tense and her mind filled with trepidation. Sherrill jumped with surprise when Aunt Vicki asked, "How are you doing, Honey?"

She breathed out, "Oh, I wasn't expecting you. I was so engrossed in learning my lines that I didn't hear you coming."

Aunt Vicki carried a courtesy copy of the script in her hand, "Well, let's see how well you've learned them." She helped Sherrill out of the lounge, opened her script, and then read the lines of the other characters. Vicki hammed it up so much that Sherrill had to pause and laugh at her melodramatic delivery.

Realizing that her feelings of trepidation were gone, she leaned over and kissed her aunt on her cheek, "Aunt Vicki, I love you. You are a walking talking tonic for stage fright."

Aunt Vicki, still caught up with the acting, melodramatically raised her arm into the air, "Your Uncle Hank often points that out to me. He says, 'Victoria Jean, you don't have a bashful bone in your body! It's frightening how much you delight in center stage.'" Sherrill smiled and nodded in agreement; Vicki's face feigned surprise at being slighted. They laughed good-naturedly then continued with their impromptu rehearsal.

Dressed in his dinner jacket, Uncle Hank walked up as they were finishing a third reading. He looked at his watch, "Our table is reserved for nine o'clock; you girls have only got forty-five minutes to get dressed before the limo picks us up."

During dinner at the Café de la Paix, Sherrill was surprised to discover that Gary Binger, who played the part of Don Luke, had an excessively developed narcissistic personality. He frequently used his hands to slick back his hair and often peered into his water glass to glimpse a partial reflection of his face. He boringly talked about himself, embellishing minor accomplishments into great deeds of endeavor.

She was further disillusioned because in previous episodes of "The Dons of Eldorado," he had projected a character that was young and rebellious, often roguish with the young ladies, but ever heroic in character. Moreover, he had always endeared himself to the audience by his devotion to his adopted mother Doña Broderick, who had taken in the three-orphaned cousins.

By contrast, Laura Blevins was beautiful, amiable, and gregarious. However, her television character Belinda Broderick was beautiful, but was flawed with *indulgence* and *petulance*, often resorting to immature tirades on the screen to get her way.

Sherrill realized that in her naivety, she had always considered the good guys as *good* and the bad guys as *bad*—on and off stage. Now she realized that the essence of acting was assuming the qualities, *good* or *bad*, of the character, and then authentically projecting that image to the audience.

The revelation of this newly found knowledge caused her to blush at her naivety. Aunt Vicki noticed and felt her forehead. She asked, "Are you okay, Honey?"

Sherrill sheepishly revealed, "I just figured out something that every five year old in Hollywood already knows—people aren't always who they appear to be."

While they were dining, several photographers approached their table and asked permission to take their picture. When reporters asked for a statement, Brad merely handed them a communiqué that the studio and Uncle Hank had already cleared for release. The communiqués varied in sentence structure, but basically stated the same information in all the press promos.

Sherrill turned to Brad, "I noticed that the front of the menu stated that this restaurant specializes in *nouvelle cuisine*. What does that mean?"

"The Café de la Paix's fare is nouvelle cuisine—low in calories. Many stars prefer this type of dining because they frequently dine out and need to watch their diet."

Sherrill responded with pleasure, "Well, by any name, it is delicious." She was thankful that Brad was here to counteract the pomposity of Gary Binger. At least, Brad's conversation was interesting and informative.

Uncle Hank and Aunt Vicki were good conversationalists, but they felt that it would be rude to break into Gary's monologue about himself. Brad did not share their inhibition. He checked his watch, "Okay, onward to the comedy club."

At Demeche's Comedy Club, they were seated at a table up front. The comedians appeared distracted by Sherrill's presence, since they tried, somehow, to include her in their skits. Awed by her beauty and popularity in the news media, the simple act of acknowledging her seemed to throw them out of their rhythm of delivering their canned comedy skits. However, instead of diminishing the audience's enjoyment, the comedians' obvious faux pas seemed to warm up the crowd. The spectators laughed at the comedians' most droll and hackneyed jokes.

Bill Notes, a comedian who was just starting out in comedy, capitalized on the good humor of the audience: "Good evening, I'm Bill **Notes**—. Hey, looks like we've got a great crowd tonight. All of you just sit back and enjoy the show, 'cause I've got someone checking you out and taking *notes—if you don't laugh at the 'Notes jokes' then you got stuck with the 'Bill.'*"

(Audience applauds)

Bill continued, "Unusual names, like my own, can sometimes open doors for people. For instance, my *moniker*, Bill Notes, landed me a job while I was in college. *Dining Card* hired me to write the fine print at the bottom of their monthly statement—*bill notes*."

(Audience chuckles)

Bill shaded his eyes against the bright lights and motioned toward Sherrill's table, "Speaking of notes—I think that it is noteworthy to mention that Sherrill, the new starlet you all have seen so much of on TV, is with us tonight."

(The spotlight swings to Sherrill, followed by loud applause with whistles & cheers)

Bill continued his monologue, "Names even seem to affect the types of jobs that people do. My brother, *Mark Notes,* is a schoolteacher and spends many hours *grading papers*." (Audience moans) "Mark has been *engaged* five times—his ex-girlfriends refer to him as *Promissory Notes*."

(Laughter & applause & whistles)

"Mark and I have an uncle with a *bad disposition* and an aunt that *sings off-key*—our family refers to them as the s*our notes*."

(Audience moans)

"We also have two cousins who are what you might call *promiscuous*—you know—they occasionally sleep around. We refer to them as the *Loose Notes*."

(Guffaws & snickers)

"Like everyone, our family has a *skeleton in the closet*—(whispering) it's referred to as *The Family Secret Notes*."

(Giggles and chuckles)

"Coincidently, on the very same day, my wife's *obstetrician* and my personal *banker* gave me the same exact news...***Notes Overdue***."

(Loud laughter)

"Our Grandpa Notes sometimes drinks too much. Grandma says he's the *High Notes*."
(Whistles and loud laughter)

"Uncle Louie sings songs—you guessed it—he's the *Musical Notes*."
(Snickers & chuckles) "Uncle Louie once was married to a woman that *yodeled*—now she's no *relation,* so we referred to her as *ululation*."
(Audience missed the connection and only chuckled)

"I sometimes use a pet name for my sweet, but nagging wife—*Reminder Notes*."
(Cheers & whistles—boos from women in the audience)

"We have a nickname for a cousin who wears a *size-sixteen shoe*—*Footnotes*. His brother has a low IQ—*Marginal Notes*.
(Mixed moans & laughter)

"Couple of cousins work for the *IRS*—you guessed it—*Treasury Notes*."
(Laughter)

"Our Grandpa Notes doesn't refer to his *descendants* as a family tree—he refers to us as a *Compendium of Notes*."
(Mixed whistles & moans & laughter)

"I want you to know how tough it's been going through life with the name, Bill Notes.... I even thought of changing my name to *John Notes*—but then people would think of me as *graffiti on the bathroom walls*."
(Loud laughter)

Bill blew kisses toward the audience, "You've been a great audience. Thank you—thank you—thank you very much!"
(The audience gave him a standing ovation and whistled to show their approval.)

Gary Binger scrunched his lips and cynically remarked, "They went easy on him tonight. Any other night, and they would have booed him off the stage."

Aunt Vicki finally took exception with Gary's negativism, "Well, I thought he was very funny. It's not often you hear *noteworthy jokes.*" Her dining companions moaned at the pun, and then laughed with her.

Bill Notes stopped at their table, "Hi, Sherrill. I'm a fan of yours." He handed her a photograph that he had coaxed from the club photographer, "May I have your autograph?"

"Sure, Bill. I enjoyed your skit, tonight. You have a nice delivery."

Bill's face lightened, "Did you really like my material?"

Sherrill replied, "You had some fairly good puns, but I kept looking for the stalks."

Bill, with a quizzical look, asked, "What stalks?"

Sherrill smiled, "You know, the ones that *corn* grows on." She smiled and laughed lightly to show that no offense was meant.

Gary interjected, "I thought that your jokes were two-thirds of a pun—you know, P—U (phew).

Bill's face blanched and Brad interjected, "Don't mind Gary. God gave him an over abundance of good looks and vanity, but left him a little shy on humility and finesse."

Gary stared at Brad, as though he couldn't comprehend the meaning of the statement.

Sherrill handed Bill the autographed picture, "Good luck, Bill. I think you have a great future."

"Thank you, Sherrill. I think you have a great *presence.*"

The party moved on to Lowe's Dance Club. Gary stood up, bowed deeply, and asked, "Sherrill, would you care to dance?" Sherrill took his hand and followed him to the dance floor. She was pleasantly surprised; Gary danced divinely. He was so light on his feet that Sherrill and he appeared to glide across the dance floor as a single entity. Their movements were synchronized and fluid, causing other couples to stop dancing to watch the performance. Cameras flashing in the audience were the dancer's applause.

Gary obviously had a background in dancing. Sherrill's background was "Poetry in motion on the basketball court," as she had moved efficiently and gracefully to the rhythm of the game.

After forty-five minutes of dancing, they walked off the dance floor with a new appreciation and respect for each other's abilities. Aunt

Vicki bubbled to Hank, "She danced like a princess at the grand ball." A reporter overheard her comment and used it for the next day's headlines.

Brad remarked to Sherrill, "I would ask you to dance, but I'm afraid that my performance would be anticlimactic. Let's leave while the audience still has visions of grandeur."

The partygoers arrived back at her hotel with Sherrill feeling like Cinderella. Tonight had been such a unique wonderful experience for her that she didn't want it to end. However, filming of her first episode would start anew tomorrow and she saw the need for a good night's sleep.

The said their goodnights and Sherrill solo danced through the rooms of her suite onto the lanai where the radiation heaters were still warming the night air. She stopped at the edge of the balcony and gazed at the sparkling lights of the city. She breathed in the brisk night air from the ocean. She thought of Randy and called out into the night, "Paradise would be perfect, Darling, if only you were here to share it with me."

The director, Emile Fabio, met Sherrill as she walked onto the set. "Have you memorized your lines?"

"Yes, I believe so," she replied.

He took her by the arm and guided her to the storyboard. He spent the next fifteen minutes showing and describing each scene that they would shoot today. She stood studying the storyboard for a long time after the director had left.

Sherrill understood what was required of her, but she was unsure of the nuances of projecting her body language while delivering her lines. Laura Blevins walked up beside her, "How do you feel about your first day?"

Sherrill explained her dilemma and Laura assuaged her concerns, "Your feelings of inadequacy are normal for your first episode." She spent the next hour demonstrating the use of gestures, eye movement, and facial expressions to project authenticity and realism into the scenes.

Sherrill studied the storyboard with a new confidence as she pantomimed the actions in the scenes. Feeling that she was as ready as she would ever be for the challenge, she entered her dressing room and submitted herself to the magic of the make-up artist.

The first scene opened:

Don Luke is sitting on a rail fence, staring into the distance. His adopted mother (named Donna by her father Don and addressed as Doña—a Spanish courtesy title) approaches him, "What's wrong with you, Luke? You have been moping around here for days like a lovesick calf."

Luke replies because he has to share his feelings with someone, "I think that I am in love, Mother Doña. I saw a girl; you remember the girl in the carriage in town?"

Doña Broderick rebuffs him, "I've seen lots of girls in town riding in carriages."

Luke explains, "Well, I found out that her name is Annabelle Lee and that she is from Virginia. She is the grandniece of the famous general and her father is the president of our town bank."

Doña interrupts him, "You said that her father is the president of the bank? I know him and his wife very well. His name is James Lee and they live on a ranch about five miles on the other side of town. Amelia Lee is much younger than he is; I didn't know that he had a daughter close to your age."

Luke shook his head; "I just can't seem to get her out of my mind. I've keep expecting to see her at the Saturday night dance in town, but she's never been there."

His mother enlightens him, "Young ladies from back East, with proper breeding, just don't show up at a dance unescorted. If they do meet someone there then it's because they have already been properly introduced."

Luke moans, "I know, but how can we get properly introduced if I never see her?"

His mother thinks for a moment. Luke is her favorite of the three boys and she indulges him almost as much as her petulant daughter Belinda. "Well, I know how; we'll throw a ranch barbecue party. I'll have Belinda send out invitations to all the single girls in the valley, and you can invite all the single men. I'll invite some families that are my close friends, so it won't look like we are trying to be matchmakers."

Luke swings his legs around and nimbly jumps down off the fence. He hugs his mother, "Thanks, Mother; you are the greatest—now I get

326

to meet her." He leaps up on his horse and rides off to help his two brothers with the ranch chores.

Annabelle's stepmother, Amelia, knocks on her door and enters the room. She reprimands, "Annabelle, you can't just stay in your room and read all the time. You need to get out and meet some young people."

Annabelle complains, "I don't know why Daddy sent for me to live here in this dusty dirty little town that doesn't even have bricks on the streets, when I was perfectly happy living with Grandma and Grandpa back in Richmond."

Amelia softly touches Annabelle's shoulder, "You know that your father loves you and wants you to live with us now that you're educated. Before now, he felt that your schooling was more important, so he let you live with your grandparents. He feels the time is right for you to see some of the world and get reacquainted with us."

"I don't care," pouts Annabelle. "There's nothing here, except for miles and miles of nothingness. The town doesn't even have a theater and my social life is non-existent. The only entertainment that I have is the little library in my room."

Since previous discussions had always ended this same way, Amelia Lee has been waiting for this moment,. She pulls out the invitation, "Belinda Broderick has invited you to a barbecue next Saturday afternoon at the Broderick's Ranch."

Annabelle jumps up and snatches the invitation from her stepmother's hand. She reads the invitation and scowls; "Belinda sent this invitation to me—personally—why are you opening my mail?"

Amelia patiently replies, "Because the envelope was addressed to 'The Lees.' There were two invitations in the envelope. Belinda's mother, Doña Broderick, invited your father and me." She shows the front of the envelope and the second invitation to Annabelle.

Annabelle's face blushes with embarrassment because of her false accusation. She steps forward and kisses her stepmother on her cheek, "I'm sorry, Mother; I shouldn't have jumped to conclusions. I know that you've always tried to treat me like a daughter." Her face brightens and she runs over to her closet and flings open the doors, "Now, I finally get to wear some of my party dresses. I will be formally introduced and there will be a dance in town afterwards."

Emile called out, "Cut—that's a take."

He walked over to Sherrill, "Very good, Sherrill; just the right tone and energy." Sherrill was elated and walked away on clouds. She could hardly believe that she had just gotten through her first scene without a retake.

Laura Blevins met her off-stage and hugged her; "You were great. You've just gotten over your first big hurdle. It's always the worst one for every actor."

They walked arm in arm toward Sherrill's dressing room. Brad Thurman popped out of Laura's dressing room door with a magnum of champagne and three glasses. He glowed with enthusiasm, "Time for a toast to our newest starlet."

The cast and crew, with glasses in hand, gathered around Sherrill. Brad sloshed a swallow of champagne into everyone's glass and made a toast, "To Sherrill—a star is born and shines brightly among us." The cast and crew repeated the toast and tipped their glasses.

Sherrill held up her empty glass, "Thank you. It was your warm support and professionalism that gave me the confidence to get past my first scene without my knees buckling." The cast and crew laughed lightly to acknowledge the compliment and to show their empathy.

Emile barked, "OK, celebration is over—filming the next scene begins in five minutes.

The next scene:

Annabelle is seated at the dinner table with her mother and father. The family is discussing Saturday's barbecue. The dinner ends with her father announcing, "Annabelle, your mother and I will be returning to our ranch after the barbecue."

Annabelle asks with alarm, "But, Daddy—what about the dance? I really wanted to attend the dance and have some fun."

"I know, darling. Your mother and I have decided to let you stay in our room at the hotel. We'll ask Belinda's mother if Belinda can stay in the room with you. You are eighteen and we don't want you returning to the ranch late at night, even with ol' Amos driving you in the buckboard."

Annabelle jumps up so fast that her chair tips over backward. She uprights the chair and kisses her father, "Oh, thank you, Father!" She moves quickly to the other end of the table and kisses her mother on her cheek, "Thank you, Mother. I know that father wouldn't have consented without your support." She quickly exits the room.

Annabelle's next speaking scene is introductions at the Lee's arrival to the Broderick's' home:

A servant escorts Annabelle and her parents to a large garden area at the back of the house, where a Mariachi band provides gala music in the background. Doña Broderick welcomes the Lees then beckons to her daughter to come and meet them.

Belinda is introduced to Annabelle and when the two young women catch each other's eye, the envy of the other's beauty causes their expression to have sparks in their eyes. Belinda's expression softens as she says, "I am pleased to finally meet you, Annabelle."

Annabelle's expression softens due to her finishing school training. Her haughty expression changes to a warm smile as she replies, "Thank you, Belinda. It is my pleasure to finally meet someone my own age." Her expression changes back to bland contempt as she curtsies to show her good breeding.

Belinda reaches out and takes her by the hand leading her off to a group of young people, "Come meet my friends."

The cameras panned through the introductions. Everything went well until Annabelle is introduced to Don Luke. Emile leaped out of his director's chair and screamed, "Cut—cut."

He took Sherrill aside, "Sherrill, what's wrong? You looked like you were just being introduced to a *toad*. Don't you remember the carriage scene when you first saw Luke—how you showed curious romantic interest in him?"

Emile stopped and remembered that the scene had been filmed with a stand-in for Luke. Sensing that something was wrong, he beckoned, "Laura, come here and talk to Sherrill. Okay, everybody—five minute break."

Laura led Sherrill off to an isolated corner of the scene, "Sherrill, you were doing so well; what went wrong?"

Sherrill shrugged her shoulders, "I'm not sure. I went out to dinner with Gary Binger last night and discovered that he is so narcissistic and full of himself that I can't stand him. I guess that I let my personal feelings spill over into the scene."

Laura put her arm around Sherrill's shoulders, "Don't let him get to you. It happens all the time in Hollywood, but you can't let it affect your acting." She thought a moment, "Do you remember the first time that you saw Randy?"

"I was in first grade with Randy."

Laura improvised, "Okay, then pretend that you are meeting the grown-up Randy for the first time. How would you feel then?"

Sherrill's face lit up, "I would feel that I was meeting Prince Charming!"

Laura consoled, "H'm, you don't want to put that much emotion into it. Just make the audience see and feel the electricity of girl meets potential Prince Charming. Remember, if you don't personally feel toward an actor exactly how you are supposed to feel in a scene then think of someone else that generates that needed feeling in you. Then, with that feeling, look at the actor and deliver your lines. It's an old theatrical trick known by all seasoned actors."

Sherrill hugged Laura, "Thank you. I don't know what I would do without your advice and support."

The director called "Places—Action."

The scene of Annabelle meeting Luke flowed through just as Emile had envisioned. The introductions continued, and then switched to supporting actors' scenes at the barbecue, where Annabelle was occasionally seen in the background interacting, without dialogue, with other characters in the cast.

Annabelle's next dialogue scene shows her sitting at an outdoor table across from Belinda. Belinda asks, "What was it like living in Richmond?" Annabelle perks up at the mention of the city where she grew up.

She divulges, "It is a big city that has everything that a girl would ever want to do. It has theaters that are open seven nights a week with matinees on the weekends. The shops are full of the latest Paris fashions. There are libraries with thousands of books and beautifully groomed parks where you can go to relax and read under a tree draped with Spanish Moss. On the outskirts of the city are several English riding clubs—I love horses."

Annabelle leans in closer to Belinda and whispers, "And, there are literally hundreds of suitors, who compete to take you to all those places."

Both girls giggle and Belinda says, "We don't have any of the culture you described, but we do have some handsome looking cowboys. Most of them are here at the barbecue."

Annabelle glances around and confides, "The only one that I am interested in—is your brother, Luke."

Belinda pushes her hand out and flips her fingers forward, saying with disdain conspiracy in her voice, "You can have your pick of any of my brothers, but the rest of the young men are mine."

Annabelle reaches out and grabs Belinda's extended hand. She vigorously shakes it, "Deal!"

They both laugh at their dark pact and discover that they can be friends, as long as they aren't competing for the same thing.

Annabelle pauses, as though she is thinking, and then leans in to Belinda. "There's just one thing. I may have to temporarily borrow a few of your young men to attract Luke's attention."

Belinda whispers back, "I think that you already have Luke's attention, but you can use any of my men as long as you don't rope-em and brand-em."

The two girls' loud laughter attracts the attention of the rest of the party. Amelia Lee leans over to Doña Broderick, "It looks like our daughters have hit it off."

Doña, having seen the handshake, replies, "Yes, they have agreed on something, but I'm not sure who or what—?"

Two cameras pan back to film the action at both tables. One of Belinda's beaux walks over and leans on the table, saying something to Annabelle. Both girls join in on an animated pantomimed conversation.

Doña hears both girls laugh a shrill falsetto attention-getting laugh. Annabelle places her hand on top of the young man's hand and swings her head so that her hair brushes the young suitor's arm.

Doña says, to the camera as though she is speaking to Amelia, "My suspicions are confirmed; they are up to something. Belinda would never be laughing if another girl was touching one of her beaux."

A camera zooms in on Luke with his hat pulled down to the top of his eyebrows. He sits morosely staring at Annabelle with a demoralized look on his face.

Emile hollered, "Cut—that's a take."

He addressed the cast and crew, "Okay everybody, I know that we normally don't work on weekends, but we've got a lot of filming to do. See you tomorrow morning—same time, same place—Goodnight." The

331

contract actors moaned, but the scale wage actors and filming crew cheered because overtime meant extra income.

Brad followed the director into the editing room, "Emile, what is your first take on Sherrill's performance?"

Emile sternly looked at Brad and prefaced his opinion, "As a director, I am supposed to be objective—only resorting to emotion to motivate people to do their best."

Brad urged, "Yes—go on."

Emile broke into a wide grin, "But, between you and me, Sherrill was fabulous! She exceeded my wildest expectations for someone that has never acted before. She didn't muff her lines. She only had one retake. Her interaction with the other characters was seamless. And—she projected that radiant appeal that caught my eye the first day that I met her."

Brad gleefully shook Emile's hand, "Thank you. I observed the same things, but I wanted your opinion."

Emile hedged his statement, "To be sure that the cameras caught the same thing, I am going to have to look at the film. However, I don't think that we are going to be disappointed."

Brad shook Emile's hand again, "Thanks, Emile. I'll leave you to your editing crew—see you tomorrow." Brad walked away feeling warm inside. His budding affection for Sherrill was reinforced by his admiration of her performances, last night and today.

He tried to suppress his feelings by rationalizing, *she's so young, and her heart already belongs to Randy. She's pregnant with his child and I would never be able to offer her more than she has already.*

Nevertheless, the more that he tried to suppress his feelings, the more his desire for her seethed and bubbled to the top of his subconscious thoughts and invaded his dreams at night.

Reconciliation

Sherrill walked up to the reservation desk in her hotel, "Are there any messages for me?"

The desk clerk handed her a message, "Yes, Sherrill. Your aunt and uncle left a message before they went out, but they are back now."

The receptionist handed her a set of keys, "Your car is parked in the garage on the second level in space B-27."

Sherrill was surprised. During the activities that filled her day, she had not even thought about her new Corvette. "Thank you," She replied, grasping the keys tightly in her hand.

She rode the elevator to the penthouse suites and unlocked her door. Entering her suite, she laid the keys on the ledge above the fireplace and glanced at the message. The connecting door between the suites opened and her peripheral vision caught the outline of a woman. Still reading the message, she turned, "Hello, Aunt Vic—Mother!"

Her mother rushed to her, "Oh, Honey, it's so good to see you! You look wonderful"

They embraced with tears in their eyes, and Sherrill questioned, "Where is Daddy?"

Her mother drew back, "He's on the patio; you two need to talk."

Mavis stayed back as Sherrill walked out on the patio. Her father was reclined in the chaise lounge and turned his head to stare at her. He rose slowly as his eyes filled with tears. Choking back emotion, he reached for her with open arms, "Baby, you are so beautiful. Can you ever forgive a spiteful old man that has driven you from your home, but never from his heart?"

Sherrill stood looking at her repentant father, replete with tears. His missing tooth had been replaced and his other injuries had healed. She tentatively stepped forward, and then rushed to embrace him, saying, "Oh, Daddy, I have missed you all so much. It is so good to see you and Mother again."

They hugged each other for a long time, feeling the oneness that only a father and daughter could share. Finally, Sherrill stepped back and said with reproach, "I can forgive and forget what you did to me, but I can't forgive and forget what you did to Randy. That forgiveness can only come from him."

"You're right, and I know it," replied her father. "Because of me, you two—you three are apart. If Randy were here right now, I would

333

get down on my knees and beg his forgiveness. I would explain that my blind obstinate primordial reaction against him was only because of my possessive love for you and my perceived loss of you...to him."

Charles wiped his eyes with his hand, "I realize now that my actions made a mockery of my love for you. I've told myself a thousand times, 'Had I just stopped to think about your happiness that night then I would have realized that my real love for you resides in my heart—not in my ego.' My letting you go with Randy will never take that love away from me."

Sherrill reached out for her father and hugged him tightly. She realized, for him to say the words that he had just spoken, that he must have spent long anguishing hours thinking of just the right words to say that would express the true feelings in his heart.

That night, they had dinner on the lanai. Sherrill shared with her parents all the events and impressions that she had experienced. Her aunt and uncle contributed anecdotes about Sherrill and expressed their feelings of how Sherrill had enriched their lives. The stories sounded more like an adventure than life, but after all, they agreed—*isn't life just an extension of daily adventures?*

Near the end of the dinner, Mavis placed her hand upon Sherrill's arm. She looked at her oldest daughter, "Sherrill, Honey, your father and I want you to come back home with us. You've been in a family way for 17 weeks and we want to take care of you."

Ambivalent feelings and thoughts swirled through Sherrill's mind. Finally, she said with measured words, "Mother, Father, my heart's home is now with Randy. Until we can be together again, I want to stay with Aunt Vicki and Uncle Hank. I love them dearly and I have found a new life with them. Another reason is: I am under contract with 'The Dons of Eldorado' and have to finish three episodes, plus publicity appearances.

"To go home with you now would be stepping backward in my life. I must think of the future for my baby and myself. I love you, but life back home with you would only remind me more of Randy and how much I desperately miss him."

Her parents silently sat reconciling their own thoughts. The looked at each other in silent communication and her father stood up and kissed Sherrill on the cheek. "You're right, Honey; your mother and I only want what's best for you and your baby—and Randy."

Hank lifted his glass of wine and energetically expounded, "A toast to life—to the adventures of life!"

They raised their glasses and repeated, "To life—to the adventures of life!"

Sherrill drove up to the gate of the studio and showed her pass. The gate guard greeted her, "Good morning, Sherrill. Your parking space is in front of the third building on the left, five spaces down."

Sherrill pulled into the parking space and read the sign, "*Sherrill.*" She stared at her name for a moment and thought, *In my wildest dreams, I would never have thought five months ago that I would have my own parking space at 'The Dons of Eldorado" in Hollywood.*

She entered the set and headed directly to the storyboard, saying good morning to everyone on the way. She studied the storyboard; then went to her dressing room, where her make-up artist was waiting to start the day.

The filming sequence of the barbecue picked up where it had left off the day before:

Additional suitors approach the two girls and engage in animated laughter-filled conversation. Luke stands off to one side, morosely watching Annabelle. The suitors finally drift away, leaving the two girls alone. Luke conjures up his courage and approaches his sister and Annabelle. He says, "Excuse me, Miss Lee, would you like to go for a buggy ride?"

Annabelle turns, looking intruded upon, and asks, "Excuse me, have we met?"

Belinda stifles a giggle at seeing her egotistical brother stammer, "Ya—yes, I'm Don Luke Broderick. We met when you first arrived here at the barbecue."

Annabelle blinks her eyes and brings her folded fan up to her brow as though trying to remember, "Oh, yes, I think I do remember…you're one of the hired servants—a cook, I believe."

Luke looks at her in stark disbelief and defensively corrects his station, "No, I'm Luke—Belinda's brother."

Belinda haughtily interjects, "Oh, he says that he is my brother, but I don't always claim him."

The conspirators glance at each other, giggling. Their rejection is too much for young Luke's ego to handle. He turns without replying and stomps away.

The two girls laugh and Belinda says, "Well, you've corralled him, but now you've got to rope and brand him."

Annabelle replies confidently, "That comes later..." They both giggle, anticipating further intrigue in their romantic conspiracy.

The scheduled scenes changed to the interaction of other characters in the cast and Sherrill's participation was not required on the set. She discovered, even though her presence at the studio required 10 to 15 hour days, that apart from make-up and dressing, she actually had a lot of time to herself to study for her high school classes and for memorizing her lines.

During the noon break Laura entered Sherrill's dressing room and suggested, "Let's go to Bob's Drive-in and have a burger for lunch."

"Okay, let's take my 'Vette'—you drive."

They passed Brad on the way out and he asked, "Going to lunch—where are you going?"

Laura answered over her shoulder, "Bob's."

Brad felt a warning chill go up his spine. Two beautiful young stars, from a show as popular as "The Dons," being seen together among the general public, could become a volatile situation—even in Hollywood. He decided to follow them. At the very least, it might provide a promo photo opportunity.

He quickly called Myra McDonald, "Myra, this is Brad Thurman. Grab a 'Roadie' and I'll treat you to a burger—meet you in the lobby in two minutes."

Myra, carrying a tape recorder, and accompanied by an assignment cameraman met Brad. They reached the parking lot as Sherrill and Laura were lowering the top of the convertible. Sherrill was reading the "Operator's Manual," while Laura was manipulating the controls.

Brad chuckled and stated with a chauvinistic inference, "Guys would never need to read the manual."

Myra retorted with feministic sarcasm, "Yeah, guys would rip off the top the convertible before resorting to read the manual." All three laughed at the veracity of her statement.

Brad drove while the cameraman in the passenger seat filmed through the windshield. The cameraman focused on a convertible with four teenage boys motioning to the girls in the Corvette. The boys were hollering flirtatious banter to the girls, and then one of them recognized Sherrill and Laura Blevins. The boy in the passenger seat tried to get a better view and blocked the driver's view. The car swerved and hit the curb, blowing a front tire.

Brad remarked, "That's not a good sign." The remainder of the trip to the drive-in was uneventful. The girls pulled into the drive-in and a couple of guys spotted the yellow Corvette with two foxes. They honked their horns and other people in their cars turned to see the source of the commotion. Spying Sherrill and Laura, all the drivers started honking their horns.

Brad backed his car into a parking space at the side of the parking lot. They were behind the Corvette and had a good view of the girls. He saw Laura press the order button. Her hand and mouth motions indicated that she was placing an order through the speaker.

The horns continued their incessant honking. This got the notice of other drivers on the street, who then turned into the drive-in to see what was causing the excitement. The girls finally waved back to acknowledge the attention—the honking ceased.

Nevertheless, the events for chaos had already been placed into motion. Many drivers pulled into the drive-in to see what was going on with all the cars there. The backup blocked cars in the street and quickly extended for several blocks, blocking the side streets. By the time the girls got their order delivered, the roads leading to the drive-in were in gridlock.

The cameraman climbed out of Brad's car and started panning the chaos. Myra had recorded the honking, while the two girls sat innocently in Sherrill's car. Then she recorded her own thoughts about the scene.

Laura turned to Sherrill, "What do we do? I would just as soon leave, but the parking lot is packed and I can't back up."

Sherrill replied, "Well, I guess that we just sit here and enjoy our lunch when it comes."

Police dispatches went out to investigate the gridlock. To approach the drive-in, the police had to use lights and sirens, while driving up on the wrong side of the street. Half-a-dozen traffic officers started unraveling the gridlock, while a sergeant spoke to people in the blocked cars. He quickly worked his way to the cars parked at the drive-in and fingers were pointed in the direction of the two girls eating their lunch. He walked up to Laura, and then recognized both stars. "I'm sorry, Miss

337

Blevins—Sherrill, but I am going to have to write you two a citation for creating a public disturbance."

Brad and Myra, seeing the officer pull out his citation book, got out of the car. The cameraman continued filming the action. Sherrill and Laura looked at each other with their eyes wide and Sherrill stated with disbelief, "Can you believe this?"

Brad walked up to hear Laura saying to the officer, "We just came here to have something to eat. How can you give us a ticket?"

Brad interrupted and identified himself, "Hello, Sergeant. I'm a lawyer with the studio. We have their entire trip on film for possible promo purposes. However, they did not know that we were following them.

"The two young ladies did just like Miss Blevins explained to you. They came here to have lunch just like all the other patrons you see here. If you have to write citations then you'll have to give everyone here a ticket.

"The traffic jam didn't start until the other patrons started honking their horns at the two girls. Then people on the street started pulling in to see what was happening. The traffic jam resulted from the honking, not from these two girls sitting here in their parked car and simply expecting to have a quiet lunch together."

The police sergeant looked around and saw that the traffic was starting to move. He shrugged, "I didn't want to give them a ticket anyway. If you have this on film then I can justify to my lieutenant why I didn't issue a citation."

Myra McDonald interjected, "If your lieutenant needs convincing, just have him watch the six o'clock news.

The police sergeant nodded, "Okay, I'm going to provide a police escort for you, so that you can get back to your studio without further incident." He walked away to get the parking lot cleared.

Sherrill reached across Laura and touched Brad's hand on the door, "We want to thank you, the three of you, for coming to our rescue. I was afraid that we would have to call you to post bail."

Laura laid her hand on top of Sherrill's and intoned, "Yes, thank you, Brad."

The three got back into Brad's car and Myra stated, "Brad, you were great. How did you know something like this might happen?"

"I didn't. I just know that when you mix a *BOMBSHELL* with *TNT*, then you get a *dynamite duo*—Sherrill and Laura—the situation was just waiting for someone to light the fuse."

"Well, that duo has just provided us with a terrific promo for tonight's news." Myra had an inspiration, "Say! Our department has had trouble coming up with ideas for promos for Sherrill because of her involvement with Randy. We can't play on the Hollywood girl—guy thing without alienating her fans and the general public.

"However, there is nothing wrong with promos using Sherrill and Laura together. They have excellent chemistry with each other and you saw from this incident that they can attract attention by the droves. I'll talk to my boss and see how she likes the idea. We can still show Sherrill associating with men, but we won't infer that a romance link is budding."

Brad acknowledged, "I like your idea. As a matter-of-fact, it's a terrific idea and we won't be slighting Laura by giving too much publicity to Sherrill, since both of them will be getting the same publicity."

The parking lot had been cleared, so Laura could back out. A police cruiser, with lights and siren, escorted them to the gates of the studio. The whole saga was recorded on film. Myra headed for her manager's office. The cameraman headed for the dark room. Brad headed back to the studio to watch Sherrill in her scenes.

The afternoon filming led off:

Amelia Lee approaches Doña Broderick, "James and I are leaving now. We want to let you know how much we really enjoyed the barbecue. And, thank you for allowing Belinda to stay with Annabelle in our room at the hotel tonight. Also, we appreciate your family letting her ride with them to the dance."

"Don't you worry about her; my boys will look after her." Doña kisses Amelia on the cheek. She shakes hands with James, "I'll be in next week to sign papers for the bank to transfer the gold shipment from our mines to the mint in San Francisco." She follows them to their carriage and waves goodbye as they drive off in their carriage.

The next scene shows the three Dons and the two girls, dressed for the dance, getting into the carriage:

Belinda suggests, "Luke, why don't you drive the carriage." Don Luke, not waiting for his brothers' concurrence, leaps up into the driver's seat because it is customary for a guest to sit next to the driver.

Belinda directs, "Annabelle, you sit in the back between Matthew and Mark."

Luke's heart sinks. He drives toward town with his hat pulled down and silently endures Annabelle's animated conversation and laughter with his two older brothers.

Matthew having an interested in history, requests, "Annabelle, tell us something about your famous uncle."

"Well," begins Annabelle, "General Lee had a horse named Traveler. They were in many battles together and were inseparable. On one occasion, the horse is credited with saving the general's life. They were jumping across a small ravine and the horse bucked in midair. The general never expected this, since it had never happened before, and he was launched out of the saddle.

"When he went to get back on his horse, he discovered that the saddle horn had been shot off by a Yankee sniper. If the horse hadn't bucked then the general would have received a fifty-caliber bullet right through his heart."

"That's an amazing story," interjects Mark. "How well did you know the general?"

"Not very well," replies Annabelle. "I was just a toddler during the war. After the war, my father was in banking and the general went off to teach at a college. Our families never got together much and I only got to meet the general when my Grandpa Lee died. Later, my father moved out West and I remained in Atlanta with my departed mother's parents. After schooling, my father sent for me and now I'm riding next to two of the handsomest men in California."

Luke has trouble hearing the conversation due to the sound of the horse's hooves on the road, but he hears the last part and his shoulders lower another inch. Belinda notices this; she and Annabelle exchange conspiratorial smiles. Annabelle says loudly, "That's enough about me. Now tell me about what you two big strong cowboys do on the ranch."

The cameras pan back and show Matthew animatedly gesturing as he is telling a story. Annabelle is laughing and Luke sits forlornly with the reins in his hands. The scene fades out.

The director called, "Cut. Okay that's a take. Twenty minute break, while we set up the square dance scene."

Myra telephoned Brad, "Brad, come over to the viewing room. We've just finished the press release and I want your impression."

Brad replied, "I'll be right over."

Brad entered the viewing room where several other executives were seated. Myra motioned for the viewing to begin.

"Hello—I'm Myra McDonald with 'The Dons of Eldorado.' Today, Sherrill, who has a guest role of 'Annabelle Lee' and Laura Blevins, who stars as 'Belinda Broderick,' drove to a local drive-in for lunch. When their fans spied the two highly publicized stars in Sherrill's Corvette, they started honking their cars. This caused motorists on the streets to stop to see what all the excitement was about and resulted in an unfortunate traffic tie-up.

The studio apologizes for any inconvenience to the driving public. However, we ask you, 'Were these two young women directly responsible?' We have a film clip of their lunch break—you be the judge."

The film clip was shown for the television audience, complete with audio providing the horns honking and Brad's short conversation with the police sergeant.

Myra reappeared on the screen, "Again, 'The Dons of Eldorado' apologizes for any inconvenience. I guess from now on that Sherrill and Laura will either have to eat their lunches at the studio cafeteria or not go out to lunch together."

Myra turned to Brad, "What do you think?"

"I think it's great. It gives the public a subliminal message that the two stars are immensely popular. It shows that Sherrill and Laura are innocent of any culpable wrongdoing. And, it will give the studio a lot of free press coverage."

"Exactly!" agreed Myra. "Now we need to get it out to the networks and locals on the microwave links. I just hope that they pick it up for their nightly newscast."

The Vice President of Advertising turned to Brad, "Myra says that you have a good feel for sensing when something newsworthy is going to happen. I know that you have other duties, but I would like you to oversee the promos of Sherrill and Miss Blevins."

Brad replied, "Thank you, sir, I would be happy to be involved with the promos." Brad tried to hide his excitement. He thought, *I would even do it on my own time—just to be near Sherrill.*

Filming picked up where:

Matthew, Mark, Luke, Belinda, and Annabelle arrive at the square dance. Matthew grabs Annabelle by the hand, "Come on let's join the fun."

Annabelle tosses her bonnet to Luke and her golden yellow hair flares down to her shoulders, refracting the light, as each strand becomes a miniature prism in the light. Luke gulps and stares with longing as his oldest brother squires Annabelle around the dance floor.

The dance ends and Luke walks up to ask Annabelle to dance. Mark pulls him back and possessively states, "My turn—*little* brother." Mark takes Annabelle onto the dance floor. Luke walks back dejectedly and leans against the wall, watching everyone else have fun.

The dance ends and Luke approaches Annabelle again, and says, "Would you care to dance?"

Annabelle fans her face with her hand, "I need to rest a minute, but I would like a fruit punch."

Luke turns immediately and heads toward the punch bowl. Finding it surrounded by other dancers, he impatiently waits his turn. When he returns with the punch, Annabelle is already dancing with a beau of Belinda's.

To Luke, the tune seems to last forever. Finally, the dance is over and Annabelle walks off the dance floor. Taking the punch from Luke, she purrs, "Thank you, Luke; you're so sweet." Luke stands and grins, while Annabelle sips the punch.

The fiddler announces, "Couples dance."

Luke lets his breath out in exasperation, "Now, will you dance with me?"

Annabelle looks around for Belinda or some excuse to refuse. Finding neither, she curtsies, "I would be very pleased to dance with you, Mr. Broderick." Luke leads Annabelle onto the dance floor, where other couples are already dancing. Luke and Annabelle's rhythm and synchronization flow together like a gentle breeze through a golden field of wheat.

It was not in the script, but one by one, the other couples stopped dancing to watch the performance. Emile opened his mouth to holler—cut, but the word hung in his thoughts and wouldn't come out of his mouth. Even *he* was mesmerized by their performance.

When the dance ended, Emile hollered, "Cut—that's a take!" Then he frantically waved his hand and yelled, "Rewrite." He turned to the cast and announced, "Okay, thirty minute break while we rewrite."

Sherrill walked off the set and was met by Brad, "You were beautiful out there. You seemed to dance even better than the other night. I thought that Emile was going to have a stroke when the cast broke the scene, but even he, like the rest of us, was entranced by watching you dance."

Sherrill replied demurely, "Thank you, but I was only following Gary's lead."

Brad felt the urge to tell Sherrill that she was wrong by giving all the credit to Gary Binger, but he swallowed his words. Sherrill asked unexpectedly, "Brad, are you really a lawyer?"

Brad gazed at her quizzically and explained, "After college I took a couple of semesters at UCLA, but then I latched onto a summer job here with the studio and decided, instead, to go into public relations." He scrunched his brow, "Why do you ask?"

Sherrill replied, "Well, at the drive-in, you told the policeman that you were a lawyer."

Brad remembered, "Oh, yes. The police officer had his book open to write you and Laura a ticket for creating a public disturbance. I wanted to diffuse the situation, so I told him that I was a lawyer. He is in law enforcement and I felt that he would be more cooperative, if he thought that he was talking to someone else associated with the law."

Sherrill replied, "Hummm—now I see why you chose public relations—you're good at it."

Brad smiled, "Let's go to the cafeteria and have a Coke."

Sherrill, with a teasing look in her eyes, "I need to rest a minute, but I would like a fruit punch."

Brad looked at her, detecting the tease. He punched her shoulder lightly, "There's your punch, lady." He grabbed her by the hand and pulled her toward the cafeteria, "Don't try using that line on me—it only works on Don Luke." Laughing, they walked to the cafeteria. Finding that it wasn't very crowded, they sat in an isolated area and discussed the lunch hour incident

Eyeing the radiant beauty of Sherrill, Brad took a sip of his Coke, "We released a promo about the drive-in incident for tonight's news."

Sherrill, slightly surprised, "You mean that you followed us to the drive-in on purpose."

"Yes," replied Brad. "We noticed that you and Laura have a good chemistry between you. We only followed you to get a little film footage for the archives. We never anticipated what actually happened.

We got it all on film and worked it into a promo." Sherrill was amazed, but said nothing.

Brad continued, "One of the vice presidents saw it and asked me to oversee future promos. We plan to film you and Laura together, instead of trying to match you with a romance interest, which would be a normal promo format for a budding starlet."

I like that angle," assured Sherrill. "Laura and I are best of friends and I like being seen with her."

Brad felt relieved, "I hope that you don't mind me being there."

Sherrill placed her hand on top of Brad's, "No, Brad, I don't mind you being there. Actually, I feel comforted, knowing that you are there."

Brad wanted to leap up and dance on the table, but instead he suppressed his expression and the urge. He looked at his watch, "It is time to get back to the fun and games on the set."

Emile gathered his cast and crew around him and explained the rewrites. "We were so impressed by Sherrill and Gary Binger's performance in the couples' dance that it has been increased in the episode from forty-five seconds to three minutes and fifteen seconds.

"Because the other couples stopped dancing to watch, we are going to insert a scene where the town mayor introduces the dance as a dance contest. We are going to insert a close-up scene of the mayor pointing toward the dance floor and eliminating couples. Our editing room will insert the dancers stopping and watching Annabelle and Don Luke.

"We are scrapping the rest of the scheduled dance scenes and the scenes where Annabelle and Laura continue to play mind games with Don Luke's emotions. We're going to start filming with the mayor presenting the winners with a picnic package (rented horse and buggy, blanket and picnic basket full of goodies) for a trip to Rainbow Falls.

"For those of you who have already read the complete script, you know that part of the picnic scene is one of the action scenes to be filmed on location. Okay, all dancers back on the dance floor and gather around as an audience....applaud after the mayor presents the prize.

The dancers assembled and a couple of assistants moved them into proper position. Sherrill and Gary stood next to the impromptu mayor.

The scene began:

The mayor holds up an envelope and announces, "Ladies and gentlemen, the winners of the dance contest and the picnic package are Miss Annabelle Lee and Mr. Don Luke Broderick." He hands the envelope to Luke and Annabelle. The audience applauds while Luke bows and Annabelle curtsies.

Emile yelled, "Cut—that's a take. He gathered the cast and crew around him and announced, "Tomorrow is Sunday. We are going to shoot the scheduled scenes in the afternoon—so enjoy the morning with your families. The next scene, today, is the hotel scene. Everyone else in the cast can go home."

Laura and Sherrill walked off the set together. Laura commented, "Emile hates rewrites, since it can throw-off the rhythm of the whole episode. However, he is a professional and recognizes when a rewrite is justified."

Sherrill observed, "It looked to me like it made things simpler, since he cut out a lot of the dance scenes."

Laura replied, "Yes, you are right from that perspective, but in the editing room it makes his job a whole lot tougher."

They paused in front of Sherrill's dressing room door and Sherrill shared, "I'm going to use the time between sets to study for my high school classes."

Laura walked away thinking, *I still can't believe she's still in high school: Her demeanor and actions are years beyond her age.*

The hotel scene began:

Belinda is staying all night with Annabelle. They walk together to their door and turn. The scene shows Luke carrying two valises. The two girls take their valises and both kiss Luke on the cheek at the same time. Annabelle whispers into Luke's ear, "Thank you Luke—think of me in your dreams."

Luke's facial expression changes from a smile to that of a love-smitten yokel. He turns and bounces along the wall as he stumbles away in ecstasy.

The girls enter their hotel room and shut the door. Giggling, with the look of intrigue on their faces, they hug each other and Belinda says with finality, "You've roped 'im—now you gotta brand him."

"All in good time," assures Annabelle,"—all in good time."

Emile yells, "Cut—take—call it a day."

Love Letter

Mavis heard Sherrill opening the door to the Princess Suite. She met her daughter and gave her a long motherly hug. Bubbling, she pointed, "We just saw you on TV and it looked like you had an exciting lunch."

"Yes, it was interesting, but *chaotic* is probably a better word. We were eating a hamburger at a drive-in and this cop walks up and tries to give us a citation for causing a public disturbance—can you believe that?"

Mavis replied, "Yes, I believe it; we just saw it on television. When the policeman took out his ticket book, your Father pulled off his shoe and started to throw it at the TV."

Her father, who was still watching television, turned his head to look at them when he heard "Father" mentioned.

"Thank you, Daddy, for sticking up for me," called Sherrill.

Charles turned back to the television and simply waved his hand in the air to acknowledge the praise. Sherrill and her mother stifled a giggle at his dismissive reaction.

Mavis prodded, "Who was that nice looking young man that straightened things out?"

"His name is Brad Thurman. He's in public relations, but seems to have several other functions with the studio. He was the talent agent at my news conference in Monterey and today, he was asked to be involved with my promos."

"Then, he probably would have been the one to bail you out of jail, it things hadn't worked out."

Sherrill thought for a moment on her mother's words and nodded her head in agreement as she thought of Brad always seeming to be there at the right place and the right time when she needed someone. It had begun in Monterey by his bringing in the hairdresser for her news conference, and then....

Her thoughts were interrupted by Aunt Vicki entering from the adjoining suite, "Sherrill, what do you think of all of us piling into a car and going to a drive-in restaurant for a burger?

The three women laughed and Sherrill jested, "No, it seems that when I go to a drive-in for a burger the police want to give me a ticket."

They laughed again and the husbands came up by them to see what was so funny. Hank saw from his wife's expression that whatever was funny was girl-talk, so he asked, "Hi, Sherrill, are you hungry?"

The three women flashed a grin at each other, but maintained their composure. Sherrill asked, "Does anyone here really feel like going out tonight for dinner?"

Vicki replied, "Not me. We've been out all day showing Charles and Mavis the sights of the city." The others muttered their agreement.

"Good," remarked Sherrill. "I was talking to the hotel's concierge and she mentioned that one of the *sous chefs* in the hotel's kitchen makes the best New York style deep dish pizza pies this side of the Hudson River."

"Sounds good to us," agreed everyone, except Charles. He stated, "I'm a steak and potatoes man—no pizza for me."

Vicki suggested, "Let's order the kitchen sink, with only one anchovy on the side."

The pizza, with side salads and two bottles of wine, was served on the lanai. Vicki picked up the anchovy with her fingers and waved it around two inches above the pizza, and then she discarded the anchovy onto a side plate.

Mavis declared, "Vicki, what good does that do? That little fishy didn't even touch the pizza."

Vicki replied, "It doesn't have to; I touched the anchovy with my fingers and that's all the flavor I need." Everyone laughed, thinking that she was kidding with them, but she wasn't.

Charles took a bite of his medium-rare steak, "This steak is excellent," he stated as he chewed, "it's as good as Abe's Café, back home."

The others urged him to take just one bite of the terrific pizza. He finally agreed by taking a bite off of Mavis' plate. He pushed his steak aside and took a slice of pizza. He justified his change of mind by saying, "Mavis can fry a couple of eggs in the morning, and I'll eat my steak for breakfast."

The rest of the family laughed at his obvious gambit to save face, since they had to order another pizza because Charles was still hungry. Laughing and retelling old stories, the family enjoyed their meal of pizza and wine. The meal was neither ordinary nor extraordinary, but the bonding feeling of serenity and camaraderie was remembered the rest of their lives.

Sunday morning, the family attended church. It was only then that Charles and Mavis became fully aware of Sherrill's popularity. Therefore, as her parents, they understood their own popularity, with only a few negative undertones of Charles' notoriety.

The minister took the pulpit for his sermon, "Today's sermon is 'Reconciliation' and I am struck with the coincidence that Sherrill and her family is worshiping with us this morning. For as you know from news reports, Sherrill and her family were sorely tried when her father, Charles, cast out his daughter into exile from her family, her friends, and her fiancé, who had fought him for her hand in marriage.

"However, recent newspaper accounts have documented that Charles, by confessing to his church congregation, has repented his reprehensible actions. He is a deacon in his own church and I now ask Brother Charles to come up to the pulpit to share his thoughts and feelings with this congregation."

Charles raised his eyebrows in surprise by the invitation. However, being a deacon, he had long since gotten over the fright of public speaking. As he walked down the aisle to the pulpit, Sherrill leaned over to her aunt and whispered, "I hope that he doesn't go into his 'Deacon mode,' because the minister won't have any time left for his sermon." Both women stifled a giggle.

Sherrill knew that at times her father could almost be two different people. At home, he was head of the family and interacted in daily life as a typical husband and father. However, as a deacon, he could become focused on a subject and spout 'Hellfire and Brimstone' along with the best of them.

Charles took the pulpit. He looked out across the congregation, which was ten times larger than his own, and collected his thoughts.

He began, "Thank you, Reverend Stevens, for giving me this opportunity to speak to your congregation."

Raising his arm with closed fist, he declared, "Today, I stand before you a resolute and prouder man...!" Pausing to let the effect of his words spread out over the audience, he lowered his hand to his heart: "And yet, I stand here a sorely-tried humbler man."

Pausing, while the audience contemplated the disparity of his statements, he continued: "The pride I speak of is not a self-induced egotistical pride, but the pride I feel for my family and friends, who stuck by me during my dark days of self-pity, self-denial, self-imposed isolation, and the subsequent desolation of my very soul.

349

"Through prayer and meditation, I have learned that we cannot accept forgiveness from others, until we first forgive ourselves—. Yes, you heard me right, Brethren and Sisters in Christ; **Others Cannot Forgive Us—Until We First Forgive Ourselves**.

"Yes, I know that logic would seem to dictate that it should be the other way around. Nevertheless, God's guidance has shown me that we cannot *tolerate* others until we first *tolerate* ourselves—. **Likewise, we** cannot *receive* others into our hearts until we *like* ourselves. We cannot *cherish* others until we *cherish* ourselves. And, we cannot *love* others until we first *love* ourselves—**praised be his name!**

"By the same divine insight, we cannot dishonor others without bringing dishonor upon ourselves; we cannot *hate* others without *hating* ourselves. And, we cannot *sacrifice* others without ultimately *sacrificing* ourselves....

"Consequently, we cannot seek compassion from others until we first find solace in our hearts. **To seek forgiveness from others without first forgiving ourselves only serves to *demean* our own sense of self-worth and lowers the opinion of the forgiver.**

"I realize that these words may sound confusing to you at first, because it appears that we are putting the cart before the horse—that we are projecting the path of our future without pulling from our experiences in the past.

"Let me share with you a common misperception. Most people erroneously think that we are what others tell us 'who and what we are.' That, my friends, is merely someone else's opinion and does not define 'who and what we are.' In the final analysis, 'who we are— really is 'whom we think and feel we are'—**it's how you and I fit and feel inside our own skins!**

"Obviously, other people have opinions of 'who we are and what we are'—we also have opinions about them. Nevertheless, we each mirror back, not a reflection of their myopic opinion, but the radiance of our true feelings of how we perceive ourselves. That, ultimately, is the essence of what we are—to our families, to our friends, and even to the strangers that we meet on the pathways of life.

"Only when I understood the relativity of *self-image* ingrained in *self-worth* did I ask God to give me the strength, the passion, and the compassion to forgive myself. In turn, and only then, could I ask my daughter Sherrill for *her* forgiveness. We have since reconciled and have become a much stronger loving family. I can now give her away in marriage to Randy, her fiancé; because I realize that my real love for her resides not in my mind, but in my heart. My mental capacity of love for her is merely a conduit of love drawn from its limitless resource in my heart, which allows me to express my love for her—to her—as a father for his child."

Charles' profound words and revelation awed the audience. Many sat with faces illuminated by their own newly discovered sense of awareness of *who they were—what they were.* Charles paused and observed the new self-awareness spreading across the faces of the congregation. He held up his right hand and boomed in a deep baritone voice, "**Praise be to God.**"

As he walked back to his seat, he saw that his family, including Hank, looked at him with new admiration in their eyes, supplemented with a glaze of proud tears. The minister returned to the pulpit and stood in silence, mulling through his own thoughts. Finally, he opined, "In all my training and experience, I have never heard a message so profoundly and succinctly presented. I have studied the Bible along with the great works of poets and philosophers and have been inspired by their messages. Brother Charles must have indeed received divine guidance to be able to tie together—forgiveness, reconciliation, love, self-image, and self-worth—into the message that you have just heard.

"Normally, I record the Sunday services on audio tape for future reference. Today, I will have our staff transcribe Brother Charles' message, so that all of you can have a printed copy to read for yourselves and to share his inspiration with others."

Sherrill drove her Corvette to the studio. She wanted to be early to review the storyboard and prepare herself for the next scene. As she drove, her mind flashed back to events of the morning. Hearing her father in church was not a new experience. Nevertheless, his statement to the congregation went well beyond her expectation of her father's ability. She had even requested a copy of the message from the minister.

As she continued her drive to work, she thought of her family's plans for the coming week. Her Uncle Hank would be returning to Merced this afternoon and her parents would be leaving tomorrow morning. Later in the week, she would drive to Merced and drop off Aunt Vicki, and then continue on to Yosemite National Park to shoot scenes on location. After filming was completed, she planned to return home to Merced to relax for a couple of days and complete her end of semester test at school.

Entering the studio, she walked directly to the storyboard. A large poster of a hamburger had replaced the display. At the bottom of the poster were the words: "Hamburgers—anyone?" She stopped and laughed. Apparently, the art department had watched the news on TV and had seen the "Great Drive-in Caper," starring Sherrill and Laura.

When she turned to see if anyone was looking, the entire crew came out from hiding with air-horns in their hands. The stage area resonated with a cacophony of horns blaring and people hollering frustrated *traffic-jam* phrases. Sherrill reacted at first by covering her ears, and then pushing her long blonde hair up with both hands. She released her hair and held her hands up in mock surrender.

Brad hollered, "Cut—that's a take."

Sherrill looked at Brad with feigned irritation, "I should have known that you were behind all of this."

With a twinkle in his eye, Brad retorted, "I didn't call for a *retake*— did I?" Brad and the crew laughed at Sherrill's reaction and the camaraderie generated by their own participation in the practical joke.

Emile walked through, haranguing, "Okay, people, we've got an episode to shoot. We have to wrap it up by tomorrow because, as you already know, we go on the road Tuesday." The cast and crew scattered to make their final preparation for the first scene.

Brad asked, "How was your morning off...do anything interesting?"

"Oh, I probably didn't mention it, but my parents are in town. Uncle Hank and Aunt Vicki have been entertaining them by showing them the local sights." She added, to see Brad's reaction, "My parents asked me to go back home with them."

Brad's reaction was immediate, as the color in his face faded into a chalky mask and he stood with his mouth partially open. Sherrill turned and walked away, flippantly remarking over her shoulder, "But I told them, 'No.'"

Brad was used to maintaining his composure, thereby maintaining control. However, he knew that Sherrill knew that she had just gotten through his armor plating. Her remark was a zinger that had left him speechless and emotionally naked.

The next scene began:

Annabelle and Belinda walk into the town bank. Belinda says, "While you're speaking with your father, I'm going to withdraw some money for new clothes."

Annabelle walks through the room-divider gate and kisses her father on the cheek, "Daddy, Belinda has invited me to spend the day at her ranch and I'll need some money to buy new riding clothes."

Her father stands up and walks around his desk to face her, "Annabelle, you don't need any money. I have an account at the General Store; you just tell the clerk to put your purchases on my account."

"Thank you, Daddy. Back in Richmond we always had to use money to buy things."

Her father hooks his thumbs into his vest and proudly states, "Well, out West a man's word is his bond and he can use it for money almost anywhere. Besides, I have a lot of investments in this town and I happen to own half interest in the General Store."

Annabelle knows nothing of her father's finances, but she suspects that her family is wealthy because she had wanted for nothing while she lived back East. "We also want to rent a horse and buggy. Do you own the stables too?"

"No, but I keep my horse and buggy there during the day while I'm working. You just tell ol' Joe what you need and he'll fix you up."

Annabelle leans forward and kisses her father, "Thank you, Daddy. Well, it looks like Belinda is ready to go. I'll be home tomorrow afternoon, before dark."

She turns to leave and her father calls after her, "Oh, did you meet any interesting boys at the dance last night?"

Annabelle smiles over her shoulder, "Got to go, Daddy. Say hello to Mother for me."

James sits back down in his chair and shakes his head. He watches Annabelle and Belinda laughing as they leave the bank. He turns his attention to his ledger. Shaking his head, he says to himself, "Women—?"

The scene changes to the general store where Annabelle and Belinda are buying clothes:

The clerk greets them, "Good morning, ladies. What can I do for you?

Belinda replies, "We're here to buy riding clothes, but we'll pick them out ourselves."

Annabelle reveals, "I've never worn western clothes before; I don't even know what to buy."

"Let me help." Belinda picks out a shirt, a pair of denim jeans, and a pair of boots with socks.

"Here, try these on while I find something for myself."

Annabelle leaves through a curtained door and the scene continues with Belinda looking through the selections. Annabelle returns decked out in her new clothes.

Belinda coos, "You even look great in western clothes, but the shirt is too tight and the jeans are too baggy. How are the boots?"

"I could barely get my feet in them and my toes feel like they are in a vise."

Belinda makes another quick selection, "Here, try these on."

Annabelle disappears and Belinda selects a belt, a cowgirl hat, and a gold bandanna.

Annabelle reappears wearing the new selections and Belinda critically looks her over, "You look almost like a real cowgirl. Here try these on."

Annabelle tries on the belt, and then selects a smaller size; tries on the hat and selects a different style. Belinda walks up and places the bandanna around Annabelle's neck. She steps back and nods at her approvingly, "Now you're starting to look like a real cattle ropin' cowgirl."

The scene fades out.

As the next scene unfolds, the two girls are sitting in a buggy in front of the stables. Annabelle has the reins in her hands with an unsure look on her face. She says to Belinda, "I've never driven a wagon or buggy. Maybe you'd better drive."

Belinda instructs, "Just hold the reins loosely in your hands and flip the reins once, and then say, 'Giddy-up.'"

Annabelle flips the reins, "Giddy-up." With the storefronts in the background, the buggy lurches forward and the cameras record their passage out of town.

Emile hollered, "Cut—that's a take. Okay now we want to do the close-ups of Annabelle and Belinda in the runaway buggy."

The scene begins:

From offstage a grip jerks the reins out of Annabelle's hands. The carriage jolts forward and large fans blow both of their hats off their heads.

With the wind blowing in their faces and the carriage rocking and jolting, Annabelle and Belinda react with wide-eyed panic and screams. They try to hold on to anything and each other.

They shot the scene and Emile hollered, "Cut." He walked up to the two actresses, "Your expressions and screams were fine. However, I want to re-shoot the scene with you—first, hugging each other for safety. Then, you become aware that you can't maintain your balance. You let go of each other and hang onto the seat railing for balance and continue to react with panic."

The scene was re-shot and Emile hollered, "Cut—that's a take."

The next scene showed:

Luke is on his horse, leaning over and holding onto the reins of the stopped carriage. He turns his horse and shouts to Annabelle and Belinda, "Are you all right?"

Annabelle says with strained relief, "Yes, Luke, thank you for coming to our rescue."

Luke impassively states, "You'd better let me drive. Belinda, you can ride my horse." He gets off his horse and starts adjusting the stirrups for Belinda as she steps down off the buggy.

The next scene began:

The cameras are close-in for a portrait shot of Luke and Annabelle sitting in the buggy. Annabelle places her arm through Luke's and squeezes. She smiles, "Oh, Luke, thank you, I feel much safer now."

Luke beams a smile and flips the reins, "Giddy-up."

Belinda is on Luke's horse and her body motion projects that the horse is starting to trot alongside the buggy.

Emile hollered, "Cut—take."

The rest of the afternoon's filming was spent at the ranch house with scenes showing preparation for the three actors to go for a saddleback ride, and other supporting scenes.

The time flew by for Sherrill and she was surprised when Emile announced, "Okay, people, it is seven o'clock. See you here bright and early tomorrow morning. We will finish up the rest of the episode shots in the studio. Then we'll film some preliminary scenes for episodes two and three that require close-ups of Sherrill.

"As soon as we get back from Yosemite then we will start shooting an episode where Sherrill doesn't appear. After that's done then we will pick up shooting scenes with Sherrill again. It is a busy schedule, so remember your lines. I want a minimum of retakes—Goodnight."

Sherrill walked back to her dressing room with Laura and said, "I just realized how busy filming can be. Emile is trying to do parts of multiple episodes during the same time frame."

Laura replied, "Actually the cast has it pretty easy, since there are many scenes where we don't have to appear. It's the crew that is always busy, since they have to be there for every scene."

"You're right," agreed Sherrill, with a new appreciation for the job that the crew accomplished every day. She looked around for Brad, but he had apparently already left for the day. She missed him being there and decided to apologize to him for zinging him earlier; but then again, maybe she wouldn't.

Brad sat in his car and watched Sherrill get into her car. He followed her until he saw her pull safely into her hotel garage, and then he headed to his own lonesome apartment. In the past, he had dated dozens of women and had an extended relationship with six or seven. He had even set up housekeeping with a couple of them, but those relationships had never lasted more than six months. Since Sherrill had appeared in his life, he looked at other women and found them uninteresting.

Sherrill entered her suite to find that her parents and Aunt Vicki weren't back from dinner. Opening the refrigerator door, she saw a Cobb salad with a note from her mother, "Back around ten. Love, Mother."

She changed into her swimming suit and swam for thirty minutes. After a shower, she sat in her robe, turned on the TV, and dined on the salad. Her parents came in with Aunt Vicki and they were laughing at her mother, who was a little tipsy from too much wine with dinner.

Sherrill asked, "What are you all laughing about?"

Aunt Vicki, who had also imbibed a little too much wine, tittered, "Your mother just said that she was going to stay in California and become a beach bum. She's going to surf by day and carouse by night." The three laughed again.

Sherrill, although she hadn't had anything to drink, was sobered by the words and thought; *Mother has been isolated on a farm for most of her life. Her life's routine had been boring most of the time and this was the first decent vacation she'd had in ten years.* She walked over to her mother and hugged her tightly, "Thank you Mother for all the sacrifices you've made for us kids."

Her mother looked at her with double vision, and then her body relaxed and she hugged Sherrill. "You all have been no sacrifice, Honey...you are my children; you are my life."

Sherrill, confused, said, "But you just said that you wanted to be a beach bum."

"Oh, Honey, is that what upset you? Of course, everybody likes a little excitement in his or her life. Also, the wine may make our tongues loose, but, Honey, I chose my life and it is a good life. I would never really wish that I had a different life without your father and you children."

Her profession of love moved Vicki and Charles. They all came together in a long family hug. Charles felt a deeper love for Mavis because he realized that she had endured a life of sacrifice, and he vowed to make it easier for her in the future.

The next day, Sherrill was between sets and studying school lessons in her dressing room. Brad knocked and entered. Sherrill observed, "I haven't seen you around this morning."

Brad quipped, "Well, I do like watching you act, but the studio doesn't pay me for that and insists that I dedicate at least part of my time to official duties."

"What are you doing right now?"

Brad pulled out a letter and grinned, "Well, right now, I'm a mail boy." He waved the envelope in the air and Sherrill jumped up and grabbed the letter.

It was from Randy and had her Merced address on it! She squealed and kissed Brad on his cheek. She tore the envelope apart and Brad said, "With benefits like that, I might just transfer to the mailroom."

Sherrill didn't hear him. She had sat back down and was avidly reading the letter. Brad backed out the door and with a heavy heart, went back to his office.

The letter began:

My Darling Sherrill,

I just came back to the air base after watching your press conference with my drill instructor and his wife Maria. Maria commented about you all through the interview. You've gained an avid fan in her, and her husband loved you too.

Darling, seeing you look so beautiful, yet so far from my arms, made me want to cry. But I didn't dare cry because visions of you would become blurred and I didn't want to miss a moment of seeing the most beautiful precious woman in the whole wide world.

I longed to reach out and touch you, as I do in my dreams every night. You looked like an angel that turned into a princess on earth. You are my earth angel. I remember being in your arms and you in my arms and I felt that I was in heaven.

I was so proud of your answers to all the questions. You looked so composed, like you had been doing it all your life. Your answers were so intelligent and profound. I could tell by the audience's reaction that they loved you too and I felt envious that they could be there with you—. Darling, I love you so very much.

I don't want to write about my life here in the barracks, but I know that you want to know what has been happening in my life as much as I want to know what is happening in yours.

I am the Barracks Chief for my barracks. They call me BC and I am training with a great bunch of guys. They are all giving their best. We march everywhere; I even march in my sleep.

Our day starts at 5:00 AM and ends most of the time at 9:00 PM, but they sometimes roust us out of bed during the night to clean the barracks or stand a surprise inspection. We eat regularly and I have gained seven pounds, but it has been mostly muscles in my arms and legs. My waistline is actually smaller; I've taken up a couple of notches on my belt.

We have put together a basketball team to play another barracks and we have had our first practice scrimmage—wish us luck.

I have to go, Honey, lights out. I love you so very much and I dream of the day when we can be together again, as husband and wife. Give your tummy a little pat, so our baby knows that Daddy loves him.

My undying love forever,
Randy

Sherrill looked at the postmark on the envelope and saw that it was weeks old. She crumpled the envelope in her fist and pressed the letter to her heart. Hot tears flowed from her eyes, ruining her makeup. She finally stopped crying and looked in the mirror. Her face was a mess. She pulled out a couple of tissues and started cleaning her face. The telephone rang and she picked it up, "Hello."

Hank said, "Oh, good, I was hoping that I could reach you, Sherrill. I just got off the phone with Randy. He tried to call you at the studio, but they gave him the runaround. I know that they were just trying to protect you, but I know how badly you would have wanted to talk to him.

"He asked me to tell you that he loves you and misses you terribly. He said that the air force is promoting him to be an officer—which would be a second lieutenant. I don't know how that is possible, since he doesn't have a college degree and he hasn't even completed basic training. It never would have happened when I was in the air force.

"Randy told me that it was part of a special training package and that he tried to get in touch with you to discuss it. But, seeing that he couldn't, he made the decision himself, for you and the baby's future. I think that it is a good career move."

Hank paused, and then consoled, "Sherrill, Honey, Randy said that he wouldn't be able to contact you for a long time—he didn't know how long. The air force must think that he is a very special individual because what happened to him—just has never happened before."

The line was silent, "Sherrill, are you still there?"

Sherrill replied, "Yes, Uncle Hank. My feelings and my thoughts are such a jumble right now. I just read my first letter from Randy, not three minutes ago. It was mailed weeks ago and it was the best love letter that I have ever received.

"Randy was trying to contact me while I was reading his letter. I think that my heart is going to break." Sherrill started crying again.

Hank replied, "Hold in there, Honey. I know that you love each other and you will—someday—be together."

Sherrill composed herself, "Thank you for calling, Uncle Hank—bye."

She wanted to burst into tears again and wash away her longing, but her next set was in fifteen minutes. Looking in the mirror, she steeled herself and called makeup.

Laura knocked on the door and entered. She stared at Sherrill, "Oh, Honey, you look a mess. Brad called and said that you might need a shoulder to cry on. I'll call makeup and have them come over."

Sherrill replied, "I already have."

Laura walked over and hugged her. Sherrill placed her hand against Laura's encircled arms, "Thank you for being a friend—thank Brad too, for me."

The makeup artist knocked on the door and Sherrill composed herself for her next scene.

Emile reiterated the shooting sequence for the cast, "Okay, we're going to shoot the last scene of the first episode. This is the scene with Luke and Annabelle. They talk; then Annabelle kisses Luke for saving her during the runaway horse scene. Luke is so excited and pumped up that he gets up and dives into the pool with his clothes on. Let's get it in one take."

The scene opens:

Annabelle says, "Luke, where did you learn to make a rock skip so many times across the water?"

Luke replies, "I've been skipping rocks all my life." He throws another one and it skips five times before sinking.

Annabelle picks up a rock and throws it. It skips once then sinks below the surface. She says, "You're so big and strong. I forgot to properly thank you for saving Belinda and me in our runaway carriage."

Annabelle gets up on her knees and leans in to kiss Luke. (Sherrill, remembering Laura's advice, thought of Randy) Annabelle presses her lips hungrily, hard, and long on Luke's lips.

Luke topples backward, throws his hands above his head in surrender, and lies there with his eyes closed. (Gary Binger knew they had blown the scene)

Sherrill opened her eyes and was so embarrassed that she was responsible for blowing the scene that she stood up quickly, subconsciously fanning her face with her hand because of the pounding pulse in her head. She stepped back and caught her heel on the edge of the blanket. Losing her balance, she staggered back and fell into the pool.

Emile screamed, "Cut—Cut—Cut."

The crew and cast began laughing, cheering, clapping, and hollering, "Encore—encore—encore."

Emile looked around at his cast and crew's reaction and thought; *if they liked it so much then the television audience should like it too.* He shouted, "That's a take—set up for the next scene." He waved his hand in the air and called out, "Rewrite!"

Gary Binger and a stage grip helped Sherrill out of the pool. She was so mortified from embarrassment that she couldn't cry. Laura ran up and helped her back to her dressing room. Laura said, "You two were great. Did you and Gary plan that on Emile?"

"Na—No," denied Sherrill, shivering from the cold water and embarrassment. "You told me to think of someone else when I didn't have the feeling for the scene. I closed my eyes and thought of Randy and got carried away."

Laura exclaimed, "Wow, I've got to meet this man if he has that effect on you when you are just thinking of him."

Sherrill took a shower and sat through makeup for the next scene. She got dressed and walked back to the set. Taking her place next to Gary, he flirtingly teased, "I think that was the sexiest kiss that I have ever had in my life—want to go on a date with me?"

Sherrill looked at him with disdain, "No, thank you. You're great at dancing—let's stick to that."

Gary got a quizzical look on his face. He couldn't decide whether he had just received a compliment or, impossibly, a rejection—or maybe both.

Yosemite

Sherrill and Aunt Vicki, having packed the night before, were on Route 99 headed for Merced by 5:00 AM. The air blew through their hair as she pressed the accelerator, opening up the Corvette. It hugged the curves on the grapevine with exhilarating catlike performance. The feeling was sheer power and joy.

They stopped in Bakersfield for breakfast, then hit the road again, and were in Merced before noon. Sherrill stayed long enough to drop off her aunt, check her mail, and have lunch with her aunt and uncle. She assured them that she would be returning home after filming in Yosemite.

She passed through the western gate of Yosemite National Park and continued through the park. Rising up from the valley was the majestic face of El Capitan, carved during the last ice age. This exposed monolith soared straight up from the floor of Yosemite Valley to its 3,600-foot height. She passed Yosemite Falls, where its waters fell almost 2500 feet. Nevertheless, it was Bridalveil Falls that caught her imagination. The water fell only 620 feet, but the swirling air currents splayed the fine mist into a bridal veil. She thought, *what a wonderful location to be married.*

Many scenes from previous episodes of "The Dons of Eldorado" had be filmed at the falls with the park panorama as a backdrop. A logistical crew had been on-site since Monday and Sherrill stopped by to find out where the cast would be staying for the night. She learned that she would be sharing a room with Laura Blevins at the Yosemite Village Lodge, at Laura's request.

Sherrill meandered through the filming location and paused for a moment to watch the work in progress. One of the cameramen, Carl Ryder, waved, and then walked her way. He was walking hand-in-hand with a pretty young girl with a smile on her face and awed look of excitement in her eyes. As they approached, Sherrill greeted, "Hi, Carl, who's your friend?"

Carl's expression changed to mild surprise, "Hi, Sherrill. I didn't think that you would remember my name."

"Carl, I remember meeting you when we did the carriage scene in the San Joaquin Valley."

Carl was impressed, since he had been a part of the road crew and they had only met once. Then he remembered that Sherrill had asked him about the girl with him, "Oh, this is my new bride Tiffaney. We are here on our honeymoon."

"Congratulations, when did you get married?"

Tiffaney answered for Carl, "We got married last Sunday. We decided to combine our honeymoon with Carl's assignment to the Yosemite location."

"Well, you certainly picked a beautiful place for a honeymoon."

"It is a wonderful place, but since I'm working, we haven't had much chance to see the sights. Even now, I'm just on a break. I think it must be pretty boring for Tiffaney, but she says it isn't. There's nothing for her to do except stand around and watch us set up for tomorrow's filming."

Tiffaney flashed her eyes at Carl, "Yes, but the nights are worth the long wait."

A deep red spreading blush appeared across Carl's face that caused beads of sweat to appear on his forehead. The two girls laughed at his self-conscious reaction. However, the statement caused a tight knot of loneliness in the pit of Sherrill's stomach and reminded her of how much she missed and hungered for Randy's kisses and caresses.

Sherrill offered, "This is my first time in the park and I'm driving around to see the sights. Tiffaney, why don't you come with me? There is still plenty of daylight left and we could go see the Mariposa Grove of giant sequoias that I saw in a brochure.

Tiffaney looked at Carl with a pleading look in her eye. Carl turned to Sherrill, "Are you sure that you don't mind? I like having Tiffaney watching us set up, but I want her to see more of Yosemite too."

"I would love to have her company; part of the enjoyment of sightseeing is sharing it with someone else."

Carl and Tiffaney kissed a long parting honeymoon kiss. Tiffaney turned to Sherrill, "Okay, let me grab a coat—there's snow on the higher peaks." Flirtatiously, she glanced at Carl's belt buckle and added, "But there is no snow down below." Carl blushed at the obvious inference and quickly headed back to the staging area. The two girls laughed at the innuendo and Carl's reaction, and then went to get Tiffaney's coat.

With the convertible top down they drove away in the Corvette. Tiffaney shouted above the wind noise, "I'm glad to finally meet you,

Sherrill. Carl told me about a beautiful girl walking onto the set and Emile wanting to get her on film. Then I saw you on television when you had your news conference. I must admit that I was jealous at first, but now that I have met you—you're just a real person."

Smiling, Sherrill felt honored by the compliment, "I know how you feel, Tiffaney. When I first met Laura Blevins, all my previous impressions were from watching her on television. Now I realize that she's a normal wonderful person, who has the same needs and feelings as the rest of us mortals."

Tiffaney nodded in agreement, "Laura is beautiful, but Carl said that you are more beautiful and had balls."

Surprised, Sherrill asked, "Why in the world would he say something like that?"

"Well, he was talking on the phone with someone at the studio and they told him that you and Gary Binger changed the end of the episode without first consulting with Emile. They thought it was hilarious because no one has ever dared to do that before."

Sherrill smiled at the misconception, "Well, if you don't tell anyone, I'll tell you what actually happened."

Tiffaney crossed her heart and whispered, "I promise."

"After I kissed Gary, he was supposed to dive into the pool from the exhilaration of the kiss. What really happened was that I had my eyes closed and was thinking of Randy, my fiancé, while kissing Gary. Gary tipped over backward and just laid there because he knew that we had blown the scene. I realized that it was actually I whom had blown the scene and when I stood up, I tripped on the picnic blanket and fell backward into the pool."

Tiffaney screamed with laughter, "Oh, that's funny—my promise doesn't include Carl does it?"

"Especially, Carl!"

"You're right, Sherrill. Girls do need to have their little secrets from the guys, but I would still love to tell him."

Sherrill advised, "When you two watch the episode on television, just think of the extra pleasure that you will have when they show the ending. Only you will know what really happened. If you told him then it might ruin the ending for him."

Convinced, Tiffaney agreed, "You are right—I can't wait to see you on TV and watch his reaction."

Sherrill had brought two fine cameras with her. One was a 35-millimeter Nikon SLR camera and the other was a Polaroid instant camera. While they were at the sequoia grove, she asked a tourist to take pictures of them driving their car though the carved out Wawona Tree. The huge sequoia tree was a world-renowned landmark because of the tunnel and road cut through it in the early 1880s.

Sherrill took the instant print and autographed it for Tiffaney, saying, "You can show this to your future children and they may wonder who 'Sherrill' was, but you will always have memories of driving through the tree with me."

Tiffaney stared at the picture, "Thank you, Sherrill. I will include this with our honeymoon album pictures."

They put on their coats and walked to the "Grizzly Giant" sequoia, which rose 209' and was over 2700 years old. It was late November and patches of snow were on the ground, making walking tricky. When they reached the tree and gazed upward, it appeared to scrape against the sky. Sherrill tried to put the height into perspective then remembered that a football field was 300 feet in length. She uttered in awe, "Wow, this giant tree is two-thirds the length of a football field."

Looking upward and watching the clouds scudding above the treetops induced the sensation of vertigo. Sherrill and Tiffaney had to quickly look down to keep from losing their balance. Tiffaney suggested, "Let me take a funny picture of you."

Sherrill, being game, nodded, "Okay."

Tiffaney led her away from the trees, all the while glancing back. She climbed up to a rock outcropping, "Okay, stand here and spread your feet apart."

Stepping back while looking through the viewfinder, she directed, "Face sideways like you're looking at the tree, stick out your arms, and hold them like you are giving Randy a hug. Okay, open your arms a little—wider—okay that's good. Now turn your face and look at me. Good."

She took a picture with each camera. Sixty seconds later, she handed the Polaroid print to Sherrill. Sherrill's eyes widened, "This is simply amazing; it looks like I've climbed halfway up that gigantic tree. How did you learn to do that?"

"When you date a cameraman, you pick up a few tricks. It's an illusion because the picture is two-dimensional; it tricks the eye into viewing the scene in a three-dimensional perspective."

Sherrill glanced at the sun in the western sky, "We had better go; I want to stop by the Badger Pass Ski Lodge before they close."

Stepping off the rock outcropping, she slipped on a patch of snow. Trying not to fall, she threw her weight on one foot and badly twisted her ankle. She cried out, "Oh, damn; oh, darn-darn—it hurts!"

Tiffaney knelt down, "Let me see how bad it is." She examined Sherrill's ankle and couldn't detect a break. It was already starting to swell and Tiffaney loosened Sherrill's shoelaces. Tears of pain ran down Sherrill's cheeks.

After resting five minutes, the initial sharp spikes of pain were starting to subside, replaced by a throbbing ache. Sherrill flexed her foot and there were no crunching or sharp spikes of pain. Tiffaney helped her down to level ground and Sherrill put her weight on her foot. "It feels okay until I put side pressure on my ankle. I think that I'll be okay."

She started walking and limped with discomfort. "Tiffaney, I think that it will be okay as long as I walk straight." With Tiffaney's help they were able reach the car.

"Do you want me to drive?" Tiffaney offered.

Sherrill saw the excitement in Tiffaney's eyes. "Have you ever driven a 'Vette' before?"

Tiffaney shook her head, "No."

Sherrill handed her the keys, "It has lots of power—press lightly on the accelerator. If you are in snow or ice, start out in second gear and let out slowly on the clutch—that's all there is to it."

Tiffaney had a little trouble at first, but she learned quickly and soon began enjoying the experience of driving a powerful sports car. She glanced at Sherrill and grinned, "This is just incredible."

They arrived at the lodge and went to the lounge. Selecting a table next to a large plate glass window facing the ski slopes, they ordered hot chocolate. Sipping the drink they relaxed and watched the skiers gliding down the slopes to assemble at the chair lift, stand in line, and then take the lift back up to the top.

"Have you ever skied?" asked Tiffaney.

"Yes, I've been on the slopes several times. Last winter, I went with Randy and his family to Colorado for a ski-weekend. It was a wonderful experience."

Tiffaney giggled, "Did you sleep with Randy?"

Sherrill smiled, "No. We were with his parents and I shared a bed with his sister. Besides, we had planned to wait until we were married." She added, "Obviously, that didn't happen."

Tiffaney stammered with embarrassment, "I'm—I'm sorry, Sherrill. I forgot that you are pregnant. It's just that Carl and I are on our honeymoon and making love is always on my mind."

"I understand," assured Sherrill. "I know that you didn't ask it to hurt me."

Sherrill started thinking of Randy, and then stopped herself. She knew that it would just make her envious of Tiffaney and Carl. She suggested, "Let's take the chair lift up to the top and back."

"What about your ankle?"

"I think its okay; we'll be sitting in a chair lift the whole trip."

They bought a lift ticket and were informed that admission to the lift would be closing down in ten minutes. As Tiffaney helped her walk to the lift, Sherrill commented, "Getting off my feet at the lodge did my ankle worlds of good. I can almost walk without a limp, even on this snow."

They got on the chair lift without any problems. The higher they went, the more scenic the view. However, the cold became more obvious and they huddled together to share their body warmth. The wind picked up and caused their eyes to tear, but the experience was invigorating and exhilarating. Sherrill would have liked to get off at the top, but the lift system was configured for skiers to ski out of the chair.

The chair lift went through the turn around at the top and continued a hundred feet when it jerked to a sudden stop. Tiffaney looked around and stated positively, "See they knew that we were on the chair lift and stopped it, so we could appreciate this panoramic view."

Sherrill laughed, "I don't think it was for our benefit." The chair swayed slowly in the wind and the two women watched skiers gliding down the slopes. They waved at the people that were riding up on the lift and the skiers waved back. Ten minutes passed and the cold started creeping through the thin layers their clothing; both girls were starting to shiver. Tiffaney looked back over her shoulder and saw the safety operator standing on the exit berm. She hollered, "Hey, how much longer 'til the lift starts movin'?"

The operator hollered back, "I don't know. A coupling broke in the drive assembly and the automatic safety locks kicked-in."

Tiffaney hollered back, "We didn't dress for skiing and we are getting cold."

367

The operator hollered back, "We may have to have you jump down into the snow and climb up the slope. You can get warm in the ski patrol chalet."

Sherrill and Tiffaney looked down. It was at least twenty feet to the snow and they didn't know what was below the surface. Sherrill stated with alarm, "No way; I'm not going to risk hurting my baby by jumping."

Tiffaney hollered up at the operator, "It is too far to jump. The girl with me is going to have a baby and she also has a badly sprained ankle."

The operator ran back to the emergency phone and called his supervisor, "This is Bill at the top. I've got two riders stranded on the chair lift. One of them is pregnant and has a sprained ankle, so she can't jump down from the chair."

The supervisor instructed, "Jerry and Ted from the ski patrol should be in the warm-up cabin. Have them get the chair lift passengers down."

Bill called the cabin and Ted answered, "Hey, you and Jerry need to rescue two girls from the chair lift; one of them is pregnant."

The two men grabbed their rescue tackle and met Bill on the berm. Jerry spotted the girls and scrambled down the slope, "We'd better hurry, round trippers never dress warm enough for the cold at the top."

The three men stood below Sherrill and Tiffaney. Jerry looked up, "Hey, I've seen that girl on television; her name is Sherrill." Bill and Ted then recognized her and their sense of urgency increased with their desire to personally meet her.

Jerry called up, "Sherrill, we are going to throw a weighted-cord up to you. You need to pull the tackle up and hook it onto the metal eyelet just above your heads." He threw the weight up. Sherrill and Tiffaney both reached out, but it was too far out to catch. After a couple more tries, Tiffaney caught the line and pulled up the tackle. She supported the tackle in place, while Sherrill hooked the eyelet.

Jerry instructed, "Okay, one of you put your foot in the loop and put the safety strap around you, and then hold onto the rope while we lower you down."

Sherrill urged, "You go first, Tiffaney."

Tiffaney declined, "No, you go first. I can always jump down if I have to."

Sherrill followed Jerry's instructions and was lowered down. Once Tiffaney was lowered, Jerry directed, "Ted, you and Bill take the young ladies up to the warm-up cabin, while I retrieve the tackle.

Ted and Bill helped Sherrill climb up the slope; Tiffaney followed. When the girls reached the cabin, their hands and feet were numb. Their shoes and socks were soaked through with melted snow. Ted threw another log on the fire, while Bill poured two cups of hot coffee for the girls. The two men massaged the girls' feet to get the circulation flowing. Ted looked up and confided, "Normally, I would only do this for my girlfriend."

Sherrill replied, "She's a lucky girl; you have strong fingers that are gentle."

"Yeah, but she is going to be jealous when she finds out that it was your feet that I massaged today." Sherrill didn't reply. She just leaned back in the chair and enjoyed the warm invigorating massage.

The shoes were starting to steam from the heat of the fireplace when Jerry stomped the snow off his boots and entered the cabin, "No one else in the chairs near the top wants to be rescued. They all said that they would stick it out until the lift gets fixed—hope those guys at the bottom get it done soon"

He walked over to the radio and called the base, "Base, this is Jerry at the top. We've rescued the two riders. One of them is the television star, Sherrill. You may want contact the supervisor and see what he wants us to do in the meantime."

Bill reluctantly picked up his mittens, "I need to get back to my station, in case the lift starts up. I'll see you guys later."

Sherrill reached out, took Bill's hand, and stood up; Tiffaney also stood up. Sherrill said, "Thanks, Bill, for helping us; we feel a lot better now." Instead of shaking his hand, she kissed him on the cheek and Tiffaney followed suit.

Ted good-naturedly jostled Bill out of the way, "Bye, Bill." He put his face in between the two girls and was rewarded with a kiss on the cheek. Jerry bumped Ted out of the way and was likewise rewarded with a kiss on the cheek. They all laughed at the flirtatious macho-man antics, and waved as Bill went out through the door.

The supervisor called on the radio, "Jerry, I want you and Ted to bring Sherrill and the other girl down on the rescue litters. I'm dispatching another team up the mountain to replace you. They will take a snow-cat up to the top with replacement litters. We should have the lift going in another twenty minutes and I need you two to take the lift back up to make sure everyone else is able to ski down okay."

Jerry replied, "Roger—boss. We'll bring the girls down."

Ted remarked, "Looks like fun times are over—duty calls."

The shoes and socks were nearly dry. Jerry taped Sherrill's ankle and put her shoes and socks back on for her. Tiffaney managed for herself. The ski patrol placed the girls sitting and facing backward on the litter and skied down the mountain.

Sherrill watched the scenery flash past and it reminded her of riding in a rear-facing seat in the back of her dad's station wagon. Her litter was in front of Ted and Tiffaney. She watched as Ted expertly maneuvered the steep slopes and the moguls. She felt confident that Jerry was doing the same.

When they got to the lodge, the ski lodge general manager and the supervisor met them. The manager apologized, "I'm sorry, Sherrill, that you and your friend were stranded on the chair lift. Is there anything we can do to make it up to you for your inconvenience?"

Sherrill replied, "No, we're fine. Jerry, Ted, and Bill were very professional and turned our little misadventure into a pleasant experience." She added, "Oh, there is one thing you could do."

She turned to her companion, "Tiffaney, would you get the cameras out of the car?"

Tiffaney returned with the cameras. Sherrill handed the cameras to a woman in the crowd that had gathered to catch a glimpse of Sherrill. "Would you mind taking a couple of pictures of us?"

Feeling flattered to be singled out, the woman agreed, "Oh, I'd love to." The four men grouped together with the girls. She took a couple of pictures with the Nikon camera, and then emptied the cartridge in the Polaroid camera.

Sherrill autographed a print for each of them, plus one for the woman who had taken the pictures. The manager and supervisor helped Sherrill up the stairs to the lodge; she turned and waved good-bye to the ski patrol. The supervisor excused himself, "I've got to get back and see how the repairs on the lift are coming along."

Tiffaney looked at her watch, "I need to contact Carl; he's going to be worried sick."

The manager gestured toward a door, "Please, use the phone in my office."

Sherrill looked around and spied the sign for the ladies' room. "I'll meet you back here, Tiffaney."

Sherrill walked back from the restroom and stopped at the large plate glass windows. She saw that the chair lift was operational and a few stranded skiers were already coming down the slope. Tiffaney walked up to her, "I couldn't get in touch with Carl, but Laura Blevins was just checking into the lodge. I gave her a message from us and told her not to worry, to let everybody know that we're okay."

The manager walked up and handed each of them a weekend ski package, explaining, "We want you to come back to visit us again and enjoy our facilities. The ski package is good for the rest of this season."

Sherrill and Tiffaney thanked him, and then left to walk to the car. "Why don't you drive, you seem to really enjoy it."

Tiffaney gleefully accepted the keys, "Oh, thank you." She got into the driver's seat and opened her package. It included two all day lift tickets and lodging at the Yosemite Village lodge, plus dinner for two.

Sherrill handed her ski package to Tiffaney, "I won't be able to use this because my baby is due in April and the season will be over by then."

Tiffaney accepted the gift, "I sure wish that you and Randy could have used it with us, but you are right, the season will be over and you don't want to ski while you're pregnant. Maybe we can come up here over New Year's with another couple—Carl will be so excited."

They drove back to the Yosemite Village and linked up with the cast and crew at the lodge. Their adventures of the day were told and retold many times before the evening ended.

The next morning the adventure of their rescue from the chair lift hit the front pages and newscasts across the United States. Myra McDonald, in Hollywood, walked up to Brad and laid the paper in front of him, "It looks like Sherrill is creating her own promos."

Brad opined, "Yes, I already know about this. I just wish that I had been there to take charge of the situation."

Myra retorted with light sarcasm, "Yes, but if you had taken charge, then it may not have been so newsworthy."

Brad grinned at the rebuff, "Yeah, maybe you're right. But, I still wish that I had been there."

Myra remarked, "I must say that her timing was excellent. Last night's episode of "The Dons of Eldorado" was the one with her bit part in the carriage scene."

"I know," said Brad. "I watched it and saw why Emile wanted her on film."

Brad and Myra had once dated, but found that it caused too many complications at work; in addition, they were competitive with each other. They both still had feelings for each other and Myra teased, "Brad, if I didn't know better, I would say that you are falling for our little starlet."

Brad winced at the statement and confessed, "It wouldn't matter, would it? She is in love with another man and is pregnant with his baby."

Myra softened and gave Brad a hug. "Oh, Brad, I didn't know...I like Sherrill and wish that she was available for you. You deserve someone special because you are a special man. You know that you will always be special to me."

"Thanks, Myra. I sometimes wish that you and I could have been more compatible off the job because you are great at work."

Sherrill found that filming on the road was less demanding than filming in the studio. In many of the scenes, a stunt double or a body double was used to insure that the *star* was not unduly exposed to injury.

She only had to appear in scenes that required dialogue or close-up shots. She used much of her spare time to learn the art of movie making and getting to know the cast and crew on a personal basis.

Due to Tiffaney's tales of adventure with Sherrill, Carl became more interested in Sherrill as a person. With both Tiffaney and Sherrill watching, he explained, "Look at the scene of the runaway horse. What do you see?"

Sherrill replied, "A man on a horse chasing after two stunt women in a buggy."

"You see some action, but not a lot of excitement—right."

Tiffaney and Sherrill agreed and Carl continued, "Okay, I've focused the camera, now look at the horse's legs and the wagon wheels—move the camera with this handle to follow the action."

Sherrill looked at the scene through the camera viewer and saw the up-close flailing of the horse's legs and hooves and the buggy wheels turning so fast, they looked like a blur. Tiffaney took a look and saw the same thing.

Carl continued, "Mix close-up sound and high tempo music with that scene, splice it together in the editing room and 'Voila,' you've got a full blown action scene with a lot of suspense and drama."

A flashbulb of comprehension flashed in Sherrill's mind. She had seen a lot of chase scenes in movies and on television. She knew that the scenes had generated a realism that caused her heart to beat faster and she sometimes held her breath—now she knew why. "Now I understand. The images and sounds saturate our *sight* and *hearing*, causing us to subconsciously *taste* and *smell* the dust in the air and *feel* the jolts of the buggy as it bounces over the road."

"Exactly," confirmed Carl. "You have just discovered some of the magic of making movies." This insight took some of the mysticism out of movies for Sherrill, but instilled in her a greater appreciation for the talented artists behind the scenes.

While watching Emile direct, he explained, "Distant shots require exaggerated movement of the main body parts—arms, legs, head—to project a state of emotion. While close-up shots only require subtle movements—a raised eyebrow, a pointed finger, a pouting lip, or a particular look in the eyes to project the intended emotion." Sherrill recalled scenes of Vivien Leigh in "Gone With the Wind" and understood exactly what Emile was telling her.

David Jacobs, the master sound mixer, explained, "The sounds are recorded on the tape at a level just below saturation. In the editing room, the technician can then adjust a volume control to lower the sound volume to the proper level. The importance of proper sound recording can be explained by: If we recorded the sound level too low then we would get static and hiss in the sound if we tried to increase the volume above a certain level. If we recorded the sound above saturation then the sound becomes clipped and flat."

Sherrill had often wondered why she had to go back to the make-up artist between scenes. Ella Martin explained, "I have to apply brighter shades of make-up for distant or dark scenes to keep your face from looking washed out. If I didn't change your make-up for close-up scenes then your face would appear on film as bloated and blotchy."

Sherrill marveled at her newly found knowledge. She now understood why Emile spent so much time in the editing room and why he always stated, "I have to find out what the camera sees, because, what the camera sees is what the viewing audience will see, which may be different from what a person sees while the scene is being filmed."

This newly found awareness allowed Sherrill to become a better actress and it gave her the needed confidence that she was projecting the correct body language in a scene. Before, she had merely reacted and recited her lines. Now, she felt that she could proactively act by properly projecting her actions relative to the requirements of the scene.

By the end of the third day of on-location filming, Emile confided to his producer, "I was happy with Sherrill in prior scenes, but now, after such a short time, I have seen a marked transition in her acting. I see greatness in her future."

The producer viewed the edited film and simply nodded, "Emile, I agree with you."

The on-location filming was completed in the afternoon on the fourth day and the entire cast and crew gathered at the lodge for hors d'oeuvres and wine. Sherrill had a small glass of wine, and then switched to ginger ale. The cast and crew had liked Sherrill from the beginning, but as she intermingled with them, a bond of camaraderie developed that drew her into the sanctuary of the extended family. Her unaffected charm and grace impressed even the most stoic individuals.

The executive producer of the series stood up, clinking a spoon against his water glass, and announced through a microphone, "The board of directors has decided to do something that is unprecedented in a television series. Normally the episode that we just completed would not be shown for four or more weeks. But due to the press coverage and extraordinary fan mail that we have received, this episode will be shown on the network next Tuesday." His announcement was followed by loud applause.

He continued, "I want to congratulate Emile Fabio for discovering Sherrill and working with her and the cast to get an outstanding performance by her as the Annabelle Lee character." Everyone applauded. The producer motioned, "I would like Sherrill to come up and say a few words to the cast and crew."

Sherrill approached the microphone with happy tears on her cheeks. She leaned into the microphone, "I don't know what to say. I feel like I have just received an Oscar or Emmy or something."

She paused for a moment to collect her thoughts. Then, with a mischievous gleam in her eyes she spoke into the microphone, "First off, I would like to thank my cast and crew—."

She pulled back from the microphone and flashed a radiant smile. Her co-workers were caught off guard, and then realized that she had started a mock acceptance speech. They broke out in loud applause and whistles of approval. The applause died down and she leaned into the microphone, "Seriously though, I do want to thank all of you for your professionalism and personal support, without which I would have not been able to finish this first episode.

"During the last eight days, I have learned that filming an episode is not just a one-person show. It requires the concerted efforts of all the people in front of and behind the cameras. Working with you, I have learned more about filming than if I had watched all the movies made during the last fifty years.

All of you are special to me for your personal contribution to the success of 'The Dons of Eldorado.' However, if I were to pick out three people for special recognition, they would be: Emile Fabio, for discovering me and giving me the opportunity to be a part of "The Dons of Eldorado. Brad Thurman, who is not with us tonight, but has been a staunch supporter in promoting me and being my earthly guardian angel. Lastly, Laura Blevins for being such a wonderful role model and inspiring me to reach for the stars in my performance.

She turned to the producer, "Thank you, Mr. Zimmerman, for allowing me the opportunity to say the words that have been on my mind and in my heart."

She blew a kiss to the audience and gleefully shouted, "I love you all—thank you—thank you." Sherrill stepped away from the microphone and received an enthusiastic applause.

The producer stepped up to the microphone and mused, "Now I wished that I had really given Sherrill some kind of award. He winked, "Sherrill, if you ever get tired of acting, you can always get a job writing acceptance speeches." The audience laughed and applauded, feeling a special kinship toward their newest cast member.

Sherrill made her way to Laura, stopping to hug or shake hands with the cast and crew that congratulated her on completing her first episode. Laura smiled brightly and with extended arms, she drew Sherrill into a hug. "Thank you, Sherrill, for including me in your recognition. I'm so glad that you came into my life and consider me as one of your special friends."

Sherrill reconfirmed, "I owe you so much. You will always be my special friend."

They hugged each other again and Sherrill looked at her watch, "It's starting to get dark outside. I called Aunt Vicki and told her that I would drive back home tonight."

Laura cautioned, "Are you sure that you want to drive back home alone."

Sherrill laughed, "It's not a long drive; I'll be home by eight."

Accosted

The sun dropped below the Western sky and night closed in on the dark lonely curvy road. Sherrill held her speed down as the curves were poorly marked and she had to brake quickly to negotiate some of the twist and turns. Her mind was preoccupied with events back in Yosemite, when she heard a loud metallic clatter in the left front of her Corvette. She heard a pop-whoosh and the steering wheel jerked to the left as she wrested control of the car and stopped on the right shoulder. Two cars whooshed by while she sat contemplating the difficulty of changing a tire in the dark. Resigning herself, she got out of the car and confirmed that the left front tire was flat.

Having grown up on a farm, she was familiar with the procedure of changing a tire. Leaving the lights on, she retrieved the spare tire from the trunk, rolled it up front, and let it fall to the ground in front of the headlights. As she was walking back to retrieve the jack, a car passed her then braked to a stop. She paused by her car door and watched as the car backed up and then stopped in front of her car.

The driver got out. He was a big burly man with hulking shoulders, almost as tall as Randy, but heavier. He had left his car door open with the motor still running. He smiled as he approached, but she felt an uneasy chill run down her back and the hair stood up on her arms. Although, he was handsome beneath his unshaven face, his eyes were cold and staring. In a forced friendly voice he nosed around, "I see you've got some car trouble 'little lady'—I don't see anyone else around; are you all alone?"

Sherrill steadied the tremor in her voice, "It's just a flat tire. You needn't bother; I know how to change it myself."

The man grinned, exposing yellowed crooked teeth, "I'm only here to help you, if I can, little lady. No use someone as pretty as you gettin' your nice clean little hands dirty." Abruptly, he stopped with an expression of recognition, and growled in surprised accusation, "I know you; you're one of them TV people.

Further alarmed by his patronizing words and hulking demeanor, Sherrill grabbed the car door handle and slightly opened it. She considered getting into her car, but a cloth-top convertible offered little protection against someone wanting to get inside. She felt rising panic and the adrenaline rush made her want to flee into the darkness. However, her sprained ankle prevented her from running fast and she rationalized the futility of trying to escape. If the man wanted to, he would catch her eventually and she would be away from the road and away from possible help from a passing motorist.

The man started forward and his pace carried him ever closer. She could see the sinister purport in his eyes that bored through her. From behind him in his belt, he pulled a hidden Bowie knife from its sheath. His grin changed into a menacing snarl as his eyes altered into predatory slits. His shoulders hulked forward as he extended his hand waving the knife blade back and forth to intimidate and freeze her from reacting.

"Don't think about running 'cause you'll never live to tell anybody what I done to you—the last one did and I got eight years in Folsom Prison." He pulled the tip of the knife blade across his throat to emphasize his intentions.

Sherrill focused on the knife and heard the words as an implied death sentence—for her and her baby. Her mind raced as she was considering her situation. She admonished herself for not having gotten the jack handle out of the trunk; she could have at least used it as a weapon.

The assailant lurched toward her with his arms extended and the knife balanced in his hand for a quick thrust. Seemingly without thinking, Sherrill placed her fingers tightly around the edge of the car door and braced herself. Just before the man was upon her, she pulled on the heavy door with all her strength and felt something pull in her stomach.

The low door slammed into the assailant's knees. He flipped over the door, breaking the glass. Half twisting in the air he slashed out with the knife, cutting Sherrill across her left shoulder with the blade. He landed on his back, knocking the air from his lungs and losing his grip on the knife. His right foot landed inside the car on the floorboard. With all her strength, Sherrill slammed the heavy door and heard the bones break in his leg.

The assailant sucked in air and screamed in agony. Without consciously thinking, she swung her foot with the vigor of survival and drove it up into his groin—reinjuring her ankle. The assailant twisted in agony, pulling his leg out of the door as he attempted to roll over.

Sherrill kicked the knife away, but he reached out and grabbed her ankle. She tried to jump away and fell backward. To break her fall, she grabbed the door handle and her falling weight pulled the door around, catching the assailant across his elbow, causing him to release his grip to keep from breaking his arm.

Sherrill rolled to the ground and was momentarily stunned. She lolled her head over to see her attacker reaching for her again. Scrambling to rise and get away, her hand brushed across a rock. She hurled the stone as hard as she could. The rock made contact at the base of his nose, breaking out two top teeth and peeling back the cartilage between his nostrils. Screaming, he grabbed his mutilated face with both hands.

Sherrill scrambled on her knees and retrieved the knife. She stood up and limped to the front of her car. Feeling momentarily safe by having the knife, she glanced at her shoulder in the illumination of the headlights and was relieved that the knife-cut was superficial. The knife had cut through her blouse and ridden up on the metal adjustment clasp on her bra-strap. The strap was severed, but the clasp had saved her from a more serious wound.

She heard the assailant moaning and grunting. He was grasping the top of the car door and attempting to get up on his feet. Sherrill looked around to find someplace to flee, and then saw the open car door and heard the motor still running. Favoring her sprained ankle, she hop-skipped to the car, tossed the knife onto the passenger's seat, slid into the driver's seat, and floored the accelerator.

The car fishtailed onto the highway, throwing large chunks of gravel back toward her car. Chunks of gravel broke her Corvette's windshield and a headlight. It also blasted into the assailant's face, hitting him in his right eye. Screaming, he fell down writhing and squirming on` the ground.

She raced toward Modesto and away from danger. As the adrenaline subsided, she became aware of the pain in her stomach and the feeling of wetness between her legs. Reaching down inside her slacks, she pulled her hand back up. In the glow of the headlights, she saw blood on her fingers. A swooning sensation droned in her ears and her vision dimmed. She shook her head, trying to throw off the effects of shock. "*I must get to a hospital for my baby.*"

With choking sobs, the assailant leaned his back against the car trying to get air back in his lungs. Several minutes passed, and then self-preservation overcame his desire to rest and he painfully raised himself to a standing position. Holding onto the side of the car, he jumped on one leg to the trunk and retrieved the jack, handle, and base plate. He stood on his one good leg for a minute getting his breath and tried to blink the tears of pain from his eyes. It was then that he realized that he could only see out of one eye. He screamed out into the blackness of the night, "I'll get that bitch for doing this!"

He grabbed the jack in his left hand and stuck the handle and base plate under his left armpit. Supporting himself with his right hand, he jumped on his good leg to the edge of the rear bumper. As he tried to navigate the turn, the heavy base plate of the jack dropped edge-on against his toes. Losing his balance, he extended the hand holding the jack and felt his left wrist snap back as he hit the ground. He lay there, cursing and writhing with pain. Crawling on his side, he retrieved the jack pieces and dragged them to the front of the car.

Using the jack handle, he popped off the hubcap, and even with his weight, he had trouble loosening the lug nuts. Bracing his left arm against the base of the wrench, he pushed against the end of the handle with his good hand. After several tries and repositioning his body for maximum leverage, he felt the first lug nut break loose.

After twenty minutes of cursing his bad luck, while several cars slowed then passed by without stopping, he had the spare tire in place. Disregarding the raised jack, he crawled to the driver's door and got into the car. The car was a stick shift and he sat, assessing his injuries.

He had a badly sprained wrist, two missing teeth, a broken nose and broken toes, a broken leg, and only one good eye. He rested for a minute from the exertion, and then realized that the keys were still in the trunk lid. Cursing and screaming at the world, he hobbled out of the car and retrieved the keys.

Sherrill saw the lights of Modesto and finally entered the city. Looking for a hospital sign, she saw a sign pointing to the police. Sliding into the turn, she accelerated the car, and then screeched to a stop in front of the police station.

Limping up the steps and through the door, she saw a desk sergeant, and sobbed, "Please call an ambulance for my baby."

The desk sergeant saw the blood stains on her blouse, but no baby. Looking for a baby and seeing none, the desk sergeant leaned forward to see if she was pregnant. She didn't look pregnant, "Where is your baby, Ma'am?

Frustrated by the delay, Sherrill screamed, "I'm pregnant—I was attacked by a man with a knife on the highway and I need an ambulance—now!"

The desk sergeant quickly called for an ambulance, "Hello, this is Sergeant Mulroney with the police department. I have an emergency transport for a female Caucasian, who is pregnant and has been attacked. Send an ambulance to the East Precinct—immediately."

He hung up the phone and informed, "The ambulance should be here in a couple of minutes Ma'am. Can you tell me where the knife attack took place?

Sherrill cleared her thoughts and steadied her voice, "About ten miles east of here on the highway from Yosemite. I left the attacker with my yellow Corvette: license number RGB-747. I left him with a broken leg and drove here in his car. He's in his mid-forties, about six feet tall and weighs around two hundred pounds—oh, I remember glancing at the mirror; the left front headlight on my car went out as I sped away."

Mulroney got a bemused look on his face, picked up the phone, and called the highway patrol office. "Hello, this is Sergeant Mulroney with the Modesto Police Department. We have a female that was attacked by a man on Highway 108. Location of the incident is about ten miles east of Modesto. The suspect was last seen with the victim's yellow Corvette, California license plate number RGB-747. The Corvette has a broken left front headlight and the suspect has a broken leg. Please put out an APB on the car and detain the driver."

The sergeant called the county sheriff, the Modesto Police Headquarters, and the Oakdale, California Police, giving them the same information.

The ambulance siren was heard approaching in the distance. Mulroney said, "Now, Ma'am, I need some more information from you, "What is your name?"

"Sherrill, my name is Sherrill Lind—"

The astonished expression on Mulroney's face stopped her as he interjected, "Sherrill—the movie star—now I recognize you. It's just that I never expected to meet you here…like this!"

He pressed the button on the intercom, "Pollard, I know that you and Skelly just finished your shift, but I need you to run interference for an ambulance transporting a VIP to the hospital. We need a statement from her after she comes out of ER."

Pollard and Skelly appeared at a side door and recognized Sherrill.

Sherrill stated, "I can walk—it's just that I am concerned about my baby." She leaned against the counter to support herself.

The two officers saw the spreading red stain at the crotch of Sherrill's white slacks, and then noticed the bloodstains on her blouse. They heard the ambulance pull up in front of the station and quickly helped Sherrill into the rear door of the ambulance. "Follow us," they shouted, and then ran to their patrol car. The medics placed Sherrill on a gurney inside the ambulance. One of the medics got into the driver's seat and followed the police car to the hospital. The medic with Sherrill took her vital signs and started an IV drip.

Cars were dispatched from all four police agencies. Moments later a highway patrolman passed a parked yellow Corvette on the other side of the road. It fit the description of the APB and the officer flicked on his lights and siren. He spun his car around in a 180-degree turn and spoke into a microphone, "This is highway patrol car 63; just located the suspect eight miles east of Modesto on Route 108. I am now headed west and pulling up behind the parked car." The officer started to get out of his car; the Corvette lurched forward off the jack.

The officer grabbed the microphone and announced, "This is car 63, the suspect is running; I repeat he is running. I am in pursuit, headed west on highway 108 from my last location."

The assailant had trouble shifting, but the high performance sports car soon put some distance between him and the patrol car. A bad eye, a broken headlight, and a cracked windshield limited his vision. He slid into the curves, but the car sprinted forward on the straightaway.

The interagency dispatchers took control and set up roadblocks ahead of and behind the pursued car. They allowed cars ahead of the pursuit to pass through slowly on the shoulder. The assailant rounded a curve and spotted the roadblock. He was on parole from two previous convictions of assault and rape and vowed never to be arrested again.

As he approached the roadblock, he slowed down as though he was going to stop. Spying the open shoulder, he gunned the car and accelerated. As he hit the graveled shoulder, he felt the car start to slide. He hit the brakes with his good foot and the car went into a side skid. The right rear wheel slid off into the ditch and caught on a culvert. The assailant was catapulted out of the car and slammed against the ground, breaking three ribs. The car rolled four times and landed on his good leg—breaking it.

The pursuing officer called in, "The suspect has just crashed and rolled over. Send an ambulance to the western roadblock's location."

Sherrill was admitted to emergency where the ER doctor made a preliminary examination, and then sent her to obstetrics. The OB doctor came in with a warm smile and introduced himself, "Hello, Sherrill, I am Doctor Mackey." Glancing at the clipboard in his hand, he asked, "Which trimester are you in?"

"My second trimester; I am in my nineteenth week."

After the examination, Sherrill entreated, "Is my baby going to be okay?"

Doctor Mackey smiled, "I think that you're both going to be fine. You had some hemorrhaging in the uterine wall, but the bleeding has already stopped. Your shoulder has a superficial wound that only required butterfly bandages. You are going to be confined to bed rest for a couple of days, but the amniotic sac is still intact and your baby's heart rate is just fine."

He placed the earpiece of his stethoscope to Sherrill's ears and the diaphragm to her stomach. Sherrill heard for the first time, the steady quick rhythmic beat of new life inside her. Her eyes filled with tears and she murmured with relief, "Oh, thank you, Doctor—thank you."

Doctor Mackey asked, "There are a couple of policemen in the waiting room. Do you feel up to giving them a statement?"

Sherrill resolutely answered, "Yes, please send them in. I want that creep caught and locked up so that he doesn't have a chance to attack anyone else."

Pollard and Skelly entered the room. Technically, they were both off duty, but both wanted a chance to see and speak with the new starlet, who had been in the headlines weekly, if not daily for the past month. Pollard said, "The doctor says that you and your baby are going to be okay. Do you mind if we ask you some detailed questions of what happened during the assault?"

"No, I don't mind. I know that man would have killed me and my baby if I hadn't gotten away from him."

"Okay," said Pollard, pulling out his statement folder. "Just start from the beginning and tell us what happened."

Sherrill began with the tire blowing out on her Corvette—. She described the events as they had occurred and quoted the assailant's threat that was burned into her memory.

"I know you, you're one of them TV people…you'll never live to tell anyone what I done to you—the last one did and I got eight years in Folsom Prison."

She ended the statement with the two officers walking up to her in the police station.

Skelly shuddered, "You are a very lucky young lady to be alive. As I see it, the only reason that you're here telling us this story is due to your quick thinking and quicker actions."

Pollard smiled, "Knowing what you deservedly did to the bad guy makes us thankful that we're the good guys." All three managed a chuckle that dissolved the goose bumps on their arms.

Sergeant Mulroney walked into the room, "I'm on my dinner break, but I thought you would like to hear that they caught your assailant. He made the mistake of trying to run the police roadblock and rolled your car, Sherrill. Right now, he's in pretty bad shape, but after he mends he's going to be behind bars for a long time."

Sherrill replied, "I don't care about the car. I just wanted him caught."

"Have they ID'ed him yet?" asked Skelly.

Mulroney replied, "His name is Larry Dean Caine. He's out on parole from two previous convictions, one for assault, and another for assault and rape."

Sherrill asked, "How can they put someone like that back on the street to assault and possibly kill other people?"

Pollard replied, "I don't know; we ask ourselves that same question all the time. Sometimes, it seems that the justice system is just one big revolving door."

Then he noticed the concern on Sherrill's face and added soothingly, "But don't worry your pretty head about him. This is his third offense and he'll be in prison for a long time—you'll probably be a grandmother before he gets out of prison."

Sketchy news reports started appearing on the wire services. Initial information stated that a man with a knife had assaulted Sherrill on the highway, as she was returning home from filming on location in Yosemite National Park. She was in a hospital in Modesto, but the hospital was unnamed. Within the hour an update hit the wire service that the assailant had been apprehended and was also in a hospital, but that hospital was also unnamed.

Thousands of phone calls started coming into all the hospitals and law enforcement agencies in the area. This resulted in critical telephone circuits being tied up. The affected institutions contacted the media and begged people not to call unless it was an emergency. At one point, intrastate and long-distance telephone trunks to the city had to be disabled to allow emergency calls to get through inside the city.

The media frenzy began again. There was much speculation and many false reports. Finally, the police unofficially released an unidentified confirmed source's account of Sherrill's statement.

The gist of the story was an account of a brave young girl using her intelligence and athletic ability to save her unborn baby from a knife attack by a more powerful male assailant, who was a twice-convicted felon. Similar headlines in all the media stated: *"Starlet Attacked— Saves Her Baby."*

Brad, hearing the news in Los Angeles, caught a jet to San Francisco and a commuter flight to Modesto.

Bill Payson, hearing of the attack, called Sherrill's home and relayed the news to her Aunt. Vicki hung up the phone and revealed with astonishment to her husband, "Sherrill's school counselor just heard on the news that Sherrill is in a hospital in Modesto!"

Hank leaped out of his chair and excitedly asked, "What happened?"

"He didn't know, but he said that he was going to drive there."

Hank reacted, "Grab your coat and purse; we're going there too."

There was a large gathering of reporters when Sherrill's guardians walked into the main police station. Hank walked to the front of the line, displaying his identification, "We are Sherrill's guardians; which hospital did they take her to?"

The desk sergeant stonewalled the inquiry, "I can't give that information out. Everybody around here claims to be somebody that needs to talk to her."

Hank demanded, "Okay, then let me speak with your shift captain—because we will find her."

One of the local reporters stepped forward, saying to the desk sergeant, "They really are Sherrill's guardians. I remember seeing them on television with Sherrill."

The desk sergeant thought for a moment then wrote on a slip of paper, "Memorial Hospital." He slid the folded note to Hank, "Don't tell anyone that I gave this to you."

"Thank you, I won't," assured Hank.

The reporter turned to Hank and asked, "Mr. Casson, can you tell us anything about Sherrill's condition."

Hank replied, "We don't know anything more than that she is in a hospital." He looked at the group of reporters and knew that they would likely follow him to the hospital and cause problems. He raised both of his hands to get their attention, "Listen up; I'll make a deal with all of you. I know that you're concerned about Sherrill and want to share the news with the rest of the world. If you don't follow us then I'll come back here and make a statement after we visit her to see if she is all right—deal?"

The reporters all nodded their heads in agreement. For insurance, Hank turned to the desk sergeant, "Don't let anyone leave here for five minutes." The sergeant nodded and called to a backroom for an officer to come up front and stand guard at the door.

Hank and Vicki entered the emergency entrance to avoid reporters in the hospital lobby. He walked up to the receptionist, "Hello, please call your head of security and tell him that Sherrill Lindstrom's guardians would like to speak with him."

The receptionist, seeing that she didn't have to make any decisions, called security.

A man appeared and Hank asked, "Can we talk in private?"

The security officer motioned them through a door. In the hallway, Hank produced identification, and explained, "My wife Vicki and I are Sherrill's guardians. We saw the crowd in your lobby and knew that you didn't need any more problems. We are here to see Sherrill."

The head of security responded, "Thank you for not adding to the chaos. Phone calls and people trying to speak to Sherrill have inundated us. She is in the OB ward; I'll take you there."

They entered Sherrill's room and Aunt Vicki ran forward and hugged her niece. She asked, "Oh, Honey, are you all right? We were worried sick about you when we heard the news."

Sherrill, hugging her aunt, said, "I'm so glad you came. Yes, I'm going to be all right. The doctor assured me that the baby has not been hurt, and all I need is bed rest to make sure that there are no complications."

Hank took her hand, "Tell us what happened, Honey."

The security officer stayed in the background because he too was curious to hear what had happened. Sherrill related the same information that she had given the police officers. In addition, she added that she had been told that the assailant had wrecked her new car and had been apprehended.

Hank was moved by her heroism and quick intelligent action. "You were very brave, Darling. I don't know if I would have even been able to fend off a knife attack."

"At the time, I wasn't thinking about being brave. I just knew that I had to protect my baby."

Hank turned to the security officer, "Would you get me a hospital pass. I have to go back to the police station. I promised the reporters that if they didn't follow me here then I would give them a statement after we saw Sherrill."

The two men left the room, while Vicki stayed with Sherrill.

Hank walked into the police station. There were many more reporters than before. He asked the desk sergeant, "Is there a conference room or a briefing room that we can use for about ten minutes?"

The sergeant wanting to clear the lobby readily agreed, "Yes, through that door and all the way to the end of the hall."

The group followed a patrolman to the room, where Hank addressed them from the lectern:

"Many of you may have seen me on television with Sherrill, but don't remember me—I don't blame you."

The reporters laughed because they had indeed concentrated on Sherrill.

Hank continued, "My name is Hank Casson. I am Sherrill's uncle and legal guardian. As her professional agent, I authorize public appearances and approve press releases.

"I did have an opportunity to speak with Sherrill in the hospital and she related the events that resulted in her being hospitalized. I am not at liberty to divulge the exact details, as this case may go to trial as a felonious assault, but here's a summary of what happened…:

As Hank shared the story, he noticed the reporters grimacing and fidgeting as the related events unfolded. He closed the statement by adding, "When I told Sherrill that she was very brave, she answered, 'At the time, I wasn't thinking about being brave. I just knew that I had to protect my baby.'"

The reporters remained silent for a long moment, contemplating what they personally might have done under similar circumstances—and found themselves lacking.

387

Finally, one reporter asked, "Mr. Casson, what is the extent of Sherrill's injuries?"

Hank replied, "Sherrill has a minor shoulder wound from the knife attack and while she was defending herself she ripped something inside her. She was bleeding and afraid that she might lose the baby. That is why she had the police call an ambulance."

Another reporter asked, "Was Sherrill sexually molested?"

"No," replied Hank. "What I summarized for you was the basic sequence of events. She was able to disable her assailant, before he could complete his intentions. And, considering the assailant's previous convictions, I have no doubt in my mind that his intention to commit a heinous crime that would have ended with Sherrill and her baby losing their lives."

This information sobered all the reporters and they didn't ask any more questions.

The uproar that followed the media release caused the authorities to move the prisoner to another city to keep him from getting lynched. Medical personnel were so incensed by the callous intent of the crime that some said during interviews, "I would have told the public where the assailant was, if I only knew." Sherrill's ordeal became the focus of women's rights groups that spearheaded legislation for tougher laws against predators and sex offenders.

Brad Thurman made the rounds searching for Sherrill. With a bouquet of flowers in his hand, he walked into the reception area of Memorial Hospital and noticed that there were many more reporters here than the other hospitals. He concluded that Sherrill had to be here. He walked up to the receptionist and identified himself. "Hello, I'm Brad Thurman, Sherrill's agent with 'The Dons of Eldorado.' Could you tell me which room she's in, please?"

She replied, "I'm sorry, sir, but all the hospitals have been instructed to neither confirm nor deny that Sherrill is a patient."

Brad, seeing the futility of questioning the receptionist further, looked around and spied another man with flowers. He walked up and introduced himself, "Hello, I'm Brad Thurman with 'The Dons of Eldorado.' Are you trying to find Sherrill too?"

Bill showed surprise on his face, and then saw the flowers Brad was holding. He shook Brad's hand and said, "I'm Bill Payson, Sherrill's school counselor. I've tried to see Sherrill, but got the runaround. I thought I might wait and see Sherrill's aunt and uncle walking through."

Brad replied, "If I know Hank, he has found another entrance."

Bill gulped, "Of course. I just didn't think logically."

The statement caused Brad to reassess the man. He was here for personal reasons, not as a representative of the school. He suggested, "Bill, let's go to the cafeteria and have a cup of coffee."

"I could use one." He walked with Brad to the cafeteria.

After thirty minutes, the two men had gotten acquainted and both detected that the other was not only a friend, but an admirer of Sherrill. Instead of creating animosity between them, the knowledge gave them a sense of camaraderie.

Brad suggested, "Let's go see the man in charge of security."

Brad identified himself and Bill. The head of security led the two men back to his office. Instead of asking to see Sherrill, Brad asked, "Are Hank and Victoria Casson with Sherrill now?"

The head of security paused for a moment, and then answered, "Yes."

"Would you mind having Hank see us in your office?"

Again, the head of security paused. He picked up the phone and called Sherrill's room. Vicki answered the phone and the head of security said, "Mrs. Casson, would you ask Hank to come down to the security office? Thank you."

Five minutes later Hank appeared through the door. He recognized Brad and shook his hand, saying, "Hi, Brad. Why am I not surprised to see you here."

Hank's question in the form of a statement surprised Brad, but he turned and said, "Hank, this is Bill Payson, Sherrill's school counselor."

The two men shook hands and Hank stated, "I assume that you two are here to see Sherrill."

He turned and saw the head of security's nameplate on his desk, *Raymond Borger*, and said, "Ray, you don't mind if these two young men see Sherrill for ten minutes—do you? I'm sure that their visit would cheer her up."

Ray considered the request, and then opened his drawer, and pulled out two passes. "Visiting hours are over, but ten minutes is not unreasonable. Just give the passes to the receptionist on your way out."

Hank opened the door and beckoned to Vicki. "Vicki, come go with me to the cafeteria. I'll buy you a cup of coffee."

Vicki grumbled as she accepted his offer, "You know that I don't drink coffee at night." Exiting the door, she saw the reason for her husband's request.

Brad and Bill walked into the room. Sherrill's face lit up and a genuine smile spread across her face. "Brad—Mr. Payson—I'm so glad to see you. Brad gave her the flowers and hugged her. Bill hesitantly offered the flowers in his hand. Sherrill extended her arms to him and he stepped forward into them and hugged her for a long moment. Finally pulling back, "We were so concerned for you, Sherrill. Are you okay?"

Sherrill smiled again, "The doctor says that I'm going to be fine. However, I had the scare of my life at the thought of losing my baby."

Bill said, "We promised to only stay for ten minutes. Would you feel okay to tell us what happened?" Sherrill retold the statement that she made to the police.

His face drained of color, Bill stated in awe, "You are lucky to be alive!"

Brad corrected him, "I would say that Sherrill's quick thinking made her own luck. Had she frozen and not reacted then I dread to predict the outcome." Bill nodded his head in agreement. Sherrill blanched at the reality of what truly could have happened.

Brad apologized profusely, "I'm sorry; I was just thinking out loud. I didn't mean to frighten you. The fact that you are here speaks for itself. We are so proud of your bravery and presence of mind." He couldn't resist giving her another hug and Bill followed suit.

Brad asked, "Did the police catch the guy?"

Sherrill replied, "Oh, I forgot to tell you about that. He tried to run a police roadblock and rolled my Corvette. I guess that it is totaled, but it doesn't matter since they caught the man. They told me that he has broken bones and they took him to a hospital, but I don't know where. The police said that this was his third offense and promised that he would be put away for a long time."

Brad thought, *yes, but there are still other creeps out there.* He would see that the studio provided additional protection for her. "Sherrill, do you mind me calling you here in the hospital?"

"I would like for you to call me; that goes for you too, Mr. Payson."

Bill implored, "Please—away from school, could you address me as just Bill?"

"Sure, 'Just Bill,'" said Sherrill cheerily. The three laughed at the name play and from relief that everything had turned out the way it had.

Brad looked at the extension number on the phone dial and said it out loud for Bill, "Extension 1227."

He hugged Sherrill and kissed her on the cheek, "We hate to go, but you've had enough excitement for today."

He took out his business card and wrote a phone number on the back. "Here is a special number. If you ever need me, they will know how to track me down. I will call you back as soon as possible."

Bill hugged her and Sherrill informed, "I've completed all my assignments for this semester, but my papers were in the car."

Bill replied, "Don't worry about it; I know that you know the material. You just get better first, and then you can take the final test without handing in your assignments."

"Thank you, Bill. You and Brad are both very special friends."

Bill turned to leave, hesitated, and then turned back to Sherrill, "I listened to every detail of your story and everything fits except for one thing, 'why were you on highway 120 out of Yosemite to Modesto, instead of the more direct route of 140 to Merced?'"

Sherrill, with a twinkle in her eye, stated, "Because I was told that route 120 was uphill and curvy. I wanted to find out how my 'Vette' performed on that kind of road."

"Oh," replied Bill, accepting the logic of the statement. The two men waved goodbye to Sherrill and left the room.

Outside the room Brad said, "Well, 'Just Bill,' how about a tall cold glass of beer?"

Bill looked at his watch; seeing that it was late, but he capitulated, "What the heck. That's the best offer I've had today—I'm buying."

They found a local pub a block away and Bill raised his glass," A toast to Sherrill, a marvelous woman."

Brad clicked his glass against Bill's and agreed, "Yes—simply marvelous."

Ratings

On Sunday, Brad checked Sherrill out of Memorial Hospital. He explained, as he signed for the charges, "The studio's insurance paid the entire hospital bill, so you don't have to worry about finances."

"That was very nice of them," remarked Sherrill. "I don't remember anything in the contract that stated that I would be covered by hospitalization."

"It wasn't in the original contract," remarked Brad. "I appended a rider to your contract after you and Laura had your little excursion at the drive-in restaurant. Both of you are now insured. However, it doesn't cover your pregnancy, since that was a pre-existing condition."

Sherrill blushed. She didn't know why, since Brad obviously had not intended to embarrass her with the remark. To change the subject, she asked, "Is my first episode still scheduled to be shown, Tuesday night?"

"Yes," reassured Brad. "The studio has released promos on the network and has bought space in all the major newspapers. You have been front-page news for the last two days and most of the newspapers reference our promos as related stories.

"Our executives are anticipating a rise in the ratings, but we aren't sure how much, since we have never had this much publicity regarding one of our stars."

A nurse's aide wheeled Sherrill to a waiting limo. Sherrill looked up at Brad, "I was expecting you to have a rental car."

"It is a rental car—for a princess. Besides, I wanted to be able to talk with you without distractions during our drive to Merced."

The limo pulled away from the hospital and Sherrill thought back on Brad's statement in the hospital lobby. "Brad, do you really think of me as a star?"

"No," replied Brad with feigned sincerity. "But what does my opinion count against your millions of fans?"

Sherrill's eyes focused on his, searching to see if he really meant what he had just said. Finally, he couldn't hold the deception any longer and broke into a broad grin. "Of course, I think that you are a star. Don't you know that I am the president of your fan club?"

Sherrill smiled back when she realized that he had been teasing her. "Your opinion carries more weight with me than all the other fans. I know you and value your opinion. I know only a few of my other fans, although they all act as if they had known me all my life."

Brad mused over her naive statement. He knew that one-sided familiarity was a phenomenon created by the news media. Fans developed an intense level of adulation because they knew personal information about the object of their affection, even though they may never have met the person.

"I'm not a philosopher," Brad qualified his statement. "Nevertheless, as I see it, being a fan is a *free form* of love. We love someone and naturally delude ourselves that the other person loves us back. We express our love and expect the other person to reciprocate in form.

"That reciprocal form may manifest itself as a simple statement from the star to the adulating masses, 'I love all of you,' or it may be an autographed photograph, or it may be a self-indulgent form of just viewing the star as personifying the perceived ideals of the perfect person.

"We, as human beings, usually believe and feel what we want to believe, instead of relying on the sterile facts of life. This belief generates hope that someday, someway, somehow, we will attain the unattainable."

A chill ran up Sherrill's spine and across her shoulders. She felt her nipples become hard and realized that Brad was not speaking for other fans, but for himself. His tone of voice, his demeanor, his sincerity, his choice of words was all a profession of love for her.

Her perception was confirmed when he added, "So now, Sherrill, you can see why I am your number one fan."

Sherrill looked away, staring blankly at the passing continuous hedge of Oleander bushes that divided U.S. 99. She thought of Randy, so far away, but ever present in her heart. She felt his child move inside her womb, as though it was reacting to her thoughts. She longed for Randy to be here beside her, so that she wouldn't feel the need to suppress the emotions generated by Brad's words.

She turned to Brad, a tear slipped down her left cheek, "Brad, I do love you back. I thought of you a lot while I was in the hospital. You have always been there for me and I adore you as a person. I am also your number one fan."

She blinked the tears away and continued, "In another world, in another life, we might have had a chance to act upon our mutual love, but our real world is that I love Randy and am going to be the mother of his child.

"This does not diminish my love for you, but neither does my love for you supercede my love for Randy."

Sherrill leaned over and touched her long tapered fingers against Brad's cheek. She leaned forward and Brad met her halfway. Their lips touched lightly and then harder with the resolve that this would be their first and last kiss as lovers. Passion rose in Brad, and then waned as their lips parted. He saw the flush in Sherrill's cheeks and felt the heat of passion on his own cheeks.

Taking her hand and holding it gently, "Sherrill, I understand. You confirmed with your kiss that you love me and that will have to suffice for the rest of my life.

"Though, I long to be your lover, I will content myself to being your friend. I will not broach the subject nor make you feel self-conscious of my love again."

He released her hand and they both stared out at the passing vista, not focusing on anything, but lost in their own thoughts and feelings. They viewed themselves as star-crossed lovers. Had they known Randy's coined phrase for this human emotion phenomenon, they might have accepted it as describing their own feelings—"*stellar-dysrhythmia*"—Star-crossed Lovers.

The chauffeur announcing, "We are on the outskirts of Merced," interrupted their thoughts.

Sherrill directed, "Turn left at the first traffic light, and then right on Teaberry Lane. The house number is 9763"

The limo pulled up in front of the house and Aunt Vicki rushed out to meet them. She hugged Sherrill as though she hadn't seen her in months, instead of just last night.

Vicki bubbled, "Oh, Honey, it is so good to have you home. Hank is on the phone with a producer of one of those talk shows, or he would have been out to meet you."

The women walked arm-in-arm toward the house; Brad signed the chauffeur's trip ticket and handed the driver a cash tip. He picked up Sherrill's small overnight case and followed the women into the house.

Hank hung up the phone and grimaced, "Hi, Brad, you won't believe the number of talk show hosts that want Sherrill to appear on their shows.

"I even got a call from Ed Sullivan in New York—you know the Beatles and Elvis premières. He wants Sherrill on his show, but I don't know what she would do to entertain a television audience."

Brad smiled and stated flatly, "He wants her for ratings. If Ed wants her then we know that he doesn't care what she does. He just wants her to be on display in front of his audience—suggest to him that Sherrill co-host his show and introduce his other guests."

"That's a great idea!" replied Hank. "I'll call him back, right now."

Brad interjected, "No, call him back after Tuesday's showing of 'The Dons of Eldorado.' If he still wants her then we will know that Sherrill's performance in that episode was as superb as we expect it to be."

Vicki appeared with coffee and croissants. "Where would you like these?"

Brad suggested, "Why don't we have them on the patio. I need to talk over some business with Hank, and then I have to catch a flight back to LA."

Hank took the tray from Vicki and led Brad to the patio. He motioned for Brad to have a seat and cautiously stated, "You seem mysterious, Brad. You know that Victoria likes to be included, when she can."

"I know. But I felt that some of what we have to discuss has to be agreed upon by you and me, first."

He took a sip of coffee and continued, "I know that the attack on Sherrill deeply disturbed Vicki and you. It deeply concerned me, too. I have spoken with the studio heads and they have agreed to hire a bodyguard for Sherrill.

"He will be her primary protection when she is out among the public. That includes personal appearances, on-location filming, and traveling between performances. However, we don't want to stifle Sherrill's sense of freedom and there will be times when she is vulnerable.

"For added security, we are going to put a two-way radio in her car for immediate communication. It can even send out a locator beacon, but still we don't feel entirely comfortable with just that precaution.

"To supplement her security, we want to give her a small caliber pistol to carry in her purse. She will have another pistol, with a quick release carrier, installed in her car."

Hank thought seriously for a moment, and then nodded, "I hate for it to come to this, but you're right. Something needs to be done to protect her. When we first heard that Sherrill was in the hospital from an assault, our first reaction was to keep her home and lock the doors.

"That wouldn't be a realistic solution, but I also hate to resort to her carrying a gun. I think that it will stifle her sense of freedom and constantly remind her of the danger of being alone. Also, I don't think that I could ever convince Victoria that Sherrill should tote a gun."

Brad got a perplexed expression on his face, "You're right, Hank. I was looking at it strictly from a male point of view. Nevertheless, we must protect her. I still want to install a gun in her car in a secret compartment that pops open by a hidden button. When she is alone in her car is when she will be the most vulnerable.

"The radio will allow her to call for help, but it's the minutes before help arrives that she may need backup protection. Only during dire emergencies, will she need access to a gun. I hope that she will never have to use it, but if she does then it will be there to save her and her baby.

"So, instead of a gun in her purse, she could carry a container of Mace (pepper spray) and a whistle. That should allow her extra minutes to escape a potential assailant. If she is near her car, like in a dark parking lot, she will still have the gun, as a last resort."

Hank pondered Brad's plan, and then stated, "I think that I can convince Victoria of that option. A gun will be available only as a last resort. It will also give us peace of mind to know that Sherrill will be safer."

"Good. We'll proceed with the conversion in her car."

Hank looked at Brad, questioningly, "What car? Sherrill's car was totaled by the assailant."

"I know. The producers have already bought her another one—insurance covered most of the cost. I plan to drive the new car up here, Tuesday. I would like to watch Sherrill's first episode with you and your family—if that's all right with you and Vicki."

"Certainly, that's all right with us," assured Hank. Come for dinner, and then we will watch the episode together."

Brad pulled a small 32-caliber pearl handled semi-automatic pistol out of his pocket and handed it to Hank. "Sherrill needs to know how to use this, even if she never has to use it."

Hank stared at the innocent looking weapon in his hand. He thought, "The pearl handle makes it look like a toy." Then he stated, "Thanks, Brad. I never would have thought that a studio agent could be so concerned and caring."

Brad swallowed hard; he did care. His next words were hard for him to say, but he forced them out, "The other matter that I wanted to discuss with you is about getting Sherrill and Randy together. They need to be married—for themselves and for the baby to have a name when it is born. Do you ever hear from Randy; do know where he is based?"

"No," replied Hank. "My one and only conversation with him was when he told me that he had been promoted to 2nd lieutenant, that he was going to be taking special training, and that he wouldn't be able to contact Sherrill for a long time. I can only surmise that he is going to be involved with *black operations*."

"Black operations—what does that mean?"

"It means espionage—CIA stuff."

"That sounds dangerous," observed Brad.

"It could be. Randy said that he couldn't elaborate anymore on the subject and to tell Sherrill that he loved her."

Brad winced at Hank's words. He resolved to himself, "If I really love Sherrill then her happiness comes before mine."

"Do you know of anyone that we could contact to see if Randy's training schedule has an opening for Sherrill and him to be married?"

Hank thought for a minute then replied, "I don't know anyone personally, but he received a field promotion. The only person who would have that authority would have been his commanding general at Lackland Air Force Base. I guess that you could start there."

"Do you know the general's name?"

"No, but I have some contacts at Castle AFB. They could provide that information for me."

"Good—that's a start. Now, is there any place in LA where you think Sherrill would like to have the ceremony performed? I know that the cast and crew would like to attend the wedding."

Hank thought a moment, "Yes, there is a church that we attended with Sherrill and her parents. It is 'The First Ecumenical Church of Hollywood' and the minister's name is Pastor John Stevens.

"Sherrill's father gave a very short, but excellent speech on forgiveness and reconciliation. Sherrill has a copy; have her show it to you sometime."

"I will," assured Brad. "Do you and Vicki think that you can handle the wedding preparations—I'm not very good at that type of public relations?"

"Sure, Victoria loves to plan and organize. You just let us know when Randy will be available and we will handle the rest."

Brad continued with his plan, "Also, like it or not, the news media is going to demand to be there. If we don't allow them to be involved then they can become quite fickle.

"We want the ceremony to be a surprise for Sherrill and Randy, but there will be many people in attendance. If the media finds out beforehand then they might leak the story for spite."

Hank assured, "Everyone that we contact will be told that the wedding is going to be a surprise. How are you going to get Sherrill and Randy there, without them becoming suspicious?"

"Well, as far as Sherrill is concerned, we will pretend that she, as Annabell Lee, is going to marry Don Luke. We'll have cameras there and Sherrill will be told that it is an on-location scene.

"As far as Randy is concerned, I'll have to work that out later, when I find out when he can attend his own marriage—which he won't know about."

Hank chuckled, and offered lightly but with conviction, "Maybe Randy should take lessons from you on running covert operations before he goes into harm's way."

Brad smiled at the compliment, "If he is indeed involved with covert operations then I'm thankful that I will be in Hollywood, instead of wherever he will be going."

Hank nodded in agreement and Brad stood up. "Well, it looks like we've got our work cut out for us. Don't tell Sherrill that I will be back, Tuesday. I want her new car to be a surprise for her."

The men walked into the living room and Vicki, feeling left out, looked up, saying, "You two *men* must have had a lot to talk about. Did you get everything settled?

Hank replied, "Pretty much so. He motioned to Vicki, "Come out on the patio with me. Brad needs to call for a taxi. Then he needs to talk with Sherrill about her filming schedule."

Vicki followed Hank, while Brad used the phone. He requested a taxi to the airport then turned to Sherrill, "Emile is going to shoot scenes around you until Thursday. Do you think that you will be ready to do your scenes then?"

Sherrill replied, "Yes, I feel fine. I could start even earlier, if he wants me."

Brad replied, "No, we want you to see your first episode with your family—Thursday will be fine. I'll be in contact with you."

He walked over and offered his hand for Sherrill to stand. He gave her a tender hug, "I'll see you later. Tell Hank and Vicki good-bye for me."

They heard the taxi honk out front. Brad observed, "That was fast." Sherrill agreed, "Yes, remember, this is small town, USA."

Brad grinned as he opened the door. He walked out to the curb and waved as he entered the taxi. Sherrill waved back, feeling a strange loneliness as the taxi disappeared down the street. She whispered to herself wistfully, "Another world—another time," as she closed the door.

Hank and Vicki were on the patio a long time. When they finally came back in, Sherrill could see that Vicki's face was flushed, as though they had been arguing. Sherrill asked, "Is there anything wrong?"

"No," replied Vicki. "We just had a reality check. Hank has something to discuss with you."

Hank sat down and explained the studio's plan for a bodyguard. He pulled out the pistol and expressed, "Though you won't be carrying a gun, we feel that you should have one in your car."

Sherrill replied, "I don't have a car anymore."

Hank covered his and Brad's surprise by adding, "Well, when you get another one."

Sherrill reached out and took the gun in her hand. Her eyes narrowed and she stated, "I don't like the idea of needing a gun. However, if I'd had one when that man attacked me, I would have used it—not to kill him, but to wound him in the legs." She felt the heft of the gun in her hand and continued matter-of-factly, "If I'm going to have a gun then I need to learn how to use it properly."

Hank suggested, "I can take you to the pistol range and teach you." Vicki interjected wisely, "Won't loud noises scare the baby?"

Hank realized that he hadn't thought about that. He mused for a moment then said, "We'll have earplugs to protect our ears. If Sherrill wears a heavy leather butcher's apron wrapped around her then it should muffle the sound for the baby."

"Good, when do we start?" urged Sherrill.

"Right after lunch," replied Hank. He and Vicki looked at each other with mild amazement on their faces; they hadn't expected Sherrill's open acceptance of having a gun.

Vicki walked over to Sherrill and hugged her, "That man must have really frightened you, Honey."

"He did. I never want to feel totally helpless again. After the baby is born, I plan to take a martial arts class in self-defense."

She smiled mischievously and asked light-heartedly, "Doesn't the air force teach judo to Randy? We could grapple with each other."

Vicki's mouth gaped opened in surprise as she gasped, "Girl, you are—wicked!"

They all three laughed at the vision in their own mind of Sherrill and Randy, in the nude, circling each other...waiting for that one moment when one of them copped an advantageous hold and the other blissfully conceded.

Vicki shook the thought from her head and giggled, "We're all bad. I can tell by the expressions on your faces that you two were thinking the same thing that I was thinking."

Hank, with a glint in his eye, agreed, "You may be right, Vicki." Then he inferred, "Sherrill, don't you need to go for a walk, while Victoria and I practice a little *t'ai chi*?"

Vicki retorted, "No, we don't, *Mr. Kung Fu*. We are going to have lunch, and then you are going to take Sherrill to the pistol range." They laughed again. The jovial bantering and innuendoes had somehow made them feel that the world was back in balance again.

Tuesday evening, Vicki asked Sherrill, "Honey, would you set the table for four? We are going to have a guest for dinner.

"Who?"

Vicki replied vaguely, "Oh, just one of our friends."

Sherrill mused, as she placed an extra setting on the table, "Maybe, Bill Payson." She couldn't think of anyone else in Merced. Most of Uncle Hank and Aunt Vicki's friends were married and that would require two extra place settings.

At seven o'clock, the doorbell rang and Hank offered, "I'll get it."

Sherrill and Vicki were putting the final touches on the meal, when Hank entered the dining room, followed by Brad. Sherrill looked up in surprise, "Hi, Brad. Aunt Vicki didn't say that you would be the guest for dinner." She glanced at her aunt and tried to detect a reason for the intrigue.

Brad replied, "We wanted to surprise you."

"Seeing you never surprises me," replied Sherrill. Then she thought, *that sounded insensitive*. She modified her statement, "What I really meant is that you are always welcome in our home."

Brad replied, "Thank you, but you didn't have to explain. I knew what you meant.

Sherrill was flustered and she didn't know why. Brad, seeing her dilemma, replied soothingly, "Don't worry about it. Every new starlet is nervous when she knows that everyone in her world is going to be watching her on television."

Sherrill thought on his statement, and then exhaled a sigh, "You are right. In front of the camera, I knew that people were watching me, but I was too busy to think much about it. Tonight, not only will I be watching myself on television, but I will be aware of other people's reaction while they are watching me."

Brad laughed disarmingly, "By golly—I think you've got it."

Aunt Vicki interrupted, pointing as she announced, "Okay, dinner is ready. Brad you sit at the end of the table, next to Sherrill.

The dinner lasted almost an hour. They had light conversation. Hank spoke of the booming business at his real estate company. Brad updated them on what was happening at the studio. Sherrill told of meeting new people at school, when the superintendent had called a special assembly and asked her to speak in front of the student body and faculty. Aunt Vicki, not to be outdone, told of the mayor inviting her to speak in front of the city council regarding beautification of the city.

Most of the news was old news to the family, but Brad was an attentive listener and they received pleasure from sharing their lives with him. Hank looked at his watch and announced with a mischievous smile, "Time for a little entertainment. What program should we watch on television, tonight?"

His question produced only passive smiles from Sherrill and Brad, but Vicki stuck her tongue out at him. He chuckled at her reaction, "Okay, if no one has a preference then I am going to watch that beautiful new starlet on 'The Dons of Eldorado.'"

They followed him into the living room. Brad and Sherrill sat on the chesterfield. Hank and Vicki had their own recliners. As the program came on, Sherrill nervously reached over and took Brad's hand. He smiled at her and squeezed her hand to show support. Sherrill watched the program progress. She had seen all the scenes on the storyboard, and intimately knew the scenes where she had appeared, but now realized that she was caught up in the magic of television.

She watched the story as it unfolded, as though experiencing it for the first time. The music and soundtrack had been added to enhance the action and drama. She found herself mildly disliking Annabelle Lee and Belinda Broderick for their petulance and conniving against Don Luke.

She floated in her thoughts through the dance scene, felt breathless during the runaway carriage scene, felt drawn in by the panoramic vista of Yosemite, and almost wanted to applaud when the beautiful Annabelle fell into the pool—a just reward for her antics against the established character, Don Luke.

Sherrill continued a mesmerized stare at the TV, even when the closing commercials appeared. Hank got up and turned off the television. Brad was the first to speak, "I watched most of that episode being filmed. Emile and his crew did a great job of blending and fitting it together. Nevertheless, the star quality of the Annabelle Lee character made the episode the best that I have ever watched. I think that the polls will show that the rest of America agrees with me."

Sherrill looked seriously at Brad, "Brad, you're not saying that just because—?"

"No," assured Brad. "I've learned that you have to be objective in this business. You can't let your heart rule your head."

Hank walked over and kissed Sherrill on the cheek, "Vicki and I may not be as objective as Brad, but I also thought that you were stunning in your performance. You evoked so much emotion in me that I wanted to turn your character over my knee and give her a good paddling. But when you fell into the pool, I instantly forgave all your indiscretions."

"But, that scene was an accident," corrected Sherrill. "It wasn't supposed to have happened."

Brad iterated, "Accident or not, it was a stroke of genius that 'The Dons' scriptwriters wished they had written. It changed your whole character perception from a priggish foible to a swooning heroine."

They turned to look at Vicki to get her reaction. She sat staring at the television set, with tears streaming down her cheeks. Snuffling, Vicki glanced up at them, "I'm so proud of you, Sherrill, that I don't have anything to say. And, you know that I'm impressed when I don't have anything to say." She giggled through her snuffles and the others laughed with her at her giggle-snuffles.

Brad surprisingly suggested, "Hank, I think that you should renegotiate Sherrill's contract."

Hank looked at Brad, the studio's agent, with surprise. He saw that Brad was serious and just as seriously replied, "No, the studio has been more than fair with Sherrill's contract. However, I do appreciate your candor in even bringing the subject up. I think that additional revenue will be generated from Sherrill's guest appearances."

Vicki suggested, "Let's have some dessert to celebrate. Oh, Sherrill, would you and Brad run to the store? I don't have any fresh ice cream to serve with the cherry pie."

"Sure," replied Sherrill with a puzzled look. She knew that Vicki had a half-gallon of vanilla in the freezer. She asked, "What flavor would you like?"

Vicki absently replied, "Oh, I don't care; you and Brad decide."

Her reply further confused Sherrill because Aunt Vicki always insisted on vanilla ice cream with cherry pie. She turned to Brad, "Would you mind driving me to the supermarket?"

"I would like very much driving you to the supermarket," replied Brad, with a wink to Hank and Vicki.

He opened the front door for Sherrill and almost collided with her when she stopped so quickly. Parked at the curb was a brand-new pale yellow Corvette with cream-tan leather upholstery. It looked exactly like her other car, except for the barely perceptible eight-inch antenna extending from just in front of the hatch.

Brad held out the keys, "Maybe you would like to drive, after all."

The shock of surprise was total. Sherrill missed driving her Corvette, but had resolved in her mind that it was just an inanimate object. Now seeing its reincarnation, she was more excited than when she had received her first one. She whispered urgently, "Excuse me; I need to go to the bathroom."

Brad grinned as she ducked under his outstretched arm and hurried toward the bathroom. Her unabashed reaction had made his long drive from LA worth every mile.

Sherrill returned with a little more composure and requested with slight embarrassment, "Okay, the keys, please."

Brad smiled with empathy and dropped the keys into her upturned hand. They got into the car and Brad reviewed the functions of the radio with her. He explained, "This is the top of the line business-class two-way radio. It has ten frequencies and ten pre-programmed numbers to cover all the regions in California. It contains its own backup battery, so that it will work even if your car battery is dead.

"This little recessed button activates a locator beacon. The police can locate your car anywhere. The radio is waterproof in case it rains, if and when you forget to put your top up.

"Oh, there is one other feature. Press 888, and then the enter button. Now push in on your clutch pedal."

Sherrill followed Brad's instructions and the car started. She exclaimed, "Hey, that's neat—no keys. How do I turn it off?"

Brad replied, "Press 888—Enter."

Sherrill did and the motor stopped. She exclaimed again, "I like this. No more digging in my purse for the keys."

Brad cautioned, "You should only use that procedure during an emergency. You don't want anyone else to know the procedure. If the wrong someone learns this then you may walk out some morning to find that you're car is missing."

Sherrill nodded. Brad showed her a radio directory and placed it back into the console. He reached over next to the driver's seat and pressed a small chrome strip on the side of the console. A compartment sprang open and a pistol appeared just in front of the strip. Sherrill reached down and easily retrieved the gun. She asked, "It's loaded, isn't it?"

Brad replied, "All guns should be considered loaded, until you confirm that they are empty."

"That's the same thing Uncle Hank told me. She pulled back on the action and spied a bullet in the chamber. She made sure that the safety was on and placed the pistol back into the compartment. The compartment closed with a click and became invisible to the casual glance.

Sherrill started the car with the key and proceeded to the store. She observed, "The steering feels slightly different."

"Yes, it will. The tires are heavy duty and puncture resistant; they are also wider. Press on the accelerator."

The car leaped forward in 3rd gear. Brad smiled at Sherrill's surprised reaction, "It has a turbo-charged interceptor engine, but don't try to outrun the cops—just the bad guys."

She turned onto U.S. 99, went to the Atwater interchange, and then headed back toward Merced. The car purred at 70 mph. "Is there anything else?"

"Yes, it has a removable hardtop for winter and cross-country driving, but I left that in LA. We figured that the hardtop would also give you an extra measure of security."

Sherrill pulled into the supermarket parking lot; it was almost empty. They went into the store and picked out a half-gallon of ice cream. At the checkout stand, Sherrill asked the clerk, "Where is everybody? You're open until eleven aren't you?"

The clerk smiled, "It's been this way all evening, Sherrill. They stayed home to watch you on television."

The statement stunned Sherrill into silence and the clerk continued, "I wished that I could have watched it. The few customers that we've had in the last thirty minutes said that it was the best episode of the series. They said that you went for a swim—then they'd laughed."

Brad paid for the ice cream and said, "Thank you. Maybe you will get a chance to see the episode during reruns."

"I sure hope so," replied the clerk, "I'm looking forward to it."

They walked to the parking lot and Sherrill stated with temperance, "They must have watched it because I'm from here."

"I don't think so," replied Brad. "I think that we have just gotten the first poll results. We'll find out for sure tomorrow."

The next morning, Brad called Myra McDonald at the studio from his motel room. "Hi, Myra—Brad here. What's the report on the ratings?"

Myra excitedly reported, "Brad, we swept the network ratings! Over twenty million viewers watched 'The Dons' last night. Our producers are ecstatic from the results. The switchboard has been inundated with request for *more Annabell Lee—more Sherrill* episodes with Belinda and Don Luke."

Brad had trouble getting a word in edgewise. Finally, he interjected, "Okay, okay, Myra. I get your drift. You've giving me exciting news that I can share with Sherrill. We'll drive down to LA this afternoon. Let Emile know that Sherrill will be on the set, bright and early tomorrow morning."

Sherrill answered the door. Brad calmly inquired, "Can a guy get a cup of coffee here?"

"Sure, come on in. I'll make some fresh. Uncle Hank is on the phone as usual and Aunt Vicki is out on the patio. I'll bring it out there."

By the time that the coffee was ready, Hank was off the phone. He and Brad were standing, while Vicki reclined in a lounge chair, listening to their conversation. Brad took the serving tray from Sherrill and placed it on the table. He stared at her without expression.

Finally, Sherrill couldn't stand it any longer, "Well—?"

Brad swooped forward and scooped her off her feet. He swung her around, while holding her in his arms. He broke out in a broad grin, "We swept the ratings. Twenty million people watched your performance on television last night—they loved you!"

Sherrill breathed in awe, "Twenty million!" She placed her arms around Brad's neck and held on, "Don't put me down yet. I don't think that I could stand up."

Aunt Vicki leaped up from her lounge chair and hugged her. Hank stepped over and hugged them all.

Sherrill wiggled her legs and Brad let her down. She sat in a patio chair, trying to visualize twenty million—the number was simply incomprehensible.

Finally, she asked, "What does all this mean?"

Brad answered, "It means that you are *a legitimate super-star.*"

Hank answered simultaneously, "It means that you are going to be a very busy girl. I just got off the phone with Ed—he called me! He wants you to appear on his Christmas show. You will co-host and announce his other guests' appearances. It means that you will be contacted for endorsement of products. It means that you will become—well—wealthy."

Sherrill stared into space and catatonically uttered, "I don't care to be wealthy—I just want Randy."

Vicki hugged her again, "That will happen too, Honey. You just have to give it time."

Brad thought, "God! I would have laid down my life, for her only to have said—*Brad.*"

Planning

Brad arrived at Lackland AFB, Texas and entered the base headquarters building. He handed his business card to the general's secretary, "Hello, my name is Brad Thurman with 'The Dons of Eldorado' television program. I would like to speak with the general for about five minutes."

Ten minutes later, Mrs. Feingold nodded to Brad, "You may see the general now, Mr. Thurman."

Brad walked into the general's office and introduced himself. "Good morning, General, my name is Brad Thurman; thank you for seeing me."

General Thurman glanced at Brad's business card, "We have the same last name. Where are you from, Brad?"

"I was born in California, sir, but my forefathers settled in South Carolina."

"So did mine," informed the general. "We must have a common ancestor back there somewhere. What can I do for you?"

"Well, sir, I thought of telephoning you, but I need information that may be considered sensitive, so I wanted to meet with you in person."

The general's eyelids lowered slightly as he tried to assess this young man's cautious approach. "Go on."

"Are you acquainted with Sherrill, a television star with 'The Dons of Eldorado?'"

"I wouldn't say acquainted, but everyone is aware of Sherrill. I watched her on television last Tuesday. I might add that she came across with an excellent performance."

"Thank you," replied Brad. "The polls and news media agree with your assessment."

Brad became more focused, "Are you also aware that she and her fiancé are expecting a baby?"

"Yes, I am aware that *Randy* and Sherrill are expecting a baby," replied the general.

"Bingo!" thought Brad. A general would never use a given name for one of his officers, unless he was intimately acquainted with that person.

Brad cut to the point, "General, we know that Randy is in training and we have been unable to contact him. I want to assure you that we do not want to interfere with his training in any way.

"The dilemma is that Sherrill and Randy's family and friends, myself included, want to coordinate a surprise wedding for them before their baby is born. In order for us to accomplish this, we need to know when the bride and groom will be available for the ceremony.

"Hmmmm," mused the general.

Encouraged, Brad continued, "I assume that military training is modularized and there possibly might be a couple of days between modules when Randy would be available to attend his own wedding."

"A surprise shotgun wedding, eh" the general envisioned.

"It's a formal shotgun wedding, sir, so we plan to use a *white* shotgun."

The general laughed at Brad's analogy. "Yes, I would like to help you. I am no longer Randy's commanding general, but I do know his present commander. I'll contact him and have him get in touch with you—if he buys off on the idea."

Brad handed two more business cards to the general, "Thank you, General Thurman. I'll be looking forward to a call from him."

Brad paused in thought then added, "The wedding is going to be in Hollywood and is planned to be a gala event due to Sherrill's popularity. Would you and your wife consider being on the guest list?"

"Yes, we would feel honored," replied the general. "If you have the space, there are a few other people that were close to Randy that might like to be invited."

"Good," replied Brad, "I'll be in contact with you for mailing addresses after we determine the date of the wedding."

Brad flew back to Los Angeles to meet with the executive board of directors of the studio. He presented his plan: "Due to the tremendous ratings of Sherrill's first episode, I would like to create an elaborate promo of her. The polls indicate that Sherrill is one of the most popular celebrities in television, today.

"However, the polls also show that conservative America is disturbed by the fact that Sherrill is going to have a baby out of wedlock. After the baby is born, a fickle audience may turn against her. This would mean lost advertising revenues that could be counted in the millions of dollars."

Brad noticed that the mention of lost revenues got the board's attention, so he continued, "What I propose is an elaborate wedding with all the bells and whistles—nothing held back. We will invite the couple's families and friends, of course, but my plan is also to include celebrities in both the movie and television industries. Famous faces at the wedding and reception will draw additional free press coverage, which will stimulate audience interest in upcoming presentations of 'The Don's of Eldorado.'"

"How do you get the movie industry to support a television celebrity event?" asked the production director.

"That's the other part of my plan," replied Brad. "I propose that we form 'The Dons' Production Company' to feature Sherrill in a starring role in a full length movie. We'll release the information before the wedding, and I think that people in the movie industry will clamor to be a part of a gala wedding event."

"Where's the hook here?" asked the advertising director. "Even with Sherrill's popularity, how are you going to generate interest in someone getting married?"

"Because," replied Brad, "Sherrill and her fiancé Randy are not going to know that it is going to be *their* wedding. In addition, people will come to see if Randy and Sherrill's father get into another big brawl.

"You also know how Hollywood likes intrigue. When they find out that the bride and groom don't know that they are getting married then we will have to turn people away from attending."

"That sounds pretty far-fetched," observed the president of the board. "You know that Hollywood can't keep a secret."

"That's almost true," replied Brad. "They can't keep a secret about anything—*except* from the person that the secret is about."

The rest of the board nodded in agreement. Each of them could recall previous examples of this phenomenon. The production manager remarked, "Still, Sherrill is a very bright girl. She is going to be in a church and a wedding dress. Why wouldn't she suspect something?"

Brad smiled, "Because, she is going to think that she is doing a studio promo to marry the character 'Don Luke.'

"Randy, her fiancé, is an officer in the air force. He is in training and as soon as his training is completed, he will be flown in for the wedding. I still have to work out the logistics of that one, but I have the cooperation of his former commanding general. I'm sure that we can concoct a plausible reason for him coming here."

The board members warmed to the intrigue. The financial director stated, "I'm starting to feel confident that you might just pull it off, Brad. Nevertheless, how much is this gala event going to cost us?"

Brad replied, "About five-percent of the potential lost revenues if we don't do it. However, I estimate that we can make another five million dollars on Sherrill's movie, as long as her popularity stays high."

The board saw dollar signs and all nodded in agreement. The president of the board stated, "Brad! If you can successfully pull this off, then I for one will vote that you be made president of the new 'Production Company.'"

Brad reeled from the offer as he saw the rest of the board members nod in agreement. He replied enthusiastically, "Consider it done." The board didn't see the confident Brad cross his fingers behind his back—for luck.

Brad was sitting at his desk when his secretary notified him that Lieutenant Colonel Mark Hadley was on the line. Brad picked up the phone, "Colonel Hadley, thank you for calling. I assume that General Thurman gave you some preliminary information."

"Yes, he did. However, why don't you explain exactly your expectations for Lieutenant Ferris being in California."

Brad spent the next twenty minutes explaining his plans for the wedding. Closing, he emphasized, "So you can see, Colonel, without Randy, there will be no surprise wedding."

Colonel Hadley thought for a moment, "Understand that Randy has to successfully complete this phase of his training in order for him to be available."

"I fully understand," assured Brad. "Sherrill indicated that Randy is a very capable man. Is there any doubt that he won't complete this phase?"

"Not really," replied Hadley. "It was a little touch and go when Sherrill was assaulted, but when Randy learned that she was safe, he settled down and has exceeded expectation."

"I know how he felt," replied Brad. "Everyone close to her was shocked by the attack and concerned for her safety. Security measures have been implemented to substantially reduce her exposure to harm by misguided individuals."

Hadley, feeling reassured that this man had no other ulterior motives, stated, "Lieutenant Ferris will be available the first week-end in February."

"That's great!" replied Brad. We'll make all our plans around that time frame. We want to include Randy's friends in the air force. The

410

studio will pay all travel expenses. I hope that I can include you and Mrs. Hadley."

Colonel Hadley now felt a personal obligation to the success of the venture. "Yes, you can put us on the guest list. I will supply you a list of other people that would like to attend."

"Thank you," replied Brad. "I'm looking forward to meeting you at the reception afterwards."

Brad hung up the phone and smiled. He thought, "This is great news; now preparations can start *rocking* and *rolling*."

He called the Cassons, "Hello, Vicki—Brad. The wedding is on for the first weekend in February. You choose either Saturday or Sunday and get back with me."

"I've got a long list of guests," asserted Vicki.

Brad paused, "Before you mail out invitations, we need to prioritize our list for the seating capacity of the church. The overflow will be invited to the reception at the Malibu Palisades Country Club."

Vicki stated excitedly, "This is going to be so much fun. I can't wait until the wedding day gets here."

Brad closed by saying, "Vicki, I want to check with you every three days. If I can't get through to you for some reason, please contact me. I'll have my secretary immediately put your call through to me."

The following weeks were a torrent of activity for Brad, Sherrill, and Aunt Vicki. Sherrill's popularity prompted many personal appearances. She worked them between filming scenes of her second episode and schoolwork.

A bodyguard had been hired for her. His name was Hugo Dalton and Sherrill soon developed a comfort level with him being around. The man looked fierce, but Sherrill found that his temperament was as gentle as a lamb. His presence was unobtrusive, but he was always within earshot of Sherrill. Slowly the trauma of her attack receded into the background of her mind.

On Christmas Day, Sherrill and Hugo were in New York City for her appearance on the Ed Sullivan Show. They took a ride on the subway, where a couple of obnoxious puckish characters ogled at Sherrill until Hugo caught their eye. They jumped out of their seat and ran to another car to escape the "Wrath of Hugo."

New Year's day, Vicki answered the phone and heard Randy say, "Hello, Aunt Vicki. This is Randy. May I speak with Sherrill, please?"

Vicki replied, "Oh, Randy, she'll be so happy to finally hear from you."

Aunt Vicki opened the patio door and called, "Sherrill, one of your admirers is on the phone."

Pausing to think whom it might be, Sherrill slowly closed her schoolbooks and walked to the phone. "Hello, this is Sherrill."

She heard, "Hello, beautiful, how's my angel?"

Sherrill squealed, "Randy! Is that really you? Where are you? What are you doing? Oh, my, what am I saying? Darling, I love you. I miss you terribly. It's so good to hear your voice!"

Randy laughed, and chided, "Had I known that I would create such a reaction then I might have called you sooner."

Sherrill sobered and feigned hurt, "You rat, you mean that you could have called before—and didn't?"

"No—no, Sweetheart! I was just teasing you."

Sherrill pouted, "Then you're not a rat. An' don't tease me. I miss you so much that I could start bawling, just hearing your voice."

"Sherrill, I only have five minutes for this call. I can't tell you where I am located or anything else about what I am doing. I don't know when I'll get to call you again. Just remember that I love you and yearn for the day when I can hold you in my arms again."

"Oh, Randy," sobbed Sherrill.

"Sherrill, how are you and the baby? I mean, how are you— *really?*"

Sherrill sniffled, clearing her nose, and composed herself, "We are just fine, Honey. Really, everything is fine. In three days, I will be six months along. The doctor says that everything is normal. I can feel the baby move—I can even heard his heartbeat!

Randy glowed with the news. "Oh, Baby, you don't know how I wished that I could be there with you and the baby!"

"I understand, Honey. I want you here, too. But, I know how important your training is for our future. Just remember that we love you and pray for the day that we can be together as a family."

Randy was starting to choke-up. There were other men standing in line to use the pay phone and he forced himself to change the subject. "How are Uncle Hank and Aunt Vicki? I'm really looking forward to meeting them."

Sherrill sensed the reason for the change and replied, "Uncle Hank and Aunt Vicki have been wonderful to me. I know that you worry about us, but don't. I'm sure that whatever you are doing requires your full concentration. Just do good and come back to us as soon as you can."

Randy breathed relief, "Thank you, Darling. I know that you are trying to be brave. I will be with you. I just have to complete my training, and then we can start having a life together. Honey, I've got to go. I love you."

"I love you, Randy. Please keep safe for me. Goodbye, Darling."

Sherrill hung up. She stared at the phone and hot tears ran down her cheeks. She wiped the back of her hand across her eyes and resolved, "I will be brave because I have his love to sustain me."

Panama

Randy arrived at Fort Bragg, North Carolina, home of the "Green Berets" since 1956. He had tried to find information on what to expect regarding training, but found very little information for public consumption. The "Green Berets" was an elite organization that specialized in special operations.

He did learn that many soldiers waited three or more years to be selected as a candidate for the training. The dropout rate was more than 50% and only the best graduated—to be entitled to wear the "Green Beret."

At the orientation, Lieutenant Colonel Hadley had explained that due to the nature of the air force mission, the initial training would be modified, condensed, and accelerated. Specific supplemental training would take place at other locations.

Randy had been in the service for a month and had just received a field promotion to second lieutenant in the U.S. Air Force. He wondered how his peers would receive his youth and inexperience, but resolutely resolved that he would be in the graduating class. His own pride was at stake. Needless to say, more importantly, Sherrill and the baby's future would be affected by his completion of the training for the "Special Intelligence Group."

Panama Canal Zone: (eight weeks later)

A water snake slithered across Randy's neck. He fought back a scream of paranoia. He was in a swamp or river somewhere in the Panama Canal Zone or possibly in another adjoining country—he didn't know.

His group of six officers had been ferried in by helicopter at night. During the flight, they had been blindfolded and their hands were tied behind them. As the helicopter hovered over the water, they had been unceremoniously shoved out the door. Randy wanted to scream as he momentarily felt the free fall through space. He slammed face down into the water. The water was only waist deep, but he hunkered down with the water up to his neck to lower his profile from human eyes that could be lurking nearby.

He had spent eight *hellish* weeks at Fort Bragg and had been one of the survivors. Following graduation from the "Green Beret" ranger training at Fort Bragg, this training exercise was a test under simulated combat conditions. The adversary's bullets were real, though his teammates' bodies wouldn't be targets. Nevertheless, a person could still die by accident or other lethal means.

The objective, here in Panama, was to covertly gather intelligence on 'Red Company', comprised of U. S. Army personnel and somehow get the information back to their U. S. Air Force Headquarters—wherever that might be from here.

Randy paused and listened. He could hear the sounds of the jungle, but due to the blindfold, there was little else that his senses could tell him. His primary concern was to regain sight by removing the blindfold—but how—his hands were tied behind him.

He would have to use his intelligence to overcome the obstacles. He started duck walking in the water; suddenly it became deeper. Reversing his direction, the water became shallower. He felt the rough grating edges of reeds against his face; this meant that a shore was near.

Pushing through the reeds, he finally felt dry ground. Still duck walking to keep a low profile, he bumped into a tree. Feeling the surface of the trunk with his cheek, he found a snag and worked off the blindfold.

After total darkness from the blindfold, the light from the half moon was surprisingly bright. Seeing a cloud moving to cover the moon, he quickly looked around to check the topography of the land before it was obscured by darkness. A hundred feet away, he spotted one of his teammates aimlessly duck walking.

Estimating where his teammate would be if he continued in a straight line, Randy started duck walking to that location. Halfway there, the cloud obscured the moon. By now, he was close enough to hear the soft sound of water squishing in the other man's boots. Heading toward the sound, he finally bumped into his teammate. Randy heard a muffled grunt and whispered, "It's Ferris. Try to untie my hands."

The two men positioned their backs together and his teammate frantically worked at the knot of the wet rope. After long moments, the knot was still tight. Randy quickly flipped his fingers across his teammate's fingers, indicating for him to stop.

Randy started to work on the other man's rope. Feeling the shape of the knot, he found a loose end and started rotating the weave tighter as he pushed on the rope. This caused the diameter of the rope to decrease and the wetness acted as a lubricant. The knot finally worked free.

415

Once free, his teammate removed his own blindfold. He used his knife to quickly free Randy's hands. He pulled Randy close to him and whispered directly into his ear, "Captain Jensen." Pushing on Randy's shoulder, he whispered, "You go that way; I'll go the other. Ten minutes—come back upstream to meet me."

Randy crawled along the shoreline next to the reeds. Three minutes later, he found 1st Lieutenant Sean O'Rorke. He sliced through his ropes and they silently continued the search.

Five minutes later they found 2nd Lieutenant Chet Taggart. The clouds moved past the moon and the area was again dimly illuminated. Randy hugged the ground and saw the silhouette of two men crawling into the reeds. He motioned for his two teammates to follow him into the reeds.

Moving upstream, they found 2nd Lieutenant Rick Medford at the edge of the reeds. Two minutes later they met up with Captain Greg Jensen and 1st Lieutenant Tom Derring.

Captain Jensen motioned them into the reeds. They formed a tight circle in the reeds and Jensen whispered, "Is everyone okay?" They had prearranged earlier in training that a silent response was a tacit "Yes." A finger in the chest was a definitive "No" answer.

Silence prevailed and Jensen continued in a whisper, "Derring, Medford, O'Rorke, Taggart; north, east, south, west; Ferris—upstream. Rendezvous back here in one hour." Jensen lifted the cover on his tritium-illuminated wristwatch and whispered, "It's now 0316."

The men departed and Jensen used his knife to cut a two-foot square at the river's edge of the reeds, two inches below the waterline. He cast the cut reeds into the reed-bed, so they wouldn't float down river. This would give his men a reference for the rendezvous, but a casual observer on the river wouldn't detect the small swath of missing reeds.

Randy pushed upstream, with just his head above water. He stopped for a moment to listen to the sounds of the night, and then continued upstream. All his senses were on edge, but his mind started recalling the circumstances of how he had gotten to this point in his training.

Randy had arrived at Fort Bragg with great expectations. Checking onto the army base had been routine; that was where the routine had ended.

On the first day of training, Lieutenant Colonel Mark Hadley had given an orientation of the training. He then turned the eighty-one air

416

force personnel over to the army trainers—forty-three officers were to survive this unnatural ordeal.

Thirty-eight had been returned to their original bases after having resigned by placing their bayonet onto their rifle and sticking it into the "resignation circle" in front of their barracks. They had placed their helmet on the vertical butt of their rifles and simply walked away—never to be seen again at Fort Bragg.

Randy had been junior in almost all categories, except intelligence, athletic ability, and determination. He was younger than most by at least four years.

Most of the men in his group had either gone to college and become officers through OTS (Officers Training School); distinguished themselves as airmen and completed OCS (Officers Candidate School); or had attended the Air Force Academy and were commissioned to 2nd lieutenants upon graduation.

Petty jealousies toward Randy had existed during his first weeks of training. It was rumored, yes, even accusations made by some of his army trainers that the only reason that he was in the training program was due to his being Sherrill's fiancé. These accusations had stung his ego, but instead of giving up, they had only made him more determined to succeed.

His tenacity had finally been rewarded. By the end of his training, his trainers and peers had accepted him on his own merits. He had graduated with top honors and was now a member of the first elite air force team to go through an actual assignment under simulated combat conditions.

The object of this exercise was to induce terror and uncertainties into the team members, and then see how they functioned in achieving their objective. To further stress the team, they had been provided with only a knife, a wristwatch, and a compass.

Captain Jensen, who was the leader of the team, had been provided a locator beacon. He would only activate this beacon if the team gave up and requested evacuation. Randy knew that this would never happen, unless circumstances were so dire that to go on would be useless.

Randy came to an opening in the reeds, where the river turned right. The swirling current had scrubbed away the reeds from the shoreline. In the dim light of the half moon, he could see animal tracks and combat boot prints. He crawled up the shore to higher ground and found an animal trail that led off into the dark jungle.

Crawling back to the river, he cut three reeds below the waterline and crawled back to the trail. Standing and holding the three reeds ahead of him, he walked like a blind man with a white cane into the canopied forest. He knew that the trail might have a booby-trap tripwire. The reeds would bend without tripping a signal grenade that might have been set up by the adversarial forces.

Two hundred paces up the trail, his reeds hit something. He raised the reeds in front of him and felt something else. He reached out and found a trip wire installed chest high. Reaching down, he found another tripwire. Following the wires, he found two grenades. He detached the grenades, coiled the wire, and placed them in his fatigue pockets.

Using the reeds to feel in the dark, he continued up the trail. A hundred paces further, he found another booby trap. Carrying the additional grenades, he continued up the trail for another one hundred paces and found a third booby trap.

Following the trail further, he came out into a small clearing. He found a large tree that extended above the forest canopy. Depositing the reeds and four of the six grenades next to the tree, he started climbing up the vines that wrapped upward around the tree. The climbing went fast because he could follow the vines in the dim moonlight. More than a hundred feet up, he rose above the forest canopy.

Looking around, he saw the silver reflection of the river bending and twisting in the distance. About five kilometers upstream Randy saw what looked like a bridge, but at this angle, it could be just another bend in the river.

Grasping what looked like just another vine, he started to climb higher. The perceived vine was cold with scales and wiggled in Randy's grasp. His toe slipped off a limb and he swung away from the tree, holding on by only one hand. His reflexes to keep from falling wouldn't allow him to let go of the snake until he knew that he wouldn't fall.

Randy clutched a sturdy vine with his other hand and his right foot was secure on a limb. As he swung around and let go of the snake, his momentum caused the snake to be slung out over the forest canopy. It went crashing down through the trees and he heard human screams and shouts, followed by gunfire.

Flashlight beams immediately appeared at the edge of the clearing. Randy knew that he would be discovered within seconds. His primary concern was to warn his team. Almost without consciously thinking, he pulled the pin on one of the grenades and cast it in the direction of where the snake had fallen.

The babble of human voices covered the sound of the grenade falling through the trees. There was a diffused flash followed by a loud boom that resonated through the forest. Randy heard someone say, "You idiots! One of your bullets must have hit a grenade. Now they (Randy's group) will never come this way. Let's get back to the company and report to the captain."

Randy saw the lights of eight flashlights disappear into the far side of the clearing. He quickly descended the tree and retrieved the four grenades and the reeds left at the base of the tree. As he entered the trail, he saw light off to his right where the snake had fallen.

The grenade had started a small fire, which illuminated an abandoned backpack leaning against a tree. He grabbed the backpack and stomped out the fire. Back on the trail, he used the reeds to feel his way back to the river.

He opened the cover on his watch and saw that it was 0421—he was already late for the rendezvous and it would be daylight soon. He entered the river with the backpack held over his head and floated with the current down the river. In the moonlight, he spotted the cutout in the reeds and angled toward it.

A hand grabbed his wrist and he felt a knife at his throat. Jensen's whispered voice demanded, "Identify yourself."

Randy whispered back, "It's Ferris."

"Ferris—we thought that you had been captured. What were the gunshots and loud boom?"

Randy moved into the reeds and explained to his teammates the events of his reconnaissance. He ended with, "I recovered a backpack, but I didn't have time to see what was inside."

"Good work, Ferris," complimented the captain. "And good heads up thinking; how did you know to use reeds to feel your way through the game trail—they didn't teach us that in training?"

"I don't know. I must have seen it in a movie or something. It just seemed the obvious thing to do."

Jensen felt inside the pockets of the backpack and found a pair of binoculars, a bottle of quinine tablets, a rain slicker, canned rations, a first-aid kit, a pair of woolen socks, a container of matches, and a plastic container of maps.

419

His men held the backpack just above the water and the captain spread out one of the maps across it. He studied the map for a moment with the light of the matches shielded by his helmet and announced, "There is a circle on the map. This must be where the soldiers are bivouacked (camped).

"From Randy's report, we know their strength is a company of soldiers. However, we don't know if they are mechanized. We must get that information before we try to get back to our base to make our report."

Randy interjected, "Captain, I think that we should try to make that report now."

Randy's teammates were dumbfounded by the suggestion and the silence lasted almost twenty seconds. 2nd Lieutenant Chet Taggart finally broke the silence, stating cynically, "What do you suggest, Ferris—sending up smoke signals?"

"Well, sort of," replied Randy. "I was thinking of using the locator beacon to send Morse code."

"That won't work," stated Captain Jensen. "The beacon generates a continuous radio signal. You need modulated pulses to send Morse code. Besides, HQ is not expecting us to contact them via radio. The locator beacon is to only be used if we give up and want to be picked up."

"I realize that," responded Randy. "Therefore, they will be watching for the beacon signal. If we hold down on the activate button and just touch the battery leads then we can send pulsed signals. They will see an intermittent flashing light and hear an intermittent audio beep in the speakers."

1st Lieutenant Tom Derring stated in an excited whisper, "Hey, Ferris might have just hit on something. I had to learn the Morse code when I got my ham radio license in college. I'm a little rusty; I haven't used it since then, but if we write it out beforehand then I can send it."

Captain Jensen agreed, "Okay, let's get to the clearing that Randy described. It should be daylight by then. Red Company won't expect us to go there after the signal grenade exploded."

Randy eased back into the river and led his team upstream. At the river edge, they cut reeds to feel for new trip wires. Ten minutes later, they were at the clearing.

Jensen instructed, "O'Rorke, you and Medford keep following the trail and check for trip wires. See if you can get close enough to "Red Army" to find out if they are mechanized."

O'Rorke and Medford headed across the clearing and disappeared into the jungle. Twenty minutes later there was enough daylight to write a message on the back of the map.

Jensen handed the message to Derring and he encoded it from memory. When he had finished it, he vacillated, "I'm not sure if I coded it right—it's been a long time."

Randy looked at the code and observed, "You've got your *R's* and *L's* switched around. *R* is (dot dash dot); *L* is (dot dash dot dot)."

Jensen looked at Randy, "Are you sure? You never said that you knew Morse code."

"Yes, I'm sure. I memorized the Morse code in one day when I found it on the back cover of a Webster's Dictionary, but I have never used it to send or receive real messages. I just pretended that I was sending messages to Sherrill, when I was bored out of my gourd on the farm. Sherrill's name has two (R's) and two (L's)."

"Randy's right!" exclaimed Derring. I remember now sending a practice message 'ROBERT E. LEE IS UP A TREE. THE SOUTH HAS LOST WITH NO PLACE TO FLEE.'"

Derring had just completed the corrections to the coded message when O'Rorke and Medford returned from their reconnaissance. "What did you find?" asked Jensen.

"There were no more trip wires on the trail, so we must be inside their defensive perimeter," reported O'Rorke. It is a mechanized company with sixteen tanks, eight half-tracks, ten trucks, and probably 110 to 120 men.

"They were eating breakfast and joking around like they were safe in their numbers. I don't think that they consider us a real threat. I heard one of them say that they would be thirty clicks away from here even if they were spotted by the *air force blue balls*, sir."

"That does it," stated Jensen with a grim set to his jaw. "Maybe Lieutenant Ferris' idea will work. We've got nothing to lose by trying."

He added to the message on the back of the map. "Mechanized—launch air attack—home on beacon."

Lieutenant Tom Derring encoded the words and removed the cover from the battery. Taggart held the transmitter with the activate button pressed while Derring tapped out the message by touching the wires to the battery.

The message was sent three times in succession. They waited ten minutes and resent the message three more times. Jensen ordered, "O'Rorke, you and Medford get as close to the mechanized company as

421

possible and tie this transmitter high enough up a tree that no one will spot it. Meet us back at the river." He pressed the activate button on the transmitter and handed it to O'Rorke.

Lieutenant Colonel Mark Hadley sat in the Operation's Center. He half-heartedly sipped his eighth cup of coffee since arriving at 0100. He had watched Captain Jensen's team being loaded into a Huey and ferried off over the jungle.

At Fort Bragg, the army training instructors had thrown away the book and hammered his men relentlessly. Hadley had not interfered, since their lives and the lives of countless other men would depend on their success behind enemy lines.

Regarding the Panama exercise, he knew that blindfolding his men and tying their hands behind their back was unrealistic for a normal training exercise, but he had to find out in a very short period of time if they would crack under pressure.

They were all good men that had been handpicked for special operations. Still, this was something new for the air force. The other services had a long established record of successes behind enemy lines, but his superiors at the Pentagon wanted actual air force personnel to be a part of this special force that had been created by presidential decree.

An army sergeant interrupted his thoughts, "Excuse me, Colonel Hadley. Captain Jensen's locator beacon just went off. That is the signal for giving up and requesting a pickup."

Hadley glanced at his watch; it was only 0523. His heart sank and he exclaimed, "Damn, they have only been on the mission for less than three hours."

Hoping against hope, he asked, "Are you sure that it was Captain Jensen's beacon?"

"Yes, sir, all the beacons for the exercise were labeled and tested before the mission began. I'll show you."

Hadley followed the sergeant to an adjoining room. The sergeant pointed to the receiver labeled, "Jensen — Blue Team."

Hadley stared at the intermittently blinking light and heard the low volume intermittent squawk from the speaker. He stared at the light, wishing that it would go away. Then something clicked in his mind, "Sergeant, isn't that light supposed to be on steady."

"Yes, sir, maybe it is malfunctioning."

Hope leaped in Hadley's mind, but he shook his head, "No, that's no malfunction—look at the rhythm. Listen to the sound coming out of the speakers. It sounds like a Morse code transmission."

The sergeant agreed, "You're right, sir. It does look and sounds like a code, but we don't use Morse codes during practice operations. There is too much chance for error, so we rely on voice communications."

Hadley stoically pointed out, "Yes, but Captain Jensen's team doesn't have a radio. Maybe, just maybe, they are trying to send a message to us by using their beacon."

He looked up at the sergeant, "Quickly, find someone that knows Morse code and have him report here, immediately!"

The sergeant left and Hadley sat staring at the light. He had never learned Morse code because he always had someone in the signal corps to decipher messages. He smacked his fist against the palm of his hand, "Damn, now I wished that I had the knowledge of code." The words were no sooner uttered than the light stopped blinking and remained off. Hadley stared at the receiver in disbelief. "Where in hell is that sergeant?"

Ten minutes passed and the light on the beacon receiver started blinking again—still no sergeant. Minutes passed and the sergeant finally arrived with a corporal in-tow. The corporal started writing on a notepad, and then the light stayed on solid with a constant carrier signal emanating from the speaker. He looked up, "Sorry, sir, but I was only able to get a partial message. I got a latitude and longitude location, plus the message 'MECHANIZED—LAUNCH AIR ATTACK—HOME ON BEACON.'"

Colonel Hadley smiled. He thought, "This wasn't part of the mission plan. My men are showing initiative and even testing the Command Post to see if we are on our toes. Well, I'll act on that information, but I'll need confirmation of the message to justify my decision."

He called up Flight Operations and said into the phone, "Hello, this is Lieutenant Colonel Mark Hadley. Launch the two F-102s on 'Tango Alert.' Have them fly thirty seconds apart and have the flight leader confirm the location of 'Red Company.'

"Upon confirmation have the second F-102 drop blue dye on 'Red Company.' That will simulate a kill and we will end the exercise. The coordinates are 'latitude - 9°12'6" N', 'longitude - 79°30'8" W'. Have them home in on beacon frequency 199.3 MHz (Megahertz). I'm at extension 109. Call me when you get a report from the pilots."

Hadley sat back in his chair to relax, but his nerves were tense. His superiors would review the operation and probably state that he was rash to rely on a partial message for a simulated bomb drop. Hadley knew in his own mind that what he had done was right, but the army brass would cry foul.

They had even argued that air force personnel didn't have the proper mindset to succeed in this type of operation that historically was carried out by the army and navy.

He instructed the army sergeant, "Get me the 'OIC of Monitoring' at Fort Huachuca, Arizona on the phone."

Three minutes later, the sergeant said, "Colonel Clark is on the line, sir."

Hadley picked up the phone, "Colonel Clark, this is Air Force Lieutenant Colonel Mark Hadley in Panama. We are running a military exercise down here and one of our teams has sent a Morse code message using their locator beacon. We weren't expecting them to use their beacon in that manner and weren't set up for decoding, so we only got a partial message. I wonder if your people might have picked it up."

Colonel Clark replied, "We have automatic scanners that record a wide spectrum of frequencies on tape. What frequency and time did they transmit?"

"They started transmitting at 0523 (1023 Zulu time) on 199.3 MHz and again around 0540."

Clark assured, "I'll have my people check it out. How do you want me to contact you?"

"Send me a telex. My number here in operations is 12-110783.

He thought of asking Clark to rush the request but then thought better of it. He knew that the army would automatically put a rush on it to impress the air force boys with their efficiency. He simply said, "Thank you, Colonel Clark," then hung up.

Hadley sat drumming his fingers on the desk. Ten minutes passed and the Teletype came to life. He thought, "It's too early," but he looked anyway. The message was normal traffic. He reached for a cigarette then remembered that he had given up smoking three years ago.

His phone rang and he picked it up, saying "Lieutenant Colonel Hadley."

"Yes, Colonel Hadley," stated the voice on the other end of the line. "This is Captain Steve Bosley at flight operations. The F-102s found 'Red Company' and doused them with pool chalk (blue powered dye).

It looks like your team *'brought in the bacon with their beacon'* on this exercise."

"Thanks, Captain Bosley. Thank the pilots, too."

He hung up the phone and wanted to dance and yell, but that would be unprofessional in front of an army sergeant. Therefore, he satisfied himself with a wide grin as he telephoned army operations. "Hello, this is Lieutenant Colonel Mark Hadley. Have a crew pick up Captain Jensen's 'Blue Team' and have them report to me at 'Mission Operations' when they land."

"Just a moment sir," stated the voice on the other end. "Colonel Brenson would like to speak with you."

Brenson came on the line and screamed, "Colonel Hadley, what kind of bullshit are you pulling over there. I just got a call from 'Red Company' and they said that your jets just dropped blue dye on them. There is no way that your pilots could have known their location unless you told them. My general is going to have a meeting with your general and there is going to be hell to pay for you violating the parameters of this mission."

Hadley stated evenly, "There were no violations, Colonel. My team reported the location coordinates of 'Red Company.' The F-102 pilots confirmed the target and dye was dropped to mark a successful air strike. You are welcome to read my report after I prepare it."

Colonel Brenson retorted, "You can forget about the army picking up your team. They were supposed to hoof it in and report the location. I'm going to have the whole regiment out looking for your men. When they make their report to you, they will be in the custody of my soldiers."

Hadley heard the line click and go dead. He slammed the receiver down, "Damn his ego; I hate a sore loser." He stared at the silent Teletype, wishing that it would deliver the collaborating information that would validate his action.

He turned to the sergeant, "I'm going to the latrine. Watch the Teletype for me. I'm expecting a message and I don't want it distributed to anyone else."

"Yes, sir," responded the sergeant.

Five minutes later, the sergeant handed the confirmation telex to Hadley. He scanned the message, folded it, and placed it in his pocket. He thought, *now let Brenson scream all he wants.*

O'Rorke and Medford slipped out of the forest and back into the reeds. Captain Jensen summarized, "We have to get back to HQ without being detected. I've studied the map and there is a bridge upstream on the *Rio Indio* about five clicks, but it may be guarded. Medford reported that there was a trail leading off into the forest on the other side of the river. That's the general direction to *Aerodrome Madden*, where Colonel Hadley is located, so let's shake a leg."

Jensen's team had just crossed the river when they heard the thunder of jets. Screened by the undergrowth at the edge of the jungle, they watched an Air Force F-102 make a low-level run and drop a load of blue dye.

Minutes later, they saw scores of men wearing green fatigues with blue spots jump into the river to wash off their blemishes of defeat. Jensen glanced around and saw his men raise their fists in a salute of triumph. He whispered, "Okay, let's get up this trail."

They had gone about two kilometers when Lieutenant Derring tapped Jensen on the shoulder, "Captain, what if they follow us? They're bound to be pissed off at us and may try to capture us."

"I realize that," replied Jensen. "That is why we have been hoofing it up this trail."

Derring continued, "Yes, but it would be nice to know for sure. Ferris has some signal grenades. Why don't we booby-trap the trail? They won't be expecting it and I, personally, would like to know for sure if we are being followed."

"Good idea," replied Jensen.

The rest of the team had overheard the conversation and Randy pulled a grenade from his pocket. He walked back down the trail where it had taken a bend and stretched the tripwire, ankle high, across the trail. He attached the grenade on the backside of a large tree so that the blast wouldn't injure anyone. The deep shadows of the rain forest would prevent anyone from seeing the black trip-wire.

He hurried back to his team and they jogged up the trail. After they had gone about a kilometer, they heard the muffled blast of the grenade.

Jensen ducked into the undergrowth and his team formed a circle around him. "Okay, that confirms that the army boys are pissed. They don't intend for us to get back to HQ. Anybody got any good ideas on how we are going to complete our mission?"

1st Lieutenant Tom Derring, second in rank by time in grade, suggested, "I think we should beat it to hell up the trail. They've got radios and will try to outmaneuver us—every second counts."

Medford, O'Rorke, and Taggart nodded in agreement. Captain Jensen noticed that Randy did not nod. He asked, "Lieutenant Ferris, I see that you don't agree, why?"

"As Lieutenant Derring stated, they have radios and will try to outmaneuver us. I think that the best way to elude them is to backtrack to the river and float down it tonight. The map indicates that it dumps into Lago (lake) Alajuela and the Rio Chagres drains into Lago Gaten, which is part of the Panama Canal. The army would never suspect that we would approach from that direction."

Captain Jensen studied the map and said, "I like your idea, except there is a road from the Lago Alajuela to HQ at Aerodromo Madden."

"I agree, sir, but don't you think that the army would have roadblocks or patrols on that road. The fact that they are pursuing us indicates that they mean to capture us or prevent us from reaching our headquarters.

"We are not only on a specific training mission, but we are also being scrutinized by the top brass that a unit like ours should even exist in the air force. You know, as well as I that Colonel Hadley expects us to report directly to him as a team that has completed a successful mission.

"Our tactical mission was completed when the jets took out the mechanized company, but you can be sure that some army colonel or general is going to try every way he can to prevent us from reporting directly to Colonel Hadley."

"Randy's right," intoned the other lieutenants.

"Yes," agreed Jensen. "I like his logic." He added wistfully, "I just wish that I really knew what the army was thinking."

Randy, feeling that he had their confidence, suggested, "Then why don't we find out. When I was up that tree and threw the grenade, it caused a lot of confusion. Men were shouting, instead of whispering. Why don't we set another grenade and see if we can pick up some Intel of their plans?"

Jensen nodded, "You do it. I'm going to take the rest of the team back down the trail a hundred meters and we'll hide in the jungle. Find out what you can, and then come down and meet up with us."

Captain Jensen left with the team and Randy strung another booby-trap low to the ground. He put the grenade on the far side of the trail then moved back into the undergrowth to wait.

Ten minutes later the patrol point man jogged across the wire and continued up the trail. Thirty seconds passed and the rest of the squad appeared. Randy sat in concealment with his hands covering his ears. The first three men passed over the wire without tripping it and Randy felt a twinge of doubt—had he set it too low? The fourth man stumbled on the wire and there was pandemonium as the loud blast caught the patrol by surprise.

They scattered into the underbrush and one man was two feet away from Randy. He held his breath; the man was so near. Flies settled on the sweat that covered his face and neck. He wanted to swat at their stings, but tensed himself and remained silent. Finally, after torturous long minutes, the man rose and joined the rest of the squad that had reassembled back on the trail.

Randy heard someone scream, "Lieutenant, those air force sons-of-bitches are still using our own signal grenades against us."

"I know," replied the Lieutenant, "but it means that we are on the right trail. We need reinforcements in case the trail splits. Helmann, give me the radio, so that I can contact HQ."

Randy listened to the one-sided conversation, and then the squad moved on up the trail. He waited until the rear guard was out of sight then he moved out of his cover and jogged back down the trail.

Medford signaled from his cover, "Pssttt, Randy, over here." Randy dove into the undergrowth and found his teammates.

"What did you find out?" asked Captain Jensen.

"They're not happy that we are using their signal grenades against them. They are confident that they are on the right trail and have called for another squad to reinforce their search. They should be along here in about fifteen minutes."

Jensen smiled, "Well, Lieutenant Ferris, it looks like your plan is starting to work."

"Yes, sir," replied Randy grimly. "But, while we were waiting, I reviewed our options. I've rethought our situation and feel that there's got to be a better way."

"What!" stated Jensen as he stared incredulously at Randy. "What do you mean 'rethought'? Your plan sounded very plausible when you presented it."

"I know. It sounded good to me too at the time. However, after I reviewed all the options in my mind, there are too many unknown variables in the plan."

He continued, picking his own original plan apart, "We would be going back into the main concentration of 'Red Company.' We would be forced to spend all day undercover. We would have to enter an unknown river in complete darkness and feel our way until the moon rose. After the moon comes up, we could see them, but they could also see us. We would have to travel over 60 kilometers in the open to get back to our base."

Randy paused, and then added for emphasis, "I don't know about the rest of you, but I had a snake crawl across my neck in the dark this morning when we were dropped into the river. I certainly don't want to give it or one of its cousins another chance to make me or one of my teammates a casualty on a training mission."

In the dim jungle light, Randy saw the futility of his original plan register on the faces of his teammates. "You are right," Jensen finally acknowledged. This is a training mission—not actual combat. We can't chance having someone killed or badly injured just to evade capture."

The silence hung as each man thought on Randy's words and their unrealistic situation.

Finally, Lieutenant Derring asked, "Well then, what do you suggest, Doctor Vet? Are we supposed to just quit and give ourselves up?"

"No, that's not an option," replied Randy. "My uncle, who was a Major in the army, had a saying, 'If you are not part of the *answer* then you've become part of the *problem*.'"

He went on to describe an alternate plan, "The army has radios, and can instantly communicate with each other. As the crow flies, our base is only 10 kilometers away. We can be there in an hour, maybe two, if we continue up the trail.

"Let's set a grenade with the tripwire waist high so that the reinforcement squad can see the wire. Even if they don't, then they will set it off. They will radio the squad that just passed us that we have doubled back to the river. When the squad, which we know has eleven men, comes back down the trail then we will hustle up the trail."

Taggert pointed out, "What if the reinforcements continue up the trail, thinking that the first squad missed the tripwire?"

"They won't," reassured Randy. "That is why we are putting the wire waist high. They will know that the first squad would have had to trip it and conclude that we must have doubled back."

O'Rorke interjected, "Randy's right—Randy's wrong—Randy's right. I agree that his second plan is brilliant. Hell, I wish that I had thought of it, myself. I hate slimy snakes and the thought of meeting one in the dark makes my skin crawl. Besides, I'm getting hungry and would just as soon dine in the officers' mess tonight."

429

The rest of the team chuckled lightly and Captain Jensen confirmed, "Yes, your second plan has a lot of merit. We'll go up the trail another click then hide in the bush. If the patrol comes back down the trail then we will know that they have fallen for the ruse."

"Medford, you take the point. Randy, you set the grenade and come up as rear guard. Okay, let's get moving."

Randy set the charge and followed them up the trail. He had gone about a kilometer, when Jensen stepped onto the trail and motioned him into the undergrowth.

As the minutes drug on, the team listened intently, anticipating the sound of the grenade going off. Flies settled on their sweat and bored into their flesh, extracting droplets of blood that attracted mosquitoes and more flies. Finally, they heard the clomping of combat boots as ten men from the lead squad hurried back down the trail. The ruse had apparently worked, but there was still one more man to pass before the trail was clear.

Finally, the soldier carrying the radio appeared. He stopped right in front of them. With his back to them, he proceeded to take a piss. Jensen felt an urge to ambush him and gain access to the radio, but he let the urge slip away.

This was a covert operation and the radioman would quickly be missed. If they took him down now then the army would know that the air force team had not doubled back. The army wouldn't be fooled a second time.

Jensen saw, out of the corner of his eye, O'Rorke crouching to spring on the radioman. He reached out and pushed him back down. He looked around and motioned to the rest of his team to stay in cover.

The radioman picked up the handset, "This is Corporal Helmann with a radio check. So far, so good, the flyboys haven't taken the bait. They must still be below my position—out."

Jensen breathed a quiet sigh of relief. The radioman had indeed been a decoy. O'Rorke looked over, acknowledging with a salute that Jensen had made the right decision. The rest of the team relaxed because they too had wanted to get the radio.

The radioman disappeared down the trail and Jensen led his men up the trail. Randy was designated rear guard while they were jogging up the trail. His mind was alert of his surroundings, but he couldn't help thinking of Sherrill.

He had only been able to speak to her once while at Fort Bragg—that was New Year's Day. He had wanted to call her on Christmas Day, but he and the other men in his training group had been on an eighty-mile hike with full packs. They had bivouacked in a cold ice covered swamp. There was no Santa Claus with presents; just cold army rations and a cold wet ground to sleep upon.

As he had lain gazing at the stars, he had thought up four more lines of a ballad that was forming in his mind:

> Lingering moments of ecstasy
> Bonding our spirits throughout eternity.
> Life is unique—an endless mystery
> A boundless cosmos in a fathomless sea.

Five of his group had washed out on that march. Every man was tempted to hang it up, but the rest had survived, only to be subjected to even greater misery and abuse for the remainder of his training.

He was proud when he had received his "Special Forces Badge." His group had completed similar training as the "Green Berets" but he knew that his group had received an extra dose of *army sadism* because they were the first air force group to go through the training.

After five kilometers Jensen's group reached the top of a ridge overlooking the airport. Jensen pointed in the direction of the airfield, "Okay, Lieutenant Ferris, there is our destination. You seem to be the strategist on this mission. Any ideas on how to get to Colonel Hadley without being detected?"

Randy looked around, not ignoring Jensen's question, but taking in the panorama of the landscape. He had not thought of what to do because he didn't know the terrain. Now that he looked down into the valley, he could see the airport and the adjoining army post with its tanks and helicopters and the air force detachment with its squadron of air force jets.

The two services shared common facilities, but in philosophy, they were worlds apart. He knew that the army provided the military security, except on the flight line. There, air police were responsible for the security of airplanes.

Randy stated seriously, "Well, Captain, being that you asked my opinion; I think that we should call up the army and request a bus to transport us to Colonel Hadley."

Randy's teammates laughed in amazement. Lieutenant Derring opined, "Ferris must of come down with jungle fever; he sounds delirious."

Captain Jensen, noting that Randy hadn't laughed with them to reveal that he was joking, stated, "Surely, you must be joking, Randy."

"Actually, I'm not. I think that the direct way is the best way. The army will be expecting us to try sneaking onto the base at night.

"O'Rorke said that he was hungry—we're all tired of listening to his stomach growling. The objective is to get him something to eat. Therefore, we need to move the schedule up to fit our needs—not the army's expectations."

Perplexed, Jensen admonished, "Okay, continue, but this plan had better be damn good."

Randy elaborated, "Do you remember when we landed here that we landed at the civilian airport, not the air force runway? The army sent over a bus from their motor pool to pick us up and we weren't even stopped at the gate by the guard. The bus driver is going to be an enlisted man and won't even question us because we are all officers."

"Jesus," cried Derring. "That just seems too simple. But you know—Randy could be right; it might just work. The army will never dream of us riding in from the airport on an army bus in broad daylight."

Two hours later, the team boarded an army bus. The driver was a PFC (Private First Class) and had only given them a cursory glance as they entered the bus. He had made this same trip hundreds of times and had seen all sorts of passengers during that time.

However, when the bus stopped at the sentry gate, an army sergeant boarded the bus. He looked at the air force officers and stated, "We have to check everybody that enters the post. Where are you coming from, Captain?"

Without batting an eye, Captain Jensen lied, "We are a new ranger team from Fort Bragg, North Carolina. We were supposed to be here yesterday, but a thunderstorm forced our plane down over Costa Rica. It cracked its landing gear and we had to fly in on Costa Rican Airlines."

The sergeant glanced across the runway and saw a Costa Rican passenger plane parked at the terminal. He looked at the rumpled and stained uniforms and asked, "Captain, why are your uniforms in such poor condition."

Jensen smoothly lied, "During the layover, we watched the Costa Rican National Soccer Team practicing. They challenged us to a game. Our baggage was still on the other plane, so we couldn't change uniforms."

The sergeant smiled, "Did you beat them?"

"Nah," replied Jensen. "They kicked our butts, 6 to 2."

The army sergeant grinned, "I've got some more bad news for you. One of your ranger teams is out on an exercise right now. They will never get back because our Colonel has the whole post alerted for them. I guess that your team will be next, so good luck—you'll need it." The sergeant got off the bus and waved them through.

O'Rorke leaned forward and whispered into Jensen's ear, "Sir, that was way too smooth. I never ever want you to ask my sister out on a date. I want her to remain a virgin."

Jensen smiled at the compliment and gazed straight ahead.

Five minutes later they exited the bus in front of "Mission Operations." Walking directly into Colonel Hadley's office, they saluted him. Captain Jensen stated, "Blue Team reports mission accomplished, sir."

Colonel Hadley's facial expression changed from total surprise to undisguised pride. He returned the salute, and then jumped up, and shook hands with each team member.

He looked at his watch—it was 1400. The mission had started just twelve hours before and he really hadn't expected them back for two or three days; even at that, the army had sworn that his team would be returned in captivity.

Shaking his head, he uttered, "I still can't believe that you guys are standing here. The whole army regiment is out looking for you. I want to know what happened—make your report Captain Jensen."

Thirty minutes later, Captain Jensen finished his report. Colonel Hadley looked directly at Randy for a long moment, but said nothing. He glanced at the rest of the team and stated, "Get cleaned up and have something to eat. Be back here in an hour. I want you to make your report to the army brass and I want you to appear in your 'Class A's.'"

Jensen led his team out the door and Colonel Hadley picked up the phone. "Hello, Colonel Brenson. This is Lieutenant Colonel Hadley. You can call off your search for the Blue Team. They just reported in at my office—all six of them."

433

Brenson interrupted, "Dammit—that's utterly impossible! I just got a report from my field commander that he has them surrounded down by a river—the Rio Indio. He's tightening the noose right now."

Hadley replied, "You've seen my team; you even know who they are by sight. They will be back in my office at 1530—that's a promise."

"I'll be there with the general," snorted Brenson, and then he slammed the phone down.

Hadley clicked the receiver and placed a call, "Hello, General Colwell. Blue Team has just completed their mission. Army General Howard and Colonel Brenson will be in my office at 1530. I know that you wanted to be kept up to date on their progress, so I hope that you can attend that meeting."

"Yes, yes, my staff and I will to be there; will your team be there too?"

"They will be here, sir. They looked pretty grubby, so I've asked them to clean up and wear their tropical Class A's."

"Good," replied the general.

Hadley hung up, put his feet on his desk, and leaned back. His team had just accomplished the *impossible*; well, almost impossible, being that they were here. They had made the mission look like a Sunday afternoon cakewalk, and the army wasn't at all pleased by his men's success against them. Feeling the afterglow of success, he smiled, and then remembering the never-ending daily reports, he swung his feet down and dug into the reports with the resignation of an indentured desk jockey.

At 1525, Blue Team arrived back at Mission Operations, and was directed to the briefing room. When they entered, they found the room filled with people, some were standing. They took the six empty seats up front and sat uneasily. They were on display and none of the brass was below the rank of major.

Hadley smiled; his men were a little early and they looked sharp in their Class "A" uniforms. He stood behind the briefing podium and addressed the audience. "As most of you know, the President through the Secretary of Defense has mandated the formation of an elite group of officers to engage in information gathering activities behind enemy lines. The first group of air force officers has completed their Ranger training at Fort Bragg, and today, has completed their first simulated combat mission.

"The mission started at 0200 hours this morning. They were ferried by helicopter to a location unknown to them. Blindfolded, with their hands tied behind their backs, they were dropped into the Rio Indio. Their only resources were a wristwatch, a knife, a compass, and their brains.

"Under those controlled conditions, we felt that they would have little chance for success. If they did succeed in getting back, we estimated that it would take two to three days. The main goal of the mission was to stress them and see how they would react under the pressure of simulated combat conditions."

Looking in the direction of his men, Hadley proudly smiled, "You can imagine my surprise when they appeared in my office—just twelve hours after the mission began. They not only got back undetected, but also called in a successful air strike on Red Company two hours after they were dropped into the river. Captain Greg Jensen will now give you a report of his team's activities during that time."

Jensen approached the podium, "Thank you, Colonel Hadley, general staff, and fellow officers." He related the story as it unwound, adding pertinent statements, and describing the terrain and environment.

Almost an hour later, he closed by stating, "We had a team effort, and I am proud to have been on the mission with each of my teammates. Nevertheless, I think that every mission has a key player. On our mission, the key player was our youngest member, 2nd Lieutenant Randall T. Ferris. His uncanny tactical savvy of a combat situation, his innovative idea of using our locator beacon to send Morse code, his use of seized signal grenades to fool our adversary, and his ballsy plan to get back on the base undetected were the main reasons that our mission was accomplished so quickly and successfully."

Randy's teammates held their fists in the air and shouted in unison, "Hoo-ah—*Doctor Vet!*" Then they pounded him on his back and shoulders to show their wholehearted support for Captain Jensen's statements. The rest of the audience applauded their approval because they too had been impressed by Blue Team's performance.

Army General Howard rose from his seat. Looking around to insure that he had the attention of everyone, he expounded, "I came here to this meeting feeling insulted and violated. Colonel Brenson and I both felt that, somehow, the air force had cheated in accomplishing their mission. We were prepared to take names and chew on some asses. Now I realize that even the army can learn some new tactics from the

'Men in Blue.'" He turned to Air Force General Colwell and Lieutenant Colonel Hadley, "Your men are to be commended for their outstanding performance in accomplishing their mission. I don't want to take anything away from their team's effort, but I do want to remind you that they were trained to be Rangers by army Green Beret instructors." He smiled and the audience chuckled. The General's statement had made it a win-win situation for both the air force and the army.

General Colwell stood, nodding to his army counterpart, "Thank you, General Howard. Now that we understand each other, we will look forward to working with you on other combined missions in the future." The army and air force officers applauded the pact, and then rushed forward to personally congratulate the members of the air force Blue Team.

Lieutenant Colonel Hadley stood at the podium until the clamor had settled down. Finally, He spoke, "Gentlemen, I must remind you that these men will be used on covert operations in the future, so you must not divulge their real names. I know that you will tell their story to others, but use only the reference 'Blue Team'. Do not use their real names as that knowledge may allow our country's enemies to put their lives in jeopardy. Thank you for your attendance; this meeting is adjourned."

The visiting brass left the room and Colonel Hadley approached his team. "Captain Jensen, your team has performed above all expectations. You are still scheduled to be here for another five days. However, I can't see you and your team having to cool their heels here on base. File your mission report, and then you and your team take the next three days off. Do a little sightseeing and explore Panama; it's a beautiful country. Right now, though, I want you to take them to the Officers Club. Buy them a couple of rounds of well-deserved drinks— put it on my tab."

Blue Team entered the Officers Club and lined up at the bar. They were in high spirits and ordered hard drinks; Randy ordered a Coke. Jensen asked, "Hey, Ferris, is that your preference?"

"No, sir. It's just that I'm underage."

Jensen snorted, "No officer in the United States Air Force that has been through what we have been through is underage. Hey, bartender, bring this lieutenant a fresh coconut filled with a double piña colada."

After being served, they all held up their drinks and Jensen toasted, "To the Blue Team."

The team repeated, "To the Blue Team." They laughed together and were finally able to relax after over two months of virtual hell. The bonds of friendship that were made during their time of trial and tribulation would serve them well in the years to come.

Nirvana

Randy and his team spent the next three days relaxing and touring Panama. Captain Jensen had grown up on the Connecticut shores and had become an adept sailor, so the team opted to rent a large sailboat with auxiliary motor power. They spent the first day sailing on the Pacific Ocean side of the Isthmus of Panama until all the crew was versed in sailing. Then they queued up to sail through the locks to the Atlantic Ocean.

The first locks on the Panama Canal were the Miraflores Locks, which raised them to the level of Lake Miraflores. The Pedro Miguel Locks raised them to the level of Gatún Lake, which was eighty-five feet above the Atlantic sea level. Lastly, the Gatún Locks lowered them to the Caribbean Sea.

They spent the night partying on a yacht with a group of college students from the University of San Diego. There were more girls than guys aboard the yacht, so the airmen were a welcome addition to the party. Randy enjoyed the party, but when it was bedtime, he chose to sleep alone on the sailboat.

The next morning, they waved goodbye to their new friends and sailed the Caribbean. That evening, they checked-in their sailboat and toured the nightspots of Colón. The following morning, they took the train back to Panama City and spent the day sightseeing. Arriving back at their base at midnight, they fell into their beds feeling tired, but rejuvenated in body, mind, and soul.

The next morning Captain Jensen met with Lieutenant Colonel Hadley. Hadley asked, "How was your R & R?"

"Just what the doctor ordered," answered Jensen. "I can't remember having a better three days to kick back and just unwind."

He related their adventures to Colonel Hadley and closed by saying, "Lieutenant Ferris enjoyed himself, but he was true-blue to Sherrill. There were over fifty beautiful girls on that yacht that could have tempted even the devil, himself."

Hadley came to the point, saying, "Randy's the main reason that I wanted to meet with just you. Your team's next training assignment will be Language School at Fort Ord in California, but your team is going to be involved in one more covert operation before then. There are a group of individuals, myself included, that want to see Sherrill and

438

Randy married before their baby is born. The covert phase of this mission is that we want it to be a surprise to both Sherrill and Randy."

Captain Jensen got a mischievous glint in his eye, "This sounds too good to be true; tell me more."

"Who in your group would like to be Randy's best man?"

"Heck—all of us! However, in this case, I'm going to have to pull rank. I will claim the honor of being Randy's best man."

Hadley smiled; he was encouraged by Jensen's juvenile enthusiasm. He continued, "Okay, that's settled. You and your team will transfer off this base and fly via Guantánamo Naval Base into March AFB in California. There you will stay the night in the officers' transient quarters. Saturday, you will be dressed in your Class "A" uniforms, and your team will be in General Collier's VIP stand to revue a late morning parade. You will have lunch in the Officers Club with the general, and then smuggle Randy's suitcases into a limo.

"The limo will take you to the church where the wedding will be held. There you will enter the south side entrance and remain in room #3 until an usher comes for you. You will lead your team to the altar, replacing the stand-ins. When you switch places with Randy, he won't know that the bride is Sherrill because of her veil. From there on, you play it by ear."

Jensen laughed and iterated, "I wouldn't miss this for a thousand dollars."

"Neither would I," remarked Hadley. "I'll be in attendance with my wife and see you at the reception afterward."

Hadley passed Jensen a small case containing Sherrill's wedding ring, "Give this ring to Randy at the appropriate time. He passed a manila envelope to Jensen, "This contains a typed copy of what I just reviewed with you, plus contingency phone numbers in case something happens to your time schedule or you have additional questions."

"Is it all right to tell the rest of the team?"

"Of course—anticipation is seventy-five percent of the enjoyment when you have a surprise."

Jensen winked, "Except for Randy. Participation will be one hundred percent of the enjoyment." The two men chuckled at thought of nuptial consummation.

Jensen rose and saluted, "This is one assignment that I look forward to, sir."

Two days later, Blue Team boarded a military C-54 transport plane bound for Guantánamo Naval Base on the southeast corner of Cuba, where a detachment of naval personnel would disembark. After refueling, the plane would continue to Eglin Air Force Base in Florida and then on to March AFB in California.

Randy leaned back and relaxed as the drone of the engines lulled him into fitful naps. Three hours into the flight, the pilot announced over the intercom, "This is the Captain speaking. We are flying into a large tropical storm; please fasten your seatbelts and prepare for heavy chop."

Captain Jensen offered a barf bag to Randy. He held up his hand, deferring obstinately, "Give it to Medford; I won't need one."

Five minutes later the plane was pitching and yawing like a bucking Brahma bull at a rodeo. After twenty minutes of continual violent updrafts and downdrafts, the stench of fear and this morning's breakfast permeated the cabin of the plane. Randy rued his decision to pass up a bag. He forced back down the rising bile and focused on the release knob of the tray table in front of him.

The plane hit a wind shear and the nose was flung vertical for half a minute, and then flung nose down for almost three minutes. The frame of the plane shuddered and the whine of the engines rapidly increased in pitch as the plane plunged ever closer toward the ocean.

Loose items rose up and tumbled toward the back of the aircraft, ricocheting off the passengers. The plane slammed into a layer of calm air and the nose was flung vertical from the change in momentum. Randy tightened his stomach muscles, but the G-forces caused him to black out momentarily.

When his vision cleared, he saw flames coming from the left outboard engine. Finally, a white mist blew from the cowling and the flames were extinguished. The propeller feathered to a stop and the engine dangled at a precarious angle from the wing.

Randy uttered a quick prayer of thanks for their still being alive, and then looked around to see if anyone was hurt. Several sailors were bleeding from collisions with the flying debris, but all of the Blue Team had miraculously come through the near tragedy without a scratch. A navy corpsman moved down the isle, giving first aid to the passengers needing medical attention.

As the commotion settled down, Randy glanced out the window. Thunderstruck by the sight, he exclaimed aloud, "My God, look at that!"

People around him craned their necks to see out the windows. O'Rorke exclaimed, "Heavens, I've never seen a round rainbow before!"

Medford cut in, "And the shadow of our airplane is smack dab in the middle of it."

Jensen and Taggart chimed, "Lord, what a fantastic sight!"

Derring with mouth agape just stared in silent awe. The reflective ice crystals in the cloud became millions of tiny prisms refracting the colors of red, orange, yellow, green, blue, and violet. The rainbow seemed to come alive with the strobe effect of the color spectrum as the vivid colors danced across the face of the cloud at the speed of the aircraft.

Passengers from the other side of the aircraft crowded over to see what caused all the commotion. As all the weight shifted, the center of gravity of the plane suddenly changed. The plane winged over and went into a dive.

The Captain came on the intercom and exclaimed, "We must have hit a CAT (clear air turbulence); everyone buckle your seatbelts!"

The passengers quickly retook their seats and the plane leveled back out.

Randy stared at the unique sight of the silhouette in the rainbow. His thoughts flashed to Sherrill and he murmured to the *icon in the sky*, "Sherrill, darling, this is God's promise that someday, someway, we will be together."

He watched another three minutes as the rainbow danced across the face of the cloud formation. He felt an inner peace that hadn't existed since the first time that Sherrill and he had made love.

Two long hours later, the plane limped in to land at Guantánamo. The passengers and crew were bussed to the dispensary for a medical examination. Six of the passengers and two of the crew, having received serious injuries, were sent to the naval hospital.

The Blue Team received a clean bill of health, checked into transient quarters, and then headed to the Officers Club for a drink to sooth their jangled nerves. After a couple of Crown Royal shots, Captain Jensen opened his flight bag and removed a manila envelope. Excusing himself, he explained, "I need to find out how long we are going to be here."

An hour later, he returned with an agitated look on his face. He cursed, "Damn, it looks like we might be stuck on this God forsaken place for another three days.

"That won't work!" interjected O'Rorke. "What's happening?"

Jensen explained, "The plane that we flew in on has to go through major repairs and there won't be another scheduled transient flight until Sunday—we'll never get to California on time."

Randy noticed the rest if his team glancing at each other with wrinkled brows. They quickly glanced at him, than averted their eyes.

"We don't have a lot of options," continued Jensen. "I checked with the navy and they have a light cruiser leaving tonight, but it won't make port for another four days. As you know, we can't catch a commercial flight out of Cuba because of the political situation that has existed since the 'Cuban Missile Crisis'"

Randy noticed that the rest of the team glanced at their wristwatches, as if they had a bus to catch. O'Rorke interjected, "But how's that going to affect our—?" He was cut-off from finishing his question by Jensen's raised hand.

"All may not be lost; I was able to get through to Colonel Hadley. He's working on a contingency plan and said that he would get back to me."

Randy, oblivious to the reason for the tension and anguish felt by his teammates, cheerfully interjected, "Where's the fire, Guys? It just means that we are stuck here for a couple more days. What's the big deal about missing a parade at March Air Force Base in California?"

More furtive glances were exchanged among his teammates. No one answered his questions and their mood remained glum throughout their meal. Randy had the feeling of being excluded from something important. Moreover, when he pressed them to explain the intrigue, they conveniently changed the subject.

At breakfast the next morning, Jensen, approached them with a cheery smile. "Gentlemen, I got an update—we're getting out of here today. Colonel Hadley contacted me last night. A civilian plane piloted by air force pilots will fly us to March Air Force Base. We won't arrive in time to attend the parade, but we still will be able to have lunch with General Collier."

The news had an instant euphoric effect on Randy's teammates. Their mood changed from despondency to one of jubilation and

442

anticipation. Each time Randy caught their eye, they broke out in a wide grin and their eyes twinkled with mirth.

The mood swing prompted Randy to wonder out loud, "What's the special attraction of having lunch with an air force general in California. I don't see anything wrong with being stuck on a perfectly good tropical island in the Caribbean?"

Medford winked at the group and asked Randy, "Have you ever had lunch with a general, before?"

"Well, no," confessed Randy.

"Good!" exclaimed Medford. "This will be a new experience for you."

As the navy bus approached the civilian aircraft at the end of the flight line, Randy noticed that it was a twin Beech D18S, the same type aircraft that he had flown in Texas. He looked at the tail number TBZ-194. Like a tape recorder in his mind, he remembered Colonel Sommers asking for clearance in Texas, "San Pedro tower, this is Beech, Tango Baker Zebra one-niner-four, requesting permission to taxi." *Why*, wondered Randy

When he entered the airplane's cabin, seeing Colonel Sommers wasn't surprising, but recognizing General Thurman in the co-pilot seat was a total surprise. Gordon called out, "Welcome aboard, Randy— headed for California."

Randy shook hands with the two officers, "You always seem to be around to bail me out—sirs."

The two officers chuckled and Colonel Sommers stated lightly, "No problem. General Thurman and I were on our way to a VIP wedding in California and heard that you and your team were stranded. It was on our way, so we decided to give you a lift."

Randy took his seat and buckled in. He mused to himself, "On our way to California—! Guantánamo Bay has to be at least two thousand miles in the opposite direction." He leaned back in his seat and dozed off; the thought brushed through his mind, "I wonder who the VIP is—zzzzzzz?

The following day Blue Team was having lunch with General Nathan Collier at March AFB, California. Lieutenant O'Rorke was embellishing their experiences in Panama and had just mentioned that everyone had gotten lucky with the co-eds, except for Lieutenant Ferris. The general knowingly smiled his approval as he glanced at the

443

young lieutenant who would this day be married to the lovely Hollywood star Sherrill.

Randy marveled that his teammates were in exceedingly high spirits after the dooms day looks on their faces at Guantánamo. He found it odd that they laughed and joked around like a bunch of college students on spring break, instead of seasoned officers in the air force.

Much of their bantering was in the form of inferences and innuendoes, mostly directed at Randy. Even though he played along with their games of verbal parry and thrust, his zinger retorts only provoked good-natured laughter and slaps on his back or nonaggressive punches to his shoulders.

The group had just finished their luncheon, when an aide walked up, "General Collier, there is a phone call for you, sir."

The general left the table and returned moments later with a perplexed look on his face. He asked, "Do you young airmen have anything special planned for this afternoon?"

Captain Jensen volunteered, "No, sir, our afternoon is entirely open to the whims of opportunity."

Acknowledging with a smile, the general explained seriously, "My niece is getting married this afternoon to an Air Force Officer from Edwards AFB. The best man and the groom's attendants were traveling in a van that blew its engine. They won't be able to arrive until two hours after the wedding is scheduled to start. I wonder if you men would mind filling in for them."

"We'd be happy to accommodate, General," Jensen volunteered for all of them.

"Very good," replied the general. "I knew that I could count on you. I have a limo waiting out front. It's too small for all of us, so you men take it. My wife and I will use my car to drive over to the wedding."

Randy thought that it was strange that Greg had committed the team without discussion, but he discarded further suspicion because a general had made the request—a general's request is always interpreted as an implied order.

The team arrived at the church at ten minutes before two. They were met by an usher and shown to an anteroom. The young man instructed, "Please wait here until someone comes for you."

Sherrill had arrived at the church at one-fifteen with her parents, brother, and sister. Brad met her and took her to an anteroom. He left

444

after explaining that someone from make-up and costume would be in shortly.

Sherrill's entire family had shown up unexpectedly a couple of days before. Aunt Vicki had suggested to Brad in front of Sherrill, "Wouldn't it be quaint to have Sherrill's father give her away to Don Luke in the promo. Sherrill's sister could even be one of the bridesmaids and her brother could be an usher."

Brad had casually replied, "I'll check with Emile. If he thinks that it is a good idea then I have no objection."

Aunt Vicki had disarmingly intoned, "It will even be good practice for Charles, for when Sherrill and Randy get married."

Sherrill had been kept very busy with personal appearances, filming segments of another episode, and filming endorsement commercials. She never gave the conversation further thought. Brad was in charge of promos and to Sherrill, the wedding was just another promo.

However, she did think it odd that Brad had chosen contemporary dress, instead of nineteenth century era clothing worn in the TV episodes. Moreover, she dismissed even this doubt from her mind because she trusted Brad implicitly.

The makeup artist, Alice, entered the room, and asked lightly, "Well are you ready to get all gussied up?"

Sherrill laughed, "I guess so. After all—as the bride, I do need to look prettier than the groom."

Alice chuckled knowingly, since Gary Binger's narcissistic feelings for himself were well known on the set. She completed her usual routine, and then quickly combed Sherrill's hair, divided it, pulled it up, and layered it in swirls on top. She locked the swirls together with a couple of well-placed bobby pins, and then pulled out a tendril of hair on each side of her face. The result accented Sherrill's long neck and framed her face.

Next, Alice opened a jewelry case and picked up a matching pair of diamond-studded earrings, each with a pendent teardrop pearl. She asked, "Do you want to put these in, or do you want me to?"

Reaching out, Sherrill replied, "I will."

While Sherrill was looking in the mirror at herself wearing the earrings, Alice exhorted, "Hold still and I will fasten your pearl necklace."

Connie from costumes entered, "Are we ready for the gown?"

Alice advised, "Just a moment. We don't want to mess up what I just did."

She took a long strip of gauze, eight inches wide and wound it lightly around Sherrill's face and head. Then she and Connie helped Sherrill into her wedding gown. When Alice unwound the gauze, Sherrill exclaimed, "Whew! Now I know how a fish feels when it is caught up in a net."

Alice patted down a couple of strands of hair that had been pulled out of place, "There, now you are more beautiful than any of those brides in magazines."

Sherrill modestly replied, "Thank you for thinking so."

Alice and Connie left the room. Sherrill turned to the full-length mirror and observed her ensemble:

Embroidered lace medallions with sequins and pearls added sparkle to the Empire waist-style bodice, silk tulle sleeves, train, and hem. The bodice, with a modified princess-line concealing her pregnancy, was shaped with a scalloped neckline. Princess seaming allowed a free flowing flare from the bodice to the base of the silk satin gown.

Giving the gown structure and form were a nylon lining and a nylon net underskirt. The back featured a row of decorative buttons and the semi-cathedral train extended from the waist.

The floral jeweled tiara had breathtaking satin rosettes set among clusters of seed pearls interleaved with quarter-carat diamonds. An enameled metal comb held in place the tiara and the tiered fingertip-length nylon veil.

Sherrill had just slipped on a pair of satin slippers, when her mother and Aunt Vicki popped in to take a peek at the bride. Aunt Vicki chirped, "Sherrill, you make the most beautiful bride that I have ever seen."

Her mother's eyes filled with tears. "Oh, darling, you are so beautiful in your wedding gown."

Vicki prompted, "Come on, Mavis. Let's go take our seats before your eye-liner starts running."

They left and Sherrill looked again at herself in the mirror, thinking, *it is a beautiful gown. I don't even look pregnant, much less 7 months along. I hope that I can wear one just like it when Randy and I get married.*

At two-fifteen, Sherrill's father knocked on the door. She opened the door and Charles stared at her with pride, "My little girl—you look so beautiful."

Sherrill kissed him on the cheek, "Thank you, Daddy. To listen to you and Mother, you would think that this was a *for real* wedding." She adjusted her veil and was ushered out of the room.

Waiting at the top of the aisle, Sherrill was surprised that the entire seating of the church was filled. She estimated that there were over six hundred extras in the promo. She thought, *Brad must have crashed his budget on this one.*

Sherrill knew that Laura Blevins was the maid of honor and that her sister, Rosemary, was one of the bridesmaids. The other three bridesmaids looked strangely familiar, but she discounted this because she was viewing them through her veil.

She glanced at the groom. Gary Binger, as Don Luke, was standing at the altar with his characteristic narcissistic smile. She shuttered, thinking of having to kiss him again at the end of the sham ceremony. Larry Meyers and Fred Buckley, the characters of Don Matthew and Don Mark, were standing next to Gary, but she didn't recognize the three extras.

The organist started playing the bridal march. The attendees rose to face the bride. Sherrill stared straight ahead and glided forward in rhythm with the music, just as she had rehearsed.

Randy heard the music begin and stood up to go to the door. The rest of his team remained nonchalantly in their seats. Finally, he queried anxiously, "Aren't we supposed to be at the altar now?"

Jensen chided, "Hey, relax ol' boy; they said that they would come for us at the proper time. Settle down ol' man! You're acting like this is your own wedding." The rest of the team laughed knowingly, but Randy failed to see the humor in Greg's remarks.

Finally, a knock came at the door and it opened. Jensen rose, "Well, I reckon they're ready for us now." He went to the door. The rest of the team held back, allowing Randy to follow Greg, and then they followed in-line.

The usher opened the door that led to the altar and motioned them to take their places at the altar. The men, who had been standing at the altar, turned and exited past the airmen.

Sherrill was three-fourths of the way down the aisle when she saw the groom and his attendants leave the altar area. Six men in military uniforms took their places. The first man switched places with the second man.

She stopped cold in recognition, and then screamed, "Randy!"

Due to Greg's switching places distracting him, Randy had not looked at the bride,. At the same moment that he glanced toward the bride, he heard his name shouted. Vertigo almost overcame him as he recognized Sherrill's voice. He shouted back, "Sherrill!"

They stared at each other for a second; Sherrill not believing her eyes and Randy not believing his ears, they broke running toward each other. Their movements played out in slow motion. Sherrill tripped on her gown and was falling. Randy reached out and caught her up in his arms. He swung her around, causing the bridal train to wrap around his legs.

Sherrill flung up her veil and they kissed hungrily. She held his face between her two hands, kissing him again and again.

Tears of joy were in their eyes, blurring their vision. Sherrill touched his cheeks, nose, mouth, chin, ears, with her fingertips; making sure that he was real, and not a dream.

The organist had stopped playing and the attendees were standing and enthusiastically applauding, caught up in the romantic display of unbridled love. The audience's continuous applause finally brought the two lovers back from their dreamy oblivion to the glaring reality that they were surrounded by hundreds of people.

They blushed deep crimson as Randy twisted and turned to unwrap the bridal train from around his legs. He placed Sherrill lightly on her feet then hugged her tightly to him.

Randy squared his shoulders, offering his arm to Sherrill, and rapturously escorted her to the altar. Surrendering to the situation, Charles threw up his hands, palms up, and shrugged his shoulders. The audience chuckled at his reaction of abandonment. He sheepishly followed his daughter and Randy to the altar.

Randy stood for a moment next to Sherrill, unable to take his eyes off her. Then he realized that he was on the bridesmaids' side of her. Blushing, he exchanged places with her. The attendees reacted to his faux pas with gleeful giggles.

Pastor Stevens paused until the sanctuary was totally quiet. He quipped, "The two of you haven't seen each other for a long time—have you?" The audience responded with empathetic laughter.

He dryly added, "Normally, the bride gets kissed at the end of the ceremony. I think you two may have already used up your allotment." In response, gleeful laughter echoed through the chapel.

The minister paused, smiling, and then became serious, "Who gives this woman to this man?"

The boom microphone picked up Charles' retort and carried it throughout the PA system. He stated with feigned wonderment, "I feel like they've already eloped." The remark generated spontaneous unrestrained laughter.

Several moments passed before Charles could say seriously, "Her mother and I." He took his seat next to his wife and the ceremony continued in solemn tones.

For Sherrill and Randy, their pulses throbbed in their heads, their hearts pounded in their chests, and their breathing came in short gasps. Every few seconds they squeezed each other's hand reassuring themselves that the other was really beside them.

They listened to the minister's words spoken in a séance staccato intonement; they responded in kind. They were dreaming in a dream world and didn't want to be awakened, lest the dream disappear.

When it came time to exchange rings, Randy unconsciously patted the pockets of his uniform, feeling for a ring. Then he realized that Greg was trying to hand him the ring for Sherrill. The audience reacted with polite giggles, but the volume of their sheer numbers sounded like a cacophony of laughter to Randy. His ears turned red and his hands shook, as he placed the ring on Sherrill's left-hand ring finger and repeated the minister's words.

Laura handed Randy's ring to Sherrill. Her hands shook as she placed the ring on his left-hand ring finger and timorously repeated the minister's words.

The minister offered a prayer of bonding and then led Randy through his vows, "Randy, do you take Sherrill to be your lawful wedded wife...?

Randy responded, "I do."

The minister turned to Sherrill and asked, "Sherrill, do you take Randy to be your lawful wedded husband...?

Sherrill responded, "I do."

The minister stated, "By the power vested in me by the State of California, I now pronounce you husband and wife. Let no man put asunder that which God has blessed."

The minister paused for a long moment for effect, and then quipped; "Dare I suggest that you kiss the bride?"

A ripple of laughter went through an audience of tear-filled eyes. Sherrill raised her veil. She and Randy stood gazing into each other's eyes. Randy leaned forward and their lips touched lightly, lingering as the organist played notes of tinkling crystal, which invoked visions of magical stardust falling through the air.

The organist switched to grand finale music as Randy and Sherrill turned and proceeded up the aisle as husband and wife.

They formed a reception line and Randy realized for the first time that his three sisters had been Sherrill's bridesmaids. His parents and grandparents were there, along with a large contingency of high school friends and teachers. The school board had declared a holiday for those that wanted to attend the celebrity wedding.

Randy was further surprised to see General Collier, General Thurman, and Lieutenant Colonel Hadley with their wives. Now he understood the reason for the intrigue and odd behavior of his team during the last three days.

A dozen other generals introduced themselves. They had heard of some of the exploits of the young second lieutenant and all wanted to meet the celebrity, Sherrill.

Sergeant Stark and Maria moved up in the reception line. Randy's former DI grinned wickedly and sarcastically quipped, "Well, is this really the same calm cool 2nd lieutenant that inspected my barracks and caused me to prematurely age ten years?"

Randy grinned warmly at seeing his friends. Appealing for their understanding, he quipped, "Basic training didn't prepare me for anything like this, DI, sir."

They both laughed and Randy introduced them to Sherrill, quipping satirically, "This is Staff Sergeant Dwayne Stark, who taught me everything—that I *don't* know. And this is his lovely wife, Maria; she is your number one fan in Texas."

Sherrill shook their hands, "I'm pleased to finally meet you. Randy wrote me about you."

Maria stated, "I'm also Randy's number one fan—we just love him."

Stark retorted, "What do you mean, love? I just like the guy—but, quite a lot."

The line of well-wishers continued and Casio strolled up, introducing Gloria as his fiancée. Randy remarked, "Congratulations, Casio. You two make a great looking couple. I'll try to talk with you more at the reception."

Abbott was next in line; he grinned, "I wouldn't have missed your wedding for all the tea in China. Sorry, I won't be at the reception; I have to fly back to Illinois to continue tech school on Monday."

Randy turned to Sherrill with praise, "This is Bart Abbott, one of the most solid guys that I have ever met. He and Casio were my area chiefs in basic. Abbott saved my butt more than once."

Abbott grinned and returned the compliment, "Sherrill, you married a true leader. I would follow Randy to the ends of the world."

The line continued and Sherrill glanced down it and saw a beautiful girl with tears in her eyes. She met a few more well-wishers, and then the girl approached Randy and kissed him lightly on the lips, saying, "Oh, Randy, your and Sherrill's wedding was so beautiful." Sherrill felt the electricity between the girl and Randy.

Randy turned to Sherrill, "This is Suzette Sommers and her parents, Colonel Gordon Sommers and his wife, Anne. They befriended me in Texas and literally 'Got me to the church on-time' by flying me here in their private airplane!"

Sherrill extended her hand and an ionic electric spark snapped between Suzette and her fingertips. Sherrill stated, "I'm pleased to meet you. Friends of Randy are friends of mine."

Suzette stated sincerely, "Sherrill, you are even more beautiful than on television. Randy is the luckiest man in the world to have you as his wife."

Her words were disarming, but Sherrill couldn't shake the feeling that something more existed between this girl and Randy. She replied, "Thank you, Suzette. I'll have to ask Randy sometime about how you *befriended* him."

Anne Sommers interjected, "No, it was the other way around. Randy befriended us by saving a valuable Thoroughbred foal. He has a vested interest of twenty-five percent in the horse."

Gordon added, "Sherrill, it's a beautiful horse and is really doing well and shows great promise for racing. You and Randy will have to visit us sometime to see it."

Sherrill replied, "It has been a pleasure meeting you. I look forward to the trip."

She turned to see Randy's reaction, but he gazed back with only love in his eyes for her. She thought, "I must be imagining things. Why am I so sensitive?" Then she realized that the day had progressed far beyond her wildest dreams.

The long line dwindled down and Brad stepped up and introduced himself to Randy, saying with a warm smile and a firm handshake, "Hi, Randy; I'm Brad Thurman. I guess that you can partially blame this surprise wedding on me, but Sherrill's Aunt Vicki did most of the work."

Randy shook his hand, "Well, you must be the *master* of surprises. I would never have dreamed in a thousand years that I would be getting married to Sherrill, today."

"Nor I," chimed Sherrill. "This was supposed to be just a promo production, so that certainly makes you, Brad Thurman, the 'Master Deceiver.'"

Flashing a broad grin, Brad quipped, "Oh, that's what all of my old girlfriends tell me."

Randy detected a furtive glance between Sherrill and Brad after the remark. He thought, "Does Brad consider Sherrill an old girlfriend?" He glanced at Sherrill and saw only love in her eyes for him. He resolved that he was just shaken at having seen Suzy again and reading his own thoughts into the situation.

Brad extracted himself by saying, "Well, I've got to get moving. We want this promo to get on the ten o'clock news. I've got a lot of work to do, but I'll see you at the reception later."

Pastor Stevens brought up the 'Marriage Certificate' for Randy and Sherrill to sign. He remarked, "I've performed a lot of marriage ceremonies, but never one quite as unique as this one. You two are obviously very much in love and I want to wish you the very best in your journey through life."

They signed the certificate and thanked the minister. Randy took out his wallet to pay the minister for his services. Pastor Stevens declined, saying, "It has already been taken care of...you two just enjoy your honeymoon."

Randy's Blue Team brought up the end of the line. They were introduced to Sherrill and Jensen jokingly bantered, "Randy, if any one of us had met Sherrill first, you wouldn't have stood a chance."

O'Rorke ribbed Randy about his surprised reaction, "Is this an indication of how you're going to react under real combat conditions?"

Randy responded, "Yeah, this is my team, my buddies, with whom I have been to hell and back. They knew all along about this surprise wedding. How can you trust guys that can keep a secret like that?"

Sherrill defended them, "Only men that respected and cared deeply for you could be capable of such a secret."

Greg Jensen quipped, "See, Randy, we finally meet a woman that appreciates our tender nature and you had to go and marry her."

They all laughed and started to leave. Jensen, remembering that he was holding Randy's air force hat, handed it to him, saying, "Here, this will keep the rice out of your hair."

After they left, Randy gently pulled Sherrill against him. Kissing her, he whispered, "Darling, I love you. You've made me the happiest man in the world."

Randy's grandfather, having waited by the door, called out, "Dammit, Boy, come on, you two. You'll have plenty damn time for that mushy stuff on your honeymoon."

Randy looked up and realized that he hadn't even had a chance to say hello to his family, especially his loveable crotchety old grandfather who cussed as though it was a virtue. He called after them as they were filing out the door, "Sorry—folks, I guess I'll have to say hello at the reception."

Sherrill and Randy followed them out the door and were instantly pelted with rice. They ran down the pathway to the waiting limo. Randy was inside the limo before he looked around and saw the hundreds of reporters and dozens of camera trucks recording the event for the nightly news.

He turned to Sherrill and said in awe, "I really did marry a movie star!"

Sherrill kissed him, "No, you married a woman that loves you with all her heart—I just accidentally happen to be a star. I would have given up all this just to be Mrs. Randall Ty-Ron Ferris—to be with you."

Randy remembered that she had said this before in public. She kissed him again, a long and tender confirmation kiss, as the limo pulled away.

Randy asked, "Do you know where the reception is being held?"

Sherrill shook her head, "I have no idea. This was just as much a surprise for me as you."

Randy dismissed it, "Well, I'm sure that the driver knows."

Sherrill stretched her legs out across the seat and lay in his arms. He placed his hand across her stomach and felt the roundness of her pregnant tummy. He thought, "She is my little *Matryoshka* (Russian doll). She is my doll with another doll inside of her. He wrapped his arms around Sherrill and felt the intoxicating thrill of just being able to hold her close to him.

All too soon, they arrived at the Malibu Palisades Country Club. Aunt Vicki met them, "Now, don't you two worry about a thing. Everything has been planned, just enjoy yourselves."

She led them through throngs of reporters and well-wishers; they numbered in the hundreds. In the gardens overlooking the Pacific Ocean were thousands of other people. Radiant heaters warmed the gentle breeze blowing off the ocean.

Sherrill was even surprised by the enormity of the event. She asked Aunt Vicki, "With all these people here, how could you keep this a secret from me?"

Vicki quipped, "It's Hollywood; they can't keep a secret, except from the person that the secret's about. I don't know how to explain it...it's just some Freudian thing."

Randy was in awe. He had recognized dozens of celebrities on his way into the club, and here in the garden he recognized hundreds more. "I didn't think that movie stars and television stars moved in the same social circles."

Aunt Vicki replied, "Oh, didn't Sherrill tell you that she is going to be in a full length movie after the baby is born?"

"No. We haven't had a chance to talk about anything."

Aunt Vicki mused, "Oh, I guess not. Well, anyway, I want you two to lead off the dancing. There are so many people here to organize. I want them mostly to entertain themselves."

Randy escorted Sherrill onto the dance floor and the dance orchestra started playing. He took her in his arms and waltzed her around the floor. She floated in his arms as they gracefully flowed across the dance floor.

Sherrill felt Randy's body with her free left hand, "Your body is as hard as a rock. I can feel the outline of each muscle through your uniform."

Randy laughed, "Uncle Sam is good at making hard bodies."

Sherrill pressed closer to him, she whispered, "Darling, this is the happiest day of my life. There were times that I thought it would never happen."

"I know," replied Randy. "There were some pretty bad days when I thought that it would never happen either. Having you here in my arms as my wife is the answer to all my prayers and dreams."

They kissed lightly and Randy continued swirling her around the dance floor, displaying her grace and poise for all to see.

Charles met them coming off the dance floor, "I believe it is customary for the bride's father to have the next dance. Randy—may I?"

Randy felt the hackles rise on the back of his neck. He saw the appeal in Sherrill's eyes, "Certainly, Charles." Charles danced away with Sherrill.

Randy's father met him with a glass of champagne, "Son, I think that it is time that you and Charles bury the hatchet. I've talked with him and he is truly repentant. He has apologized for his actions to everyone in the world—except you."

Randy nodded, "Dad, I've already rationalized that Sherrill and I wouldn't be where we are in our careers, except for Charles. Nevertheless, I've cursed him for keeping Sherrill from me.

"However, now that we're finally married, I might be able to see the world in a different light."

Charles said to his daughter as they were dancing, "Sherrill, I want to apologize to Randy, but I don't know how or where to start."

Sherrill squeezed her father, "Daddy, Randy is a wonderful man. He is intelligent and sensitive. Though you've hurt him badly, I think that he is just waiting for your apology."

The dance ended and they walked back to Randy and his father. Frank said, "Sherrill, I think that this dance is mine." He escorted her onto the dance floor.

Charles and Randy stood evaluating each other's action or reaction. Both were proud men that had fought the fight for Sherrill. Charles was sweating, partly from the exertion of dancing, but mostly at confronting Randy. The murmur of the crowd became quiet in anticipation...the music died off as everyone focused on the adversarial potential of the two men.

Electricity filled the hushed silence. Breaths became breathless. Hands of the onlookers unconsciously touched their chest in anticipation—. Finally, Charles' eyes softened and he extended his right hand, palm up, "Randy—Son, I beg your forgiveness for what I've done to you and Sherrill." The audience gave a collective sigh as they expelled the air from their lungs, and then breathed a collective gasp as they filled their lungs with new air.

The simpleness and sincerity of Charles' proclamation moved Randy. He smiled and took the extended hand in friendship, "Dad, there is nothing left to forgive. Sherrill and I are married—that is all we wanted to do in the first place. Sherrill has forgiven you—and so shall I."

They hugged and pounded each other on the back. The tense moment that all of the guests had anticipated had come and gone.

455

Dozens of flashbulbs went off and the guests applauded the pact of friendship. The orchestra struck up lively music, acknowledging the armistice between father-in-law and son-in-law.

Randy's teammates vied for the honor of dancing next with Sherrill. Greg Jensen won out since he had been best man. The others lined up for their turn.

Since Sherrill was occupied, Randy had a chance to visit with his family and old friends from back home. As he danced with his mother, he caught up on the local news and learned that his sister Leta, and his best friend David, were engaged.

Later, Coach Martin mentioned, "Our basketball team has had a dismal year without you as their captain."

Randy examined his ambivalent feelings and simply replied, "I'm sorry that I wasn't there to help them out."

His old coach replied, "Don't worry about it. I saw your air force game on television. I was so proud of you and proud for myself at having been a part of your basketball training."

"I owe you for more than a game, Coach Martin. Your formula for teamwork has influenced every accomplishment that I've attained in the air force."

The coach beamed with a wide smile, "It's seeing the development of men like you, Randy, that makes my life's work worthwhile."

Lieutenant Medford, the last of Randy's team to dance with Sherrill, returned her to Randy and said, "Ferris, you're lucky that Sherrill hadn't met one of us first. Otherwise, you would have been a best man, instead of the groom." He smiled and slapped Randy on the back, adding, "You lucky devil!"

Randy handed Sherrill a cup of punch, "Did those guys wear you out dancing?"

"Almost. I am ready for a break now."

They started to sit down and Brad appeared. "Randy, I need to borrow Sherrill for a short press conference. The media is clamoring for a photo-shoot and a statement from her."

Randy asked tentatively, "Does that include me?"

Brad replied sympathetically, "No, I'm afraid not. You see, Colonel Hadley asked me to shield you from the press as much as possible. I don't know why, but he must have his reasons."

Randy nodded disappointedly, "I understand."

Brad led Sherrill off to the commons' area of the country club. Randy stood wistfully gazing after them. Suzette walked up beside him and asked neutrally, "Hey, Good Lookin', someone steal your girl?"

Randy looked at her, "Hi, Suzette! You are the *last* person in the world I expected to be here."

Suzy's expression showed hurt as she replied, "If you knew me better then you would have said that I was the *first* person in the world that you expected to be here."

"How do you mean?"

Suzy replied in a whisper that only Randy could hear, "I still love you, but I don't possess you. I love you so much that your happiness is more important to me.... Who do you think pleaded with my father to fly in and rescue you as a castaway on a far off island?

She paused; then added charitably, "Although, Daddy probably would have done it anyway—because of his high regard for you."

Randy glanced around and noticed that some of the people nearby had edged closer, drawn to the whispered conversation.

He asked in a stage whisper, "Would you care to dance, Miss Sommers?"

Suzette curtsied melodramatically, "Why, thank you, Lieutenant Ferris. I'd love to."

Randy escorted her onto the dance floor, which was more public, but they could move with their conversation. "How have you been, Suzy?"

She sighed, "My heart is still broken, but I now have some direction to my life. I'm taking journalism in college and doing quite well. The sun still rises—the sun still sets, except it's not as bright since you're not there. And you—Randy. How have you been?"

"I'm okay, now. There were moments in my training that I felt like giving up and saying, 'To hell with being an officer,' but I toughed it out and now I'm here."

"Your tan indicates that you must have toughed it out in the tropics," observed Suzy.

"Partially, but the tan is mostly from three days of R & R. My team rented a sailboat and we sailed the Caribbean."

"Sounds like fun. Did you meet any girls?"

"Yes, a whole boatload," answered Randy, slightly bemused at Suzy's straightforwardness.

"Well, I can see that none won your heart," appraised Suzy.

"No, but they sure made the rest of my teammates' hearts palpitate."

Suzy laughed aloud and drew closer to Randy.

At that moment, Brad was walking back from the news conference with Sherrill. He heard the girl laugh and saw her draw closer to Randy. Sherrill tensed and stopped. Brad offered, "We haven't danced together yet. Would you care to dance?"

"Thank you, Brad. I'd love to dance with you."

As they danced, Sherrill kept glancing in the direction of Randy and Suzy. Brad observed, "That is a very beautiful woman dancing with Randy."

Sherrill perked up, "Would you like to meet her?"

"Yes, very much." They started dancing slowly in the direction of Randy and Suzette.

Both Randy and Suzy had seen Sherrill and Brad come onto the dance floor. Suzy felt rigidity in Randy's normally fluid movement. She remarked, "That is a very handsome man dancing with Sherrill. Who is he?"

"His name is Brad Thurman. He must have helped organize this surprise because he knows Colonel Hadley."

Randy added, enticingly, "He could be *the* Mr. Right."

Suzy's interest stirred and she replied coyly, "Yes, I would like to meet him."

Randy danced Suzy slowly in the direction of Sherrill and Brad. When the couples met and stopped dancing, Sherrill interjected, "Miss Sommers—Brad Thurman. Brad—Suzette." She placed herself in Randy's arms and danced off with him.

Sherrill pressed against Randy and he whispered, "Eliminating the competition, my Sweet?"

Sherrill looked up, surprised, "How come you always know what I am thinking?"

Randy chuckled, "Because I love you; we are soul mates—remember? You said so yourself."

Sherrill pressed her temple against his cheek and whispered, "Yes, Darling, I remember. I also remember you saying it too."

They danced together as one. Randy remembered his analogy of *their* free-floating bubbles. He held Sherrill closer to him. Their separate bubbles had at last merged into one. As he looked into her eyes, he soothingly crooned a song of verse in rhythm with the flow of the dance music.

458

Fame and fortune—kith and kin
Touching our lives as fickle friends.
For those of us inclined to pray
Counting our blessings day by day.
Seeking love from the day we're born
Sans l'amour leaves us lonely and forlorn.
Lingering moments of ecstasy
Bonding our spirits throughout eternity.
Life is unique—an endless mystery
A boundless universe in a fathomless sea.
Discovering our love unique and true
Creating that celestial bridge from me—to you....
—"My Sherrill"—*ma chérie.*

Randy hummed the tune softly as their bodies flowed together in a synchronized expression of their being in harmony with each other. As the dance ended, he lightly kissed her ear and whispered, " *Je t'aime; je t'adore—ma chérie*—I love you; I adore you—my darling."

THE BEGINNING—TR

Outtakes: Prologue

A blinding flash of light, diffused slightly by veiled curtains, created a momentary day glow in the room shocked by an instantaneous double-clap of thunder jouncing the walls. A crash-shatter-tinkle reverberating from the master bedroom coincided with the computer screen momentarily blinking off—then it began rebooting.

"Sheez—that was close," Randy reacted with sibilating oath. *I should have shut down the computer before the storm hit.*

Drumming his fingers on the keyboard, he impatiently awaited the desktop display to reappear on the screen. He quickly clicked the Start button then selected Shut Down. Two seconds later the screen displayed: *It's now safe to turn off your computer.* He toggled the power switch—off, and then rose from his chair to investigate the source of the calamitous sound that had come from the bedroom.

Feeling a tingling vacillation, he discovered a large picture resting on-edge against the wall and floor. Shards of shattered glass menacingly extended from the splintered frame. The hair prickled on his arms and he had an ominous uneasy feeling, backed by an unexplained twinge of superstition that someone or something close to him had been hit by the lightening.

Leaving the picture where it fell, he stepped outside to shake off the feeling. Gazing from the bedroom patio, he observed a fast moving summer shower receding in the distance. In the east a rainbow arched across the sky. The clean crisp pungent odor of negative ozone from the lightning permeated the air.

Stretching and breathing in deeply, he thought, *Ah, life is good, but too much idleness can be boring—nothing like a quick summer shower to stir the spirits.*

Returning to his computer, he turned it on, dialed up the Internet, and sought distraction by finding some remote corner of the "World Wide Web." Not finding solace from this diversion, he shut down his computer.

Remembering the broken picture frame, he retrieved a canister vacuum cleaner from the closet and cleaned up the broken glass. Leaving the picture on the coffee table, he racked back into his recliner. Palming the TV clicker to channel surf, he pressed the "On" button and heard a *zzzitt-pop-twee*—the television screen remained dark.

Slowly, realization crept through his mind. It was not *someone*, but *something*, close to him that had been damaged by the lightning bolt—his big screen TV. "That's ludicrous," he uttered to himself. "No one can foretell when a TV is going on the fritz."

Staring at the defective TV and disbelieving his own senses, the blank screen reflected the astonishment on his face. His mind, not being stimulated by sight and sound, began generating its own diversion as he focused on his reflection in the screen.

With middle age approaching, his body had put on a few extra pounds and his diffused-silhouetted outline was reflected back from the darkened screen. He had heard the term "couch potato," but never really thought much about it until now. Seeing his reflection, he realized that the human torso, when not regularly exercised, could sometimes resemble a rotund "Idaho Potato."

In retrospect, his thoughts dreamily drifted back...back...back—to when his body had been young and virile—age seventeen centered in his mind. Life had been simple then and every day had brought new wonders and delights.

Chapter 1

*"Oh, **hail**, ye bane with innocent white crystal purity. You turn the storm clouds green with envy and pummel sweet nature's mirth.*

All creatures seek refuge from your fury, for you are the dark side of raindrops that wont to bring life to God's green earth."—TR

Chapter 3

He recognized in her statement the need to develop the proper atmosphere before discussing important events. Sherrill realized, probably more than he that:

"To jump into a serious discussion, without first clearing the air, was a little like making love without foreplay. You may go through the motions, but probably won't come up with the ultimate climax that you desired."

"A town without pity is not necessarily a bad town, it's just the mores of the people that live here. They may appear bigoted and unforgiving, but they grew up in the same atmosphere with the same rules.

"Anyone that strays from this mind-set becomes '*not one of them.*' We can't change that mentality in a day, but I hope that it will evolve to where it's not so intractable in the future."

Chapter 8

A man sets his pace to the beat of his own drum. A father's good intentions and intervention would only serve up as a reminder to his son, how much the young lad is out of step with the rest of the world.— TR

Chapter 10

Casio— *During the smoke break, people gathered around him to hear what he had to say. He had a smoldering hatred in his eyes that denotes pent-up energy looking for a release.*

The curious onlookers used the table as a line of demarcation.

Chapter 15

Sherrill shivered, not from being cold, but from the realization of the "duality of self and the multiplicity of human personalities." At her young age, she had known herself, as—just herself. Now she realized that even *she* had the capacity to be perceived as a different person to many different people.

She marveled at the many permutations, combinations, and interactions of these perceived personalities. Yet to herself—she was still—*just* herself.

In her mind she drew the analogy that the mirrorball represented the radiated aura of a person—i.e. a movie star. The adulating gazes of the people around them were the sources of light; each person receiving back a part of their own reflected light, but at the same time perceiving the aura of light reflected from emanations of other people. This phenomenon generated the general illusion that the person (movie star) was the light source of their own brilliance and the eyes of the public were ever drawn to them.

Chapter 16

Stark caught the directed innuendo, which was lost on Randy since he was formulating a definition in his mind. Staring into space, he hyperbolized, "Self-pride is internal and bloats the ego; whereas, love too comes from within, but has to be given freely in order to survive and thrive in the heart.

Stark cut in, "Hey, you two are getting way too *deep*. Christ, next thing you know, you'll be debating whether the sun circles the earth or vice-versa."

Maria and Randy glanced at each other then laughed because they both realized that Stark had been left out of the conversation and that he was feeling, *too alone and not in control.*

The three men had more of a bounce in their step as they continued their walk to HQ; each feeling a sense of discovery—*of temperate elation at having vicariously touched the hem of fame and fortune.*

Chapter 19

When are life and a game not merely the game of life? Living life to its fullest is the fulfillment of being alive. The ominous possibility of losing sweetens the flavor of victory when it is finally won. The essence of those moments flow through our veins and recharge our soul. The lessons learned from defeat may build character, but the sweet moments of victory rejuvenate our earthly being, which is a part of the universal spirit that weaves through the cosmos fabric of time. — TR

Chapter 27

The events of mortal men are like a reel of movie film. We see life one frame at a time; unaware of future events until they are illuminated by the brilliant klieg light of the living sun.—TR

Chapter 28

She started the engine and drove away—to seek fulfillment of her own destiny.

A blink of time in the whispered mist
Our souls torn asunder by a parting kiss
Anguished emotions, we contemplate—Were our choices premature or were they too late
Have we ultimately changed our destiny
By countermanding God's intent for thee and me? —TR

Chapter 29

"People sometimes ask me, 'Bill Notes, what *denomination* are you...?' Do they think I'm Catholic or possibly insinuating that I'm as queer as a three dollar bill?"

(Stifled snickers)

"Once had an uncle that was *kidnapped* by the mafia—never saw him again. News reports referred to him as the *Missing Notes.*"

(Moans and sporadic chuckles)

"My Uncle Otto Mottle Notes has a *car advertising business.* His company slogan is Otto Mottle Notes'-*Auto Motto Notes.*"

(Laughter and guffaws)

"I have another uncle who is a *philosopher*—what else could he be with a name like *Max .M.* (maxim) *Notes.*"

(Delayed moan & intermittent snickers)

"A cousin in England won the *Pulitzer Prize* and got **knighted** for it— we're very proud of him and refer to him as *Your Noteworthiness.*"

(Light laughter)

"It's been tough going through life with the moniker of Bill Notes— I've been thinking of changing name to—*George* or *Mortimer*— anything, but *Bill.*"

(No audience response)

Chapter 32

Sherrill thought philosophically for a moment. *The realities of life sober us—the illusions of life entertain us.*

Jerry pulled on the take-up rope until the two pulleys closed, which tripped an ingenious mechanism that automatically detached the hook. The tackle fell down into the snow.

Jerry hollered to the other people within hearing distance, "Does anyone else need to be rescued?"

The skiers waved him off, "No, we'll ski down after the lift starts again."

Chapter 33

Life often reads like a Greek Tragedy.
Man finds a woman that epitomizes his ideal.
His heart is lost to her in every way
He walks in a dream world only to awaken to the reality that her heart belongs to another.—TR

Chapter 34

Fate weaves a wobbly wicker basket and fills it with things we take for granted. When fate finally supplies our heart's desires, our insatiable human nature opens the lid and peers inside—still seeking the unattainable.—TR

Chapter 35

Parting is such sweet sorrow, but being apart has no sweetness, only sorrow. The salty taste of tears gives us temporary solace from the pain in our hearts and bathes the deserts of our lonely desiccated souls.—TR

Chapter 36

Were I to choose a friend to weather a firestorm, it would be with a friend with whom I had been to hell and back—TR